DIABLO®

ARCHIVE

TALES IN THE WORLDS OF BLIZZARD ENTERTAINMENT:

NOVELS:

DIABLO®: LEGACY OF BLOOD by Richard A. Knaak
DIABLO: THE BLACK ROAD by Mel Odom
DIABLO: THE KINGDOM OF SHADOW by Richard A. Knaak
DIABLO: MOON OF THE SPIDER by Richard A. Knaak
DIABLO: THE SIN WAR, BOOK ONE—BIRTHRIGHT by Richard A. Knaak
DIABLO: THE SIN WAR, BOOK TWO—SCALES OF THE SERPENT
by Richard A. Knaak
DIABLO: THE SIN WAR, BOOK THREE—THE VEILED PROPHET
by Richard A. Knaak
WARCRAFT®: DAY OF THE DRAGON by Richard A. Knaak
WARCRAFT: THE LORD OF THE CLANS by Christie Golden
WARCRAFT: THE LAST GUARDIAN by Jeff Grubb
WARCRAFT: WAR OF THE ANCIENTS, BOOK ONE—THE WELL OF
ETERNITY by Richard A. Knaak
WARCRAFT: WAR OF THE ANCIENTS, BOOK TWO—THE DEMON SOUL
by Richard A. Knaak
WARCRAFT: WAR OF THE ANCIENTS, BOOK THREE—THE SUNDERING
by Richard A. Knaak
WORLD OF WARCRAFT®: CYCLE OF HATRED by Keith R. A. DeCandido
WORLD OF WARCRAFT: RISE OF THE HORDE by Christie Golden
WORLD OF WARCRAFT: TIDES OF DARKNESS by Aaron Rosenberg
WORLD OF WARCRAFT: BEYOND THE DARK PORTAL
by Aaron Rosenberg & Christie Golden
STARCRAFT®: SPEED OF DARKNESS by Tracy Hickman
STARCRAFT: SHADOW OF THE XEL'NAGA by Gabriel Mesta
STARCRAFT: LIBERTY'S CRUSADE by Jeff Grubb
STARCRAFT: QUEEN OF BLADES by Aaron Rosenberg
STARCRAFT GHOST™: NOVA by Keith R. A. DeCandido
STARCRAFT: THE DARK TEMPLAR SAGA, BOOK ONE—FIRSTBORN
by Christie Golden
STARCRAFT: THE DARK TEMPLAR SAGA, BOOK TWO—SHADOW
HUNTERS by Christie Golden

COLLECTIONS

THE WARCRAFT ARCHIVE
by Richard A. Knaak, Christie Golden, Jeff Grubb, Chris Metzen
THE STARCRAFT ARCHIVE
by Jeff Grubb, Gabriel Mesta, Tracy Hickman, Micky Neilson
THE WARCRAFT: WAR OF ANCIENTS ARCHIVE
by Richard A. Knaak

**FROM POCKET BOOKS
AVAILABLE WHEREVER BOOKS ARE SOLD
ALSO AVAILABLE AS EBOOKS
WWW.SIMONSAYS.COM**

DIABLO®

ARCHIVE

Richard A. Knaak

Mel Odom

Robert B. Marks

POCKET BOOKS
New York   London   Toronto   Sydney

Pocket Books
A Division of Simon & Schuster, Inc.
1230 Avenue of the Americas
New York, NY 10020

First Pocket Books trade paperback edition July 2008

POCKET and colophon are registered trademarks of Simon & Schuster, Inc.

For information about special discounts for bulk purchases, please contact Simon & Schuster Special Sales at 1-800-456-6798 or business@simonandschuster.com

Cover art by Glenn Rane

Manufactured in the United States of America

10 9 8 7 6 5 4 3

ISBN-13: 978-1-4165-7699-0
ISBN-10:   1-4165-7699-1

These titles were previously published individually by Pocket Books.

Contents

✻

LEGACY OF BLOOD

RICHARD A. KNAAK

ONE

❋

The skull gave them a lopsided grin, as if cheerfully inviting the trio to join it for all eternity.

"Looks like we're not the first," Sadun Tryst murmured. The scarred, sinewy fighter tapped the skull with one edge of his knife, causing the fleshless watcher to wobble. Behind the macabre sight, they could just make out the spike that had pierced their predecessor's head, leaving him dangling until time had let all but the skull drop to the floor in a confused heap.

"Did you think we would be?" whispered the tall, cowled figure. If Sadun had a lean, almost acrobatic look to his build, Fauztin seemed nearly cadaverous. The Vizjerei sorcerer moved almost like a phantom as he, too, touched the skull, this time with one gloved finger. "No sorcery here, though. Only crude but sufficient mechanics. Nothing to fear."

"Unless it's your head on the next pole."

The Vizjerei tugged at his thin, gray goatee. His slightly slanted eyes closed once as if in acknowledgment to his partner's last statement. Whereas Sadun had a countenance more akin to an untrustworthy weasel—and sometimes the personality to match—Fauztin reminded some of a withered cat. His nub of a nose, constantly twitching, and the whiskers hanging underneath that nose only added to the illusion.

Neither had ever had a reputation for purity, but Norrec Vizharan would have trusted either with his life—and had several times over. As he joined them, the veteran warrior peered ahead, to where a vast darkness hinted of some major chamber. Thus far, they had explored seven different levels in all and found them curiously devoid of all but the most primitive traps.

They had also found them devoid of any treasure whatsoever, a tremendous disappointment to the tiny party.

"Are you sure there's no sorcery about here, Fauztin? None at all?"

The feline features half-hidden by the cowl wrinkled further in mild offense. The wide shoulders of his voluminous cloak gave Fauztin a foreboding, almost supernatural appearance, especially since he towered over the brawnier Norrec, no small man himself. "You have to ask that, my friend?"

"It's just that it makes no sense! Other than a few minor and pretty pathetic traps, we've encountered nothing to prevent us from reaching the main chamber! Why go through all the trouble of digging this out, then leave it so sparsely defended!"

"I don't call a spider as big as my head *nothing*," Sadun interjected sourly, absently scratching his lengthy but thinning black hair. "Especially as it was *on* my head at the time . . ."

Norrec ignored him. "Is it what I think? Are we too late? Is this Tristram all over again?"

Once before, between serving causes as mercenaries, they had hunted for treasure in a small, troubled village called Tristram. Legend had had it that, in a lair guarded by fiends, there could be found a treasure so very extraordinary in value, it would make kings of those fortunate enough to live to find it. Norrec and his friends had journeyed there, entering the labyrinth in the dead of night without the knowledge of the local populace . . .

And after all their efforts, after battling strange beasts and narrowly avoiding deadly traps . . . they had found that someone else had stripped the underground maze of nearly anything of value. Only upon returning to the village had they learned the sorry truth, that a great champion had descended into the labyrinth but a few weeks before and supposedly slain the terrible demon, Diablo. He had taken no gold or jewels, but other adventurers who had arrived shortly thereafter had made good use of his handiwork, dealing with the lesser dangers and carrying off all they could find. But a few days' difference had left the trio with nothing to show for their efforts . . .

Norrec himself had also taken no consolation in the words of one villager of dubious sanity who had, as they had prepared to depart, warned that the champion, so-called the Wanderer, had not defeated Diablo but, rather, had accidently freed the foul evil. A questioning glance by Norrec toward Fauztin had been answered at first with an indifferent shrug by the Vizjerei sorcerer.

"There are always stories of escaping demons and terrible curses," Fauztin had added at the time, complete dismissal of the wild warning in his tone. "Diablo is generally in most of the favorites whispered among common folk."

"You don't think there's anything to it?" As a child, Norrec had grown up being scared by his elders with tales of Diablo, Baal, and other monsters of the night, all stories designed to make him be good.

Sadun Tryst had snorted. "You ever seen a demon yourself? Know anyone that had?"

Norrec had not. "Have you, Fauztin? They say Vizjerei can summon demons to do their bidding."

"If I could do that, do you think I would be scrounging in empty labyrinths and tombs?"

And that comment, more than anything else, had convinced Norrec then to chalk the villager's words down as yet another tall tale. In truth, it had not been hard to do. After all, the only thing that had mattered then to the three had been what mattered now—wealth.

Unfortunately, it seemed more and more likely that once again those riches had eluded them.

As he peered down the passage, Fauztin's other gloved hand tightened around the spell staff he wielded. The jeweled top—the source of their light—

flared briefly. "I had hoped I was wrong, but now I fear it is so. We are far from the first to delve this deep into this place."

The slightly graying fighter swore under his breath. He had served under many a commander in his life, most of them during the crusades from Westmarch, and from surviving those various campaigns—often by the skin of his teeth—he had come to one conclusion. No one could hope to rise in the world without money. He had made it as far as captain, been broken in rank thrice, then finally retired in disgust after the last debacle.

War had been Norrec's life since he had been old enough to raise a sword. Once, he had also had something of a family, but they were now as dead as his ideals. He still considered himself a decent man, but decency did not fill one's stomach. There had to be another way, Norrec had decided . . .

And so, with his two comrades, he had gone in search of treasure.

Like Sadun, he had his share of scars, but Norrec's visage otherwise resembled more that of a simple farmer. Wide brown eyes, with a broad, open face and a strong jaw, he would have looked at home behind a hoe. Yet, while that vision occasionally appealed to the sturdy veteran, he knew that he needed the gold to pay for that land. This quest should have led them to riches far beyond his needs, far beyond his dreams . . .

Now, it seemed as if it had all been a waste of time and effort . . . again.

Beside him, Sadun Tryst tossed his knife into the air, then expertly caught it at the hilt as it fell. He did this twice more, clearly thinking. Norrec could just imagine what he thought about. They had spent months on this particular quest, journeying across the sea to northern Kehjistan, sleeping in the cold and rain, following false trails and empty caves, eating whatever vermin they could find when other hunting proved scarce—and all because of Norrec, the one who had instigated this entire fiasco.

Worse, *this* quest had actually come about because of a dream, a dream concerning a wicked mountain peak bearing some crude resemblance to a dragon's head. Had he dreamt of it only once, perhaps twice, Norrec might have forgotten the image, but over the years, it had repeated itself far too many times. Wherever he had fought, Norrec had watched for the peak, but to no avail. Then, a comrade—later dead—from these chill northern lands had made mention of such a place in passing. Ghosts were said to haunt it and men who traveled near the mountain often disappeared or were discovered years later, all flesh stripped from the shattered bones . . .

There and then, Norrec Vizharan had been certain that destiny had tried to call him here.

But if so—why to a tomb already vandalized?

The entrance had been well hidden in the rock face, but definitely open to the outside. That should have been his first clue to the truth, yet Norrec had refused to even see the discrepancy. All his hopes, all his promises to his companions . . .

"Damn!" He kicked at the nearest wall, only his sturdy boot saving him from a few broken toes. Norrec threw his sword to the ground, continuing to curse his naïveté.

"There's some new general from Westmarch hiring on mercenaries," Sadun helpfully suggested. "They say he's got big ambitions . . ."

"No more war," muttered Norrec, trying not to show the pain coursing through his foot. "No more trying to die for other people's glory."

"I just thought—"

The lanky sorcerer tapped the ground once with his staff, seeking the attention of both his earthier partners. "At this point, it would be foolish not to go on to the central chamber. Perhaps those who were here before us left a few baubles or coins. We did find a few gold coins in Tristram. Certainly it would not hurt to search a little longer, would it, Norrec?"

He knew that the Vizjerei only sought to assuage his friend's bitter emotions, but still the idea managed to take root in the veteran's mind. All he needed were a few gold coins! He was still young enough to take a bride, begin a new life, maybe even raise a family . . .

Norrec picked up his sword, hefting the weapon that had served him so well over the years. He had kept it cleaned and honed, taking pride in one of the few items truly his own. A look of determination spread across his visage. "Let's go."

"You've a way with words for one using so few," Sadun jested to the sorcerer as they started off.

"And you use so many words for one with so few things worth saying."

The friendly argument between his companions helped settle Norrec's troubled mind. It reminded him of other times, when, between the three of them, they had persevered through worse difficulties.

Yet, the talk died as they approached what surely had to be the last and most significant chamber. Fauztin called a halt, staring briefly at the jewel atop the staff.

"Before we proceed inside, the two of you had better light torches."

They had saved the torches for emergencies, the sorcerer's staff serving well until now. Fauztin said no more, but as Norrec used tinder to light his, he wondered if the Vizjerei had finally noted sorcery of some significance. If so, then perhaps there still remained some sort of treasure . . .

With his own torch lit, Norrec used it to set Sadun's ablaze. Now surrounded with more secure illumination, the trio set off again.

"I swear," grumbled the wiry Sadun, a few moments later. "I swear that the hair on the back of my head's standing on end!"

Norrec felt the same. Neither fighter argued when the Vizjerei took the lead. The clans of the Far East had long studied the magical arts and Fauztin's people had studied them longer than most. If a situation arose where sorcery had to take a hand, certainly it made sense to leave it to the thin spellcaster. Norrec and Sadun would be there to guard him from other assaults.

The arrangement had worked *so* far.

Unlike the heavy boots of the warriors, the sandaled feet of Fauztin made no sound as he walked. The mage stretched forth his staff and Norrec noticed that, despite its power, the jewel failed to illuminate much. Only the torches seemed to act as they should.

"This is old and powerful. Our predecessors may not have been so fortunate as we first believed. We may find some treasure yet."

And possibly more. Norrec's grip on the sword tightened to the point that his knuckles whitened. He wanted gold, but he also wanted to live to spend it.

With the staff proving unreliable, the two fighters took to the front. That did not mean that Fauztin would no longer be of any aid to the band. Even now, the veteran knew, his magical companion thought out the quickest, surest spells for whatever they might encounter.

"It looks as dark as the grave in there," Sadun mumbled.

Norrec said nothing. Now a few steps ahead of both his comrades, he became the first to actually reach the chamber itself. Despite the dangers that might lurk within, he almost felt drawn to it, as if something inside called to him . . .

A blinding brilliance overwhelmed the trio.

"Gods!" snapped Sadun. "I can't see!"

"Give it a moment," cautioned the sorcerer. "It will pass."

And so it did, but as his eyes adjusted, Norrec Vizharan at last beheld a sight so remarkable that he had to blink twice to make certain it was not a figment of his desires.

The walls were covered in intricate, jeweled patterns in which even he could sense the magic. Precious stones of every type and hue abounded in each pattern, blanketing the chamber in an astonishing display of refracted and reflected colors. In addition, below those magical symbols and no less eye-catching were the very treasures for which the trio had come. Mounds of gold, mounds of silver, mounds of jewels. They added to the overall glitter, making the chamber brighter than day. Each time either fighter shifted his torch, the lighting further altered the appearance of the room, adding new dimensions equally as startling as the last.

Yet, as breathtaking as all this looked, one shocking sight dampened Norrec's enthusiasm greatly.

Strewn across the floor as far as he could see were the many mangled and decaying forms of those who had preceded him and his friends to this foreboding place.

Sadun held his torch toward the nearest one, an almost fleshless corpse still clad in rotting leather armor. "Must've been some battle here."

"These men did not all die at the same time."

Norrec and the smaller soldier looked to Fauztin, who had a troubled expression on his generally emotionless countenance.

"What's that you mean?"

"I mean, Sadun, that some of them have clearly been dead for far longer, even centuries. This one near your feet is one of the newest. Some of those over there are but bones."

The slight warrior shrugged. "Either way, from the looks of it, they all died pretty nasty."

"There is that."

"So . . . what killed them?"

Here Norrec answered. "Look there. I think they slew each other."

The two corpses he pointed at each had blades thrust into one another's midsections. One, with his mouth still open in what seemed a last, horrified cry, wore garments akin to the other mummified body by Sadun's feet. The other wore only scraps of clothing and only a few strands of hair covered an otherwise clean skeleton.

"You must be mistaken," the Vizjerei replied with a slight shake of his head. "The one warrior is clearly much older than the other."

So Norrec would have supposed if not for the blade thrust into the other corpse's torso. Still, the deaths of two men long, long ago had little bearing on present circumstances. "Fauztin, do you sense anything? Is there some sort of trap here?"

The gaunt figure held his staff before the chamber for a moment, then lowered it again, his disgust quite evident. "There are too many conflicting forces in here, Norrec. I can get no accurate sense of what to seek. I sense nothing directly dangerous—yet."

To the side, Sadun fairly hopped about in impatience. "So do we leave all of this, leave all our dreams, or do we take a little risk and gather ourselves a few empires' worth of coin?"

Norrec and the sorcerer exchanged glances. Neither could see any reason not to continue, especially with so many enticements before them. The veteran warrior finally settled the matter by taking a few steps farther into the master chamber. When no great bolt of lightning nor demonic creature struck him down, Sadun and the Vizjerei quickly followed suit.

"There must be a couple dozen at least." Sadun leapt over two skeletal corpses still trapped in struggle. "And that's not counting the ones in little pieces . . ."

"Sadun, shut your mouth or I'll do it for you . . ." Now that he actually walked among them, Norrec wanted no more discussion concerning the dead treasure hunters. It still bothered him that so many had clearly died violently. Surely *someone* had survived. But, if so, why did the coins and other treasure look virtually untouched?

And then something else tore his thoughts from those questions, the sudden realization that beyond the treasure, at the very far end of the chamber, a dais stood atop a naturally formed set of steps. More important, atop that dais lay mortal remains still clad in armor.

"Fauztin . . ." Once the mage had come to his side, Norrec pointed to the dais and muttered, "What do you make of that?"

Fauztin's only reply was to purse his thin lips and carefully make his way toward the platform. Norrec followed close behind.

"It would explain so much . . ." he heard the Vizjerei whisper. "It would explain so many conflicting magical signatures and so many signs of power . . ."

"What're you talking about?"

The sorcerer finally looked back at him. "Come closer and see for yourself."

Norrec did just that. The sense of unease that had earlier filled him now amplified as the veteran peered at the macabre display atop the platform.

He had been a man of military aspirations, that much Norrec could at least tell, even if of the garments only a few tattered remains existed. The fine leather boots lay tipped to each side, pieces of the pants sticking out of them. What likely had once been a silk shirt could barely be seen under the majestic breastplate lying askew on the rib cage. Underneath that, blackened bits of a formerly regal robe covered much of the upper half of the platform. Well-crafted gauntlets and gutter-shaped plates, vambraces, gave the illusion of arms still sinewy and fleshbound; whereas other plates, these overlapping, did the same for the shoulders. Less successful was the armor on the legs, which, along with the bones there, lay askew, as if something had disturbed them at some point.

"Do you see it?" Fauztin asked.

Not certain what exactly he meant, Norrec squinted. Other than the fact that the armor itself seemed colored an unsettling yet familiar shade of red, he could see nothing that would have—

No head. The body on the dais had no head. Norrec glanced past the dais, saw no trace on the floor. He made mention of that to the sorcerer.

"Yes, it is exactly as described," the lanky figure swept toward the platform, almost too eager in the veteran's mind. Fauztin stretched out a hand but held back at the very last moment from touching what lay upon it. "The body placed with the top to the north. The head and helm, separated already in battle, now separated in time and distance in order to ensure an absolute end to the matter. The marks of power set into the walls, there to counter and contain the darkness still within the corpse . . . but . . ." Fauztin's voice trailed off as he continued to stare.

"But what?"

The mage shook his head. "Nothing, I suppose. Perhaps just being so near to him unsettles my nerves more than I like to admit."

By now somewhat exasperated with Fauztin's murky words, Norrec gritted his teeth. "So . . . who is he? Some prince?"

"By Heaven, no! Do you not see?" One gloved finger pointed at the red breast plate. "This is the lost tomb of Bartuc, lord of demons, master of darkest sorcery—"

"*The Warlord of Blood.*" The words escaped Norrec as little more than a gasp. He knew very well the tales of Bartuc, who had risen among the ranks of sorcerers, only to later turn to the darkness, to the demons. Now the redness of the armor made perfect and horrible sense; it was the color of *human blood*.

In his madness, Bartuc, who even the demons who had first seduced him had eventually come to fear, had bathed himself before each battle in the blood of previously fallen foes. His armor, once brilliant gold, had become forever stained by his sinful acts. He had razed cities to the ground, committed atrocities unbounded, and would have continued on forever—so the stories went—if not for the desperate acts of his own brother, Horazon, and other Vizjerei sorcerers who had used what knowledge they retained of the ancient, more natural magics to defeat the fiend. Bartuc and his demon host had been slaughtered just short of victory, the warlord himself decapitated just in the midst of casting a dire counterspell.

Still untrusting of his brother's vast power even in death, Horazon had commanded that Bartuc's body forever be hidden from the sight of men. Why they had not simply burned it, Norrec did not know, but certainly he would have tried. Regardless, rumors had arisen shortly thereafter of places where the Warlord of Blood had been laid to rest. Many had sought out his tomb, especially those of the black arts interested in possible lingering magic, but no one had ever claimed to truly find it.

The Vizjerei likely knew more detail than Norrec, but the veteran fighter understood all too well what they had found. Legend had it that for a time Bartuc had lived among Norrec's own people, that perhaps some of those with whom the soldier had grown up had been, in fact, descendants of the monstrous despot's followers. Yes, Norrec knew very well the legacy of the warlord.

He shuddered and, without thinking, began to back away from the dais. "Fauztin . . . we're leaving this place."

"But surely, my friend—"

"We're *leaving*."

The cowled figure studied Norrec's eyes, then nodded. "Perhaps you are right."

Grateful, Norrec turned to his other companion. "Sadun! Forget everything! We're leaving here! Now—"

Something near the shadowed mouth of the chamber caught his attention, something that moved—and that was *not* Sadun Tryst. The third member of the party presently engaged himself in trying to fill a sack with every manner of jewel he could find.

"Sadun!" snapped the older fighter. "Drop the sack! Quick!"

The thing near the entrance shuffled forward.

"Are you mad?" Sadun called, not even bothering to look over his shoulder. "This is all we've dreamed about!"

A clatter of movement caught Norrec's attention, a clatter of movement from more than one direction. He swallowed as the original figure moved better into view.

The empty sockets of the mummified warrior they had first stepped over greeted his own terrified gaze.

"Sadun! Look to your back!"

Now at last he had his partner's attention. The wiry soldier dropped the sack instantly, whirling about and pulling his blade free. However, when he saw what both Norrec and Fauztin already faced, Sadun Tryst's countenance turned as pale as bone.

One by one they began to rise, from corpse to skeleton, those who had preceded the trio to this tomb. Now Norrec understood why no one had ever left alive and why he and his friends might soon be added to the grisly ranks.

"*Kosoraq!*"

One of the skeletons nearest to the sorcerer vanished in a burst of orange flame. Fauztin pointed a finger at another, a half-clad ghoul with some traces of his former face still remaining. The Vizjerei repeated the word of power.

Nothing happened.

"My spell—" Stunned, Fauztin failed to notice another skeleton on his left now raising a rusted but still serviceable sword and clearly intending to sever the mage's head from his body.

"Watch it!" Norrec deflected the blow, then thrust. Unfortunately, his attack did nothing, the blade simply passing through the rib cage. In desperation, he kicked at his horrific foe, sending the skeleton crashing into another of the shambling undead.

They were outnumbered several times over by foes who could not be slain by normal means. Norrec saw Sadun, cut off from his two friends, leap to the top of a mound of coins and try to defend himself from two nightmarish warriors, one a cadaverous husk, the other a partial skeleton with one good arm. Several more closed in from behind those two.

"Fauztin! Can you do anything?"

"I am trying a different spell!"

Again the Vizjerei called out a word: this time the two creatures battling with Sadun froze in place. Not one to miss such an opportunity, Tryst swung at the pair with all his might.

Both ghouls shattered into countless pieces, their entire top halves scattered on the stone floor.

"Your powers are back!" Norrec's hopes rose.

"They never left me. I fear I have only one chance to use each spell—and most of those still remaining take much time to cast!"

Norrec had no chance to comment on the terrible news, for his own situation had grown even more desperate. He traded quick strikes with first one, then two of the encroaching ranks of undead. The ghouls seemed slow in reaction, for which he gave some thanks, but numbers and perseverance would eventually pay off for these ghastly guardians of the warlord's tomb. Those who had planned this last trap had planned well, for each party that entered added to the ranks that would attack the next. Norrec could imagine where the first undead had come from. He had remarked to his friends early on that although the three had come across sprung traps and dead creatures, no bodies had been found until the skull with the spike in its head. The first party to discover Bartuc's tomb surely had lost some of its numbers on the trek inside, never knowing that those dead comrades would become the survivors' greatest nightmare. And so, with each new group, the ranks of guardians had grown—with Norrec, Sadun, and Fauztin now set to be added.

One of the mummified corpses cut at Norrec's left arm. The veteran used the torch in his other hand to ignite the dry flesh, turning the zombie into a walking inferno. Risking his foot, Norrec kicked the fiery creature into its comrade.

Despite that success, though, the horde of unliving continued to press all three back.

"Norrec!" shouted Sadun from somewhere. "Fauztin! They're coming at me from everywhere!"

Neither could help him, though, both as harried. The mage beat off one skeleton with his staff, but two more quickly filled in the space left. The creatures had begun to move with more fluidity and greater swiftness. Soon, no advantage whatsoever would remain for Norrec and his friends.

Separating him from Fauztin, three ghoulish warriors pressed Norrec Vizharan up the steps and finally against the dais. The bones of the Warlord of Blood rattled in the armor, but, much to the hard pressed veteran's relief, Bartuc did not rise to command this infernal army.

A flash of smoke alerted him to the fact that the sorcerer had managed to deal with yet another of the undead, but Norrec knew that Fauztin could not handle all of them. So far, neither of the fighters had managed much more than a momentary stalemate. Without flesh for their blades to penetrate, without vital organs that could be skewered, knives and swords meant nothing.

The thought of one day rising as one of these and moving to slay the next hapless intruders sent a shiver down Norrec's spine. He moved along the side of the dais as best he could, trying to find some path by which to escape. To his shame, Norrec knew that he would have happily abandoned his comrades if an opening to freedom had abruptly materialized.

His strength flagged. A blade caught him in the thigh. The pain not only made him cry out, but caused Norrec to lose his grip on his sword. The weapon clattered down the steps, disappearing behind the encroaching ghouls.

His leg nearly buckling, Norrec waved the torch at the oncoming attackers with one hand while his other sought some hold on the platform. However, instead of stone his grasping fingers took hold of cold metal that offered no support whatsoever.

His wounded leg finally gave out. Norrec slipped to one knee, pulling the metallic object he had accidentally grabbed with him.

The torch flew away. A sea of grotesque faces filled the warrior's horrified view as Norrec attempted to right himself. The desperate treasure hunter raised the hand with which he had tried to garner some hold, as if by silently beseeching the undead for mercy he could forestall the inevitable.

Only at the last did he realize that the hand he had raised now had somehow become clad in metal—a gauntlet.

The very same gauntlet that he earlier had seen on the skeleton of Bartuc.

Even as this startling discovery registered in his mind, a word that Norrec did not understand ripped forth from his mouth, echoing throughout the chamber. The jeweled patterns in the walls flared bright, brighter, and the unearthly foes of the trio froze in place.

Another word, this one even less intelligible, burst free from the stunned veteran. The patterns of power grew blinding, burning—

—and exploded.

A fearsome wave of pure energy tore through the chamber, coursing over the undead. Shards flew everywhere, forcing Norrec to fold himself into as small a bundle as possible. He prayed that the end would be relatively quick and painless.

The magic consumed the undead where they stood. Bones and dried flesh burned as readily as oiled tinder. Their weapons melted, creating piles of slag and ash.

Yet, it did not touch any of the party.

"What's happening? What's happening?" he heard Sadun cry.

The inferno moved with acute precision, sweeping over the tomb's guardians but nothing else. As their numbers dwindled, so too did the intensity of the force, until at last neither remained. The chamber became plunged into near darkness, the only illumination now the two torches and the little bit of light reflected by the many ruined stones.

Norrec gaped at the devastating results, wondering what he had just wrought and whether somehow it heralded an even more terrible situation. He then stared down at the gauntlet, afraid to leave it on, but equally fearful of what might happen if he tried to remove it.

"They . . . they have all been devoured," Fauztin managed, the Vizjerei forcing himself to his feet. His robe had been cut in many places and the thin mage held one arm where blood still flowed from a nasty wound.

Sadun hopped down from where he had been battling. Remarkably, he looked entirely uninjured. "But how?"

How, indeed? Norrec flexed his gloved fingers. The metal felt almost like a second skin, far more comfortable than he could have thought possible. Some of the fear faded as the possibilities of what else he might be able to do became more obvious.

"Norrec," came Fauztin's voice. "When did you put that on?"

He paid no attention, instead thinking that it might be interesting to try the other gauntlet—better yet, the entire suit—and see how it felt. As a young recruit, he had once dreamed of rising to the rank of general and garnering his riches through victory in battle. Now that old, long-faded dream seemed fresh and, for the first time, so very possible . . .

A shadow loomed over his hand. He looked up to see the sorcerer eyeing him in concern.

"Norrec. My friend. Perhaps you should take off that glove."

Take it off? Suddenly, the notion of doing so made absolutely no sense to the soldier. The gauntlet had been the only thing that had saved their lives! Why take it off? Could it . . . could it be that the Vizjerei simply coveted it for himself? In things magic, Fauztin's kind knew no loyalty. If Norrec did not give him the gauntlet, the odds were that Fauztin might simply just take it when his comrade could not stop him.

A part of the veteran's mind tried to dismiss the hateful notions. Fauztin had saved his life more than once. He and Sadun were Norrec's best—and only—friends. The eastern mage would certainly not try something so base . . . would he?

"Norrec, listen to me!" An edge of emotion, perhaps envy, perhaps fear, touched the other's voice. "It is vital right now that you take that gauntlet off. We shall put it back on the platform—"

"What is it?" Sadun called. "What's wrong with him, Fauztin?"

Norrec became convinced that he had been right the *first* time. The sorcerer wanted *his* glove.

"Sadun. Ready your blade. We may have to—"

"My blade? You want me to use it on Norrec?"

Something within the older fighter took control. Norrec watched as if from a distance as the gauntleted hand darted out and caught the Vizjerei by the throat.

"Sa-Sadun! His wrist! Cut at his—"

Out of the corner of his eye, Norrec saw his other companion hesitate, then raise his weapon to attack. A fury such as he had never experienced consumed the veteran. The world grew to a bloody red . . . then turned to utter blackness.

And in that blackness, Norrec Vizharan heard screams.

Two

In the land of Aranoch, at the very northern fringe of the vast, oppressive desert which made up much of that land, the small but resolute army of General Augustus Malevolyn remained encamped. They had set up camp some weeks previous for reasons that still mystified most of the soldiers, but no one dared question the decisions of the general. Most of these men had followed Malevolyn since his early days in Westmarch, and their fanaticism to his cause remained without question. But in silence they wondered why he seemed unwilling to move on.

Many felt certain that it had to do with the more gaudy tent pitched not far from the commander's own, the tent belonging to the witch. Each morning, Malevolyn went to her, evidently seeking portents of the future and making his decisions based upon those. In addition, each evening Galeona made her way to the general's tent—for more personal matters. How much influence she had over his choices, none could truly say, but it had to be substantial.

And as the morning sun began to peek over the horizon, the slim, well-groomed figure of Augustus Malevolyn emerged from his quarters, his pale, clean-shaven features—once described by a now-deceased rival as "the very visage of Lord Death without the kindness inherent"—entirely without expression. Malevolyn stood clad in armor of the darkest ebony save for the crimson border running along every edge, especially around the neck. In addition, the symbol of a red fox over three silver swords decorated the breastplate, the only reminder of the general's far-flung past. Two aides attended the general as he put on ebony and crimson gauntlets that looked as if they had just been forged. In fact, Malevolyn's entire suit looked to be in perfect condition, the result of nightly cleanings by soldiers trained to understand what even a single hint of rust might mean to their lives.

Fully covered save for his head, Malevolyn marched directly toward the sanctum of his sorceress, his mistress. Resembling something of a tentmaker's nightmare, the abode of Galeona looked as if it had been put together like a quilt, with patches of more than two dozen shades of color sewn together over and over. Only those like the general, who saw beyond the facade, might have noticed that the various colors created specific patterns and only those cognizant of the inner workings of sorcery would have known the power inherent in those patterns.

Behind Malevolyn the two aides followed, in the arms of one a covered burden that vaguely resembled something akin in shape to a head. The officer carrying the object moved uneasily, as if what he held filled him with distrust and not a little fear.

The commander did not bother to announce himself, yet just as he reached the closed flap of the witch's tent, a feminine voice, both deep and taunting, bid him enter.

Even though sunlight now toyed with the encampment, the interior of Galeona's tent appeared so dark that, if not for the single oil lamp dangling from the middle of the ceiling, the general and his aides would not have been able to see more than a foot beyond their noses. Had that been so, they would have missed quite a sight, indeed.

Pouches and flasks and items unnamed hung everywhere. Although once offered a case in which to house her wares, the sorceress had declined, finding some purpose in hanging each piece by noose in carefully preselected locations. General Malevolyn did not question this idiosyncrasy; so long as he received his desired answers, Galeona could have hung dry corpses from the ceiling and he would have made no comment.

She nearly did just that. While many of her prizes remained thankfully hidden within containers, those that dangled free included the desiccated forms of several rare creatures and various components of others. In addition, there were a few items that looked to have come from human sources, although full identification would have required too close an inspection.

To further add to the uneasiness her sanctum engendered in all save her commander and lover, the single lamp somehow created shadows that did not move in conjunction with normal reasoning. Ofttimes, Malevolyn's men would see the flame flicker in one direction, but a shadow move in another. The shadows in general also made the tent seem much larger inside than its outer dimensions warranted, as if by stepping in, the newcomers had entered a place not entirely set in the mortal plane.

And as the centerpiece to this unsettling and distracting chamber, the sorceress Galeona presented the most arresting and yet also disturbing vision of all. As she rose from the multicolored pillows covering the patterned carpet below, a fire stirred within each man. Lush, cascading black hair fell back to reveal a round, enticing countenance marked by full red and inviting lips, a generous but pleasing nose, and deep, so very deep, green eyes matched only by the sharp emerald ones of the general himself. Thick lashes half-draped over those eyes as the witch seemed to devour each newcomer in turn simply by looking at him.

"My general . . ." she purred, each word a promise.

Built voluptuously, Galeona displayed her assets as she did every weapon at her command. Her gown had been purposely cut as low as it could without failing its most basic function, and glittering jewels accented the edges near her chest. When she moved, she moved as if the wind gently pushed her along, her thin garments billowing seductively around her.

The visible effect of her charms on Malevolyn proved to be little more than a slight touch of his gloved hand on her deep-brown cheek, which the sorceress accepted as if he caressed her with the softest fur. She smiled, revealing teeth perfect save that they had a slight catlike sharpness to them.

"Galeona . . . my Galeona . . . slept you well?"

"When I actually slept . . . my general."

He chuckled. "Yes, the same myself." His very slight smile faded abruptly, "Until I had the dream."

"Dream?" The momentary intake of breath before she spoke signaled well enough that Galeona took this comment not at all lightly.

"Yes . . ." He moved past her, staring at without actually seeing one of the more macabre pieces of her collection. He toyed with it, moved one of the joints, while he spoke. "The Warlord of Blood arisen . . ."

She swept over to him, a dark angel now at his shoulder, her eyes wide with anticipation. "Tell me all, my general, tell me all . . ."

"I saw the armor without the man struggle from the grave, then bone filled the armor, with muscle and tendon joining afterward. Then flesh covered the body, but it was not Bartuc as his images have shown." The ebony-clad officer seemed disappointed. "A rather mundane face, if anything, but artisans were never known for carvings such as those. Perhaps this was the face of the war-lord, although he seemed more a frightened soul in my dream . . ."

"Is that it?"

"No, I saw blood then, on his face, and after it appeared he marched off. I saw mountains give way to hills and hills to sand and then I saw him sink into that sand . . . and there the dream ended."

One of the other officers caught sight of a shadow in one far corner of the tent. It moved, shifting toward the general. Trained by experience not to speak of such things, he swallowed and held his tongue, hoping that the shadow would not, at some later point, turn in his own direction.

Galeona draped herself against General Malevolyn's breastplate, looking up into his eyes. "Have you ever had this dream before, my general?"

"You would have known."

"Yes, I would've. You know how important it is to tell me everything." She separated from him, returning to the pile of plush pillows. A glimmer of sweat covered every revealed portion of her body. "And this most important of all. . . . For this is no ordinary dream, no it is not."

"I suspected as much myself." He waved one negligent hand toward the aide who carried the cloth-covered object. The man stepped forward, at the same time ripping away the material in order to reveal what lay beneath.

A helmet with a ridged crest glistened in the weak light of the single lamp. Old but intact, it would have covered most of the head and visage of its wearer, leaving but two narrowed gaps for the eyes, a slight passage for the nose, and a wider but still narrow horizontal gash for the mouth. The back of the helmet hung low, protecting the neck there, but leaving the throat itself completely open.

Even in the dim illumination one could clearly discern that the helmet had been colored bloodred.

"I thought you might need Bartuc's helm."

"You may be right." Galeona separated herself from Malevolyn, reaching out for the artifact. Her fingers brushed the aide's own and the man shivered. With the general facing away from her and the second officer unable to see from his angle, the sorceress took the opportunity to let one hand briefly caress the aide's wrist. She had tasted him once or twice when her appetite had demanded some change of pace, but knew that he would never dare tell his commander of their encounters. Malevolyn would be more likely to have *him* executed rather than his valued witch.

She took the helmet and placed it on the ground near where she had origi-nally been sitting. The general dismissed his men, then joined Galeona there, placing himself directly across from her.

"Do not fail me, my dear. I am adamant in this."

For the first time, a bit of Galeona's confidence dissipated. Augustus had always been a man of his word, especially when it came to the fates of those who did not live up to his expectations.

Hiding her concern, the dark sorceress placed her hands palm down on the top of the helmet. The general removed his gauntlets and did the same.

The flame in the lamp flickered, seemed to shrink to nearly nothing. The shadows spread, thickened, and yet somehow also seemed more alive, more independent of the frail light. That they had a surreal, unworldly sense to them did not bother General Malevolyn in the least, though. He knew of some of the powers with which Galeona conversed and suspected others. As a military man with imperial ambitions, he saw all as useful tools to his cause.

"Like calls to like, blood to blood . . ." The words slipped readily from Galeona's full lips. She had uttered this litany many times for her patron. "Let that which was his call to that which was his! What the shadow of Bartuc wore must be linked again!"

Malevolyn felt his pulse quicken. The world seemed to pull back from him. Galeona's words echoed, became the only focus.

At first he saw nothing but an eternal gray. Then, before his eyes, an image coalesced in the grayness, an image somewhat familiar to him. He saw again Bartuc's armor and the fact that someone wore it now, but this time the general grew certain that the man before him could not possibly be the legendary warlord.

"Who?" he hissed. "Who?"

Galeona did not answer him, her eyes closed, her head bent back in concentration. A shadow moved behind her, one that Malevolyn vaguely thought resembled some large insect. Then, as the image before him grew, he threw his attention wholly back into identifying and locating this stranger.

"A warrior," the sorceress murmured. "A man of many campaigns."

"Forget that! Where is he? Is he close?" The warlord's armor! After so very long, so many false trails . . .

She twitched from effort. Malevolyn did not care, willing to push her to the very limits and beyond if necessary.

"Mountains . . . cold, chill peaks . . ."

No help there, the world was filled with mountains, especially the north and across the Twin Seas. Even Westmarch had its share.

Galeona shuddered twice. "Blood calls to blood . . ."

He gritted his teeth. Why repeat herself?

"Blood calls to blood!"

She teetered, nearly losing her grip on the helmet. Her link to the spell all but broke. Malevolyn did his best to maintain the vision on his own even though his own magical skills paled in comparison to Galeona's. Yet, for a moment, he managed to fix better on that face. Simple. Nothing at all like a leader. In some ways, panic stricken. Not cowardly, but clearly far out of his element. . . .

The image began to falter. The general silently swore. The armor had been found by some damned foot soldier or deserter who likely had no idea of either its value or its power. "Where *is* he?"

The vision faded away with such abruptness that it startled even him. At the same time, the dark witch let out a gasp and fell back onto the many pillows, completely shattering the spell.

A tremendous force threw Malevolyn's hands from the helmet. A string of harsh epithets burst from the general's mouth.

With a moan, Galeona slowly rose to a sitting position. She held her head with one hand as she looked at Malevolyn.

He, in turn, considered whether or not to have her whipped. To entice him with the fact that the armor had been found and then to leave him without the knowledge of where it was.

She read his dark look and what it likely meant for her. "I haven't failed you, my general! After all this time, Bartuc's legacy is yours to fulfill!"

"Fulfill?" Malevolyn rose, barely able to keep his frustration and fury in check. "Fulfill? Bartuc commanded demons! He spread his power over much of the world!" The pale commander gestured at the helmet. "I bought that from the peddler as a memento, a symbol of the might I sought to gain! A false artifact, I thought, but well done! The Helmet of Bartuc!" The general let out a harsh laugh. "Only when I put it on did I realize the truth—that it *was* the helmet!"

"Yes, my general!" Galeona quickly rose and put her hands on his chest, her fingers caressing the metal as if it were his own flesh. "And you began to have the dreams, the visions of—"

"*Bartuc* . . . I've seen his victories, seen his glories, seen his strength! I've lived them all—" Malevolyn's tone grew increasingly bitter "—but only in my *dreams.*"

"It was fate that brought the helmet to you! Fate and the spirit of Bartuc, don't you see? He means for you to be his successor, trust me," the witch cooed. "There can be no reason, for you're the only one to see these visions without my aid!"

"True." After the first two incidents, each during a period in which Malevolyn had worn the helmet, the general had commanded a few of his most trusted officers to try the artifact on for themselves. Even those who had worn it for several hours had admitted to no subsequent dreams of their own. That, to Augustus Malevolyn, had been proof enough that he had been chosen by the spirit of the warlord to take on his glorious mantle.

Malevolyn knew all that any mortal man could know of Bartuc. He studied every document, researched every legend. While many in the past have shrunken away from the warlord's dark and demonic history—fearing some taint spreading to themselves—the general had devoured each scrap of information.

He could match Bartuc in strategy and physical strength, but Malevolyn himself wielded only the least bit of magic. Barely enough to light a candle. Galeona had provided him with more sorcery—not to mention other pleasures—but to truly be able to emulate the warlord's glory, Malevolyn needed some manner by which to summon and command not one demon, but *many*.

The armor would open that path for him, of that he had become obsessively certain. Malevolyn's extensive research had indicated that Bartuc had imbued the suit with formidable enchantments. The general's own meager powers had already been augmented by the helmet; surely the complete, ensorcelled suit would give him what he desired. Surely the shade of Bartuc wanted that. The visions had to be a sign.

"There is one thing I can tell you, my general," the sorceress whispered. "One thing to encourage you in your quest . . ."

He seized her by her arms. "What? What is it?"

She grimaced momentarily from the pain of his grip. "He—the fool who wears the armor now—he comes nearer!"

"To us?"

"Perhaps, if the helmet and the rest are meant to be with one another, but even if not so, the closer he comes, the better I'll be able to specifically locate him!" Galeona pulled one arm free, then touched Malevolyn's chin. "You can wait just a little longer, my love. Just a little longer. . . ."

Releasing her, the general considered. "You will check each morning and each evening! You will spare no effort! The moment you can identify where this cretin is located, I must know! We shall march immediately after! Nothing must stand between me and my destiny!"

He seized the helmet and, without another word, departed from her tent, his aides quickly falling into line behind him. Malevolyn's mind raced as he pictured himself in the ensorcelled armor. Demonic legions would rise to his command. Cities would fall. An empire spanning . . . spanning the *world* . . . would spring up.

Augustus Malevolyn hugged the helmet almost protectively as he returned to his own quarters. Galeona had the right of it. He only had to be a little more patient. The armor would come to him.

"I will do as you once dreamed of doing," he whispered to the absent shade of Bartuc. "Your legacy *will* be my destiny!" The general's eyes gleamed. "And soon . . ."

The witch shuddered as Malevolyn vanished through the tent's flap. He had grown more unstable of late, especially the longer he wore the ancient helm. On one occasion she had even caught him speaking as if he were the Warlord of Blood himself. Galeona knew that the helmet—and likely all the armor—contained some mysterious magical force, but as of yet she had been able to neither identify nor control it.

If she could control it . . . she would not need her lover any longer. A pity in some ways, but there were always other males. Other more *malleable* males.

A voice broke the silence, a scratchy, deep voice that even to the witch sounded something akin to the buzzing of a thousand dying flies. "Patience is virtue . . . this one should know! One hundred twenty-three years on this mortal plane in search of the warlord! So long . . . and now it comes together . . ."

Galeona looked around at the shadows, searching for one in particular. She finally noticed it in a far corner of the tent, a wavering, insectlike figure only visible to one who truly looked close. "Be silent! Someone may hear!"

"No one hears when this one chooses," the voice rasped. "Know you that well, human—"

"Then quiet your voice for my sanity, Xazax." The dark-skinned sorceress stared at the shadow but did not approach it. Even after all this time, she did not entirely trust her constant companion.

"So tender the ears of a human." The shadow took more form, now resembling a specific insect, a *praying mantis*. Yet, such a mantis would have been more than seven feet tall, if not more. "So soft and failing their bodies—"

"You'd do well not to talk of failures."

A low, chittering noise spread throughout the tent. Galeona steeled herself, knowing that her companion did not like to be corrected.

Xazax moved, shifting closer. "Tell this one of the vision shared."

"You saw it."

"But this one would hear it from you. . . . Please . . . indulge this one."

"Very well." Taking a deep breath, she described in as good detail as she could the man and the armor. Xazax surely had seen everything, but for some reason the fool always made her go over the visions. Galeona tried to hurry matters by ignoring the man for the most part, going more into the armor itself and the landscape vaguely seen in the background.

Xazax suddenly cut her off. "This one knows that the armor is true! This one knows that it wanders this mortal plane! The human! What about the human?"

"Perfectly ordinary. Nothing special about him."

"Nothing is ordinary! Describe!"

"A soldier. Plain of face. A simple fighter, probably the son of farmers, from the looks of him. Nothing extraordinary. Some poor fool who stumbled onto the armor and, as the general clearly thinks, has no idea what it is."

Again the chittering. The shadow withdrew slightly. When Xazax spoke, he sounded extremely disappointed. "Certain that this mortal journeys nearer?"

"So it seems."

The murky form grew still. Xazax clearly had something in mind. Galeona waited . . . and waited some more. Xazax had no concept of time where others were concerned, only when it came to his own needs and desires.

Two flashes of deep yellow momentarily appeared where the head of the shadow seemed to be. What might have been the outline of an appendage ending in three-clawed digits shifted momentarily into sight, then quickly vanished again.

"Let him come, then. This one will have decided by then whether one puppet is better than another . . ." Xazax's form grew indistinct. All semblance of a mantis, of any creature, faded away. "Let him come . . ."

The shadow melted into the darkened corners.

Galeona swore to herself. She had learned much from the foul creature, increased her power in so many ways because of his past guidance. Yet, much more than Augustus she would have preferred disposing of Xazax, being rid of his horrid self. The general could be manipulated to a point, but not so her secret companion. With Xazax, the sorceress played a continual game of cat and mouse and too often she felt like the latter of the two creatures. However, one did not simply break a pact with Xazax's kind; if done without precautions, Galeona might find herself minus her limbs and her head—all before he finally let her die.

And that made her consider at last something new.

He who wore Bartuc's armor certainly looked to be a warrior, a fighter, and, as she had also described him, a simple man, too. In other words, a fool. Galeona knew well how to manipulate such. As a man, he would be defenseless against her charms; as a fool, he would never realize that fact.

She would have to see how matters went with both the general and Xazax. If it seemed one or the other still worked to her advantage, Galeona would do what she could to tip the balance that way. Malevolyn with the armor his to command could certainly deal with her shadowy partner. However, if Xazax gained the ensorcelled artifacts first, truly he would be the one to follow.

Still, the stranger remained a possibility. Certainly he could be led around by the nose, told what to do. He presented potential where the other two presented risk.

Yes, Galeona intended to keep an eye on this fool for her own good. He would be far more susceptible to her desires than an ambitious and slightly mad military commander—and certainly far less dangerous than a *demon*.

Three

Blood.

"By all that's holy, Norrec? What've you done?"

"Norrec. My friend. Perhaps you should take off that glove."

Blood.

"Damn you! Damn you!"

"Sa-Sadun! His wrist! Cut—"

Blood everywhere.

"Norrec! For god's sake! My arm!"

"Norrec!"

"Norrec!"

The blood of those closest to him. . . .

"Nooo!"

Norrec raised his head, screaming before he even knew he had awakened. A chill wind snapped him to full consciousness and for the first time he noticed the intense pain in his right cheek. Without thinking much, he put a hand to that cheek.

Cold metal brushed his skin. With a start, Norrec looked at the hand—a hand clothed in a crimson gauntlet, a reddish liquid now staining the fingertips.

Blood.

With great trepidation, he returned his hand to his cheek, touching the flesh with one finger now. By that means, Norrec discovered that he bled in three places. Three valleys had been gouged in his cheek, as if some animal had clawed him.

"Norrec!"

A flash of memory sent shivers through the veteran. Sadun's face, contorted in fear not witnessed by Norrec outside of the most horrible field of battle. Sadun's eyes pleading, his mouth open but no more words escaping.

Sadun's hand . . . tearing desperately at his friend's face.

"No . . ." It could not be as Norrec remembered it.

Another image.

Fauztin on the floor of the tomb, blood pooling on the stones nearby, its source the gaping hole where the Vizjerei's throat had once been.

The sorcerer, at least, had died relatively quickly.

"No . . . no . . . no . . ." Growing more horrified by the moment, the half-mad soldier struggled to his feet. Around him he noticed tall hills, even mountains, and the first glimmers of sunlight. Yet, none of them looked at all familiar. None of them at all resembled the peak in which he and his friends had discovered the tomb of Bartuc. Norrec took a step forward, trying to get his bearings.

An unsettling creaking accompanied every motion.

Norrec looked down to discover that not only his hands were clad in metal.

Armor. Everywhere he stared, Norrec only saw the same blood-colored metal plates. He had thought that his shock and horror could not possibly grow worse, but simply gazing at the rest of his body nearly threw the formerly steady soldier into complete panic. His arms, his torso, his legs, the same crimson armor now hid all. To add to the mockery, Norrec saw that he even wore Bartuc's ancient but still serviceable leather boots.

Bartuc . . . Warlord of Blood. Bartuc, whose dark magic had apparently saved the helpless soldier at the price of Sadun and the sorcerer's lives.

"Damn you!" Gazing down at his hands again, Norrec tore at the gauntlets. He tugged as hard as he could on first the left, then the right. Yet, regardless of

which Norrec sought to remove, the metal gloves slid no more than an inch before seeming to catch.

He peered within and, after seeing no impediment, tried once more—but still the gauntlets would not come off. Worse, as the sun rose, for the first time Norrec could see that the blood from his injured cheek had not been the only stains upon the metal. Each finger, even most of each palm, looked as if it had been bathed in a rich, red dye.

But it was not dye that covered them.

"Fauztin," he murmured. "Sadun . . ."

With a roar of outrage, Norrec swung one fist at the nearest rocks, perfectly willing to break every bone in his hand if only it would mean the release of his hand. Instead, though, the rock itself gave way in part, the only damage to Norrec being a violent throbbing throughout his entire arm.

He dropped to his knees. "Nooo . . ."

The wind howled, seeming to mock him. Norrec remained where he was, head cast down, arms dangling. Fragments of what had happened in the tomb flashed through his mind, each painting a scene most diabolic. Sadun and Fauztin, both dead . . . both dead by his hands.

Norrec's head jerked up again. Not exactly by his hands. The damned gauntlets, one of which had saved him from the ghoulish sentinels, had done this. Norrec still blamed himself much for those deaths, for perhaps he might have altered matters if he had removed the first gauntlet immediately, but by himself he would have never slaughtered his friends.

There had to be a way to remove the gloves, even if he had to peel them off piece by piece, taking some of his skin off with the metal.

Determined to do something for himself, the veteran fighter rose again, trying to better identify his surroundings. Unfortunately, he saw little more now than he had on first glance. Mountains and hills. Forest stretching to the north. No sign of habitation, not even a distant plume of smoke.

And, again, nothing resembling the peak in which Bartuc's tomb lay.

"Where in Hell—" He broke off quickly, uneasy at even mentioning that dark and supposedly mythic realm. Even as a child and certainly as a soldier, Norrec had never believed much in either demons or angels, but the horror to which he had been a part had changed some of his opinions. Whether or not demons and angels truly existed, the Warlord of Blood had certainly left a monstrous legacy—a legacy of which Norrec hoped to rid himself quickly.

Hoping that perhaps he had simply been too upset the first time he had tried to remove the gauntlets, Norrec decided to inspect them in yet greater detail. However, as he looked down, he made yet another horrific discovery.

Not only did blood soil the gloves, but it did so the breastplate, too. Worse, on closer study, Norrec saw that the blood had not accidentally splattered the armor but had been purposively and methodically spread across it.

Again he shuddered. Quickly returning to the gauntlets, he sought some latch, some catch, even some dent that might have caused the gloves to stick. Nothing. Nothing held the gauntlets fast. By rights, they should have slid off his hands with a simple shake toward the ground.

The armor. If he could not remove the gauntlets, surely he could unfasten the other pieces. Some had catches readily seen and even with the gauntlets he surely would not have that much trouble undoing them. Other pieces would not have any catches, having been simply designed to slide on and off . . .

Bending down, Norrec tried one leg. He fumbled at the catches at first, then saw how best to secure his hold. With great care, the soldier forced the catch open.

And immediately it snapped shut.

He forced it open again, only to have the same result. Norrec cursed, attempting the catch a third time.

This time, it would not even open.

Attempting several others resulted in the same frustrating results. Worse, when he tried to at least remove the boots—that despite the cold—they, like the gauntlets, slid only so far before refusing to give way.

"This can't be possible . . ." Norrec tugged harder, but again with no visible success.

Madness! These were only garments, pieces of metal and a pair of old if sturdy boots! They had to come off!

Norrec's desperation rose. He was a common man, a man who believed that the sun rose in the morning and the moon at night. Birds flew and fish swam. People wore clothes—but clothes never wore people!

He glared at the bloody palms. "What do you *want* of me? What do you *want*?"

No sepulchral voice arose from around him, telling him of his dark fate. The gauntlets did not suddenly draw words or symbols in the earth. The armor simply would not let go of its new wearer.

Scattered images of his companions' gruesome ends once more tumbled about in his thoughts, making it hard for Norrec to focus. Norrec prayed—pleaded—for them to go away, but suspected that they would forever torment him.

Yet, if he could never be rid of the nightmares, there still might be something he could do about the cursed suit he wore. Fauztin had been a sorcerer of some reputation, but even the Vizjerei had admitted that there were many practitioners more skilled, more knowledgeable, than he.

Norrec would just have to find one of them.

He looked east, then west. To the east he saw nothing but tall and menacing mountains, whereas the west seemed a bit more gentle in scope. True, Norrec knew he might be working under false assumptions, but his best hope, he decided, had to be the latter direction.

The cold wind and moisture already chilling him to the bone, the weary veteran started off on his tremendous trek. It might be that he would die of exposure before he even made it out of the mountains, but some part of him suspected that such would not be so. Bartuc's armor had not seized him simply to let him die in the middle of the wilderness. No, it likely had some other notion in mind, one that would make itself known with time.

Norrec did not look forward to that revelation at all.

The sun vanished into an overcast sky, turning the weather even colder. A wetness also hung in the air. Breathing heavily, Norrec pushed on despite everything. As of yet he had not so much as seen a glimpse to hint that he traveled the right direction. For all the weary veteran knew, he had headed in the exact opposite of where he should have gone. Some mountain kingdom could have been just past the next peak to the east.

Thoughts like that, however frustrating, managed to keep Norrec from completely going mad. Each time he let his thoughts wander, they ever returned to the tomb and the horror of which he had been a part. Fauztin's and Sadun's faces haunted him and every now and then Norrec imagined he saw the pair condemning him from this shadow or that.

But they were dead and, unlike the bloody warlord, they would stay so. Only Norrec's guilt continued to condemn him.

Around midday, he began to stumble. It finally occurred to him that he had neither eaten nor drunk since waking and the day before he had last supped early. Unless he planned to fall over soon and die, Norrec had to find sustenance of some sort.

But how? He had no weapon, no trap. Water he could find simply by scooping up some of the snow topping the nearby rocks, but actual food looked to be hard to come by.

Deciding he could at least assuage his thirst, Norrec walked over to a small outcropping where the coolness of the shadows had kept a small bit of snow and ice still unmelted. He scooped up what he could and greedily sucked on it, not caring at all about the bits of dust and grass that came with it.

In moments, his head seemed to clear a bit. Spitting out a few fragments of dirt, Norrec pondered what to do next. Not once had he seen any wild animal other than a bird. Without a bow or slingshot, he had no chance to bring down one of the creatures. Yet, he needed food—

His left hand suddenly moved without any regard as to his wishes. The fingers separated and bent inward, almost as if now Norrec clutched an invisible sphere. The gauntleted hand then turned until the palm faced the landscape just before the stunned fighter.

From his lips burst a single word, *"Jezrat!"*

The ground a few feet ahead buckled. Norrec at first thought that a tremor had struck the area, but only a small crevice, perhaps six feet by three, actually formed. The rest of his surroundings did not so much as shiver in the slightest.

His nose wrinkled as noxious fumes arose from the minute but apparently deep fissure. The air burned where yellow tendrils of smoke spread.

"Iskari! Woyut!" The new words came out of his own mouth with great ferocity.

From within the fissure came a horrid, chattering sound. Norrec sought to back up, but his feet would not move. The chattering increased, now a babble of high-pitched, animalistic sounds.

Norrec barely stifled a gasp as a grotesque tusked face thrust itself somewhat unwillingly into the overcast day. A pair of jagged, curved horns rose from the top of the scaly head. Round, yellow orbs with blazing red pupils shied away from the sky, finally focusing with clear bitterness on the human. The creature's squat, porcine nose twitched as if smelling something terrible—something that the fighter realized likely was him.

Twin sets of three-digited talons seized hold of the sides of the fissure as the horrific beast pushed itself up to the surface. Squat, oversized feet with curved nails planted themselves on the ground. Norrec stared down at a thing surely out of the underworld, a vaguely humanoid, hunchbacked denizen of the depths who, while barely reaching his waist, revealed surprising muscle under skin both scaled and furred.

And then a second of the creatures joined the first . . . . he immediately followed by a third, a fourth, a fifth . . .

The frightful pack ceased growing in numbers after the sixth, a half a dozen more than Norrec certainly desired. The demonic imps chattered in their incomprehensible language, obviously upset with being here and very clear upon whom they blamed this entire situation. A few opened toothy maws and hissed at Norrec, while others simply scowled.

"Gester! Iskari!" The strange words once more startled him, but their effect on the monstrous pack proved even more astonishing. All signs of defiance faded abruptly as the imps groveled before him, some fairly burying themselves in the ground to prove how lowly they were.

"Dovru Sesti! Dovru Sesti!"

Whatever the phrase meant, it sent the horned brutes scurrying in outright panic. Squealing and chattering, they headed off in different directions as if their very lives depended upon it.

Norrec exhaled. Each time unknown words sprang from his lips, it felt as if his heart stopped. The language sounded akin to that used by Fauztin and other Vizjerei with whom the veteran had made acquaintance over the years, but it also sounded harsher, darker, than anything Norrec's murdered friend had ever spouted, even in the worst of battles.

He had no time to think any more on the subject, for suddenly chattering arose in the distance. Norrec peered to the south, saw two of the monstrosities loping back—the bloody, torn remains of a goat dragging behind them.

He had been hungry and now the suit provided him with its idea of sustenance.

Norrec blanched at the sight of the carcass. He had, of course, often slaughtered animals for food, but the imps had taken some delight in capturing and slaying the unfortunate goat. The head had nearly been ripped from the body and the legs dangled as if all broken. A portion of the goat's flank had been torn away, the blood flowing from that massive wound leaving a stream of crimson behind.

The grotesque creatures dropped the animal in front of Norrec, then backed away. Even as they did so, a third member of their pack returned, this one carrying a small, bloody carcass with vague similarities to a rabbit.

Eyeing the grisly offerings, the wary veteran looked for anything he himself might still consider edible. Exceptional hunters the tusked beasts might be, but their handling left much to be desired.

The other three imps returned within moments, each bearing their own prizes. One, a tattered-looking lizard, Norrec immediately dismissed. The others, a pair of rabbits, he finally chose in preference to what had been first given to him.

As he reached for them, his left hand again rebelled. The gauntlet passed over the rabbits and as it did, incredible heat threatened to sear Norrec's fingers.

"Damn you!" He managed to stumble back a step. The heat faded quickly again, but his hand still throbbed from the near burning. From where they gathered, the imps chattered, this time sounding quite amused at his discomfort. However, a quick and furious glance silenced them.

His hand nearly normal again, Norrec returned his attention to the rabbits— and found them completely cooked. The scent that arose from them even smelled of certain spices, all enticing.

"So . . . don't think I'm going to thank you for this," he muttered to no one in particular.

Hunger overtaking his good sense, the graying warrior tore into the surprisingly well-prepared meat. He devoured not only one, but both rabbits with great ease. Large, they eventually silenced the cry in his stomach, leaving him to ponder what to do with the rest. Norrec waited, expecting the suit to make the decision for him, but nothing happened.

The pack still watched him, but their gazes often slipped to the meat, finally giving Norrec his own answer. He raised his hand, indicated the goat and the other slaughtered creatures, and waved toward the imps.

They needed no further invitation. With a manic glee that made the seasoned veteran push away, the tiny horde fell upon the meat. They tore into the flesh, sending gobbets and blood flying everywhere. Norrec's own meal grew queasy in his stomach as he watched the demons strip the bones of anything they could devour. He imagined those same claws and teeth on him . . .

"*Verash!*" So disturbed by the sight before him, Norrec barely reacted to the harsh word bursting from his mouth.

The imps recoiled as if struck. Cowed, they seized what remained of the goat's carcass and dragged it toward the fissure. With some effort, the grotesque creatures deposited the remains in the crevice, then, one by one, followed after it.

The last gave the human a quick and highly curious glance, then vanished into the bowels of the earth.

Before Norrec's wondering eyes, the crevice sealed itself, leaving no trace of its existence.

Walking dead. Haunted armor. Demons from the underworld. Norrec had witnessed magic in the past, even heard tales of dark creatures, but nothing could have ever prepared him for all that had happened since he had first entered that cave. He wished that he could go back and change events, make the decision to leave the tomb before the guardians had risen to slay his band, but Norrec knew he could no more do that than peel the cursed suit from his body.

He needed rest. The trek had been an arduous one and with food in his stomach the desire to go on had faded, at least for the time being. Better to sleep, then continue on refreshed. Perhaps his thoughts would also clear, enable him to better think how to extricate himself from this terrifying situation.

Norrec leaned back, stretching out. After so many years on the battlefield, any spot served as good as another when it came to finding a bed. The armor would make matters uncomfortable, but the tired soldier had suffered worse in that respect.

"What in—?"

His arms and legs pushed him back up to a standing position. Norrec tried to sit down, but no part of his body beneath his neck obeyed.

His arms dropped, swinging from the shoulders as if every muscle had been cut. Norrec's left foot stepped forward; his right followed after.

"I can't go on, damn you! I need some rest!"

The suit cared not a whit, picking up the pace. Left. Right. Left. Right.

"An hour! Two at the most! That's all I need!"

His words echoed uselessly through the mountains and hills. Left. Right. Whether the hapless veteran liked it or not, he would continue his arduous journey.

But to where?

This should never have happened, Kara nervously thought. *By the will of Rathma, this should never have happened!*

The emerald sphere that she had conjured earlier in order to see gave the entire tableau an even more unsettling appearance. Her face, already pale in color, paled further. Kara pulled her lengthy black cloak about her, taking some comfort from its warmth. Under thick lashes, silver, almond-shaped eyes surveyed a scene that her masters surely could never have envisioned. *The tomb is forever safe,* they had always insisted. *Where Vizjerei elemental sorcery falters, our own trusted skills will make the difference.*

But now both the more materialistic Vizjerei and the pragmatic followers of Rathma had apparently failed in their trust. That which they had sought to forever bury from the sight of men had not only been discovered, but had actually been stolen.

Or was there more to it? How powerful could the intruders have been to not only eliminate the undead guardians, but also shatter the unbreakable wards?

Not so powerful that two of them had not died in very violent fashion. Moving with such grace that she seemed almost to glide, the black-clad woman went to the nearest of the corpses. Kara leaned down and, after pushing back several tresses of lengthy, raven-colored hair, inspected the remains.

A wiry man, a battle-scarred war veteran. From one of the distant western lands. Not a pleasant-looking man, even before someone had completely twisted his head around and nearly torn off his arm. The dagger in his chest, surely an exercise in excess, looked to be his own. Which had killed him, even the necromancer could not say—not yet. The gaping wound had bled well, but not as much as it normally should have. Yet, why cut the victim open after snapping his neck?

As silent as death, the slim but curvaceous young woman made her way to the other body. This one she immediately recognized as a Vizjerei, which did not surprise her in the least. Always meddling, always seeking methods by which to gain advantage over one another, the Vizjerei made untrustworthy allies at best. If not for them, this entire situation would never have occurred. Bartuc and his brother had followed the early teachings of the Vizjerei, especially their reckless use of demons for more powerful spells of sorcery. Bartuc had especially excelled in that respect, but his constant interactions with the dark ones had twisted his own thinking, making him believe that demons were his allies. They, in turn, had fed off his growing evil, kindred spirits from both the mortal and infernal planes.

And although Horazon and his fellow mages had slain Bartuc and defeated his demon host, they had found it impossible to destroy the warlord's very corpse. The armor, known to bear several sinister enchantments, had continued to try to serve its function, protecting its master even in death. Only the fact that Bartuc had failed to cover his throat properly had even allowed his foes to decapitate the villain in the first place.

Left with a head and torso that they could not readily burn, the Vizjerei had come to Kara's own people, searching the dense jungles for the reclusive practitioners of a sorcery that balanced life and death, a sorcery that caused their wielders to be branded *necromancer*. Together the two diverse orders worked hard to make certain that Bartuc's remains forever vanished from the face of the world, hopefully even the warlord's enchantments fading to nothing with time.

Kara touched the crimson-soaked throat of the dead sorcerer, noting how most of it had been ripped away with a savageness beyond that of most animals. Unlike the fighter, the mage had died very quickly if still brutally. His eyes stared up at her, the horror of what had happened to him still evident. His expression remained a mix of shock and disbelief, almost . . . almost as if he could not believe who his murderer had been.

Yet, how could some force slay a Vizjerei and still fail to stop the other thieves? Had they just been fortunate, barely escaping? Kara frowned; with the undead guardians gone and the wards shattered, *what* had remained that could have hunted the intruders? What?

She wished the others had come with her, but that had not been possible. They had been needed elsewhere—*everywhere,* it seemed. A general ground swelling of forces so very dark had been sensed not only throughout Kehjistan, but also Scosglen. The faithful of Rathma had been spread thinner than in any other period of their existence.

And that left only her, one of the youngest and less-tested of her faith. True, like most of those who followed the path of Rathma, she had been trained to be independent almost from birth, but now Kara felt she entered territory for which no amount of teaching or experience could have prepared her.

Perhaps . . . perhaps though, this Vizjerei could still teach her something about what she now faced.

From her belt, Kara removed a delicate-looking but highly resilient dagger, the blade of which had been fashioned in a back-and-forth serpentine manner. Both the blade and the handle had been carved from purest ivory, but there again appearances deceived. Kara would have willingly pitted her own knife against any other, knowing full well that the enchantments placed on it made it stronger and more accurate than most normal weapons.

With neither distaste nor eagerness, the necromancer touched the point to one of the bloodiest areas on the dead Vizjerei's ravaged throat. She turned the blade over and over until the tip had been completely covered. Then, holding the dagger hilt down, Kara muttered her spell.

The deep red splotches on the tip flared bright. She muttered a few more words, concentrating.

The splotches began to change, to grow. They moved as if alive—or remembering life.

Kara, called Nightshadow by her teachers, flipped the dagger over, then thrust the point into the floor.

The blade sank in halfway, not at all impeded by the hard rock surface. Stepping back quickly, Kara watched as the ivory dagger became engulfed by the swelling splotches, which then melded together, creating a vaguely *human* form little taller than the weapon.

Drawing patterns in the air, the necromancer uttered the second and final part of her incantation.

In a blaze of red light, a full-sized figure materialized where the ivory dagger had stood. Completely crimson from head to toe, skin to garments, he stared at her with vacant eyes. He wore the clothes of a Vizjerei sorcerer, the same clothes, in fact, that the corpse on the floor behind him wore.

Kara eagerly beheld the phantasm bearing the likeness of the dead mage. She had done this only once before and under conditions much more favorable. What stood before her most mortals would have called a ghost, a spirit—but in doing so they would have been only partially correct. Drawn forth from the life's blood of the victim, it indeed bore some traces of the dead's spirit, but to fully summon a true specter would have taken more time and trouble and Kara had to act in haste now. This phantasm would surely serve to answer her questions.

"Name yourself!" she demanded.

The mouth moved but no sound came from it. Nonetheless, an answer formed in her mind.

Fauztin . . .

"What happened here?"

The phantasm stared, but did not answer. Kara cursed herself for a fool, realizing that it could only answer questions in a simple way. Taking a breath, she asked, "Did you destroy the undead?"

Some . . .

"Who destroyed the rest?"

Hesitation, then . . . *Norrec.*

Norrec? The name meant nothing to her. "A Vizjerei? A sorcerer?"

To her surprise, the spectral form shook his crimson head ever so slightly. *Norrec . . . Vizharan . . .*

The name again. The last part, *Vizharan,* meant *servant of the Vizjerei* in the old tongue, but that information helped Kara little. This path led her nowhere. She turned to a different and far more important subject. "Did this Norrec take the armor from the dais?"

And again the phantasm shook his head ever so slightly. Kara frowned, recalling nothing in her teachings mentioning this. Perhaps Vizjerei made for more unusual summonings. She pondered her next question with care. With the limitations of the phantasm, the necromancer realized that she could spend all day and night asking and yet still receive no knowledge of value to her mission. Kara would have to—

A sound came from the passage behind her.

The young enchantress whirled about. For just the briefest of moments, she thought she saw a slight bluish light deep within, but it vanished so quickly that Kara had to wonder if she had imagined it. It could have simply been a glow bug or some other insect, but . . .

Cautiously approaching the tunnel, Kara warily peered into the darkness. Had she been too hasty in heading directly to the main chamber? Could this Norrec have been hiding outside, waiting for someone to come?

Absurd, but Kara *had* heard a noise. Of that she felt certain.

And at that moment, she heard it again, this time much farther into the passage.

Muttering a spell, Kara formed a second emerald sphere, which she immediately sent fluttering down the rocky corridor. As it darted along, the dark-haired woman followed after for a few steps, trying to make out what she could.

Still no sign of another intruder, but Kara could not take a chance. Anyone who could so readily slay a Vizjerei certainly offered deadly threat. She could not simply ignore the possibility. Taking a deep breath, the necromancer started down the rocky passage—

—and froze a moment later, swearing at herself for her carelessness. Kara had left her prized dagger behind, and she dared not face a possible foe without it. Not only did it provide her with protection both in the mundane and magical senses, but by leaving it behind, the dark mage even risked possibly losing it to whomever might be stalking the tomb.

She quickly stepped back into the chamber, already preparing in her mind the spell to dismiss the phantasm, only to find that the crimson figure had *already* vanished.

Kara managed but one more step before a further realization struck her just as hard. With the phantasm had vanished her precious *dagger,* yet that alone did not leave her now wide-eyed and unable to even speak.

Both the body of the sorcerer Fauztin and his slighter companion had also disappeared.

FOUR

The sand snake wound swiftly along the shifting desert, its constant undulations keeping the heat of the ground from burning it underneath. Hunting had been poor today but with the sun rising higher, the time had come, like it or not, for the snake to temporarily seek shelter. When the sun had descended some it could come out again, this time hopefully to snag a mouse or beetle. One could not go long in the desert without food, where hunting had always been a difficult business.

Pushing itself hard, the snake traveled up the latest dune, aware that only minutes separated it from shade. Once over this one impediment, it would be home free.

The sand beneath the snake suddenly erupted.

Mandibles more than a foot in length snapped tight around the midsection of the serpent. The snake flailed desperately, trying to slither out. A monstrous head burst through the sand, followed by the first pair of needlelike legs.

Still struggling, the snake struck at its attacker, hissing and trying to use its venom. The fangs, however, could not penetrate the chitinous exoskeleton of the huge arthropod.

One leg pinned down the rear half of the snake. The beetlelike head of the massive predator twisted sharply, at the same time the mandibles squeezing tight.

Flailing, the bloody front half of the serpent dropped to the ground, the head still hissing.

The black and red arthropod emerged completely from its hiding place, turning now to the process of dragging its meal to where it could eat in leisure. With its front appendages, the nearly seven-foot long predator began prodding the back half of the serpent.

A shadow suddenly loomed over the hideous creature. Immediately it turned its bulky head and spat at the new intruder.

The corrosive poison splattered against the somewhat ragged silk robe of a bearded and rather wild-eyed elderly man. From above a long, almost beaklike nose, he gazed down briefly at the sizzling mess, then waved one gnarled hand over it. As he did this, the acidic poison and the damage it had already caused completely vanished.

Watery blue eyes focused on the savage insect.

Plumes of smoke arose from the exoskeleton. The beetlelike creature let out a high-pitched squeal, its spindly legs teetering. It tried to flee, but its body seemed no longer to work. The legs buckled and the body crumpled. Parts of the monstrous insect began to drip away, as if the creature was no longer made of shell and flesh, but rather runny wax now melting in the hot sun.

The squealing arthropod collapsed in a molten heap. The mandibles, so deadly to the snake, dissolved into a pool of black liquid that readily sank into the sand. The cries of the dying creature finally cut off and, as the ragged figure watched, what remained of the once-savage predator utterly vanished, draining away like the few drops of rain that annually sought to soothe this parched land.

"Sand maggot. Too many of them about now. So much evil about every-where," the white-haired patriarch muttered to himself. "So much evil even out here. I must be careful, must be very careful."

He walked past the savaged snake and its just as unfortunate pursuer, heading to another dune just a short distance away. As the bearded hermit neared, the dune suddenly swelled, growing higher and higher, finally form-ing a doorway within that seemed to lead directly into the underworld itself.

Watery blue eyes turned to survey the oppressive landscape. A momentary shiver ran through the elderly man.

"So much evil . . . I must definitely be careful."

He descended into the dune. The sand immediately began to pull inward the moment he passed through the entrance, filling the passage behind in rapid fashion until no sign remained at all of any opening.

And as the dune settled to normal again, the desert winds continued their shifting of the rest of the landscape, the snake and the sand maggot already joining countless other hapless denizens in a dusty, forgotten burial.

The mountains lay far behind him, although how he had journeyed so far Norrec only half-recalled. At some point he had passed out from exhaustion, but evidently the suit had gone on and on. Despite the fact that none of the effort had actually been his own, every muscle in the veteran's body screamed and every bone felt as if it had broken. His lips were parched from the wind while sweat covered much of his body. Norrec yearned to peel off the armor and run free, but knew the hopelessness of that dream. The armor would do with him as it chose.

And now he stood atop a ridge, staring at the first sign of civilization he had seen in many a day. An unsavory inn, a place that more befitted brigands and highwaymen rather than honest warriors such as himself. However, with darkness about to befall and Norrec nearly done in, the suit seemed to finally register that it had to once more deal with the frailties of its human host.

He marched without desiring to toward the building. Three glum horses stood tethered nearby and at least one more sounded its displeasure from a wretched stable just beyond. Norrec found himself wishing that he had his sword; the armor had not bothered to take that when it had walked out of the tomb with him.

Just before he reached the doorway, the veteran's legs suddenly buckled under him. Norrec quickly caught himself, realizing that Bartuc's damnable armor had granted him the dubious gift of entering on his own, likely in order to avoid notice of anything strange.

Hunger and rest more important to Norrec at the moment than his own pride, the soldier pushed the door wide open. Grimy, suspicious faces looked up, the onlookers a mixture not only of the eastern races, but those on the other side of the Twin Seas as well. Mongrels, all four of them, Norrec saw, and although he certainly held no man's background against him, this group did not look at all like men next to whom he desired to sit.

Kind of place where you gotta watch your back even around the serving wench! Sadun Tryst would have jested. Tryst, of course, would have sat with anyone who would have offered him a drink.

But Sadun was dead.

"Shut the door or go back out!" snarled the one seated nearest.

Norrec obeyed, desiring no confrontations. Forcing himself to act as if he had just ridden in, the weary fighter kept his head high as he walked smartly through the room. His body screamed as he moved, but no one there would know of it. Give these men even the slightest hint of weakness and Norrec suspected that they would make dire use of that fact.

He approached what he assumed to be the innkeeper, a towering heavy-set figure more frightful than his patrons, who stood behind a worn and scratched counter. A bush of dirty brown hair fought its way from under an old travel cap. Beady eyes stared from a round, canine face. Norrec had noted a peculiar odor in the room when he had first entered and now he knew it to originate from the man before him.

Had he thought that the armor would let him leave, Norrec would have walked right out regardless of his needs.

"What?" the innkeeper finally muttered, scratching his extravagant belly.

His shirt had been decorated with a variety of stains and even a rip under the arm.

"I need food." That, more than anything else, Norrec had to have quickly.

"I need good coin."

Coin. The desperate soldier fought back growing frustration. Another item that had been left behind with the bloodied corpses of his companions.

His left hand suddenly shot forward, the gauntlet slapping down so hard on the counter that the innkeeper jumped. The men seated at the tables leapt to their feet, some reaching for weapons.

The gauntlet pulled away . . . leaving behind an old but clearly *gold* coin.

Recovering before the rest, Norrec said, "And a room for that, too."

He could feel every pair of eyes avidly staring at the coin. Once more Norrec silently cursed the damnable armor. If it could produce wealth from thin air, it could have at least produced something less conspicuous than gold. Again he wished that he still carried his sword or at least a good, solid knife.

"Got some stew in the pot back there." With a tip of his head the ursine giant indicated the kitchen. "Got a room up the second floor. First on the right."

"I'll eat in there."

"Suit yourself."

The innkeeper vanished in back for a few moments, then returned with a stained bowl containing something that smelled even worse than he did. Nevertheless, Norrec gratefully accepted it, his hunger so demanding now that, if offered to him again, he would have even eaten the goat the imps had mutilated.

With the bowl in the crook of his arm, Norrec followed the innkeeper's directions to the room. As he walked up the creaking wooden stairway, he heard low muttering down in the common area. His free hand tightened. The gold coin had burned itself into the minds of the men below.

The room proved as dismal as the veteran had expected, a dark, dusty closet with a window so grimy it gave no view of the outside. The bed looked ready to collapse and what had once been white sheets now were permanently gray. The single oil lamp shed barely enough light to illuminate its immediate surroundings, much less the rest of the room.

With no table or chair in the place, Norrec gingerly sat on the bed and began spooning the contents of the bowl into his mouth. If anything, it tasted more vile than he could have imagined, but seemed at least fresh enough not to kill him.

The need to sleep grew more urgent as food filled his stomach. Norrec had to struggle to remain awake long enough to finish and the moment he had the bowl emptied, he dropped it gently on the floor and settled back. In the back of his mind, Norrec continued to worry about those below him, but exhaustion soon overcame even that significant concern.

And as he drifted off to sleep, Norrec began to dream.

He saw himself shouting commands at an infernal army of grotesque horrors his imagination could have never created on its own. Scaled, fiery, nightmarish abominations thirsting for blood—blood Norrec seemed all too willing to give them. Demons they were, but under his complete control. They would raze cities for him, slaughter the inhabitants in his name. Even Hell respected the power of the Warlord of Blood, he . . . *Bartuc.*

At that thought, the soldier finally fought to escape the dream. He could never be Bartuc! Never demand such horror for the sake of his own desires! Never!

Yet such absolute power had its seductive side.

Norrec's internal battle with himself thankfully came to an abrupt halt as a noise suddenly awoke him. Eyes flashing open, he listened for more. What he had heard, the fighter could not say. A small, somewhat insignificant sound, but one that had registered even in his subconscious.

He heard it again, just barely audible through the closed door. The creak of someone slowly and, it seemed, very cautiously ascending.

There were other rooms, true, but the men below had hardly struck Norrec as so polite that they would tread so carefully in order not to disturb him. Had they tromped up the steps without concern, he would have thought nothing of it. However, such caution indicated to the soldier that perhaps they had something else in mind, something not at all to his liking.

If a weary traveler had *one* gold coin, surely he had more . . .

Norrec's hand slipped to where his sword should have been. No hope there. That left him entirely dependent on the armor itself, not necessarily a path he could trust. Perhaps the suit would find one of the thieves more to its liking, opening the way for the soldier's easy slaughter . . .

The creaking ceased.

Norrec pushed himself up as silently as he could.

Two men with drawn knives broke through the dilapidated door, instantly diving toward the figure before them. From behind the pair came a third villain, this one wielding a curved short sword. Each of the attackers matched the rising fighter in height as well as in muscle, and they had the advantage of trapping him in a room with a window too small for Norrec to try to fit through.

He raised a fist, ready to make them pay—

And the fist suddenly held a long, sable sword with wicked teeth set in the edge. Norrec's hand came down with the blade, moving so swiftly that he and his first adversary could only gape.

The blade ripped into the attacker, tearing flesh and sinew without effort. A gaping wound spread across the robber's entire chest as if by magic, blood spilling so fast from it that it took the victim a moment to realize he had been slain.

The first attacker finally slumped to the floor even as his companions came to grips with this sudden, dismaying turn of events. The one with the dagger sought to back away, but his partner pushed forward, daring to match blades. Norrec might have warned the brigand of the foolishness of that, but by then they were locked in combat.

Once, twice—that proved to be all the effort the suit would allow its opponent. As the intruder brought his sword up for a third strike, Norrec's gauntleted hand twisted sharply. The sable blade turned in a mad, zig-zag fashion.

His life fluids spilling from a horrendous slit running from his throat to his waist, the second villain staggered. He dropped his sword as he desperately tried to prevent the inevitable.

As if impatient to end matters, Norrec's hand came up again.

The head of his foe struck the floor, rolling to a corner and coming to rest— all before the torso even began to tip over.

"Gods!" the soldier managed to gasp. He had been trained to fight, not to slaughter.

Clearly aware of what chance he had, the third intruder had already hurried to the doorway. Norrec wanted to let him go, desiring no more bloodshed, but the suit chose otherwise, leaping over the two bodies and chasing after.

At the bottom of the steps, the last of the trio struggled to get around the innkeeper, who appeared to be demanding to know why his friends had failed in their task. Both men looked up to see the crimson figure above them, the dark blade flaring. The innkeeper drew a prodigious long sword from his waist, a weapon so massive Norrec momentarily feared that the suit had overestimated its invulnerability. The other man tried to continue his flight, but a fifth outlaw who suddenly appeared from behind the innkeeper pushed him back toward the fray.

If they expected to meet him on the stairs, they were sorely mistaken. Norrec found himself leaping feet first toward the trio, their astonished faces no doubt matching his own. Two of them managed to back away just in time, but the lone survivor of the earlier debacle stood too horrified to move quickly.

The sinister weapon made short work of him, the blade pushing through until it came out the back, then immediately retracting.

"His right!" snarled the heavy-set innkeeper. "His right!"

The other swordsman obeyed. Norrec knew exactly what the leader planned. Attack from opposite sides, keep the soldier distracted. One of them would surely land a blow, especially the innkeeper, whose weapon had nearly twice the reach of the black one.

"Now!" Both men struck at once, one aiming for Norrec's throat, the other for his legs, where the armor did not cover everywhere. These two had evidently battled side-by-side before, just as Norrec had with Sadun and Fauztin. Had it been his effort alone, the soldier knew that he would have perished there and then. Bartuc's armor, however, fought with a speed and accuracy that nothing human could match. Not only did it force down the larger adversary's gargantuan blade, but it also managed to come up in time to deflect the second villain's strike. More amazing, it followed through with a savage thrust that sank into the throat of the latter man.

And as his companion fell, the innkeeper's iron reserve suddenly melted. Still wielding his sword before him, he began to back toward the doorway. The suit pushed Norrec forward, but did not harry the last of its foes.

Flinging open the door, the innkeeper turned and fled into the night. Now Norrec expected Bartuc's armor to pursue, but instead the suit turned around and marched him over to where one of the other bodies lay. As Norrec knelt beside the corpse, the sable blade dissolved, leaving both hands free.

To his horror, one gauntleted finger thrust into the mortal wound, pulling back only when blood covered much of the upper portion of the digit. Moving to the wooden floor, the finger drew a pattern.

"Heyat tokaris!" his mouth suddenly blurted. *"Heyat grendel!"*

The suit backed away and as it did, a plume of rank, greenish smoke arose from the bloody pattern. It quickly formed arms, legs—and tail and wings. A reptilian visage with too many eyes blinked in disdain, disdain that vanished when the demon saw what stood before him.

"Warrrlorrrd . . ." it rasped. The bulbous eyes looked closer. "Warrrlorrrd?"

"Heskar, grendel! Heskar!"

The demon nodded. Without another word, the monstrous being headed toward the open door. In the distance, Norrec heard the frantic beats of several fleeing horses.

"Heskar!" his mouth demanded again.

The reptilian horror picked up its pace, departing the inn. As it stepped outside, it spread its wings and took off, disappearing into the night.

Norrec did not have to guess its purpose. On the command of Bartuc, it had gone hunting.

"Don't do it," he whispered, now certain that whatever spirit lurked within the armor could hear him. "Let him go!"

The suit turned back toward the first corpse.

"Damn it! Leave him be! He's not worth it!"

Seemingly ignorant to his pleas, it forced him again to bend down near the body. The hand that had earlier touched the wound with but one finger now planted all of them there, letting the blood stain the entire palm.

Outside, a frantic human scream rose high—then cut off with harsh finality.

In Norrec's other hand, a new weapon appeared, this time a scarlet dagger with a double point at the end.

The flapping of wings warned him of the demon's return, but Norrec could not twist his neck enough to see. He heard the heavy breathing of the creature and even the folding of its leathery wings as it settled down in the common room.

"Nestu veraki . . ." The dagger shifted toward the corpse's throat. *"Nestu ver-akuu . . ."*

The veteran soldier shut his eyes, now praying for himself. Enough of his memories concerning his friends' deaths had come back to him to give him indication of what would happen next. Norrec had no desire to face it, would have fled if he could.

"*Nestu hanti . . .*"

But he could do nothing now except try to preserve both his sanity and his soul.

"*Nestu hantiri . . .*"

The dagger plunged into the throat of the brigand.

General Augustus Malevolyn arose from the sea of pillows, leaving Galeona to whatever dreams a sorceress of her ilk had. Without making a sound, he donned some clothes and stepped out of his tent.

Two sentries snapped to attention, their eyes straight ahead. Malevolyn gave them the slightest of nods, then moved on.

A city of tents spread out to the west, the only homes for the general's dedicated minions. Despite being a landless noble, he had managed to raise a fighting force virtually unequaled in the Western Kingdoms. For a price, he had served the causes of any ruler, garnered for himself the money he had needed for his future ambitions. Now, however, the point had come when he had sworn never to serve another, that some day he, Augustus Malevolyn, would be master of more than this worthless patch of ground.

The general turned his eyes to the south, where the vast desert of Aranoch lay. For some time now, he had felt drawn in that direction, drawn to more than the fact that a tremendous prize, the rich, lush city of Lut Gholein, lay some distance within. Lut Gholein, despite its proximity to the desert, also bordered the Twin Seas. Because of that and the fertile strip of land on which it stood, the kingdom had prospered well. Several times would-be conquerors had thought to add its riches to their coffers, but each attempt had met with total disaster. Lut Gholein had not only proven to be well defended, but it appeared to have a bit of a charmed existence. In fact, in Malevolyn's mind, that charm bordered on outright sorcery. Something watched over the city.

And that something was what most tantalized the commander now. Somehow it had some link to his desire to seize Bartuc's legacy and make it his own. Malevolyn dreamed about it, found himself constantly turning his thoughts toward it.

"Soon," he whispered to himself. "Soon . . ."

And what will you do with that legacy? came the sudden thought in his head. *Emulate Bartuc? Repeat his mistakes as well as his victories?*

"No . . ." He would not do that. For all the warlord's power, for all his command of demon hosts, Bartuc had had one failing that the general could not overlook. Bartuc had not been a career soldier. The fabled Warlord of Blood had been first and foremost a sorcerer. Mages had their uses, especially Galeona, but they were unstable and too focused on their arts. A true commander had to be able to keep his attention on the field of battle, on the logistics and the sudden shifts. That had been part of the reason Augustus Malevolyn had been unable to achieve any true skill with his own sorcerous abilities; his military career had been his true passion.

But with the armor, with the magic of Bartuc, you could be more than him, the perfect fusion of soldier and sorcerer! You could be more than Bartuc, even eclipsing him . . .

"Yesss . . . yesss . . ." The general pictured his image forever engraved in the hearts and minds of those in the future. General Augustus Malevolyn, emperor of the *world*!

And even demons will bow to you, call you master.

Demons. Yes, with the armor his, the ability to summon demons would surely follow. The dreams he had had since first wearing the helm had all pointed to that. Reunite helm with suit and the enchantments within would give him the power.

The suit. . . . His brow furrowed. He needed the suit!

And some fool had it.

Malevolyn would find him, find the witless wretch and peel off the armor piece by piece. Then, he would reward the cretin with the honor of being the first to die at the hands of the new Warlord of Blood.

Yes, the general would make the fool's death a memorable one.

Augustus Malevolyn walked on, dreaming of his glory, dreaming of what he would do with the dark powers he would soon wield. Yet, while he walked and dreamt, he still paid meticulous attention to the encampment, for a good leader always watched to make certain that slovenliness did not spread among his forces. Empires were won and lost because of overlooking such seemingly minor things.

Yet, while Malevolyn noted the care with which his loyal warriors performed their tasks, he failed to notice a shadow not caused by the flickering torches. He also failed to notice that this selfsame shadow had stood behind him moments prior, whispering what the general had believed had been his own thoughts, his own questions.

His own dreams.

The shadow of the demon Xazax shifted toward Galeona's tent, his work this night more than to his satisfaction. This human presented some interesting possibilities, ones that he would explore. It had occurred to him long ago that the armor of Bartuc would never accept an actual demon as its master, for, while the warlord had come to believe in the ways of Hell, he had also carried a basic distrust of anyone but himself. No, if the spirit of Bartuc remained even in part in the ancient armor, it would demand a more susceptible human host, however fragile and temporary their bodies might be.

The general desired to play warlord. That suited Xazax well. The witch had her uses, but a *successor* to the bloody Bartuc—Xazax's lord, Belial, would reward his humble servant well for such a find. Not only had the civil war in Hell against Azmodan not gone well of late, but troublesome rumors had reached even there that the Prime Evil Diablo had made good his escape from his mortal prison. If so, he would seek to free his brothers Baal and Mephisto from theirs as well, at which point they would then attempt to regain their thrones from Azmodan and Belial. The three would not deal well with demons who had so loyally served their rebellious lieutenants. If Belial fell, so too would Xazax . . .

"What've you been doing?"

The shadow paused just within the entrance of the sorceress's abode. "This one has many tasks and cannot always be at your beck and call, human Galeona . . ." He made a clacking sound, much like a sand maggot might have done just before crushing its prey in its mandibles. "Besides, you slept . . ."

"Not deep enough to not sense your magic in the air. You promised you wouldn't cast any spells around here! Augustus has some skill; he might notice it and wonder what it means!"

"There is no danger of that, this one promises."

"I ask again, demon! What were you doing?"

"Making a little study of the helmet," Xazax lied, shifting to another part of the tent. "Searching for our fool who knows not what he wears . . ."

Her anger turned to interest. "And did you find out where he is? If I could tell Malevolyn more . . ."

The demon chuckled, a scratchy sound like furious bees trapped in a jug. "Why, when we agreed that the armor will never be his?"

"Because he still has the helmet, you fool, and until we find the armor, we still need Augustus because of his connection to the helmet!"

"True," mused the demon. "His ties to it run deep . . . this one would say *blood* deep."

Her chin went up as she flung her hair back, signs that Xazax had long ago learned meant that the human had grown angry. "And what does *that* mean?"

The shadow did not waver. "This one only meant a jest with that, sorceress. Only a jest. We speak of things concerning Bartuc, do we not?"

"A demon with a sense of humor." Galeona looked not at all amused. "Very well, I'll leave the jesting to you; you leave Augustus to me."

"This one would not seek to take your place in the general's bed . . ."

The sorceress gave the shadow a withering glance, then left the tent. Xazax knew she would hunt down Malevolyn, begin reinforcing her hold on him. The demon respected her abilities in this matter even if he felt confident that in a struggle between Galeona and himself, the witch woman would surely lose. After all, she was mortal, not one of the foul angels. Had she been such, Xazax might have been more concerned. Angels were conniving, working behind the scenes, playing tricks instead of confronting their foes directly.

The shadow of the demon pulled back, secreting himself in the darkest corner. No angels had interfered so far, but Xazax intended to remain wary. If one showed itself, he would take it in his claws and slowly pluck its limbs from it one at a time, all the while listening to the sweet song of its screams.

"Come to me if you dare, angels," he whispered to the darkness. "This one will greet you with open arms . . . and teeth and claws!"

The dim flame from the single oil lamp suddenly flared, briefly illuminating Galeona's tent far more than normal. In that sudden light, the shadow hissed and cringed. The outline of a massive emerald and crimson insect briefly flashed into sight, then quickly faded again as the flame dimmed.

Xazax chittered furiously, grateful that Galeona had not witnessed his reaction. Oil lamps often flared; he had only been taken by surprise by a mundane act of nature. Nonetheless, the shadow of the demon pressed deeper into the comforting recesses of the tent. There he could safely plot. There he could safely use his power to seek out the human wearing Bartuc's armor.

There he could better watch for cowardly angels.

FIVE

✵

Rumbling storm clouds turned the day as nearly as black as the night had been, but Norrec hardly noticed. His mind still sought to come to grips with the terror of the previous evening and his own limited part in it. More men had died brutally because of Norrec's damned quest for gold; although unlike Sadun and Fauztin these had likely deserved execution for past crimes, their deaths had been too awful as far as the soldier had been concerned. The innkeeper especially had suffered a horrible demise, the returning demon bringing back far too much proof of its thorough handiwork. Norrec only gave thanks that the hellish beast had returned to the nether realm shortly thereafter with its prize.

That, of course, had not enabled Norrec to escape the suit's own monstrous actions afterward. As the desperate fighter moved on, he tried not to look down at the armor, greatly stained by the night's activities. Worse, each passing second Norrec remained aware that his own face still bore a few smudges despite his best attempts to rub everything off. The armor had been very thorough in its foul work.

And while he fought off the horrors in his thoughts, the suit pushed him unceasingly west. Thunder rumbled again and again and the wind howled, but still the armor moved on. Norrec had no doubt that it would keep on moving even if the storm finally broke.

He had been granted one slight boon at least, the garnering of an old, dusty travel cloak hanging on a peg in the common room. The odds had been that it had belonged to the thieving innkeeper, but again Norrec tried to avoid thinking of such things. The cloak obscured much of the armor and offered him a bit of protection should the rains come pouring down. A very small blessing, but one for which he was truly grateful.

The more he headed west, the more the landscape changed, the mountains giving way to smaller hills and even flatlands. Now much farther down in altitude, it also grew increasingly warm. The plant life turned lush, becoming more and more reminiscent of the dense jungles the fighter knew existed farther south.

For the first time, Norrec could also smell the sea. What he recalled of the maps he and his companions had carried indicated to him that the more northerly of the Twin Seas could not be that far away at this point. Norrec's original hope had been to head southwest to find one of the Vizjerei, but he had suspicions that the cursed suit had other plans in mind. A fear briefly erupted within him that it might actually try to walk the breadth of the sea, dragging a helpless Norrec into the inky depths. However, so far Bartuc's armor had kept him alive, if not completely well. It apparently needed him breathing in order to achieve its mysterious goals.

And after that?

The wind continued to pick up, nearly buffeting Norrec about despite the determination of the cursed suit to keep on its course. No rain had yet fallen, but the air grew thick and moist and fog began to develop. It became impossible to see very far ahead and although that did not seem at all a bother to the armor, now and then Norrec still feared that it would walk him right off a cliff without ever realizing it.

At midday—which almost might as well have been midnight for all the sun failed to penetrate the cloud cover—imps again came in summons to the unintelligible words spouted unwillingly by Norrec. Even despite the growing fog, it took them but minutes to bring back prey, this time a deer. Norrec ate his fill, then gladly allowed the small, horned demons to drag the rest of the carcass back to their infernal abode.

On and on he trudged, the smell of the sea growing stronger. Norrec could barely see in front of him, but knew that he could not be that far from it—and whatever destination the infernal armor had in mind.

As if reading his thoughts, a building abruptly materialized in the mist . . . followed almost immediately by another. At the same time, he heard voices in the distance, voices clearly of those hard at work.

His hands his own for the moment, the exhausted traveler pulled his cloak tight about him. The less any of the locals saw what he wore underneath, the better.

As he wandered through the town, Norrec sighted a dim but vast shape in the distance. A ship. He wondered whether or not it had just arrived or now prepared to disembark. If the latter, it likely would be the armor's destination. Why else would he have been brought to this specific place?

A figure in mariner's garb came from the opposite direction, a bundle under one arm. He had eyes and features somewhat akin to Fauztin, but with much more animation in his face.

"Ho, traveler! Not a good day to be making your way from the interior, eh?"

"No." Norrec would have walked past the man without another word, his concern that the mariner might become the next of the suit's victims, but his feet suddenly stopped.

This, in turn, caused the other to also halt. Still grinning, the seaman asked, "Where do you hail from? Look to be a westerner to me, though it's a little hard to tell under all that stubble!"

"West, yes," the soldier returned. "I've been on a . . . a pilgrimage."

"In the mountains? Not much up there but a few goats!"

Norrec tried to move his legs, but they would not budge. The armor expected something of him, but would not indicate what. He thought fast and furiously. He had arrived in a harbor town toward which the armor had purposely headed. Norrec had already assumed that it needed transport to some location, possibly even the ship in the distance—

The ship . . .

Pointing toward the murky shape, Norrec asked, "That vessel. Is it heading out soon?"

The mariner twisted his head back to look. "The *Napolys*? She's just come in. Be another two, maybe five days even. Only ship leaving soon's the *Hawksfire*, just down that way." He pointed toward the south, then leaned close—far too close, in Norrec's anxious opinion—and added, "A word of caution there. The *Hawksfire* is not a good vessel. She'll be at the bottom of the sea one of these days, mark me. Best to wait for the *Napolys* or my own fine girl, the *Odyssey*, though that'll mean a week or more. We've need for a little refitting."

Still his legs would not move. What more did the armor want?

Destination? "Can you tell me where each sails to?"

"My own, we're heading for Lut Gholein, but it'll be awhile before we can leave, as I said. The *Napolys* now, that heads for far Kingsport, a long journey but a part of your Western Kingdoms, eh? Get you home faster, I think! That'd be the one for you, eh?"

Norrec noticed no change. "What about the *Hawksfire*?"

"Leaves tomorrow morn, I think, but I warn you against it. One of these days, she'll not make it all the way back from Lut Gholein—and that's if she makes it there in the first place!"

The soldier's legs suddenly started moving again. The suit had finally found out what it wanted to know. Norrec gave the mariner a quick nod. "Thank you."

"Heed my warning well!" the seaman called. "Best to wait!"

Bartuc's armor marched Norrec through the small town, heading to the southern part of the harbor. Mariners and locals glanced at him as he walked by, his western looks not as common here, but none made any comment. For all its tiny size, the port apparently handled a steady business. Norrec supposed that it would have looked more impressive in the sunshine, but doubted that he would ever have the opportunity to see it so.

A sense of unease touched the veteran as he entered the southernmost part of the port. In contrast to what Norrec had seen so far, the area here looked to be in some disrepair and those few figures he noticed nearby struck Norrec as almost as unsavory as the unfortunate fools who had tried to rob him. Worse, the only vessel in sight looked to be most appropriate for a journey desired by a cursed suit of armor.

If some dark spirit had dredged up a long-lost ship from the black depths of the sea, then failed afterward in a half-hearted attempt to make it pass for something still from the land of the living, it would have looked little more baleful than the *Hawksfire* did at that moment. The three masts stood like tall, skeletal sentinels half-wrapped in the shroudlike sails. The figurehead at the bow, once probably a curvaceous mermaid, had been worn down by the elements until it now resembled more an aquatic banshee in midshriek. As for the hull itself, something had long-ago stained the wood nearly to pitch and scars raked the sides, making Norrec wonder if at some point in its colored past the vessel had either served in war or, more likely, had been used more than once as a freebooter.

He saw no crew, only a single, gaunt figure in a worn coat standing near the bow. Despite the uncertainty of taking a voyage on such a ghastly ship, Norrec had no choice but to do as the armor forced him. Without hesitation, it walked its unwilling host up the gangplank toward the rather haggard figure.

"What you want?" The skeleton coalesced into an older man with parchment skin and absolutely no flesh and sinew beneath the thin veil of life. One eye stared sightlessly to a point just to the left of Norrec, while the other, bloodshot, glared suspiciously at the newcomer.

"Passage to Lut Gholein," replied Norrec, trying to end this matter as quickly as he could. If he cooperated, then perhaps the warlord's garments would give him some freedom of movement for awhile.

"Other ships in port!" the captain snapped, his accent thick. Under a broad-rimmed hat he wore his ivory-white hair in a tail. The faded green coat, clearly once that of a naval officer from one of the Western Kingdoms, had likely gone through several owners before this man had laid claim to it. "No time to serve passengers!"

Ignoring the fetid breath, Norrec leaned closer. "I will pay well to get there."

An immediate change came over the captain's demeanor. "Aye?"

Trusting the armor to do as it had done at the inn, the soldier continued. "All I need is a cabin and food. If I'm left alone for the duration of the journey, so much the better. Just get me to Lut Gholein."

The cadaverous figure inspected him. "Armor?" He rubbed his chin. "Officer?"

"Yes." Let him think Norrec some renegade officer on the run. Likely it would raise the price but make the captain more trusting. Norrec obviously needed to be away from here.

The elder man rubbed his bony chin again. Norrec noted tattoos running from his thin wrist down into the voluminous sleeve of the coat. The notion that this ship had served as a freebooter gained merit.

"Twelve draclin! Bed alone, eat away from crew, talk with crew little! Leave ship when docked!"

Norrec agreed with everything except the price. How much was a draclin worth compared to the coin of his own land?

He need not have bothered worrying. The left hand stretched out, several coins in the gauntlet's palm. The captain eyed them greedily, scooping each from the proffered hand. He bit one to make certain of its worth, then poured all into a ragged pouch on his belt.

"Come!" He hobbled past Norrec, for the first time revealing that his left leg had splints running down each side all the way to the boot. From the extensive binding he saw and his own experiences with field surgery, the veteran suspected that his host could not even stand on the leg without those large splints. The captain should have had the limb better looked at, but both the bindings and the splints appeared as if they had been put on quite some time ago and then forgotten.

However much twelve draclin might be in Norrec's own land, his first viewing of the cabin led him to believe it far too great a price for this. Even the room at the inn had looked more hospitable than what he now confronted. The cabin barely outspanned a closet; only a rickety bunk whose side had been nailed to the back wall represented anything in the way of amenities. The sheets were stained and looked as if they had been crudely cut from the sails, so dark and coarse were they. A smell like rotting fish pervaded the cabin and marks on the floor hinted of some past violence. In the upper corners, spiderwebs larger than Norrec's head wiggled in the breeze let in by the open door and near the edge of the floor, moss of some sort had taken a foothold.

Knowing he had no choice, Norrec hid his disgust. "Thank you, captain—"

"Casco," the skeletal figure grunted. "Inside! Eat at bell! Understand?"

"Yes."

With a curt nod, Captain Casco left him to his own devices. Heeding the man's advice, Norrec shut the door behind him and sat down on the dubious bed. To his further regret, the cabin did not even have a porthole, which might have offered some relief from the stench.

He flexed his hands, then tested his legs. Movement had been granted to him for his cooperation, but for how long, Norrec could not say. He supposed that aboard the *Hawksfire,* the armor expected little trouble. What could Norrec do except step over the rail and sink to the bottom of the sea? As terrible as his situation had grown, he could not yet bring himself to try to end his life, especially in such horrifying fashion. Besides, Norrec doubted that he would be allowed to do even that, not so long as the suit required his living body.

With no notion as to what else to do with his time, he tried his best to go to sleep. Despite the stench—or perhaps because of it—Norrec managed to doze off. Unfortunately, his dreams proved again to be troubled ones, in great part because they did not even seem his own.

Again he lived as Bartuc, taking relish in the dreadful acts he performed. A settlement that hesitated too long in accepting his domination felt the full force of his righteous wrath, the town elders and several other chosen fools drawn, quartered, then flayed for the good of the rest. A Vizjerei caught spying became the centerpiece for a macabre candelabra that illuminated not only the warlord's quarters, but even caused his demonic servants to shudder. A bell sounded . . .

—stirring a grateful Norrec from his sleep. He blinked, finally registering that he had actually slept until the bell for evening meal. While he doubted the food would be anything to his liking, his hunger had become so great that Norrec could not avoid the matter any longer. Besides, he did not want to risk the suit summoning imps to feed him. There was no telling *what* they might decide could be edible . . .

Pulling his cloak tight around him, the fighter stepped out to see several worn, bitter-looking men heading down into the bowel of the ship. Assuming that they, too, planned to eat, Norrec followed them down to a rather seedy-looking mess. In silence the former soldier stood in line, receiving hard bread and a questionable meat dish that almost made him yearn for the thieving innkeeper's fare.

One glance at the surly group convinced Norrec to retire to his room. Carrying his food up to the deck, he paused at the rail for a moment to inhale some of the relatively fresh sea air before going back into the cabin.

A figure standing in the fog-enshrouded dock caught his eye.

The food slipped from his hands, spilling all over the deck, but Norrec did not even notice.

Fauztin. Even with his robes wrapped around him, it could be no other.

The dead eyes of his former comrade stared back at him. Even from where the fighter stood, he could see the gaping hole where the Vizjerei's throat once had been.

"Fool!" Casco roared from behind Norrec. "What mess! You clean up! No help!"

The startled veteran looked over his shoulder at the angry captain, then down at the spilled food. Some of the meat dripped over the toes of Bartuc's boots.

"Clean up! No help! No more food tonight!" Casco limped off, muttering in his native tongue something no doubt derogatory about foreign devils.

Despite the fury of the captain, Norrec immediately forgot the spilled meal, instead quickly returning his gaze to the dock in search of—

Nothing. No sepulchral figure stood staring back at him. The ghastly shade had vanished—if it had ever even been there in the first place.

Hands trembling, he stumbled back, unmindful of anything but the terrifying sight he thought he had just beheld. Fauztin, so clearly dead, condemning him with those empty eyes . . .

Still ignoring Captain Casco's earlier demand that he clean up the mess, Norrec hurried back to his cabin, slamming the door tight behind him and not daring to breathe until he sat once more on the bunk.

He had lost the struggle. The sorcerer's ghost had been the first obvious sign. Norrec had lost the struggle for his sanity. The horrors the cursed armor had put him through had finally torn away the last barriers protecting the veteran's mind. Surely now, the downward spiral into complete madness would be swift. Surely now, he had no hope of saving himself.

Surely now Bartuc's legacy would claim not only his body—but his soul, too.

An exhausted Kara Nightshadow inspected the miserable little port town with some distaste. Accustomed to the beauty of the jungle and the carefully cultivated ways of her kind, she found the port, Gea Kul, reeking of too many unwashed bodies and far too much devotion to materialistic things. As a necromancer, Kara saw the world in balance between the actions of life and that which occurred after death and believed that both aspects should be dealt with accordingly with as much dignity as a soul could muster. What she had so far witnessed in her few minutes here had revealed very little dignity.

It had taken her great effort to reach this place as quickly as she had, effort that had worn her out physically, spiritually, and very much magically. Kara dearly wanted to get some sleep, but she had come to this place for reasons that even she did not completely understand and so needed to at least survey the area in the hopes of finding some answers.

After the unsettling loss of not only the warlord's armor but also both her prized dagger and the two corpses, the young necromancer had used her training to try to ferret out the locations of all—and that had unerringly led her to this most unassuming place. What ties the port might have to all, she could not say, but it clearly did not bode well. Kara wished that she could have consulted with her teachers, but time had been of the essence and she had been trained to rely on herself as much as possible. Delaying the chase only meant it becoming more difficult to track everything later on. That, she could not afford. If the thieves planned on taking the armor overseas, she had to stop them now.

As for the revenants . . . she had no idea what to do about that unsettling pair. They acted like nothing spoken of in her studies.

Ignoring the unsavory glances from the sailors she passed, Kara headed for the first inn she found. On the one hand, the ebony-tressed enchantress needed food, while on the other, she hoped to garner useful information.

Surely those who carried Bartuc's suit had needed a meal or a drink after such an arduous trek.

The Captain's Table, as the inn had been titled, proved to be a bit better in appearance than she expected. Although the building looked old and worn, the gray-haired, imposing man in charge kept it clean and orderly. Kara immediately knew that he had once been an officer in some naval force, from his features likely one of the wealthier Western Kingdoms. Cheerful for the most part, the gigantic figure with muttonchop sideburns brooked no argument from one patron who believed he could depart without paying. Despite his advanced age, the innkeeper handled the much younger seaman with ease, not only retrieving the money owed him but also depositing the culprit out in the fog and mud.

Rubbing his hands on his apron, the owner noticed his newest guest. "Good evening, milady!" He bowed graciously despite his growing girth, his entire expression lighting up at the sight of her. "Captain Hanos Jeronnan, your humble servant! May I say you grace my little place!"

Unaccustomed to such open displays toward her, Kara did not answer at first. However, Captain Jeronnan, clearly realizing that he had overwhelmed her, patiently waited for her to recover.

"Thank you, captain," she finally responded. "I seek some food and, if you have the time, the answers to a few questions."

"For you, my lovely little one, I'll make the time!"

He walked off, humming to himself. Kara felt her face reddening. Captain Jeronnan obviously meant nothing forward in his comments, but none of the dark mage's intense training had taught her how to take compliments on her appearance. She knew that some of her brethren found her attractive, but among the followers of Rathma such matters were treated with the formality with which they treated everything.

Seating herself in a side booth, Kara glanced around at the other patrons. Most went about the business of drinking and eating, but a few had other matters in mind. She saw a woman in scandalous garments leaning over a sailor, her offer to him needing little actual conversation. To her right, a pair of men dickered over some deal, babbling in a language of which the necromancer had no knowledge. There were also a few males among the clientele who eyed her with more open interest than Captain Jeronnan had and without his tact. One who showed far too much interest for her own tastes received a stony glare from her silver eyes, a sight so unsettling to him that he quickly turned away, burying his head in drink and visibly shivering for several seconds.

The innkeeper returned with a plate bearing broiled fish and some sea vegetable. He placed that and a mug in front of the necromancer. "Cider in the mug. 'Tis the simplest drink I've got here, milady."

Kara considered telling him something about the strong herbal concoctions developed by the Rathma faithful, but chose to graciously accept the mild drink. She looked at the fish, the spices giving it a very enticing scent. Of course, at this point Kara almost would have been willing to eat it right out of the sea. Still, it pleased her to find such civilized fare here. "What do I owe?"

"Your company alone's worth the price."

She bristled, thinking of the woman plying her wares on one of the customers. "I am no—"

He looked chagrined. "No, no! 'Tis just that I don't get such fair visitors much, lass! I only meant sitting here and answering your questions! No harm meant—" Jeronnan leaned closer, whispering, "and I know better than to try forcing myself on one who follows the ways of Rathma!"

"You know what I am and still you desire to sit with me?"

"Milady, I sailed every sea and all over the Great Ocean. I've seen many a magic, but the most trustworthy of mages were always the faithful of Rathma . . ."

She rewarded him with a slight smile that proved enough to redden his already ruddy cheeks. "Then perhaps you are the man with whom I can trust my questions."

The captain leaned back. "Only when you've first tasted my specialty and given me your fine opinion."

Kara cut into the fish, tasting a small bite. Immediately she cut a second, downing it as quickly as the first.

Jeronnan beamed. "'Tis to your liking, then?"

Indeed, it was. The jungles of the east contained a variety of marvelous spices, but the necromancer had never eaten anything like this fish. In less time than she could have imagined, Kara had devoured a good portion of her meal, so much so that she finally felt like herself again.

Captain Jeronnan had excused himself now and then to deal with his other customers, but by the time she had finished, there remained only two others, a pair of dour-looking sailors clearly too weary to do anything but nurse their ales and food. The innkeeper settled in across from her and waited.

"My name is Kara Nightshadow," she began. "You know what I am."

"Aye, but I've never seen one that looked like you, lass."

Kara pushed on, unwilling at this point to be detoured by niceties. "Captain, have you noticed anyone out of the ordinary here?"

He chuckled. "In Gea Kul? It'd be more extraordinary to see someone ordinary!"

"What about . . . what about a man traveling with armor probably strapped to the back of an animal?" The necromancer paused to consider the implications further. "Or a man wearing armor?"

"We get some soldiers here. Not uncommon."

"In crimson plate?"

Jeronnan's brow wrinkled. "I'd recall that—but, no. No one."

It had been a desperate hope. Kara wanted to ask another, very particular question, but feared that if she did, the captain's easy manner would change.

He might be familiar with her kind, but some subjects could be too dark even for him to accept. Walking corpses would certainly be one of those subjects.

Kara opened her mouth with the intention of trying a different track, yet what escaped from her lips proved not to be words but rather a long yawn.

Her companion looked her over. "Pardon me for being blunt, milady, but you look even more pale than you likely usually are. I think you need some good rest."

She sought to dissuade him, only to yawn again. "Perhaps you are right."

"I've got a couple of rooms available, lass. For you, no charge—and nothing expected, if you're worried about it."

"I'll pay you." Kara managed to retrieve some coins from the purse on her belt. "Is this enough?"

He shoved most of it back. "That is . . . and don't go showing all that money around. Not everyone's a kind soul like me!"

The necromancer could barely move. Her legs felt like lead. The spellwork she had utilized to quicker get her to her destination had taken too much from the dark mage. "I think I will go to it immediately, if you will forgive my leaving."

"Best give me a few minutes, lass. I fear that with the help I hire here, it might not be ready for you. Just remain here and I'll be back shortly!"

He hurried off before she could protest. Kara straightened, trying to keep awake. Both the spellwork and her own physical efforts naturally had drained her much, but this exhaustion seemed far more oppressive than it should have been, even taking those matters into account. It almost made her believe—

She pushed herself to her feet, turning to the door at the same time. Perhaps Kara had misjudged Captain Hanos Jeronnan. Perhaps his congenial manner hid a darker side.

Aware that her thinking might well be too muddled, the necromancer stumbled her way toward the entrance, not at all caring what the two sailors in the corner might think. If she made it outside, then perhaps she could clear her mind enough to reconsider. Yes, for all the odious smells of the port itself, the sea air would still no doubt help her regain her balance.

Kara nearly fell through the doorway, so weak had her legs become. Immediately she inhaled. Some of the heaviness in her head evaporated, enough at least for her to get some general sense of her surroundings, but the raven-haired enchantress needed more. She could not decide what to do about the innkeeper until she could think clearly again.

Once more she inhaled, but as her head cleared a bit more, a sense of immediate unease struck Kara.

She looked up into the dark fog and saw a figure in a worn travel cloak standing just a few feet from her. His face remained obscured by the hood of his cloak, but lower Kara could make out one pale hand emerging. In that hand, the figure held a dagger that gleamed even in the mist-enshrouded night.

An ivory dagger.

Kara's dagger.

Another pale hand reached up and pulled back the hood slightly, revealing a face the necromancer had seen but once before. The Vizjerei from Bartuc's tomb.

The Vizjerei who had had his throat torn out.

"Your spell . . . should've worked . . . better on her," a voice croaked from behind her.

Kara tried to turn, her body still moving far too slowly. At the same time, it occurred to her that all her training, all her spellwork, had failed to enable her to notice not one attacker, but two.

A second pale face smiled grimly at her, the man's head tipped slightly to one side as if not entirely connected to his body.

The second corpse from the tomb. The wiry man whose neck had been snapped.

"You leave us . . . no choice."

His hand had been raised, in it another dagger held hilt up. Even as this fact reached her sluggish brain, the hand of the ghoul came down, swinging hard.

The blow caught Kara Nightshadow on the temple. She spun around once and would have surely cracked her head on the stone path save that the undead creature who had hit her now caught her in his arms. With astonishing tenderness, he lowered the stunned woman to the ground.

"You . . . really . . . leave us . . . no choice."

And with that, she blacked out.

Six

Norrec did not leave his cabin again until time came to retrieve his morning meal. No one spoke to him, especially Captain Casco, who had not forgiven his passenger for leaving the mess near the rail. Norrec actually appreciated the lack of conversation, wanting nothing to slow his return to the safety of his room.

He had slept fitfully during the night, not only haunted by dreams of Bartuc's glory, but now also dread images of Fauztin's vengeful spirit come to claim him. Not until the *Hawksfire* finally set sail did the veteran fighter calm at all. Out on the sea, troubled spirits could certainly not pursue him. In fact, as the ship pushed out onto the stormy waters, it finally began to sound reasonable to Norrec that he had imagined the dreadful vision, that what he had taken for Fauztin had either been but another Vizjerei—for certainly the port lay near enough to their eastern lands—or the complete figment of his own troubled mind.

The latter seemed more and more likely. After all, Norrec had been both physically and mentally torn apart by the demands of the cursed armor. The memories of not only the tomb but the slaughter at the inn remained with him. In addition, the warlord's suit had pushed his endurance to the limits and beyond, forcing the soldier to traverse a rough landscape without hardly any rest and at a pace that would have killed many men. If not for the fact that only part of the effort had been his own, Norrec suspected that he would definitely have died along the way.

The waves grew choppier as the *Hawksfire* entered deep waters. With each groan of the hull, Norrec became more and more convinced that at some point the sea would crush the worn ship like tinder. Yet, somehow, the *Hawksfire* continued on, riding one wave to the next. In addition, for all their motley outer appearance, Captain Casco and his crew proved quite adept at managing the vessel. They scurried up the ropes, raced across the decks, ever keeping their ship ready to meet the elements.

What they could not entirely keep at bay, though, was the storm. It struck but a few hours out, the sky blackening and lightning flashing all about. The winds picked up, bending the masts and trying to rip the sails. Norrec, who had finally stepped out, quickly gripped the rail as the sea tossed the *Hawksfire* to the side.

"Starboard!" called Casco from the deck. "Starboard!"

The man at the wheel worked to obey, but wind and water battled against him. A second crew member came to his aid, the pair managing to fulfill the captain's orders after great effort.

Rain at last fell, a torrent that forced Norrec back into the cabin. Not only did he know nothing about sailing, but, clad in armor, he risked his life every time he neared the rail. It would take only one strong wave to toss him over the side.

A soiled lantern swinging violently from the ceiling tried desperately to keep the cabin illuminated. Norrec planted himself on the inside corner of the bunk and tried to think. He had not yet completely given up hope of escaping the cursed armor, but so far had no idea as to what to do. It would require powerful sorcery and he knew no one with such abilities. If only he could have asked Fauztin—

The memory of what he had thought he had seen on the dock returned full blown, sending renewed chills through Norrec. Best to forget about Fauztin— and Sadun, too. They were dead.

Night came and still the storm did not abate. Norrec forced himself down to the mess, where he noticed for the first time some of the crew eyeing him with more than disinterest and disdain. Now a few gazes seemed almost hostile, hostile and yet frightened. Norrec had no doubt that it had to do with the armor. Who was he, they must be wondering? The armor spoke of power, of command. Why did such a one as he travel on a miserable vessel such as the *Hawksfire*?

Again he took his meal to the cabin, preferring the solitary atmosphere.

This time he found the food slightly more palatable or perhaps the previous meals had just burned away his tongue. Norrec devoured it, then fell back and tried to go to sleep. He did not look forward to sleep, both the dreams of Bartuc and the nightmares surrounding the tomb not at all enticements. However, exhaustion quickly set in and, as a veteran campaigner, Norrec Vizharan knew better than to try to fight it. Even the violent rocking of the *Hawksfire* could not keep his eyes from closing . . .

"It would be . . . nice to rest," came a cracking yet still familiar voice. "But, after all, they say . . . no rest for the wicked, eh?"

Norrec bolted to his feet, eyes wide. Barely any light shone from the lantern, but even with what little he had the soldier could see that no one else stood in the room.

"Damn!" Another nightmare. Staring at the lantern, Norrec realized that he must have fallen asleep without realizing it. The voice had been in his head, nowhere else. The voice of a comrade now lost . . .

Sadun's voice.

Thunder crashed. The *Hawksfire* shivered. Norrec gripped the side of the cot, then started to ease himself back onto it.

"You should've . . . listened to Fauztin . . . Norrec. Now it . . . may be too late."

He froze where he was, gaze shifting to the door.

"Come to us, friend . . . come to Fauztin . . . and me."

Norrec straightened. "Sadun?"

No reply, but some of the planks just outside the cabin creaked as if someone walked upon them and paused now before his door.

"Someone out there?"

The *Hawksfire* dipped, nearly sending him tumbling. Norrec flattened himself against a wall, eyes never leaving the doorway. Had he imagined Tryst's cracking, laboring voice?

The days since the horror of the tomb had tested the veteran's nerve more than any battle in which he had fought, yet still something within urged Norrec toward the door. Most likely when he opened it there would be nothing. Sadun and the Vizjerei could not be out there, awaiting the friend who had so terribly murdered them. Such things did not happen save in tales spoken in whispers around late night campfires.

But such things as the dreadful armor Norrec wore did not happen outside of those tales, either.

Again the planks creaked. Norrec gritted his teeth, reached toward the latch . . .

The gauntleted hand suddenly twitched—and began to glow a sinister red.

Norrec drew the glove back, watching in wonder as the glow now faded. He reached forward once more, but this time, nothing happened. Steeling himself, Norrec undid the latch, then swung open the door—

Rain and wind battered him, but no fearsome shade stood outside the cabin, bony finger outstretched in condemnation.

Seizing his cloak, Norrec hurried outside, his gaze immediately shifting first to the left, then the right. Toward the bow he saw the dim shapes of men struggling to keep the sails in order, but of the supposed phantoms, he found not a trace.

The hard tramping of feet made him look in the direction of the stern again, where he saw one of Casco's men running toward the bow. The man would have passed Norrec without a glance, but the soldier seized him. Ignoring the sailor's fierce glare, he shouted, "Did you see anyone out here before you? Anyone standing by my cabin?"

The sailor spat something in another tongue, then pulled away from Norrec as if just touched by a leper. Norrec watched the man run off, then shifted his own attention to the rail. A notion filled his head that he found entirely ludicrous, but still it made him risk fate by actually stepping to the edge and peering over the side.

Waves shattered unceasingly against the timeworn hull of the *Hawksfire*, doing their best, it seemed, to pound through the wood and send the vessel and its occupants to their watery dooms. The sea beyond churned wildly, sometimes rising so high that Norrec had trouble seeing the heavens.

But of his supposed visitor, he saw no sign. No vengeful ghoul clung to the side of the hull. The unforgiving shades of Sadun Tryst and Fauztin had not, after all, been standing outside his cabin door. He had imagined them, just as he had first believed.

"You! What you do out? Inside! Inside!" The hobbling form of Captain Casco closed in on Norrec from the bow. Casco seemed completely outraged that his sole passenger had dared the elements. Norrec doubted it had to do with concern for the veteran's well-being. As with the rest of the crew, a hint of fright tinged Casco's angry words.

"What is it? What's wrong?"

"Wrong?" the cadaverous mariner barked back. "Wrong? Nothing wrong! Back to cabin! Storm outside! You fool?"

Half-tempted to respond "yes" to Casco's question, Norrec did not bother to argue with the man. With the crippled mariner watching, he returned to the cabin, closing the door on Casco's scowling visage. After a moment, Norrec heard him stump away.

The thought of trying to fall asleep again did not at all appeal to Norrec, but he nonetheless tried. At first, questions raced through his thoughts, all but one of which the veteran could answer. That lone question concerned the crimson gauntlet and why it had begun to glow just prior to his going outside to search. If no danger had lurked beyond the door, what reason would the armor have for such a protective measure? True, it had not seized control of him, but still its actions had appeared to have purpose . . .

Norrec fell asleep still pondering the suit's reaction. He did not stir again until a crack of thunder that shook the cabin nearly caused him to tumble out of the makeshift bunk. Disoriented, the soldier tried and failed to calculate just how long he had been asleep. The storm still blew strong, which to Norrec meant that it could not have been more than a few scant hours. Rarely had a storm that he had suffered through lasted more than a day, although he supposed that on the high sea it could be different.

Arms and legs stiff, Norrec stretched, then tried to go back to his slumber.

A long, cracking sound far different from thunder again brought him to his feet. He recognized that sound, even if he had not heard it often. It had been the sound of *wood* breaking.

And on a ship in the midst of a wild storm, that could spell doom for everyone.

Norrec burst out of the cabin, heading toward the bow. Shouts informed him that the crew already struggled to deal with whatever danger threatened, but he knew how difficult their task would be if what he suspected had truly occurred. Bad enough for the ship to suffer damage, but to try to repair it during such chaos . . .

A moment later, his worst fears had been realized. Just ahead, several sailors fought to keep one of the masts from entirely cracking in two. They pulled on ropes, trying to force the upper portion in place while other men attempted to strengthen the ruined area with planks, nails, and more rope. Norrec, however, could already tell that theirs had become a struggle in futility. More and more the mast leaned dangerously, and when it went the others would surely soon follow.

He wanted to do something, but none of the skills he had learned would have been of aid to the more experienced mariners. Norrec stared at the gauntleted hands, the crimson coloring making them look so mighty, so full of strength. Yet all the vaunted power of Bartuc's legacy would avail him nothing now.

The thought faded as an unsettling blue aura formed without warning around each glove.

Norrec suddenly found himself rushing forward, the suit again in command of his actions. For once, though, the veteran fought little against it, certain of its intentions if not its methods. The armor desired to reach its distant destination, and it could not if it and Norrec sank to the bottom of the sea. For Norrec's life alone, it needed to act.

"Away! Away!" shouted Captain Casco, no doubt certain that his clumsy passenger would just make a terrible situation worse. Norrec, though, barged past him, nearly bowling the crippled mariner over.

The mast creaked ominously, a sure sign that only seconds remained before it toppled into the next. Norrec took a deep breath, anxiously waiting for the suit to act.

"Kesra! Qezal irakus!"

Lightning punctuated each word thrust from the soldier's mouth, but Norrec paid it little mind. What he did notice, what all those around him also surely noticed, was that several shimmering green forms suddenly surrounded, even *clung* to, the ruined mast. They had strong, sleek arms that ended in suckered fingers, but where there should have been legs, the monstrosities had bodies reminiscent of gigantic slugs. The creatures hissed and crawled, their half-seen faces akin to some demented artist's idea of a bat made up like a clown, face paint and all.

The sailors fled in panic, releasing their grip on the ropes and wood. The mast started to fall . . .

The shimmering horde pushed it back in place. While some held it there, others started to crawl around and around the ruined area. As they moved, they left trails of slime over the cracks. At first Norrec had no idea what they intended, but then he noticed that the slime almost immediately hardened, strengthening and stabilizing the mast. Over and over the creatures crawled, a madcap race with no finish line. Their brethren, no longer needed to support the mast, watched and waited, hissing in what seemed encouragement to the ones circling around the pole.

"Kesra! Qezal ranakka!"

The demons quickly crawled from the mast, grouping together. Norrec pulled his gaze from the horrific band, looking over their completed hand-iwork. Despite the storm, the mast now swayed as if only in a gentle breeze. Not only had they repaired it, but they had reinforced it in such a manner that the odds were it would better survive this voyage than the other two.

As if also satisfied, the suit waved a negligent hand at the demons. A burst of light so bright that Norrec had to shield his eyes covered the foul pack. The creatures' hissing grew stronger, harsher, until, with what seemed a sigh, the light faded out—leaving no trace of the sluglike beasts, not even a single trail of slime.

Seemingly unimpressed, the storm battled on, tossing the *Hawksfire* about. Yet, despite the continued threat of it, the crew hesitated to return to their posts, only doing so when the captain finally shouted at them. The sailors who passed Norrec gave the fighter a wide berth, their fear of him quite clear in their expressions. True, their lives had probably been spared because of the demons summoned, but to know that one who could call forth such horrific apparitions journeyed with them surely shook the men to the very core of their souls.

Norrec, however, did not care, so weary his legs threatened to collapse underneath him. Even though it had been the suit that had cast the spell, he suddenly felt as if he had just rebuilt the entire mast singlehandedly. Norrec waited for the armor to guide him back to the cabin, but now that the danger had been dealt with, apparently it had left matters to him.

The metal plate felt like a thousand pounds as he turned and walked from the deck. Around him, Norrec continued to feel the uneasy stares of the crew of the *Hawksfire*. No doubt they would soon even forget that they owed their lives to his presence and begin to consider what it meant to have a master of demons aboard. Fear had a way of turning to violence . . .

Yet, despite that knowledge, Norrec sought only his bed. He very desperately needed sleep. Even the storm would not be able to keep him awake now. Come the morrow, he would do what he could to explain what had happened.

Norrec only hoped that, in the meantime, none of the crew would attempt anything foolish . . . and fatal.

Darkness. Warm, enveloping darkness.

Kara nestled in it, dwelled in it, found it so comforting that for the longest time she had no desire to leave it. Yet, there came a point when something—an uneasy feeling, a sense of foreboding—made her turn, shift . . . and try to wake.

She also heard a voice.

"Kara! Lass! Where are you?"

The voice had a familiarity to it, one that slowly drew her up from oblivion. As she tried to awaken, Kara Nightshadow's own will aided in the task. This darkness, this nothingness, held her prisoner. The comfort it offered was a smothering one, an eternal sleep.

"Kara!"

It no longer even comforted. Now it scratched, crushed, felt more akin to a casket than a soft bed . . .

"Kara!"

The necromancer's eyes flew open.

She stood imprisoned in a tomb of wood, her limbs seemingly frozen.

Somewhere a hound barked. The necromancer blinked, trying to focus better. A few cracks of dim light shone through, just enough to enable her to better understand what had become of her. Wood tightly surrounded her on all sides, a hollow tree without major openings. Somehow, she had been placed here, sealed in here—to die?

A sense of claustrophobia nearly overwhelmed her. Kara struggled to move her arms, but could not. They had been pinned to her sides and wrapped by vegetation growing in the hollow tree. Worse, moss also covered her mouth, sealing her lips together. She tried to make a sound, but, muffled by both the moss and the thick trunk, Kara knew that no one outside would hear her.

More hounds barked, this time nearer. She fixed on a voice, Captain Jeronnan's voice, calling her name.

"Kara! Lass! Can you hear me?"

Her legs also could not move, likely for the same reasons as her arms. Physically, Kara had been left completely helpless.

The sense of claustrophobia grew. Although the necromancer had lived much of her short life in seclusion, she had always had freedom of movement, freedom of choice. Her ghoulish attackers had left her without either. Why they had not slain her outright, the desperate dark mage could not say, but if she did not soon escape, her demise would be just as certain . . . and in a far slower, grislier fashion.

And that thought, accompanied by her growing feeling that the tree trunk closed in on her from all sides, pushed Kara as none of her teachers had ever. She wanted to escape, to be free, to not suffer the slow tortures of starvation . . .

Bound as she was, with even her mouth sealed, no sophisticated spell could save her. Yet, raw emotion, so generally kept under control by the followers of Rathma, now bubbled up, demanded to overflow. Kara stared at the wood before her, seeing it as her nemesis, her own tomb.

She would not die this way, not through the dark magic of an undead sorcerer . . .

Not die this way . . .

The interior of the trunk grew hot, stifling. Sweat dripped over the necromancer. The vegetation seemed to tighten around her limbs.

Not die . . .

Her silver eyes flashed bright . . . *brighter* . . .

The tree exploded.

Fragments of wood flew in all directions, bombarding the nearby landscape. Somewhere, Kara heard men swear and dogs whine. She could do nothing for them, though, and, in truth, could do no more for herself. The necromancer fell forward, her arms and legs no longer hindered. The instinctive reaction to put her hands out to save herself kept Kara from striking the ground head first, but did not prevent the jolt when her body hit from causing her to momentarily black out.

Vaguely she heard voices that seemed to draw near. A beast sniffed the ground near her head, its cold nose briefly rubbing against her ear. She heard a command, then felt strong but gentle hands touch her shoulders.

"Kara! What in the name of the Sea Witch happened to you, lass?"

"Jeron—" she managed to utter, the effort nearly doing her in again.

"Easy, lass! Here, you fool! Take the dogs' leashes! I'll see to her!"

"Aye, captain!"

Kara barely noticed the journey back to Gea Kul, save for one moment when the innkeeper, who carried her in his arms, swore at one of his companions for nearly letting the dogs trip him. She drifted into and out of consciousness, now and then recalling her short glimpses of the two undead. Something about them had greatly disturbed her, more than she would have imagined possible.

Even in her present state, it went through Kara's mind that they had been invisible to her senses, that they had played her, not the other way around. Necromancers manipulated the forces of life and death, not the other way around. Yet, the Vizjerei and his grinning companion had toyed with Kara as if she had been less than a first-year novice. How? More to the point, why did they walk the world at all?

The answer had to deal with her earlier error in the tomb. Somehow, although her training had never covered such astounding occurrences, when she had left the phantasm alone, it had been able to seize full control of the body. Then, it must have summoned the companion it had known in life, the pair vanishing by magic before she returned.

A simple explanation, and yet not at all satisfactory. Kara missed something; she felt sure of it.

"Enchantress?"

The word echoed in her skull, drowning out her thoughts. She forced her eyelids open—which Kara had not even realized until now had been closed—and stared up at the concerned visage of Captain Hanos Jeronnan. "What . . . ?"

"Easy, lass! You've gone two days without food and water! Not enough to do you any real harm, but still too much for your own good!"

Two days? She had been trapped in the tree for two days?

"When you vanished that night, I started a search right away, but not until morn came did I find this pouch near the side of the inn." He held up a small, leather pouch in which Kara stored some of the herbs necessary for her calling. Necromancer spells required other ingredients besides blood, although most outsiders never knew that.

Odd, though, that she should lose that pouch. It would have almost required her captors to spend precious time to tear it off, so securely had the young spellcaster generally kept it fastened. Of course, that made even less sense, since the only reason that they would bother to do that might be to actually leave a clue to her kidnapping, hardly something either ghoul would have done.

But, then, they *had* left her alive, if buried in the heart of a dead tree.

She felt so confused. Her irritation must have shown, for the innkeeper immediately sought to aid her. "What is it? Need more water? Blankets?"

"I'm . . ." Her words sounded more akin to the croaking of a frog—or too much like her more vocal assailant. Kara gratefully accepted water, then tried again. "I am all right, captain . . . and I thank you for your care. I will, of course, pay you—"

"I don't like foul language in my establishment, milady! There'll be no more talk of that!"

He truly was a curiosity to her. "Captain Jeronnan, most folk, especially westerners, would rather have left one of my kind to rot in that tree, much less put together a search party. Why do this?"

The huge man looked uncomfortable. "Always watch over my guests, lass."

Despite the aches throughout her body, she pushed herself up to a sitting position. Jeronnan had given her a room such as she could not have imagined in Gea Kul. Clean and comfortable, with no odor of fish, either. Truly a marvel. Yet, Kara did not let her pleasant surroundings deter her from her question. "*Why* do it, captain?"

"I had me a daughter once," he began with much reluctance. "And before you think it, she looked not a bit like you save in also being pretty." Jeronnan cleared his throat. "Her mother was higher born than me, but my naval successes let me rise to where we could wed. Terania was born to us, but her mother never lived much beyond carrying her." A daring tear emerged from the gruff man's eye, one the innkeeper quickly brushed out of existence. "For the next decade and more, I couldn't stand my life because it tore me away from the only one left to me. Finally, I resigned my commission when she was just beginning to blossom into a fair maiden and took her across the sea to a place I remembered being so beautiful. Bless her, Terania never complained, even seemed to thrive here."

"Gea Kul?"

"Don't sound so surprised, lass. Was a much nicer, cleaner place a decade ago. Something foul's touched it since, just as it's touched every other place I hear of these days."

Kara carefully kept her expression neutral. As one of the faithful of Rathma, she knew well that dark powers had begun to spread over the world. The ransacking of Bartuc's tomb only exemplified that fact. The necromancers feared that soon the world would slip out of the delicate balance it needed to maintain, that the tide would shift toward the Lords of Hell.

That demons already walked the world again.

Captain Jeronnan had been talking while she had considered all of this and so Kara had missed his past few words. However, something at the end caught her attention, so much so that she had to blurt, "What?"

By now his face had turned grim, so very grim. "Aye, that's what happened, all right! Two years we lived here, happy as could be possible; then one night I hear her scream from her room, a place no man could get without passing me first! Smashed through her door, I did—and found *no* trace of her. Her window remained locked, her closet I searched well, but she'd somehow vanished from a room with no other good exit."

Jeronnan had searched high and low for his daughter, several of the locals more than willing to join the hunt. For three days, he had looked and for three days he had failed . . . until one night, as he tried to sleep, the captain had heard his daughter calling to him.

A cautious man despite his desperate hopes, he had taken with him the ceremonial blade awarded to him by his admiral. With it, the innkeeper had gone out into the wilds, following the call of his child. For more than an hour he had trekked through the woods and hills, seeking, searching . . .

Finally, near a crooked tree, he had caught sight of his beloved Terania. The girl, her skin so oddly pale—even more so than Kara's—had stood waiting for her father with arms outstretched.

She had called out to him again and Jeronnan had, of course, responded. Sword in one hand, he had taken his daughter close—

Her fangs had nearly ripped out his throat.

Captain Jeronnan had sailed the world, had seen many a marvelous and disturbing thing, had fought pirates and villains in the name of his masters, but no experience in his life had meant more to him than raising his only child.

And nothing had ripped at his soul more than running the creature she had become through the heart.

"It hangs downstairs," he muttered, finishing. "A fine piece of craftsmanship and designed to be practical, too." Almost as an afterthought, the captain added, "Plated in silver or else I'd not be here with you today."

"What happened to her?" Kara knew such tales, but the causes varied.

"The damned thing is, I never found out! Finally managed to push it to the back of my mind until you vanished. Feared that it had come back for you!" A daring tear escaped his eyes. "I still hear her cries . . . both the one when she vanished and the one when I *slew* her."

Jeronnan's unknown horror had not stalked Kara, but the two undead tomb robbers had certainly been waiting, which drew her at last back to her own immediate situation. "Forgive me, captain, for sounding so uncaring about your great loss, but can you tell me if any ships departed during the time I was lost?"

Kara's question caught the grieving man off guard for a moment, but he quickly recovered. "Only ship that's sailed off so far has been the *Hawksfire*, a cursed vessel if I've ever seen one! Surprised it hasn't sunk yet."

Only a single ship had departed. It had to be the one she wanted. "Where was it heading?"

"Lut Gholein. It always sails to Lut Gholein."

She knew the name. A prospering kingdom on the western side of the Twin Seas, a place where merchants from all over the world bought and sold.

Lut Gholein. The Vizjerei and his grinning friend had trekked all the way here from the tomb, moving at a pace only those who felt no exhaustion could maintain. They had specifically come to Gea Kul, whose only good purpose served as a point by which to reach other realms. But why?

There could be only one reason. They pursued the remaining members of their party, the ones who also carried with them Bartuc's armor. Kara suspected that might be only one man, but she had to keep in mind the possibility of more in mind.

So this *Hawksfire* carried either the survivors or the revenants. If the latter, the pair would have to have secreted themselves carefully in order to avoid detection, but she had heard tales of the undead doing whatever they needed while pursuing their victims. Crossing the sea would be difficult, but not impossible.

Lut Gholein. It might yet be only another brief stop, but at least Kara had a particular destination.

"Captain, when is the next ship sailing there?"

"Lass, you're barely able to sit up, much less—"

Silver eyes fixed unblinking at him. "When?"

He rubbed his chin. "Not for a time. Maybe a week, maybe more."

Much too late. By then, both the revenants and those they pursued would be long gone, the armor with them. Even more important than her dagger remained the fact that the bloody warlord's suit moved about. The enchantments within would certainly call out to the ambitious, the evil.

Even those not necessarily human.

"I have funds. Can you recommend a ship I could hire?"

Jeronnan eyed her for a moment. "This is that important?"

"More than you can imagine."

With a sigh, the innkeeper replied, "There's a small but sleek vessel, the *King's Shield*, near the northernmost end of the port. She can sail at any time. Just need a day or two to gather the crew and supplies together."

"Do you think you can convince the owner to hear me out?"

This caused Jeronnan to laugh hard. "No need to worry about that, milady! He's a man who used to follow many a cause, so long as it was a good one!"

Her hopes rose. Already she felt nearly well enough to travel. The *Hawksfire* had a few days head start, but with a good ship, Kara might be able to arrive in Lut Gholein in but a short time after. Her unique skills, combined with a few careful questions, should enable her to follow the trail from there.

"I need to talk with him. I must be able to leave by tomorrow morning."

"Tomorrow morn—"

Again she gave him that gaze. Kara regretted pushing, but more than her health and the patience of this other captain were at stake. "It must be so."

"All right." He shook his head. "I'll get everything ready. We'll set sail in the morning."

Kara was touched by his sudden offer. "It is more than enough that you can convince the *King's Shield*'s captain to take this journey, but you need not tear yourself from your beloved inn! This is no longer your concern."

"I don't like when my guests are nearly killed . . . or worse, lass. Besides, I've been too long on dry land! Be good to feel the sea again!" He leaned nearer, giving her a smile. "And as for convincing the captain, I don't think you understand me yet, enchantress! *I'm* owner of that fine vessel and by all that's holy, I'll see that she sets sail in the morning—or I promise you that there'll truly be hell to pay!"

As he hurried off to see to arrangements, Kara slumped down, caught by his last words. *Hell to pay?*

Captain Hanos Jeronnan had no idea just how fateful his oath just might end up being.

SEVEN

"My men grow restive and I can truly understand their positions, Galeona. Greatness beckons and we have sat here on the edge of the desert!"

" 'Twas by your command that we remained yet longer, my dear Augustus."

He towered over her. "Because you said that soon we would better know the location of Bartuc's armor! We would soon know where this fool brings it!" Malevolyn seized her hair, pulling her up until their faces nearly touched. "Find him, my darling. Find him—or I may have to find myself mourning your passing!"

She let him see no fear. Those who showed fear to the general became much reduced in his eyes, nevermore respected, forever expendable. Galeona had worked long and hard to make certain that she remained invaluable and she would not let that change now.

"I will see what I can do, but it must be accomplished without you this time."

He frowned. "You always required my presence in the past. Why the change now?"

"Because what I must do will require me to delve deeper than I ever have before . . . and if for any reason I am disturbed at the wrong point, not only will it kill me, but it may also perhaps slay anyone nearby."

This clearly impressed even the general. Brow raised, he nodded. "Very well. Is there anything you require of it?"

A voice suddenly spoke in Galeona's head. *There must be . . . some sacrifice.*

The sorceress smiled, wrapping one arm around Malevolyn and putting her lips to his. As she pulled away from the kiss, she absently asked, "Who's failed you most of late, my love?"

His mouth set into a straight edge, unyielding and unforgiving. "Captain Tolos has proven something of a disappointment of late. I think his dedication is slipping."

Her hand stroked Malevolyn's cheek. "Then perhaps I can make him more useful to you."

"I understand. I'll send him to you immediately. Just give me *results.*"

"I think you'll be pleased."

"We shall see."

General Malevolyn marched out of the tent. Galeona immediately turned to the shadows, one in particular. "You think it'll be enough?"

"This one can only try," replied Xazax. The shadow separated from the others, moving nearer. Part of the shadow crossed over the sorceress's foot, sending a sensation like approaching death through her.

"I must find him this time! You see how impatient the general gets!"

"This one has waited much longer than the mortal," chittered the shade. "This one desires the finding far more than even him."

They both heard footsteps outside her tent. Xazax's silhouette immediately sank back into the rest of the shadows. Galeona brushed back her hair, then adjusted her arresting garments for best viewing.

"You may enter," she cooed.

A young officer, his helm in the crook of his arm, entered. Red-haired, with a slight beard and eyes too innocent, he looked like a lamb coming to the slaughter. Galeona remembered his face and the interesting notions that had crossed her mind more than once. "Come closer, Captain Tolos."

"The general sent me," the officer returned in a voice that held just a hint of uncertainty. No doubt he knew well of the sorceress's reputation . . . not to mention her appetites. "He said you had a task for me."

She went to the table where she kept wine for the general, pouring Tolos a cup of the finest. Galeona held it up for him to see, beckoning the man to come to her. Like a fish to the lure, he did just that, his expression still confused.

Pressing the cup into his hand, Galeona led it to his mouth. At the same time, her other hand followed the course of his body, which further increased his anxiety.

"Lady Galeona," Tolos stammered. "the general sent me here for a purpose. It would not do for him to discover—"

"Hush . . ." She pushed the drink to his lips, making him sip. The fiery-tressed soldier swallowed once, twice, before the enchantress lowered the cup again. With her free hand, she brought his lips to hers, keeping them there long. He hesitated for the first few seconds, then pressed hard, lost in her charms.

Enough of frail pleasures, came the demon's voice in her head. *We have work to do . . .*

Behind the enamored officer, the shadow grew, solidified. A sound akin to a dying swarm of flies arose, enough of a noise to finally snap Captain Tolos from the enchantment Galeona had woven over him. The light of the oil lamp let part of a new shadow cross his field of vision, a shadow shaped like nothing human.

Tolos pushed her away, then sought his sword as he turned to face his supposed assassin. "You'll not take me so—"

Whatever words he planned failed him. Captain Tolos gaped, his skin turning completely white. His fingers still fumbled for the sword, but the overwhelming fear enveloping him made his hand shake so much that he could not maintain any grip on the hilt.

And looming before him, the demon Xazax surely represented a sight capable of instilling such horrific fear. More than seven feet in height, Xazax resembled most a praying mantis, but a mantis as only Hell could create. A mad mix of emerald and crimson colored a body upon which pulsated great golden veins. The head of the demon looked as if someone had peeled off the outer shell of the insect, seeking the equivalent of a skull beneath. Oversized, yellow pupilless orbs stared down at the puny mortal and mandibles wider than a soldier's head—with smaller yet equally savage ones nearer the actual mouth—opened and closed with terrible eagerness. A stench like decaying vegetation pervaded the area surrounding the monstrous creature and even began permeating the tent.

The middle appendages, skeletal arms with three-fingered claws, reached out with lightning speed, dragging the petrified officer near. Tolos finally tried to scream, but the demon spat first, covering his victim's face with a soft, sticky substance.

Xazax's main appendages rose high, two jagged scythes ending in needle-like points.

He thrust both lances through the breast plate of the unfortunate officer, skewering Tolos like a fish.

The body quivered violently, something that seemed to amuse Xazax greatly. Tolos's hands feebly clawed at both his chest and his face, succeeding in freeing neither.

Galeona frowned at the sight, trying to cover her own dread of the demon's physical presence with anger and sarcasm. "If you're done playing, we do have *work* to do."

Xazax let the still-quivering body slide free. Tolos dropped to the ground, his blood-soaked carcass splayed out like some stringless marionette. The hellish mantis prodded the officer's corpse toward her. "Of course."

"I'll draw the patterns. You be ready to channel."

"This one will be prepared, make no mistake about it, human Galeona."

Touching Tolos's chest, the witch began to shape the patterns needed. She drew first a series of concentric circles, afterwards placing a pentagram in the midst of the largest. Galeona then traced in crimson both the marks of summoning and the wards that would protect her and even Xazax from being overwhelmed by the forces of the spell.

After a few minutes' work, Galeona had everything prepared. The sorceress glanced up at her demonic companion.

"This one is ready, as promised," came the raspy reply to her unspoken question.

The mantis approached, his scythelike arms reaching out to touch the center of Galeona's main pattern. A sound that grated the sorceress's ears erupted from Xazax, the demon speaking in a tongue with no earthly origins. She gave thanks that her protective spells kept anyone outside from hearing the creature's unholy voice.

The tent began to shake. A wind arose inside, one that lifted Galeona's hair and blew it back. The oil lamp flickered, at last dousing, but another light, a dank, poison-green aura, emerged from the blood-soaked chest of the dead soldier.

Xazax continued muttering in his demonic tongue, at the same time the mantis drawing new variations in the crimson pattern. Galeona felt forces both natural and hellish come forth, then mix in a combination otherwise impossible in the real world.

She reached out, adding to the demon's variations on the patterns. Now the interior of the tent crackled with energies both in flux and in conflict.

"Speak the words, human," commanded Xazax. "Speak before we are *engulfed* by our own creation . . ."

Galeona did, the ancient syllables spilling from her lips. Each word made her own blood burn, made the horrific veins coursing over her partner flare over and over. The dark sorceress spoke more quickly, knowing that if she faltered, Xazax's fear might yet prove true.

A thing the color of mold and fleshed almost like a toad formed above the body of Captain Tolos. It struggled, twisted, tried to cry out with a mouth not completely formed.

Let . . . me . . . ressssst! it demanded.

Deformed beyond even the manner of demons, the grotesque creature sought to swipe first at Galeona, then Xazax. However, the wards that she had set into place caused a blue spark whenever the monstrosity reached out, a spark which clearly hurt the thing much. In frustration, it finally pulled within itself, wrapping spindly, taloned limbs about it as if trying to fold itself up enough to utterly disappear.

"You are ours to command," she told the imprisoned creature.

I . . . must . . . rest!

"You cannot rest until you complete the task we've set for you!"

Nightmarish eyes that dangled loose yet also seemed in some ways human peered at her in open malevolence. *Very well . . . for a time, anyway. What would . . . you have . . . of me?*

"No magic binds your eyes, no barriers block your vision. See for us what we seek and tell us where it is."

The horror above Tolos's cooling body quivered, rumbled. Both Xazax and Galeona bent back at first—until both realized that the thing only *laughed* at their demand.

That . . . is all? For this . . . I am tortured . . . forced to wake and even . . . forced to remember?

Recovering, the witch nodded. "Do it and we'll return you to your sleep."

The eyes swung toward the demon. *Show . . . me what . . . you seek.*

The mantis drew a small circle in the midst of the main pattern. A haze of orange filled the area in which the trapped creature floated. The eyes stared into the haze, seeing what even Galeona could not see.

It becomes . . . clearer . . . what you . . . seek. It will . . . be requiring . . . of a price.

"The payment," interjected Xazax. "you have already tasted a portion of."

Their prisoner gazed down at the body. *Accepted.*

And with but that—a force struck Galeona so hard within her mind that the sorceress fell back, collapsing onto her pillows.

She sailed aboard a vessel of dubious means and reputation, a vessel fighting a storm she found not at all natural. The storm had already ripped apart some of the sails, yet still the ship pressed on.

Curiously, Galeona saw no crew aboard, almost as if only ghosts manned this vessel. However, something tugged at her, demanded she look beyond the deck. Without even moving her feet, the sorceress shifted position, the door of a cabin now before her. Galeona raised one transparent hand, trying to push open that door.

Instead, she drifted through it, entering the cabin like one of the specters she had imagined sailing the ship. Yet, the lone occupant of this sad excuse for a room in no manner resembled the dead. In fact, up close he looked like far more than Galeona had first believed. Very much a soldier. Very much a man.

The witch tried to touch his face, but her hand went through his flesh. Nevertheless, he shifted slightly and almost smiled. Galeona glanced down at the rest of his body, noting how Bartuc's armor fit him well.

Then, a shadow in the corner caught her attention, a shadow with a familiar feel to it. Xazax.

Knowing that she had to tread carefully now, Galeona focused on what she and the demon sought. Once more acting as if she caressed the fighter's cheek, the witch murmured. "Who are you?"

He turned slightly, as if unsettled.

"Who are you?" she repeated.

This time, his lips opened and he mumbled, "Norrec."

She smiled at her success. "On what ship do you sail?"

"Hawksfirrre."

"What is its destination?"

Now he began to turn. A frown appeared on his slumbering visage and he seemed unwilling to answer, even in his dreams.

Determined not to fail in this, the most important of the questions, Galeona repeated herself.

Again, he did not answer. The witch looked up, saw that Xazax's shadow grew stronger. She did not trust the demon to take care, though. In fact, his presence even threatened to jeopardize matters.

The sorceress turned her attention back to Norrec, looming over him and speaking to him now in the seductive tone she generally reserved most for Augustus. "Tell me, my brave, handsome warrior . . . tell Galeona to where you sail . . ."

His mouth opened. "Lut—"

At that moment, the demon's shadow crossed his face.

Norrec's eyes flew open. "What in the name of all—"

* * *

And Galeona found herself back in the tent, her eyes staring toward the ceiling, her body covered in a chill sweat.

"You imbecile!" she roared, picking herself up. "What were you thinking?"

Xazax's mandibles snapped open and close. "Thinking that this one could find answers much more quickly than a much distracted female human . . ."

"There are much better ways than fear for discovering secrets! I had him answering everything! A few moments' more and we would have had all we needed to know!" She thought quickly on the subject. "Maybe it's not too late! If—"

She hesitated, staring down at where Tolos lay—or rather, *had* lain.

The body, even the blood that had splattered the carpet, had vanished.

"The dream one has taken his prize," Xazax remarked. "This Captain Tolos will suffer a terrible afterdeath . . ."

"Never mind him! We have to get the Dreamer back—"

Here the mantis vehemently twisted his head back and forth, the closest he could come to shaking it. "This one will not defy a Dreamer in his own domain. Their realm is beyond even that of Hell or Heaven. Here we may command them, but, break the link, and they may take what is theirs." The demon leaned forward. "Do you think your general might part with another soul?"

Galeona ignored his suggestion, thinking what she could say to Malevolyn. She had the names of both the man and his vessel, but what good did that do her? The ship might be sailing anywhere! If only he had managed to blurt out his destination before the demon had fouled matters much! If only—

"He said 'Lut—,'" the witch gasped. "It has to be!"

"You have a thought?"

"Lut Gholein, Xazax! Our fool journeys to Lut Gholein!" Her eyes widened in satisfaction. "He comes to us, just as I first said!"

The monstrous yellow eyes flashed once. "You are certain of this?"

"Very much!" Galeona let out a throaty chuckle, one that would have stirred many a man, but did nothing for the demon. "I must go tell Augustus at once! This will keep him in line for the time being!" She considered further. "Perhaps I can finally convince him to dare the desert. He wants Lut Gholein; this gives him even more reason to want to take it!"

Xazax gave her what for the mantis appeared a puzzled look. "But if the human Malevolyn throws his men at Lut Gholein, he will certainly fail—aah! This one understands! How clever!"

"I don't know what you mean . . . and I've no more time to argue with you! I must tell Augustus that the armor sails toward us as if summoned by our very hand."

She swept out of the tent, leaving the demon to his own devices. Xazax glanced at the spot where the unfortunate officer's body had lain but a short time before, then again at the tent flaps through which the dark-skinned sorceress had passed.

"The armor sails toward us, yes," the mantis chittered, his form beginning to fade back into shadow. "Curious what your general would think of you, though . . . if it did not reach Lut Gholein."

Norrec's eyes flew open. "What in the name of all—"

He paused, already half out of his bunk. Even though the lamp had gone out, Norrec could see well enough to know that he remained the only occupant of the cabin. The woman leaning over him—a sight he would certainly not soon forget—had evidently been the product of his dreams. What exactly she had been doing, the veteran could not say, only that she seemed interested in talking with him.

A beautiful woman who only wants to talk is certain to be after your purse, Fauztin had once pointed out to Sadun Tryst after the latter had nearly lost his meager pay to a female thief. Yet, what harm could a woman in a dream do to Norrec, especially considering his already dire situation?

He wished that he had not awakened. Perhaps if the dream had gone on longer, it would have proved more enticing. Certainly it had been an improvement over his recent nightmares.

Thinking of nightmares, Norrec tried to remember what had actually made him call out. Not the woman. Some sense of foreboding? Not quite right, either. More the feeling that something horrific had been encroaching upon him even as the dark-skinned temptress had leaned nearer . . .

A violent shift in the *Hawksfire* suddenly sent Norrec tumbling. He fell against the cabin door, which swung open without warning.

On his own, Norrec would not have reacted swiftly enough, but one gauntleted hand shot out of its own accord, seizing hold of the door frame and preventing the helpless soldier from crashing through the outside rail and plummeting into the stormy sea. Norrec dragged himself to safety, then pulled himself to his feet, his hands once more his own.

Did Captain Casco no longer have any control over his crew? If they were not careful, they would end up letting the waves and wind tear the *Hawksfire* apart!

He seized a handhold and began fighting his way toward the bow. The roar of the waves and the constant rumble of thunder made it impossible to hear the mariners, but certainly Casco had to be berating them for their carelessness. Certainly the captain would see to it that his crew—

Not a soul stood on the deck of the *Hawksfire*.

Still unwilling to believe his eyes, Norrec glanced up at the wheel. Using strong rope, someone had lashed it into one position, giving at least a semblance of control. However, there any concern for the ship ended. Already some of the lines for the sails fluttered loose, whipping about madly in the storm. One sail had tears in it that threatened to widen quickly unless someone did something.

The crew had to be below. No one would have been insane enough to abandon a serviceable ship, even the *Hawksfire,* in the midst of such violence. Casco had likely summoned them to the mess in order to discuss some drastic measure. Surely that had to be—

The lifeboat that should have been hanging near to where he stood had vanished.

Norrec quickly peered over the rail, but saw only loose ropes battering the hull. No accident had occurred here; someone had definitely lowered the boat into the water.

He ran from rail to rail, confirming his greatest fear. The crew *had* abandoned the *Hawksfire,* leaving both it and Norrec at the mercy of the storm . . .

But why?

It was a question to which he already knew the answer. He recalled the expressions of the crew after the suit had summoned the demons to repair the mast. Fear and horror—and both aimed not at the armor, but rather the man who wore it. The crew had been afraid of the power they believed Norrec wielded. Even from the start of the voyage, there had been a wariness whenever he had entered the mess. They had known even then that he had been no ordinary passenger and the incident involving the mast had more than proven them correct.

Ignoring the rain and wind, he returned once more to the rail, trying to make out any sign of the crew. Unfortunately, they had likely left hours before, making good use of his exhaustion after the summoning. Never mind that they had probably condemned themselves to death on the sea; the mariners had feared more for their eternal souls than their mortal bodies.

But where did that leave Norrec? How could he hope to sail the *Hawksfire* to land by himself, much less even steer a course to Lut Gholein?

A creaking noise directly behind him made the desperate soldier quickly turn.

Looking much bedraggled and not at all pleased to see Norrec, Captain Casco emerged from below deck. He had appeared cadaverous before, now he looked almost like a ghost.

"You . . ." he muttered. "Demon man . . ."

Norrec closed in on him, seizing Casco by the shoulders. "What happened? Where's the crew?"

"Left!" the captain snapped, pulling free. "Drown on sea rather than sail with demon master!" He shoved past Norrec. "Too much work to do! Away!"

The dismayed soldier watched as Casco moved to tighten some lines. His entire crew had abandoned ship, but the captain insisted on not only trying to keep the *Hawksfire* seaworthy, but also on route. It seemed like a mad, pointless exercise, but Casco looked determined to try as best he could.

Following after, Norrec called out, "What can I do to help?"

The soaked mariner gave him a contemptuous glance. "Jump over!"

"But . . ."

Casco ignored him, moving on to the next ropes. Norrec took one step, then realized how futile it would be to get the captain to listen. Casco had reason to both fear and hate him, and the veteran could not blame the man. Because of Norrec, Casco would likely lose both his ship and his life.

Lightning flashed, this time so near that Norrec had to turn away in order to keep from being blinded. Frustrated by his inability to do anything, he headed to the doorway leading below deck. Perhaps out of the storm he could better think.

A few lanterns still provided light as he descended into the bowels of the *Hawksfire,* yet their illumination did not help keep Norrec from being unsettled by the emptiness around him. Everyone but Casco had left the ship, daring certain death in order to be rid of the demon master in their midst. Likely if they had thought that they could have slain him, they would have tried that, but the display of power by the suit had clearly convinced them otherwise.

Which left Norrec wondering how long the *Hawksfire* had before the waves and wind tore it apart.

He glared at the gauntlets, the parts of the armor he most associated with his plight. If not for the suit, he would have never been in this predicament.

"Well?" Norrec nearly spat. "What do you plan to do now? Are we to start swimming if the ship sinks?"

At first he regretted even making the suggestion, fearful that the armor would choose to attempt to do just that. Norrec tried not to picture the heavy armor trying to stay afloat. To him, who had rarely taken to the sea save for short voyages, drowning seemed the most horrible of fates. To suffocate, to have his lungs fill with water as the dark sea engulfed him . . . better to run a blade through his gut instead!

The *Hawksfire* shook, this time in so violent a manner that the hull moaned ominously. Norrec gazed toward the ceiling, wondering if Captain Casco had finally lost what little control of the ship he had briefly had.

Again the vessel shook, the planks literally bending. A few more moments of this and the soldier felt certain that all his darkest fears would soon come true. Already he could feel the waters closing in.

Determined not to fall victim to panic, Norrec raced to the stairway, fighting to keep his footing as he rushed back up on deck. Whatever the mariner might think of him, Norrec had to try to somehow help Casco regain mastery of the *Hawksfire*.

He heard Casco shouting something in his native tongue, an unending litany of curses, from the sound of it. Norrec looked around, trying to find the captain in the storm.

He found Casco—along with a gigantic nightmare rising from the sea.

A gargantuan horror with what seemed a hundred tentacles and one vast red orb had the bow of the *Hawksfire* in its clutches. The aquatic behemoth resembled a giant squid, but only if some great force had first ripped away its skin and put in place wicked barbs everywhere. Worse, many of the smaller tentacles had, not suction cups, but rather tiny, clawlike hands that grasped and pulled at whatever part of the ship they could reach. Sections of the rail came away readily, as did some of the deck itself. Several hands and tentacles sought for the sails.

Captain Casco ran about the deck, ducking one attacking appendage and swatting at others with a long, hooked pole. On the deck near him, one ripped end of a tentacle flopped around, dark ichor pouring from the torn section. Defying the danger all about him, the mariner continued to try to fend off the monstrous sea creature. The sight looked as absurd as it did terrifying, one lone man trying to stop the inevitable . . .

Once more, Norrec looked down at the gloves, shouting, "Do something!"

The suit did not react.

With nothing else left for him, Norrec looked around, seeking a weapon. Seeing another of the hooked poles, he immediately seized it and ran to Casco's side.

His actions proved most timely for at that moment a pair of clawed hands rose behind the battling captain, reaching for his back. One hand managed to dig into Casco's bony shoulder, causing the captain to cry out.

Norrec brought the hooked pole into play, burying the point in the monstrous hand and pulling with all his might.

To his amazement, the hand tore off, dropping to the deck. At the same time, though, the second appendage, inhuman claws outstretched, turned toward Norrec. In addition, two tentacles with suction cups darted in from the veteran fighter's right.

Bringing the pole around again, Norrec tore into one of the tentacles, sending it retreating. The hand snapped at him, talons as long as the fingers trying to rip into Norrec's face. He swatted at it with the side of the pole, but missed.

What sort of monster had risen up from the depths? Although he would have willingly admitted that he knew little about life in the Twin Seas, Norrec Vizharan had heard no tales of any creature akin to this ungodly abomination. It looked more like a thing out of a tale of horror, a beast more at home with the demonic imps the suit had earlier summoned.

Demons? Could this creature be some sort of demonic force? Could that explain why the armor had not reacted? It still left so much unexplained, yet . . .

More than a dozen new tentacles, some with the bizarre clawed hands and some not, erupted from the sea, assaulting anew both Casco and Norrec from various directions. More adept at using the hooked pole, the lanky captain disproved his sickly appearance by swiftly tearing into two of the tentacles. Norrec proved not so fortunate, managing to push back a few of the horrors but doing damage to none.

More and more tentacles turned from the task of ripping the ship to pieces to now dealing with the only resistance. One managed to seize Casco's pole, pulling it free with such force that the captain fell to the deck, his bad leg giving out on him at last. Several clawed tentacles encircled him, dragging Casco toward the great behemoth.

Norrec would have helped, but his own troubles grew worse than those of the mariner. Tentacles wound around both legs, then his waist. Two more tore the pole from his hands. The soldier found himself hoisted up into the air, his breath slowly being squeezed out of him despite the enchanted armor.

He screamed as a set of claws raked his left cheek. Somewhere beyond his limited field of vision, Norrec heard Casco uttering oaths even as death prepared to welcome both men.

A serpentine shape curled around Norrec's throat. In desperation, he tugged at it, already aware that his strength would not prove sufficient to save him.

The gauntlet flared a fiery red.

The tentacle instantly uncoiled from his throat, but the glove would not release it. Norrec's other hand, also glowing furiously, came up, seizing the tentacle holding him by the upper part of the waist.

The rest of the behemoth's limbs pulled away, leaving the startled veteran dangling by his hands high above the *Hawksfire*. The storm whipped him about, but Bartuc's armor refused to give up its hold on the gargantuan monster, even when the beast sought to separate the captured tentacles. Norrec screamed, his arms feeling as if they would soon be torn from their sockets.

"Kosori nimth!" his mouth shouted. *"Lazarai . . . lazarai!"*

A bolt of lightning struck the leviathan.

The creature shuddered, nearly succeeding in freeing itself of Norrec simply due to its throes of pain. Yet, even then the gauntlets fought to retain hold, clearly the warlord's suit was not finished yet.

"Kosori nimth!" the soldier's mouth repeated. *"Lazarai dekadas!"*

A second bolt caught the sea monster directly in its terrifying eye. The bolt burned away the orb with little trouble, sending a shower of hot fluids over Norrec and the ship.

"Dekadas!"

The areas of the tentacles under Norrec's fingers turned a pasty gray. Serpentine flesh grew stony, petrified with startling swiftness.

The leviathan stiffened, its many appendages remaining in whatever position they had been just after the last of the magical words had been spoken. The pasty gray coloring spread rapidly down the two tentacles the hapless soldier held, then coursed along in every direction, covering the giant's body and other limbs in mere seconds.

"Kosori nimth!" Norrec shouted for the third and—so he suspected—final time.

A flash of lightning more intense than either of the others struck the graying sea demon directly in the ruined eye.

The horrific behemoth *shattered*.

The gauntlets released their grip on the crumbling tentacles, at the same time returning control of the hands to Norrec. Suddenly bereft of any hold, the startled fighter frantically grabbed at one of the massive limbs, only to have the piece he seized break off.

He plummeted toward the ship, his only hope that he would die crashing into the hard deck rather than sinking beneath the violent waters.

EIGHT

✹

"Very curious," Captain Jeronnan muttered, peering far ahead. "Seems like a lifeboat in the distance."

Kara squinted, seeing nothing. The captain evidently had miraculous eyesight. "Is there anyone in it?"

"No one visible, but we'll take a closer look. I'll not risk a single sailor's life just to spare a few minutes . . . hope you understand that, lass."

"Of course!" She felt grateful enough that Jeronnan had arranged this voyage in the first place. He had put his ship and his crew at her disposal, something the necromancer would not have expected from any person. In return, he had accepted such payment as would cover her expenses, but no more. Each time she tried to press, a dark expression would cover his countenance, warning the raven-tressed enchantress that she threatened to tread on the memory of the former naval officer's daughter.

It had taken two days at sea, in fact, before Kara had come to realize that he truly needed this voyage as much as she did. If the tall innkeeper had seemed boisterous before, he now seemed at times ready to burst. Even the constant hint of less than fair weather on the western horizon did nothing to dampen his spirits.

"Mister Drayko!" At Jeronnan's cry, a slim hawk-faced man in perfectly kept officer's garments turned and saluted. Drayko had not acted at all bitter when his master had declared that he would be taking command of this voyage. Clearly Jeronnan's second had great respect and devotion for the innkeeper. "Lifeboat ahead!"

"Aye, captain!" Drayko immediately gave commands for the sailors to prepare for survivors. The crew of the *King's Shield* reacted in quick and orderly fashion, something Kara Nightshadow had already come to expect. Those who served Jeronnan served a man who had lived much of his life following the strict dictates of discipline. This did not mean that he ruled with an iron hand. Jeronnan also believed in the humanity of each of his men, a rare quality in any leader in these times.

The *King's Shield* came up to the lone craft, two sailors immediately preparing lines to draw her in. Jeronnan and Kara stepped down to watch them at work, the necromancer beginning to feel uneasy about this discovery. They followed the same general route that the *Hawksfire* would have used; could this be a boat from that vessel? Had Kara's quest ended so soon, her quarries at the bottom of the sea?

"There's one aboard her," Captain Jeronnan muttered.

True enough, one sailor did lie in the boat, but even as the crew worked to secure the life craft, Kara already noted telltale signs that, for this man, they had arrived too late.

Mister Drayko sent a pair of men down to investigate. Sliding down the ropes, they gingerly turned over the body, which had been lying face down.

Eyes that no longer saw stared up into the heavens.

"Been dead a day," called up one of the men. He grimaced. "Permission to send him to his rest, sir."

Kara did not have to ask what he meant. Out here, there were limitations to what they could do for a corpse. A ceremony . . . and then a watery burial.

Jeronnan nodded his permission, but Kara quickly put a hand on his arm. "I need to see the body . . . it may tell us something."

"You think it's from the *Hawksfire*?"

"Don't you, captain?"

He frowned. "Aye . . . but what do you plan to do?"

She dared not explain in full. "Find out what happened . . . if I can."

"Very well." Jeronnan signaled for the men to bring the body up. "I'll have a cabin set aside for you, milady! I don't want anyone else witnessing what you plan. They wouldn't understand."

It took but a short time to bring the body to the cabin Jeronnan had chosen. Kara had expected to work with the corpse by herself, but the captain refused to leave. Even when she gave him a rather cursory explanation of what she intended, the former innkeeper refused to depart.

"I've watched men torn apart in battle, seen creatures I doubt you've even heard of, viewed death in a thousand forms . . . and after what happened to my daughter, nothing can ever make me flee again. I'll watch and I'll even help, if it comes to that."

"In that case, please bolt the door. We will not want anyone else seeing this."

After he had obeyed, Kara knelt beside the body. The sailor had been a middle-aged man who had not lived a gentle life. Recalling what little she had learned of the *Hawksfire,* the dark mage grew more suspicious that the boat had been indeed from that desperate vessel.

The men who had brought the body had quickly closed the eyes, but Kara now opened them up again.

"What in the Sea Witch's name are you doing, lass?"

"What has to be done. You may still leave if you wish, captain. It is not necessary that you subject yourself to any of this."

He steeled himself. "I'll stay . . . it's just that a dead man's stare is said to be bad luck."

"He certainly had enough of that." She reached into her pouch, searching for components. Without the dagger, she could not readily summon a phantasm as she had done in Bartuc's tomb. Besides, attempting to do so might have even made Jeronnan change his mind about letting her continue. No, what she had in mind would work well enough, provided that in the process it did not turn the captain against her.

From one tiny pouch Kara pulled forth a pinch of white powder.

"What's that?"

"Ground bone and a mix of herbs." She reached toward the dead sailor's face.

"*Human* bone?"

"Yes." Captain Jeronnan made no noise, no protest, which relieved the necromancer. Kara held the powder over the eyes, then sprinkled both sightless orbs with the white substance.

To his credit, Jeronnan kept his tongue still. Only when she next retrieved a tiny black vial, then reached for the corpse's mouth, did he dare interrupt again. "You're not going to pour that down his gullet, are you, lass?"

She peered up at him. "I mean no desecration, captain. What I do, I do to find out why this man perished. He looks dehydrated, starved, almost as if he has had neither food nor water for more than a week. A very curious state for him to be in if, indeed, he is from the ship we pursue. I would assume the captain there would keep his crew fed, would he not?"

"Casco's a mad, foreign devil, but, aye, he'd still see that his men were fed."

"As I thought. And if this poor soul is not from the *Hawksfire,* it behooves us to find out exactly which vessel he *is* from, too. Don't you agree?"

"Your point's made, lass . . . forgive me."

"There is nothing to forgive." With the top of the vial now removed, she used one hand to open the jaws of the sailor. That accomplished, Kara immediately tipped the vial so that half the contents would quickly drain down into the throat. Satisfied with that, she stoppered the bottle again and leaned back.

"Maybe you could at least tell me how you hope to find out anything."

"You'll see." She would have explained, but Jeronnan did not realize how swiftly she now had to work. In conjunction with the powder, the liquid Kara had used would have an effect lasting but a very short time and the necromancer still had the final part of the spell to cast. Any interruption from here on might waste crucial seconds.

With her finger, Kara drew a circle over the sailor's chest, then extended a line from there along the length of the throat, up the jaw, and finally ending at the mouth. At the same time, she whispered the words of the spell. Once that had been done, Kara tapped the corpse on the chest, once, twice, thrice. All the while, the dark mage kept track of each passing second.

The dead mariner let out an audible gasp as his lungs sought to fill with air.

"Gods above!" blurted Jeronnan, taking a step back. "You've brought him back!"

"No," Kara curtly answered. She had known that the captain would mistake this for a resurrection. Outsiders never understood the many facets of a necromancer's work. The faithful of Rathma did not toy with death as some believed; that went against their teachings. "Now, please, Captain Jeronnan, let me proceed."

He grunted, but otherwise remained silent. Kara leaned over the sailor, looking into the dead eyes. A faint hint of gold radiated from them, a good sign.

She leaned back. "Tell me your name."

From the cold lips emerged a single word. *"Kalkos."*

"From what ship do you hail?"

Another gasp of air, then, *"Hawksfirrrre."*

"So, he *is* from the—"

"Please! No speaking!" To the corpse, she asked, "Did the ship sink?"

"Noooo . . ."

Curious. Then why would this man have abandoned it? "Were there pirates?"

Again a negative response. Kara estimated the time she had remaining and realized that she had better push to the point. "Did everyone abandon ship?"

"Noooo . . ."

"Who remained behind?" The necromancer tried to keep the anticipation out of her voice.

Once more, the corpse inhaled. *"Casco . . . captain . . ."* The mouth shut, something not at all normal. The mariner's body almost seemed reluctant to add more, but then it finally gasped, *"Sssorcererrrr . . ."*

A sorcerer? The answer caught Kara off guard for a moment. She had expected to hear him speak of either the thieves who had stolen the armor or, in view of the crew's desperate act, the two revenants who had attacked her. Certainly their presence would have sent hardened sailors fleeing to the dangers of the sea.

"Describe him!"

The mouth opened, but no words came out. Like the phantasm, this spell allowed only for simple answers. Kara cursed quietly, then altered her question. "What did he wear?"

Inhaling . . . then, *"Armorrrr . . ."*

She stiffened. "Armor? Red armor?"

"Yesss . . ."

Something she had not expected. So, apparently one of the survivors of the tomb had been a sorcerer after all. Could it be this Norrec Vizharan of which the earlier phantasm had spoken? She repeated the name to the mariner, asking him if he knew it. Unfortunately, that did not prove the case.

Still, Kara had found out much of what she wanted to know. The last time this man Kalkos had seen the *Hawksfire*, it had not only been afloat, but the armor she sought remained aboard.

"Without a crew," she commented to a silent Captain Jeronnan. "The ship cannot sail far, can it?"

"More than likely to go in circles, if only its master and this spellcaster remain aboard." Jeronnan hesitated, then asked, "Haven't you more questions?"

She did, but none that the corpse could answer. Kara dearly wished that she still had her dagger. Then she could have taken more time and summoned up a true spirit, something that could have answered with longer, more coherent statements. Older, more skilled necromancers could have performed such a fantastic feat without the use of a tool, but Kara knew it would still be a few years before she reached that point.

"What about him?" insisted the former naval officer. "What *happened* to him . . . and the rest, for that matter, lass? One day on a rough sea's enough to kill many a man, but there's something unsettling about the look of him . . ."

Feeling somewhat ashamed that Jeronnan had found the need to remind her, Kara quickly leaned over the corpse again. "Where are your comrades?"

No answer. She quickly touched the chest, felt it sink under the slight pressure of her fingers. The liquid component of her spell had begun to wear off.

The necromancer had one chance. The eyes of a dead man often retained the last few images he had witnessed. If the powder she had placed on them still had some potency, then Kara might be able to see those images for herself.

Without looking back at the captain, she said, "Under no circumstances must I be interrupted for the next step. Is that understood?"

"Aye . . ." but Jeronnan said it with much reluctance.

Kara positioned her gaze directly over the sightless orbs, then began muttering. The gold tint to his eyes seized her, pulled her in. The necromancer fought back the instinctive desire to flee from the world of the dead, instead throwing herself fully into the spell she now cast.

And suddenly Kara sat in a boat in the midst of a stormy sea, pulling at the oars with all her might as if the three Prime Evils themselves chased the tiny vessel. The necromancer looked down, saw that her hands were thick, rough, seaman's hands—the hands of Kalkos.

"Where's Pietr's boat?" a bearded man called out to her.

"How would I know?" her own mouth snapped back, the voice deep and bitter. "Just row! Got us a chance if we keep headin' east! That hellish storm's got to end somewhere!"

"We shoulda taken the captain with us!"

"He'd never leave her, not even if she sank! He wants to ride with the demon master, let 'im!"

"Watch out for that wave!" someone else shouted.

Her head turned toward that direction, epithets such as Kara had never imagined men using spitting from her lips. In the distance, she saw two other lifeboats, each crammed tight with desperate men.

The bearded man suddenly stood up, not the wisest thing in such conditions. He gaped at something behind her—behind Kalkos—and pointed frantically. "Look out! Look out!"

Kalkos's gaze shifted as best it could. The sailor continued to man the oars.

At the edge of the the mariner's field of vision emerged a vast, serpentine tentacle.

"Turn about! Turn about!" Kalkos called. "Sit down, Bragga!"

The bearded man dropped to his place. Those able to work the oars desperately tried to turn the boat around.

Over the roar of the waves and the crash of thunder, Kara heard the distant screams of men. Kalkos looked that direction, revealing the horrific sight of scores of tentacles overwhelming one of the other boats. Several men were lifted into the air, some by the suction cups of the tentacles, others by macabre, grasping claws—almost hands—that plucked sailors from the boat as if they were flowers.

Kara expected the sailors to be drawn to the cavernous opening that she now witnessed in the center of a massive, monstrous form, a creature much like a gigantic squid, but with only one massive orb and horrid flesh that marked it as no denizen of this mortal plane. Instead, however, the monster simply held them aloft, using its clawed appendages to attach other sailors to various suckers. The victims cried out, pleading to those in the distance to save them.

"Row, damn you!" Kalkos roared. "Row!"

"I told you he wouldn't let us go! I told you!"

"Be quiet, Bragga! Be—"

A vast wave washed over them, throwing one shouting man overboard. Next to the tiny vessel, an array of tentacles rose from the water, surrounding Kalkos's companions on all sides and reaching hungrily for each.

"At 'em with your blades! It's the only—"

Yet although the men managed to parry the assaults of a few of the demonic arms, one by one they were picked off the boat, screaming—until only Kalkos, one oar used as a weapon . . . remained.

Kara felt a chill as wet tentacles seized her legs, grabbed her arms. She felt the suction cups attach to her body . . . No! This had all happened in the past! This had happened to Kalkos, not her!

Despite recalling that, however, she still felt the mariner's own horror as a new and terrible thing happened. Even despite his clothing, Kalkos felt weaker, drawn—as if the very life were being sucked from his body. His flesh wrinkled, dried despite the wetness all around him. He felt like a water sack whose contents were being swiftly drained . . .

And then, just as all life seemed stolen from him, when his body felt like no more than a dry husk, the tentacles suddenly dropped Kalkos back into the boat. Too late for the sailor to survive, Kalkos already knew that, but better to spend his last few moments of life back in the boat rather than in the gullet of such a hellish beast.

Only when talons dug into his arms and dragged him to a standing position did he come back from the brink enough to register that someone else had joined him in the lifeboat.

No—not someone—but some thing.

It spoke in a voice reminiscent of a thousand buzzing insects in agony; although Kara strained to make its form out clearly, the eyes of Kalkos no longer saw well. The enchantress could only perceive a terrifying, emerald and red shape looming over the dying sailor, a shape that did not conform to any human standard. Oversized eyes of deep yellow that seemed to have no pupils fixed on the unfortunate Kalkos.

"Death is not your pleasure yet," it chittered. "This one has things it must know! Where is the fool? Where is the armor?"

"I . . ." the mariner coughed. His body felt so very dry, even to Kara. "What . . . ?"

His inhuman inquisitor shook him. A pair of needle-tipped spears came from nowhere, pressing against Kalkos's chest. "This one has no time, human. Can offer you much pain before life flees. Speak!"

From somewhere within, Kalkos found the strength to obey. "The s-stranger . . . armored . . . blood . . . still on . . . Hawksfire!"

"Which way?"

The mariner managed to point.

The demon, for Kara knew it to be one, chittered to itself, then demanded, "Why flee? Why run?"

"He—demons on ship."

The murky creature made a sound unlike any Kara would have expected from one of his kind, a sound that she recognized instantly as a sign of consternation. "Impossible! You lie!"

The sailor did not answer. Kara felt him slipping away. His last attempt to respond to the monstrous figure had drained him of what little he had left of life.

The half-seen creature dropped Kalkos, a jolt of pain coursing through the necromancer as the body struck. She heard the demon chitter again, then spout one comprehendible word.

"Impossible!"

Kara had a lone brief glimpse of the inner side of the lifeboat and the sailor's fingers twitching—and with that, the vision faded.

Inhaling, Kara clutched herself tight, eyes still fixed on the corpse's own.

She felt the nearby presence of Captain Jeronnan. The former naval officer put comforting hands on her shoulders. "Are you all right?"

"How long?" the necromancer murmured. "How long?"

"Since you started whatever you've been doing? A minute, two maybe."

So short a time in the real world, but so long and violent in the memories of the dead. The necromancer had performed this spell before, but she had never faced a death time so horrible as what this Kalkos had suffered.

The *Hawksfire* sailed a day or two ahead of them, no crew left to man the ship save the captain and this sorcerer, Norrec Vizharan. The last name should have warned her: "Servant of the Vizjerei"? More like one of the untrustwor-thy mages themselves! He had the armor, even had the audacity to wear it! Did he not understand the danger?

Without a crew, even he would have trouble keeping the ship on course. Kara had a chance to catch him after all, provided that neither the revenants nor the demonic forces she had witnessed in Kalkos's death time had not caught up with the murderer already.

"So," continued Jeronnan, helping her to her feet. "Did you find out any-thing?"

"Little more," she lied, hoping her eyes would not give her away. "About his death, nothing. However, the *Hawksfire* is definitely still afloat, both the captain and my quarry aboard."

"Then we should catch up to them soon enough. Two men can't do much to keep a ship like that going."

"I believe it is only two days ahead at most."

He nodded, then glanced down at the corpse. "Are you done with him now, lass?"

She forced herself not to shiver at the memories she had shared with the late Kalkos. "Yes. Give him a proper burial."

"He'll get that . . . and then we'll be on our way after the *Hawksfire*."

As he departed the cabin to summon a pair of hands, Kara Nightshadow pulled her cloak about her, her gaze still on the body, but her mind on to what she had just committed herself—herself and every man aboard the *King's Shield*.

"It must be done," the necromancer muttered. "He must be caught and the armor returned to hiding. No matter what the cost . . . and no matter how many *demons*."

"Xazax!"

Galeona waited, but the demon did not respond. She looked around, search-ing for the telltale shadow. Sometimes Xazax played games, games with dark intentions. The sorceress had no time for games, especially ones that occasion-ally proved fatal for others than her partner.

"Xazax!"

Still no reply. She snapped her fingers and the lamp blazed brighter—yet still the shadow of the demon did not reveal itself.

Galeona did not care for that. Xazax in the tent, she understood. Xazax else-where generally spelled trouble. The mantis sometimes forgot who aided him in secretly walking the mortal plane.

No matter. She had far too much to do. The dark-skinned sorceress turned her fiery gaze on a massive chest positioned in one corner of the gar-ish tent. Taken as it appeared, the chest, made of iron and good strong oak and standing on four stylized leonine paws, would have required two sturdy soldiers to drag it to her and that with much effort on their part.

However, as with the demon, Galeona had no time to go searching for strong arms, especially when the enchantress knew that they were all busy packing up the rest of the camp. No, she could handle her own needs at this juncture.

"Come!"

The lower corners of the great chest shone. The metallic paws twitched, the leonine toes spreading, stretching.

The chest began walking.

The massive box wended its way toward Galeona, looking almost like a hound summoned by its mistress. It finally paused within a few inches of the witch, awaiting her next command.

"Open!"

With a long, creaking noise, the lid swung up.

Satisfied, Galeona turned and put her hand under one of the many pieces of her hanging collection. The piece unlatched itself, dropping gently into her waiting palm. The sorceress placed it in the chest, then went on with the next.

One after another, she dropped the items inside. An onlooker who had observed the entire time would have begun to notice that, no matter how many things Galeona put in the chest, it never seemed to completely fill. Always the witch found room for the next and the next . . .

But as she neared completion of her task, a slight chill went up and down her spine. Galeona turned and, after some searching, found a shadow that had not been present before.

"So! You finally come back! Where've you been?"

The demon did not answer at first, his shadow sinking deeper into the folds of the tent.

"Augustus has commanded that the entire camp be struck down. He desires we leave immediately after, whether preparations are completed in daylight or night."

Still Xazax did not answer. Galeona paused, not liking the silence. The mantis tended to babble, not hold his tongue. "What is it? What's gotten into you?"

"Where does the general seek to go?" the shadow abruptly asked.

"You have to ask? Lut Gholein, of course."

The demon seemed to consider this. "Yes, this one would go to Lut Gholein. Yes . . . that might be best . . ."

She took a step toward the shadow. "What's the matter with you? Where've you been?" When he did not answer, the witch walked up to the corner of the tent, growing more furious by the moment. "Either answer me or—"

"*Away!*"

The demon burst forth from the shadow, his full monstrous form looming over the human. Galeona let out a gasp and stumbled backward, at last falling over the pillows still covering much of the floor.

Death in the form of a hellish insect with burning yellow orbs and rapidly snapping mandibles hovered. Claws and sicklelike appendages came within an inch—no more—of Galeona's face and form.

"Cease your chattering and keep from this one! Lut Gholein is our agreed destination! We will talk no more until I choose!"

With that . . . Xazax pulled back into the dark corner, his physical form fading, his shadow growing dimmer. In but a few seconds, the only sign of his continued presence remained just the hint of a monstrous shape among the folds of fabric.

Galeona, however, did not move from where she had fallen until absolutely positive that the mantis would not leap out again. When the sorceress did finally rise, Galeona did so making certain that she rolled away from where the shadow lurked. She had come very close to death, very close to a lingering, *agonizing* death.

Xazax made no more sound, no more movement. Galeona could not recall when she had ever seen the horrific demon act as he had just done. Despite the pact between them, he had been more than willing to slay her if she had not obeyed instantly—something she swore not to forget. The pact should have been impossible for either to break, the only reason they could tolerate one another on such a long-term basis. If Xazax had been willing to risk the consequences of doing away with both that pact and her, then it behooved Galeona more than ever to find a way to rid herself of him . . . which very well meant either the general or the fool. At least with men, she always knew she had some control.

The sorceress turned back to the task of loading the contents of her tent into the chest, but her mind never left the demon's actions. Besides the danger she now perceived in his willingness to risk the consequences of breaking their covenant, his near attack of her had left a question behind to which she dearly desired an answer. It alone would give reason not only for Xazax's unnerving reaction, but also the revelation of an emotion she had never witnessed in him before.

What, Galeona wondered, could possibly have *frightened* the demon so?

Πίπε

The agonizing pain coursing through Norrec Vizharan proved to be the first sign that he had not, after all, perished. That he could breathe also indicated immediately to him that he had not dropped into the sea and that, therefore, he had struck the deck. Why he had not snapped his neck nor broken several other bones, Norrec could only suspect had to be the fault of Bartuc's cursed armor. It had already saved him from the demonic behemoth; a simple, short fall likely had been child's play to it.

Yet, in his heart, the veteran soldier half-wished that it had failed. At least then he would have been rid of the nightmares, the horrors.

Norrec opened his eyes to see that he lay in his cabin. Outside, the storm raged unceasingly. Only two forces could have dragged him back in here, one being the suit. Yet, after what it had done to the tentacled monstrosity, it had seemed weaker, unable to perform any feat. Norrec himself felt so drained, he marveled that he could even move. The weakness felt so odd that the weary soldier wondered if either the armor or the beast had somehow sucked part of his life from him.

At that moment, the door swung open, Captain Casco hobbling into the tiny cabin with a covered bowl in his hand. A scent that Norrec found both enticing and repulsive drifted from the bowl.

"Awake? Good! No waste of food!" Without waiting for the soldier to rise, the cadaverous mariner handed him the bowl.

Norrec managed to right himself enough to eat. "Thank you."

In return, the captain merely grunted.

"How long have I been out?"

Casco considered the question for a time, possibly wanting to make certain that he understood it. "Day. Little more."

"How's the ship? Did the creature damage it much?"

Again a pause. "Ship always damaged . . . but can still sail, yes."

"How can we possibly sail in a storm with no crew at all?"

The captain scowled. Norrec suspected that he had finally asked the question for which Casco had no good answer. Of course, they could not sail without a crew. Likely the *Hawksfire* went around and around, tossed in random directions by the winds and waves. They might have survived the attack by the monster, but that did not mean that they would reach Lut Gholein.

The monster . . . Norrec's memory of what happened seemed so outrageous that he finally had to ask Casco if what he had seen had been truth.

The captain shrugged. "Saw you fall . . . saw the Sea Witch fall."

The foreign mariner had evidently decided that what he had confronted had been the legendary behemoth mentioned by so many sailors. Norrec believed different, certain after his encounters with the imps and the winged creature at the inn that this had been yet another demonic force—but not one, this time, summoned by the enchanted armor.

Legend spoke of Bartuc's rise to dark glory, first as a pawn of hellish powers, then as a sorcerer both respected and feared by them, and how he had led a legion of demons in his quest to overwhelm all else. No one, though, ever spoke of how the greater demons might have felt about that usurping of their power. Had they now noted the armor's escape from the tomb and so feared that the ghost of Bartuc sought to reestablish his hold over their kind?

His head pounded at such outlandish thoughts. Best he concern himself with his own situation. If the *Hawksfire* remained unmanned, it would continue to meander over the Twin Seas, either sailing on long past the deaths of the only two aboard or finally sinking due to some aspect of the endless storm.

"I'm no seaman," he commented to Casco between bites of food. "But show me what I can do and I'll help. We've got to get the ship back on course."

Now Casco snorted. "Done enough! What more? What more?"

His attitude not only struck Norrec as peculiar, but it also stirred the fighter's own ire. He knew that much of this situation could be blamed on him—or rather, the armor—but his offer to help the captain had been an honest one. Norrec doubted that the suit would prevent him from helping; after all, it had been the one that had truly wanted to reach Lut Gholein, not him.

"Listen! We'll die if we don't get the *Hawksfire* under control! If the storm doesn't take us, then we'll either eventually starve when the supplies go bad or, more likely, strike some rocks and sink like a stone! Is that what you want for your ship?"

The gaunt figure shook his head. "Fool! Fall crack skull?" He had the audacity to seize Norrec by the arm. "Come! Come!"

Putting aside the nearly empty bowl, he followed Casco out into the storm. His legs took a few steps to again get used to the rocking of the ship, but the captain waited for him to catch up. Casco seemed caught between hatred, respect, and fear when it came to his passenger. He did not offer any assistance, but neither did he try to force Norrec along faster than the weakened man could go.

Reaching the open deck, the mariner let Norrec move past him. The veteran fighter held tight to what handrail remained, peering through the heavy rain and trying to see what it had been that Casco sought to show him. All Norrec could make out was the same empty scene he had confronted earlier. No sailors manned the ropes, no helmsman stood at the wheel.

And yet . . . the wheel *turned*. Ropes no longer held it in place. Norrec squinted, certain that the wheel should have been spinning wildly, yet it barely moved, sometimes turning one direction, then adjusting to the other, as if some invisible sailor kept it under control.

A movement to the side caught his attention. Focusing, Norrec at first had the horrible fear that one of the main lines had suddenly untied, only to have it *reloop* itself before his very eyes, then tighten the new knot.

And all around him he began to notice subtle shifts, subtle changes. Ropes adjusted according to the needs of the sails. The sails themselves adjusted as necessary. The wheel continued to counter the churning waves, fixing the *Hawksfire* on a particular route—one that Norrec expected would turn out to be almost directly west.

No crew manned the vessel, but it seemed to the *Hawksfire* not to matter in the least.

"What's going on?" he shouted at the captain.

Casco only gave him a knowing glance.

The armor! Again its power astounded him. It had dealt with the gargantuan demon and now it ensured that its own journey would continue regardless of the mutiny of the crew. The *Hawksfire* would reach port one way or another.

Norrec stumbled away, heading not for his cabin but down into the mess. Casco trailed behind, a captain with no purpose on this voyage. Both men shook off the rain. Casco dug into a chest, pulled out a dusty bottle whose contents he did not offer to his companion. Norrec thought of asking for a drink—he certainly needed one—but thought better of it. His head pounded enough at the moment and he preferred to try to let it clear.

"How long until we reach port?" he finally asked.

Casco put down the bottle just long enough to answer him. "Three. Four days, maybe."

Norrec grimaced. He had hoped for less than that. Three or four more days aboard a vessel where wheels and ropes moved by themselves and his only companion remained a wild-looking captain who thought him a devil in human form.

He rose. "I'll be in my cabin until it's time to eat."

Casco made no move to stop him, the lanky mariner quite content to be alone with his bottle.

Stepping out into the storm, Norrec battled his way back to the tiny cabin. He would have preferred to stay in the much more spacious—not to mention drier—area below deck, but in Casco's presence, the guilt over the troubles Norrec's being here had caused the man ate at the soldier. It amazed him that Casco had not just slit his throat when he had come across the unconscious figure. Of course, after seeing what Norrec had supposedly done, then discovering that even the fall had not killed his unsettling passenger, the captain likely had suspected that any attempt to slay the stranger would end up with Casco the dead party.

He would have probably not been far from wrong.

The rain continued to not only soak Norrec but tried to beat him to the deck. In all his years fighting for one master or another, the veteran had faced harsh weather of all sorts, including blizzards. However, to him this storm had no equal and he could only pray that it would at last end when the *Hawksfire* reached Lut Gholein's port.

That assumed, of course, that the ship *would* reach the port.

The intense rain kept visibility limited, not that there had ever been much to see either aboard ship or among the waves beyond. Nevertheless, Norrec had to continually blink away moisture just to see a few yards ahead of him. Never had the cabin seemed so far away as it did this moment. The heaviness of the armor did not help, either, the metal plate seeming twice its normal weight. Still, at least Norrec did not have to worry about rust settling in; the enchantments cast by Bartuc had clearly kept the suit as new as the day the demon master had first donned it.

Not for the first time, Norrec stumbled. Cursing the weather, he straightened, then wiped his eyes clear again so that he could see just how far away the door to his quarters remained.

A murky figure stared back at him from the aft section of the walkway.

"Casco?" he called out, realizing only afterward that the captain could not have possibly rushed all the way to the stern, not with his bad leg. More to the point, this figure stood taller than the mariner and wore a broad-shouldered cloak reminiscent of a Vizjerei sorcerer—

Reminiscent of *Fauztin's* cloak.

He took a step forward, trying to see better. The figure seemed half mist and Norrec wondered if what stood before him could be only the result of his own tortured, weary mind.

"Fauztin? Fauztin?"

The shadow did not answer.

Norrec pushed another step forward—and the hair on the back of his neck suddenly stiffened.

He whirled around.

A second, somewhat shorter figure near the bow drifted in and out of sight, his wiry form hinting of an acrobat or, more likely, a thief. What looked to be a travel cloak fluttered in the wind, enshrouding and obscuring most of the second figure's detail, but Norrec imagined a dead, still-grinning face, the head cocked slightly to the side because the neck had been broken.

"*Sadun . . .*" he blurted.

His hands suddenly tingled. Norrec glanced down, barely catching a slight red aura about them.

A bolt of lightning struck so near that it lit up the entire ship—so near, in fact, that the stunned fighter almost swore that it touched the *Hawksfire* yet did not damage it in any way. For a moment, the blinding brilliance surrounded Norrec, making him even briefly forget the two specters.

His eyesight finally returned to normal. Blinking, Norrec glanced toward both the bow and stern and saw no sign whatsoever of either of the dire shades.

"Sadun! Tryst!" the frantic fighter shouted. Turning back to the stern, he yelled, "Fauztin!"

Only the storm answered him, rumbling with renewed fury. Unwilling to give up yet, Norrec headed back toward the bow, shouting Sadun's name over and over. He made his way across the open deck, scanning every direction. Why he desired to confront either of his two dead comrades, even Norrec Vizharan could not actually say. To try to apologize? To explain? How could he do that when, even knowing that it had been the armor that had claimed their lives, the former mercenary still blamed himself for not having heeded Fauztin a few precious seconds earlier. Had he done so, he would not be where he was now.

Had he done so, neither of his friends would be dead.

"Tryst! Damn you! If you're real—if you're there—come to me! I'm sorry! I'm sorry!"

A hand fell upon his shoulder.

"Who you call?" demanded Casco. "What you call now?"

Even in the darkness and the rain, Norrec could see the fear rising in the captain's watery eyes. To Casco, either his passenger had gone completely mad or, more likely, Norrec planned to summon yet new demons. Neither choice obviously thrilled the mariner.

"No one . . . nothing!"

"No more demons?"

"No more. None." He pushed past Captain Casco, wanting nothing more than rest, but no longer interested in his cabin. Looking back at the perplexed and frustrated sailor, Norrec asked, "Are there bunks for the crew below?"

Casco nodded glumly. Likely he slept in a cabin near those bunks and did not like the direction of the question. Bad enough he had to share the ship with a summoner of hellish creatures, but now that same demon master planned to sleep nearby. No doubt Casco expected various monsters to go wandering around below deck if that happened . . .

"I'll sleep in one of them." Not caring how the captain surely felt, Norrec headed below deck. Perhaps the battle against the demonic behemoth had taken too much out of him, resurrecting his guilt over the deaths of his comrades. Perhaps he had imagined both of them. That seemed so very likely, just as it seemed likely that he had imagined Fauztin on the dock in Gea Kul. The mutilated bodies of his two friends still lay in the tomb, there to be found by the next eager treasure hunters.

Yet, as he shook off the rain and headed in search of the bunks, a stray thought disturbed him. Norrec stared at his gloved hands, flexed the fingers that, for the moment, obeyed his will. If he had imagined it all, if the shades of Fauztin and Sadun Tryst had not confronted him out on deck, why had the gauntlets glowed, even if only for a moment?

In the dead of night, the army of General Augustus Malevolyn went on the move, entering the vast, terrible desert of Aranoch. Many of the men did not look forward to this march, but they had been given an order and knew no other course of action but to obey. That some of them would surely perish before they reached their destination—assumed to be the lush prize of Lut Gholein—did not deter them in the least. Each hoped that he would be one of the fortunate survivors, one of those who would lay claim to some portion of the wealth of the port kingdom.

At the head of the army rode the general himself, the helmet of Bartuc worn proudly. A faint sphere of light conjured by Galeona floated just ahead of him, marking the path for his steed. That it might also identify him as the most desired target by ambushers did not bother Malevolyn in the least. Clad in the ancient helmet and his own spell-enshrouded armor, the general sought to show the ranks that he feared nothing and that nothing could defeat him.

Galeona traveled beside her lover, outwardly indifferent to everything, but all the while quietly utilizing her sorcery in order to detect any possible threat to the column. Behind the witch came a covered wagon loaded with Malevolyn's folded tent, the various personal items from within it, and— seeming almost as an afterthought—Galeona's wooden chest.

"At last . . . the armor will soon be within my grasp," the general murmured, staring ahead into the darkness. "I can already sense its nearness! With it, I shall be complete! With it, I shall command a host of demons!"

Galeona considered, then dared ask, "Can you be certain that it'll do all this for you, my general? True, the helmet has enchantments and the armor is said to be even more bespelled, but so far the helmet has left us all baffled! What if the armor acts much the same? I pray not, but the secrets of Bartuc may demand more of us than we're able to—"

"No!" He snapped at her with such vehemence that his guards, situated just behind him, immediately drew their swords, perhaps thinking that the sorceress had sought to betray their leader. Augustus Malevolyn signaled them to resheathe their weapons, then glared at Galeona. "It will not be so, my dear! I have seen the glorious visions brought forth by the helmet, the shade of Bartuc surely calling to me to add to his victories! I have seen in each of those visions the power of the armor and helm combined! The spirit of the bloody warlord lives on in the suit, and it is his desire that I become the mortal bearer of his standard!" He waved a hand at the desert. "Why else does the fool who wears it now come to me? He does so because it is destined! I will be Bartuc's successor, I tell you!"

The witch cringed, taken aback by his outburst. "As you say, my general."

Malevolyn abruptly calmed, once more a self-satisfied smile across his face. "As I say. And after that, yes, Lut Gholein will be mine to take. *This* time, I shall not fail."

Galeona had ridden with the commander from Westmarch for some time, likely knew him better than any under his command. Yet, in all that time, the only mention of Lut Gholein had been as an eventual target, one that Malevolyn had dreamed of conquering. She had never heard him speak of it as a past defeat. "You've been there . . . before?"

With something akin to devotion, he gently adjusted the helmet, turning away from her and preventing the sphere from illuminating what of his expression the armor did not already hide. "Yes . . . and if not for my brother . . . it would have been mine for the taking . . . but this time . . . this time, *Viz-jun will fall!*"

"*Viz-jun?*" she blurted, her tone incredulous.

Fortunately, General Malevolyn paid her no mind, attention concentrated on the darkened, shifting sands. Galeona did not repeat the name again, preferring to immediately drop, if not forget, the subject. Perhaps it had been a slip of the tongue, just as something else he had just said had to have been an innocent mistake. After all, the general had much on his mind, so very much . . .

She knew that he had never been to the fabled Kehjistani temple-city, had never yet been across the sea to that land. In addition, Augustus Malevolyn had been an *only* child—and an unwanted bastard at that.

Yet . . . someone else Galeona knew of had not only been to fabled Viz-jun, but had sought to conquer it, to destroy it, only to be thwarted in the end by his own brother.

Bartuc.

With a surreptitious glance, the witch studied the helmet, trying to divine its intentions. The visions that the western commander had experienced had clearly been for his benefit alone; even when she had secretly tried the artifact on, no such images had been shown her. Yet, it appeared that the more Augustus wore it, the more he had trouble differentiating between his own life and that of the monstrous warlord.

Did the helmet perform some sort of enchantment each time these incidents happened? Galeona casually touched a black-jeweled ring on one of the fingers of her left hand, turning the gem in the direction of her lover's head. She mouthed two forbidden words, afterward cautiously glancing to see if the general had noticed her lips moving.

He had not, nor did he now notice the invisible tendrils extending from that ring, tendrils that reached out to touch the helmet in various places. Only Galeona knew that they were there, seeking, probing, trying to detect whatever forces permeated the ancient armor.

Perhaps if she finally discovered how they affected the general, the witch could take the first step toward using those powerful enchantments for her own goals. Even some slight bit of new knowledge would go far toward extending her own abilities—

A flash of crimson light flared from the helmet, illuminating for a stunned Galeona each of the magical tendrils rising from her ring. A surge of power coursed toward her with lightning speed, eating away at the tendrils and converging on her finger. Fearing for herself, the sorceress reached to pull the ring free.

Only mortal, she moved too slow. The streams of crimson light devoured the last of the tendrils, then came together at the black jewel itself.

The gemstone sizzled, turned molten in less than the blink of an eye. The liquefied stone dripped over her finger, burning at her skin, searing her flesh . . .

Galeona managed to bite back a scream, transforming her reaction to the intense pain into a barely audible gasp.

"Did you say something, my dear?" General Malevolyn casually asked, his eyes never leaving the landscape.

She managed to keep her voice calm and assured despite her suffering. "No, Augustus. Just a slight cough . . . a bit of desert sand in my throat."

"Yes, that's a risk here. Perhaps you should cover it with a veil." He said no more, either focused on his duties as commander or lost once more in Bartuc's past.

Galeona carefully looked around. No one had noticed the astounding display of powerful energies in conflict. Only she, with her magical senses, had been witness to both her failure and her punishment.

Giving silent thanks for that bit of fortune at least, she cautiously investigated the damage. The ring had turned to slag, the rare and resilient gem a black, burning stain on her finger. The band she finally managed to remove, but the melted jewel left a permanent and painful ebony blot on her otherwise unmarred hand.

The injury meant little to her overall. She had endured much worse for her craft. No, what bothered Galeona more concerned the helmet's violent reaction to her probing. None of her spells in the past had caused it to respond with such vehemence. It almost seemed as if something within the armor had awakened, something with distinct intentions of its own.

It had always been her assumption that the ancient warlord had cast numerous enchantments of tremendous power on his armor, the better to aid him in battle. Such precautions would have made perfect sense. Yet, what if she had only guessed a part of it? What if even those who had slain Bartuc had not realized the full extent of his mastery of magicks demonic?

Did enchantments alone possess the helm and plate—or had Galeona discovered more?

Did Bartuc himself seek to return from the dead?

Ten

The *King's Shield* entered the storm late into its fifth day out of Gea Kul. Kara had hoped that the foul weather would break up before they confronted it, but, in truth, those who manned the ship had only themselves to blame for this new situation. Captain Jeronnan commanded an excellent crew, one that understood well the idiosyncrasies of the turbulent sea. The necromancer doubted that any other vessel could have plied the waters as efficiently and with such remarkable speed as this one, which, unfortunately, had virtually guaranteed that the *King's Shield* would outrace even this swiftly moving tempest.

The unfortunate Kalkos had been given a formal burial at sea, Kara adding to the ceremony with a few words of respect based on the funeral traditions of her people. In her eyes, Kalkos had only transcended to another plane, where, in his new existence he and those before him would work to maintain the balance of all things. However, she still felt some guilt, some misgivings, about the prayer she had said, for the pale enchantress had not forgotten her own deep desire to live when she had found herself entombed in the tree. Kara's only way so far to reconciliate that with her general beliefs had been to decide that, if she had perished, it would not only have upset the balance, but it would also have left no one who could have tracked down the missing armor. That could not be allowed to happen.

Almost immediately upon entering the storm-tossed waters, Kara Nightshadow took it upon herself to spend much of her time watching the wild seas from the bow. Jeronnan questioned the sanity of this, but she refused all suggestions that she return to the safety of her cabin. He thought that she watched for the *Hawksfire*—in part the truth—but what actually concerned her more had been the possibility that the demons of Kalkos's memories might possibly return, especially the aquatic leviathan that had slain the majority of the other vessel's crew in such a horrible manner. Having still not mentioned its existence to the captain, Kara felt honor-bound to at least keep watch. She also believed that, of all of them, she had the best chance of doing something to either scare it off or possibly distract it while the *King's Shield* attempted to escape.

Even though caught between the harsh rain and the mad sea, Jeronnan's crew remained determined and—to her—quite polite. For a time, Kara had feared that the stories she had always heard about sailors would mean her having to deflect unwanted attention. However, although several of the men clearly admired her—and that despite now knowing her true calling—they did not press. In fact, only Mister Drayko had attempted anything resembling an advance, and he had done so in so formal and cautious a manner that it had almost been as if one of her own had made entreaties. She had kindly and quietly rejected his advance, but had found his attention flattering.

Captain Jeronnan himself had long ago erased any lingering question as to whether he had designs on his passenger. When he did not treat Kara like an aristocratic client, he acted as if at some point she had been adopted into his house. Now and then the former naval officer fussed over her just as Kara suspected he had fussed over Terania. She allowed him to do that, not only because it kept him in good spirits, but because the necromancer also found it made her feel some comfort as well. Growing up, she had not been without parental love, but once her adult training had begun, the faithful of Rathma were expected to put such emotions aside for the better good of learning how best to protect the balance of the world. The balance had to come before all else, even family.

The *King's Shield* leapt up a particularly high wave, crashing down into the water a second or two later. Kara held the rail tight, trying to see past the rain and mist. Although day had begun to give way to night, her eyes, more accustomed to seeing in the dark, let her better view what might lay ahead than any of the more experienced mariners. By now they had surely reached—even *passed*—the waters in which Kalkos and his comrades had perished and that meant that at any moment the entire vessel might be under attack by forces unnatural.

"Lady Kara!" Drayko called from behind her. "It's getting worse! You should really get below!"

"I am fine." Although certainly no highborn lady, the dark mage could not get the men to simply call her by her name. That had been the fault of Jeronnan, who had, on first introducing her to the crew, emphasized the title and, most important, his respect for her. What served their captain well served the crew.

"But the storm—!"

"Thank you for your concern, Mister Drayko."

He already knew better than to argue with her. "Just be careful, my lady!"

As he battled his way back, Kara decided that the consideration she had received from Jeronnan and his men would certainly spoil her for Lut Gholein. There, she knew, she would face the prejudices far more common toward her kind. Necromancers dealt with death and most folk did not like to be reminded of their mortality nor the fact that their spirits could perhaps be affected by those like her afterward.

Despite her refusal to Drayko, the necromancer soon decided that she could not stay at the bow much longer. The coming night, combined with the horrific weather, reduced visibility with each passing second. It was quickly coming to the point where even she would be of no use. Yet, she remained determined to stand her post as long as humanly possible.

Up and down the waves flowed, their continual rise and fall in some ways a monotonous sight despite the spectacle of such raw power at work. Once or twice, she had spotted what she believed some sea creature and much earlier a piece of rotting wood had momentarily broken the cycle, but, other than that, Kara had little to show for her efforts. Of course, that also meant that there had been no sign of the demons, something for which the enchantress could feel grateful.

She wiped the spray and rain from her eyes, turning her gaze one last time to the port side of the *King's Shield*. More waves, more froth, more—

An arm?

Shifting her position, Kara peered into the dark waters, every sense alert.

There! The arm and part of the upper body of a man. She could make out no detail—but swore she saw the waterlogged limb rise of its own accord.

Kara had no quick spell for such a situation and so turned instead back to the deck . . . and the dwindling figure of Jeronnan's second. "Mister Drayko! A man in the sea!"

Fortunately, he heard her immediately. Calling to three other men, Drayko rushed up to where the necromancer stood. "Show me where!"

"Look! Can you see him?"

He studied the mad waters, then nodded grimly. "A head and an arm, and I think it might be moving!" Drayko shouted to the helmsman to bring the ship about, then, in a much more subdued voice, told her, "It's unlikely that we'll be able to save him at this point, but we'll try."

She did not bother to reply, more aware of the odds than even he could be. If the nature of the balance dictated the man's survival, he would be rescued. If not, then, like Kalkos, his soul would go on to the next plane of existence, there to fulfill another role for the balance, as taught in the teachings of Rathma.

Of course, that same balance also dictated that where there remained hope of life, those that could had to struggle to save it. Rathma taught pragmatism, not coldheartedness.

The storm made for rough going, but despite that the *King's Shield* still managed to close in on the feebly struggling form. Unfortunately, the coming of night made the task more and more difficult as the vague figure vanished and reappeared with every new wave.

By this time, Captain Jeronnan had joined his crew, taking over control of the situation. To Kara's surprise, he commanded two sailors to bring bows, sailors Drayko informed her were exceptionally skilled with the weapons.

"Does he mean them to end the man's suffering?" she asked, startled by this side of the former officer. Kara had at least expected him to try to save the unfortunate mariner.

"Just watch, my lady."

Her eyes narrowed in belated understanding as the archers quickly tied rope to their shafts. Rather than trying to simply toss a line to the man in the water, they hoped to use the shafts to better get the ropes within reach. Even with the storm, they could get more precision from using the bows than relying on hands only. A risky venture still, but one with more chance of success.

"Hurry, blast you!" Jeronnan roared.

The two men fired. One arrow soared far past its target, but the second came within a short distance of the rolling form.

"Grab hold!" Drayko shouted. "Grab hold!"

The figure made no move toward the line. Taking a terrible risk, the necromancer leaned over the rail, trying to will the floating rope closer. Perhaps if it actually touched him, he would react. Kara knew elders who could move objects simply by thinking of them, but, as with so much else, her studies in that respect had not yet reached such a point. She could only hope that her desperation combined with what abilities she had already learned might prove enough at this dire moment.

Whether due to her desperate thoughts or merely the whims of the sea, the line came within inches of the man's arm.

"Grab it!" the captain encouraged.

Suddenly, the body jerked. A wave washed over it and, for a few nerve-wracking seconds, the hapless figure vanished. Kara sighted it first, now several yards from either line.

"Damn!" Drayko pounded his fist on the rail. "Either he's dead or—"

The floating form jerked again, almost going under.

The first officer swore. "That's not the waves doing that!"

In growing dread Kara and the crew watched as the body bobbed twice more, then went under again.

This time, it did not reappear.

"The sharks've gotten 'im," one of the sailors finally muttered.

Captain Jeronnan agreed. "Draw in the lines, lads. You did what you could. Odds were he was already dead, anyway, and we've got ourselves to worry about more, eh?"

The mood dampened by the futility of their efforts, the crew slowly returned to their tasks. Mister Drayko stayed behind for a moment with Kara, who still sought some last glimpse of the lost mariner.

"The sea claims its own," he whispered. "We try to learn to live with it."

"We see it as part of an overall balance," she returned. "but the loss of a life that might have been saved is still to be mourned."

"You'd best come away from there, my lady."

Touching the back of his hand very briefly, Kara replied, "Thank you for your concern, but I wish to remain for a moment. I will be all right."

With reluctance, he left her once again. Alone, the necromancer reached into her cloak and removed from around her throat a small, red icon shaped in the likeness of a fearsome dragon with blazing eyes and savage teeth. The followers of Rathma believed that the world sat upon the back of the great dragon Trag'Oul, who acted as a fulcrum and, as such, helped maintain the celestial balance. All necromancers gave their full respect to the fiery leviathan.

Under her breath, Kara prayed that Trag'Oul would see the unknown man to the next plane of existence. She had prayed the same for the sailor Kalkos, although none of the *King's Shield*'s crew had noticed. Outsiders did not readily comprehend the place of Trag'Oul in the world.

Satisfied that she could do no more, the slim, silver-eyed woman returned to her cabin below deck. Despite her dedication to her task, Kara entered the room with much relief. Standing lookout for demons, then watching the rescue attempt fail, had drained her of much of her strength. During the enchantress's self-imposed task, she had taken only minimal breaks for her meals and had, in truth, been longer on her feet than any of the men. Now all Kara wanted to do was sleep and sleep and sleep some more.

The cabin offered to her by Hanos Jeronnan had been originally set aside for his daughter and so the more austere Kara had to deal with ladylike frills and too-soft pillows. Unlike the crew, she also had a true bed, one secured very well to the floor in order to prevent it from sliding across the room. To further ensure her safety while she slept, the bed also had short, padded rails on each side to keep the occupant from rolling off onto the hard, wooden floor during the worst storms. Kara had already found herself grateful more than once for those rails and especially appreciated them now, so exhausted did she feel.

The necromancer doubted that tonight she would have had the strength to hold on by herself.

Throwing off the wet cloak, Kara sat on the bottom edge of the bed, trying to collect her thoughts. Despite the cloak, her garments, too, had been thoroughly soaked, from her jet-black blouse down to her leather pants and boots. The dampness of the blouse made it cling tight, chilling her further. Jeronnan had been dismayed that the necromancer had not brought any other garments with her and had insisted before the voyage on locating at least one more set of clothes. Kara had only relented when he had agreed that they would resemble her own black garments as much as possible. The teachings of Rathma did not include interest in the latest fashions; the necromancer sought only functional, durable clothing.

Grateful now that she had given in even that much, Kara changed quickly into the second set, hanging the others to dry. She had performed the exact same ritual each night of the voyage, doing what she could to keep everything clean. Because one dealt with blood and death did not meant that cleanliness no longer became an option.

For once, the young woman found the so soft bed a very welcome thing. The captain would have been dismayed had he known she slept fully clothed, but on a journey of this nature, Kara could take no chances. If the demons of Kalkos's memories did materialize, she had to be ready for them immediately. Her only compromise to comfort concerned her boots, which, out of respect for Jeronnan and his daughter, she left by the bottom of the bed.

Lantern doused, Kara Nightshadow sank deep into the bed. The wild waves actually worked to more quickly send her drifting off to sleep, rocking the weary mage back and forth, as if in a cradle. The troubles of the world began to recede . . .

Until a faint blue light seeped through her eyelids, pulling her back from slumber.

At first she thought it a figment of some peripheral dream, but then the gradual realization that Kara still sensed it through closed eyes even while awake set every nerve on edge. The dark mage tensed—then spun about in the bed, rising to a kneeling position with her hands pointed toward the source of the surreal illumination.

Situated in a cabin below the waterline, Kara at first imagined that somehow the sea had finally broken through the hull. However, as the last vestiges of sleep faded from her mind, she saw instead something far more unsettling. The blue light from her dreams not only existed, but it now covered a fair portion of the side of her cabin. It had a hazy look to it, almost as if the wall had turned to mist, and pulsated continually. Kara felt her entire body tingle . . .

Through the magical haze stepped not one but *two* water-soaked figures.

She opened her mouth, whether to cast a spell or call out for help, even Kara could not be completely certain. In either case, her voice—and her body as a whole, in fact—failed her. The necromancer did not understand why until one of the dark figures held up a familiar ivory dagger, a dagger that blazed an unsettling blue each time Kara even thought of attempting anything.

The dripping and quite *dead* figure of the Vizjerei sorcerer Fauztin—the gaping hole where his throat had once been only partially obscured by the collar of his cloak—grimly stared at her, his unblinking eyes silently warning Kara of the foolishness of any defiance.

Next to him, his grinning companion shook off some of the seawater. Behind them the blue light faded away, the revenants' magical portal vanishing with it.

The smaller of the two undead took a step toward her, performing a mocking bow. As he did, Kara realized that it had been *his* body she and the crew had seen; *he* had been the helpless mariner. Fauztin and his friend had tricked her and the crew in order to arrange this monstrous visitation.

The ghoul's smile widened, yellow teeth and rotting gums now adding to the initial image of peeling skin and the wet, putrefying flesh beneath. "So . . . very good . . . to see you . . . again . . . necromancer . . ."

If the storm did not end by the time the *Hawksfire* at last reached the harbor of Lut Gholein, then at least it finally eased to something approaching tolerable. For that, Norrec Vizharan gave thanks, just as he gave thanks that the ship had arrived just prior to sunrise, when most of the kingdom would still be asleep and, therefore, would not so much notice the sinister peculiarities of the dark vessel.

The moment the *Hawksfire* docked, the spell cast by the armor ceased, leaving Captain Casco and Norrec to do the best they could to finish matters. The ship drew the stares of those few about, but, fortunately, it seemed that no one had noticed lines adjusting themselves nor sails lowering without physical aid.

When finally the gangplank had been lowered, Casco made clear with his expression if not words that the time had come for his passenger to disembark—and, hopefully, never return. Norrec reached out a hand in an attempt to make some sort of peace with the skeletal, foreign mariner, but Casco glanced down at the gauntlet with his good eye, then set that same eye unblinking on the soldier's own gaze. After a few seconds of unease, Norrec lowered the hand and quickly walked down the gangplank.

However, a few yards from the *Hawksfire,* he could not help but look back one last time—and therefore saw the captain still watching him closely. For several seconds, the two stared at one another, then Casco slowly raised one hand Norrec's way.

The veteran fighter nodded in return. Seemingly satisfied by this minor exchange, Casco lowered his hand and turned away, now seeming intent only on inspection of his badly damaged vessel.

Norrec had barely taken a step when someone called down to him from another direction.

"The *Hawksfire* tricks fate again," an elderly looking sea captain with almond-shaped eyes, a white tuft of beard, and weathered features remarked from the deck of his own vessel. Despite the early hour and the foul weather, he greeted Norrec with a cheerful smile. "But looks like barely, this time! Rode along with this storm, did ye?"

The soldier only nodded.

"Word to the wise; ye've been fortunate! Not every man that's sailed her has finished the voyage! She's bad luck, especially to her captain!"

More so than ever, thought Norrec, although he dared not tell the other captain. He nodded again, then tried to move on, but the elderly mariner called out once more.

"Here now! After a trip like that, ye've no doubt the need for a tavern! Best one's *Atma's!* The good lady herself still runs it, even what with her husband gone now! Tell 'em Captain Meshif said to treat ye well!"

"Thank you," Norrec muttered back, hoping that the short answer would satisfy the much-too-cheerful man. He wanted to be away from the docks as quickly as possible, still fearful that someone would not only recognize something amiss with the arrival of the *Hawksfire* but also link Norrec to it.

Cloak drawn about him, the weary veteran hurried on, after several anxious minutes at last leaving ships and warehouses behind and entering the true, fabled Lut Gholein. He had heard tales about the kingdom often over the years, but had never visited it before. Sadun Tryst had said of it that anything a man could buy he could find here . . . and in great quantities. Ships came from all over the world, bringing in goods both legal and not. Lut Gholein represented the most open of markets, although those who ruled made certain that order was still constantly maintained.

At no time did the entire city sleep; according to Sadun, one only had to look long enough and one would find a place willing to let those seeking exotic entertainments spend their coin no matter what the hour. Of course, those who could not keep their entertainments confined to the facilities provided still risked running afoul of the watchful eye of the Guard, who served the cause of the sultan with great fervor. Tryst himself had told some quite lurid tales of Lut Gholein's dungeons . . .

Despite all that had happened to him since the tomb, Norrec's interest stirred almost immediately as he walked through the streets. All around him, gaily-decorated buildings of mortar and stone rose tall, the banners of the sultan atop each. Along the astonishingly clean, cobblestone streets that stretched in every direction, the first wagons of the day began to emerge. As if sprouting from the very shadows, quick-moving figures in flowing robes began opening tents and doors in preparation for new business. Some of the wagons paused at these tents, suppliers delivering new goods to the vendors.

The storm had dwindled now to a few dark, rumbling clouds, and with its continued lessening, Norrec's mood lightened yet more. So far, the armor had not demanded anything more of him. Perhaps he could, for a time at least, seek his own path. In a place as vast as Lut Gholein, surely there had to be sorcerers of some repute, sorcerers who could help free him of this curse. Under the pretext of admiring the sights—an easy enough thing to do—Norrec would try to keep his eye out for any sign of possible help.

Within moments of the dawn, the streets filled with people of all shapes, sizes, and races. Travelers from as far away as Ensteig and Khanduras walked among dark-clad visitors from Kehjistan and beyond. In fact, there seemed more outsiders than locals. The varied crowd worked in Norrec's favor, enabling him to fit in without much suspicion. Even the armor did not overly mark him, for other figures clad akin to him appeared everywhere. Some of them had clearly disembarked from ships not all that long ago, while others, especially those with the turbaned helms and elegant silver capes fluttering behind their blue-gray breastplates, obviously served the masters of this fair kingdom.

Overall the architecture remained consistent, with the lower floors of buildings a smooth, rectangular shape while quite often the tops tended toward small towers resembling minarets. A peculiar design, especially to one born and raised among the high, turreted castles of lords and the lowly, thatched domiciles of the peasantry, but one with an exotic quality that caused Norrec to marvel over it again and again. No two buildings were exactly the same, either, some being broader, even squat, while others appeared to be making up for the lack of space on the ground by stretching thinner and higher.

A horn sounded and the street around Norrec suddenly emptied of people. Following suit, he narrowly missed being run over by a mounted patrol clad in the same turbaned helms and breastplates he had seen earlier. A lively, active city Lut Gholein might be, but, as Sadun had said, it also looked to be well policed. That made it all the more curious that no one had stopped Norrec on the docks for at least some questioning. Most major seaports kept security strong day and night, but he had seen no one. Despite Lut Gholein's open reputation, it puzzled him.

Hunger and thirst slowly crept up on him as he wandered along. He had eaten some food aboard the *Hawksfire*, but his interest in reaching the docks had kept him from taking his fill. Besides, it had been Norrec's secret hope to find something in the city rather than stomach yet another portion of Casco's unsettling concoctions.

The armor had provided funds before and so with some confidence the veteran looked around. Several taverns and inns of various demeanor dotted the area, but one in particular instantly caught Norrec's eye.

Best one's Atma's! *Tell 'em Captain Meshif said to treat ye well!* That same tavern stood but a few yards from the soldier, the wooden sign with its bleary-orbed mascot hanging directly over the entrance. A hardy, weathered place, but one still honest enough in looks for him to risk without worry. With as much determination as he could still muster, Norrec headed toward it, hoping against hope that the armor would not suddenly turn him elsewhere.

He entered in peace and of his own free will, something which, along with his new surroundings, raised Norrec's hopes further. Despite the early hour, *Atma's* had a good business going, most of its customers seamen, but a few merchants, tourists, and military figures partaking of its offerings as well. Not wanting to draw too much attention to himself, Norrec chose a booth in one corner and sat down.

A slip of a girl, likely too young to be working in any such establishment, came up to take his order. Norrec's nostrils had already pinpointed something cooking in the back and so he risked ordering whatever it might be, plus a mug of ale to rinse it down. The girl curtsied, then hurried off, giving him the opportunity to look around.

He had spent far too much of his life in taverns and inns, but at least this one did not look as if the cooks would be broiling whatever they could catch in their floor traps. The servers kept the tables and floors relatively clean of refuse and none of the customers had so far choked on either their meals or drinks. Overall, *Atma's* verified his opinion of Lut Gholein as a kingdom in the midst of tremendous prosperity, where everyone appeared to be benefiting, even the lower castes.

The girl returned with his food, which actually looked as good as it smelled. She smiled at him, asking for what seemed to him reasonable coin. Norrec eyed his gloved hand, waiting.

Nothing happened. The gauntlet did not slam down on the table, leaving the proper amount. Norrec tried not to show his sudden anxiety. Had the armor let him trap himself? If he could not pay, at the very least they would throw him out. He glanced toward the door, where two brawny enforcers who had not bothered to look at him on his way in now seemed more than interested in his discussion with the serving girl.

She repeated the amount, this time a less friendly expression on her face. Norrec glared at the glove, thinking, *Come on, damn you! All I want is a good meal! You can do that, can't you?*

Still nothing.

"Is there something wrong?" the girl asked, her expression indicating that she thought she already knew the answer.

Norrec did not reply, closing and opening his hand in the fading hope that some coins would magically appear.

With one glance toward the two enforcers, the young server began to back away. "Excuse me, sir, I . . . I've other tables . . ."

The soldier looked past her, where the muscular pair had begun to move in his direction. The girl's actions had been a clear signal for them to do their work.

He rose, planting his hands on the table. "Wait! It's not what you—"

Under his palm, he heard the tinkle of coins as they struck the table.

She heard them, too, and the smile suddenly returned. Norrec sat back down, indicating the tiny pile now before him. "I'm sorry for the confusion.

I've not been to Lut Gholein before and had to think whether I had the right amount. Is this enough?"

Her expression told him all he needed to really know. "Aye, sir! Enough and much more!"

Over her shoulder, he saw the burly pair hesitate. The larger of the duo tapped his companion on the arm and the two men returned to their posts. "Take what you need for food and drink," he told the girl, feeling much relieved. After she had done that, Norrec added, "And the largest coin left for yourself."

"Thank you, sir, thank you!"

She nearly floated back to the counter, from the looks of things having received the largest tip of her life from him. The sight cheered Norrec briefly. At least some little good had come of the cursed armor.

He stared at the gauntlets, well aware of what had just happened. The suit had let him understand without words that *it* and not he controlled the entire situation. Norrec lived his life through *its* sufferance. To think otherwise was to play the fool.

Regardless of the reality of his dilemma, Norrec managed to enjoy his meal. Compared to Captain Casco's fare, it tasted of Heaven. Thinking of that mystical realm, the soldier pondered his next move. The armor kept a close rein on him, but surely there had to be a way to get past its guard. In a realm as vibrant as Lut Gholein, not only sorcerers but priests had to be found in abundance. Even if the former could do nothing for Norrec, then perhaps a servant of Heaven might. Surely a priest had links to forces far more powerful than the enchanted suit.

But how to speak with one? Norrec wondered if the armor could withstand being on holy ground. Could it be so simple as walking past a church and then throwing himself onto its steps? Would he be able to do even that much?

For a desperate man, it seemed worth the try. The armor needed him alive and relatively well; that alone might give him just enough of an opportunity. At the very least, Norrec had to try for the sake of not only his life, but his soul, too.

He finished his meal, then quickly downed what remained of the ale. During that time, the serving girl came back more than once to see if he needed anything, a clear sign that he had been very generous in his tipping. Norrec gave her one of the smaller coins remaining to him, which caused her smile to somehow grow even wider than before, then he casually asked her about some of the sights of the city.

"There's the arena, of course," the girl, Miram, replied quickly, no doubt having been asked this question more than once by newcomers. "And the palace, too! You must see the palace!" Her eyes took on a dreaming look. "Jerhyn, the sultan, lives there . . ."

This Jerhyn evidently had to be a handsome and fairly young man judging from Miram's rapt expression. While the sultan's palace surely had to be an intriguing sight, it had not been what he had been searching for. "And besides that?"

"There's also the Aragos Theater near the square with the Cathedral of Tomas the Repentant across from it, but the Zakarum priests only allow visitors at midday and the theater is being repaired. Oh! There's the races on the far north side of the city, horses and dogs—"

Norrec ceased listening, the information he had needed now his. If holy ground or Heaven had any power over the demonic legacy of Bartuc, then this cathedral offered the best hope. The Zakarum Church represented the most powerful order on either side of the Twin Seas.

"—and some old folk and scholars like the ruins of the Vizjerei temple outside the city walls, though there's not much to see any more after the Great Sandstorm . . ."

"Thank you, Miram. That's good enough." He prepared to leave, already trying to think of some roundabout method by which to approach the vicinity of the Zakarum site.

Four figures in the now familiar garb of Lut Gholein's Guard stepped into *Atma's,* but their interest in the tavern had nothing to do with drink. Instead, they looked directly at Norrec, their countenances darkening. He could almost swear that they knew exactly who he was.

With military precision that Norrec would have at other times admired, the foursome spread out, eliminating any hope of bypassing them on the way to the front entrance. Although they had not yet drawn their long, curved swords, each guard kept a hand near the hilt. One wrong action by Norrec and all four blades would come flying out, ready to cut him down.

Pretending to be not at all concerned, the wary fighter turned back to the serving girl, asking, "There's a friend I need to meet in a place located in the street behind this tavern. Do you have another exit in the back?"

"There's one that way." She started to point, but he gently took her hand, dropping another coin in it.

"Thank you, Miram." Gently pushing past her, Norrec moved as if heading toward the counter for one last drink. The four guards hesitated.

Halfway to the counter, he veered toward the back doorway.

Although he could not see them now, Norrec felt certain that the men knew his intentions. He picked up his pace, hoping to reach the exit as quickly as possible. Once out, he could try to lose himself among the growing throngs.

Norrec pushed the door wide, immediately darting through—

—and came to an abrupt halt as rough, strong hands seized him by both arms, holding him fast.

"Resist and it will go the worse for you, westerner!" snapped a swarthy guard with gold tabs on his cloak. He peered past Norrec, saying, "You have done your work well! This is the one! We will take it from here!"

The four who had pursued Norrec from inside stepped past the prisoner, pausing only to salute the officer in charge before wandering off. Norrec grimaced, realizing that he had walked into the most basic of traps.

He had no idea as to the intentions of his captors, but at the moment, they interested him far less than the question as to why Bartuc's armor had not reacted. Surely this situation called for something from it, but so far it seemed unwilling to try to free its host. Why?

"Pay attention, westerner!" the officer came close to slapping Norrec, but finally lowered his hand. "Come peacefully and you will not be mistreated! Resist . . ." The man's hand now slipped to the hilt of his curved sword, his meaning quite clear.

Norrec nodded his understanding. If the armor chose not to resist, he certainly had no intention of trying to fight himself free of this armed patrol.

His captors formed a square of sorts, with their leader in front and Norrec, of course, in the middle. The party headed down the street, away from the larger crowds. Several curious folk watched the procession, but no one seemed at all sympathetic to the foreigner's troubles. Likely they figured that there were always more outsiders, so what difference the loss of one?

No one had as of yet explained exactly for what reason Norrec had been arrested, but he had to assume it had something to do with the *Hawksfire*'s arrival. Perhaps he had been wrong when he had thought that no watch had been set at the port. Perhaps Lut Gholein kept a more wary eye on those who arrived by ship than appearances had suggested. It also remained possible that Captain Casco had, after all, reported the goings-on aboard his vessel and the one responsible for the loss of his crew.

The lead guard suddenly veered toward a narrow side street, the rest of the group following close behind. Norrec frowned, no longer thinking of Casco and the *Hawksfire*. His captors now journeyed through less-frequented, more disreputable-looking avenues into which even the brightest day would have had trouble shedding light. The soldier tensed, sensing something suddenly awry with the situation.

They journeyed a little farther, then turned into an alley nearly as dark as night. The band proceeded a few yards into it, then the guards came to an abrupt halt.

His captors stood at attention, seeming to barely even breathe. In fact, the four guards stood at attention with such stillness that Norrec could not help but think that they resembled nothing more than puppets whose master had ceased pulling their strings.

And as if to verify that notion, a portion of the shadows separated from the rest, shaping itself into an elderly, wrinkled man with long, silver hair and beard and clad in an elegant, broad-shouldered robe clearly fashioned in the style worn by someone Norrec had known so very well . . . Fauztin. However, this figure, this Vizjerei, had not only lived for far longer than Norrec's unfortunate friend, but by being here evidenced quite well the fact that his abilities far outstripped those of the dead mage.

"Leave us . . ." he ordered the guards, his voice strong, commanding, despite his advanced years.

The officer and his men obediently turned, marching back the way they had come.

"They will recall nothing," the Vizjerei commented. "As the others who aided them will recall nothing . . . just as I desire . . ." When Norrec attempted to speak, the silver-haired figure cut him off with but a singular glance. "And if you hope to live, westerner . . . you, *too*, will do as I desire . . . *exactly* as I desire."

ELEVEN

"Are you not feeling well, then, lass?" Captain Jeronnan asked. "You've come out of your cabin only to gather your meals, then returned there for the rest of the time."

Kara looked him directly in the eye. "I am well, captain. With the *King's Shield* nearing Lut Gholein, I must prepare for my journey from that point on. There is much for me to consider. I apologize if I appear unfriendly to you and your crew."

"Not unfriendly . . . just more distant." He sighed. "Well, if you need anything, just let me know."

She needed quite a lot, but nothing with which the good captain could help her. "Thank you . . . for everything."

The necromancer felt his eyes on her as she headed for her cabin. Jeronnan would likely have done anything he could for Kara regardless of the situation and she much appreciated that fact. Unfortunately, any aid he might have offered would not have at all helped the enchantress in her present predicament.

As she entered the cabin, Kara saw the two undead standing in the far corner, waiting with the proverbial patience of their kind. Fauztin held the gleaming dagger ready, the Vizjerei's spell upon it ensuring that the necromancer could do nothing against the pair. The yellowed eyes of the mage stared unblinking at her. Kara could never be certain what Fauztin thought, for his expression varied little.

Not so with Sadun Tryst. The other revenant continually smiled, as if he had some jest he wished to share. Kara also found herself constantly desiring to straighten his head, which ever leaned a little too far to one side or another.

The stench of death surrounded them, but so far as she could tell it had not pervaded any part of the ship beyond her cabin. As a necromancer, the foul smell bothered Kara less than most, but she still would have preferred to do without it. Her studies and her faith had ensured that Kara had dealt almost daily with the realm of the dead, but those encounters had ever been on her own terms. Never before had the tables been turned, that the *dead* made her come at their beck and call.

"The good captain . . . leaves you to . . . your self still . . . I hope," Tryst gasped.

"He is concerned for me; that is all."

The wiry ghoul chuckled, a sound like an animal choking on a bone. Perhaps when the man's neck had been broken, a part of the bone there had lodged in his wind pipe. It would explain the way he talked. Even though Sadun Tryst did not need to breathe, he needed air in order to speak.

Of course, with a gaping hole in his throat, Tryst's companion, the Vizjerei, would forever be silent.

"Let us hope . . . that his concern . . . remains distant . . . from this room."

Fauztin pointed to the edge of the bed, a wordless order the dark mage readily understood. Her food held tight in one hand, she perched there, awaiting whatever new command they had of her. So long as the Vizjerei held the dagger, his magic kept Kara Nightshadow in thrall.

Tryst's eyes blinked once, a conscious effort on the part of the corpse. Unlike Fauztin, he worked to pretend that some life remained within his decaying husk. As a mage, the gaunt Vizjerei no doubt saw the situation in more practical, realistic terms. The fighter, on the other hand, appeared to have been a man much in love with all the aspects of life. Behind the smile Kara suspected that this ungodly predicament enraged him more than it did his companion.

"Eat . . ."

Under their unwavering gazes she did. All the while, though, the necromancer rummaged through her memory, trying to recall some bit of knowledge she might use to free herself from all this. That they had not so far touched Kara, much less harmed her in any manner, did not assuage her concerns in the least. The revenants had one goal in mind—to reach their friend, this Norrec Vizharan. If, at some point, it seemed necessary to sacrifice her for the culmination of that goal, Kara felt certain that they would do so without regret.

Vizharan had been their partner, their comrade, and yet he had evidently brutally slain both, then taken off with the armor. Sadun Tryst had not exactly told her all this, but she had come to that conclusion from the fragments of information garnered from conversations with the talkative ghoul. Tryst had never actually even accused Norrec, instead only saying that they needed to find their partner, to end what had begun in the tomb—and that because Kara had not stayed behind as they had wished, *she* would now be a part of their macabre quest.

Kara ate in silence, purposely keeping her gaze from the ungodly pair as much as possible. The less she drew their attention, especially that of Tryst, the better. Unfortunately, just as she reached the bottom of the bowl, the more vocal revenant suddenly rasped, "Is it . . . does it taste . . . good?"

The peculiar question so caught her by surprise that she had to look at him. "What?"

One pale, peeling finger pointed at the bowl. "The food. Does it . . . taste . . . good?"

Some bit remained, more than Kara truly desired at the moment. She considered what she knew of undead, never recalling any with an appetite for fish stew. *Human flesh*, yes, in some cases, but never fish stew. Still, on the off chance that it might ease tensions a little, the necromancer held out the bowl and, in a steady voice, asked, "Would you like to try it?"

Tryst looked at Fauztin, who remained the immovable rock. The slimmer ghoul finally stepped forward, seized the food, then immediately returned to his favored spot. Kara had never known that a walking corpse could move with such speed.

With decaying fingers he took some of the remnants and stuck them in his mouth. Sadun tried to chew, fragments of fish dropping to the floor. Despite the fact that both he and the mage acted as if living, the dead man's body did not completely function as it had previous to his murder.

He suddenly spat out what remained, at the same time a monstrous expression crossing his rotting countenance. "Filth! It tastes . . . it tastes of . . . *death.*" Sadun eyed her. "It's too long dead . . . they should have . . . cooked it . . . less . . . a lot less." He considered this crucial matter more, eyes never leaving Kara. "I think . . . maybe they should have . . . not cooked it . . . at all . . . the fresher . . . the better . . . eh?"

The raven-haired woman did not reply at first, having no desire whatsoever to prolong a conversation that might turn to exactly what types of meat the ghoul would think tasted best uncooked. Instead, Kara tried to turn back to the subject of most concern to her—the hunt for Norrec Vizharan.

"You were aboard the *Hawksfire*, weren't you? You were aboard until whatever happened that caused the crew to abandon her."

"Not aboard . . . underneath . . . for the most part . . ."

"Underneath?" She pictured the two clutching the hull, using their inhuman strength to hold on even through the most turbulent of waves. Only a revenant could have accomplished such a harrowing effort. "What do you mean . . . for the most part?"

Sadun shrugged, sending his head wobbling for a moment. "We came aboard . . . for a short . . . time . . . after the fools jumped . . . ship."

"What made them leave?"

"They saw . . . what they didn't like to see . . ."

Not a very helpful answer, but the longer Kara could keep the conversation going, the less time the pair had to think about what else they might need of her—and what it might cost the necromancer.

Once more Kara thought about their unholy perseverance. The revenants had managed to nearly catch up with their prey, even latch themselves onto the hull of his vessel like a pair of lampreys onto a shark. The vision of the two undead clinging to the underside of the *Hawksfire* throughout the violent storm they had earlier mentioned would forever be seared into the necromancer's imagination. Truly Norrec Vizharan would not escape their brutal justice.

And yet . . . he so far had, even with them within yards of his throat.

"If you and he were alone aboard the ship, then why is the hunt not yet over?"

A decidedly grim change came over Tryst's smile, managing to make his general appearance even more ghastly than previous. "It should . . . have been."

He would say no more and when Kara looked to Fauztin, his dark visage revealed nothing. She pondered their responses as rapidly as she could, finally deciding to try to play on their failure aboard the *Hawksfire*. "I can be of more help to you, you know. Next time, nothing will go awry."

This time, Fauztin blinked once. What that meant, the necromancer could not say, but the Vizjerei's action had been for some specific reason.

Sadun Tryst's eyes narrowed slightly. "You'll be . . . of all the . . . help . . . we need. Trust on . . . that . . ."

"But I could be more than your unwilling puppet. I understand what drives you. I understand why you walk the earth. As an ally rather than a prisoner, the possibilities of what you can accomplish grow tenfold and more!"

Silent, the wiry corpse tossed and caught his own dagger a few times, something he had done often since his arrival. Apparently even death could not break some habits. Kara thought he did it whenever he had to concentrate especially hard. "You understand . . . less than you think."

"All I am trying to say is that we need not be adversaries. My spell stirred up your murdered spirits, set you on this quest, and so I feel some responsibility. You seek this Norrec Vizharan, so do I. Why can we not work as allies?"

Again the mage blinked, almost as if he might have wanted to say something—an impossibility, of course. In lieu of that, he glanced down at his companion. The two undead shared a long gaze, which made the enchantress wonder if they communicated in some manner beyond her ken.

The grating sound of Sadun Tryst's unearthly chuckle filled the tiny cabin, but Kara knew better than to hope that Captain Jeronnan or one of the crew would hear. The Vizjerei had cast a spell deadening all sounds within. As far as the men of the *King's Shield* might be concerned, the necromancer made no more noise than if she now slept peacefully.

"My friend . . . he brings up an . . . amusing point. You . . . as our good ally . . . would surely . . . expect your dagger back . . . eh?" When she had no good reply, Tryst added, "Not a bargain . . . we could very much . . . *live* with . . . if you know what I mean."

Kara understood very well. Not only did the dagger give them power over her, but it likely served as a focus for that which let them function on the mortal plane. The ritual blade had been what had first summoned the phantasm of Fauztin and the probable result of taking it from them would be that both bodies would simply collapse, the vengeful shades sent back to the afterlife forever.

This pair would have none of that.

"You'll aid us . . . as we need. You'll serve . . . as the cloak covering . . . the truth from . . . those we meet. You'll do . . . what we can't do . . . in the light of day . . . where all can see . . ."

Fauztin blinked for a third time, a very distressing sign. He had never before taken such a visible interest in their conversations, preferring everything to come from his more vocal companion.

Tryst rose, ever smiling. The more Kara Nightshadow thought of it, the more she realized that the smile never truly left the slimmer ghoul's face save when its owner forcefully chose to make it go, as when the food had so disgusted him. What she had taken for humor looked, in part, to simply be what death had frozen on his countenance. Tryst would likely be smiling even when he ripped out the heart of his treacherous comrade, Norrec.

"And as we must . . . have your cooperation . . . my good friend's suggested a way . . . to make you even more . . . amenable . . . to the situation."

Both he and the Vizjerei approached her.

Kara leapt from the bed. "You have the dagger. You need no other hold over me."

"Fauztin believes . . . we do. I am so . . . sorry."

Despite the unlikely chance of anyone hearing her, she opened her mouth to shout.

The mage blinked for a fourth time—and no sound escaped the necromancer's lips. Her seeming helplessness both horrified and infuriated the pale woman. Kara knew that there were far more experienced practitioners of her arts that could have turned both undead into silent, obedient servants. A few more years and perhaps even she would have been able to do so. Instead, the ghouls had turned her into the puppet—and now they sought to further add to her invisible chains.

Tryst's macabre grin and cold, white eyes filled her view. The breath of decay drifted to her nostrils each time the rotting figure spoke. "Give me . . . your left hand . . . and it'll be . . . less painful."

With no choice left to her, Kara reluctantly obeyed. Sadun Tryst took the hand in his own moldering fingers, caressing it almost as if he and the young enchantress had become lovers. Kara felt a chill run up and down her spine at the thought. She had heard such tales before . . .

"I miss many things . . . about life . . . woman . . . many things . . ."

A heavy hand dropped on his shoulder. Tryst nodded as best his crooked neck allowed, then backed away a step. His grip on her hand remained painfully tight, the ghoul now turning it so that the palm showed.

Fauztin plunged the gleaming dagger into it.

Kara gasped—then realized that while she felt discomfort, she did not feel actual pain. She stared in astonishment, noting and yet not quite believing the sight before her. More than two inches of the curved blade stuck out of the other side of her hand, yet nowhere did she see any trace of blood.

A brilliant yellow glow arose from the area where the dagger had penetrated, a glow that completely bathed her palm.

The Vizjerei at last tried to say something, but only a thin gasp escaped. Even rewrapping his ruined throat did not work.

"Let me . . ." snarled Tryst. Eyeing the captive necromancer again, he intoned, *"Our lives are . . . your life. Our deaths . . . are your death. Our fate is . . . your fate . . . bounded by this . . . dagger and your . . . soul . . ."*

With that, Fauztin tugged the dagger free. The Vizjerei thrust the blade toward her face, showing Kara that no blood stained it. He then indicated her hand.

She studied her palm, could not even make out the slightest scar. The murdered mage had summoned powerful sorcery for his terrible spell.

Tryst pushed her toward the bed, indicating the young woman sit. "We are . . . one now. If we fail . . . you fail. If we should perish . . . or be betrayed . . . you . . . too . . . will suffer . . . remember that always . . ."

Kara could not help but shiver slightly. They had bound her to them in a manner far more absolute than that which their possession of the dagger had previously done. If anything at all happened to the pair before they could accomplish their dreadful task, Kara's soul would even be dragged back to the underworld with them, forever doomed to wander without rest.

"You did not have to do that!" She looked for some glimmer of sympathy, but found none. Nothing mattered more than avenging what had been done to them. "I would've helped you!"

"Now . . . we can be certain you will." Tryst and Fauztin retreated to the far corner again. The ritual dagger gleamed golden. "Now . . . there'll be . . . no fear . . . of tricks . . . when you meet with . . . the sorcerer."

Despite what they had just done to her, Kara stiffened at the last words. "Sorcerer? In Lut Gholein?"

Fauztin nodded. Sadun Tryst cocked his head more to the side—or perhaps the weight on what remained of his neck simply had proven too much for the moment.

"Yesss . . . a Vizjerei like . . . my friend here . . . an old man . . . with much knowledge . . . and known by . . . the name . . . Drognan."

"My name is Drognan," the cloaked mage remarked as he swept into the chamber. "Please be seated, Norrec Vizharan."

As he gazed around the Vizjerei's sanctum, the sense of unease that had crept over Norrec earlier returned a thousand times stronger. Not only had this elderly but certainly formidable figure drawn the veteran to him with ease, but Drognan understood well exactly what had happened to Norrec—including the quest by the cursed armor.

"I always knew that the curse of Bartuc could not be contained forever," he informed Norrec as the soldier seated himself in an old, weathered chair. "Always knew that."

They had come to this dim chamber after a short trek into even less savory areas of the otherwise rich, energetic kingdom. The doorway through which the pair had entered had seemed to have led into an abandoned, rat-infested building, but once through, the interior had shifted . . . transforming into an ancient but still stately edifice which Drognan informed him had once been rumored to be the home of Horazon, the bloody warlord's brother.

It had been abandoned at some point long after the disappearance of Bartuc's brother, but the spells protecting it from curious eyes had continued to serve their designated purpose—until Drognan had outwitted them while searching for the tomb of the very one who had cast them. Deciding that no one had a more appropriate right to lay claim to the magical abode than himself, the Vizjerei had moved in, then continued his research.

Through an empty hall whose floor had been covered in a rich tapestry of mosaic patterns that included animals, warriors, and even legendary structures, they had finally reached this particular room, the one that the old mage most called his home. Shelf upon shelf bordered the walls and on each of those shelves had been arranged more books and scrolls than a simple soldier such as Norrec could have ever dreamed existed in all the world. He could read, but few of the titles had been written in the common tongue.

Other than the books, though, only a few other items decorated the shelves, among the most interesting being a single polished skull and a few jars of a dark colored liquid. As for the room itself, its decor consisted chiefly of a well-crafted wooden table and two old but stately chairs. It had all the look of a chamberlain's office such as might have been found in the sultan's palace. Hardly what Norrec would have expected from a Vizjerei or any other sorcerer for that matter. Like most common folk, he had expected to see all sorts of horrifying and grisly objects, the so-called tools of Drognan's trade.

"I am a . . . researcher," the wrinkled figure added suddenly, as if he needed to explain his surroundings.

A researcher who had been the reason why no guards had stopped Norrec on the dock. A researcher who, with but a simple use of his power, had seized the minds of a half dozen soldiers and directed them to bring the foreigner to him.

A researcher who dabbled in dark arts, knew of the deadly enchantments contained in Bartuc's armor—and who had apparently overcome most of them with ease.

And that, more than anything else, had been why Norrec had willingly followed him here. For the first time since the tomb, hope had arisen that someone could at last free him of the parasitic suit.

"It came to me in a vision little more than a week or two ago." The sorcerer ran wizened fingers along a row of books, obviously searching for one in particular. "The legacy of Bartuc rising anew! I could not believe it at first, naturally, but when it repeated itself, I knew the vision to be a true one."

Since then, Drognan continued, he had performed spell after spell to discover the meaning—and in the process had uncovered Norrec's secret and the journey the armor had forced upon him. Although he had not been able to observe the veteran during the long trek from the tomb, the elderly mage had at least been able to keep track of where that trail seemed to lead. Soon it became apparent that both man and armor would soon be in the Vizjerei's very midst, a fortuitous event as far as Drognan had been concerned.

The sorcerer pulled free one vast tome from the shelf, then placed it gently on a table in the center of the chamber. He began thumbing through it, still talking. "It surprised me not at all, young man, to find out that the armor sought out Lut Gholein. If some lingering, spectral aspect of Bartuc hoped to fulfill his last wishes, then certainly traveling to this fair kingdom makes perfect sense, especially for two particular reasons."

Norrec cared little for what those reasons might be, more concerned with that which the Vizjerei had hinted might be possible to obtain—the fighter's freedom from the suit. "Is the spell in that book?"

The aged sorcerer looked up. "What spell?"

"The one to separate me from this, of course!" Norrec banged the breastplate with one hand. "This damned armor! You said you had some way you could peel it off of me!"

"I believe my earlier words to you were closer to 'if you hope to live, you will do *exactly* as I desire.' "

"But the armor! Damn you, wizard! That's all I care about! Cast a spell! Get it off of me while it's still subdued!"

Looking down on him as a father might a whining child, the silver-haired mage responded, "Of the armor, while I cannot as yet remove it, I assure you that you need not worry about its other enchantments while I have it under my power." Reaching into one of the deep pockets of his robe, Drognan removed what at first seemed a short stick but quickly revealed itself to be much, much, *much* longer. In truth, by the time the sorcerer had it freed from the pocket, the "stick" had swollen in size and length—the latter a good four feet and more—and revealed itself as a spell staff covered in elaborate and glittering runes. "Observe."

Drognan pointed the staff at his guest.

Norrec, who had traveled with Fauztin long enough to know what it meant to be on this end of the magical staff, leapt to his feet. "Wait—"

"*Furiosic!*" shouted the mage.

Flames shot toward the soldier, flames that spread as they moved. A blanket of fire sought to envelop Norrec.

Just a few scant inches from his nose, the fire abruptly died out.

At first Norrec believed that the suit had saved him again, but then he heard the wrinkled figure chuckle. "Not to worry, young man, not even a hair singed! You see now what I mean? My control over the armor is complete! Had I so desired, I could have left you a roasted skeleton and even the suit could not have saved you! Only my canceling of the spell protected you now! Now do sit back down . . ."

The searing heat still burning his nostrils, Norrec slumped back into the old chair. Drognan's unnerving display had proven two things. The first had been that what the elderly sorcerer had claimed had been true; with his magic, he had subdued the enchantments of the armor.

The second had been that Norrec had evidently placed himself into the hands of a somewhat ruthless and likely *half-mad* wizard.

Yet . . . what else could he have done?

"There is a bottle of wine next to you. Pour yourself some. Calm your nerves."

The offer itself did little to calm Norrec down, for both the bottle mentioned and the table upon which it now sat had not been next to the veteran a second earlier. Still, he kept himself from showing any uncertainty as he first filled a goblet, then sipped some of the contents.

"That should be better." One hand spread over a page in the massive book, Drognan peered at his guest. The staff rested loosely in his other hand. "Do you know anything of the history of Lut Gholein?"

"Not much."

The wizard stepped away from the book. "One fact I will impart upon you immediately, a fact I think central to your situation. Before the rise of Lut Gholein, this region served briefly as a colony of the Empire of Kehjistan. There existed Vizjerei temples and a military presence. However, even by the time of the brothers Bartuc and Horazon, the empire had begun to pull back from this side of the sea. Vizjerei influence remained strong, but a physical presence proved too costly for the most part." An almost childlike smile spread across the dark, narrow features. "It is all quite fascinating, really!"

Norrec, who, under the circumstances cared little about history lessons, frowned.

Seeming not to notice, Drognan continued. "After the war, after Bartuc's defeat and death, the empire never regained its glory. Worse yet, its greatest sorcerer, its shining light, had suffered too much in body and, most pointedly, *mind*. I speak, of course, of Horazon."

"Who came to Lut Gholein," Norrec helpfully added, hoping by doing so that it would assist the rambling elder to reach whatever point he sought to make. Then—perhaps then—Drognan would finally get around to helping the fighter.

"Yes, exactly, Lut Gholein. Not named that yet, of course. Yes, Horazon, who had suffered so terribly even in victory, came to this land, tried to settle into a life of studious pursuit—and then, as I informed you earlier, just disappeared."

The veteran soldier waited for his host to continue, but Drognan only stared back, as if what he had just said explained all.

"You do not understand, I see," the robed sorcerer finally commented.

"I understand that Horazon came to this land and now the cursed armor of his hated brother has come here, too! I also understand that I've had to watch men slaughtered, demons rise from the earth, and know that my life's no longer my own, but that of a dead demon lord!" Norrec rose again, having had enough. Drognan could have easily raised the staff and slain him on the spot, but his own patience had come to an end. "Either help me or slay me, Vizjerei! I've no time for history lessons! I want release from this hell!"

"Sit."

Norrec sat, but this time not of his own accord. A darkness crossed Drognan's features, a darkness that reminded the hapless soldier that this man had readily taken control of not only half a dozen guards, but the damnable suit, too.

"I will save you despite yourself, Norrec Vizharan—although certainly no servant of the Vizjerei are you despite that ancient name! I will save you while at the same time you will lead me to that for which I have searched for more than half my life!"

Whatever spell Drognan used pressed the fighter so tight into the chair that Norrec could barely speak. "What . . . what do you mean? Lead you to what?"

Drognan gave him a nearly incredulous look. "Why, what must surely be buried somewhere under the city itself and what the armor must also be seeking—the tomb of Bartuc's brother, Horazon . . . the legendary *Arcane Sanctuary!*"

TWELVE
※

As he did each night, General Augustus Malevolyn marched the perimeter of the encampment. Also as he did each night, he studiously observed each detail concerning his men's readiness. Ineptitude meant severe punishment no matter what the soldier's rank.

Yet, one thing the general did different this particular night, a single change that went little noticed by most of his weary men. This night, Malevolyn made his rounds still wearing the crimson helm of Bartuc.

That it did not quite match with the rest of his armor did not concern him in the least. In fact, more and more he considered the possibility of finding some manner by which to dye his present armor a color more akin to that of the helmet. Thus far, though, Malevolyn had come up with but one method by which to possibly match the unique color, a method that surely would have caused a full-scale insurrection.

His hand touched the helm almost lovingly as he adjusted its fit. Malevolyn had noticed some discomfort on Galeona's part when he had earlier refused to remove it, but had simply chalked it up to her fear of his growing might. In truth, when both the helmet and the suit became his, the general would no longer need the witch's magical skills—and while her more earthly talents were most expert, Malevolyn knew that he could always find a more willing, more submissive female to satisfy his other needs.

Of course, such matters of flesh could wait. Lut Gholein called to him. He would not be cheated out of it, as he had been cheated out of Viz-jun.

But are you worthy of it? Are you worthy of the glory, the legacy of Bartuc?

Malevolyn froze. The voice in his head, the one that asked on a previous eve the questions that he himself feared to ask out loud, that proclaimed what he dared not yet proclaim.

Are you worthy? Will you prove yourself? Will you seize your destiny?

A faint glint of light from beyond the encampment caught his attention. He opened his mouth to summon the sentries, then made out the murky figure of one of his own men, a dying torch in one hand, coming toward him from that direction. The dim light of the flames kept the soldier's visage almost a complete shadow even when the man came within a couple of yards of the commander.

"General Malevolyn," whispered the sentry, saluting. "You must come and see this."

"What is it? Have you found something?"

The sentry, though, had already turned back to the darkness. "Better come see, general . . ."

Frowning, Malevolyn followed behind the warrior, one hand gripped on the pommel of his sword. The guard no doubt understood that whatever he had to show his leader had better be of some import or there would be hell to pay. Malevolyn did not like his routine disturbed.

The two wended their way some distance through the uneven landscape. With the sentry in the lead, they crossed over a dune, cautiously making their way down to the other side. Ahead, the dark outline of a rocky ridge loomed over the otherwise sandy region. The general assumed that whatever the guard had noticed had to be out there. If not . . .

The sentry paused. Malevolyn did not even know why the man bothered to carry the torch any longer. The pale, sickly flame did nothing to illuminate the area and if some foe lay ahead, it would only alert them to the presence of the approaching pair. He cursed himself for not having ordered it doused before, but then assumed that, if the soldier had not thought to do so, whatever he had brought the general out to see could not be an enemy.

Spitting granules from his mouth, Augustus Malevolyn muttered, "Well? What did you see? Is it near the rocks?"

"It is difficult to explain, general. You must see it." The shadowed soldier pointed at the ground to the right, "The footing is better there, general. If you'll come . . ."

Perhaps the man had discovered some ruins. Those Malevolyn would have found of interest. The Vizjerei had a long history in and around Aranoch. If this turned out to be the remains of one of their temples, then perhaps it contained some lost secrets of which he could make use.

The ground beneath his foot, the ground on which the sentry had told him to step, gave completely away.

Malevolyn first stumbled, then fell forward. Fearful of losing the helmet, he sacrificed one hand in order to keep it in place, thus losing any chance of halting his fall. The general dropped to both knees, his face but inches from the sand. His right arm, the one that had been forced to support his weight, throbbed with pain. He tried to right himself, but the loose ground at first made it difficult.

He looked up, searching for the fool who had led him into this. "Don't just stand there, you wretch! Help me—"

The sentry had vanished, even his torch nowhere to be seen.

Steadying himself, Malevolyn managed at last to rise. With great caution, he reached for his sword—and found *that* also missing.

Are you worthy? repeated the damnable voice in his head.

From the sand erupted four hideous and only vaguely humanoid forms.

Even in the darkness, the general could make out the hard carapaces, the distorted, beetlelike heads. A pair of arms ending in oversized, sharp pincers completed the look of an insect out of some nightmare, yet these manlike horrors were no product of Malevolyn's imagination. He knew already of the sand maggots, the massive arthropods that hunted for prey in the wilderness of Aranoch and also knew of one of the few hellish creatures that hunted them in turn . . . when human prey could not be found.

Yet, while scarab demons in great numbers had been rumored to be the cause of caravans lost over the years, never had the commander heard of such creatures lurking in the vicinity of as great a force as his own. While not the largest of armies—not *yet*—Malevolyn's disciplined warriors certainly represented a target not at all of temptation to creatures such as these. They preferred smaller, weaker victims.

Such as a lone warrior tricked into walking into their very midst?

Which of his officers had betrayed him he would find out when he located the traitorous sentry. For now, though, Malevolyn had more important matters to consider, such as keeping himself from becoming the scarab demons' next meal.

Are you worthy? the voice repeated again.

As if suddenly prodded to action, one of the grotesque beetles reached for him, its pincers and mandibles clacking wildly in anticipation of a bloody prize. Although not true beasts of Hell despite their name, the scarab demons were certainly monstrous enough foes for any ordinary man to face.

Yet Augustus Malevolyn considered himself no *ordinary* man.

As the savage claws came at him, the general reacted instinctively, his hand swinging forward to deflect as well it could the attack. However, to his surprise—and certainly that of the creature before him—in that empty hand materialized a blade of purest ebony surrounded by a blazing crimson aura that lit up the surrounding area more than any torch. The blade grew even as it cut an arc through the air, yet its weight and its balance remained perfect at all times.

The edge dug into the hard carapace without hesitation, completely sever-ing the pincered appendage, which went flying to the side. The scarab demon let out a high-pitched squeal and backed away, dark fluids dripping from its ruined arm.

General Malevolyn did not pause, caught up in the miraculous turn of events. With expert ease he drove the wondrous blade through the second of his attackers. Even before that monster had fallen, the general turned to the next, forcing it back with his relentless onslaught.

The two remaining creatures joined with the third, seeking to catch the commander from opposing directions. Malevolyn took a step back, reposi-tioned himself, and immediately dispatched the one whose limb he had but moments before cut off. As the other pair fell upon him, the veteran officer twisted, bringing the sword around and beheading one.

A foul-smelling liquid sprayed him as he did it, momentarily blinding the general. The final of his opponents took advantage, first dragging him to the ground, then attempted to remove Malevolyn's head by biting through his throat. Snarling like an animal, Malevolyn blocked the mandibles with his armored forearm, hoping that the plate there would protect the flesh and bone beneath long enough for him to recover.

With one knee, he managed to push his monstrous attacker up a bit, forcing the mandibles away. That gave Malevolyn the angle he needed. Twisting the sword around in his other hand, the general turned the point toward the head of the scarab demon and drove it through the thick, natural armor of the beast with all the force he could muster.

The horrific beetle let out a brief, shrill squeal and dropped dead on top of General Malevolyn.

With only a slight sense of disgust, the commander pushed the carcass away, then rose. His immaculate armor dripped with the life fluids of the scarab demons, but, other than that, they had done him little real harm. He stared at the dark, still forms, both angered at the earlier betrayal yet also feel-ing a rush of intense satisfaction for having singlehandedly slain the four hell-ish creatures.

Augustus Malevolyn touched his breastplate, which had become covered with the fluids of the scarab demons. For nearly a minute, he stared at the stench-ridden muck now covering his gauntleted hand. On impulse, Malevolyn touched the breastplate again, but instead of trying to wipe his armor clean, he began to spread the fluids further—just as Bartuc had done with the blood of his human foes.

"So . . . perhaps you *are* worthy . . ."

He spun about, at last sighting the night-enshrouded form of the traitorous sentry. However, common sense now told Malevolyn that what he had taken for one of his own men surely had to be something far more powerful, not to mention *sinister* . . .

"I know you now . . ." he muttered. Then his eyes widened slightly as truth dawned. "Or should I say . . . I know *what* you are . . . *demon* . . ."

The other figure laughed quietly, laughed as no man could. Before the astounded eyes of General Malevolyn, the sentry's shape twisted, grew, changed into that not born of the mortal plane. It towered over the human and where there had been four limbs now six materialized. The foremost appeared as great scythes with needle points, the middle as skeletal hands with deadly claws, and the last, serving as legs, bent back in a manner much like the hind limbs of the insect the demon most resembled.

A mantis. A mantis from Hell.

"Hail to you, General Augustus Malevolyn of Westmarch, warrior, conqueror, emperor—and true heir to the Warlord of Blood." The hideous insect performed a bizarre bow, the sharp points of the scythes digging into the sand. "This one congratulates you on your worthiness . . ."

Malevolyn glanced at his hand, now empty of any weapon. The magical blade had vanished the moment it had no longer been needed—and yet the general felt certain that, in the future, he could summon that blade whenever necessary.

"You're the voice in my head," the commander finally replied. "You're the voice that cajoles me . . ."

The demon tilted his own head to the side, glowing bulbous eyes flaring once. "This one did not cajole . . . simply encouraged."

"And if I had not passed this little test?"

"Then this one would have been terribly disappointed."

The creature's words caused General Malevolyn to chuckle despite the implications in the response. "Damned good thing I didn't fail, then." One hand reached up to adjust the helmet while Malevolyn thought. First had come the visions, then the increase in his otherwise limited powers—and now this magical blade and a demon to boot. Truly it had to be as the mantis had proclaimed; Augustus Malevolyn had indeed earned the mantle of Bartuc.

"You are worthy," the demon chittered. "So says this one—Xazax, I am called—but still one thing remains outside your grasp! One thing must you have before Bartuc you become!"

General Malevolyn understood. "The *armor*. The armor that fool of a peasant wears! Well, it comes to me even now from across the sea! Galeona says it approaches Lut Gholein, which is why we march there now." He considered.

"Perhaps now would be a good time to see what she can learn. Maybe with your aid . . ."

"Best to not speak of me to your sorceress, great one!" Xazax chittered with what seemed some anxiety. "Her kind . . . cannot always be trusted. They are better not dealt with at all . . ."

Malevolyn briefly mulled over the demon's statement. Xazax almost spoke as if he and Galeona shared a history, which, in retrospect, would hardly have surprised the general. The witch dealt with dark powers almost on a continuous basis. What did interest him, however, was that this creature did not want her to know what was now being discussed. A falling out? A betrayal? Well, if it served Malevolyn, then so much the better.

He nodded. "Very well. Until I decide what must be done, we'll leave her ignorant of our conversation."

"This one appreciates your understanding . . ."

"By all means." The general had no more time to concern himself with the sorceress. Xazax had raised a point of much more interest to him. "But you spoke of the armor? Do you know something of it?"

Again the foul mantis bowed. Even in the starlight, the general could see the horrendous veins coursing all over its body, veins that pulsated without pause. "By now, this fool has brought it to Lut Gholein . . . but there he can hide it within the city's walls, keep it from he to whom it truly belongs . . ."

"I had thought of that." In fact, General Malevolyn had considered it much during the journey, considered it and grown more and more enraged, although he had revealed no outward sign of that fury to anyone else. A part of him felt certain that he could seize Lut Gholein and, thus, capture the peasant who wore the armor, but a more practical part had also counted up the losses on his own side and found them far too great. Failure still remained well within the realms of possibility. Malevolyn had, in truth, hoped to keep his army beyond the sight and knowledge of the kingdom and wait for the stranger to head out to the desert on his own. Unfortunately, the general could not necessarily trust that the fool would do as he desired.

Xazax leaned closer. "The kingdom, it is a strong one, with many soldiers well versed in the art of war. He who has the armor would feel quite safe in there."

"I know."

"But this one can give you the key with which to make Lut Gholein yours . . . a force most terrible . . . a force which no mortal army can subdue."

Malevolyn could scarcely believe what he had just heard. "Are you suggesting—"

The demon suddenly looked back toward the camp as if he had heard some sound. After a momentary pause, Xazax quickly returned his attention to the human. "When but a day separates you from the city, we shall speak again. There, you must be prepared to do this . . ."

The commander listened as the demon explained. At first even he felt repulsed by what the creature suggested, but then, as Xazax told him why it must be so, Augustus Malevolyn himself saw the need—and felt the growing excitement.

"You will do this?" the mantis asked.

"Yes . . . yes, I will . . . and gladly."

"Then we shall speak soon." Without warning, Xazax's form began to grow indistinct, quickly becoming more shadow than substance. "Until then, hail to you once again, general! This one honors the successor of Bartuc! This one honors the new master of demons! This one honors the new *Warlord of Blood!*"

With that, the last vestiges of Xazax faded into the night.

General Malevolyn immediately started back to camp, his mind already racing, the words of the monstrous mantis still echoing in his head. This night had become a turning point for him, with all his dreams coming together at last. The demon's test and the manner by which Malevolyn had passed it paled in comparison to what Xazax now offered—the armor and the method that would guarantee that it and Lut Gholein fell into the general's hands with little trouble.

Master of demons, the mantis had said.

One more night to get through. One more night and the *King's Shield* would dock in the port of Lut Gholein.

One more night and Kara would be alone in the strange land, alone save for her two grotesque companions.

She had returned with her evening meal just as before and eaten it under the watchful eyes of the two undead. Fauztin had remained standing in the corner, the dour Vizjerei looking like some macabre statue, but of late Sadun Tryst had edged closer, the more talkative of the two ghouls now seated on a bench built into the wall nearest her bed. The wiry ghoul even tried to make conversation with her on occasion, something that the necromancer could have done well without.

Yet, one subject interested her enough to force her to speak with him for a time and that subject concerned the ever elusive Norrec Vizharan. Kara had noticed something odd about the way Tryst spoke of his former comrade. His words seemed to hold no malice at all for his murderer. Most of the time, he simply regaled her with tales of their adventures together. Tryst even seemed to feel some remorse for the veteran soldier despite the horrible acts Norrec had committed.

"He saved . . . my life . . . three times and more . . ." the ghoul concluded, after being coaxed once more into speaking of his treacherous friend. "Never a war . . . as bad as . . . that one."

"You traveled with him from then on?" The war mentioned by Tryst had apparently taken place in the Western Kingdoms some nine years before. For men such as these to stick together for so very long showed a powerful bond of some sort.

"Aye . . . save during . . . Norrec's sickness . . . he left us . . . for three months . . . and caught up after . . ." The rotting figure looked to the Vizjerei. "Remember . . . Fauztin?"

The sorcerer nodded his head ever so slightly. Kara had expected him to somehow forbid Sadun from going on with such stories, but Fauztin, too, seemed caught up in them. In life, both men had clearly respected Norrec highly and, from what she had heard so far, so now did the necromancer.

Yet this same Norrec Vizharan had brutally murdered the pair and revenants did not exist if not fueled by a sense of revenge and justice that went beyond mortal comprehension. These two should have harbored only thoughts of retribution, of the rending of Vizharan's flesh and the sending of his damned soul to the underworld. That they still felt anything at all other than that struck her quite strange. Sadun Tryst and Fauztin did not act at all like the revenants of which legends had spoken.

"What will you do when you find him?" She had asked this question but once before and received no clear answer.

"We'll do . . . what must be . . . done."

Again, a response that did not satisfy her. Why shield Kara from the truth? "After what he did, even your past friendship must mean little. How could Norrec commit so terrible a crime?"

"He did . . . what had to be . . . done." With that equally enigmatic reply, Tryst's smile stretched, revealing more of the yellowed teeth and the gums already receding. Each day, despite their all-consuming quest, the revenants grew less and less human in appearance. They would never completely decay, but their link to their former humanity would continue to shrivel. "You're very beautiful . . ."

"What?" Kara Nightshadow blinked, not certain that she had heard correctly.

"Very beautiful . . . and fresh . . . alive." The ghoul suddenly reached forward, caught a lock of her long, raven-colored hair. "Life's beautiful . . . more so than . . . ever . . ."

She hid a shudder. Sadun Tryst had made his intent quite clear. He still recalled too well the pleasures of life. One of those, food, had sorely disappointed him already. Now, hidden in this tiny cabin for the past couple of days in the constant company of a living woman, he seemed ready to try to relive a different pleasure—and Kara did not know how she could prevent him from trying.

Without warning, Sadun Tryst suddenly turned and glared at his friend. Although Kara had noticed nothing, clearly some communication had passed between the two, communication that did not please the wiry ghoul in the least.

"Leave me . . . at least . . . the illusion . . ."

Fauztin said nothing, his only reaction being to blink once. However, that alone seemed to quell his comrade some.

"I wouldn't have . . . touched her . . . much . . ." Tryst looked her over once before meeting her eyes. "I just—"

A heavy knocking on the door sent him hurrying to the far corner. Kara could not believe her eyes each time the ghoul moved so. She had always read that swiftness could not be termed one of the skills of the undead. In its place, they had persistence, an unholy patience.

Ensconced next to the Vizjerei, he muttered, "Answer."

She did, already suspecting that she knew who it would be. Only two men dared come to her door, one Captain Jeronnan, whom she had just spoken with but a short time before, the other—

"Yes, Mister Drayko?" the sorceress asked, keeping the door open only a crack.

He looked uncomfortable. "My Lady Kara, I realize that you've requested absolute privacy, but . . . but I wondered whether you might join me on the deck for a few minutes."

"Thank you, Mister Drayko, but, as I have said before to the captain, I have much to do before we make landfall." She started to close the door. "Thank you for asking—"

"Not even for a little *fresh* air?"

Something in his tone puzzled her, but the necromancer had no time to think about it. Tryst had made it very clear that she should spend no more time outside than needed to retrieve her food from the mess. The revenants wanted their living puppet where they could see her. "I am sorry, no."

"I thought as much." He turned to leave—then *threw* his shoulder to the door with such force that the door knocked Kara back onto the bed. The blow did not stun her, but she lay there for a moment, completely bewildered by his actions.

Drayko fell to a kneeling position just inside. He looked up, saw the ghouls, and blanched. "By the King of the Depths!"

A dagger suddenly materialized in Tryst's hand.

The mariner reached for his own knife, which Kara saw lay by his side. Drayko had clearly been holding it all along, concealing its presence while he had spoken inanities with the dark mage. All along he had acted with the knowledge that something seemed amiss in the cabin—although likely even Drayko had never imagined the sight before him.

As Sadun Tryst raised his arm, a second figure charged into the tiny room. Ceremonial blade held ready, Captain Hanos Jeronnan shielded his officer from harm. Unlike Drayko, he seemed only mildly surprised at the horrendous figures but a short distance from him. In fact, Jeronnan almost looked pleased to see the two ghouls.

"I won't let it happen again . . ." he murmured. "You'll not take this one . . ."

Kara immediately understood the captain's words. In his mind, the undead represented that invisible monster that had not only taken his daughter from him, but had turned her into a vile creature he had been forced to destroy. Now he thought to wreak his vengeance on them.

And with the silver-plated sword, he had the potential to do just that.

Tryst threw his dagger, again moving with a speed his decrepit form belied. The smaller blade sank into Jeronnan's sword arm, sending the captain staggering. However, the former naval commander did not retreat. Blood dripping down, the ghoul's weapon still half-buried in his flesh, Captain Jeronnan attacked, slicing at his unliving adversary.

His macabre smile seeming to mock, Sadun Tryst reached for the blade, clearly intending to grab it in his hand. As one beyond death, no normal blade could touch him.

The edge of the captain's weapon severed off the lower two fingers.

Pure agony abruptly coursed through Kara, the pain so great that she doubled over, nearly collapsing.

With a hiss, Tryst pulled his maimed hand back. Glaring at Jeronnan, he gasped to his partner, "Do something . . . while I still have . . . a head on my . . . shoulders . . ."

Her eyes blurry from tears, the necromancer nonetheless saw Fauztin blink once.

"Look out!" she managed to cry.

A wall of force erupted from her ceremonial dagger, sending both Jeronnan and Drayko flying against the opposite wall. At the same time, the Vizjerei put his other hand on the wall behind him.

A blue haze spread behind the ghouls, a blue haze that grew rapidly in both height and width.

The two mariners struggled to their feet. Mister Drayko started forward, but Jeronnan pushed him back. "Nay! The only weapon that's good for them is this one! I swear I'll slice them both into fish bait—that is, if even the fish'll take something so rotten! You see to the girl!"

The officer obeyed instantly, hurrying to the Kara's side. "Can you stand?"

With help, Kara found that she could. Although the pain did not leave her, at least it subsided enough for the enchantress to think—and realize what had happened.

Through the dagger, Fauztin had tied her life to the revenants' continued existence. The blow that Jeronnan had landed had not been felt by Sadun Tryst, who had been long past such mortal weaknesses. However, each successful strike against them would, so it appeared, be suffered by *her*.

And so, with a sword gilded in silver, Captain Jeronnan had the capability of not only slicing the undead into the bait he had mentioned, but also in the process slaying the very one he sought to save.

She had to warn him. "Drayko! Jeronnan must stop!"

"It's all right, my lady! The captain knows what he does! His silver blade's just right for dealing with the likes of those! In such close quarters, he'll make quick work of them before the one can cast another spell!" Drayko wrinkled his nose. "Gods, what a stench in here! After you started acting so strangely, Captain Jeronnan finally recalled what had happened to you back in Gea Kul and felt certain that something was up! He summoned me to his cabin after dinner, related his suspicions, then told me to come with him and be prepared for Hell itself—although how close to the truth he meant that even I didn't know!"

The necromancer tried again. "Listen! They've cast an enchantment on me—"

"Which is why you couldn't say anything, aye!" He started to pull her toward the open doorway, where several of Jeronnan's men had gathered. Some had their weapons drawn, but none had yet dared enter, far more fearful of facing the undead than either the captain or his second. "Come on! Let's get you away from them!"

"But that's not the—" Kara stopped as her body suddenly twisted free of its own accord from the officer.

He reached for her arm. "Not that way! You'd better—"

To her dismay, the necromancer's hand folded into a fist—then *struck* her protector hard in the stomach.

While not that harsh a blow, it nevertheless caught Drayko completely by surprise. Jeronnan's second fell back, more startled than injured.

Kara turned toward the undead . . . and saw the grim Vizjerei beckoning her to join them.

Her limbs obeyed despite her best attempts to counter his summons. Behind the ghouls the blue haze had spread to encompass most of the wall. Discovered by the living, the undead now sought to retreat—but with them, they hoped to take their prize.

Kara tried to resist, knowing not only that she had no desire to go with the duo, but that the only thing beyond that wall lay the dark sea. Tryst and his companion did not need to breathe, but Kara surely did.

Come to me, necromancer . . . she suddenly heard in her head. The eyes of Fauztin stared unblinking into her own, drowning out her own thoughts.

Unable to control herself any longer, Kara ran toward the undead.

"Lass, no!" Captain Jeronnan seized her arm, but his wound kept his grip from tightening much. She tore herself free, then reached forth to take Sadun Tryst's mutilated hand.

"I . . . have her!" the smiling ghoul gasped.

Fauztin grabbed his companion by the shoulder, then purposely fell backwards—vanishing through the blue haze and pulling Tryst with him.

And with Tryst went Kara.

"Grab hold of her!" the captain shouted. Drayko called out something, possibly her name, but by then they were both too late to do anything.

The dark mage fell through the haze—and into the suffocating embrace of the sea.

THIRTEEN

The tomb of Horazon . . . the Arcane Sanctuary . . .

Norrec Vizharan struggled through a thick, gray webbing, forcing his way down a winding, confusing arrangement of corridors.

Horazon . . .

Ancient statues lined the wall, each the face of someone familiar to him. He recognized Attis Zuun, his fool of an instructor. Korbia, the far too innocent acolyte he had later sacrificed for his goals. Merendi, the council leader who had fallen prey to his well-crafted words of admiration. Jeslyn Kataro, the friend who he had betrayed. Buried behind the webs he found everyone he had ever known—except one.

Everyone except his brother, Horazon.

"Where are you?" Norrec shouted. "Where are you?"

Suddenly, he stood in a darkened chamber, a vast crypt before him. Skeletons in the garb of Vizjerei sorcerers stood at attention in a series of alcoves lining the right and left walls of the room. The symbol of the clan, a dragon bent over a crescent moon, had been carved in the center of the great sarcophagus directly before the armored intruder.

"Horazon!" Norrec cried. "Horazon!"

The name echoed throughout the crypt, seeming to mock him. Angered, he marched up to the stone coffin and reached for the heavy lid.

As he touched it, a moaning arose from the skeletons on each side of him. Norrec almost shrank back, but fury and determination won out over all other emotions. Ignoring the warnings of the dead, the soldier wrenched the lid from the sarcophagus and let it drop to the floor, where it shattered in a thousand pieces.

Within the coffin, Norrec beheld a shrouded form. Sensing victory, he reached to tear the cloth from the face, to see the withered and failing countenance of his cursed brother.

A hand covered with rotting flesh and burrowing maggots seized his own at the wrist.

He struggled, but the monstrous fingers would not release him. Worse, to Norrec's horror, the corpse began to sink deeper and deeper into the coffin, as if the bottom had suddenly given way to an endless abyss. Try as he might, Norrec could not keep from being pulled into the sarcophagus, into the pit of darkness below.

He screamed as the world of the dead closed in around him—

"Awaken."

Norrec shook, his gauntleted hands reaching to fend off nightmares. He blinked, gradually realizing that he still sat in the old chair in Drognan's sanctum. The dream about his brother's crypt—no, *Bartuc's* brother—had seemed so real, so horribly real.

"You slept. You dreamed," the elderly Vizjerei commented.

"Yes . . ." Unlike most dreams, however, the veteran recalled this one quite vividly. In fact, he doubted that he would ever be able to forget it. "I'm sorry about falling asleep . . ."

"No need to apologize. After all, I am the one who, with the aid of some wine, made you sleep . . . and dream as well."

Sudden anger made Norrec try to leap up from the chair—only to have Drognan stop him in his tracks with but a warning hand. "You will sit back down."

"What did you do? How long have I been out?"

"I placed you under shortly after you sat down. As for how long you slept . . . nearly a day. The night has come and gone." The sorcerer came closer, the spell staff now used as a cane. Norrec, however, did not read Drognan's use of it as any sign of weakness. "As for why I did it, let us just say that I have taken the first step toward both our goals, my friend." He smiled expectantly. "Now, tell me, what did you see in the dream?"

"Shouldn't you know?"

"I made you dream; I did not decide *what* you dreamed of."

"Are you saying I made up that nightmare myself?"

The ancient mage stroked his silver beard. "Perhaps I had some influence on the choice of subjects . . . but the results were yours alone. Now tell me what you dreamed."

"What's the point of it?"

All friendliness faded from Drognan's tone. "The point is your life."

Aware that he had no true choice in the matter, Norrec finally gave in and told the sorcerer what he wanted to know. In nearly perfect detail, the soldier described the scene, the events, and even the faces and names of the statues. Drognan nodded, quite interested in all of it. He asked questions, dredging up minor details that Norrec had initially forgotten to mention. Nothing seemed too insignificant to the listening mage.

And when it came time to relate the horrifying events taking place in the crypt, the Vizjerei paid very close attention. Drognan seemed to take special delight in having Norrec describe the skeletal mages and the opening of the sarcophagus. Even when Norrec began to shake in recollection of his descent into the abyss, the sorcerer pushed him to continue, to not leave out the most minute bit of information.

"So fascinating!" Drognan burst out when Norrec had finished, completely oblivious to the agony he had just forced the veteran to relive. "So vivid! It must be truth!"

"What . . . must be?"

"You actually saw the tomb! The *true* Arcane Sanctuary! I'm certain of it!"

If he expected Norrec to share in his delight, the wrinkled mage had to have been disappointed. Not only did the soldier not believe that what he had seen could be real . . . but if such a place could exist, Norrec wanted no part of it.

After Bartuc's lair, the notion of entering the crypt of his hated brother chilled the otherwise steadfast fighter. He had suffered nothing but misery and terror since this had all begun; Norrec only desired to be free of the enchanted armor.

He said as much to Drognan, who replied, "You will have that chance, Vizharan . . . if you are willing to face the nightmare one more time."

Somehow, Norrec found himself not at all surprised that this would be the sorcerer's response. Both Bartuc and Drognan shared the history of a culture focused much on ambition regardless of the consequences. The Empire of Kehjistan had been founded on that principle and the Vizjerei, its backbone, had delved into demon summoning as a method by which to garner power over all others. Only when those demons had turned upon them had they willingly given up that course—and even these days there existed stories of corrupt Vizjerei who had turned again to the forces of Hell for their might.

Even Fauztin had, at times, hinted of a willingness to take steps beyond what his craft would have deemed safe. However, Norrec liked to believe that his friend would have been less inclined than Drognan to force another to suffer such horrific nightmares not once, but twice—and all for simple gain.

Yet, what choice did the soldier have now? Only Drognan kept the cursed suit from running off with Norrec to who knew what new monstrous destiny . . .

He gazed around at the multitude of books and scrolls gathered over the years by the elderly Vizjerei. Norrec suspected that they represented only a part of Drognan's storehouse of knowledge. The sorcerer had kept him to this one chamber, but surely hid some of his other secrets from the fighter. Truly, if anyone could free him, the Vizjerei could—but only if Norrec proved willing to pay the price.

Again, what other choice did he have?

"All right! Do what you must . . . and do it soon! I want an end to this!" Yet, even as he said it, Norrec knew that there would never be an end to the horrible guilt he felt.

"Of course." Drognan turned from him, reaching for another massive tome. He perused the pages for a few moments, nodded to himself, then shut the book. "Yes, that should do it."

"Do what?"

Replacing the book, the mage answered, "Despite the enmities between them, Bartuc and Horazon are forever bound together, even in death. That the suit has brought you here to Lut Gholein shows that bond remains strong even after all this time." He frowned. "And your bond with the armor is nearly as great. An unexpected plus, I might add, but one I find myself curious about. Perhaps after this is over, I shall make a study of it."

"You still haven't told me what you want to do," reminded the veteran, not wanting Drognan to become distracted again. He vaguely understood what the sorcerer had said about the bond between the brothers and how the suit had a link to that, but the rest made no sense to him and Norrec did not wish to pursue it any further. His own connection with the armor had begun with entering Bartuc's tomb and would end when Drognan helped him strip the metal from his body. After that, the Vizjerei could do what he wanted with the suit—preferably *melting* it down to make farm tools or some other such harmless items.

"This time I will cast a spell that should enable us to find the actual physical location of the tomb, which I have always believed might very well be under the *city*!" Drognan's eyes lit up at the possibility. "It will require you to go back into the dream . . . but this time you will do so in a waking state."

"How can I dream if I'm awake?"

The mage rolled his eyes. "Preserve me from the uninitiated! Norrec Vizharan, you shall dream while awake because of my *spell*. Rest assured that you need to know nothing more."

With great reluctance, the weary fighter nodded. "All right, then! Let's get it done!"

"The preparations will take but a few moments . . ."

Coming closer, the elderly Vizjerei used the tip of his staff to draw a circle around the chair. At first Norrec saw nothing of interest in this, but the moment Drognan completed the circle, it suddenly flared to life, glowing a furious yellow and pulsating over and over. Again, the fighter would have jumped out of the chair if not for the warning glance his host gave him. In an attempt to calm down, Norrec reminded himself of the ultimate goal of all of this—freedom. Surely he could face whatever Drognan might put him through for that.

The sorcerer muttered something, then reached out with his left hand to touch Norrec's forehead. The soldier felt a slight jolt, but nothing more.

With his finger, Drognan began drawing symbols in the air, symbols that flashed into and out of existence each time he finished one. Norrec caught only glances of each, although at least one reminded him of one of the wards he had seen in Bartuc's tomb. That made him more wary again, but the time for retreat had already passed and he knew that he had to face whatever resulted from the spellcasting.

"*Shazari . . . Shazari Tomei . . .*"

Norrec's entire body stiffened, almost as if the armor had once more taken control. However, the veteran soldier knew that it could not be that, for Drognan had long ago proven his mastery over the enchanted suit. No, it had to be just another part of the spell.

"*Tomei!*" the silver-haired mage cried, raising his spell staff high above his head. Despite his advanced years, he looked more terrible, more powerful, than any man Norrec had ever met, even on the battlefield. A white, crackling aura surrounded the Vizjerei, causing Drognan's beard and hair to fluttered about almost as if with a life of their own. "*Shazari Saruphi!*"

Norrec gasped as his body shook violently. A force pushed him hard against the chair. The mage's sanctum suddenly receded from him with such speed it made the fighter dizzy. Norrec felt as if he floated, although neither his arms nor his legs could move at all.

An emerald haze formed before him, a haze with a vaguely circular shape to it. Far, far away, Norrec heard Drognan shout something else, but it seemed drawn out and unintelligible, as if for the Vizjerei time had slowed to a crawl and even sound could move no swifter than a snail.

The haze refined itself, forming a perfect circle now. The emerald mist within that circle then dissipated—and as it did, an image, a place, formed within.

The crypt.

But something about its appearance immediately troubled Norrec. Details seemed altered, incorrect in many ways. The Vizjerei skeletons now wore elaborate armor instead of robes and appeared not to be true dead, but rather cleverly carved from stone. The massive cobwebs gave way instead to tattered tapestries depicting magical creatures such as dragons, rocs, and more. Even the symbol of the brothers' clan had transformed, now a vast bird clutching in its talons the sun.

Norrec tried to say something, but his voice did not work. Once more, though, he heard the painfully belabored words of Drognan. The mage sounded farther away than before.

Suddenly, the image of the crypt receded. Faster and faster it rushed away from Norrec. Although he still sat in the chair, it felt to the fighter as if he ran backwards through the musty corridors leading to Horazon's tomb. Row upon row of statue darted in front of Norrec, vanishing as quickly as the crypt had. Although most faces appeared as little more than blurs, some few he recognized, but not as those from the warlord's dark past. Instead, they were faces from Norrec's own life—Sadun Tryst, Fauztin, Norrec's first commander, some of the women he had loved, and even Captain Casco. A few he did not recognize at all, including a pale but attractive young woman with hair the color of night and eyes so arresting not only for their exotic curve, but for the simple fact that they gleamed silver.

But even the statues finally receded from sight. Now he saw but earth and rock, all tumbling about him as if he burrowed in reverse. Drognan called out something, but he might as well have been silent for all Norrec understood him.

At last, the earth and rock gave way to a more powdery substance . . . *sand*, he belatedly realized. A glimmer of light, perhaps the light of day, spread around the edges of the images.

Norrec!

The veteran shook his head, certain that he had imagined someone calling his name.

Norrec! Vizharan!

It sounded like Drognan, but Drognan as he had never heard the sorcerer. The Vizjerei sounded almost anxious, possibly even fearful.

Vizharan! Fight it!

Something within Norrec stirred, a fear for his very soul . . .

His left hand rose of its own accord.

"No!" he shouted, his own voice seeming distant, disconnected from him.

His other hand rose, his entire body following suit.

He had barely left the chair when a physical force suddenly attempted to halt his unwilling progress. Norrec saw the distorted form of Drognan, staff in both hands, trying to drive the soldier back, away from the vision of the Arcane Sanctuary. He also saw his own gauntleted hands meet those of the Vizjerei, Norrec gripping the staff as if he sought to rip it free.

The staff crackled with energy where the two men held it tight, brilliant yellow bursts where Drognan touched, bloody crimson flashes where Norrec's fingers sought a hold. Norrec could feel powerful sorceries flowing through his very being——

Fight it, Vizharan! called Drognan from somewhere. His mouth never seemed to move, but his expression matched the stress in the words in Norrec's head. *The armor is stronger than I believed! We have been tricked all along!*

No more need have been said. He understood exactly what the mage meant. The enchanted armor had obviously never been under the Vizjerei's control; the suit had simply bided its time, waiting for Drognan to discover that for it which it had so very long sought.

The location of Horazon's tomb.

In some things, then, Drognan had been correct. He had said that Bartuc and his hated brother remained linked forever. So now did Norrec see why the armor had dragged him from one side of the world to the other. Something pulled it toward the final resting place of Horazon, something so powerful that even death had been unable to stop the quest.

The armor had a mind of sorts; certainly it had shown far more cleverness than either Norrec or anyone else he had so far met. Likely when the *Hawksfire* had approached Lut Gholein it had even sensed Drognan's spellwork . . . and somehow knew that it could make use of the Vizjerei in order to further its own sinister goals.

Incredible, unbelievable, improbable—but more than likely the absolute truth.

Energy sizzled between Norrec's gauntlets. Drognan let out a cry and fell back, not dead but obviously stunned. The gloves released their hold on the spell staff, then the right reached for the image before Norrec.

However, as it did, the vision began to shift, to pull away, as if some other force now sought to defeat the suit's evil purpose. The image faded, twisted——

Undeterred, the armor placed the right gauntlet into the very center. A crimson aura appeared around the hand.

"*Shazari Giovox!*"

As the undesired words fell from his lips, Norrec's body lost all substance. He cried out, but nothing would stop the process. As if a creature of smoke, his form stretched, contorted—and finally *poured* into the dwindling vision.

Not until both Norrec and the magical circle had both vanished did his screaming stop.

This day they had lost one man to sand maggots and another to the heat of the desert itself, yet Galeona noticed that, if anything, Augustus Malevolyn acted more and more cheerful, almost as if he already had not only the armor of Bartuc but the power and glory he dreamed it would give him. That bothered the witch, bothered her more than she would have thought it could. Such a display was hardly like the general. If his disposition had lightened so much, he surely had good reason for it.

Galeona suspected that reason had something to do with Xazax. She had not seen much of the demon of late and that never meant anything good. In fact, since the other night, when Malevolyn had evidently lost his common sense and taken a walk alone in the dark desert, the mantis had acted distant. Twice when the sorceress had found excuses to separate herself from the party and talk with him about their plans, Xazax had remained suspiciously remote in his comments. It almost seemed as if everything for which they had worked together no longer mattered.

Xazax wants the armor, she considered. *But he can't make use of its enchantments himself.*

Yet, if he could not, surely a human dupe could . . . and Augustus presented a quite a distinct possibility there. Already the witch had suspected Xazax of trying to manipulate her lover. Now she felt certain that she had underestimated the mantis.

Galeona had to regain her influence over the general. If not, she risked losing more than her station—the sorceress risked losing her head.

Malevolyn had called for a rest. They had made surprisingly good time and had overall suffered scant losses to their harsh surroundings. A pack of leapers—monstrous, hopping terrors somewhat reptilian in appearance and with spikes along their spines—had harried them for a time, but never had the troops allowed the creatures to come near enough to make use of their long claws and savage teeth. Slaying one had left the others fighting over the carcass. Like most desert creatures, the easy meal, even if it happened to be one of their own, ever won out over battling with something that battled back.

If anything, the sand and heat continued to be their greatest nemesis, which had been why the general had finally relented. Had the choice been solely his, he would have kept going, even if it meant riding his mount to death and then walking on from there.

"I can almost see it," he remarked as she rode up next to him. Malevolyn had taken his horse and moved on a short distance ahead of the column. Now he sat in the saddle, surveying the emptiness ahead. "I can almost taste it. . . ."

She edged her own mount nearer, then extended one hand in order to touch his. General Malevolyn, Bartuc's bloody helm still in place, did not so much as look at her, not a good sign at all.

"And well deserved," she cooed, trying to garner his interest. "Imagine how you'll look when you bear down on Lut Gholein clad in the crimson helm of the warlord! They'll think you to be him come back to life!"

She regretted the words almost at once, recalling how his memories and those of the helmet had earlier melded together. He had not suffered another bout since that last, sinister event, but Galeona still wore the burning reminder of that time on her finger.

Fortunately, Augustus appeared to have his own mind for the moment. He finally looked Galeona's way, sounding pleased with what the sorceress had said. "Yes, that *will* be a wondrous sight—the last one they will ever behold! I can almost picture it now . . . the cries of fear, the looks of horror as they realize their doom and who it is who delivers it."

Perhaps now she had the opportunity for which she had been looking. "You know, my love, while if we still have time, I can cast another search spell for you. With the helmet, it wouldn't be—"

"No." As simple as that. His gaze leaving her, Malevolyn added, "No. That will not be necessary."

He did not see the shiver that coursed through her. With those few words, he had verified her deepest fears. The general had even been adamant about taking any opportunity they could to seek out with sorcery the rest of Bartuc's legendary garb. When the helmet had fallen into his hands in an act even she would have called providential, he had spared no effort in letting her use the artifact to aid in hunting for the suit. Even when they had discovered that this Norrec now walked the earth clad in Malevolyn's prize, he had insisted she still use the helmet at regular intervals to keep track of the wanderer's route.

Now he talked as if he hardly cared, as if he had become so certain of the inevitability of retrieving the armor that he no longer even needed to maintain a magical eye on it. This did not at all sound like the Augustus she had known so inside and out, and Galeona felt it did not entirely have to do with the influence of the helmet. Surely the enchanted artifact had already solidified its hold over him enough to survive a few moments' separation.

And that brought her back to Xazax.

"As you wish," Galeona finally replied. "How soon before we move on again, my love?"

He glanced up in the direction of the sun. "A quarter hour. No more. I will be ready to meet my destiny at the proper time."

She did not ask him to elaborate. A quarter hour would suffice for her work. "I shall leave you to your thoughts, then, my general."

That he did not even nod in dismissal did not surprise her in the least. Yes, Xazax had definitely made his move, likely had even contacted the commander directly. By doing so, the demon had taken the first step toward not only severing his pact with the witch, but seeing her *dead*.

"We'll see whose head lies atop a pike," she muttered. With no shadows in which to hide, Xazax had to remain far from the column until the fall of night. That meant that Galeona could cast her spell with little worry that the treacherous mantis would know of it.

The sorceress found an ideal location behind a dune just beyond the column. She herself had no fear of sand maggots and the like, protective measures cast by her before the journey's beginning still strong. It had been within the limits of her power to do the same for the rest of those in the column, but that would have left Galeona without any ability to cast other spells. She had seen no reason to be so magnanimous. A few less soldiers would not make a difference to her . . .

Dismounting, she took her water flask, then knelt on the hot sand. From the flask the witch poured several precious mouthfuls of the cool liquid onto the parched ground. The moment she felt satisfied with the amount, Galeona shut the flask, then quickly went to work.

Her slim, tapering fingers molded the damp sand into a vaguely human figure the size of a doll. As she refined the form, Galeona muttered the first portion of her spell, attuning her creation to what she desired. The sand figure took on a more male aspect, broad of shoulder with indentations along the torso showing it to be wearing armor.

Knowing that the moisture would not last long, Galeona quickly took out a tiny vial. Still whispering, the sorceress poured a few drops of its contents onto the chest of the sand doll. The vial contained a liquid most precious to her; a small bit of blood that she had sacrificed from her body, then preserved for certain, delicate spellwork.

A representation involving Bartuc's armor needed blood to mark it and, more important, to link Galeona to the figurine she had created. That, in turn, she hoped would enable her to reach out to this Norrec, touch him as she had on the ship. As distant as he had earlier been when she and Xazax had summoned the Dreamer, such a spell cast then would have required far too much of her life's fluids for her to survive the effort. The soldier sacrificed in the tent had served in her place the last time. Now, though, Galeona felt certain that what she attempted here *would* succeed—and with minimal effect on her.

She drew a circle around the effigy, then placed her hands—palms down and fingers splayed—on the left and right sides of her creation. Leaning low, she stared at where the face would have been, whispering the final segment of her spell while intermittently muttering the soldier's name.

"Norrec . . . Norrec . . ."

The world around her receded. Galeona's view shifted, flew along the desert as if she had been transformed into an eagle who soared the skies with the swiftness of the wind. Faster and faster it raced, until she could no longer even see what landscape lay beneath her.

Her spell had worked. Through her own memories of her brief encounter with the fool, she further strengthened the magic by concentrating on his face, his form.

"Norrec . . . show me . . . show me where you are . . ."

Her view suddenly shifted, turned completely black. The abrupt change so caught Galeona by surprise that she nearly broke the spell. Only quick thinking enabled her to maintain the precious link; she would not have time to try again if she failed now. Even this long away from the column might make Augustus suspicious.

"Norrec . . . show me . . ."

His face appeared before her, eyes closed, mouth slack. For a moment, the witch wondered if he had somehow perished, but then she realized that her incantation could not have worked in the first place if that had been the case. The sand effigy demanded a living target.

If not dead, then what had happened? Galeona probed deeper, entered the frame in which Norrec existed. By doing so, she lost all but the thinnest thread of contact with the true world, but, by doing so, she also stood to gain so much more.

And at last, the sorceress saw where her quarry lay.

The knowledge so stunned her that *this* time she could not help but lose her link to him. His face pulled away, receded with such shocking speed that it gave her vertigo. The darkness reappeared, then Galeona found herself falling backwards across the desert, a complete reversal of her journey.

With a gasp, the exhausted witch fell back onto the burning sand.

She ignored the discomfort, ignored everything. The only thing that mattered to her was what she had just learned.

"So . . ." Galeona whispered. "I have you, my pretty puppet."

FOURTEEN

❋

A harsh rumbling shook Kara Nightshadow, dragging her from the darkness enveloping her. She inhaled, only to quickly start choking. The necromancer tried to breathe, but her lungs would not work properly.

She coughed, suddenly expelling an ocean of water. Over and over, Kara coughed, each time trying to empty her lungs so that she could then fill them up with life-saving air.

At last it became possible to breathe, albeit somewhat raggedly. The necromancer lay still, inhaling again and again in an attempt to regain some balance. Gradually, matters returned near enough to normal for her to begin to sense other things, such as the chill around her and the moisture saturating all her clothes. A gritty substance in her mouth forced her to spit, and she slowly realized that she lay face down on a sandy beach.

Again the world rumbled around her. Forcing her head up, Kara saw that the heavens above had begun to fill with storm clouds much like those of the tempest through which the *King's Shield* had sailed. In fact, she suspected the clouds above to be the precursor of the same storm, now ready to assail much of the eastern coast.

Memories began to return, memories of Captain Jeronnan in battle with the revenants, then the two undead dragging the necromancer through the portal and into the raging sea. After that, however, she could recall nothing whatsoever. How Kara had survived, she could not say. The enchantress did not even know what fate, if any, might have befallen Jeronnan and his men. It had seemed as if the portal had not had any effect on the hull, so if the *King's Shield* had survived that incident, then the odds were good that the vessel would soon make Lut Gholein—if it had not done so already.

Kara blinked, thinking of the city. The fate of the *King's Shield* aside, where by Rathma had *she* ended up? With great effort, the soaked necromancer pushed herself to a kneeling position and peered around.

Her first glimpse of her surroundings told Kara little. Sand and a few hardy plants typical of a coastal environment. She saw no signs of civilization, no signs of any human touch. Ahead of her lay a high ridge, making observation further inland impossible without a bit of a climb. Kara tried to avoid the inevitable by looking left, then right, but neither of those directions offered her more hope. Her only true option remained the ridge.

Still feeling as if she had just expunged both of the Twin Seas from her system, Kara forced herself to her feet. She knew that she should have removed most of her cold wet clothing, but the notion of being discovered by any locals while without much to wear did not appeal to her. Besides, other than the wind, the day itself seemed fairly warm. If she moved around for a while, surely her garments would dry.

Of either Sadun Tryst or Fauztin she saw no sign, but by no means did Kara think herself rid of the two ghouls. Most likely they had all become separated in the fearsome waters. For all she knew, the duo had washed up farther down the coast. If so, it behooved the necromancer to reach Lut Gholein as quickly as possible, perhaps even look for this Vizjerei they had mentioned, this Drognan. She doubted that he willingly worked with the undead; likely they sought the use of his knowledge in order to find their former friend. Whatever the case, Drognan also represented her best chance of not only freeing herself from any bond to the revenants, but also locating Norrec Vizharan and the armor.

With some struggling, the enchantress made it to the top of the sandy ridge—and there discovered a well-worn road. Better yet, as she looked to the south, she noticed a dim shape on the horizon, a shape Kara believed resembled a city.

Lut Gholein?

With as much eagerness as her weary mind could muster, she started south. If, as she suspected, Lut Gholein lay ahead, it would likely take her a good day to travel that far, especially in her condition. Worse, hunger already gnawed at her stomach, a condition that only grew worse with each step she took. Nevertheless, Kara did not even think of giving in to her weaknesses. So long as she could walk, she would continue on with her mission.

However, Kara had journeyed only a short distance when a clatter behind her made the weary necromancer pause to look over her shoulder. To her relief, she spied two well-laden wagons making their way from the north, a bushy-bearded old man and heavy-set woman in the first, a younger, wide-eyed youth and a girl most likely his sister guiding the second. A family of merchants no doubt on their way to sell their wares in the thriving metropolis. The exhausted necromancer paused, hoping that they would have pity on a bedraggled wanderer.

The elderly man might have driven his team past Kara, but his wife took one look at her and made him stop. They exchanged words with one another for a few moments, then, in the common tongue, the woman asked her. "Are you all right, young one? What's happened? Are you in need of help?"

Almost too tired to answer, the necromancer pointed toward the east. "My ship, it——"

She need not have said anything more. A sad look came over the elderly woman's round face and even the man gave her sympathy. Anyone living or traveling this near the sea surely knew of its violence. No doubt this had not been the first time the merchants had learned of some seafaring disaster.

The husband leapt down with an agility that belied his age. As he approached, he asked, "Is there anyone more? You the only one?"

"There is . . . no one else. I was . . . the ship may be all right . . . I was . . . washed overboard."

His wife made a tsking sound. "You're still soaked, too, young one! And your clothes are in tatters! Hesia! Find her a blouse and a warm blanket! Those, at least, she must have at once! Hurry!"

Unwilling to accept any charity, Kara fumbled at her belt. To her tremendous relief, the pouch in which she kept her money had somehow managed to remain intact. "I will pay for everything, I promise."

"Rubbish!" remarked the husband, but when she insisted on thrusting some coins in his hand, he nonetheless took most of them.

Hesia, daughter of the merchants Rhubin and Jamili, brought garments that Kara could only believe had to belong to the girl herself. Clearly with an eye toward respecting the stranger's dour garb, she had chosen a black blouse and even a gray knit blanket with which Kara could cover herself. Out of eyesight of Rhubin and his son, Ranul, she changed, feeling much better to be out of the soaked and ruined clothing.

Kara regretted the loss of her cloak even more once she had put on the blouse. Although in keeping with her taste in color, it fit too tight and had been cut too low. Yet, she said nothing, knowing that it had been the best choice available and, more important, something offered to her out of genuine concern. That she had insisted on paying for it did not take away from that.

To her relief, Jamili had Kara ride in the first wagon. Old enough to appreciate women, Ranul had eyed her with casual interest in the beginning and far more pointed interest once the enchantress had dried herself off and changed clothing. She expected no harm from him, but did not want to encourage anything that might cause dissension between herself and her rescuers.

And so, with the help of the kind merchant family, Kara Nightshadow managed to actually reach Lut Gholein more than an hour before sunset. She thought of immediately going to the port to see if Captain Jeronnan had arrived, but the urgency of her quest finally made her decide against it. The hunt for Norrec Vizharan and Bartuc's armor remained paramount.

In the gaily-colored bazaar, she bid farewell to Jamili and her family. Kara returned the blanket with thanks, then searched the marketplace for someone from whom she could buy an inexpensive but serviceable cloak. Doing so used up another valuable hour, but with the hooded garment the necromancer no longer felt so vulnerable. Kara would have replaced some of her other clothes as well, but her funds, much depleted, needed to be preserved now for food.

Questioning the locals carefully brought the dark mage some information concerning the mysterious Drognan. He seemed to live in an old building some distance into the massive city. Few visited him save to purchase elixirs and such. The only time Drognan left his sanctum looked to be when he made excursions to various scholars, seeking information on some pet passion of his.

Following the directions of a vegetable seller who had, on occasion, supplied the Vizjerei with supplies, Kara wended her way through the mazelike streets. The multitude of noises and bright colors wreaked some havoc on her senses, but she managed to not lose her way more than twice. Every so often the necromancer asked a passerby if he or she had seen a man clad in red armor, but not once did anyone say that they had.

Her kidnapping and near drowning in the sea had left her bereft of nearly all her belongings. Other than the pouch in which she had kept her money, only two others had survived. Unfortunately, the powders and chemicals in both had been ruined, save for a couple of vials of no use to her at present. Amazingly enough, the icon of Trag'Oul remained around her throat, for which she thanked the great dragon. It gave her some comfort in this strange land.

The loss of her belongings did not mean that Kara could no longer cast spells, but it did limit her somewhat. Fortunately, her change in garb had so far kept anyone from realizing her calling, even if it had encouraged one or two vendors to try to offer her more than information. Necromancers were not favored in Lut Gholein. The Church of Zakarum, powerful in the kingdom, frowned on their existence even more than it did that of the Vizjerei, who were evidently tolerated here by the young sultan. One or two acolytes from the Church had crossed her path so far, but, other than brief glances, they had not paid any attention to the slim young woman.

With much of what remained of her funds, Kara had purchased enough to carry along with her so that she could eat while she searched for Drognan. The notion of confronting a skilled, experienced Vizjerei bothered her enough, but to do so nearly ready to collapse would have been foolhardy at best. She could not assume that their encounter would necessarily be a friendly one. Animosity had long existed between the two callings.

A trio of soldiers on mounted patrol rode past, their eyes stern and their swords always near at hand. The foremost, evidently the officer in charge, rode a magnificent white stallion while his two subordinates each had brown, well-muscled beasts of their own. Kara had ridden little in her life, but realized as she watched them that, if the trail led outside of Lut Gholein, she would have to find some means of obtaining a horse. The dark mage could not rely on any travel spell out in the desert of Aranoch. Even in her far-off homeland Kara had heard tales of its deadly nature.

Her surroundings suddenly grew decrepit and dank, a complete contrast to the well-kept areas she had first encountered. Kara cursed herself for not having parted with her remaining coins for a usable dagger. The one that Captain Jeronnan had loaned her while aboard the *King's Shield* had been lost at sea. The enchantress began concentrating on her spells, inwardly hoping that she would still have the strength to cast them should the situation prove dire enough.

The necromancer came at last to the old building the vendor had somewhat vaguely described. Despite its decayed appearance, Kara immediately sensed forces at work in and around it. Some felt extremely ancient, surely even more ancient than the edifice itself. Others seemed more recent, including a few that had to have been summoned not all that long ago.

Climbing the outer steps, Kara looked over the ruined doorway, then stepped inside——

——and found herself standing in a timeworn but still magnificent hall that spoke of the glories of another time, another place. While also projecting a sense of long-ago abandonment, the high-columned hall had nothing else in common with the decrepit exterior, so much so that Kara even felt tempted to step outside again to see if perhaps she had somehow entered the wrong building. Here stood no ruin, but rather an ancient wonder still filled with the memories of greatness, of a splendor that even modern Lut Gholein had not yet approached.

The necromancer walked slowly through the hall, her mission still in mind but her attention distracted by the awesome marble columns, the imposing stone fireplace that covered nearly all of of one far wall, and the massive mosaic floor upon which she cautiously tread.

The floor, in fact, ensnared her attention more and more as Kara walked. In it, the artisan had captured intricate images both fanciful and real. Dragons curled around trees. Lions gave chase after antelope. Fearsome, stony warriors clad in breastplates and kilts did battle with one another.

Something clattered further down the hall.

Kara froze, her gaze shifting that direction. Yet, despite her excellent night vision, she could only make out a shadowed doorway at the far end. The necromancer waited, hesitant to even breathe too loudly. However, when no new noise came, Kara exhaled, realizing that in this ancient edifice bits of marble and stone would, on occasion, fall free. Even the slightest sound echoed here.

And at that moment, something behind her scraped across the marble floor.

She spun about, suddenly certain that the revenants had followed her here and now had chosen to reveal themselves. Against them, Kara could truly do nothing, but that did not mean that she would not struggle. They had already done too much, taken too much.

However, instead of the ever-grinning Sadun Tryst and his sorcerous companion, what greeted her eyes proved to be even more startling.

The gray figure wielding the sturdy blade moved slowly but surely toward her, his intention quite clear. Kara might have taken him for some brigand who had waited in the shadows for her, if not for the fact that she recognized him from but a few seconds earlier. Of course, even if Kara had not recognized the newcomer, she certainly could still make out the many tiny squares of stone composing not only his entire breastplate and kilt—but also his very skin.

The mosaic warrior stalked her, his savage expression exactly the same as when he had existed only as a decoration set in the floor. He swiped at her with the blade—revealing then that while he had the height and width of a living creature, he had no more depth to his form than the tiny stones from which he had been created.

Not for a moment, though, did Kara think this any weakness. The magic that had created such a guardian would not have made him so fragile. Physically striking the mosaic warrior would likely be just like striking a stone wall. She also suspected that the blade would cut just as well as, if not better than, a real one freshly sharpened.

But what had set him into action? Surely Drognan did not set out such a welcome for everyone who walked through the door. No, more likely Kara had been identified by some hidden spell as a necromancer, a dark mage of unknown loyalties. She knew of such detection spells and knew also that many mages utilized them for their own safety. Had Kara not suffered through so much of late, the enchantress felt certain she would have recalled such information earlier—when it might have prevented this deadly encounter.

Rattling came from the floor just behind her macabre assailant, and to the necromancer's consternation, a second warrior arose to join the first. Kara then turned quickly to her right, where yet more noise marked the awakening of a third.

"I mean no harm," she whispered. "I seek your master." Did they even serve Drognan? Kara only assumed that she had come to the right place. Perhaps someone the enchantress had talked to earlier had recognized her for what she was and had sent her here to *die*. Many, especially those of the Zakarum faith, would have considered the loss of a necromancer no loss at all.

The first of the mosaics had nearly come within the striking range of his sword. Kara saw no other choice but to take the offensive.

The words of the spell tripped off her tongue as the necromancer clutched the icon of Trag'Oul and pointed at her first attacker. At the same time, Kara stepped back as a precaution. If her spell worked, the incredible forces she summoned might not be contained to the destruction of the magical guardian.

A swarm of toothy projectiles formed from thin air, then rained down on the nearest of the mosaic warriors. The *Den'Trag*, or *Teeth of the Dragon Trag'Oul*, ripped through the stone body of the guardian, scattering small squares everywhere. The warrior tried to move, but his legs and arms, now missing so many pieces, crumbled. Still wearing his scowl, he attempted one last thrust at her, then collapsed in a shower of stone.

Kara exhaled, relieved to be rid of at least one adversary but praying she still had the strength to deal with the others. Summoning the Den'Trag had taken much out of the already-weary necromancer. Yet, if Kara could do it twice more and thus completely eliminate her unliving foes, then perhaps she could rest afterward.

Once again the necromancer clutched the icon tight, muttering the spell. A few words more and—

An intense rattling all around her caused Kara to falter. She glanced down, saw the many bits of mosaic stone from the fallen warrior now rolling toward one another, gathering in a swiftly growing pile behind the others. To her horror, first the feet, then the legs reformed. Bit by bit the stone warrior rebuilt himself, none the worse for her destructive spell.

The Teeth of Trag'Oul had failed her. Stepping back, Kara entered the darkened hall leading to the doorway. She had other spells at her command, but, combined with her weakness and the enclosed surroundings, none of them seemed likely to help her quickly enough without risking her own life further.

"Verikos!" a voice called. *"Verikos . . . Dianysi!"*

The ungodly trio paused at the cry . . . then each warrior abruptly collapsed, the individual stones dropping to the ground with a harsh clatter that echoed throughout the ancient structure. The stones, however, did not rest where they lay, but rather began to quickly roll back to where the figures had originally been set in the ground, each bit of mosaic returning to its precise location. One by one, they fell into place. Within seconds, the menacing fighters had not only retreated from their attack but had completely reformed as images on the elegant floor.

Kara turned to thank her rescuer, certain that it had to be the enigmatic Drognan. "I thank you for your aid——"

The figure that stood before her could hardly be the venerable, elegantly clad Vizjerei the vendor and others had described. Advanced age seemed the only thing this wild-eyed beggar with long white hair and beard had in common with the mage in question, although even Drognan could not be as old as this man looked. While still somewhat firm of body, his skin had grown so wrinkled and his watery blue eyes so weary that surely he had to be the oldest human alive in all the world.

He put a gnarled finger to thin lips. "Hush!" the beggar whispered much too loudly. "So much evil about! So much danger! We shouldn't have come here!"

"Are you . . . are you Drognan?"

The elderly man blinked, looked confused, then patted his worn, silk robe as if looking for something. After several seconds of this, he finally looked up and replied, "No . . . no, of course not! Now hush! There's too much evil about! We've got to be careful! We've got to be on guard!"

Kara considered. This man had to be a servant or something similar to the mage. Perhaps Drognan even kept him here out of pity for the beggar's madness. She decided to get to the point. Perhaps enough sanity remained within the man so that he could help her with the Vizjerei. "I have to see your master, Drognan. Tell him it concerns something of interest to him, Bartuc's——"

"*Bartuc?*" A ghastly change came over the beggar as he shouted the dead warlord's name. "*Bartuc!* No! The evil's come! I warned you!"

At that moment, another voice called out from the entrance of the building. "Who is it? Who has invaded my sanctum?"

The necromancer turned to speak, but the ragged man moved with amazing swiftness. He clamped a hand over her mouth, then whispered, "Hush! We mustn't be heard! It might be Bartuc!"

Instead, the newcomer proved to be a Vizjerei—and likely the one for whom Kara had been searching. Curiously, he looked as if he had been in some accident, for he had bruises over much of his face and seemed in discomfort each time he put pressure on his right leg. In the crook of one arm, the elderly mage carried a small package. She had no doubt that here stood Drognan, newly arrived from some errand.

"Norrec?" he called. "Vizharan?"

He knew the man Kara hunted! She tried to speak, but for a rather spindly figure, the beggar had incredible strength.

"Hush!" her unwanted companion whispered. "So much evil about! We must be careful! We mustn't be seen!"

Drognan stepped closer, surely able to see them now—and yet, he peered *past* both intruders as if seeing only air.

"Curious . . ." He sniffed the air, then frowned. "Smells as if a necromancer was about . . . but that's absurd." Drognan glanced at the floor, at the warriors in particular. "Yes . . . absurd."

He continued to stare, as if lost in thought. Not once did the mage so much as notice the struggling woman or her odd captor. At last, the sorcerer shook his head, muttered to himself about another lost trail and the need to keep searching, then—much to Kara's dismay—walked past her and the madman. Drognan continued on, heading into the darkness, heading toward the doorway she had earlier sought.

Heading away from someone in desperate need of his aid.

Only when he vanished behind the door did the tattered figure pull his hand from her lips. Planting his face next to hers, he whispered, "We've stayed too long! We'd better go back! Been out much too long! He might find us!"

She knew that he did not mean Drognan. No, judging by his earlier reaction, her captor could only mean one other—*Bartuc.*

He led her along the sculpted floor, to the very center, where the unknown artisan had built out of mosaic tiles an intricate temple like those that might have existed in legendary Viz-jun. Kara would not have followed him that far, but, as with the revenants, the choice of what her body did no longer remained hers. The necromancer could not even call out.

"Soon we'll be safe!" the madcap figure muttered to her. "Soon we'll be safe!"

He stomped down once with his right foot—and suddenly the doorway of the temple opened, *deepened,* becoming an oval hole in the floor in which the necromancer could see a set of steps leading to—to *where?*

"Come, come!" her captor chided her. "Before Bartuc finds us! Come, come!"

Unable to do otherwise, she followed him down into the earth, down toward a distant, yellowish light. As Kara stepped below the level of the floor, the enchantress sensed the stones shifting, the image of the Vizjerei temple returning to its prior state.

"We'll be safe down here," the mad hermit assured her, seeming somewhat more calm now. "My brother will never find us here . . ."

Brother? Had she heard right?

"Horazon?" Kara blurted, surprised not only by her conclusion but that she could now articulate it. Evidently her captor had no concerns about anyone hearing her underneath layers of rock and earth.

He looked right at her, the watery eyes focusing hard for the first time. "Do we know each other? I don't think we know each other . . ." When she did not respond immediately, he shrugged and continued on with the trek, still mumbling. "I'm sure we don't know each other, but we might know each other . . ."

Kara Nightshadow still had no choice but to follow, not that she much noticed at the moment. Her thoughts reeled, her world entirely turned upside-down.

She had come in search of the Warlord of Blood's armor and had found instead—even despite the many centuries that had passed since their time—Bartuc's living, breathing, and much hated *brother*.

Incredible heat assailed Norrec as he at last came back to his senses. At first he imagined that a fire must have started in Drognan's sanctum, perhaps through the arcane powers of the sinister armor. However, gradually the veteran became aware that the heat, while harsh, did not burn and, in fact, surely had to be from the sun itself.

Rolling over onto his back, Norrec shielded his eyes and tried to get his bearings, only to find a sea of sand in every direction. He grimaced, wondering where he had landed now. In the distance, Norrec thought he noticed darkness, as if a storm approached from that direction. Could Lut Gholein lay somewhere underneath those clouds? It seemed wherever he went, the storm followed. If that were the case now, then at least he knew that he had materialized somewhere west or northwest of the coastal kingdom.

But why?

Drognan had said something about the armor having tricked them. How true those words had been. It had played both the Vizjerei and him for fools, no doubt seeking the mage's aid in locating its goal. Could that have been Horazon's tomb, as Drognan believed? If so, why had Norrec ended up out here in the middle of nowhere?

With great effort, the battered and worn soldier rose. Judging by the sun, he had a little more than an hour or two before nightfall. The walk back to Lut Gholein would take far longer than that, likely two days—and that providing Norrec actually survived the trek. More important, he could not even be certain that the suit would let him return. If what it sought lay out here, it would do everything it could to remain in the desert.

Norrec took a few steps, testing the armor's resolve. When it did nothing to prevent him from heading toward the city, he increased his pace as best he could. At the very least, Norrec needed to find some shelter for the night and the only hope of that lay in a twisted hill of rock barely visible ahead. It would take him until sunset to reach the hill, if not longer, which meant that, despite the heat, he had to move even quicker.

His legs ached horribly as Norrec pushed on. The loose sand and high dunes made it tough going and often Norrec lost sight of his goal for quite some time. He even found himself turned around at one point, the swirling dunes shifting in size and direction even as he tried to cross them.

Yet, despite all that, the hill soon became an aspiration possible to achieve. Norrec prayed that he would find moisture of some sort there; his short time in the desert had already parched him. If he did not find water soon, it would not matter whether he made it to the hill or—

A large, winged shadow crossed over his own . . . followed immediately by a second.

Norrec looked up, trying to see against the sun. He caught glimpses of two or three airborne forms, but could not make them out. Vultures? Quite possible in Aranoch, but these looked much larger and not quite avian in some ways. Norrec's hand slipped to where his sword would have been and once more he cursed Bartuc's armor for putting him through such horrors without a decent weapon of his own.

Despite his flagging strength, the veteran doubled his pace. If he could reach the rock, it would provide him with some defense against the marauding birds. Vultures tended to be scavengers, but this flock looked more aggressive and, in some way he could still not define, unsettling.

The shadows passed over him again, this time much larger, much more distinct. The creatures had descended for a better look.

He barely sensed in time the feathered form dropping on him from behind. With instincts honed on the battlefield, Norrec threw himself to the ground just as talons as great as his hand scraped across his armored back and managed to briefly snag his hair. The hardened fighter grunted as he rolled over, ready to face the birds. Surely he could scare off a few vultures, especially once he let them see he would not simply lie down and die for them.

But *these* were no vultures . . . although their ancestry had certainly come from those desert scavengers.

Nearly as tall as a man and with the wings and head of the avian they so resembled, the four grotesque creatures fluttered just above him, talons on both their feet and their almost human hands ready to tear his head from his body. Their tails ended in whips that lashed out at Norrec as he desperately tried to back away. The demonic birds let out harsh cries as they tried to surround their would-be victim, cries that made Norrec's pulse pound.

He waited for the suit to do something, but Bartuc's armor remained dormant. Swearing, Norrec braced himself. If he had to die here, he would not die like a lamb because he had come to depend on the armor for so much. Nearly all his life, he had served in one war or another. This battle represented little different.

One of the monstrous vultures came within his grasp. Moving with more speed than he thought himself capable of at this point, Norrec seized it by one of its legs and threw it to the ground. Despite their size, the desert terrors were astoundingly light, no doubt because, like their ancestors, their bones were designed for flight. He took advantage of that, using his own considerable mass to pin the shrieking creature down, then twisting the head as hard as he could.

The three survivors harried him even harder as he rose from the limp form, but a different Norrec faced them now, one who had, for the first time in many days, fought a battle of his own and won. As the second dove at him, he grabbed a handful of sand and threw it in the vulpine horror's eyes. The demonic bird blindly whipped its tail at him, giving the veteran soldier the chance to seize the deadly appendage in both hands.

Squawking, the creature tried to fly free. However, Norrec spun the massive avian around again and again, driving back the other pair at the same time. The talons of his captured foe scraped futilely on his gauntleted hands, Bartuc's armor well protecting its host.

Norrec's blood surged. His attackers had come to represent to him more than simply the dangers of the desert. In many ways, they now became the brunt of all his frustration and fury. He had suffered through too many terrible events, suffered too many horrors, and not once had been able to do anything about them. Powerful enchantments saturated the warlord's armor and yet none of it obeyed him. Had it been his to command, he would have used the sorcery of the suit to roast the demonic beast he now held, turn it and its dire companions into fireballs.

His gloves suddenly glowed bright red.

Eagerly, Norrec eyed them, then stared at the vulture demon. Yes, a blazing inferno . . .

He grabbed the furious avian by the neck. The savage beak tried to tear out his face, only increasing his determination to end this battle as quickly and decisively as possible.

Norrec glared at the monster. *"Burn!"*

With a garbled shriek, the winged terror burst into flames, perishing in an instant.

Wasting not a second, the fighter threw the fiery carcass into the nearest of the two survivors, setting that one aflame, too. The last of the avians quickly turned about, flying away as if the hounds of Hell pursued. Norrec paid its retreat no mind, content to finishing off the third.

Its feathers seared away, it tried to emulate its sole surviving comrade, but it had already suffered too much injury. Unable to do more than rise a foot or two above the ground, it could not escape the vengeful fighter. Norrec seized it by one wing, letting the now-pathetic monster claw at his breast plate while he took it by the head.

With one quick jerk, Norrec snapped its neck.

In truth, the battle had taken only a minute or two, but in that short span the veteran soldier had transformed. As he dropped the feathered corpse to the sand, Norrec felt a thrill such as he had never experienced in any war. Not only had he triumphed against the odds, but for once the cursed armor had *obeyed* him. Norrec flexed the fingers, truly admiring the workmanship of the gloves for the first time. Perhaps the encounter with Drognan had changed everything; perhaps now that which had driven the armor to such lengths had finally given in, had even accepted its host as its master . . .

Perhaps he could test it. Surely after all he had seen it do, the armor could perform one basic task at his command.

"All right," he growled. "Listen to me! I need water! I need it now!"

His left hand tingled, twitched slightly, as if the armor wanted to take control—but sought *permission*.

"Do it. I order you!"

The glove pointed to the ground. Norrec knelt, allowed his index finger to draw a circle in the sand. It then drew a looping pattern around that circle, with small crosses in each loop.

Words of power erupted from his lips, but this time Norrec welcomed them.

The entire pattern suddenly crackled, miniature arcs of lightning playing between one end of the design and the other. A tiny fissure opened in the center . . .

Clear, sparkling water bubbled to the surface.

Norrec eagerly bent down, sipping his fill. The water felt cool, sweet, almost as if instead he drank wine. The thirsty fighter savored each swallow until at last he could sip no more.

Leaning back, he took a handful and spilled it on his face. The soothing moisture trickled down his chin, his neck, and into his hot garments.

"That'll be enough," he finally said.

His hand waved over the tiny spring. Immediately the ground healed itself, sealing the fissure and cutting off the flow of water. What remained on the sand quickly sank out of sight.

A feeling of jubilation washed over Norrec, causing him to laugh loud. Twice now, the armor had served him. Twice now, he had been the *master,* not the slave.

Spirits lifted, he headed again for the hill. Now Norrec no longer worried about whether he would survive the desert. What could he not survive, if the enchantments obeyed him? For that matter, what could he not accomplish? No one had seen such might as the armor wielded since the days of Bartuc! With it, Norrec could make of himself a commander instead of a foot soldier, a leader instead of a follower . . .

A *king* instead of a peasant?

The image enticed him. *King Norrec,* ruler of all he surveyed. Knights would bow before him; ladies of the court would seek his favor. Lands would come under his control. Riches beyond belief would be his to spend . . .

"King Norrec . . ." he whispered. A smile once again spread across his face, a smile not at all like any Norrec Vizharan had evinced before in his life. In fact, although he could not know it, Norrec's smile resembled almost exactly the smile of another man, one who had lived long, long before the former mercenary.

A man named Bartuc.

Fifteen

Night enshrouded Aranoch and with its coming also returned the demon Xazax to Augustus Malevolyn. The general had been waiting most anxiously for the past hour, pacing back and forth inside his tent. He had dismissed all his officers and ordered that even his guards depart from the vicinity of his quarters. As an added precaution, he had also not permitted any tents within hearing distance. What transpired between Malevolyn and the mantis would be for their ears alone.

Even Galeona had been forbidden to set up her abode nearby, but she had protested little when he had told her. The general had not given that lack of protest much thought, more concerned with the offer made by his new ally. As far as he was concerned, the witch could now pack her things back up and ride off. If she did not, he would likely have to have her slain. Some sort of animosity existed between Xazax and her and, at the moment, Malevolyn needed the demon far more than he needed a very mortal sorceress, whatever her other charms.

Women could be easily replaced; moments of immortality generally could not be.

By Malevolyn's choice, only a single lamp lit the tent. He did not know if the demon cast shadows, but, if so, the less chance of one of his men noticing, the better for the general. Had they known what he and the mantis wished to discuss, they would have all likely fled into the dark desert heedless of the dangers lurking out there.

A flickering movement caught his attention. Augustus Malevolyn turned, noticing that one shadow moved in defiance of the lamp's flame.

"You are here, aren't you?" he murmured.

"This one has come as promised, oh great one . . ."

The shadow deepened, grew substantial. In moments, the hideous form of the hellish mantis loomed over the human. Yet despite the presence of a creature who looked capable of ripping him apart limb by limb, General Malevolyn felt only anticipation. In Xazax, he saw the first of many such monsters who would eventually serve him in every way.

"Lut Gholein lies little more than a day from you now, warlord. Have you changed your mind?"

Changed his mind about gaining the armor? Changed his mind about his destiny? "You waste my time on useless prattle, Xazax. I am firm in my choice."

The bulbous, yellow orbs flared. The mantis's head twisted slightly, as if the demon tried to peer through the closed tent flap. "We spoke briefly of the witch, great warlord. This one has considered that matter much since then and believes still that she must not be part of this . . . or perhaps anything else."

Augustus Malevolyn pretended to brood over this. "She's been of value to me for some time. I would hate to lose her assets."

"She would not agree with what this one has proposed to you, warlord. You may trust this one on that . . ."

The general had not missed Xazax's continual use of the new title and while it pleased Malevolyn to hear it, the demon in no way succeeded in playing to his ego. Malevolyn still considered each detail by its own worth, even Galeona. "What lies between you and her?"

"An agreement made foolishly—and one this one wishes to break."

Not the most clear of answers, but enough to give the general what he needed. He had a possible bargaining chip. "You will give me all I demand? All we discussed?"

"All—and gladly, warlord."

"Then you may have her now, if you wish. I will wait here while you do what you must."

If the demon could possibly ever looked disconcerted, then he did so now. "This one most graciously declines your kind offer, warlord . . . and suggests that perhaps you take the honor *yourself* at some point soon."

The mantis would not or *could* not touch Galeona, just as Malevolyn had expected. Still, to him the matter seemed moot. It would not change his other decision, not in the least. "I will send a detachment to her tent to see that she remains under control. That will at least prevent her from causing any disturbance during our efforts. Perhaps after, I will decide what to do about her. In the meantime, unless there is something else you need to tell me—I would like to begin."

The eyes of the demon flashed again, this time in what seemed immense satisfaction. In that voice that reminded the general of a dying swarm of flies, Xazax replied, "Then . . . you will need *this*, warlord . . ."

In the two skeletal hands, the hellish mantis held a large, twin-bladed dagger made of a black metal, a dagger with runes etched not only in the handle but along the flat sides of the blades. Also in the handle had been embedded two stones, the larger as red as blood, the other as pale as bone. Both stones had a slight gleam to them that came from no outside source.

"Take it . . ." urged the demon.

Augustus Malevolyn did so with eagerness, hefting the massive knife and noting its fine balance.

"What must I do with it?"

"Prick the skin. Let a few drops of blood flow." The mantis cocked his head. "A simple matter . . ."

Dagger in hand, the general hurried to the flap of the tent. He shouted for one of his officers, then glanced over his shoulder at Xazax. "You'd better fade back into—"

But the demon had already anticipated his request, Xazax melting once more into shadow.

A thin, mustached soldier with silver tabs on his shoulders appeared out of the darkness. He rushed up to the tent, then saluted his commander. "Yes, general?"

"Zako." One of his more competent aides. Malevolyn would miss him, but the potential glories outweighed any concern for a single person. "The witch is to be placed under protective arrest. She is not to be allowed to touch any of her belongings nor is she to even so much as raise a finger until I say so."

A grim smile crossed the other soldier's face. Like most of Malevolyn's officers, Zako had no love for this sorceress who had, up until now, influenced their leader so much. "Aye, general! I'll do that, all right!"

Something occurred to the commander. "But first . . . but first bring the guards chosen for this task here. Be quick about it!"

With a swift salute, Zako vanished into the dark, only to return a short time later with four sturdy-looking warriors. Zako ushered them into Malevolyn's tent, then took up his place at the forefront.

"All present, general!" he called out, snapping to attention.

"Very good." Malevolyn gave the small troop a brief inspection, then faced them. "You have all served me loyally time and time again." His fingers stroked the hilt of the dagger, to which none of the five had so far paid much attention. "You have sworn your lives to me more than once . . . and for that I thank you. However, with a prize such as the one awaiting us, I must ask of you one last show of your willingness to serve me unto *death . . .*"

To one side, General Malevolyn noticed a shadow move. Xazax no doubt grew impatient, not understanding the need for the short speech. These men would be the first; therefore, from them would spread word of why their leader now demanded this new proof from them.

"Tomorrow begins a day of glory, a day of destiny, and each of you shall play an integral part! I ask now, my friends, that you verify my faith in you, my hopes in you, with this one last oath!" He held up the dagger for all of them to see. A couple of the guards blinked, but no one otherwise reacted. "Zako! I give you the honor of being the first! Show me your bravery!"

Without hesitation, the mustached officer stepped up and thrust out his ungloved hand. This had not been the first time he had sworn a blood oath to his commander and, of the five, only he no doubt thought that he understood why Malevolyn desired to reemphasize to the men the loyalty they owed the general.

"Palm up." After Zako had obeyed, Malevolyn held the dagger points-down over the fleshiest part—then jabbed his officer's palm.

Zako stifled a gasp, the man keeping his eyes straight ahead, as had been expected of him. Because of that, he did not notice something strange about both the knife and where it had punctured his skin. The two gems in the hilt briefly flashed the moment the points pierced his hand. More curious, although blood flowed from the tiny wounds, little of it actually spread over the palm, most of it seeming drawn toward the black blade—where it then disappeared.

"Have yourself a sip of wine, Zako," Malevolyn offered, pulling back the dagger. As his aide stepped away, the general signaled to the next man, upon whom he repeated the same process.

After all five had been bled, Augustus Malevolyn saluted them. "You have given me your lives. I promise to treat them as the valuable gifts they are. You are dismissed." As the soldiers departed, he called to Zako, "Before you deal with the witch, have Captain Lyconius bring every man under his command to my tent, will you?"

"Aye, general!"

When the others had gone, the voice of Xazax drifted from the shadows. "This goes too slow, warlord. It will take days at this rate."

"No, now it will go much faster. These five have been given an honor, so they see it. Zako will tell Lyconius and he, in turn, will tell his men and so on. I will order the officers to give a ration of drink to each soldier who shows them he has once more sworn his life to my cause. The pace will quicken incredibly, I promise you."

A few seconds later, Lyconius, a thin, fair-haired man older than the general, asked to be admitted. Outside, every soldier under his command awaited. Malevolyn bled the captain first, then had him line the men up. The mention of a ration of drink afterward made each fighter all the more eager to be there.

However, only a few of Lyconius's men had been dealt with when Zako, looking much perturbed, burst into the tent. He knelt on one knee before the commander, head down in shame.

Somewhat irritated at this costly interruption, General Malevolyn barked, "Speak! What is it?"

"General! The witch—she is nowhere to be found!"

Malevolyn tried to conceal his annoyance. "Her belongings; are they still in the tent?"

"Aye, general, but her horse is missing."

Even Galeona would not ride out into the vast desert at night. Taking a casual glance over his shoulder, Malevolyn noticed the shadow of the demon shift. No doubt Xazax did not find this news pleasant either, but at the moment neither man nor demon could afford to waste time on her. If the sorceress had somehow learned of their intention and had chosen to flee, it truly mattered little in the long run to her former lover. What harm could she do? Perhaps, once he wore the armor, he would hunt her down, but now Malevolyn had more important concerns.

"Never mind her, Zako. Return to your normal duties."

Relief in his voice, the aide thanked him, then hurried from the tent.

General Malevolyn turned back to his task, bleeding the next man, then commending him for his bravery.

The pace did indeed quicken, just as he had told the mantis it would. The combination of honor and drink caused a line to spread throughout the entire encampment, each man anxious to prove his worth to his master and his fellows. Tomorrow, they felt, the general would lead them to a glorious victory and riches beyond their wildest dreams. That they might be too few to take a stronghold such as Lut Gholein did not occur to them; General Malevolyn would not have made the sudden decision—so *they* assumed—if he did not already have some battle plan ensuring success.

And deep into the night, the last man proved his loyalty, hand out, the dagger already pricking his palm.

The final soldier and the officer who had guided him in both departed after saluting their trusted leader. From without, Augustus Malevolyn could already hear the sounds of celebration, as each of his men savored their ration of drink and toasted their future good fortunes.

"It is done," rasped Xazax, emerging from the shadowy corners. "Each and every one has tasted the dagger's bite and of each and every one the dagger has sipped . . ."

Turning the ceremonial weapon over and over in his hands, the general commented, "Not a single drop, not the tiniest stain. Where did all the blood go?"

"Each to its own, warlord. Each to the one it must go. This one promised you an army against whom even Lut Gholein could not defend long, remember?"

"I recall . . ." He touched the helmet, which he had not taken off once since camp had been made. It seemed so much a part of him now that he swore it would never leave his side, that he would only remove it for necessity's sake. "And I say again, I *accept* the consequences of our deal."

The mantis's body dipped in what might have been an acknowledging bow. "Then, there is no reason not to proceed immediately . . ."

"Tell me what must be done."

"In the sand at your feet, you must draw this symbol." Using one of the skeletal hands, Xazax traced the mark in the air. The general's eyes widened slightly as the demon's gaunt finger left a fiery, orange trail behind, highlighting the symbol.

"Why don't you just do it?"

"It must be done by he who will command. Would you prefer it to be this humble one, warlord?"

Seeing Xazax's point, Malevolyn bent down and drew the mark as it had appeared in the air. To his surprise, as he completed it, strange words suddenly burst from his lips.

"Do not hesitate!" urged the mantis eagerly. "The words were known to him; they will be known to you!"

His words . . . *Bartuc's* words. Augustus Malevolyn let them flow, savoring the power he felt from their use.

"Hold the dagger over the center." When the general had done that, the demon added, "Now . . . speak the name of my infernal lord! Speak the name of *Belial!*"

Belial? "Who is Belial? I know of Baal and Mephisto and Diablo, but not of this Belial. Do you mean Baa—"

"Speak not that name again!" Xazax nervously chittered. The mantis twisted his horrific head left and right as if he feared discovery by someone. Evidently finding nothing upon which to base that fear, the demon finally responded in calmer tones, "There is no master in Hell save *Belial*. It is he who offers you this wondrous gift! Recall this always!"

More familiar with the magic arts than the mantis might think him, Malevolyn knew that Hell had once been described as being ruled by the Three Prime Evils. Yet, he also knew of legends which had told of the three brothers cast up onto the mortal plane, their rule over Hell a thing of the past. In fact . . . one of the more obscure legends mentioned Lut Gholein as the possible location of *Baal's* tomb, although even the general doubted the veracity of such a fantastic tale. Who would build a city on top of a demon lord's tomb?

"As you say, Xazax. Belial, it is. I simply wanted to get the name correct."

"Begin again!" the monstrous insect snapped.

Once more the words spilled from Malevolyn's tongue. Once more he held the vampiric dagger high above the center of the symbol—Belial's symbol, the general now realized. At the end of the incantation, the eager commander called out the demon lord's name . . .

"Plunge the dagger into the center—exactly!"

General Malevolyn drove the twin-tipped blade deep into the sand, catching the center of the image perfectly.

Nothing happened. He looked up at the looming horror.

"Step back," Xazax suggested.

And as the would-be conqueror did, a grim, black haze arose around the dagger. While the two watched, the haze rapidly grew, first expanding above the weapon, then finally spreading toward the tent flap. As it drifted outside with what seemed definite purpose to Malevolyn's trained eye, the foreboding haze took on the shape of what looked to be a huge, clawed hand.

"It will not be long now, warlord."

Unconcerned, Malevolyn sought out a goblet of his finest wine. For this night, he chose a new bottle, one that had been packed carefully for countless journeys over desperate landscapes. The general opened it, sniffed the contents, and, with much approval, poured himself a full cup.

At that point, the first of the screams began.

Augustus Malevolyn's hand shook at the sound, but not because of any fear or regret. It was just that he had never heard such a soul-tearing cry, not even from those he had tortured, and the suddenness of it had simply startled the hardened veteran. When the second, the third, and fourth arose, Malevolyn found them not at all disconcerting. He even raised his goblet toward the half-buried dagger and Xazax's unseen lord.

And as he did, the shrieks outside became a chorus of the damned, scores of men crying out at the same time, pleading for some escape. From all around the camp the agonized screams assaulted the general, but he took each in stride. The men—*his* men—had each sworn more than one oath that they would serve him in all things in all ways. Tonight, he had taken that oath to heart, accepting their sacrifices—quite literally—for the better of his quest.

He turned toward the tent flap again. Mistaking the human's reaction, the mantis warned, "It is too late to save them. The pact has been accepted by this one's infernal lord."

"Save them? I merely wished to toast them for what they have given in order to garner me my destiny!"

"Aaah . . ." responded the demon, clearly seeing the true General Malevolyn for the first time. "This one is mistaken . . ."

And on went the screams. A few sounded quite distant, as if some of the men had tried to flee, but they could not flee from something eating away at them from within their very souls. Some, obviously very loyal, called out to their commander, pleading for help. Malevolyn poured himself another goblet, then sat down to wait for the finish.

Gradually, the last of the screams died down, leaving only the nervous whinnying of the horses, who could not understand what had happened. That, too, though, ceased as the heavy silence of the camp affected them as well.

The sudden clank of metal against metal made him look at the demon again, but Xazax said nothing. Outside, the clanking increased, growing both in intensity and nearness. General Malevolyn finished the last of his wine and stood up.

The noise outside abruptly stopped.

"They await you . . . warlord."

Adjusting his armor, especially his helmet, General Augustus Malevolyn stepped outside.

They did indeed wait for him, their ranks perfect. Several held torches, so he could see their faces, the faces he had come to know so well over their years of service to him. They all stood there, Zako, Lyconius, and the rest of the officers, each with their men behind them.

As he stepped into their sight, a cry of salute rose up among the throng, a cry monstrous, brutal, in its tone. It made Malevolyn smile, just as a somewhat closer glance at the foremost visages further enthused the commander. No matter how dark or light their skins had been before, they now had a pale, pasty look to them. As for their mouths, their battle cry had revealed teeth now fanged and tongues long and forked. The eyes—

The eyes were completely red—blood red—and burned with such evil desire that they could be seen even without the aid of a torch. They were not human eyes, but rather eyes that, at least in malignance, more resembled those of the mantis.

Garbed in the very husks of his loyal soldiers, these horrific warriors would be his new legion, his path to glory.

Xazax joined him outside the tent, the hellish mantis no longer needing to be concerned about secrecy. After all, here he stood among his own.

"All hail Malevolyn of Westmarch!" Xazax called out. "All hail, the *Warlord of Blood!*"

And once again, the demonic horde cheered Augustus Malevolyn.

So far from the encampment, Galeona heard nothing, but the witch did sense the striking of the sinister spell. Long associated with the darker aspects of her art, she knew that such incredible emanations of hellish sorcery could only mean that her fears had come to fruition. She had been right to depart when she had or else the enchantress would have certainly joined the fates of Augustus's unsuspecting warriors.

Xazax had underestimated her for the last time. The mantis would have used others to deal with her in order to break the blood pact that they had made some years back. He had chosen the general for his new ally, the demon having always hinted that a new warlord would be of more interest than simply gaining empty armor. Galeona should have realized months ago that he had never intended to continue with their own alliance any longer than necessary.

Yet, what had made him so suddenly choose Augustus over her? Could it really have been fear? Ever since that night when the monstrous insect had nearly done the unthinkable—slain her outright despite the repercussions of directly breaking their pact—the witch had tried to think of what could so disturb a creature of Hell. What fear had sent him scurrying straight to Malevolyn?

In the end, it did not matter. Both Xazax and Augustus could have one another for all she cared. After what she had discovered during her brief spell-work earlier, Galeona had decided that she, in turn, needed neither of the two treacherous creatures. Why settle for always looking over her shoulder when she could be the one who truly commanded?

The sorceress glanced down at her hand as she rode, not the first time she had done so. In her left palm, Galeona held a small crystal which through spells she had tied to her intended destination. So long as the crystal glowed, the enchantress knew that she remained on the right track.

So long as it glowed, she knew that she could find the fool she intended to make her puppet.

In betraying her, Xazax had made one terrible error in judgment. For some reason that she could not yet fathom, the demon could not by himself detect the ancient warlord's armor. He needed human assistance, which had been one of the foremost reasons the two of them had first joined together. That had been why, when he had believed that he knew where the prize lay, the cursed mantis had abandoned her for General Malevolyn. It should not have been at all surprising to her since Galeona had considered doing much the same, but for Xazax, the error would prove a costly one.

The demon no doubt believed that the armor could be found now in nearby Lut Gholein, the location they had last determined it would head toward. Even she had assumed that much until her last spell. Where else could it be but within the coastal kingdom? A lone traveler either needed to find a caravan there willing to take him on or wait instead for a ship heading on from Lut Gholein to one of the more western lands. Either way, Norrec should have still been within the city walls.

But he was not. At some point, he had left, choosing to forego sanity and apparently ride out into the desert at a pace that surely had killed his mount. When Galeona had discovered his new location, it had stunned her; the veteran fighter practically stood under Augustus's very nose. If the general had agreed to letting her cast a search spell when she had originally offered, the armor might very well even now be his. He could have already been approaching Lut Gholein clad in the crimson garb of Bartuc, his loyal witch at his side.

Instead, Galeona now hoped to convince this other fool that *he* should use it . . . under her masterful guidance, of course. He looked to be a manageable sort of oaf, one she should readily be able to wrap around her finger. He also had a not unreasonable countenance, one in some ways the witch preferred to her former lover. That would make the task of maintaining control of her new puppet not so great a chore.

Of course, if Galeona found some better method by which to harness the astonishing power of the enchantments, it would also not bother her much if she had to do away with this Norrec. There were always other men, other fools.

On and on she rode, her only concern that Xazax might choose to interrupt his activities with Augustus to pursue his former partner. Of course, that would go against their pact, too, which would endanger the demon as well as her. More likely the hellish mantis would forget her for now, satisfied that he had his grand prize. Later he would no doubt find the means by which to sever their ties—not to mention her head and limbs.

He would be too late, though. Once she had her pawn ensnared, Galeona would see to it that Xazax, not she, would soon lay scattered over the landscape. Perhaps she would even have Norrec bring the insect's head to her, a pretty trophy with which to begin to rebuild the collection that the sorceress had been forced to leave abandoned tonight.

She peered around, looking for some sign of her prey. In order to lessen the risk of riding around nearly blind because of the darkness, the witch had cast a spell enhancing both the visions of her horse and herself. It enabled the animal to pick a path that would avoid accidents and predators while giving Galeona the ability to better hunt for the soldier.

There! Reining her mount to a halt, the sorceress stared at the distant, shadowed form of a rocky hill. The crystal indicated that her path continued directly that way. Galeona rose in the saddle for a moment, searching for any other likely spot and finding none. As a seasoned warrior, the fool certainly had enough sense to look for reasonable shelter and the small hill before her looked to be the only such choice for many miles around. He had to be there.

Eager now, Galeona urged the horse on. As they neared, she thought she saw a figure just to the left of the hill. Yes . . . most definitely a man seated under an outcropping, his knees drawn up to his chest, his arms resting atop the knees.

He jumped up as the witch approached, for one clad in heavy armor his agility and speed surprising her. Galeona could see him peering back, trying to make her out in the darkness and so far failing. No, not an unpleasant face at all, the guileful sorceress thought. Better than she had recalled from their encounter on the ship. If he would just prove himself to be reasonable, to listen to her, then they would have no troubles with one another and she would not have to so soon begin the search for his eventual replacement.

"Who is it?" Norrec called. "Who are you?"

She dismounted a short distance from him. "Only a fellow wanderer . . . no one who means you harm." Now Galeona simply used the crystal to illuminate the area, let him see the good fortune that had just stepped into his miserable little life. "Someone looking for some warmth . . ."

The witch manipulated the gleaming stone, letting its light cross both her face and torso. She saw his interest immediately. So much the better. He looked to be one readily led around by the nose in return for a few readily given pleasures. The perfect dupe.

His expression suddenly changed and not for the better. "I know you, don't I?" He approached, towering over her. "I need to see your face again."

"Of course." Galeona held the crystal nearer to her features.

"Not enough light," Norrec muttered. "I need more."

He held up his left hand—and in the palm of the gauntlet there suddenly formed a tiny fireball that outshone the crystal a hundredfold.

Galeona could not stifle a gasp. She had expected an uninitiated fool, a fighter with no grasp of sorcery. Instead, he had summoned flame without so much as an effort, something still beyond many well-schooled apprentices.

"That's better . . . I *do* know you . . . your face, anyway! On the *Hawksfire*!" He nodded in immense satisfaction. "I dreamed of you there!"

Recovering, Galeona quickly replied, "And I dreamed of you, too, that time! Dreamed of a warrior, a champion, who could protect me from the evils pursuing me."

As she hoped, her words and tone had an immediate effect on the man. His look of distrust did not completely fade, but now she saw also sympathy—and pride that she looked at him as her savior. The witch pressed nearer to Norrec, staring adoringly into his eyes with her own, half-lidded ones. She surely had him enticed by this point.

"You're in danger?" A protective look crossed his face. He peered beyond Galeona, as if already expecting to see the villains who chased after her.

"They don't know I escaped them just yet. I . . . I dreamed of you again last night, knew that you had to be near, waiting for me." Putting a hand on his breastplate, Galeona leaned forward, but inches between her full lips and his own.

He did not rise to the tempting bait, instead considering some other matter. "You're a sorceress," Norrec finally responded. "What's your name?"

"Galeona . . . and I know from my dreams that my knight is called Norrec."

"Yes . . ." The fighter smiled at the title she had given him. "Are you a powerful sorceress?"

The witch let her hand trace the seams on the armor. "I have some talent in that . . . and other fields as well."

"I could use a sorceress," he muttered almost to himself. "I wanted one to help me deal with this armor . . . but that's not so important any more. I've had time to think, time to put matters in their proper order. There's things I need to do before I go on any further."

Galeona only half-paid attention, already planning ahead. Norrec definitely did not sound as simple a man as the enchantress had first imagined, but he had at least taken her story to heart and accepted her as a companion, if nothing else. As she learned more about him, Galeona would strengthen that tie. He had already revealed some weakness to her charms; the rest of what she desired the witch would gain soon enough.

Of course, if she could help Norrec with whatever concerned him, show her puppet of what valuable assistance she could be, that would shorten her own task. While Galeona did not understand his statement concerning the armor itself, these other matters he had mentioned—whatever they might be—she could surely aid him in accomplishing.

"Of course, I'll help you in any way I can, my knight! I ask only in return that you protect me from those who would do me harm." She turned her gaze briefly to the desert. "They're powerful and have dark arts at their command."

Galeona had wanted to test his reserve, to see the extent he felt sure of the power he apparently wielded. Yet, even to her surprise, Norrec shrugged, then almost casually answered, "Warriors, magic, demons . . . I've no fear of any of them. Those under my protection will come to no harm."

"You've my gratitude," she whispered, leaning up and kissing him hard.

He pulled her away, not out of any disgust, but because he seemed not to have any interest at the moment in what she had offered him. Instead, Norrec appeared once more lost in his other concerns.

"I've thought about it," the fighter finally told the witch. "Thought about why I ended up here of all places. It has to be somewhere near. It tries to keep hidden and from me it can do it . . ." He looked down at her again, something in his eyes suddenly unnerving Galeona a little. "But *you* might be able to find it! You found me, after all! You can probably succeed where Drognan failed."

"I'll do what I can," the dark-skinned enchantress returned, curious as to what so demanded the man's attention. Something of value to her, too, perhaps? "What are we looking for?"

His expression indicated that he found it surprising that she did not already know. "*Horazon's tomb*, of course!" Something in his face changed as he spoke, something that made Galeona look at him again—and this time see a face that she did not entirely recognize. "My *brother's* tomb."

SIXTEEN

An entire world existed beneath Lut Gholein.

No, corrected Kara, not a world, but something that seemed at least as large as, if not *larger* than, the regal kingdom far above her. The curious and unsettling figure she had identified as an impossibly old Horazon had led her down one confusing corridor to the next and to the next and so on until the necromancer had actually gotten dizzy trying to keep track of her path. She had climbed up and down stairs, walked through door after door, and passed room after room until at last Horazon had brought her to this single chamber, this well-lit and well-furnished bedroom, and told her to sleep.

Kara did not even remember lying down, but now she found herself atop the soft bed, staring up at the intricately-sewn canopy there. She had imagined her quarters aboard the *King's Shield* to be the finest she would ever use, but these set even those to shame. Curiously, the elegant furnishings, while clearly of another time, another place, looked as if they had been made only yesterday. The great wooden bed appeared perfectly polished, the sheets crisp and clean, and the marble floor beneath spotless. The same went for the nightstand next to the bed and the chair in the far corner. On the walls had been hung richly-woven tapestries of decidedly Vizjerei tastes, fantastic creatures and images of astonishing spellwork, all crafted by an expert artisan. If not for the fact that she was presently a prisoner in the lair of a possibly dangerous madman, the enchantress would have felt quite comfortable indeed.

She dared not stay here. While legend had always spoken of Horazon as the brother considered the lesser of two evils, he nonetheless not only remained an ambitious Vizjerei who had once, too, commanded demons to serve him, but who also clearly had lost his sanity over the centuries. Kara wondered how he had even survived for so long. The only records of such extensive life-extending spells had always included the summoning of unearthly powers to help cast them. If Horazon had turned again to demons for his needs—despite his constant mutterings to the contrary—then that would not only explain his present condition but also gave Kara even more reason to find her way out before he returned.

Still clothed, the anxious dark mage slipped out of the bed, heading immediately to the door. It did no good to try to see if Horazon had cast any spells upon it, for his entire sanctum emanated magic to such a staggering degree that she wondered why every spellcaster for hundreds of miles around could not have sensed its presence. Then again, perhaps that same magic explained why they did not. If even a portion of that might had been directed toward hiding Horazon's domain, then the greatest mages in all the world could have stood at its very doorstep and still not noticed the wonder at their feet.

Deciding to take the risk, the necromancer tugged at the handle, only to find the door unmoving. She tried again, with equally dismal results.

It hardly surprised her that she had been locked in, but the truth nevertheless frustrated Kara immensely. The necromancer had been trapped time and time again since beginning this chase and now she wondered whether or not she would be able to escape this prison. Unwilling to give up, Kara touched the handle and muttered a spell of opening. It was a minor incantation, one that actually had its roots in Vizjerei elemental sorcery, but the followers of Rathma had found it one of the few useful creations of the rival calling. That it almost certainly would fail did not escape her, but Kara could think of no other way out of the room that would not require a spell likely to bring the ceiling down on her as well.

The handle *turned*.

Startled by her unlikely success, the necromancer nearly flung open the door. Instead, taking a deep breath, Kara cautiously opened it a crack, then surveyed the outer hallway. Seeing no sign of danger, the dark mage quietly stepped out. She peered both directions, trying to recall by which she had earlier come. After a brief mental debate, Kara turned to the right and ran.

The corridor ended at a stairway that led up, a hopeful sign. Kara pushed herself up the steps, certain that if she kept going the direction she did, the desperate spellcaster would eventually find her way out.

The stairway stopped two flights later, opening up into a much wider corridor. Making certain that Horazon did not seem about, the necromancer crept down the larger hall. Although the room in which she had slept had been well-decorated, the halls themselves seemed positively austere, with only the occasional door breaking the monotony. The one consistently odd element of her surroundings proved to be the yellow light, whose source never proved evident. It came from everywhere at the same time. There were no torches nor anywhere even to put them.

As she hurried along, Kara occasionally felt tempted to try one of the doors, but knew that it behooved her more to find the way out as soon as she could. Any lingering might give Horazon time to discover that she had gone missing. While the necromancer dearly wanted to know more about the mad mage and his sanctum, she desired to do so on her own terms, not his.

Just ahead, the corridor took a hard right turn. Kara stepped up her pace, hoping that the change in direction meant that she had found a passage to the outside. The frustrated enchantress cut around the corner as quickly as she could, praying that somewhere at the end would be another stairway or, better yet, the true exit.

Instead, she found herself facing a blank *wall*.

The hallway simply ended just a few yards after it had begun. Putting both hands to it, the necromancer checked the wall for illusions, magic, even a false front. Unfortunately, for all practical purposes, the barrier before her seemed as solid as it looked even though she could find no good reason at all for its existence.

Stepping back, Kara studied the only other direction. To return to the stairway made no sense, but that left to her only the doors. Surely they did not represent a path out of Horazon's domain.

She went to the first, cautiously opening it. With her luck as it had been so far, Kara feared that her choice would turn out to be the ancient Vizjerei's very own chambers.

Behind the door stood a long, curving passage.

"Is that the trick, then?" she whispered to herself. Did the true way out depend on opening the doors and not following the regular corridors? Trust her demented host to design his underground lair in such an improbable manner!

Eagerly Kara Nightshadow hurried down the hidden corridor, not even bothering to shut the door behind her. Somewhere at the end, she would find escape. Somewhere she would find the way back to the old building or some other secret entrance into Lut Gholein.

Instead, the necromancer found yet *another* door.

She had no choice but to open it. There had been no other passage, no other entrance. However, at least this time Kara opened the door with some hope of success. She had journeyed for some distance. Horazon's mazelike sanctum had to come to an end here and now.

Another hallway greeted her.

That it resembled the wide one Kara had long left behind did not bother her. Of course, the design would be similar. After all, the same man had created it all.

Then she saw the open door just a short distance to her left.

With great trepidation, the weary necromancer walked over to it. She peeked inside, hoping her guess to be wrong.

The same curved corridor Kara had just traversed greeted the weary woman.

"Trag'Oul, guide me out of the madness!" What point had there been to a corridor that returned to the same hall? Kara blinked as another realization hit her. This door and the one she had returned by had been located on *opposite* sides of the hall. How could she possibly have looped around like that? The corridor would have had to cut through the hallway, a complete impossibility!

Without hesitation Kara headed for the lone door left to her. If it did not lead somewhere other than this hallway, then Horazon's bizarre realm had finally defeated her.

To the necromancer's relief, though, the doorway opened into a vast chamber in which two sets of wide, bannistered staircases flanked a pair of high bronze doors decorated with intricate dragon motifs. A well-preserved marble floor covered the entire expanse of the room and more tapestries covered the stone walls.

Kara stepped into the massive room, debating whether to choose the doors or one of the staircases. The doors looked most tantalizing, being directly across from her, but the stairs, too, enticed the necromancer, either one possibly leading to an exit above ground.

A slight sound above her head made Kara look up—then gasp at what she saw.

Far, far up, Horazon sat in a chair, the white-haired sorcerer mumbling to himself while he ate at a long dining table. The noise Kara had heard had been the madman laying his knife on what looked to be an elaborate gold plate filled with rich meat. Even though so far below, Kara could still smell its succulent flavor. As she watched, Horazon reached for a goblet of wine, the elderly Vizjerei taking a long sip without spilling so much as a drop. That feat especially amazed her, not because she had not thought the insane mage capable of simple table manners—but because he did so while he sat *upside down* on the ceiling.

In fact, the entire tableau was upside down and yet nothing fell toward Kara. The chair, the table, the plates full of fresh food, even Horazon's lengthy beard—all defied basic nature. Gazing around the ceiling in astonishment, the dark mage even saw doors and other staircases that would have suited the mage well in his present position. If not for Horazon and his elaborate meal, it would have been as if she stared at a mirror image above her,

Still drinking, Horazon cocked his head up—or rather *down*—and at last caught sight of the startled young woman.

"Come! Come!" he called to her. "You're late! I don't like people late!"

Fearful that he might use his considerable power to drag her up to the ceiling, perhaps forever eliminating her hopes for escape, Kara rushed across the great hall, heading to the bronze doors. They had to lead somewhere out of his reach! They had to!

With one last look up at her captor, Kara flung open the nearest of the doors and darted through. If she could just keep ahead of him—

"Aaah! Good! Good! Sit there! Sit there!"

Horazon watched her from the other end of a long, elegant table identical to the one at which she had just seen him sitting, only this time it stood not on the ceiling, but rather in the center of the room she had just now entered. The exact same meal, even down to the wine, lay spread before him. Beyond the mage, doorways and staircases just like the necromancer had seen atop the other chamber now served as backdrop to Horazon and his meal.

Unable to prevent herself from doing so, Kara looked up at the ceiling.

Staircases and doorways, all upside down, greeted her gaze.

One of the latter, a bronze giant, stood open—as if someone had flung it aside in haste.

"Rathma, protect me . . ." Kara murmured.

"Sit, girl, sit!" commanded Horazon, totally oblivious to her dismay. "Time to eat! Time to eat!"

And with nothing more she could do to save herself, the necromancer obeyed.

A storm covered the desert, a vast ocean of black, churning clouds that spread all the way from the east to as far west as Augustus Malevolyn could see. Dawn had risen, but it might as well have been just after sunset, so dark had the day begun. Some might have taken such a threatening sky for a bad omen, but the general saw it instead as a sign that his time had come, that his day of destiny was at hand. Lut Gholein lay just ahead and in it he knew cringed the fool who wore the glorious armor—*his* glorious armor.

Xazax had assured him of the last. Where else would the stranger have gone? The winds blew strong, ensuring that no ship would be heading out to sea this day. He *had* to still be in the city.

The general studied Lut Gholein from atop a massive dune. Behind him and entirely invisible to the eyes of the enemy, Malevolyn's demonic host patiently awaited his word. Because of the particular spell utilized, the sinister creatures still wore the shells of his men, although eventually they would be able to discard those. They had needed them to make the passage from Hell to the mortal plane and would yet require them for some time to come. That need, though, did not bother Malevolyn. For the moment, it served better that the enemy thought this tiny army simply mortal. It would make the commanders in Lut Gholein overconfident, arrogant. They would commit themselves to tactics which would expend their might early for a quick victory—but in doing so they would merely be setting themselves up for a slaughter that Malevolyn already much savored.

Xazax joined the human, the mantis finally creeping into sight after being gone far too long. Something about that struck the general as curious. Of all the demons now with him, Xazax clearly had to be the most dominating, yet the insidious insect moved about as if fearful that, even on such a dark day, someone might see him.

"Why do you lurk about? What are you afraid of?" Malevolyn asked, growing a bit suspicious. "Are you expecting something I should know about?"

"This one is afraid of nothing!" the mantis snapped, his mandibles working furiously. "Nothing!" However, in a slightly lower voice, he added, "This one is merely . . . cautious . . ."

"You act as if you fear something."

"No . . . nothing . . ."

General Malevolyn again recalled both Xazax's reaction to the name *Baal* and the fact that Lut Gholein had been said to house underneath it the demon lord's tomb. Could there then be some fact after all to that outlandish tale?

Deciding he could investigate the demon's anxieties later, General Malevolyn turned his gaze back to Lut Gholein. The city lay unsuspecting. Even now, a contingent of the sultan's forces rode out of the gate on early morning patrol, the riders' attitudes plain to see even from this distance. They did their rounds with the notion that no one would have the audacity to attack, especially by way of the desert. Lut Gholein more feared attacks by sea and on a day as fierce as this one looked to be, the odds of that appeared infinitesimal.

"We will let the patrol come as near as possible," he informed the mantis. "Then we shall take them. I want to see how your warriors act before we seek the city itself."

"Not this one's warriors," corrected Xazax. "*Yours . . .*"

The riders swept out, crisscrossing the land beyond the walls. Malevolyn watched and waited, knowing that their course would soon enough take the patrol to where he wanted them to be.

"Prepare the archers."

A rank of figures stepped forward, inhuman eyes eager. Although they wore but the husks of Malevolyn's men, the demons somehow retained the knowledge and skills of their victims. The faces Augustus Malevolyn glanced at had been the faces of his best archers. Now the demons would prove whether or not they could do as well—or, preferably, better.

"On my mark," he commanded.

They readied their bows. Xazax spoke a single word—and the tips of the arrows blazed.

The turbaned riders drew nearer. Malevolyn shifted his mount, the better to be seen by them.

One of the defenders noted him and called out to the others. The patrol, an estimated forty and more in strength, turned toward the outsider.

"Be ready." He urged his horse a few steps in the direction of the other riders, as if he intended to meet them. They, in turn, rode at a pace that suggested that they were wary, but not very much so.

And at last, the soldiers from Lut Gholein came near enough for General Malevolyn's tastes.

"Now!"

Even the howling wind could not overwhelm the terrible shrieks of the feathered shafts in flight. A rain of death undaunted by the gale fell upon the enemy.

The first of the arrows landed, some missing, some striking well. Malevolyn saw a bolt hit one of the lead riders dead on, the shaft burning through his breastplate as if the latter did not exist, then burying itself deep in the man's chest. Even more shocking, that rider suddenly burst into *flames*, his terrible wound the point of origin. The corpse fell off the frightened horse, colliding with another mount who then shied, throwing his own rider to the ground.

Another shaft caught a guard in the leg, but what seemed a bad wound at best became a new terror as that, too, erupted in fire. Screaming, the soldier frantically slapped at a limb entirely engulfed by quickly spreading flames. His animal, too, shied, sending the unfortunate man to the ground. Even there, the flames would not cease, already spreading up and around the victim's waist.

Of the forty or so riders in the patrol, at least a third lay either dead or near to it, all the bodies afire. Several horses, also lay stricken. The rest of the soldiers fought for control of their panicked steeds.

A smile on his face, Augustus Malevolyn turned back to his deadly horde. "Second and third ranks . . . advance and attack!"

A war cry that would have chilled most men but only served to thrill the general erupted from the throats of those summoned. The demonic warriors poured over the dune. As with Malevolyn's late soldiers, they kept their ranks tight and orderly, yet still he could see the savagery in their movements, the inhuman lust in their continual shouts. In numbers, they more than surpassed those of the riders, but not enough that, under normal circumstances, the patrol could not readily fight their way to freedom.

One of the officers spotted the marauding band and called out a warning. Immediately the survivors of the patrol turned toward Lut Gholein. However, Malevolyn had no intention of letting them go. Glancing at the archers, he ordered another volley.

This time the shafts flew far over his adversaries, just as intended. Moments later, the sand in front of the retreating patrol exploded with fire as the arrows struck the ground. For a few precious seconds, a wall of flame cut off all hope of escape.

Those few precious seconds were all the demons needed to reach their foes.

They swarmed around the riders, swords and spears up. Several riders and horses fell quickly, pin-cushioned. The defenders fought back, thrusting at their assailants. One managed to strike what should have been a mortal blow, only to have Malevolyn's unholy warrior completely ignore the blade in his side while he pulled the stunned soldier off his mount.

An officer from the patrol attempted to organize better resistance. Two of the demons dragged him down. Abandoning their weapons, they tore his armor from his body, then tore into the flesh underneath.

"They are . . . enthusiastic . . ." Xazax remarked with some amusement.

"Just so long as they recall what I said this morning."

"They will do so."

One of the few remaining defenders made a mad break for Lut Gholein. A demon grabbed at his leg and would have brought him down, but another suddenly tore his comrade's clawing fingers from the hapless rider, enabling the human to make good his escape.

"You see? This one promised you that they would obey your orders, warlord . . ."

"Then, as soon as the rest have been dealt with, we'll move forward. You'll remain behind, I trust?"

"For now, warlord . . ." Xazax had suggested that, without a true human form, he would be too obvious a sight for this first struggle. In daylight, the demon could not apparently create sufficiently the illusion of a man, as he had done that night. In fact, had General Malevolyn inspected the shadowed face better during that encounter, he would have seen that no true features had actually existed—just hints of them.

The mantis's explanation for his hesitation had a few holes in it that the general would discuss with him further, but he knew that such a conversation could wait. The armor called to Malevolyn; all he had to do was take the city to get it.

Below, the slaughter of the patrol took but a few short minutes more, the defenders' ranks dwindling with each passing second. More and more the true nature of Malevolyn's force became evident as the demons fell upon the soldiers, drenching the sand with blood.

By this time, the lone survivor had reached the gates of Lut Gholein. Horns blared behind the walls, warning being given to all that the kingdom had been attacked.

"All right! Let's let them see us!" He raised his hand high in the air—and in it formed the fiery, ebony sword that he had used on the scarab demons. "Advance!"

The clouds rumbled and lightning flashed as General Malevolyn's army came out of hiding. Below, the first and second rank formed up, their lines a little more ragged than before. The feast of bloodletting had stirred up the demons there, making them forget some of the human traits they had stolen. Still, so long as they obeyed his commands to the letter, the general could forgive the slight error.

The howling wind whipped Malevolyn's cloak around. He adjusted his helmet, bent his head slightly down to avoid the sand blown into the air. As of yet, the sky had not given any indication of rain, but even that would not stop him now.

Panic must be spreading among the common folk within. The soldiers, however, would, at this moment, be studying his advancing force and determining that, despite the wholesale slaughter of the patrol, this new foe lacked the numbers to be a true threat to them. They would make one of two choices; either defend the walls only—or send out a much larger force seeking retribution for the horrific deaths of which the one surviving guard would speak.

Understanding human emotions, Augustus Malevolyn predicted that they would choose the latter.

"All ranks into line formation!"

The hellish horde spread out, gradually creating two larger, imposing rows. To the commanders in Lut Gholein, it would be clear that the invaders sought to make their force look more impressive. Yet, those same commanders would also think how foolish the newcomers had to be to try such an apparent trick.

Lut Gholein would also wait to see if a second force followed after the first. They would judge the possibility of that by how near to the walls Malevolyn dared lead his troops. The commanders would then decide whether the risk was worth it to crush the first wave, then retreat back inside before any aid might arrive.

The demons began to lose some of the order in their ranks, but for the most part they held as they should. Their new warlord had promised them much blood, much mayhem, and that alone kept them in control. They had but one order to obey once the walls of the city had been breached; the man clad in the crimson armor had to be brought to Malevolyn immediately.

All others they could deal with as they desired.

As he and his force reached the point midway between the mangled bodies of the unfortunate patrol and the very gates of the fabled realm, a long row of turbaned figures with bows suddenly arose at the battlements. In quick fashion, they loosed a storm of arrows, all arced perfectly to wipe out the first line of attackers—including the general himself.

However, as each shaft neared Malevolyn, a brief flash of light erupted around every single one . . . obliterating them before they could touch even his horse. More than a score of arrows vanished in such a way, the archers evidently determined to slay the enemy's leader quickly if they could.

Yet, around him, his warriors fell one after another, shafts sticking out of throats, in sides, even in heads. One by one, the rain of arrows whittled down the first row and even many in the second, leaving the would-be warlord with visible losses of nearly *half* his followers.

Lightning played above Lut Gholein as if marking the next phase of the defenders' intended vengeance. The gates opened, a vast legion of hardened, bitter fighters on both horseback and foot charging in perfect order toward what remained of the murderous invaders. The turbaned warriors spread out, creating a series of rows not only longer than Malevolyn's but also several times thicker. As he had surmised, defending from the battlements had not been satisfying to his adversaries. They would make him and his pay for the butchered riders at the same time garnering some glory for themselves.

"Fools," he muttered, trying hard to hold back a smile. "Impetuous fools!"

General Malevolyn made no move to retreat. In normal combat conditions that would have proven even more costly than his suicidal advance. At least his men could die knowing that they took more of the enemy with them—or so Lut Gholein's commanders must also be thinking.

And as the opposing sides converged, he signaled to one of the few surviving warriors next to him, the one to which had been given the battle horn.

The hellish soldier raised the horn to his lips and blew, sending out a mournful cry throughout the field of combat.

From the sand arose the supposed dead, General Augustus Malevolyn's demons charging forward regardless of the wounds the arrows had inflicted. Armored figures with shafts sticking out of their throats or their eyes moved to meet the stunned defenders, some of whom let out horrified cries and tried to back away only to collide with those advancing behind them. The turbaned lines slowed, faltered, as the horrific sight registered with each man in front.

In a voice that smothered the thunder, Malevolyn roared, "Slay them! Slay them all!"

The demons roared and fell upon their more numerous but merely mortal foes.

They tore into the humans, with their hellish strength completely severing limbs and even heads from those nearest. The foremost of Lut Gholein's defenders perished horribly, several split open completely by swords, others ripped apart by hand while they screamed. Swords and lances had little effect on the general's troops, although occasionally a demon would indeed fall. Yet, despite these one or two losses, the balance of the battle clearly had begun to turn. The bodies of the defenders began to pile up as those in back, still somewhat ignorant of the terrible truth, forced their comrades into the unyielding maw of death.

A horn within the walls sounded and suddenly a new rain of arrows fell upon the invaders. Unfortunately, the new volley had little hope of success and even contributed to the continual slaughter of the defenders on the ground, many of them now falling victim to their own archers. Almost immediately after the first wave of shafts, the horn sounded again, but by that point scores more had perished.

Out among the demons, Malevolyn fought as possessed as the rest of his infernal legion. The ebony blade cut a bloody swathe through his foes, neither armor nor bone slowing it in any fashion. Soon, even his monstrous horde gave him room, the general's viciousness approaching their limits. Malevolyn's black armor had been stained from head to foot in crimson, but, if anything, it spurred him on to harsher, more brutal acts.

The ground around him abruptly exploded. His horse fell hard, dying instantly. More fortunate, General Malevolyn landed a few yards away. The explosion, which would have killed any normal man, did little more than stun him for a few seconds.

Rising, he looked up at the walls to see a pair of robed figures, Vizjerei no doubt in the service of the young sultan. Malevolyn had expected Lut Gholein to throw sorcery at him, but had become so caught up in the massacre that he had forgotten.

A fury such as he had never experienced took hold of him. He recalled Viz-jun, recalled how Horazon and the others had tricked him, led his hellish horde into a trap . . .

"Not *this* time!" Augustus Malevolyn held up a fist, shouted words he had never known before. Above him, the heavens appeared ready to explode.

A fierce wind struck the battlements, but only where the sorcerers stood. Those who watched saw the pair pulled high into the air, where they help-lessly flailed about, no doubt trying to cast counterspells.

The warlord brought his fist down hard.

With wild shrieks the two Vizjerei plummeted to the ground as if shot from great bows.

When the sorcerers hit, even the demons backed away, so startled were they by the terrible force with which the pair hit. Only Malevolyn watched with great satisfaction, his first step toward avenging *his* loss at Viz-jun now taken. That his memories had so mingled with Bartuc's that he could no longer tell them apart did not even occur to him any more. There could be only one Warlord of Blood—and he stood nearly at the gates of this trembling city.

His quick eyes caught sight of one among the failing defenders, an officer of high rank. A demon stood before the bearded warrior, the black-clad creature forcing the enemy commander to his knees.

General Malevolyn acted swiftly, summoning the magical sword and driv-ing it through the back of the stunned demon. The monstrous warrior shrieked and the body within the black armor shriveled until nothing remained but a thin, papery layer of dried flesh over bone. A wisp of green smoke rose from the collapsing corpse, smoke that dissipated in the wind.

Stepping over the pile of bones and metal, Malevolyn headed for the officer he had just saved. The general had known that the demon would not have paused in time and the loss of one of his minions meant little to him. After Lut Gholein, he would be able to summon every beast in Hell.

The weakened officer tried to fight him, but with a gesture of his hand, Malevolyn sent the man's own weapon flying—into the throat of one of the other defenders.

He seized the hapless officer by the throat, dragging him up to a standing position. "Hear me and you may live, fool!"

"You might as well slay me now—"

Tightening his grip, Malevolyn held on until the fighter nearly suffocated. At the last, he loosened his fingers slightly, allowing the man to breathe again. "Your life—the life of everyone in Lut Gholein, is mine! Only one thing will save you for the time being! One thing!"

"W-what?" his prisoner gasped, now much more sensible.

"There is a stranger in the city! A man dressed in armor the color of the blood that covers both of us and that you might yet keep running through your veins! Bring him to me! Bring him out through the gates and send him to me!"

He could see the commander calculating the advantages and disadvantages. "You'll—you'll put an end to this battle?"

"I'll put an end to it when I have what I want . . . and until I see him, Lut Gholein will know no peace! Think well on this, for you can already see that your walls will be of little good against me!"

It did not take the man long. "I—I will do it!"

"Then go!" General Malevolyn contemptuously threw the officer back, waving away a pair of demonic soldiers ready to strike the man down. To the enemy commander, he added, "Call a retreat! Any who pass through the gates will not be slaughtered! Any who fail to follow quick enough will serve as fine food for the carrion crows! This is all I grant you—be grateful you get this much!"

The officer fled from him, stumbling in the direction of Lut Gholein. Malevolyn watched him signal to someone up on the walls. A few moments later, a pitiful wail went up from one of the war horns in the city.

An armored figure with eyes that matched the blood on Augustus Malevolyn's armor came up to him. The face had once belonged to Zako. "Let them go, warlord?"

"Of course not. Beat them to the ground, let none survive who do not make it to the gates. Any who do, though, you do not touch and none of you are to enter the city!" He glanced in the direction of the enemy commander, who had not bothered much to wait for his men. "And make sure that *he* survives! He'll have much to tell them."

"Yes, warlord . . ." The Zako demon bowed once, then hesitated. "Not to enter the city? We leave Lut Gholein alone?"

"I want the armor! We will harass them, even do what we can to damage their defenses, but until I have the armor and the head of the one who dared keep it from me, the city will not be touched!" General Malevolyn—*Warlord* Malevolyn—smiled grimly. "I promised them an end to the battle, that Lut Gholein would not know peace until I had the armor. Once I have it, I will give to them exactly what I promised. A *final* end to the battle . . . and the peace of the *grave*."

Seventeen

"What's that sound?" Norrec asked, looking up from the pattern he had drawn in the sand.

Close to his side, Galeona shook her head. "I hear only thunder, my knight."

He rose, listening again. "Sounds like battle . . . from the direction of the city."

"Perhaps a celebration. Maybe it's the sultan's birthday."

Norrec frowned to himself, suspicious of her continual denial of what he certainly recognized. Although his memories and those of Bartuc had intermingled to the point where it had become hard to tell one from the other, both sets of memories now aided him in determining that he heard correctly. The clatter, the shouts . . . they all spoke of violence, of bloodshed . . .

A part of him felt tempted to join in.

No . . . he had more important things to do. Horazon's tomb, what the beguiling witch evidently called the Arcane Sanctuary, had to lie somewhere near, perhaps even beneath where he presently stood.

He knelt down again, ignoring Galeona's momentary look of relief. Something about the pattern he had drawn—an upside-down triangle with circles around each corner and three crescents beneath—did not look right. That the fighter should not have even known of such spells no longer bothered him. Bartuc had known them; therefore, Norrec Vizharan did.

"What's missing?"

The witch hesitated. "One of two things. To search for a person, you would need a pentagram in the middle of the triangle. To search for a place, you would need a larger pentagram surrounding all the rest."

She made perfect sense to him. Norrec grimaced at having forgotten something so simple. He rewarded her with a smile. "Very good."

Despite the fact that her magical skills augmented his own growing abilities and her physical charms enticed his baser nature, not for a minute did the veteran soldier trust his new companion. She told half-truths and hid much from him. He could sense her ambition. The enchantress saw him as useful to her own ends, just as he saw the same where she was concerned. So long as she aided his efforts, Norrec had no trouble accepting her lies. However, if she tried to betray him later on, he had no compunction about dealing with her as he would have any traitor.

Some part within him still did battle with what he had become. Even now, Norrec sensed that such thoughts as he had just had about Galeona went against what the veteran had believed in most of his life. Yet, it seemed so easy to accept those thoughts now.

His mind shifted back to his task. He had to find Horazon's tomb, although *why* still remained a mystery to him. Perhaps when he did discover its whereabouts, then the reason for the quest would finally become clear.

He drew the larger pentagram, choosing to try to find the sanctuary rather than the man. Horazon would be little more than bones, making it somewhat more difficult to fix upon him. The edifice itself represented a larger, more distinct target for the spell.

"Have you cast anything such as this before?"

Galeona gave him a proud look. "Of course, I have!" Her look faltered slightly. "But I've never seen the Arcane Sanctuary nor do I have anything from it."

"That'll be no problem." Norrec already had a plan in mind. He felt certain that he could have both uttered the necessary incantation and focused on the location, but that would have forced him to spread his thoughts and will too much, likely increasing his chance for failure. The Arcane Sanctuary had already appeared to be a place quite unwilling to reveal itself. Even after the armor had fought off Drognan, some other force had pushed Norrec away from his goal. As with Bartuc's own tomb, Horazon's resting place had probably been built with much security in mind. The creators had obviously not wanted it defiled or ransacked and had cast powerful protective measures such as those the soldier had encountered in Drognan's chamber.

But with Galeona casting the spell, Norrec could focus fully on their destination. Surely that would work. If not . . .

He explained it to the witch, who nodded. "It can be done, I think. We must be of one mind, though, or else our own thoughts might work against us."

She reached out her hands. Norrec placed his own in hers. Galeona smiled at him, but something about that smile repelled the veteran rather than attracted him. Again he saw raw ambition in her eyes. The sorceress thought that by proving her usefulness to her companion, she could eventually control him. That, in turn, brought more dark thoughts of his own, thoughts of what he would do to any who believed that they could do such. There could be only one master—and that had to be Norrec.

"Picture it," she muttered. "Picture where you want us to go . . ."

In his mind, Norrec imagined the tomb as he had seen it the first time. He felt certain that the initial vision had been the true one, that the force trying to keep him from the sanctuary had afterward attempted to confuse his memory. The robed skeletons, the stone coffin with the symbol of the dragon over the crescent moon . . . these surely had to be the true images of the tomb.

Holding tight, Galeona leaned back, her eyes closed and her face toward the sky. She swayed as she muttered the incantation, pulling at her companion's gauntleted hands.

Norrec shut his own eyes, the better not to be distracted by the witch's body while he pictured Horazon's resting place. An eagerness swelled within him. This *would* work. He *would* be transported to the Arcane Sanctuary.

And then what?

Norrec had no time to divine an answer to that question, for suddenly he felt his entire body lighten, as if he had become more spirit than flesh. The only tug of weight he felt at all came from his hands, where the sorceress still gripped him tight.

"*Nezarios Aero!*" cried Galeona. "*Aerona Jy!*"

The fighter's body crackled with pure energy.

"*Aerona Jy!*"

A great sense of displacement shook Norrec—

—and in the next moment, his feet landed on *hard stone*.

Eyes immediately opening wide, Norrec Vizharan looked around. Web-enshrouded walls greeted his gaze and within those walls he saw a line of statues, each distinct in face and form, staring back. Not all of them had names that he could recall, but among them he spotted more than one who had known him well—and known his brother, Horazon, too.

But no—Horazon was *not* his brother! Why did he keep thinking that?

"We've done it!" Galeona cried, having at last registered their surroundings. She flung herself on him, kissed him with a fury that could almost not be denied—yet, Norrec desired nothing more than to push her away.

"Yes, this is it," he replied, once he had managed to peel her tentacles from his body.

"There is nothing we can't accomplish *together*," she cooed. "No one who could stand in our way . . ."

Yes, Galeona definitely sought to seal their alliance. The seductive witch understood full well the power he wielded, the power the suit had at last given to him. If she could have, Norrec had no doubts that she would have tried to wear the armor herself—and thereby cut out any need for a partner. The sooner he rid himself of her, the better.

Turning from the devilish woman, Norrec looked down the ancient, musty corridor. A peculiar, yellowish light illuminated the abandoned edifice, a light seemingly without source. He could not recall it from his first incursion into this dark realm, but since everything else looked as it should, Norrec paid the one difference little attention. His goal was at hand.

"This way." Without waiting to see if the sorceress followed, Norrec stomped down the corridor in the direction he felt certain that the sarcophagus lay. Galeona hurried to catch up, the dark-skinned woman slipping an arm around his own as if the two were lovers in the midst of a moonlit walk. He did not struggle free, aware that this way he could also keep *her* under watch.

Now and then a face familiar to him stared out from the dust-ridden statues. Norrec marked each with satisfaction, remembering their order from the vision. Not only did they prove that he headed in the correct direction but particular faces indicated to him that the final chamber had to be only a short distance farther.

And yet . . . and yet something about the statues also caused the veteran some unease, for although outwardly they seemed identical to those he recalled, minute alterations in detail began to haunt him. Certain features on some of the faces looked ever so slightly off—the shape of a nose, the curve of a mouth, the strength of a jaw. Most of all, the eyes tended toward different appearances. Never completely, but enough to make Norrec finally pause at one in order to look.

"What is it?" Galeona whispered, anxious to move on to their ultimate destination.

The face he stared at, the face of one Oskul, a round-headed, officious mage who had briefly been Horazon's sponsor to the Vizjerei council, resembled much the visage as Norrec's memory recalled it . . . but the eyes should have been narrower and the artisan had also given the orbs a sleepy look, not at all in keeping with the ever-active personality of the man. Nothing else about the statue seemed out of place, but the eyes proved to be enough to disturb him yet more.

Still, Norrec had been in the tomb for only a short time and had spent only a fraction of it among the ghostly sculptures. Whatever mistakes he now recalled likely had more to do with the artist's failing rather than anything else.

"Nothing," the soldier finally remarked. "Come on."

They journeyed on for a few minutes more—and at last entered the crypt. Norrec smiled as he studied the ancient site. Here, everything looked as it should. In the niches on the left and right, the skeletal figures of the Vizjerei sorcerers silently greeted the newcomers' arrival. The vast stone coffin atop the dais matched perfectly his vision.

The coffin . . .

"*Horazon* . . ." he whispered.

With growing eagerness, Norrec dragged Galeona toward the sarcophagus. The horror he had suffered during his dream visit to this place had been all but forgotten. All Norrec wanted to do now was open the coffin. He left the witch to the side, then reached up to take hold of the lid.

At that moment, his gaze slipped down to the clan markings again, something about them snaring his attention.

The dragon remained as it had been—but now below it lay a fiery star.

He stepped back, the truth dawning slowly on him. There had been too many errors, too many differences in detail . . .

"What's wrong? Why didn't you open it?"

Glaring at the traitorous markings, the veteran fighter snapped, "Because it's not real!" He waved his hand at the legion of dead mages. "I don't think *any* of this is real!"

"But that's mad!" Galeona touched the coffin. "It's as solid as you or I!"

"Is it?" Norrec extended his hand—and as he had hoped, in it he now held the sinister ebony sword. "Let's see what exactly the truth is!"

As Galeona watched in both astonishment and dismay, the soldier raised the sword high above his head, then brought it down hard on the massive sarcophagus.

The blade cut through without pause and yet no line appeared in the coffin. The two halves of the great stone monument did not separate and collapse . . . and the tattered bones of Horazon did not tumble to the floor.

"Illusion . . . or something akin to it." He turned to the horrific throng lined up against the walls, glaring at the dead as if they were to blame. "Where is he? Where's Horazon?"

"Perhaps down another passage . . ." suggested Galeona, her tone indicating she did not completely trust his sanity at the moment.

"Yes, maybe so." Without waiting for her, he charged out of the crypt. For some distance, Norrec followed the single corridor, looking for a side passage, a doorway. Yet, not once could he recall having seen one. In both versions of his dream, it had always been only this single passageway. The great Arcane Sanctuary had always consisted of only this and the actual burial chamber itself. Hardly the immense edifice one would have expected.

Unless what he had seen had been designed simply for the benefit of curious and greedy intruders—and the rest lay hidden elsewhere.

The frustrated fighter paused to glare at the statue of one of his—no, Bartuc's—former rivals. The bearded man smiled in what Norrec felt a very mocking manner.

That brought him to a decision. He raised the black blade again.

"What do you plan to do this time?" snapped Galeona, her patience with him having finally gotten thin. Great power he might wield, but so far Norrec had evidently not impressed her with his running about in circles.

"If there're no passages, I'll make one of my own!"

He glared at the statue, desiring very much to wipe the condescending smile off its face. Here would be the perfect location to begin cutting his way out. Norrec held the sword ready, determined to bring down the mocking effigy with his first blow.

But as he swung, as the blade came within inches of beheading the smiling statue, Norrec's entire surroundings fragmented. The floor rose and the walls pulled away, the rows of statues seeming to fall back as if fainting. The enshrouding webs folded in on themselves, utterly vanishing. Stairs bloomed like flowers, twisting and turning. Part of the floor ceased rising and instead dropped lower, leaving the two standing near a precipice. The only thing that remained consistent through the growing anarchy was the yellowish illumination.

"What've you done?" Galeona cried. "You fool! It's all falling apart!"

Norrec could not answer her, unable even to keep his footing. He fell back, the heavy armor dragging him down. His weapon flew from his grip and as it did, it faded away. The ground shook, keeping him from rising and, worse, rolling him toward the edge.

"Help me up!" he called to the sorceress, growing desperate. The gauntlets tore at the stone floor but could not get a grip anywhere. Around him, the Arcane Sanctuary continued to transform itself without any noticeable rhyme or reason, almost as if the tomb had gone into convulsion as a human might.

Galeona looked his way, hesitated, then looked to her right, where a stairway had suddenly formed.

"Help me, damn it!"

She sneered at him. "What a waste of my time! You, Augustus, Xazax—all of you! Better I relied only on myself! If you can't even pick yourself up, you might as well stay here and die, fool!"

With one last contemptuous glance at Norrec, Galeona started toward the steps.

"No!" Anger and fear vied for supremacy in him, anger and fear of the likes the fighter could never have imagined. As the witch fought her way to what might be freedom—abandoning Norrec to whatever fate awaited him—the urge to strike out, to punish her for her betrayal grew almost overwhelming.

Norrec pointed at her with his left hand. Words of power gathered on his lips, ready to be spoken. With one quick phrase, he would rid himself of the treacherous woman.

"Damn it! No! I won't!" He turned from her, pulled down his hand. Let her flee without him if she liked. He would not have *another* death on his hands.

Unfortunately, the armor did not agree.

The hand rose again, this time against Norrec's will. He struggled to lower it, but as since almost from the beginning of this terrible quest, the soldier found himself not the master, but simply the means. Bartuc's armor sought retribution for Galeona's failing—and it would have that retribution regardless of what its host wanted.

The gauntlet flared crimson.

Their surroundings still in complete flux, the dark-skinned enchantress had only now made it to the twisting staircase. To her misfortune, however, it shifted to the side, forcing her to readjust her path. As Norrec's hand came up, Galeona managed at last to set a foot on the first and second steps.

"No!" shouted Norrec at the gauntlet. He looked at the fleeing woman, who had not bothered to take even the slightest parting glimpse at her struggling companion. "Run! Hurry! Get out of here!"

Only after he had blurted out the warning did Norrec realize what he had done. Those words more than anything else caused Galeona to pause and look over her shoulder, costing her the precious seconds she had needed.

The dark words that the fighter had struggled not to say burst free.

Galeona saw what he did and reacted, striking back. She pointed at the prone figure, mouthing a single harsh word that some memory not of Norrec Vizharan's past recognized as a spell most foul.

Brilliant blue flames surrounded the witch even as she finished speaking. Galeona raised her head and howled once in utter agony—then burned away to ash in the blink of an eye.

Norrec, though, had no time to acknowledge her terrible demise, for suddenly his entire body became wracked in pain, as if each bone within sought to break apart. Norrec could feel even the tiniest of them slowly but inexorably cracking. Although the armor's magic had destroyed her, Galeona had succeeded in her own spellcasting. He screamed, shaking uncontrollably. Worse, despite his agony, the armor did nothing to help and instead appeared to be trying to rise so that it now could use the very staircase upon which the sorceress had perished.

Yet although the suit made it to the steps, it could go no farther. Each time it tried, an invisible force buffeted it back. Norrec's fist slammed against air, sending new shockwaves through the already-suffering man.

"Please!" he croaked, not caring that only the armor could possibly hear him. "Please . . . help . . ."

"Norrec!"

Through tear-drenched eyes, he tried to focus on the voice, a woman's voice. Did the ghost of Galeona call to him to join her in death?

"Norrec Vizharan!"

No . . . a different voice, young but commanding. He managed to turn his head some, although the action caused more torture within. In the distance, a vaguely familiar woman pale of skin but black of hair futilely reached out to him from what appeared to be a crystalline doorway at the top of yet another flight of stairs. Behind her stood another figure, this one male and with long, wild hair and a beard, both as white as snow. He looked suspicious, curious, and frightened all at the same time. He also looked even more familiar than the woman.

To Norrec he could be only one person.

"Horazon?" the soldier blurted.

One of the gloved hands immediately came up, the gauntlet ablaze with magical fury. Bartuc's armor had reacted to the name—and not with pleasure. Norrec could feel the formation of a spell, one that would make Galeona's death seem a peaceful end.

But as if reacting in turn to the armor, an awful moaning arose, as if the very building itself took offense to what it saw. Horazon and the woman suddenly disappeared as the stairway shifted a different direction and new walls formed. Norrec discovered himself suddenly standing in a high-columned hall that looked as if a grand ball had just ended. Yet, even that changed quickly.

No matter what the room, no matter where the woman and Horazon had gone, the armor did not care. Another spell erupted from the fighter's mouth and a ball of molten earth flew from his hand, exploding seconds later against the nearest wall.

The moaning became a *roar*.

The entire sanctuary shook. A tremendous force buffeted Norrec from every side. Worse, he realized that not only did the air close in on him—but so did the walls and the ceiling. Even the floor rose.

Norrec raised his arms, now evidently his own again, in a last futile effort to staff off the onrushing walls.

The meal had been a sumptuous one, better by far than any Kara could have imagined, including those which Captain Jeronnan had served her. If not for the fact that she was the prisoner of an insane mage, she might have enjoyed it even more.

During the meal, the necromancer had tried on more than one occasion to pluck some bit of reason from the white-haired sorcerer, but from Horazon she had only received babbled words and inconsistent information. At one point he had spoken of having discovered by accident the Arcane Sanctuary—the name by which legend called Horazon's tomb—then he had told Kara that he had built it all by himself through masterful sorcery. Another time, Horazon had told his prisoner that he had come to Aranoch to study the massive convergence of spiritual ley-lines centered in and around the city's present location. Even she had heard that mages could tap the mystical energies of this region far better than in any other spot in all the world. However, afterward he had spoken, with great trepidation, of fleeing to this side of the seas in fear that his brother's dark legacy still followed him.

Gradually Kara came to feel as if she spoke to two distinct men, one who truly *was* Horazon and another who simply thought he was. She could only think that the terrible trials through which Bartuc's brother had suffered, especially the horrific war against his own sibling, had combined with his centuries-long seclusion to tear apart his already-fragile mind. The necromancer grew somewhat sympathetic to his plight, but never did she forget that not only did this mad sorcerer still keep her in his underground labyrinth against her will, but also that, in times past, his magic had, on occasion, been as black as Bartuc's had ever been.

One other thing Kara had noted that unnerved her as much as her host's sanity. The Arcane Sanctuary itself acted as if more than simply an extension of Horazon's tremendous power. Many times, she could have sworn that it, too, had a mind, a personality, even. Sometimes she would note the room around her shift subtly, the walls moving and the general design transforming even when the wizard paid it no mind. Kara had even noticed that the table and the food changed. More to the point, when the necromancer had tried to push Horazon on the matter of Bartuc, a peculiar darkness had slowly begun to pervade her surroundings—almost as if the edifice itself wished an end to the troubling topic.

When they had finished, Horazon had immediately bid her to rise. Here in his sanctum, he had not babbled too much about 'the evil,' but still the watery-eyed figure acted with caution in all things.

"We must be careful," Horazon had muttered, standing. "At all times we must be careful . . . come . . . there is much to do . . ."

Her thoughts more on escape than his constant warnings, Kara had also risen—only to see a sight so startling that it had made her knock her chair over.

From the table itself had emerged a hand completely formed of the wood. The hand had seized her empty plate and had dragged it down *into* the table. At the same time, other hands had materialized, each seizing an object and dragging it, too, into the table. Still stunned, Kara had stepped back, only then discovering that the reason she had not heard her chair strike the floor had been because two more appendages formed from the marble at her feet had caught the piece of furniture before it could hit.

"Come!" Horazon had called, his expression now somewhat peevish. He seemed not at all disturbed by the unsettling appendages. "No time to waste, no time to waste!"

While the dining hall had worked to clear itself, he had led her up a flight of stairs, then through a polished, oak door. Behind the door lay another stairway, this one going back down. Despite having wanted to question the trustfulness of their path, the young dark mage had quietly followed even when that set of steps had ended at yet another doorway which seemed to lead back to the vast hall again. Only when Horazon had opened the door and instead of the great hall she had been confronted with a wizard's laboratory had Kara finally blurted out something.

"This is impossible! This room shouldn't be here!"

He had looked at her as if she had been the mad one. "Of course, it should be! I was looking for it, after all! What a silly thing to say! If you look for a room, it should be where you want it, you know!"

"But . . ." Kara had ceased her protest, unable to argue with the facts before her very eyes. Here should have stood the grand room in which she and Horazon had eaten, but instead this imposing if disorderly chamber had greeted her. Thinking back to the impossible journeys she had already made in the sanctuary, the dark-haired spellcaster had finally come to the conclusion that the ancient mage's home could not possibly completely exist on the mortal plane. Even though no architect could have ever solved the physical problems she had encountered, it had been said of the most powerful Vizjerei that some had learned to actually manipulate the very fabric of reality itself, to create for their use what some called "pocket universes" where the laws of nature were what their masters decided it should be.

Could that have been what Horazon had accomplished with the Arcane Sanctuary? Kara could find no other explanation for everything she had experienced. If so, he had created a marvel such as not ever seen before in all the world!

Despite his ragged robe and otherwise unkempt appearance, in this chamber Horazon had taken on a more formidable look. When he had stepped to the center of the room, raising his arms and beckoning to the ceiling, Kara had expected fire and lightning to play from his fingers. She had expected winds to rise from nowhere and perhaps even the Vizjerei's body to glow bright.

Instead, he had simply turned back to her and said, "I brought you here . . . but I don't know *why*."

After taking a moment to register this odd statement, the necromancer had replied, "Is it because of the armor? Your—brother's—armor?"

He had stared up at the ceiling again. "Is it?"

The ceiling, of course, had not answered.

"Horazon . . . you must remember what they did with your brother's body, your people and mine."

Again, the ceiling. "What was done with it? Ah, yes, no wonder I don't remember."

Feeling as if she might as well have been talking to the ceiling herself, Kara had pressed, "Listen to me, Horazon! Someone managed to steal his enchanted armor from the tomb. I've followed them all the way here! He may even be in Lut Gholein at this moment! We need to find him, to take the armor back! There's no telling what evil still lurks within it!"

"Evil?" His eyes had taken on a wide, animalistic look. "Evil? Here?"

Kara had bitten back a curse. She had stirred him up again.

"So much evil about! I must be careful!" A condemning finger had pointed at her. "You must go!"

"Horazon, I—"

It had been at that moment that something had happened, something that passed between the wizard and his lair. Seconds later, she had felt the entire sanctum shiver, a shiver more that of a living thing, not simply a structure caught in some shockwave.

"No, no, no! I must hide! I must hide!" Horazon had looked completely panic stricken. He might have even fled from the chamber, but the room again transformed. The sorcerer's tables of equipment and chemicals receded from the two and from the floor a gigantic, crystalline sphere arose to eye level, a huge hand formed from the stone below keeping it there.

In the center of the sphere, a vision had coalesced, a vision of a man whom Kara Nightshadow had never truly seen but had still been able to identify immediately—thanks to the crimson armor he wore.

"It's him! Norrec Vizharan! He has the armor!"

"Bartuc!" her mad companion had snapped. "No! Bartuc's come for me!"

She had seized him by the arm, daring death in the hopes of finally bringing a conclusion to this dangerous quest. "Horazon! Where is he? Is that part of the sanctuary, too?"

In the sphere, Norrec Vizharan and a dark-skinned woman had rushed through a web-enshrouded corridor filled with ancient statues carved in the fashion of the Vizjerei. Norrec had carried a monstrous black sword and had looked ready to use it. Kara had wondered then if Sadun Tryst had spoken too well of his former friend. Here had looked a man who had seemed very capable of the outrageous murders.

Regardless of the answer to that, Kara had known she could not come this close and fail. "Answer me! Is that part of the sanctuary? It must be!"

"Yes, it is! Now leave me be!" He had torn free from her, headed to the door—only to be stopped there by hands sprouting from the floor and walls, hands that had kept him from abandoning the necromancer.

"What——?" She had been able to say no more, startled by what seemed the vehemence in the hands' actions. Horazon's very stronghold had seemed in rebellion, forcing him to return to Kara.

"Let me go, let me go!" the mad sorcerer had cried out to the ceiling. "It's the evil! I mustn't let it get me!" As the raven-tressed woman had watched, a sullen expression had finally crossed Horazon's wrinkled face. "All right . . . all right . . ."

And so he had returned to the sphere, pointed at the image. By this time, Norrec had confronted one of the statues, shouted something in anger that the crystal did not relay, then raised the black blade as if prepared to strike.

At the same time, Horazon cried, *"Greikos Dominius est Buar! Greiko Dominius Mortu!"*

Chaos had erupted in the scene with walls, floors, and stairs shifting, materializing, or disappearing. In the midst of the madness, the two figures had struggled to survive. However, Norrec Vizharan had been unable to save himself, falling near an edge and then being unable to rise because of the constant motion all around him. The woman—a witch, in Kara's mind—had completely abandoned the helpless fighter, choosing instead to head toward what seemed a fairly stable set of stairs.

"Greiko Dominius Mortu!" her companion snapped.

Something in his tone had made Kara look at Horazon and in his eyes she had read nothing but death for the pair. So, this had been how it would end. Not by the hands of the revenants nor through her own sorcery, but by the fatal spells of Bartuc's own crazed brother. For the witch she had felt nothing, but because of Tryst's tales of the veteran fighter, a spark of sadness had still touched her. Perhaps there had been a good man there once.

But not at that moment. The scene had revealed Norrec determined to slay his wayward partner. He had pointed one gauntleted hand at her, shouted something——

Only then had Kara noticed the look of horror and regret on his face. No satisfaction, no dark intent, only fear for what he would do to the fleeing woman.

But that had made no sense, unless . . .

"What did he say, Horazon? Do you know what he said? I need to know!"

From the crystalline sphere had suddenly burst a man's fearful voice. *"Damn it! I won't!"* Then, *"No! Run! Hurry! Get out of here!"*

Not the bitter shouts of a vengeful murderer and yet the image had still shown him ready to strike down his fleeing companion. However, his expression had continued to belie that notion. Norrec Vizharan had actually appeared as if he battled for control of himself or—or—

Of course! "Horazon! You must stop this! You must help them!"

"Help them? No, no! Destroy them and I destroy the evil at last! Yes, at last!"

Kara had glanced at the sphere again—just in time to witness not only the witch's awful demise, but the woman's own last attack on the fighter. Norrec's cries had filled Horazon's chamber, the sphere apparently still fulfilling the necromancer's previous request.

"Listen to me! The evil is in the armor, not the man! Don't you see? His death would be a travesty, a tipping of the balance!" Frustrated at Horazon's unyielding expression, she had glared up at the ceiling. The wizard seemed to consult some power up there, some power that did not merely exist in his mind. To it she had cried, "Bartuc was the monster, not the one clad in his armor and only Bartuc would take a life so!" Once more gazing at the mad mage, she concluded, "Or is Horazon just like his brother?"

The reaction to her desperate declarations had startled even Kara. From every wall, from even the ceiling and the floor, *mouths* had formed in the stone. Only one word had issued from each, the same word over and over,

"*No . . . no . . . no . . .*"

The crystalline sphere had suddenly expanded and, even more startling, *opened* up. Within it had arisen a stairway, which Kara had imagined had to lead somehow—as impossible as it had seemed—directly to the struggling Norrec.

Horazon had refused to aid her, but the Arcane Sanctuary had not.

The necromancer had immediately rushed to the crystal, pausing only when she came to the first step. Despite having offered her this path, the enchanted sanctum had continued to assault Norrec, making rescue difficult. Momentarily uncertain, Kara had initially chosen to call to the fighter, to see if he could perhaps make it to her without her having to enter the chaos.

He had responded to the second call—by shouting Horazon's name. Confused, Kara had withdrawn the hand she had offered, a symbolic gesture intended to let him know she had meant only help. As she had done that, he, in turn, had reacted oddly, moving as if he intended not to come to the necromancer—but to slay her.

"The evil awakens . . ." a voice had muttered behind her.

Horazon. She had not realized that he had stepped into sight. Kara had assumed that the mad mage had stayed far from the danger. She had known then why Norrec—or rather the *armor*—had reacted so. The enchanted armor had yet sought to fulfill its creator's greatest desire, to slay the accursed brother.

But before it had been able to strike, the sanctuary had chosen once more to take command of the situation. Norrec and his surroundings had regressed, pulling farther and farther back, almost vanishing from sight. Kara had seen the walls there begin to converge, as if the astonishing edifice had sought to box its adversary in . . . and worse. It had occurred to her only at the last that, with the armor seeking Horazon's imminent destruction, the best choice for the Arcane Sanctuary had been to end this once and for all, even if it meant, after all, the death of an innocent. Better to destroy both the armor and Norrec Vizharan than give Bartuc's legacy another chance to succeed.

But such a death went against the balance that Kara Nightshadow had been trained to preserve. Now, with Norrec's doom looming, the necromancer *leapt* into the chaos within the crystalline sphere, hoping that Horazon's apparently sentient domain would do for her what it would not for the hapless fighter.

Hoping that it would not decide that Kara, too, was expendable.

Eighteen

Norrec could not move, could not even breathe. It felt as if a giant hand had taken hold of him and sought to crush his entire body to a tiny pulp. In some ways he welcomed it, for with his death would at least end his guilt. No one else would die because he had sought to rob a tomb and instead unearthed a nightmare.

Then, just as he prepared himself to die, a tremendous force threw him upward. Norrec flew hard, almost as if he had been fired off by a catapult. So, instead of a crushing death, he would eventually fall to his doom. Unlike the short drop aboard the *Hawksfire*, Norrec felt certain that this time he would not survive.

But something—no, *someone*—caught him by one arm, slowing his flight. Norrec tried to see who it might be, but turning his head toward his would-be rescuer brought about an overwhelming sensation of vertigo. He lost all sense of direction, no longer even able to tell up from down.

Without warning, Norrec struck the ground, the sand doing very little to prevent the jolt from knocking him nearly senseless.

For some time, the battered veteran lay there, cursing the fact that he seemed to end up in such a position more often than necessary. His body ached to his bones and his vision revealed nothing to him but blurs. Yet, despite all that, he at least felt less pain. Whatever spell Galeona had cast before her death had at some point ceased and with it had also gone the crushing suffocation.

He heard thunder and knew from the general grayness his unfocused eyes could make out that he had returned to the storm-swept desert near Lut

Gholein. Norrec also sensed that he had not come here alone, that even now, someone stood over him.

"Can you stand?" a familiar female voice asked gently.

He almost told her that he had no desire to, but instead forced himself as best he could to a sitting position. Doing so made his head spin, but at least Norrec felt some pride at accomplishing the simple task by himself.

His vision finally cleared enough for him to see who had spoken. It proved to be the dark-haired woman he had not only seen just before the walls had closed in, but also now recalled as one of the faces on the statues he had passed during his second sojourn into the dream version of Horazon's tomb.

Horazon. Thinking of Bartuc's brother made him recall who he had seen standing near the pale woman. Horazon—still alive after *centuries.*

She mistook his momentary shaking as a part of a possible injury. "Be careful. You have been through much. We do not know how it may have affected you."

"Who are you?"

"My name is Kara Nightshadow," she replied, kneeling so as to get a better look at his face. One slim hand gently touched his cheek. "Does that hurt you?"

In truth, her hand felt good, but he knew better than to tell her so. "No. Are you a healer?"

"Not exactly. I am a follower of Rathma."

"A necromancer?" Surprisingly, the admission did not shock him as much as it once might have. Everything around Norrec of late had concerned death—or worse. A necromancer certainly fit well into the pattern, although he had to admit he had never seen an attractive one before. The few others of her faith that he had come across had been dour figures little different from the dead with whom they communed.

He realized that although she had told him her name he had not introduced himself. "My name's Norrec—"

"Yes. Norrec Vizharan. I know."

"How?" He recalled that she had used his name earlier, yet the two had never actually met as far as he knew. Certainly he would have remembered.

"I have been hunting for you ever since you left Bartuc's tomb with the armor."

"You? But why?"

She leaned back, apparently satisfied that he had not suffered much from their ouster from Horazon's bizarre domain. "Along with the Vizjerei, my people took the responsibility for hiding the warlord's ensorcelled remains. We could not destroy either the body or the armor at that time, but we could keep them from those who might find a use—either corrupted mages or deadly demons."

Norrec remembered the monstrous creature in the sea. "Why demons?"

"Bartuc started out as a pawn of theirs, but even you must know that by the time of his death, even the lords of Hell looked in awe at his power. Although only a portion of his total might, what remains in the armor itself would be enough to entirely upset the delicate balance of life and death in the world . . . and even, perhaps, beyond."

After all that he had seen, he had little trouble believing her. Norrec struggled to his feet, Kara assisting him. He looked down at her, thinking back to what had just happened. "You saved me."

She looked away, almost seeming embarrassed. "I had some part in it."

"I would've died otherwise, right?"

"Very likely."

"Then you saved me—but *why* did you do it? Why not simply let me die? If I had, the armor would've been left with no *host*. It would've been powerless!"

Kara stared him in the eyes. "You did not choose to wear Bartuc's accursed armor, Norrec Vizharan. It chose you, although I do not know why. Whatever it has done, whatever foul deeds it has performed, I felt you innocent of them—and therefore deserving of a chance of life."

"But more might die because of that!" The bitterness must have shown in his expression, for the necromancer withdrew slightly. "My friends, the men at the inn, the *Hawksfire*'s crew, and just now that witch! How many more must perish—and most before my eyes?"

She put a hand on his own. Norrec feared for her, but the suit did nothing. Perhaps whatever fueled its evil task lay dormant for a time—or perhaps it simply awaited the best moment to strike. "There is a way to end this," Kara replied. "We must remove the armor."

Norrec burst out laughing. He laughed long and hard—and with no hope. "Woman, don't you think I've tried? Don't you think the first chance I had I pulled at both gloves, attempted to peel off every bit of plate? I couldn't even remove the damned *boots*. They're all sealed to my body, as if a very part of my flesh! The only way you'll be able to remove the suit is if you take my skin off with it!"

"I understand the trouble. I understand also that, under most circumstances, no spellcaster would have the power to undo what the armor has done—"

"Then what could you possibly hope to accomplish?" the frustrated soldier snapped. "You should've let me die just now! It would've been better for all!"

Despite his outburst, the raven-haired woman remained calm. She glanced around before answering, as if looking for someone or something. "He did not follow. I should have known."

"Who . . . Horazon?"

Kara nodded. "So you recognized him, too?"

Exhaling, Norrec explained, "My memories . . . my memories are confused. Some of them I know are mine, but others . . ." He hesitated, certain she would find him mad for what he believed. ". . . the others belonged to Bartuc, I think."

"Yes, very likely they did."

"That doesn't surprise you?"

"In legend, the warlord and his crimson suit seemed as one. Over time, he imbued it with one mighty enchantment after another, transforming it into more than simply pieces of metal. By the time of his death, it had been said that the armor acted as if a loyal dog, its own magic protecting and fighting for Bartuc as hard as he himself would. Small wonder that his life has been imprinted upon it . . . and that some of those vile memories have seeped into your *own* mind."

The weary veteran shuddered. "And the longer I wear it, the more I'll succumb. There's been times I actually thought I *was* Bartuc!"

"Which is why we must remove it." She frowned. "We must try to convince Horazon to do it. I feel he is the only one who has the capability."

Norrec did not exactly like that notion. The last time he and the bearded elder had seen one another, the armor had reacted instantly and with clear malice. "That may stir up the suit again. It may even be why it's being so quiet now." Something suddenly struck him. "It *wants* him. It wants Horazon. All this damn distance, all the things it's put me through—it's all been because it wants to slay Bartuc's brother!"

Her expression indicated that she had come to much the same conclusion. "Yes. Blood calls to blood, as they say, even if the blood between two is bad. Horazon helped slay his brother at the battle of Viz-jun and the armor must have preserved that memory within it. Now, after all this time, it has risen and seeks to repay the deed—even though Horazon should have been dead centuries ago."

"But he isn't. Blood calls to blood, you said. It must've known he was still alive." Norrec shook his head. "Which doesn't explain why it waited so long. Gods! It's all insane!"

Kara took him by the arm. "Horazon must have the answer. Somehow we must find our way back to him. I feel that he is the only hope by which we can put an end to the warlord's curse."

"Put an end to it, someone says?" rasped a voice of no human origin. "No . . . no. . . . This one desires otherwise, he does . . ."

Kara stared past Norrec, who immediately began to turn.

"Look—" was as far as the necromancer got.

What resembled a sharp, needlelike lance darted down toward him. It would have caught Norrec through the head, but at the last, Kara pushed him aside. Unfortunately for both of them, the wicked lance continued its downward thrust unabated—and buried itself in the woman's chest.

The lance quickly withdrew. Kara gasped, collapsing. Blood spilled over her blouse. Norrec froze momentarily, then, knowing he could do nothing for her if he, too, perished, the veteran fighter turned to confront their attacker.

Yet, what greeted his horrified eyes proved to be no warrior, but rather a thing born of nightmares. It most resembled a towering insect, but one clearly spawned in more hellish climes. Pulsating veins crosscrossed its grotesque form. What he had taken for a lance had actually been one of the creature's own appendages, a lengthy, sicklelike arm ending in a deadly point. Beneath the sickles, savage skeletal hands with claws opened and closed. Somehow, the massive horror managed to support itself on two lengthy hind limbs bent back in the manner of the mantis it so resembled.

"This one came in search of a treacherous, wandering witch, but such a prize will serve better! Long has this one hunted for you, for the power you wield . . ."

Even dazed, Norrec knew that the demon—for what other creature could this be—meant the armor, not the man.

"You killed her!" he managed to reply.

Blood dripping from one sickle, the mantis dipped his head. "One less mortal makes no difference. Where is the witch? Where is Galeona?"

He knew her? Norrec did not find that at all surprising. Even half under the spell of the armor, he had known that much of her story had been lies. "Dead. The armor killed her."

An intake of breath indicated to him that the demon found this startling. "She is dead? Of course! This one sensed something amiss—but did not suspect that!"

He began to emit a peculiar, rattling noise which the soldier at first thought anger. Only after a time, however, did it become clear that the monstrous insect *laughed*.

"The bond is severed, yet still this one roams the mortal plane! The tie is broken, but the blood spell preserves! This one could have slain her all along! What a fool Xazax has been!"

Norrec took the demon's enjoyment as a chance to look at Kara. Her entire chest had turned crimson and from where he stood he could not tell if she even breathed. It pained him to have her, the one who had tried to save him, die before his very eyes without being able to do anything about it.

Spurred on by anger, Norrec took a step toward the mantis—or at least *tried* to do so. Unfortunately, his legs, his entire body, refused to obey him.

"Damn you!" he roared at the suit. "Not now!"

Xazax ceased laughing. The deep, yellow orbs fixed on the helpless human. "Fool! Think you to command the greatness of Bartuc? This one thought to peel the armor off your cold corpse, but now Xazax sees this would have proven a terrible blunder! You are needed—at least for the time being!"

The mantis raised one spearlike tip toward the breast- plate. Immediately, Norrec's left hand reached out, but not in defense. Instead, to his horror, it touched the demon's own appendage as if in acknowledgment.

"You would be whole, would you not?" Xazax asked of the suit. "You would desire the return of the helm separated from you so long ago? This one can take you to it . . . if you like."

In response, one booted foot stepped forward. Even Norrec knew what the lone movement meant.

"Then go we shall . . . but it must be done quickly." The mantis turned and started off.

Norrec had no choice but to follow, the armor soon marching alongside the demon. Behind the desperate soldier, Kara bled away the last drops of her life, but he could do no more for her than he could for himself. In some ways, Norrec envied the pale woman. The necromancer's suffering had already all but ended; his would only get worse. His last hope had been crushed.

"Heaven help me . . ." he whispered.

The mantis apparently had sharp hearing, for he immediately fell upon the hopeless words. *"Heaven? No angel will there be to help you, fool of a human! Too afraid, they are! Too cowardly! We walk the world in numbers, the demon master awakes, and the human stronghold of Lut Gholein prepares to suffer a horrific end! Heaven? You would do better to pray to Hell!"*

And as they continued on toward their destination, Norrec could not help but think that on this the demon might just speak the truth.

Kara felt her life ebbing away, but she could do nothing about it. The demonic creature she had seen had moved with inhuman swiftness. Perhaps she had saved Norrec, but even that the necromancer doubted.

She drifted along, each drop of blood leaving her body bringing her close to taking her next step in the overall scheme of the balance. Yet despite her deep beliefs, Kara wanted nothing more at the moment than to return to the mortal plane. She had left too much undone, had left Norrec in a position that he could not possibly survive without her aid. Worse, demons walked her world, further evidence that every follower of Rathma was badly needed. She *had* to return.

But such choices were generally not given to the dying.

"What should we do?" a voice in the distance asked, a voice that Kara felt she knew.

"He said that we should give it back when we felt we must. I feel we must."

"But without it—"

"We will still have time, Sadun."

"He may have said so, but I don't trust him!"

A brief, throaty chuckle. *"Trust you to be the only one capable of not trusting one of his grand kind."*

"Save the remarks . . . if it's got to be done, let's do it."

"As you say."

Kara suddenly felt a great weight upon her chest—a weight that felt so good that she eagerly welcomed it, took it into her very being. It had a tremendous familiarity to it that caused her to reminisce about little things, such as her mother feeding her fruit, a butterfly the color of rainbows landing on her knee while she studied in the forest, the smell of Captain Jeronnan's freshly cooked meals . . . even a brief glimpse of Norrec Vizharan's weathered but not unhandsome face.

The necromancer suddenly gasped as *life* enfolded her again.

She blinked, feeling the sand, the wind. Thunder rumbled and somewhere distant she heard what seemed the sounds of battle.

"It did . . . as he said . . . it would. I should've . . . used it . . . on myself."

Kara knew that voice now, although it had changed some from just a few seconds before. Now it sounded more as she would have expected it to sound—the rasping words of a dead man.

"I know . . . I know . . ." Sadun Tryst retorted to some silent response. "Only her . . ."

Opening her eyes, the enchantress stared up at the solemn forms of the grinning revenant and his Vizjerei companion. "What—how did you find me?"

"We never lost . . . you. We let you . . . go . . . and followed." His eyes narrowed. "But here in . . . Aranoch . . . we knew you . . . were around, but . . . could not see . . . you . . . until now."

They did not know exactly where she had gone when Horazon had led her down into his underground sanctum. The spell binding her to them had kept them in the general area, but both the sanctuary's location and its incredible magic had left the revenants baffled. She could have been directly underneath and neither would have noticed.

Her strength returning, the dark mage tried to push herself up a bit. Something slid from her chest. Kara instinctively caught it with one hand and marveled. Her dagger!

Tryst's smile had taken a decidedly bitter turn. "The bond is . . . broken. The life force . . . we took . . . is yours. . . ." He looked frustrated. "We have . . . no more . . . hold . . . over you."

The necromancer looked down at her chest. Blood covered most of the blouse, but the horrible wound inflicted on her by the demon had sealed over, the only sign of its earlier presence a circular mark, as if someone had tattooed Kara there.

"Looks . . . much healed."

She covered the area up again, glaring at the undead, despite the fact that he and Fauztin had just gifted her with a second chance at life. "How did you do that? I've never heard of such a feat!"

The wiry corpse shrugged, his head tipping to the other side. "He—my friend . . . said that the dagger . . . was a part . . . of you. When you were . . . bound to us . . . some part of you . . . came with. We returned it . . . to make you alive." He grimaced as best he could. "Nothing keeps . . . you tied to . . . us any more."

"Except one thing. Norrec." Kara forced herself up. Tryst stood back, but, to her astonishment, Fauztin lent a hand. She hesitated at first, but realized that the revenant only meant to help. "Thank you."

Fauztin blinked . . . then rewarded her with a brief, tight-lipped smile.

"You bring life . . . to the deadest of . . . the dead . . . now . . . we're even . . ." Sadun Tryst jested.

"What about Norrec?"

"We think . . . he nears . . . Lut Gholein."

Even though they had saved her, the necromancer could not let them slay their former friend. "Norrec is not responsible for your deaths. What happened to you he could not prevent."

The two stared back at her. At last, Fauztin blinked again and Tryst replied, "We know."

"But then why—?" Kara stopped. All along she had assumed that they hunted their murderer, who, naturally, could only be Norrec. Only now, looking at the duo, did she understand that her misconceptions had led her astray.

"You do not pursue Norrec in order to exact revenge on him—you pursue Bartuc's *armor*." Although they did not answer her, she knew that she had not been wrong. "You could have told me!"

Tryst did not reply to that, either, instead abruptly announcing to Kara, "The city is under . . . siege."

Under siege? When had that happened? "By who?"

"One who . . . also seeks . . . to raise the dead . . . or at least . . . the bloody specter of . . . Bartuc."

Where did all these madmen come from, Kara wondered—and that made her think of the ragged figure from whom she had most recently escaped. Turning around, she looked for some sign of the Arcane Sanctuary, but to no avail. The desert sands swirled in the wind, the dunes looking as if they had remained untouched for years. Yet, somewhere around here the earth had opened up and deposited her and Norrec on the ground.

Not caring what the revenants might make of her peculiar actions, Kara called out, "Horazon! Listen to me! You can help us—and we can help you! Help us save Norrec—and put an end to Bartuc's legacy!"

She waited, the wind whipping her hair and sand stinging her face. Kara waited for Horazon to materialize or at least send her some sign that he listened.

But nothing happened.

At last, Sadun Tryst broke the silence. "We can't . . . wait here any longer . . . while you call . . . more ghosts . . ."

"I'm not calling—" the necromancer stopped. Of what use trying to explain to the revenants that Horazon had survived the centuries and lived, albeit as a madman, under their very feet? For that matter, why had she even hoped that Bartuc's brother would join with them in this dire venture? He had already shown that, if it had been up to him alone, Norrec would have perished along with the armor. Some legends concerning Horazon had painted him as a hero in comparison to his brother, but this same hero had also summoned demons, bending them to his will. Yes, his war against Bartuc had definitely been about self-preservation as much as anything else. There would be no aid from the ancient Vizjerei.

"We go . . ." Tryst added. "You come . . . or not . . . your choice, necromancer."

What else could Kara do? Even without Horazon, she had to go after Norrec. The demon must have taken him to the one besieging Lut Gholein, but for what reason? Did they hope to destroy what remained of the veteran fighter's own mind, enabling the ghostly memories of the Warlord of Blood to completely take over? A terrifying thought for all people everywhere, not simply poor Norrec. Many scholars had assumed, quite rightly, that, had he defeated his brother, Bartuc would have wreaked his evil upon the rest of the world until it had all fallen under his heel. Now, it seemed, like Kara, he had a second chance to succeed.

As a follower of Rathma, she could not permit that—even if it meant having to kill the armor's host. The thought left her cold, but if the balance after all required Norrec to be slain, then so be it. Even her own life did not matter if only it meant that she put an end to the danger.

"I will come with you," the necromancer finally replied.

Fauztin nodded, then pointed in the direction of Lut Gholein.

"Time is . . . wasting . . . he says."

The revenants flanked Kara as the trio set off, a fact which did not escape her. The wind had already wiped clean much of Norrec's trail, but Tryst and the Vizjerei had no apparent trouble following. The bond to what had murdered them enabled the pair to follow anywhere, any place.

"What about the demon?" Kara asked. He had designs on the armor, too, and would certainly fight anyone who sought to take it away from him.

Tryst pointed at her dagger, which now hung from the dark mage's belt. "That . . . is our best bet."

"How?"

"Just use it . . . and pray." He looked as if he intended to say more, but Fauztin gave him a glance that silenced the smaller of the ghouls immediately.

What secret did they still hold from her? Had she underestimated them? Did they still plan to use her as a puppet? Now was certainly not the time to hold back anything that might mean the difference between victory and death.

"What do you—"

"We'll deal . . . with the armor . . ." Sadun commented, cutting her off, "and Norrec."

His tone indicated that there would be no further conversation on this or any other subject. Kara considered trying anyway, but decided not to aggravate relations with the duo. The revenants acted in no manner she could readily predict, going against everything she had been taught about their kind. Half the time, they acted as if they still had hearts that pumped, blood that flowed. The rest of the time, they moved on with the silent determination for which such undead had been fabled. Truly, a unique situation. . . but then, everything about this matter had been unique.

Deadly, too.

She pictured Norrec in her mind, wondering what he must be going through at the moment. The image of the demon overshadowed the fighter, causing the necromancer to bite her lip in concern. There also appeared in her mind the shadow of a third figure, the one who now led the assault on the coastal kingdom. What part did he play? What did he gain in all this? He could not simply desire to have Norrec become a second Bartuc—that would be the same as signing his own death warrant. Bartuc had never either willingly served nor allied himself with any other mortal.

She would have the chance to discover the answers to her many questions soon enough. As to whether she would live long enough to appreciate those answers—Kara had severe doubts.

Nineteen

More than an hour had past and still Lut Gholein had not given up the armor. General Malevolyn barely contained his righteous anger, wondering if they had already found it and thought that somehow they could use its magic against him. If so, they would be sorely mistaken. The armor would never work for their cause and, if tampered with, would likely strike out at those investigating it. No, Bartuc's legacy belonged to him and him alone.

In keeping with his threat, his demon horde continued to assault the walls. The grounds near Lut Gholein had been littered with the mangled remains of not only those who had earlier failed to reach the gates, but also several who had fallen from above. The demon archers had proven in many ways superior shots to even the men whose bodies they now inhabited. In addition, the six catapults that he had brought along now wreaked more havoc in the city itself. Protected by demonic sorceries, the siege machines, in turn, suffered no damage from Lut Gholein's return fire.

He watched as those at the nearest catapult prepared yet another fiery gift for the inhabitants. General Malevolyn had saved the weapons for just this, showing his adversaries that he would permit them no respite. Either they gave him what he desired or even their high walls would not save them—not that he would let such limited barriers save them in the end, anyway.

And the end was very near. Lut Gholein, the general decided, had just run out of time. He would let the catapults fire their present volley, then give the command for his full forces to strike. The people within thought that their gates would hold against the invaders, but even now they underestimated the might of demons. It would be a simple matter to remove the one obstacle to the horde's entrance into the city . . . and from there would begin a day of death so bloody that Lut Gholein's fall would be spoken of in terrified whispered by all other men for years to come.

Once more, the crimson armor of the Warlord of Blood would cast the shadow of fear across the entire world.

Augustus Malevolyn suddenly stiffened as an unsettling sensation filled him. He quickly turned to look behind him, certain that he *had* to see who—or what—approached from the rear.

And over a dune came a familiar sight, Xazax moving along the sand. That the demon had dared come so near to Lut Gholein during the day puzzled the general—until he saw who walked beside the monstrous insect.

"The armor . . ." he whispered almost reverently.

Forgetting his demon soldiers, forgetting Lut Gholein, Malevolyn charged toward the oncoming pair. In all his life he had never experienced so glorious a moment. Bartuc's armor came toward him. His greatest desire had at last come to fruition!

Why the simpleton who had stolen it from the tomb still lived to wear it, only Xazax could say. It amazed Malevolyn that the mantis had let the man live this long. Perhaps Xazax simply had not wanted to bother with carrying the suit back himself and had forced the fool to bring it along. Well, for that deed, the least the general could do would be to grant the armor's present wearer a relatively quick and painless death.

"And what prize is this you bring, my friend?"

The mantis sounded quite pleased with himself. "A gift surely proving this one's intentions match those of the warlord. This one gives you one Norrec Vizharan—mercenary, tomb robber, and host for the glorious armor of Bartuc!"

"Mercenary and tomb robber . . ." General Malevolyn chuckled. "Perhaps I should hire you on for your expertise. Certainly I should congratulate you for bringing to me at last the final step in my ascension to glory!"

"You—want this suit?" The fool sounded incredulous, as if he, who had worn it so long, could not comprehend its majesty, appreciate its power . . .

"Of course! I want nothing more!" The general tapped his helmet. He saw that Norrec Vizharan instantly recognized the link between them. "I am General Augustus Malevolyn, late of Westmarch, a land, from your looks, I think you know. As you see, I wear the helm, lost when Bartuc's head and body were separated by the fools who by fluke managed to slay him. So fearful—and rightly so!—of his tremendous power, they placed body and head on opposite sides of the world, then secreted both in places from which they thought no one would be able to take them!"

"They were wrong . . ." muttered the mercenary.

"Of course! The spirit of the Warlord of Blood would not be denied! He called to his own, awaited those whose links to him would stir the powers to life, to new horizons!"

"What do you mean?"

Malevolyn sighed. He supposed he should have slain the fool out of hand, but the commander's mood had grown so light that he decided to at least explain what Norrec had obviously never understood. Reaching up, General Malevolyn gently removed the helmet. He felt at some slight loss as it left his head, but assured himself that soon it would be back in place again.

"I did not know its secret then, but I know now . . . for the artifact itself revealed it to me. Even you, I daresay, do not know the full truth, friend Xazax."

The mantis performed a mock bow. "This one would be delighted to be enlightened, warlord . . ."

"And you shall!" He grinned at Norrec. "I would wager to say that many died in the tomb before you came along, eh?"

Vizharan's expression darkened. "Too many . . . some of them were friends."

"You'll be joining them soon, have no fear . . ." The ebony-clad officer let Norrec get a better view of the helmet. "I daresay it was the same with this. The same fate for every minor tomb robber until one—one with a very special, *inherent* trait that gave him just enough of an advantage." Malevolyn's hands suddenly began to shake slightly. Quickly but still with an air of casualness, he replaced the helm. An instant feeling of relief washed over him, although he made certain not to let either the man or the demon know. "Can you guess what you and he had in common?"

"A cursed life?"

"More a magnificent heritage. In both of you, the blood of greatness flowed, albeit in quite a watered state."

This explanation only made Norrec frown. "He and I—were related?"

"Yes, although in his case that bloodline had become even more diluted. It gave him the right to take the helmet, but he proved too weak to be of use and so it let him be slain. With his death, it grew dormant again, waiting for one more worthy . . ." The general proudly indicated himself. "And it finally found me, as you see."

"You share the same blood, too?"

"Very good. Yes, I do. Far less tainted than that which flowed through that fool and, I have no doubt, far less tainted than you. Yes, Norrec Vizharan, you might say that you and I and he who discovered the head and helm are all *cousins*—several times removed, of course."

"But who—" the soldier's eyes widened, truth at last dawning. "That's not *possible!*"

Xazax said nothing, but clearly he still did not understand. Demons did not always comprehend human mating and the result of it. True, some of their kind knew the process and, indeed, bred rapidly at times through its use, but they bred as animals, without any concern for bloodlines.

"Oh, yes, cousin." Malevolyn smiled broadly. "we are all the progeny of the grand and noble *Bartuc* himself!"

The mantis clacked his mandibles together, rightly impressed. He looked even more pleased with himself, likely because he had chosen rightly in joining forces with Augustus Malevolyn.

As for Norrec, he took no evident pleasure in the revelation, like so many lesser mortals not at all understanding what Bartuc had nearly accomplished. How many men had earned the respect and fear of not only their fellows, but Heaven and Hell, too? It disappointed the general slightly, for, as he had said, the two were indeed cousins of a sort. Of course, since Norrec only had a few moments left to his life, the disappointment was not all that great. A fool removed was still a fool removed, always a plus in the world.

"Blood calls to blood . . ." Norrec muttered, staring down at the sand. "Blood to blood, she said . . ."

"Indeed! And that was why with you, the armor could act as it could not for so many centuries. Great power lay dormant within it, but power without life. In you flowed the life that had given that sorcery a spark. It was as if two halves, separated for so long, came together to create the whole!"

"Bartuc's blood . . ."

Augustus Malevolyn pursed his lips. "Yes, we've gone over that . . . you mentioned 'she'? My Galeona, perhaps?"

"A necromancer, warlord," Xazax interjected. "Quite dead now." He lifted one sickle limb up, indicating the cause. "But as for the witch—she is also no more."

"A pity, but I suppose it had to be, anyway." Something occurred to the slim commander. "Excuse me a moment, will you?"

He turned back to where his hellish warriors harassed Lut Gholein, picturing the demon who wore the face of Zako.

In the distance, the ghoulish minion suddenly turned from his task at the lead catapult and rushed toward Malevolyn. The moment he reached the general, the demon went down on one knee. "Yes, warlord—" A sharp intake of breath escaped the false Zako as he suddenly noticed Norrec and the armor. "Your— your command?"

"The city has no more value. It is yours to play with."

A savage, toothy grin spread an impossible distance across the dead man's features. "You're very gracious, warlord . . ."

General Malevolyn nodded, then waved him off. "Go! Let no life be spared. Lut Gholein will serve as notice of what hope any other kingdom, any other power, has against me."

The thing with Zako's face rushed off, fairly bouncing up and down with glee as he hurried to tell the others. The horde would ravage the city, leave nothing standing. In many ways, it would assuage the warlord for what had happened at Vin-Jun.

Vin-Jun. Malevolyn's chest swelled with anticipation. Now that he had the armor, even Kehjistan, legendary home of the Vizjerei, would fall to him.

His hand traced the fox and swords crest on his own breastplate. Long ago, after he had slain his birth father and burned down the house that had never acknowledged him, Augustus Malevolyn had decided to bear the symbol of that house on his armor in order to remind himself that what he wanted he would always be able to take. Now, though, the time had come to set aside that symbol for a better one. The bloodred suit of Bartuc.

He turned back to Xazax and the mercenary. "Well, shall we begin?"

Xazax prodded Norrec forward. The man stumbled, then dared to glare at the demon. Malevolyn's opinion of his distant cousin rose a notch. At least the buffoon had some nerve.

But the words spat bitterly from Norrec's mouth did not at all please the new warlord. "I can't give it to you."

"What do you mean by that?"

"It won't come off. I've tried again and again and it won't come off, not even the boots! I've no control over the armor whatsoever! I thought I did, but it was all a trick! What I do, where I go—the armor always decides!"

His tragic situation amused General Malevolyn. "Sounds almost like a comic opera! Is there any truth to this, Xazax?"

"This one would have to say the fool speaks the truth, warlord. He could not even move to save the necromancer . . ."

"How fascinating. Still, a problem not at all difficult to solve." He raised a hand toward Norrec. "Not with the power now at my command."

The spell summoned from memories other than his own should have enabled Malevolyn to desiccate the soldier within the very armor, leaving but a dried husk easily removed. Bartuc had used the spell and used it well during his reign and never once had it failed him.

But now it did. Norrec Vizharan stood wide-eyed but untouched. He looked as if he had truly expected to die, which made the failure of so strong a spell all the more puzzling.

Xazax it was who suggested the reason. "Your spell encompasses the entire body, warlord. Perhaps the suit reacts instantly as if attacked itself."

"A good point. Then we shall just have to do something a little more personal." He stretched out his hand—and the demon blade appeared in it. "Beheading him should sever the armor's link. It needs a live host, not a corpse."

As he approached, the general noted the mercenary struggling within the suit, trying desperately to make it move. Malevolyn took the lack of reaction by Bartuc's armor as a sign that he had chosen the right method this time. One swift slash would do it. In some ways, Vizharan should have considered himself honored. Had not the first great warlord perished much the same way? Perhaps Malevolyn would keep the man's head for a trophy, a reminder of this wondrous day.

"I shall remember you always, Norrec, my cousin. Remember you for all you have given me."

General Augustus Malevolyn readied the ebony sword, taking expert aim at his target's throat. Yes . . . one swift slash. Much more elegant than simply hacking away until the head fell off.

Smiling, he performed the killing stroke—

—only to have his blade resound off an *identical* one now held in Norrec's left hand.

"What in the name of *Hell*?"

The mercenary looked as startled as him. Behind Norrec Vizharan, the monstrous demon clacked and chittered in open consternation.

Norrec—or rather the *armor*—shifted into a combat stance, the other black blade ready for any attack by the general.

A peculiar expression spread across the soldier's countenance, an expression both bewildered and bemused. After a moment's hesitation, he even dared speak to Malevolyn. "I guess it might not think you're the right choice for it, general. I guess we'll be forced to fight over it. I'm sorry, believe me, I am."

Malevolyn fought back his growing rage. He could ill afford to lose his temper now. In a calm tone, he returned, "Then fight we shall, Vizharan— and when I claim the armor, the victory will be that much the sweeter for this battle!"

He swung at Norrec.

Xazax feared that he had made a terrible error. Now before him stood two mortals clad in pieces of Bartuc's armor, two mortals who both seemed capable of wielding to some extent the warlord's ancient sorcery. Yet, the mantis had thrown in his lot with Malevolyn, who had, until now, seemed the destined successor. The suit of armor, however, clearly saw matters differently, choosing to defend its quite unwilling host.

The demon had worked hard to convince his infernal lord, Belial, to sacrifice so many hellish minions to this effort. Belial had only agreed because he, too, had thought that a new Bartuc could give him the edge he needed not only against his rival, but the possible return of any of the three Prime Evils. If Xazax had assumed wrongly, if Norrec Vizharan somehow managed to win, it would look as if Belial's lieutenant had completely mismanaged the entire affair. Belial did not suffer incompetence in his servants.

Now, watching the two prepare for the struggle, he also felt certain that the suit had played him in particular for a fool. It had come with him as if docile, as if it only wished to reunite itself with the helmet, then join the demon's cause. However, now the mantis believed that it sought the helmet only—and after that intended to turn upon *him*.

It must have known that Xazax had been the one who had brought the aquatic behemoth to the mortal plane and, who, after questioning the dying mariner, had sent that monster to attack the ship. At the time, Xazax had thought he could quicken matters, take the armor before it ever reached dry land. Galeona had guided him to a fair approximation of where Norrec

Vizharan could be found. It should have been a simple matter for the hellish beast to rip the puny wooden vessel apart, then strip the armor from the dead man's body . . .

Only . . . only the armor had not only fended off the titanic creature, it had slain the demon with hardly any effort. The result had been so startling that it had sent Xazax fleeing in panic. He had never expected the enchanted armor to unleash such overwhelming power . . .

The mantis fixed his gaze on the back of the mercenary, his decision made. With Malevolyn as the warlord, Xazax had something spectacular to show his master, an ally with whom they could crush Azmodan and, if necessary, the *three*. However, with Norrec Vizharan the unwilling host, Belial would surely not be nearly so pleased.

And when his master was displeased . . . those who failed him suffered much for it.

The demon raised one sickle, biding his time. In the heat of combat, it would take only one strike. The general might complain about his loss of glory, but he would soon come around. Then, they could return to the ravaging of Lut Gholein.

And from there . . . the rest of the mortal realm.

Norrec did not even feel a fraction of the confidence he tried to portray to General Malevolyn. While his words concerning the suit's reluctance to part from him had been true, that did not mean that he trusted in the ability of the enchanted armor to defeat the helmed officer. In truth, Malevolyn looked as if the link between him and the helmet far surpassed the questionable alliance Norrec suffered. Not only did Malevolyn share in the knowledge and skills of the Warlord of Blood, but the general also had his own not inconsiderable abilities. In combination with what the helmet offered, even the armor would likely not be able to stand long against the dedicated commander.

The general came at him, attacking with such fury that the suit had to step back in order to save Norrec. Again and again the fiery blades clashed, each time sending plumes of flame flying. Had they fought in any other domain save the sandy desert, the odds of a fire starting would have been quite likely. Norrec himself worried that some stray spark would land on his hair or blind him in one eye. Bad enough already that he had to participate in the desperate struggle without having any choice as to defense or attack, for, from what he quickly saw, the armor had some gaps in its knowledge of swordplay. True, it countered Malevolyn's strikes, but Norrec watched at least one evident opening go wasted. Had not the bloody warlord learned how to properly handle a blade?

"A bit like fighting one's self, isn't it?" sneered his adversary. Augustus Malevolyn seemed to be enjoying himself, so certain of victory did he no doubt feel.

Norrec said nothing in return, wishing that, even if he had to die, it would be through his own efforts, not the failures of the enchanted armor.

Malevolyn's blade passed within inches of his head. Norrec swore, muttering quietly to the armor, "If you can't do better than that, I should be the one leading!"

"Do you really think so?" retorted the general, expression no longer amused. "You think a simpleton like you worthier to bear the title, carry on the legacy, than I would be?"

The suit suddenly had to defend against a series of lightning-swift attacks by Malevolyn. Norrec silently cursed the general's exceptional hearing; the man believed that the mercenary had mocked him.

He had served under many a skilled officer, battled many a talented foe, but Norrec could not recall any with the adaptability of Augustus Malevolyn. Only the fact that the general fought as much with Bartuc's skills as his own enabled the suit to anticipate most of his moves. Even then, if not for the other protections of the armor, Norrec would have already been dead twice.

"You are fortunate that the enchantments protect you so well." The slim commander said as he momentarily backed away. "Else this matter would have been settled already."

"But if I'd died so quickly, it would've meant that the armor wasn't as special as you hoped."

Malevolyn chuckled. "True! You have some wits about you after all. Shall we see what they look like spilled out on the sand?"

Again he thrust up, over, and around Norrec's guard. Twice Bartuc's plate nearly failed the soldier. Norrec gritted his teeth; the ancient warlord had been a good swordsman, but his methods were those of the Vizjerei. After so many years in the company of Fauztin—who could handle a sword well despite being a mage—the veteran fighter probably knew more about the advantages and disadvantages of their fighting style than even the general here. Malevolyn appeared to have accepted that melding his skills with those of Bartuc only meant the better, yet, if Norrec himself had been combatting the man, he could have possibly threatened Malevolyn's life at least twice.

He suddenly screamed, his right ear feeling as if it had burst into flames. General Malevolyn had finally landed a blow, albeit a glancing one. Unfortunately, with the magical swords even that meant an agonizing injury. Norrec's entire ear throbbed, but fortunately, despite the wound, he could still hear with it. Yet, one more strike like that . . .

If only he could enter the fight himself. If only the suit could understand that he had a better chance. He knew the weaknesses, knew also the western styles the general used. There were some tricks that Norrec doubted that even the helmed commander had learned. As a mercenary, one picked up such tricks to make up for deficiencies in formal training—and more than once they had saved the veteran.

Let me fight . . . or at least let me fight alongside you!

The suit ignored him. It deflected Malevolyn's latest attack, then tried countering with a move recognizable to the veteran from some of Fauztin's own occasional sessions of sword practice. However, Norrec also knew that the Vizjerei people had also developed a countermove to *that* attack—and a moment later Malevolyn proved him right by using it to keep the armor from succeeding.

So far, the battle had been all the general's. It could not go on much longer. Bartuc's plate might desire Norrec as its simple, malleable host, but if matters continued as they presently did, it would soon have to bow to the skill and might of General Malevolyn and his own enchanted helmet.

Caught up in his darkening thoughts, Norrec barely noticed his foe suddenly thrust toward his face. The veteran fighter immediately raised his own sword, barely pushing Malevolyn's blade aside. Had he failed to do so, the general's weapon would have cut right through Norrec's skull, coming out the back.

And then it came to Norrec that *he* and not the armor had just defended against the nearly fatal assault.

He had no time to mull over the sudden shift, for Malevolyn did not slow his advance. The would-be warlord cut again and again at Norrec, forcing him backward in the direction of the watching Xazax.

Yet, despite the precariousness of his situation, Norrec's hopes rose. If he died, he would die his own man.

Augustus Malevolyn tried a move the soldier recognized from one of his first forays as a mercenary. The maneuver took skill and cunning and oft times succeeded, but from a willing commander Norrec had learned how it could be turned to the opponent's advantage . . .

"What?" Malevolyn's gaping expression enthused Norrec Vizharan as he turned what should have been a near-mortal blow by the general into a sudden counterattack that forced the veteran's foe to retreat or lose his own head.

Wasting no time, Norrec sought to push the general back until the soft sand made the man stumble or even fall, but at the last moment, Malevolyn succeeded in turning the duel back into a stalemate.

"Well," the helmed figure gasped. "Seems that the suit can learn like a man. Interesting. I wouldn't have thought it would've known that last move."

Norrec refrained from telling him the truth. Any advantage he had, however small, he would use. Yet, he could not help keep a slight, grim smile from briefly crossing his weary visage.

"You smile? You think it learning a trick or two enough? Then let's see how it and you fare if we change the rules a little . . ."

Malevolyn's free hand suddenly came up—and a brilliant sunburst exploded in Norrec's eyes.

He swung wildly, managing twice to parry the general—then a tremendous force ripped the sword from his grip. Norrec stepped back, lost his footing— and tumbled back onto the sand.

Through vision still suffering the aftereffects of Malevolyn's treacherous spell, the fallen fighter saw the murky form of his triumphant opponent loom over him. In each hand General Malevolyn held a black sword.

"The battle is done. I will say well fought, cousin. It only occurred to me at the last that you seemed a bit more eager than earlier—as if you had joined the duel yourself. So you finally thought that working with the armor would save you? A good notion, but clearly decided upon much too late."

"Waste no time!" snapped Xazax from somewhere behind Norrec. "Strike! Strike!"

Ignoring the demon, Malevolyn hefted the two swords, admiring them. "Perfect balance in each. I can wield both with no fear of crossing myself up. Interesting, too, that yours still exists. I would have thought it would have faded away once out of your hands, but I suppose that since I immediately grabbed it, that made all the difference. Bartuc's enchantments are full of surprises, are they not?"

Still trying to focus better, Norrec suddenly felt his left hand tingle. He knew the sensation, had experienced it before. The suit intended some ploy, but exactly what ploy the fighter did not know—

Yes, he *did* know. The knowledge filled Norrec's head, instantly enabling him not only to understand the enchanted armor's part in this, but the man's as well. For this to succeed, both would have to work together. Neither alone stood a chance of success.

Norrec fought back a grin. Instead, he satisfied himself with answering his adversary. "Yes . . . they are."

The left gauntlet flared.

Norrec's lost sword transformed into an inky shadow swarming over Malevolyn's arm and head.

Swearing, the general released his grip on his own weapon and gestured toward the hungering shadow. From his mouth came ancient words, Vizjerei words. A green luminescence radiated from his fingertips, eating away in turn at the shadow.

Yet, as Malevolyn focused his attention on this new menace, Norrec leapt up at him—just as the armor had desired. As the shadow faded away under the brunt of the general's own spell, Norrec seized Malevolyn by the hands and the two wrestled. This close, neither dared use Bartuc's sorcery unless certain.

"The battle's even again, general!" murmured Norrec, for the first time feeling as if he, not anyone else, had command of the situation. The armor and he had a common goal at last—triumph over this foul foe. Exhilaration filled him as he grappled, exhilaration at the thought of Malevolyn lying dead at his feet.

And the fact that much of that newfound determination and confidence might possibly have come from a source other than himself did not enter his mind. Nor did it occur to Norrec that, if he did slay the one who wore the crimson helm—then he had as good as cursed himself to the fate that Bartuc's armor had long chosen for him.

Xazax watched the sudden turn of events with great dismay. The shifting tide in the battle had caught even him unaware and now the mortal with whom he had chosen to ally himself risked defeat. Xazax could not take that risk; he had to ensure that this duel ended with Malevolyn as the victor.

The giant mantis poised to strike—

Twenty

Kara stepped over the winding dune—and into yet another nightmare.

In the distance, black armored warriors battered at Lut Gholein's gates, shouting with a murderous glee almost inhuman. The defenders above continuously fired down at them, but curiously their many arrows had no visible effect whatsoever as far as she could see, almost as if the invaders had somehow made themselves invulnerable to mortal weapons. Judging by what else she could see, the necromancer felt fairly certain that the straining gates would soon crash inward, gaining this savage force entrance.

However, the terrible struggle there paled in her mind in comparison to the duel taking place not far from her right. She had found Norrec again, yet with him she had also found not only the demon, but a furious figure clad in armor akin to the men attacking Lut Gholein—akin, that is, save for his crimson helmet.

The necromancer immediately recognized Bartuc's helm. Now matters made more sense. The armor of the warlord sought to reunite, but it had *two* hosts with which to contend and only one who could end up with the prize. Unfortunately for Norrec, he stood to lose everything no matter what the outcome of the combat. Slay his foe and he became the armor's puppet; fail in the struggle and he died at the feet of the new Warlord of Blood.

Kara eyed the trio for several moments, trying to consider what best to do. Unable to come up with a satisfying answer, she turned back to her decaying companions. "They're locked together and the demon's only a few yards behind him! What do you—"

She talked to the air. Both Tryst and Fauztin had completely vanished, the sand revealing no trace of their path. It was as if they had simply flown into the air and vanished.

Regrettably, that left the necromancer's decision completely up to her and time looked to be rapidly running out. Norrec had brought the battle to a more even level again, but as Kara watched, the hellish mantis began to move toward the combatants. Kara could think of only one reason why he would do so at such a juncture.

Knowing that she had no other option remaining, the dark mage leapt forward, racing for the back of the imposing demon. If she could get near enough, she had a chance.

The mantis raised one wicked limb high, awaiting the ideal moment to strike . . .

Kara realized that she would not make it—unless, of course, she took a desperate gamble. In her hand the necromancer already held her ceremonial dagger, which Sadun Tryst had suggested she might need. Until now, though, her fear of possibly losing it again had kept Kara from considering such an act. The weapon was a part of her calling, a part of her very *being*.

And the only way she could possibly save Norrec.

Without hesitation, she took aim at the foul creature—

Now! Xazax thought. *Now!*

But just as the mantis chose to attack, fire burst within him, coursing through his entire body with astonishing swiftness. The monstrous insect stumbled, nearly falling on top of the two fighting figures. Xazax swiveled his head so as to see the cause of his agony and found in his back a gleaming dagger made of something other than metal. He recognized quickly the intricate runes in the protruding handle and knew then why such a minuscule weapon could cause him so much pain.

A necromancer's ceremonial dagger . . . but the only such being Xazax had come across he had quickly murdered, so surely it could not be—

But there she came, hurtling toward him despite the fact that she should have been dead. The mantis knew where he had struck her, knew that no human could have rightly survived the blow, not even those who dealt in life and death such as she.

"You cannot be!" he demanded of her, a sense of dread building quickly within. For all their chaotic origins, demons had a very set sense of how things worked. Humans were fragile; rip, stab, cut, or tear them apart in certain ways and they would die. Once dead, they stayed so unless summoned back in the form of some ghoulish servant. This female defied the rules . . . "Dead you were and dead you should stay!"

"The balance dictates the terms of life and death, demon, hardly you." She made her right hand into a fist and pointed at him.

An incredible weakness spread through the demon. Xazax teetered, then caught himself. The necromancer's spell should not have affected him so thoroughly, but with her dagger in him, he became far more susceptible to anything she cast.

That situation could not be allowed to continue long.

Summoning what reserves he had, the mantis used his upper appendages to stir up the sand, then send it flying into the face of the enchantress. As she fought to regain her sight, Xazax's middle limbs bent back in a most impossible manner and sought out the treacherous dagger.

It burned, burned terribly, but he forced himself to seize the hilt and try to pull it free. The demon roared as he tugged at the enchanted blade, so great did the pain grow.

He would rend her into bloody gobbets for this abominable act. He would pinion her, then peel away every layer of skin, every bit of muscle—all while her heart still beat.

But just as the monstrous insect felt the blade begin to loosen, the necromancer uttered her final spell.

And before Xazax's eyes materialized a luminescent being so glorious his very presence burned the eyes of the demonic mantis. He looked manlike, but with all imperfections washed away. His hair flowed golden and the beauty of his countenance affected even the demon. However, even overwhelmed by the robed figure's presence, Xazax did not fail to notice the majestic, gleaming sword that the vision wielded with expert grace . . .

"Angel!!"

Xazax knew that what he saw had to be an hallucination. Necromancers had reputations for being able to cast such terrifying illusions directly into the minds of their enemies—and yet even that knowledge could not keep the primal fear from drowning the demon's senses. In the end, Xazax only knew that one of Heaven's imperious warriors now came for *him*.

With an inhuman cry, the cowardly mantis turned from Kara and fled. As he did, the dagger slipped from his wound, causing the escaping demon to leave a steady stream of thick, black ichor trailing behind him in the sand.

Kara Nightshadow watched as her adversary disappeared into the wastes of Aranoch. She would have preferred a more final conclusion to her encounter with the mantis, but in her present state of exhaustion, that conclusion could have just as well gone against her. The spell would keep him from any foul play for some time, at least long enough, so Kara hoped, to deal with the unholy threat of the armor.

She picked up her dagger and turned to where Norrec and his own foe still battled. The necromancer frowned. If the helmed stranger won, her course would be quick and clear. The dagger would see to a swift end to the second coming of the Warlord of Blood.

And if Norrec won?

Kara had no choice there, even. Without a host, the armor could cause no more harm. Whoever won between them—she would have to make certain that the victor did not live long enough to draw another breath.

Neither Norrec nor his adversary noticed the battle taking place beside them, so desperate had their own struggle become. The gauntleted hands of the two flared again and again as dark sorceries burst into life and immediately died. Although Malevolyn did not wear the armored suit of Bartuc, the helm alone gave him strength and power matching that now wielded by a willing Norrec. Because of that, the fight continued to be a stalemate, although both men knew that eventually the end would come for one.

"I am destined to take his place!" snarled Augustus Malevolyn. "I am more than just his blood! I am his kindred spirit, his will reborn! I am Bartuc come back to the mortal plane to reclaim his rightful place!"

"You're no more his successor than I am," returned Norrec, not at all aware that his own expression matched that of the arrogant commander. "His blood is mine as well! The armor chose me! Maybe you should think about that!"

"I will not be denied!" The general slipped one boot under the soldier's leg, forcing Norrec off balance.

They tumbled to the ground, Malevolyn on top. The sand softened some of the blow when Norrec's head hit, but still the veteran fighter lay momentarily dazed. Taking advantage of the situation, General Malevolyn forced his hand toward his rival's visage.

"I will remove your face, your entire head," he hissed at Norrec. "Let us see then who the armor thinks more worthy . . ."

The general's red and black gauntlet blazed with wild magic, Malevolyn's fingers only an inch or two from making good his dire promise. One hand pinned by his foe's own and the other trapped between their armored bodies, Norrec had little hope of preventing the sadistic general from accomplishing what he desired . . .

At that moment, though, Norrec sensed movement behind him, as if a third person had joined the fray. Malevolyn looked up at the newcomer—and the triumphant sneer on his countenance switched to an expression of utter bafflement.

"You—" he managed to blurt.

Something within Norrec urged him to take advantage. He slipped the one hand free from the general's, then immediately struck Malevolyn hard in the chin. A brief burst of raw magical energy accompanied Norrec's strike, sending the helmed figure flying back as if pulled by a string attached to his head. Malevolyn dropped to the sand some distance away with a harsh thud, the general too stunned at first to rise.

Focused only on victory now, the veteran fighter rose and charged toward his fallen foe. In his growing certainty that he had been meant all along to triumph, Norrec nearly threw himself on top of the general—an action which would have cost him his life.

In Malevolyn's hand materialized one of the black blades. Norrec barely had time to twist out of its deadly reach, dropping to the sand just beside the other fighter. General Malevolyn rolled away, ending up in a crouched position. He kept the sword between them, his mocking expression quite evident even within the bloodred helmet.

"I have you now!"

Leaping forward, he *thrust*.

The tip of the ebony blade sank deep . . . deep into the chest of *General Augustus Malevolyn*.

The sinister noble's resummoning of his enchanted sword had immediately reminded Norrec that he, too, could call his own weapon back into play. In his haste to at last be done with the mercenary, Malevolyn had evidently not considered that last part. As his sword came at Norrec, Norrec rolled forward, at the same time thinking his own demonic blade into existence.

Augustus Malevolyn's thrust had come within a hair of slicing the veteran's skull in half.

Norrec's had materialized already a third of the way through his adversary's torso.

Malevolyn gaped at his wound, the blade having skewered him so quickly that his body had not quite yet registered that death was upon it. The general dropped his own weapon, which instantly faded away.

In past battles, Norrec Vizharan had taken no pleasure in the deaths of his foes. He had been paid for a task and he had performed that task, but war had never been a pleasure for him. Now, however, he felt a chill run up and down his spine, a chill that stirred him, made him desire more of such bloodshed . . .

He stood up, and walked over to the gaping general, who only now slipped to his knees.

"You don't need this any more, *cousin*."

With great force, Norrec tore the crimson helmet from Augustus Malevolyn's head. Malevolyn screamed when he did, although not from any physical pain. Norrec understood what so troubled the man more than even the lethal thrust, understood because at that moment he would have felt the same if someone had tried to rip the armor from his body. The power inherent in Bartuc's suit seduced both of them, but in Malevolyn's case, he had lost the duel and, therefore, lost all right to that power.

Laying the helmet to the side, Norrec took hold of the hilt of his sword. With easy effort, he pulled it free, then inspected the blade itself. No blood stained it. Truly a marvel. It had served him well here, served him as grandly as it had done at *Viz-jun* . . .

A gauntleted hand grabbed at him. General Malevolyn, a manic look on his face, tried desperately to grapple with Norrec.

Norrec shoved him back and grinned. "The war's over, general." He readied the sword. "Time to retire."

One easy sweep left General Augustus Malevolyn's head rolling in the sand. The headless torso joined it a moment later.

As he reached down to retrieve the fabled helmet, a feminine voice called out to the exhausted but also exhilarated veteran. "Norrec? Are you all right?"

He turned to face Kara, pleased in more than one manner by her unexpected resurrection. In the short time since they had met, she had proven her loyalty to him by sacrificing her lesser existence for his. Had she remained dead, Norrec would have honored her memory, but now that she had some-how cheated Xazax's murderous strike he instead considered her further uses. The necromancer had shown some skill and likely had more sense than the untrustworthy Galeona. Her not unpleasing face and form also made him consider her as possibly worthy of being his consort—and what sane woman would spurn the offer of becoming consort to the *Warlord of Blood*?

"I'm well, Kara Nightshadow . . . very well!" He opened his one hand and let the magical sword fall free. As the weapon vanished, Norrec took the hel-met in both hands and raised it over his head. "In fact, I am far *better* than well!"

"Wait!" The raven-tressed woman rushed up to him, concern in her almond-shaped eyes. Pretty eyes, the new warlord decided, eyes reminiscent of another woman he had briefly known during his apprenticeship in Kehjistan. "The helmet . . ."

"Yes . . . it's mine at last . . . I'm now complete."

She pressed against him, placing one hand on the breastplate. Her eyes seemed to implore. "Is this truly what you want, Norrec? After all we spoke of earlier, do you now really desire to wear the helmet, to give yourself up to Bartuc's ghost?"

"Give myself up? Woman, do you know *who* I am? I'm his own blood! Blood calls to blood, remember? In a way, I already *am* Bartuc; I just didn't know it! Who better to carry on? Who better to bear the title, the legacy?"

"Bartuc's shade himself?" she countered. "There will not be any more Norrec Vizharan, not in mind and soul . . . and if the armor has its way, I dare-say that even in form you will begin to resemble your predecessor. It will be Bartuc who wears the suit. Bartuc who reclaims his role. *Bartuc* who slaugh-ters more innocents, just as he—not you—slaughtered your *friends* . . ."

Friends. . . . The horrific images of the mangled, blood-soaked bodies of Sadun Tryst and Fauztin blossomed once more in Norrec's beleaguered mind. They had been brutally murdered and he had suffered terrible guilt for those murders for each waking moment since then. He recalled quite succinctly how the armor had slain each—and now Kara spoke of other deaths to come.

He lowered the helmet slightly, battling with himself. "No, I can't let that happen . . . I can't . . ."

His arms suddenly rose again, holding the helmet just above his head.

"No!" Norrec roared, his denial aimed now at the enchanted suit. "She's right, damn you! I won't be a part of your bloody campaign—"

But what foolishness . . . a voice so much like his own whispered in his mind. *The power is yours . . . you can do with it what you wish . . . a world of order, where no kingdom wars, where no one is poor . . . that is the true legacy . . . that is all Bartuc sought . . .*

It sounded so very good. Simply place the helmet on his head and Norrec would be able to change the world to what it should be. The demons would even serve him in this monumental task, their wills subservient to the power of the warlord. He would create a perfect realm, one that even Heaven would *envy.*

And all he had to do was put on the helmet, accept his destiny . . .

He suddenly felt Kara shift—

One hand slipped from the helmet, seizing the necromancer's own in an iron grip that made Kara gasp. From her own hand slipped a gleaming blade of what looked like bone or ivory.

She had been about to use it on him.

"Stupid female . . ." Norrec snapped, not noticing that his voice did not entirely sound as it should. He shoved her to the sand. *"Stay put! I'll deal with you in a moment!"*

Despite his warning, the dark mage tried to rise, but arms of sand arose from each side, pinning her to the ground. More sand flowed over her mouth, preventing her from casting any verbal spells.

Eyes bright in anticipation, Norrec took hold of the helmet again—and placed it on his head.

A world such as he had never known now lay open to him. He saw the might he wielded, the legions he could command. The destiny thwarted by his fellow Vizjerei could once more be attained.

The Warlord of Blood lived again.

But a warlord needed soldiers. Leaving Kara to struggle, Norrec climbed to the top of the dune and stared at Lut Gholein. With avid interest he watched the demonic warriors tear at the walls and gates. The city could not be more than a few moments from bloody destruction. He would let his horde have their fun, let them race through Lut Gholein slaying every man, woman, and child—then reveal to them his return to the mortal plane.

He imagined the blood flowing everywhere, the blood of all those who feared and hated him. The blood of those who would perish at his command—

The dune exploded around him, a pair of dark forms leaping up out of the sand. Two strong sets of hands seized his arms, twisting him back.

"Hello . . . old friend . . ." a horrifyingly familiar voice whispered on one side of him. "It's been . . . a lifetime . . . since we last . . . saw you . . ."

The hold the armor had over Norrec shattered for the moment as recognition mixed with sudden terror. "S-Sadun?"

He turned in the direction of the voice—and stared close into the peeling, decaying visage of his dead companion.

"You haven't . . . forgotten us . . . how nice . . ." The ghoulish figure smiled, revealing the blackened gums and yellowed teeth.

Unable to flee, Norrec turned his head the other way—only to find Fauztin there. The murdered Vizjerei's collar had slipped, showing the tattered, crusted gap in his throat.

"No . . . no . . . no . . ."

They pulled him back down the dune, back toward where Kara still fought to free herself.

"We tried to . . . see you on . . . the ship . . . Norrec," Tryst went on. "But you certainly . . . didn't seem . . . so willing to see . . . us . . ."

Their eyes never blinked and the stench of death became apparent the longer they held him so near. Their very presence overwhelmed Norrec so much that even the armor could not demand control. "I'm sorry! I'm so sorry! Sadun—Fauztin—I'm so sorry!"

"He's sorry . . . Fauztin," commented the wiry undead. "Did you know . . . that?"

Norrec glanced at the gaunt Vizjerei, who nodded solemnly.

"We accept . . . your apology . . . but . . . I'm afraid . . . we've no choice . . . with what we . . . now do . . . my friend . . ."

With remarkable speed and strength, Sadun Tryst tore the helmet from Norrec's head.

It felt as if the revenant had ripped the veteran's skull off as well, so great did the pain of separation feel. Now Norrec truly understood how Malevolyn had felt. He cried out, pulling at his captors with a fury even they grew hard-pressed to combat.

"Hold . . . him! Hold—"

Both gauntlets flared a furious crimson. Even caught up in the intense agony coursing through him, Norrec noted the gloves and feared . . . feared for his friends who had already died once because of his inability to do anything to stop the armor's damnable actions. That their troubled spirits had followed him, he understood completely. Such an injustice demanded retribution. Unfortunately, the armor had no intention of granting them that opportunity.

The area around Norrec exploded, sending the two undead hurtling away and ripping through the dune from which they had just descended. He stared in horror at the two bodies, fearing that once more they had perished.

"No! Not again! I won't let you do it again!" The veteran fighter seized one hand in the other and although both struggled, this time his determination proved too great even for Bartuc's legacy. Norrec tugged, using his own suffering to augment his strength . . .

The right gauntlet came free.

Without hesitation he threw it as far away as he could. Immediately the suit tried to turn that way, seek after its lost member, but Norrec would no longer be denied. He forced the armor a different direction, that of Lut Gholein, now visible through the collapsing gap in the dune.

How long he controlled the power and not the other way around, the soldier could not say. Norrec only knew that he had to try to make as much right as possible. So long as his outrage, his guilt, fueled his actions, he had the advantage—and Lut Gholein had little enough time.

He raised the free hand toward the distant city. The demons had at last torn their way past one of the gates. Norrec could hesitate no longer.

The words he spoke had never been taught to him. They had been Bartuc's words, Bartuc's magic. But Bartuc's memories—his *ancestor's* memories—had become just as much Norrec's by this point. He knew what they could do, knew what they *had* to do, and so he willingly spoke them even though that part of him still in thrall to the armor struggled to prevent it from happening.

Had he been witness to the wicked spellwork performed by Malevolyn and Xazax in the general's tent, Norrec might have noted that what he said almost sounded like Malevolyn's incantation, but chanted in reverse. As it was, he simply knew that if he did nothing, an entire city would become awash in the blood of its people.

And at the end of that incantation, the descendent of the Warlord of Blood shouted out two last words. *"Mortias Diablum! Mortias Diablum!"*

Within the gates of Lut Gholein, the defenders stood and fought, knowing already that they battled men without souls, men who were not men but something far more monstrous. Yet, the sultan's warriors braced themselves for death even as the citizens prepared to weather the dangerous storm waters and try to escape.

The captains of the ships had little hope, though, already one of their vessels swamped and another shattered against the side of the docks. The waves roared inland, making it dangerous even to stand near the water. Three men had already been washed off as they had tried to prepare the vessels for refugees.

But as all hope faded, a sight both unsettling and miraculous happened. Just within the city walls, the fiery-eyed soldiers in black stopped, turned their heads back in clear dismay—and then let loose with a chorus of unearthly, savage howls.

Then, from out of the backs of each erupted hideous, spectral forms with grotesque, inhuman faces and limbs twisted and clawed. Those who witnessed the event would later say they saw both rage and despair on those demonic faces just before the specters, screaming piteously, were cast out into Aranoch in a thousand different directions.

For a moment, the army of darkness stood at attention, weapons ready, suddenly empty eyes staring straight. Then, as if all within them had been drained away along with the phantoms, each of the monstrous soldiers began to *collapse* in on himself. One by one, then row by row, the invaders dropped— bones, faded flesh, and fragments of plate spilling into piles that left more than one of Lut Gholein's defenders unable to hold onto the contents of their own stomachs.

One of the commanders, the very one whom General Augustus Malevolyn had ordered to find Norrec Vizharan, became the first to mouth what everyone else thought. Stepping toward the nearest of the grisly sets of remains, the officer gingerly prodded it.

"They're dead . . ." he finally muttered, unable to believe he and the rest of his people would live after all. "They're dead . . . but how?"

*   *   *

"Norrec."

He turned to find Kara free, the gleaming ivory dagger ready in her hand. From his left and right came the two revenants, the determination of the dead forever tattooed on their expressions.

"Kara." He glanced at his former comrades. "Fauztin. Sadun."

"Norrec," continued the necromancer. "Please listen to me."

"No!" The mercenary instantly regretted his harsh tone. She only sought to do what even he knew had to be done. "No . . . listen to me instead. I—I've got some control over the armor now, but I can feel that already slipping away. I guess I'm just too exhausted to fight it much longer . . ."

"How could you even manage to fight it at all?"

"He is . . . Bartuc's progeny . . . after all," remarked Sadun. "Something that the . . . armor needed . . . in order to . . . fulfill its destiny . . . but that it . . . did not . . . understand worked . . . *both* ways. What other . . . answer?"

She lowered her gaze. Norrec could read the pain in them. Although a necromancer, the pale woman felt no pleasure or satisfaction in slaying one who had not chosen to cause such evil. Yet so long as he lived, all humanity lay threatened.

"You'd better do it quick. One swift thrust straight through the throat. It's the only way!"

"Norrec—"

"*Hurry*—before my mind changes!" He did not simply refer to any sudden reluctance on his part, and they all knew it. The risk remained that at any second the armor might transform him again into the ideal host for its insidious desires.

"Norrec—"

"Do it!"

"This is not . . . how it was . . . supposed to be . . ." rasped Tryst in open bitterness. "Fauztin! He swore . . . to us . . ."

The Vizjerei, of course, said nothing, instead moving toward Norrec. With great reluctance, Sadun slowly followed suit. Norrec swallowed, hoping the madness would end soon.

The hand still gloved suddenly rose.

Fauztin seized it in his own.

"Best do . . . as he says . . . necromancer . . ." a sullen Tryst murmured. "Looks like . . . we don't have . . . long . . ."

Kara came toward him, clearly steeling herself for what she had to do. "I'm sorry, Norrec. This is not how I would wish it, not as it should be . . ."

"Nor is it how it *will* be," a peculiar, almost hollow voice answered.

Horazon stood a short distance behind the necromancer, but Horazon with something different about him. The glimpse Norrec had earlier had of the ancient mage had made him think of Horazon as a cowardly looking hermit most likely bereft of most of his wits. However, this figure, while still clad in rags and with hair like uncut weeds, had a presence that made all else around him seem insignificant. Norrec had a suspicion now what had made Malevolyn look up at that most vital moment in the battle, for surely the ancient mage's appearance would have shocked the half-possessed general as well . . .

A massive, unexpected surge of bitterness and hatred welled up within the fighter, all aimed at his foul brother—

No! Horazon was not his brother! Once again the armor sought to reestablish its control, rekindle the insidious spirit of *Bartuc*. Norrec managed to fight the emotions down, but he knew that next time the suit would likely prevail.

The robed figure moved purposefully toward him and as he did, Norrec noticed a curious shimmer around him. The captive warrior squinted, trying to make out what caused it.

Horazon's entire body had been *encased* in a thin layer of glittering, almost transparent sand grains.

"Blood calls to blood," the Vizjerei murmured. His eyes stared brightly, never blinking. Even the two undead holding onto Norrec seemed taken aback by his presence. "And blood will end this travesty now."

Norrec could feel the will of the suit battering at his mind, struggling physically with his body. Only the combined efforts of he and his comrades kept it from succeeding for the moment.

"Horazon?" Kara whispered. The white-haired sorcerer glanced her way— and the woman stepped back. "No—you are *him*, but you also are *not*."

He gave her—gave all of them—a condescending smile. "This living shell is another's, a too-curious sorcerer who long ago found the Arcane Sanctuary by accident, but in the process lost his senses forever. I have watched over him ever since, feeling some responsibility . . ." Foregoing any further explanation as to what in the underground sanctum might have destroyed a mind so, the glittering figure glanced at his borrowed hands. "So fragile is flesh. More stable and lasting are earth and stone . . ."

"You!" Kara gaped, her eyes nearly as wide open as her mouth. "I know you at last! He talked to you, seemed to even obey you—the great Horazon seemed so *willing* to obey you—which made no sense until now! *You* are the presence I felt—the presence of the very *sanctuary* itself!"

He nodded, his own eyes never blinking once. "Yes . . . over time it just seemed the natural path, the natural way of things . . ."

Still battling the insidious incursions of Bartuc's enchanted armor, it took Norrec a moment longer to understand—and when he did the answer so astounded him that he nearly dropped his defenses.

Horazon and the Arcane Sanctuary were one and the *same*.

"My own mind almost shattered by what I had been through, I came here to escape the memories, escape the horror, and so I built my sanctum and dwelled underneath the sand, away from the events of the world." A smile crossed the false Horazon's face, the sort of smile attempted by someone who had all but forgotten such minor mortal practices. "And as I kept remaking my domain over and over in my own image, it became more me than the fal-tering shell I wore—until at last, one day, I gave what remained within and took upon a new, stronger, and far more durable form . . . and so I have been ever since—"

Horazon might have gone on further, but at that moment, Norrec's world turned bloodred. He felt an all-consuming rage build. He would not be denied again! Horazon had escaped his wrath at Viz-jun, but even if he had to burn away the entire desert, the *warlord* would have his final vengeance!

Horazon's puppet looked his way again, holding out one hand as if asking something of the armored figure.

A gauntlet—the same one Norrec had earlier torn off and thrown away—materialized on the aged sorcerer's own hand.

"Blood calls to blood . . . and I am calling you, brother. Our war is over. Our time is over. *We* are over. Your power negates mine. Mine negates yours. Join me now where we both belong . . . far from the sight of men . . ."

The other gauntlet tore free from Norrec, flying over to the glittering fig-ure's ungloved hand. Then, in rapid succession, each piece of armor from his legs, torso, and arms flew forth, the crimson suit quickly remaking itself bit by bit on the elder's body. Somewhere along the way, the torn, stained robe of the hermit vanished, replaced by other garments more suitable to the armor. Even the boots Bartuc had worn left Norrec to join the rest of the suit. The false Horazon raised his arms as his astonishing work went on, eyes never blink-ing, lips set grimly.

With each loss, Norrec's mind edged nearer to what it had more or less been like before the armor had claimed him. The memories and thoughts became wholly his own, not that of a murderous demon master. Yet, he could never be rid of the terrible days since the tomb, never be rid of the horrors and death of which he had played an unwilling but great part.

And when it was done, the white-haired figure stretched out a gauntleted hand again, summoning the helmet. Placing that in the crook of one arm, Horazon's puppet looked over Norrec and the others.

"It is time for the world to forget Bartuc and Horazon. You would do well to do the same, all of you."

"Wait!" Kara dared approach the enigmatic form. "One question. Please tell me—did you send this one," she indicated Horazon's host. "To find me in Lut Gholein?"

"Yes . . . I sensed something amiss and knew that a necromancer so near—a necromancer who should not be in the city above—had to be involved. I needed you closer so that I could discover why. As you slept, as you ate, I learned what I needed to know from you." He stepped back from her, from all of them. "Our conversation is at an end. I leave you on your own now. Remember this, though; the Arcane Sanctuary exists in many places, has many doorways—but I advise you now to *never* seek it again."

His darkening tone left them with no doubt as to what he meant by the last.

Horazon had no desire to be a part of the living world again. Those who would disturb him would risk much.

He suddenly seemed to lose form and substance, bits of him crumbling away as if even flesh and metal had become grains of sand. With each second, the armored mage looked less like anything mortal and more a very part of the landscape.

"Norrec Vizharan," Horazon called in that odd, echoing voice. "It is time to create your own legacy . . ."

Clad in the same garments he had worn upon entering Bartuc's tomb—even his own boots having somehow been returned to him by the astounding sorcerer—Norrec pulled free from the revenants and started forward. "Wait! What do you mean by that?"

But Horazon's host, now a man completely of sand, only shook his head. Of all of him, only the eyes remained somewhat human. Even as Norrec neared, the figure shrank, his sandy form melting into the dunes around. By the time the veteran fighter reached the area it was already too late . . . only a small lump of loose grains remained to mark Horazon's past presence.

Seconds later, even that no longer existed.

"It's over," Kara quietly remarked.

"Yes . . . it is," agreed Sadun Tryst.

Something in his tone made Norrec now turn to the two ghouls. Both undead had a peculiar look in their eye, as if they waited for something else to happen.

The necromancer guessed first. "Your quest is over, is it not? Just as with Horazon, your time in this world is at an end."

Fauztin nodded. Sadun gave what seemed a sad grin—or perhaps his failing flesh and muscle simply made it seem so. "He came . . . when he felt . . . the armor stir . . . but too late . . . so he granted us . . . this chase . . . but with . . . the promise that . . . when it finished . . . so would we."

"*He?*" Norrec asked, joining Kara.

"But it was my spell and my dagger that brought you back!"

"His trickery . . . to throw you . . . off . . ." The smaller of the undead looked around. "Sanctimonious . . . bastard . . . can't even show up . . . now that it's . . . over . . ."

However, as he finished, a brilliant blue light suddenly shone down on the four, turning their small patch of desert as bright as, if not brighter than, a cloudless day at noontime.

Sadun Tryst would have spat in disgust, if such a simple feat had been within his ability any more. Instead, he shook his head—or rather, let it rock back and forth once—then added, "Should've known . . . better . . . damned strutting . . . angel!"

Angel? Norrec looked up in the direction of the light, but found no source for it, much less an angel. Still, what else could explain so much?

The ghoul glared at it. "At least . . . show yourself . . ." When nothing happened, he glanced at Norrec and added, "Typical. Just like . . . his kind . . . hiding in the . . . shadows . . . pretending they're . . . above it all . . . but putting their hands . . . in everything."

"I know this light," Kara muttered. "I caught a glimpse of it in the tomb. It's what drew me away from your bodies."

"He likes . . . his tricks . . . the archangel does." Tryst eyed Fauztin, who nodded again. To the two living members, the wiry revenant continued, "And for his . . . last one—"

"Damn you, Sadun, no!" Norrec scowled at the heavens, scowled at the unseen archangel. "It's not fair! They had no choice in the matter—"

"Please . . . it's . . . time . . . and we . . . want it so . . . Norrec . . ."

"You can't mean it!"

Sadun chuckled, a harsh sound. "I swear it . . . on my . . . life, friend . . ."

The blue light focused suddenly on the revenants, bathing them in such brilliance that Norrec had to shield his eyes. Fauztin and the smaller ghoul became harder and harder to see.

"Time to . . . buy that . . . farm . . . you always wanted . . . Norrec . . ."

The light flared then, becoming so intense that it momentarily blinded the veteran and his companion. Fortunately for both, the burst lasted only a few seconds, but even with that, by the time their eyes recovered, it was to find that not only had the heavenly illumination completely faded away—but with it had gone the two undead.

Norrec stared at the spot, at first unable to speak.

A hand touched his own. Kara Nightshadow gave him a look of sympathy. "They have moved on to the next step in the eternal journey, on to their next role in helping to maintain the balance of the world."

"Maybe . . ." Wherever they had gone, Norrec knew that he could be of no aid to them. The best he could do was keep their memories alive in him—and do something with his own life in honor of the friendship the three had built. He glanced up again, noticed for the first time that the ever-present storm clouds had finally quieted. In fact, they had already begun to dwindle to the point where patches of clear sky could be made out.

"What will you do now?" the necromancer asked him.

"I don't know." He glanced in the direction of Lut Gholein, the only sign of civilization for days. "Go there first, I suppose. See if they need any help cleaning up. After that . . . I just don't know. What about you?"

She, too, looked to the far-off city, giving him a chance to study her profile. "Lut Gholein makes sense also. Besides, I wish to discover whether Captain Jeronnan and the *King's Shield* are there. I owe him a debt. He treated me well, as if I were his own daughter—and he probably fears I drowned at sea."

Having no desire to part from her company just yet, Norrec responded, "I'll come with you, then, if you don't mind."

That brought an unexpected smile from Kara. Norrec liked it when the dark-haired woman smiled. "Not at all."

Recalling the ways of the many nobles he had served, Norrec offered her his arm, which, after a moment's hesitation, the necromancer took. Then, together, the weary pair made their way through what remained of the ruined dune and headed back toward civilization. Neither looked behind them to where the head and body of General Augustus Malevolyn already lay half-covered by the drifting sand, where Horazon and the armor had faded into the desert itself. The weary, battered soldier especially had no desire to be reminded of what had happened—and what *could* have happened if matters had taken a turn to the dark.

The legacy of Bartuc, the legacy of the Warlord of Blood, had been buried once again from the sight and knowledge of all . . . this time hopefully forever.

EPILOGUE

Night fell upon the desert of Aranoch, a solemn, brooding night. The creatures of the day hurried to the safety of their lairs while those who hunted in the darkness came forth in search of careless prey . . .

And from beneath the sand slowly emerged a monstrous form, one that would have sent maggots, scarabs, and vulture demons fleeing in mindless panic. Mandibles snapped open and closed several times and bulbous yellow orbs that glowed faintly in the darkness carefully perused the unyielding landscape, searching . . . searching somewhat fearfully.

Xazax rose unsteadily, a pool of brackish, black fluids underneath him. The wound caused by the necromancer's dagger refused to be healed by his power and the mantis knew that he could not yet petition his lord Belial to help him. By this time, Belial would know of his failure and, worse, the decimation of the infernal horde summoned to aid General Malevolyn.

The mantis had sensed the terrible spell being cast even as he had fled. Who had been responsible for it, he could only guess, but it had meant the certain end for most of the lesser demons. Summoning such numbers in so quick a fashion had required each hellish warrior to be initially *bound* to the mortal shell they had been given. With the passing of time, even as little as a month, they would have grown more adapted to this plane, been able to fully cast off the husks. This new spell, though, had torn them from their earthly anchors far too soon. Only the strongest would survive the extraordinary forces unleashed by the abrupt separation. In human terms it would have been akin to removing a baby from the womb more than a month before its proper birth time. Only the strongest would survive . . .

The few survivors would be condemned to wander Aranoch without any guidance, unable to return to Hell without aid. Unlike Xazax, most these demons lacked sense enough to plan beyond the moment; Belial had relied on his lieutenant for their guidance.

In that lay the mantis's only hope for redemption. His dark lord might forgive him if Xazax managed to gather those who remained and sent them back to Hell. For that, the demon would need another human dupe capable of sorcery, but there were always plenty of those. Of more immediate importance, however, was the necessity of finding prey of his own, something to provide the energy he heeded to combat his wound. The mantis would have preferred a nice, ripe merchant camped out for the night, but at this point, anything he could catch would have to do.

Nervously the demon moved about on the sand. The cursed necromancer's spell still lingered, albeit with less influence than before. Illusions of angels and other fearful sights on occasion materialized before Xazax, but with effort each time he managed to fight off the urge to flee.

When he had regained his strength, recovered from his wounds, the mantis would find Norrec Vizharan and the female. He would impale each, making certain that they lived, then slowly work on peeling the flesh from first one, then the other. After that, Xazax would devour them slowly, savoring each bloody morsel—

Xazax . . .

He froze, waves of fear seeking to wash over him. *Damn the human's spell!* Would the last vestiges of it never fade away? How many illusions, how many whispering voices, would the demon have to suffer before it all stopped?

Smelled you from afar . . . knew you immediately . . .

The giant mantis looked around, but saw nothing. So, it was only in his head this time. He could suffer that well enough—

A shadow darker than the night swept across Xazax, completely startling the wounded monster.

Cunning . . . lying . . . traitorous little bug . . .

Xazax froze. None of the creations of the female's spellwork had ever spoken in his mind with such elaborate conviction.

"Who dares?" he rasped, turning in the direction from which he sensed the voice in his head somehow originated. "Who—"

And before the hellish mantis loomed the most terrible of all the nightmares he could have dreamed. The demon's mandibles stretched wide and a single, almost plaintively spoken word tried unsuccessfully to completely escape.

"Diab—"

A scream punctuated the stillness of the nighttime desert, a scream seemingly of no earthly origin. It caused the various creatures of Aranoch to pause in whatever they had been doing and listen in absolute terror. Even long after the cry abruptly cut off, they remained unmoving, fearful that whatever had preyed upon the source of the mournful sound might next be coming for them.

And among those of Belial's demons that yet survived from the debacle at Lut Gholein, that fear took a greater form. They sensed what had happened, sensed the force behind it—and knew that for them and the humans of this mortal plane the *nightmare* might just be beginning . . .

The Black Road

Mel Odom

One

Darrick Lang pulled at the oar and scanned the night-shrouded cliffs overlooking the Dyre River, hoping he remained out of sight of the pirates they hunted. Of course, he would only know they'd been discovered after the initial attack, and the pirates weren't known for their generosity toward Westmarch navy sailors. Especially ones who were hunting them pursuant to the King of Westmarch's standing orders. The possibility of getting caught wasn't a pleasant thought.

The longboat sculled against the gentle current, but the prow cut so clean that the water didn't slap against the low hull. Sentries posted up on the surrounding cliffs would raise the alarm if the longboat were seen or heard, and there would be absolute hell to pay for it. If that happened, Darrick was certain none of them would make it back to *Lonesome Star* waiting out in the Gulf of Westmarch. Captain Tollifer, the vessel's master, was one of the sharpest naval commanders in all of Westmarch under the king's command, and he'd have no problem shipping out if Darrick and his band didn't return before dawn.

Bending his back and leaning forward, Darrick eased the oar from the water and spoke in a soft voice. "Easy, boys. Steady on, and we'll make a go of this. We'll be in and out before those damned pirates know we've come and gone."

"If our luck holds," Mat Hu-Ring whispered beside Darrick.

"I'll take luck," Darrick replied. "Never had anything against it, and it seems you've always had plenty to spare."

"You've never been one to go a-courtin' luck," Mat said.

"Never," Darrick agreed, feeling a little cocky in spite of the danger they were facing. "But I don't find myself forgetting friends who have it."

"Is that why you brought me along on this little venture of yours?"

"Aye," Darrick replied. "And as I got it toted, I saved your life the last time. I'm figuring you owe me one there."

Mat grinned in the darkness, and the white of his teeth split his dark face. Like Darrick, he wore lampblack to shadow his features and make him more a part of the night. But where Darrick had reddish hair and bronze skin, Mat had black hair and was nut brown.

"Oh, but you're up and bound to be pushin' luck this night, aren't you, my friend?" Mat asked.

"The fog is holding." Darrick nodded at the billowing silver-gray gusts that stayed low over the river. The wind and the water worked together tonight, and the fog rolled out to the sea. With the fog in the way, the distance seemed even farther. "Mayhap we can rely on the weather more than we have to rely on your luck."

"An' if ye keep runnin' yer mouths the way ye are," old Maldrin snarled in his gruff voice, "mayhap them guards what ain't sleepin' up there will hear ye and let go with some of them ambushes these damned pirates has got set up. Ye know people talkin' carries easier over the water than on land."

"Aye," Darrick agreed. "An' I know the sound don't carry up to them cliffs from here. They're a good forty feet above us, they are."

"Stupid Hillsfar outlander," Maldrin growled. "Ye're still wet behind the ears and runnin' at the nose for carryin' out this here kind of work. If'n ye ask me, ol' Cap'n Tollifer ain't quite plump off the bob these days."

"An' there you have it then, Ship's Mate Maldrin," Darrick said. "No one bloody asked you."

A couple of the other men aboard the longboat laughed at the old mate's expense. Although Maldrin had a reputation as a fierce sailor and warrior, the younger men on the crew considered him somewhat of a mother hen and a worrywart.

The first mate was a short man but possessed shoulders almost an ax handle's length across. He kept his gray-streaked beard cropped close. A horseshoe-shaped bald spot left him smooth on top but with plenty of hair on the sides and in back that he tied in a queue. Moisture from the river and the fog glistened on the tarred breeches and soaked the dark shirt.

Darrick and the other men in the longboat were clad in similar fashion. All of them had wrapped their blades in spare bits of sailcloth to keep the moonshine and water from them. The Dyre River was fresh water, not the corrosive salt of the Gulf of Westmarch, but a sailor's practices in the King's Royal Navy were hard to put aside.

"Insolent pup," Maldrin muttered.

"Ah, and you love me for it even as you decry it, Maldrin," Darrick said. "If you think you're miserable company now, just think about how you'd have been if I'd up and bloody left you on board *Lonesome Star*. I'm telling you, man, I don't see you up for a night of hand-wringing. Truly I don't. And this is the thanks I get for sparing you that."

"This isn't going to be as easy as ye seem to want to believe," Maldrin said.

"And what's to worry about, Maldrin? A few pirates?" Darrick shipped his oar, watchful that the longboat crew still moved together, then eased it back into the water and drew again. The longboat surged through the river water, making good time. They'd spotted the small campfire of the first sentry a quarter-mile back. The port they were looking for wasn't much farther ahead.

"These aren't just any pirates," Maldrin replied.

"No," Darrick said, "I have to agree with you. These here pirates, now these are the ones that Cap'n Tollifer sent us to fetch up some trouble with. After orders like them, I won't have you thinking I'd just settle for any pirates."

"Nor me," Mat put in. "I've proven myself right choosy when it comes to fighting the likes of pirates."

A few of the other men agreed, and they shared a slight laugh.

No one, Darrick noted, mentioned anything of the boy the pirates had kidnapped. Since the boy's body hadn't been recovered at the site of the earlier attack, everyone believed he was being held for ransom. Despite the need to let off steam before their insertion into the pirates' stronghold, thinking of the boy was sobering.

Maldrin only shook his head and turned his attention to his own oar. "Ach, an' ye're a proper pain in the arse, Darrick Lang. Before all that's of the Light and holy, I'd swear to that. But if'n there's a man aboard Cap'n Tollifer's ship what can pull this off, I figure it's gotta be you."

"I'd doff my hat to you, Maldrin," Darrick said, touched. "If I were wearing one, that is."

"Just keep wearin' the head it would fit on if ye were," Maldrin growled.

"Indeed," Darrick said. "I intend to." He took a fresh grip on his oar. "Pull, then, boys, while the river is steady and the fog stays with us." As he gazed up at the mountains, he knew that some savage part of him relished thoughts of the coming battle.

The pirates wouldn't give the boy back for free. And Captain Tollifer, on behalf of Westmarch's king, was demanding a blood price as well.

"Damned fog," Raithen said, then swore with heartfelt emotion.

The pirate captain's vehemence drew Buyard Cholik from his reverie. The old priest blinked past the fatigue that held him in thrall and glanced at the burly man who stood limned in the torchlight coming from the suite of rooms inside the building. "What is the matter, Captain Raithen?"

Raithen stood like a mountain at the stone balcony railing of the building that overlooked the alabaster and columned ruins of the small port city where they'd been encamped for months. He pulled at the goatee covering his massive chin and absently touched the cruel scar on the right corner of his mouth that gave him a cold leer.

"The fog. Makes it damned hard to see the river." The pale moonlight glinted against the black chain mail Raithen wore over a dark green shirt. The ship's captain was always sartorially perfect, even this early in the morning. Or this late at night, Cholik amended, for he didn't know which was the case for the pirate chieftain. Raithen's black breeches were tucked with neat precision into his rolled-top boots. "And I still think maybe we didn't get away so clean from the last bit of business we did."

"The fog also makes navigating the river risky," Cholik said.

"Maybe to you, but for a man used to the wiles and ways of the sea," Raithen said, "that river down there would offer smooth sailing." He pulled at his beard as he looked down at the sea again, then nodded. "If it was me, I'd make a run at us tonight."

"You're a superstitious man," Cholik said, and couldn't help putting some disdain in his words. He wrapped his arms around himself. Unlike Raithen, Cholik was thin to the point of emaciation. The night's unexpected chill predicting the onset of the coming winter months had caught him off-guard and ill prepared. He no longer had the captain's young years to tide him over, either. The wind, now that he noticed it, cut through his black and scarlet robes.

Raithen glanced back at Cholik, his expression souring as if he were prepared to take offense at the assessment.

"Don't bother to argue," Cholik ordered. "I've seen the tendency in you. I don't hold it against you, trust me. But I choose to believe in things that offer me stronger solace than superstition."

A scowl twisted Raithen's face. His own dislike and distrust concerning what Cholik's acolytes did in the lower regions of the town they'd found buried beneath the abandoned port city were well known. The site was far to the north of Westmarch, well out of the king's easy reach. As desolate as the place was, Cholik would have thought the pirate captain would be pleased about the location. But the priest had forgotten the civilized amenities the pirates had available to them at the various ports that didn't know who they were—or didn't care because their gold and silver spent just as quickly as anyone else's. Still, the drinking and debauchery the pirates were accustomed to were impossible where they now camped.

"None of your guards has sounded an alarm," Cholik went on. "And I assume all have checked in."

"They've checked in," Raithen agreed. "But I'm certain that I spotted another ship's sails riding our tailwind when we sailed up into the river this afternoon."

"You should have investigated further."

"I did." Raithen scowled. "I did, and I didn't find anything."

"There. You see? There's nothing to worry about."

Raithen shot Cholik a knowing glance. "Worrying about things is part of what you pay me all that gold for."

"Worrying me, however, isn't."

Despite his grim mood, a small smile twisted Raithen's lips. "For a priest of Zakarum Church, which professes a way of gentleness, you've got an unkind way about your words."

"Only when the effect is deserved."

Folding his arms across his massive chest, Raithen leaned back against the balcony and chuckled. "You do intrigue me, Cholik. When we became acquainted all those months ago and you told me what you wanted to do, I thought you were a madman."

"A legend of a city buried beneath another city isn't madness," Cholik said. However, the things he'd had to do to secure the sacred and almost forgotten texts of Dumal Lunnash, a Vizjerei wizard who had witnessed the death of Jere Harash thousands of years ago, had almost driven him there.

Thousands of years ago, Jere Harash had been a young Vizjerei acolyte who had discovered the power to command the spirits of the dead. The young boy had claimed the insight was given to him through a dream. There was no doubting the new abilities Jere Harash mustered, and his power became a thing of legend. The boy perfected the process whereby the wizards drained the energy of the dead, making anyone who used it more powerful than anything that had gone on before. As a result of this new knowledge, the Vizjerei—one of the three primary clans in the world thousands of years ago— had become known as the Spirit Clans.

Dumal Lunnash had been a historian and one of the men to have survived Jere Harash's last attempt to master the spirit world completely. Upon the young man's attaining the trance state necessary to transfer the energy to the spells he wove, a spirit had taken control of his body and gone on a killing rampage. Later, the Vizjerei had learned that the spirits they called on and unwittingly unleashed into the world were demons from the Burning Hells.

As a chronicler of the times and the auguries of the Vizjerei, Dumal Lunnash had largely been overlooked, but his texts had led Cholik through a macabre and twisted trail that had ended in the desolation of the forgotten city on the Dyre River.

"No," Raithen said. "Legends like that are everywhere. I've even followed a few of them myself, but I've never seen one come true."

"Then I'm surprised that you came at all," Cholik said. This was a conversation they'd been avoiding for months, and he was surprised to find it coming out now. But only in a way. From the signs they'd been finding the last week, while Raithen had been away plundering and pillaging, or whatever it was that Raithen's pirates did while they were away, Cholik had known they were close to discovering the dead city's most important secret.

"It was your gold," Raithen admitted. "That was what turned the trick for me. Now, since I've returned again, I've seen the progress your people are making."

A bitter sweetness filled Cholik. Although he was glad to be vindicated in the pirate captain's eyes, the priest also knew that Raithen had already started thinking about the possibility of treasure. Perhaps in his uninformed zeal, he or his men might even damage what Cholik and his acolytes were there to get.

"When do you think you'll find what you're looking for?" Raithen asked.

"Soon," Cholik replied.

The big pirate shrugged. "It might help me to have some idea. If we were followed today . . ."

"If you were followed today," Cholik snapped, "then it would be all your fault."

Raithen gave Cholik a wolfish grin. "Would it, then?"

"You are wanted by the Westmarch Navy," Cholik said, "for crimes against the king. You'll be hanged if they find you, swung from the gallows in Diamond Quarter."

"Like a common thief?" Raithen arched an eyebrow. "Aye, maybe I'll be swinging at the end of a gallows like a loose sail at the end of a yardarm, but don't you think the king would have a special punishment meted out to a priest of the Zakarum Church who had betrayed his confidence and had been telling the pirates what ships carry the king's gold through the Gulf of Westmarch and through the Great Ocean?"

Raithen's remarks stung Cholik. The Archangel Yaerius had coaxed a young ascetic named Akarat into founding a religion devoted to the Light. And for a time, Zakarum Church had been exactly that, but it had changed over the years and through the wars. Few mortals, only those within the inner circles of the Zakarum Church, knew that the church had been subverted by demons and now followed a dark, mostly hidden evil through their inquisitions. The Zakarum Church was also tied into Westmarch and Tristram, the power behind the power of the kings. By revealing the treasure ships' passage, Cholik had also enabled the pirates to steal from the Zakarum Church. The priests of the church were even more vengeful than the king.

Turning from the bigger man, Cholik paced on the balcony in an effort to warm himself against the night's chill. *I knew it would come to this at some point,* he told himself. *This was to be expected.* He let out a long, deliberate breath, letting Raithen think for a time that he'd gotten the better of him. Over his years as a priest, Cholik had found that men often made even more egregious mistakes when they'd been praised for their intelligence or their power.

Cholik knew what real power was. It was the reason he'd come there to Tauruk's Port to find long-buried Ransim, which had died during the Sin War that had lasted centuries as Chaos had quietly but violently warred with the Light. That war had been long ago and played out in the east, before Westmarch had become civilized or powerful. Many cities and towns had been buried during those times. Most of them, though, had been shorn of their valuables. But Ransim had been hidden from the bulk of the Sin War. Even though the general populace knew nothing of the Sin War except that battles were fought—though not because the demons and the Light warred— they'd known nothing of Ransim. The port city had been an enigma, something that shouldn't have existed. But some of the eastern mages had chosen that place to work and hide in, and they'd left secrets behind. Dumal Lunnash's texts had been the only source Cholik had found regarding Ransim's whereabouts, and even that book had led only to an arduous task of gathering information about the location that was hidden in carefully constructed lies and half-truths.

"What do you want to know, captain?" Cholik asked.

"What you're seeking here," Raithen replied with no hesitation.

"If it's gold and jewels, you mean?" Cholik asked.

"When I think of treasure," Raithen said, "those are the things that I spend most of my time thinking about and wishing for."

Amazed at how small-minded the man was, Cholik shook his head. Wealth was only a small thing to hope for, but power—power was the true reward the priest lusted for.

"What?" Raithen argued. "You're too good to hope for gold and jewels? For a man who betrays his king's coffers, you have some strange ideas."

"Material power is a very transitory thing," Cholik said. "It is of finite measure. Often gone before you know it."

"I've still got some put back for a rainy day."

Cholik gazed up at the star-filled heavens. "Mankind is a futile embarrassment to the heavens, Captain Raithen. An imperfect vessel imperfectly made. We play at being omnipotent, knowing the potential perhaps lies within us yet will always be denied to us."

"We're not talking about gold and jewels that you're looking for, are we?" Raithen almost sounded betrayed.

"There may be some of that," Cholik said. "But that is not what drew me here." He turned and gazed back at the pirate captain. "I followed the scent of power here, Captain Raithen. And I betrayed the King of Westmarch and the Zakarum Church to do it so that I could secure your ship for my own uses."

"Power?" Raithen shook his head in disbelief. "Give me a few feet of razor-sharp steel, and I'll show you power."

Angry, Cholik gestured at the pirate captain. The priest saw waves of slight, shimmering force leap from his extended hand and streak for Raithen. The waves wrapped around the big man's throat like steel bands and shut his breath off. In the next instant, Cholik caused the big man to be pulled from his feet. No priest could wield such a power, and it was time to let the pirate captain know he was no priest. Not anymore. Not ever again.

"Shore!" one of the longboat crew crowed from the prow. He kept his voice pitched low so that it didn't carry far.

"Ship oars, boys," Darrick ordered, lifting his own from the river water. Pulse beating quicker, thumping at his temples now, he stood and gazed at the stretch of mountain before them.

The oars came up at once, then the sailors placed them in the center of the longboat.

"Stern," Darrick called as he peered at the glowing circles of light that came from lanterns or fires only a short distance ahead.

"Sir," Fallan responded from the longboat's stern.

Now that the oars no longer rowed, the longboat didn't cut through the river water. Instead, the boat seemed to come up from the water and settle with harsh awkwardness on the current.

"Take us to shore," Darrick ordered, "and let's have a look at what's what with these damned pirates what's taking the king's gold. Put us off to port in a comfortable spot, if you will."

"Aye, sir." Fallan used the steering oar and angled the longboat toward the left riverbank.

The current pushed the craft backward in the water, but Darrick knew they'd lose only a few yards. What mattered most was finding a safe place to tie up so they could complete the mission Captain Tollifer had assigned them.

"Here," Maldrin called out, pointing toward the left bank. Despite his age, the old first mate had some of the best eyes aboard *Lonesome Star*. He also saw better at night.

Darrick peered through the fog and made out the craggy riverbank. It looked bitten off, just a stubby shelf of rock sticking out from the cliffs that had been cleaved through the Hawk's Beak Mountains as if by a gigantic ax.

"Now, there's an inhospitable berth if ever I've seen one," Darrick commented.

"Not if you're a mountain goat," Mat said.

"A bloody mountain goat wouldn't like that climb none," Darrick said, measuring the steep ascent that would be left to them.

Maldrin squinted up at the cliffs. "If we're goin' this way, we're in for some climbin'."

"Sir," Fallan called from the stern, "what do you want me to do?"

"Put in to shore there, Fallan," Darrick said. "We'll take our chances with this bit of providence." He smiled. "As hard as the way here is, you know the pirates won't be expecting it none. I'll take that, and add it to the chunk of luck we're having here this night."

With expert skill, Fallan guided the longboat to shore.

"Tomas," Darrick said, "we'll be having that anchor now, quick as you will."

The sailor muscled the stone anchor up from the middle of the longboat, steadied it on the side, then heaved it toward shore. The immense weight fell short of the shore but slapped down into shallow water. Taking up the slack, he dragged the anchor along the river bottom.

"She's stone below," Tomas whispered as the rope jerked in his hands. "Not mud."

"Then let's hope that you catch onto something stout," Darrick replied. He fidgeted in the longboat, anxious to be about the dangerous business they had ahead of them. The sooner into it, the sooner out of it and back aboard *Lonesome Star*.

"We're about out of riverbank," Maldrin commented as they drifted a few yards farther downriver.

"Could be we'll start the night off with a nice swim, then," Mat replied.

"A man will catch his death of cold in that water," Maldrin grumped.

"Mayhap the pirates will do for you before you wind up abed in your dotage," Mat said. "I'm sure they're not going to give up their prize when we come calling."

Darrick felt a sour twist in his stomach. The "prize" the pirates held was the biggest reason Captain Tollifer had sent Darrick and the other sailors upriver instead of bringing *Lonesome Star* up.

As a general rule, the pirates who had been preying on the king's ships out of Westmarch had left no one alive. This time, they had left a silk merchant from Lut Gholein clinging to a broken spar large enough to serve as a raft. He'd been instructed to tell the king that one of the royal nephews had been taken captive. A ransom demand, Darrick knew, was sure to follow.

It would be the first contact the pirates had initiated with Westmarch. After all these months of successful raids against the king's merchanters, still no one knew how they got their information about the gold shipments. However, they had left only the Lut Gholein man alive, suggesting that they hadn't wanted anyone from Westmarch to escape who might identify them.

The anchor scraped across the stone riverbed, taking away the margin for success by steady inches. The water and the sound of the current muted the noise. Then the anchor stopped and the rope jerked taut in Tomas's hands. Catching the rope in his callused palms, the sailor squeezed tight.

The longboat stopped but continued to bob on the river current.

Darrick glanced at the riverbank a little more than six feet away. "Well, we'll make do with what we have, boys." He glanced at Tomas. "How deep is the water?"

Tomas checked the knots tied in the rope as the longboat strained at the anchor. "She's drawing eight and a half feet."

Darrick eyed the shore. "The river must drop considerably from the edges of the cliffs."

"It's a good thing we're not in armor," Mat said. "Though I wish I had a good shirt of chain mail to tide me through the coming fracas."

"You'd sink like a lightning-blasted toad if you did," Darrick replied. "And it may not come to fighting. Mayhap we'll nip aboard the pirate ship and rescue the youngster without rousing a ruckus."

"Aye," Maldrin muttered, "an' if ye did, it would be one of the few times I've seen ye do that."

Darrick grinned in spite of the worry that nibbled at the dark corners of his mind. "Why, Maldrin, I almost sense a challenge in your words."

"Make what ye will of it," the first mate growled. "I offer advice in the best of interests, but I see that it's seldom taken in the same spirit in which it was give. Fer all ye know, they're in league with dead men and suchlike here."

The first mate's words had a sobering effect on Darrick, reminding him that though he viewed the night's activities as an adventure, it wasn't a complete lark. Some pirate captains wielded magic.

"We're here tracking pirates," Mat said. "Just pirates. Mortal men whose flesh cuts and bleeds."

"Aye," Darrick said, ignoring the dry spot at the back of his throat that Maldrin's words had summoned. "Just men."

But still, the crew had faced a ship of dead men only months ago while on patrol. The fighting then had been brutal and frightening, and it had cost lives of shipmates before the undead sailors and their ship had been sent to the bottom of the sea.

The young commander glanced at Tomas. "We're locked in?"

Tomas nodded, tugging on the anchor rope. "Aye. As near as I can tell."

Darrick grinned. "I'd like to have a boat to come back to, Tomas. And Captain Tollifer can be right persnickety about crew losing his equipment. When we get to shore, make the longboat fast again, if you please."

"Aye. It will be done."

Grabbing his cutlass from among the weapons wrapped in the bottom of the longboat, Darrick stood with care, making sure he balanced the craft out. He took a final glance up at the tops of the cliffs. The last sentry point they'd identified lay a hundred yards back. The campfire still burned through the layers of fog overhead. He glanced ahead at the lights glowing in the distance, the clangor of ships' rigging slapping masts reaching his ears.

"Looks like there's naught to be done for it, boys," Darrick said. "We've got a cold swim ahead of us." He noticed that Mat already had his sword in hand and that Maldrin had his own war hammer.

"After you," Mat said, waving an open hand toward the river.

Without another word, Darrick slipped over the side of the boat and into the river. The cold water closed over him at once, taking his breath away, and he swam against the current toward the riverbank.

Two

Twisting and squirming, hands flailing through the bands of invisible force that held him captive, Raithen fought against Cholik's spell. Surprise and fear marked Raithen's face, and Cholik knew the man realized he wasn't facing the weak old priest he thought he'd been talking to with such disregard. The big pirate opened his mouth and struggled to speak. No words came out. At a gesture, Cholik caused Raithen to float out over the balcony's edge and the hundred-foot drop that lay beyond. Only broken rock and the tumbled remains of the buildings that had made up Tauruk's Port lay below.

The pirate captain ceased his struggles as fear dawned on his purpling face.

"Power has brought me to Tauruk's Port," Cholik grated, maintaining the magic grip, feeling the obscene pleasure that came from using such a spell, "and to Ransim buried beneath. Power such as you've never wielded. And none of that power will do you any good. You do not know how to wield it. The vessel for this power must be consecrated, and I mean to be that vessel. It's something that you'll never be able to be." The priest opened his hand.

Choking and gasping, Raithen floated back in and dropped to the stone-tiled floor of the balcony overlooking the river and the abandoned city. He lay back, gasping for air and holding his bruised throat with his left hand. His right hand sought the hilt of the heavy sword at his side.

"If you pull that sword," Cholik stated, "then I'll promote your ship's commander. Perhaps even your first mate. Or I could even reanimate your corpse, though I doubt your crew would be happy about the matter. But, frankly, I wouldn't care what they thought."

Raithen's hand halted. He stared up at the priest. "You need me," he croaked.

"Yes," Cholik agreed. "That's why I've let you live so long while we have worked together. It wasn't pleasant or done out of a weak-willed sense of fair play." He stepped closer to the bigger man sitting with his back against the railing.

Purple bruising already showed in a wide swath around Raithen's neck.

"You're a tool, Captain Raithen," Cholik said. "Nothing more."

The big man glared up at him but said nothing. Swallowing was obviously a hard and painful effort.

"But you are an important tool in what I am doing." Cholik gestured again.

Seeing the priest's fluttering hand inscribing the mystic symbols, Raithen flinched. Then his eyes widened in surprise.

Cholik knew it was because the man hadn't expected to be relieved of his pain. The priest knew healing spells, but the ones that caused injury came more readily to him these days. "Please get up, Captain Raithen. If you have led someone here and the fog has obscured their presence, I want you to handle it."

Showing restraint and caution, Raithen climbed to his feet.

"Do we understand each other?" As Cholik gazed into the other man's eyes, he knew he'd made an enemy for life. It was a pity. He'd planned for the pirate captain to live longer.

Aribar Raithen was called Captain Scarlet Waters by most of the Westmarch Navy. Very few people had survived his capture of a ship, and most ended up at the bottom of the Great Sea or, especially of late, in the Gulf of Westmarch.

"Aye," Raithen growled, but the sound wasn't so menacing with all the hoarseness in it. "I'll get right on it."

"Good." Cholik stood and looked out to the broken and gutted buildings that remained of Tauruk's Port. He pretended not to notice as Raithen left, nor did he indicate that he heard the big pirate captain's slight foot drag that told him Raithen had considered stabbing him in the back.

Metal whispered coolly against leather. But this time, Cholik knew, the blade was being returned to the sheath.

Cholik remained at the balcony and locked his knees so he wouldn't tremble from the cold or from the exhaustion he suffered from spell use. If he'd had to expend any more energy, he thought he'd have passed out and been totally at Raithen's mercy.

By the Light, where has the time gone? Where has my strength gone? Gazing up at the stars burning bright against the sable night, Cholik felt old and weak. His hands were palsied now. Most of the time he maintained control of them, but on occasion he could not. When one of those uncontrollable periods arrived, he kept his hands out of sight in the folds of his robes and stayed away from others. The times always passed, but they were getting longer and longer.

In Westmarch, it wouldn't be many more years before one of the younger priests noted his growing infirmity and brought it to the senior priest's attention. When that happened, Cholik knew he'd be shipped out from the church and placed in a hospice to help with the old and the diseased, all of them dying deaths by inches and him helping only to ease them into the grave while easing into a bed of his own. Even the thought of ending his days like that was too much.

Tauruk's Port, with Ransim buried beneath, the information gleaned from the sacred texts—those things Cholik viewed as his personal salvation. The dark forces he'd allied himself with the past few years willing, it would be.

He turned his gaze from the stars to the fogbound river. The white, cottony masses roiled across the broken land forming the coastal area. Farther north, barbarian tribes would have been a problem to their discovery, but here in the deadlands far north of Westmarch and Tristram, they were safe.

At least, Cholik mused, they were safe if Raithen's latest excursion to take a shipload of the king's gold fresh out of Westmarch had not brought someone back. He peered down at the layers of fog, but he could see only the tall masts of the pirate ships standing out against the highest wisps of silver-gray fog.

Lanterns aboard those ships created pale yellow and orange nimbi and looked like fireflies in the distance. Men's raucous voices, the voices of pirates and not the trained acolytes Cholik had handpicked over the years, called out to one another in casual disdain. They talked of women and spending the gold they'd fought for that day, unaware of the power that lay buried under the city.

Only Raithen was becoming more curious about what they sought. The other pirates were satisfied with the gold they continued to get.

Cholik cursed his palsied hands and the cold wind that swept over the Hawk's Beak Mountains to the east. If only he were young, if only he'd found the sacred Vizjerei text sooner . . .

"Master."

Startled from his musings but recovering in short order, Cholik turned. He tucked his shaking hands out of sight inside his robes. "What is it, Nullat?"

"Forgive me for interrupting your solitude, Master Cholik." Nullat bowed. He was in his early twenties, dark-haired and dark-eyed. Dirt and dust stained his robes, and scratches adorned his smooth face and one arm from an accident during the excavation only a few days ago that had claimed the lives of two other acolytes.

Cholik nodded. "You know better than to interrupt unless it was something important."

"Yes. Brother Altharin asked me to come get you."

Inside his withered chest, Cholik's heart beat faster. Still, he maintained the control he had over himself and his emotions. All of the acolytes he'd bent to his own ends feared him, and feared his power, but they remained hungry for the gifts they believed he would bestow. He intended to keep it that way. He kept silent, refusing to ask the question that Nullat had left hanging in the air.

"Altharin believes we have reached the final gate," Nullat said.

"And has Altharin halted his work?" Cholik asked.

"Of course, master. Everything has gone as you have ordered. The seals were not broken." Nullat's face creased with worry.

"Is something wrong?"

Hesitation held Nullat mute for a moment. The pirates' voices and the clangor of ships' lines and rigging against yardarms and masts continued unabated from below.

"Altharin thinks he has heard voices on the other side of the gate," Nullat said. His eyes broke from Cholik's.

"Voices?" Cholik repeated, feeling more excited. The sudden rush of adrenaline caused his hands to shake more. "What kind of voices?"

"Evil voices."

Cholik stared at the young acolyte. "Did you expect any other kind?"

"I don't know, master."

"The Black Road is not a way found by those faint of heart." In fact, Cholik had inferred from the sacred Vizjerei texts that the tiles themselves had been shaped from the bones of men and women who had been raised in a village free of evil and strife. They'd never known need or want until the population had grown large enough to serve the demons' needs. "What do these voices say?"

Nullat shook his head. "I cannot say, master. I do not understand them."

"Does Altharin?"

"If he does, master, he did not tell me. He commanded only that I come get you."

"And what does the final gate look like?" Cholik asked.

"As you told us it would, master. Immense and fearful." Nullat's eyes widened. "I've never seen anything like it."

Nor has anyone else in hundreds of years, Cholik thought. "Get a fresh torch, Nullat. We'll go have a look at what Brother Altharin has discovered." *And pray that the sacred texts were right. Otherwise, the evil that we release from behind that gate will kill us all.*

Pressed into the side of the mist-covered cliff, holding himself on his boot toes and the fingers of one hand, Darrick Lang reached for the next handhold. He was conscious of the rope tied around his waist and loins. He'd tacked the rope to a ship's spike he'd driven into the cliffside five feet below, leaving a trail of them behind him for the others to use. If he slipped and everything worked right, the rope would keep him from plunging to his death or into the river sixty feet below. If it worked wrong, he might yank the two men anchoring him to the side of the cliff down after him. The fog was so thick below that he could no longer see the longboat.

I should have brought Caron along, Darrick thought as he curled his fingers around the rocky outcrop that looked safe enough to hold his weight. Caron was only a boy, though, and not one to bring into a hostile situation. Aboard *Lonesome Star,* Caron was ruling king of the rigging. Even when he wasn't assigned aloft, the boy was often found there. Caron had a natural penchant for high places.

Resting for just a moment, feeling the trembling muscles in his back and neck, Darrick breathed out and inhaled the wet, musty smell of rock and hard-packed earth. It smelled, he couldn't help thinking, like a newly opened grave. His clothing was wet from the immersion in the river, and he was cold, but his body still found enough heat to break out in perspiration. It surprised him.

"You aren't planning on camping out up there, are you?" Mat called up. He sounded good-natured about it, but someone who knew him well could have detected the small tension in his voice.

"It's the view, you know," Darrick called down. And it amused him that they acted as if they were there for a lark instead of serious business. But it had always been that way between them.

They were twenty-three years old, Darrick being seven months the elder, and they'd spent most of those years as friends growing up in Hillsfar. They'd lived among the hill people, loaded freight in the river port, and learned to kill when barbarian tribes had come down from the north hoping to loot and pillage. When they'd turned fifteen, they'd journeyed to Westmarch and pledged loyalty in the king's navy. Darrick had gone to escape his father, but Mat had left behind a good family and prospects at the family mill. If Darrick had not left, Mat might not ever have left, and some days Darrick felt guilty about that. Dispatches from home always made Mat talk of the family he missed.

Focusing himself again, Darrick stared out across the broken land at the harbor less than two hundred yards away. Another pirate sentry was encamped on the cliff along the way. The man had built a small, yellow-tongued fire that couldn't be seen from the river.

Beyond, three tall-masted cogs, round-bodied ships built for river travel as well as coastal waters rather than the deep sea, lay at anchor in a dish-shaped natural harbor fronting the ruins of a city. Captain Tollifer's maps had listed the city as Tauruk's Port, but not much was known about it except that it had been deserted years ago.

Lanterns and torches moved along the ships, but a few also roved through the city, carried by pirates, Darrick felt certain. Though why they should be so industrious this early in the morning was beyond him. The swirling fog laced with condensation made seeing across the distance hard, but Darrick could make out that much.

The longboat held fifteen men, including Darrick. He figured that they were outnumbered at least eight to one by the pirates. Staying for a prolonged engagement was out of the question, but perhaps spiriting the king's nephew away and costing the pirates a few ships were possible. Darrick had volunteered for such work before, and he'd come through it alive.

So far, bucko, Darrick told himself with grim realization.

Although he was afraid, part of him was excited at the challenge. He clung to the wall, lifted a boot, and shoved himself upward again. The top of the cliff ledge was less than ten feet away. From there, it looked as if he could gain safe ground and walk toward the city ruins and the hidden port. His fingers and toes ached from the climb, but he put the discomfort out of his mind and kept moving.

When he reached the clifftop, he had to restrain a cry of triumph. He turned and looked back down at Mat, curling his hand into a fist.

Even at the distance, Darrick saw the look of horror that filled Mat's face. "Look out!"

Whipping his head back up, some inner sense warning him of the movement, Darrick caught a glimpse of moonlight-silvered steel sweeping toward him. He pulled his head down and released his hold on the cliff as he grabbed for another along the cliff's edge.

The sword chopped into the stone cliff, striking sparks from the high iron ore content just as Darrick's hands closed around the small ledge he'd pushed up from last. His body slammed hard against the mountainside.

"I told you I saw somebody out here," a man said as he drew his sword back again and stepped with care along the cliff's edge. His hobnailed boots scraped stone.

"Yeah," the second man agreed, joining the first in the pursuit of Darrick.

Scrambling, holding tight to the edge of the cliff, Darrick pressed his boots against the stone and tried in vain to find suitable purchase to allow him to push himself up. He gave thanks to the Light that the pirates were almost as challenged by the terrain as he was. His boot soles scraped and slid as he tried to pull himself up.

"Cut his fingers off, Lon," the man in back urged. He was a short, weasel-faced man with an ale belly pressing against his frayed shirt. Maniacal lights gleamed in his eyes. "Cut his fingers off, and watch him fall on the others down there. Before they can make it up, we can nip on down to the bonfire and warn Captain Raithen they's coming."

Darrick filed the name away. During his years as part of the Westmarch Navy, he'd heard of Raithen. In fact, Captain Tollifer had said that the Captain's Table, the quarterly meeting of chosen ships' captains in Westmarch, had suggested Raithen as a possible candidate for the guilty party in the matter of the pirate raids. It was good to know, but staying alive to relate the news might prove difficult.

"Stand back, Orphik," Lon growled. "You keep a-buzzing around me like a bee, and I'm gonna stick you myself."

"Shove off, Lon. I'll do for him." The little man's voice tittered with naked excitement.

"Damn you," Lon cursed. "Get out of the way."

Quick as a fox in a henhouse, Orphik ducked under his companion's outstretched free arm and dashed at Darrick with long-bladed knives that were almost short swords in their own right. He laughed. "I've got him, Lon. I've got him. Just sit you back and watch. I bet he screams the whole way down."

Keeping his weight distributed as evenly as possible, going with the renewed strength that flowed through his body from the adrenaline surge, Darrick swung from hand to hand, dodging the chopping blows Orphik delivered. Still, one of the pirate's attempts slashed across the knuckle of his left hand's little finger. Pain shot up Darrick's arm, but he was more afraid of how the blood flow would turn his grip slippery.

"Damn you!" Orphik swore, striking sparks from the stone again. "Just stay still, and this will be over with in a trice."

Lon reeled back away from the smaller man. "Look out, Orphik! Someone down there has a bow!" The bigger pirate held up a sleeve and displayed the arrow that had caught on its fletchings and still hung there.

Distracted by the presence of the arrow and aware that another could be joining it at any moment, Orphik stepped back a little. He drew up a boot and lashed out at his intended victim's head.

Darrick swung to one side and grabbed for the little man's leg with his bloody hand, not wanting to trade it for the certain grip of his right. He knotted his fingers in the pirate's breeches. Even though the breeches were tucked into the hobnailed boots, there was plenty of slack to seize. Balancing his weight from one hand on the cliff, Darrick yanked hard with the other.

"Damn him! Lon, give me your hand before this bilge rat yanks me off the cliff!" Orphik reached for the other man, who caught his hand in his own. Another arrow fired from below clattered against the cliff wall behind them and caused them both to duck.

Taking advantage of the confusion, knowing he'd never get a better chance, Darrick swung his weight to the side and up. He pushed his feet ahead of him, throwing his body behind, hoping to clear the cliff's edge or he would fall. Maybe the rope tied around his loins would hold him, or maybe Mat and the other men below had forgotten it in the mad rush of events.

Arching his body and rolling toward the ledge, Darrick hit hard. He started to fall, then threw an arm forward in desperation, praying it would be enough. For a gut-wrenching moment, he teetered on the edge, then the point of balance shifted, and he sprawled facedown on the ledge.

Three

Buyard Cholik followed Nullat down through the twisting bowels of Tauruk's Port into the pockets of pestilence that remained of Ransim. Enclosed in the rock and strata that were the younger city's foundation, the harbor seemed a million miles away, but the chill that had followed the fog into the valley remained with the old priest. Aches and pains he'd managed to keep warm in his rooms now returned with a vengeance as he made his way through the tunnels.

The acolyte carried an oil torch, and the ceiling was so low that the writhing flames left immediate traces of lampblack along the granite surfaces. Filled with nervous anxiety, Nullat glanced from left to right, his head moving like a fast metronome.

Cholik ignored the acolyte's apprehensions. In the beginning, when the digging had begun in earnest all those months ago, Tauruk's Port had been plagued with rats. Captain Raithen had suggested that the rats had infested the place while trailing after the camp lines of the barbarians who came down out of the frozen north. During hard winters, and last year's was just such a one, the barbarians found warmer climes farther south.

But there was something else the rats had fed on as well after they'd reached Tauruk's Port. It wasn't until after the excavation had begun that Cholik realized the horrible truth of it.

During the Sin War, when Vheran constructed the mighty gate and let Kabraxis back into the worlds of men, spells had been cast over Tauruk's Port to protect it and hide it from the war to the east. Or maybe the city had been called Ransim at that time. Cholik hadn't yet found a solid indication of which city had been ensorcelled.

The spells that had been cast over the city had raised the dead, giving them a semblance of life to carry out the orders of the demons who had raised them. Necromancy was not unknown to most practitioners of the Arts, but few did more than dabble in them. Most people believed necromancy often linked the users to the demons such as Diablo, Baal, and Mephisto, collectively called the Prime Evils. However, necromancers from the cult of Rathma in the eastern jungles fought for the balance between the Light and the Burning Hells. They were warriors pure of heart even though most feared and hated them.

The first party of excavators to punch down through the bottom layer of Tauruk's Port had discovered the undead creatures that yet lurked in the ruins of the city below. Cholik guessed that whatever demon had razed Ransim had been sloppy with its spellwork or had been in a hurry. Ransim had been invaded, the burned husks of buildings and carnage left behind offered mute testimony to that, and all among them had been slain. Then someone with considerable power had come into the city and raised the dead.

Zombies rose from where fresh corpses lay, and even skeletons in the grave-yards had clawed their way free of their earthen tombs. But not all of them had made the recovery to unlife in time to go with whatever master had sum-moned them. Perhaps, Cholik had thought on occasion, it had taken years or decades for the rest of the populace to rise.

But those dead had risen, their flesh frozen somehow in a nether point short of death. Their limbs had atrophied, but their flesh had only withered without returning to the earth. And when the rats had come, they'd funneled down through the cracks and the crevices of Tauruk's Port to get to the city below. Since that day, the rats had feasted, and their population had reached prodi-gious numbers.

Of course, when presented with prey that could still fight even though a limb was gnawed off or a human with fresh blood that would lie down and die if dealt enough injury, the rats had chosen to stalk the excavation parties. For a time, the attrition rate among the diggers had been staggering. The rats had proven a resilient and resourceful enemy over the long months.

Captain Raithen had been kept busy raiding Westmarch ships, then buying slaves with Cholik's share of the gold. More gold had gone to the mercenaries whom the priest employed to keep the slaves in line.

"Step carefully, master," Nullat said, raising the torch so the light showed the yawning black pit ahead. "There's an abyss here."

"There was an abyss there the last time I came this way," Cholik snapped.

"Of course, master. I just thought perhaps you'd forgotten because it has been so long since you were down here."

Cholik made his voice cold and hard. "I don't forget."

Nullat's face blanched, and he cut his eyes away from the priest's. "Of course you don't, master. I only—"

"Quiet, Nullat. Your voice echoes in these chambers, and it wearies me." Cholik walked on, watching as Nullat flinched from a sudden advance of a red-eyed rat pack streaming along the pile of broken boulders to their left.

As long as a man's arm from elbow to fingertips, the rats raced over the boul-ders and one another as they fought to get a closer view of the two travelers. They chattered and squeaked, creating an undercurrent of noise that pealed throughout the chamber. Sleek black fur covered them from their wet noses to their plump rumps, but their tails remained hairless. Piles of old bones, and per-haps some new ones as well, adorned the heaps of broken stone, crumbled mor-tise work, and splintered debris left from dwellings.

Nullat stopped and, trembling, held the torch out toward the rat pack. "Master, perhaps we should turn back. I've not seen such a gathering of rats in weeks. There are enough of them to bring us down."

"Be calm," Cholik ordered. "Let me have your torch." The last thing he wanted was for Nullat's ravings to begin talk of an omen again. There had been far too much of that.

Hesitating a moment as if worried Cholik might take the torch from him and leave him in the darkness with the rats, Nullat extended the torch.

Cholik gripped the torch, steadying it with his hand. He whispered words of prayer, then breathed on the torch. His breath blew through the torch and became a wave of flame that blasted across the piles of stones and debris like a blacksmith's furnace as he turned his head from one side to the other across the line of rats.

Crying out, Nullat dropped and covered his face, turning away from the heat and knocking the torch from Cholik's grasp. The torch licked at the hem of Cholik's robes.

Yanking his robes away, the priest said, "Damn you for a fool, Nullat. You've very nearly set me on fire."

"My apologies, master," Nullat whimpered, jerking the torch away. He moved it so fast that the speed almost smothered the flames. A pool of glistening oil burned on the stone floor where the torch had lain.

Cholik would have berated the man further, but a sudden weakness slammed into him. He tottered on his feet, barely able to stand. He closed his eyes to shut out the vertigo that assailed him. The spell, so soon after the one he'd used against Raithen and so much stronger, had left him depleted.

"Master," Nullat called out.

"Shut up," Cholik ordered. The hoarseness of his voice surprised even him. His stomach rolled at the rancid smell of burning flesh that had filled the chamber.

"Of course, master."

Forcing himself to take a breath, Cholik concentrated on his center. His hands shook and ached as if he'd broken every one of his fingers. The power that he was able to channel was becoming too much for his body. *How is it that the Light can make man, then permit him to wield powerful auguries, only to strip him of the mortal flesh that binds him to this world?* It was that question that had begun turning him from the teachings of the Zakarum Church almost twenty years ago. Since that time, he had turned his pursuits to demons. They, at least, gave immortality of a sort with the power they offered. The struggle was to stay alive after receiving it.

When the weakness had abated to a degree, Cholik opened his eyes.

Nullat hunkered down beside him.

An attempt to make himself a smaller target if there are any vengeful rats left, Cholik felt certain. The priest gazed around the chamber.

The magical fire had swept the underground chamber. Smoking and blackened bodies of rats littered the debris piles. Burned flesh had sloughed from bone and left a horrid stink. Only a few slight chitterings of survivors sounded, and none of them seemed inclined to come out of hiding.

"Get up, Nullat," Cholik ordered.

"Yes, master. I was only there to catch you if you should fall."

"I will not fall."

Glancing to the side of the trail as they went on, Cholik gazed down into the abyss to his left. Careful exploration had not proven there was a bottom to it, but it lay far below. The excavators used it as a pit for the bodies of dead slaves and other corpses and the debris they had to haul out of the recovered areas.

Despite the fact that he hadn't been down in the warrens beneath Tauruk's Port in weeks, Cholik had maintained knowledge of the twisting and turning tunnels that had been excavated. Every day, he scoured through all manner of things the crews brought to the surface. He took care in noting the more important and curious pieces in journals that he kept. Back in Westmarch, the information he'd recorded on the dig site alone would be worth thousands in gold. If money would have replaced the life and power he was losing by degrees, he'd have taken it. But money didn't do those things; only the acquisition of magic did that.

And only demons gave so generously of that power.

The trail they followed kept descending, dipping down deep into the mountainside till Cholik believed they might even be beneath the level of the Dyre River. The constant chill of the underground area and the condensation on the stone walls further lent to that assumption.

Only a few moments later, after branching off into the newest group of tunnels that had been made through Ransim's remains, Cholik spotted the intense glare created by the torches and campfires the excavation team had established. The team had divided into shifts, breaking into groups. Each group toiled sixteen hours, with an eight-hour overlap scheduled for clearing out the debris that had been dug out of the latest access tunnels. They slept eight hours a day because Cholik found that they couldn't be worked any more than sixteen hours without some rest and sleep and still stay healthy for any appreciable length of time.

The mortality rate had been dimmed by such action and the protective wards Cholik had set up to keep the rats and undead at bay, but it had not been eradicated. Men died as they worked there, and Cholik's only lament was that it took Captain Raithen so long to find replacements.

Cholik passed through the main support chamber where the men slept. He followed Nullat's lead into one of the new tunnels, skirting the piles of debris that fronted the entrance and the first third of the tunnel. The old priest passed the confusion with scant notice, his eyes drawn to the massive gray and green door that ended the tunnel.

Men worked on the edges of the massive door, standing on ladders to reach the top at least twenty feet tall. Hammers and chisels banged against the rock, and the sound echoed in the tunnel and the chamber beyond. Other men shoveled refuse into wheelbarrows and trundled them to the dumpsites at the front of the tunnel.

The torchlight flickered over the massive door, and it inscribed the symbol raised there for all to see. The symbol consisted of six elliptical rings, one spaced inside another, with a twisting line threading through them in yet another pattern. Sometimes the twisting line went under the elliptical rings, and sometimes it went over.

Staring at the door, Cholik whispered, "Kabraxis, Banisher of the Light."

"Get him! Get him! He's up here with us!" Orphik screamed.

Glancing up, not wanting to leap into the path of the little man's knives as he came at him on the cliff ledge, Darrick watched the pirate start for him. The hobnailed boots scratched sparks from the granite ledge.

"Bloody bastard nearly did for me, Lon," Orphik crowed as he made his knives dance before him. "You stay back, and I'll slit him between wind and water. Just you watch."

Darrick had only enough time to push himself up on his hands. His left palm, coated in blood from his sliced finger, slipped a little and came close to going out from under him. But his fingers curled around a jutting rocky shelf, and he hurled himself to his feet.

Orphik swung his weapons in a double slash, right hand over left, scissoring the air only inches from Darrick's eyes. He took another step back as the wiry little pirate tried to get him again with backhanded swings. Unwilling to go backward farther, knowing that a misstep along the narrow ledge would prove fatal, Darrick ducked below the next attack and stepped forward.

As he passed the pirate, Darrick drew the long knife from his left boot, feeling it slide through his bloody fingers for just a moment. Then he curled his hand around the weapon as Orphik tried to spin to face him. Without mercy, knowing he'd already been offered no quarter, Darrick slashed at the man's boot. The leather parted like butter at the knife's keen kiss, and the blade cut through the pirate's hamstring.

Losing control over his crippled foot, Orphik weaved off-balance. He cursed and cried for help, struggling to keep the long knives before him in defense.

Darrick lunged to his feet, slapping away Orphik's wrists and planting a shoulder in the smaller man's midsection. Caught by Darrick's upward momentum and greater weight, Orphik left his feet, looking as if he'd jumped up from the ledge. The pirate also went out over the dizzying fall to the river below, squalling the whole way and flailing his arms. He missed Mat and the other sailors by scant inches, and only then because they'd all seen what had happened and had flattened themselves against the cliff wall.

Dropping to his knees and grabbing for the wall behind him, clutching the thick root from the tree on the next level of the cliffs that he spotted from the corner of his eye, Darrick only just prevented his own plunge over the cliff's side. He gazed down, hypnotized by the suddenness of the event.

Orphik missed the river's depths, though. The little pirate plunged head-first into the shallows and struck the rocky bottom. The sickening crunch of his skull bursting echoed up the cliff.

"Darrick!" Mat called up.

Realizing the precariousness of his position, Darrick turned toward the other pirate, thinking the man might already be on top of him. Instead, Lon had headed away, back up the ledge that led to the passable areas on the mountains. He covered ground in long-legged strides that slammed and echoed against the stone.

"He's makin' for the signal fire," Mat warned. "If he gets to it, those pirates will be all over us. The life of the king's nephew will be forfeit. Maybe our own as well."

Cursing, Darrick shoved himself up. He started to run, then remembered the rope tied around his loins. Thrusting his knife between his teeth, he untied the knots with his nimble fingers. He spun and threw the rope around the tree root with a trained sailor's skill and calm in the face of a sudden squall, gazing up the rocky ledge after the running pirate. *How far away is the signal fire?*

When he had the rope secure, giving Lon only three more strides on his lead, Darrick yanked on the rope, testing it. Satisfied, he called down, "Rope's belayed," then hurled himself after the fleeing pirate.

"Get up and get dressed," Captain Raithen ordered without looking at the woman who lay beside him.

Not saying a word, having learned from past mistakes that she wasn't supposed to talk, the woman got up naked from the bed and crossed the room to the clothing she'd left on a chest.

Although he felt nothing for the woman, in fact even despised her for revealing to him again the weakness he had in controlling his own lusts, Raithen watched her as she dressed. He was covered in sweat, his and hers, because the room was kept too hot from the roaring blaze in the fireplace. Only a few habitable houses and buildings remained in Tauruk's Port. This inn was one of those. The pirates had moved into it, storing food and gear and the merchandise they'd taken from the ships they'd sunk.

The woman was young, and even the hard living among the pirates hadn't done much to destroy the slender lines and smooth muscles of her body. Half-healed cuts showed across the backs of her thighs, lingering evidence of the last time Raithen had disciplined her with a horsewhip.

Even now, as she dressed with methodical deliberation, she used her body to show him the control she still felt she had over him. He hungered for her even though he didn't care about her, and she knew it.

Her actions frustrated Raithen. Yet he hadn't had her killed out of hand. Nor had he allowed the other pirates to have at her, keeping her instead for his own private needs. If she were dead, none of the other women they'd taken from ships they raided would satisfy him.

"Do you think you're still so proud in spirit, woman?" Raithen demanded.

"No."

"You trying to rub my nose in something here, then?"

"No." Her answer remained calm and quiet.

Her visible lack of emotion pushed at the boundaries of the tentative control Raithen had over his anger. His bruised neck still filled his head with blinding pain, and the humiliation he'd received at Cholik's hands wouldn't leave him.

He thought again of the way the old priest had suspended him over the long drop from the rooms he kept in the city ruins, proving that he wasn't the old, doddering fool Raithen had believed him to be. The pirate captain reached for the long-necked bottle of wine on the small stand by the bed. Gold and silver weren't the only things he and his crew had taken from the ships they'd raided.

Taking the cork from the bottle, Raithen took a long pull of the dark red wine inside. It burned the back of his throat and damn near made him choke, but he kept it down. He wiped his mouth with the back of his hand and glanced at the woman.

She stood in a simple shift by the trunk, no shoes on her feet. After the beating he'd given her the first time, she wouldn't dream of leaving without his permission. Nor would she ask for it.

Raithen put the cork back into the wine bottle. "I've never asked you your name, woman."

Her chin came up a little at that, and for a moment her eyes darted to his, then flicked away. "Do you want to know my name?"

Raithen grinned. "If I want you to have a name, I'll give you one."

Cheeks flaming in sudden anger and embarrassment, the woman almost lost control. She forced herself to swallow. The pulse at the hollow of her throat thundered.

Grabbing the blanket that covered him, Raithen wiped his face and pushed himself from the bed. He'd hoped to drink enough to sleep, but that hadn't happened.

"Were you an important person in Westmarch, woman?" Raithen pulled his breeches on. He'd left his sword and knife within easy reach out of habit, but the woman had never looked too long at either of them. She'd known they were a temptation she could ill afford.

"I'm not from Westmarch," the woman answered.

Raithen pulled on his blouse. He had other clothing back on his ship, and a hot bath as well because the cabin boy would know better than to let the water grow cold. "Where, then?"

"Aranoch."

"Lut Gholein? I thought I'd detected an accent in your words."

"North of Lut Gholein. My father did business with the merchants of Lut Gholein."

"What kind of business?"

"He was a glassblower. He produced some of the finest glassware ever made." Her voice broke a little.

Raithen gazed at her with cold dispassion, knowing he understood where the emotion came from. Once he'd found it, he couldn't resist turning the knife. "Where is your father now?"

Her lips trembled. "Your pirates killed him. Without mercy."

"He was probably resisting them. They don't much care for that because I won't let them." Raithen raked his disheveled hair with his fingers.

"My father was an old man," the woman declared. "He couldn't have put up a fight against anyone. He was a kind and gentle soul, and he should not have been murdered."

"Murdered?" Raithen threw the word back at her. In two quick steps, he took away the distance that separated them. "We're pirates, woman, not bloody murderers, and I'll have you speak of that trade with a civil tongue."

She wouldn't look at him. Her eyes wept fearful tears, and they tracked down her bruised face.

Tracing the back of his hand against her cheek, Raithen leaned in and whispered in her ear. "You'll speak of me, too, with a civil tongue, or I'll have that tongue cut from your pretty head and let my seadogs have at you."

Her head snapped toward him. Her eyes flashed, reflecting the blaze in the fireplace.

Raithen waited, wondering if she would speak. He taunted her further. "Did your father die well? I can't remember. Did he fight back, or did he die screaming like an old woman?"

"Damn you!" the woman said. She came around on him, swinging her balled fist at the end of her right arm.

Without moving more than his arm, Raithen caught the woman's fist in one hand. She jerked backward, kicking at his crotch. Turning his leg and hip, the pirate captain caught the kick against his thigh. Then he moved his shoulders, backhanding her across the face.

Propelled by the force of the blow, the woman stumbled across the room and smacked against the wall. Dizzy, her eyes rolling back up into her head for a moment, she sank down splay-legged to her rump.

Raithen sucked at the cut on the back of his hand that her teeth had caused. The pain made him feel more alive, and seeing her helpless before him made him feel more in control. His neck still throbbed, but the humiliation was shared now even though the woman didn't know it.

"I'll kill you," the woman said in a hoarse voice. "I swear by the Light and all that's holy that if you do not kill me, I will find a way to kill you." She wiped at her bleeding mouth with her hand, tracking crimson over her fingers.

Raithen grinned. "Damn me for a fool, but you do me well, wench. Spoken like you'd looked deep inside my own heart." He gazed down at her. "See? Now, most people would think you were only talking. Running your mouth to play yourself up, to make yourself feel maybe a little braver. But I look into your eyes, and I know you're speaking the truth."

"If I live," the woman said, "you'll need to look over your shoulder every day for the rest of your life. Because if I ever find you, I *will* kill you."

Still grinning, feeling better about life in general and surprised at how it had all come about, Raithen nodded. "I know you will, woman. And if I was an overconfident braggart like a certain old priest, let's say, I'd probably make the mistake of humbling you, then leaving you alive. Most people you could probably terrify and never have to worry about."

The woman pushed herself to her feet in open rebellion.

"But you and me, woman," Raithen went on, "we're different. People judge us like we were nothing, that everything we say is just pomp and doggerel. They don't understand that once we start hating them and plotting for them to fall, we're only waiting for them to show a weakness we can exploit." He paused. "Just like you'll suffer through every indignity I pass on your way to break you, and then remain strong enough to try to kill me."

She stood and faced him, blood smearing her chin.

Raithen smiled at her again, and this time the effort was warm and genuine. "I want to thank you for that, for squaring my beam and trimming my sails. Reminds me of the true course I have to follow in this endeavor. No matter how many scraps Loremaster Buyard Cholik tosses my way, I'm no hound to be chasing bones and suffering ill use at his hands." He crossed to her.

This time she didn't flinch away from him. Her eyes peered at him as if she were looking through him.

"You have my thanks, woman." Raithen bent, moving his lips to meet hers.

Moving with speed and determination that she hadn't been showing, the woman sank her teeth into the pirate captain's throat, chewing toward his jugular.

FOUR

Darrick drove his feet against the rocky ledge, aware of the dizzying sight of the fogbound river lying below. Here and there, moonlight kissed the surface, leaving bright diamonds in its wake. His breath whistled at the back of his throat, coming hard and fast. Knowing that Mat and the other sailors were already clambering up the rope cheered Darrick a little. Plunging through the darkness and maybe into a small party of pirates encamped along the cliff wasn't a pleasant prospect.

He carried his knife in his hand but left his cutlass in its scabbard at his side.

The heavy blade thumped against his thigh. Covering his face with his empty hand and arm, he managed to keep the fir and spruce branches from his eyes. Other branches struck his face and left welts.

The big pirate followed a game trail through the short forest of conifers, but he left it in a rush, plunging through a wall of overgrown brush and disappearing.

Darrick redoubled his efforts, almost overrunning his own abilities after the long, demanding climb up the mountainside. Black spots swam in his vision and he couldn't get enough air in his lungs.

If the pirates discovered them, Darrick knew he and his group of warriors had little chance of reaching *Lonesome Star* out in the Gulf of Westmarch before the pirate ships overtook them. At the very least, they'd be killed out of hand, perhaps along with the young boy who had been taken captive.

Darrick reached the spot where the pirate had lunged through the brush and threw himself after the man. Almost disoriented in the darkness of the forest, he lost his bearings for a moment. He glanced up automatically, but the thick tree canopy blocked sight of the stars, so he couldn't set himself straight. Relying on his hearing, tracking the bigger man's passage through the brush, Darrick kept running.

Without warning, something exploded from the darkness. There was just enough ambient light for Darrick to get an impression of large leathery wings, glistening black eyes, and shiny white teeth that came at him. At least a dozen of the bats descended on him, outraged at the pirate's passing. Their harsh squeals were near deafening in the enclosed space, and their sharp teeth lit fiery trails along his flesh for an instant.

Darrick lashed out with his knife and never broke stride. The grimsable bats were noted for their pack-hunting abilities and often tracked down small game. Though he'd never seen it himself, Darrick had heard that flocks of the blood-drinking predators had even brought down full-grown men and stripped the flesh from their bones.

Only a short distance ahead, with the bats searching without success behind him, Darrick tripped over a fallen tree and went sprawling. He rolled with it, maintaining his hard-fisted grasp on the knife. The cutlass smashed against his hip with bruising force. Then he was up again, alert to the shift in direction his quarry had taken.

Breath burning the back of his throat, Darrick raced through the forest. His heart triphammered inside his chest, and his hearing was laced with the dulled roaring of blood in his ears. He caught a tree with his free hand and brought himself around in a sharp turn as the bark tore loose from the trunk.

The big pirate wasn't faring well, either. His breathing was ragged and hoarse, and there was no measured cadence left to it.

Given time, Darrick knew he could run the man to ground. But he was almost out of time. Even now he could see the flickering yellow light of a campfire glimmering in the darkness through the branches of the fir and spruce trees.

The pirate burst free of the forest and ran for the campfire.

Trap? Darrick wondered. *Or desperation? Could be he's more afraid of Captain Raithen's rage than he is that I might overtake him.* Even the Westmarch captains showed harsh discipline. Darrick bore scars from whips in the past as he'd fought and shoved his way up through the ranks. The officers had never dished out anything more than he could bear, and one day some of those captains would regret the punishments they'd doled out to him.

Without hesitating, knowing he had no choice about trying to stop the man, Darrick charged from the forest, summoning his last bit of energy. If there were more men than the one surviving pirate, he knew he was done for. He leaned into his running stride, coming close to going beyond his own control.

The campfire was set at the bottom of a low promontory. The twisting flames scrawled harsh shadows against the hollow of the promontory. Above it, only a short distance out of easy reach, the small cauldron of pitch blend that was the intended signal pot hung from a trio of crossed branches set into the ground.

Darrick knew the signal pot was in clear view of the next post up the river. Once the pirate ignited the pitch blend, there was no way to stop the signal.

Wheezing and gasping for air, the pirate reached the campfire and bent down, grabbed a nearby torch, and shoved it into the flames. The torch caught at once, burning blue and yellow because the pitch had been soaked in whale oil. Holding the torch in one hand, the big pirate started up the promontory, making the climb with ease.

Darrick threw himself at the pirate, hoping he had enough strength and speed left to make the distance. He caught the pirate knee-high with his shoulders, then slammed his face against the granite mountainside. Dazed, he felt the pirate fall back across him, and they both slid down the steep incline over the broken rock surface.

The pirate recovered first, shoving himself to his feet and pulling his sword. Light from the campfire limned his face, revealing the fear and anger etched there. He took a two-handed hold on his weapon and struck.

Darrick rolled away from the blade, almost disbelieving when the sword missed him. Still in motion, he rolled to a kneeling position, then drew his cutlass as he pushed himself to his feet. Knife in one hand and cutlass in the other, he set himself to face the pirate almost twice his size.

New agony flared through Raithen as the woman ground her teeth in his neck. He felt his own warm blood spray down his neck, and panic welled from deep inside him, hammering at the confines of his skull like a captive tiger in a minstrel show. For one frightening moment he thought a vampire had attacked him. Maybe the woman had found a way to trade her essence to one of the undead monsters that Raithen suspected Buyard Cholik hunted through the ruins of the two cities.

Mastering the cold fear that ran rampant along his spine, Raithen tried to back away. *Vampires aren't real!* he told himself. *I've never seen one.*

Sensing his movement, the woman butted into him, striking his chin with the top of her head, and threw her arms around him, holding tight as a leech. Her lips and teeth searched out new places, rending his flesh.

Screaming in pain, surprised at her maneuver even though he'd been expecting her to do something, Raithen shook and twisted his right arm. The small throwing knife concealed in a cunning sheath there dropped into his waiting palm butt-first. He wrapped his fingers around the knife haft, turned his hand, and drove it into the woman's stomach.

Her mouth opened in a strained gasp that feathered over his cheek. She released his neck and wrapped her hands around his forearm, pushing to pull the knife from her body. She shook her head in denial and stumbled back.

Grabbing the back of her head, knotting his fingers in her hair so she couldn't just slip away from him and maybe even make it through the doorway out of the room, Raithen stepped forward and trapped the woman against the wall. She looked up at him, eyes wide with wonder as he angled the knife up and searched for her heart.

"Bastard," she breathed. A bloody rose bloomed on her lips as her blood-misted word emerged arthritically.

Raithen held her, watching the life and understanding go out of her eyes, knowing full well what he was taking from her. His own fear returned to him in a rush as blood continued to stream down the side of his neck. He was afraid she'd been successful in biting through his jugular, which meant he would bleed to death in minutes, with no way to stop it. There were no healers on board the pirate ships in Tauruk's Port, and all the priests were locked away for tonight or busy digging through the graves of Tauruk's Port. Even then, there was no telling how many healers were among them.

In the next moment, the woman went limp, her dead weight pulling at the pirate captain's arm.

Suspicious by nature, Raithen held on to the woman and his knife. She might have been faking—even with four inches of good steel in her. It was something he had done with success in the past, and taken two men's lives in the process.

After a moment of holding the woman, Raithen knew she would never move again. Her lips remained parted, colored a little by the blood that had stopped flowing. Dull and lifeless, her eyes stared through the pirate captain. Her face held no expression.

"Damn me, woman," Raithen whispered with genuine regret. "Had I known you had this kind of fire in you before now, our times together could have been spent much better." He breathed in, inhaling the sweet fragrance of the perfume he'd given her from the latest spoils, then demanded that she wear to bed. He also smelled the coppery odor of blood. Both scents were intoxicating.

The door to the room broke open.

Raithen prepared for the worst, spinning and placing the corpse between himself and the doorway. He slipped the knife free of the dead woman's flesh and held it before him.

A grizzled man stepped into the room with a crossbow in his hands. He squinted against the bright light streaming from the fireplace. "Cap'n? Cap'n Raithen?" The crossbow held steady in the man's hands, aimed at the two bodies.

"Aim that damnfool thing away from me, Pettit," Raithen growled. "You can never trust a crossbow to hold steady."

The sailor pulled the crossbow off line and canted the metal-encased butt against his hip. He reached up and doffed his tricorn hat. "Begging the cap's pardon, but I thought ye was in some fair amount of rough water there. With all that squallering a-goin' on, I mean. Didn't know you was up here after enjoying yerself with one of the doxies."

"The enjoyment," Raithen said with a forced calm because he still wanted to know how bad the wound on his neck was, "was not all mine." He released the dead woman, and she thumped to the floor at his feet.

As captain of some of the most vicious pirates to sail the Great Sea and the Gulf of Westmarch, he had an image to maintain. If any of his crew sensed weakness, someone would try to exploit it. He'd taken his own captaincy of *Barracuda* at the same time he'd taken his former captain's life.

Pettit grinned and spat into the dented bronze cuspidor in the corner of the room. He wiped his mouth with the back of his hand, then said, "Looks like ye've about had yer fill of that one. Want me to bring another one up?"

"No." Controlling the fear and curiosity that raged within him, Raithen cleaned his bloody knife on the woman's clothes, then crossed the room to the mirror. It was cracked and contained dark gray age spots where the silver-powder backing had worn away. "But she did remind me of something, Pettit."

"What's that, cap'n?"

"That damned priest, Cholik, has been thinking of us as lackeys." Raithen peered into the mirror, surveying the wound on his neck, poking at the edges of it with his fingers. Thank the Light, it wasn't bleeding any more than it had been, and it even appeared to be stopping.

The flesh between the bite marks was raised, swollen, and already turning purple. Bits of skin and even the meat beneath hung in tatters. It would scar, Raithen knew. The thought made him bitter because he was vain about his looks. By most accounts, he was a handsome man and had taken care to remain that way. And it would give him a more colorful and acceptable excuse about how all the bruising had taken place around his neck.

"Aye," Pettit grunted. "Them priests, they get up under a man's skin with them high-and-mighty ways of theirs. Always actin' like they got a snootful of air what's better'n the likes of ye and me. There's been a night or two on watch when I'd think about goin' after one of them and guttin' him, leavin' him out for the others to find. Might put them in a more appreciatin' frame o' mind about what we're a-doin' here."

Satisfied that his life wasn't in danger unless the woman was carrying some kind of disease that hadn't become apparent yet, Raithen took a kerchief from his pocket and tied it around his neck. "That's not a bad idea, Pettit."

"Thank ye, cap'n. I'm always thinkin'. And, why, this here deserted city with all them stories o' demons and the like, it'd be a perfect place to pull something like that. Why, we'd find out who the true believers were among ol' Cholik's bunch fer damn sure." He grinned, revealing only a few straggling, stained teeth remaining in his mouth.

"Some of the men might get worried, too." Raithen surveyed the kerchief around his neck in the mirror. Actually, it didn't look bad on him. In time, when the wound scarred over properly, he'd invent stories about how he'd gotten it in the arms of a lover he'd slain or stolen from, or some crazed and passionate princess out of Kurast he'd taken for ransom then returned deflowered to her father, the king, after getting his weight in gold.

"Well, we could tell the men what was what, cap'n."

"A secret, Pettit, is kept by one man. Even sharing it between the two of us endangers it. Telling a whole crew?" Raithen shook his head and tried not to wince when his neck pained him. "That would be stupid."

Pettit frowned. "Well, somethin' has to be done. Them priests has discovered a door down there in them warrens. An' if the past behavior of them priests is anythin' to go by, they ain't a-gonna let us look at what's behind it none."

"A door?" Raithen turned to his second-in-command. "What door?"

The big pirate, Lon, attacked Darrick Lang without any pretense at skilled swordplay. He just fetched up that huge sword of his in both hands and brought it crashing down toward Darrick's head, intending to split it like an overripe melon.

Thrusting his cutlass up, knowing there was a chance that the bigger sword might shear his own blade but having no other choice for defense, Darrick caught the descending blade. He didn't try to stop the sword's descent, but he did redirect it to the side, stepping to one side as he did because he expected the sudden reversal the pirate tried. He didn't entirely block the blow, though, and the flat of the blade slammed against his skull, almost knocking him out and leaving him disoriented.

Working on sheer instinct and guided by skilled responses, Darrick managed to lock his opponent's blade with his while he struggled to hold on to his senses. His vision and hearing faded out, as the world sometimes did between slow rollers when *Lonesome Star* followed wave troughs instead of cutting through them.

Recovering a little, Lon shoved Darrick back but didn't gain much ground.

Moving with skill and the dark savagery that filled him any time he fought, Darrick took a step forward and head-butted the pirate in the face.

Moaning, Lon stumbled back.

Darrick showed no mercy, pushing himself forward again. Obviously employing all the skill he had just to keep himself alive, the pirate kept retreating, stumbling and tripping over the broken terrain as he tried to walk up the incline behind him. Only a moment later, he went too far.

As though from a great distance, Darrick heard the man's boots scrape in the loose dirt, then the man fell, flailing and yelling, in the end wrapping his arms about his head. Ruthless and quick, Darrick knocked the pirate's blade from his hand, sending the big sword spinning through the air to land in the dense brush a dozen yards away.

Lon held his hands up. "I surrender! I surrender! Give me mercy!"

But, dazed as he was from the near miss of the sword, mercy was out of Darrick's reach. He remembered the bodies he'd seen in the flotsam left by the plunderers who had taken the Westmarch ship. Even that was hard to hang on to, because his battered mind slipped even farther back into the past, recalling the beatings his father had given him while he was a child. The man had been a butcher, big and rough, with powerful, callused hands that could split skin over a cheekbone with a single slap.

For a number of years, Darrick had never understood his father's anger or rage at him; he'd always assumed he'd done something wrong, not been a good son. It wasn't until he got older that he understood everything that was at play in their relationship.

"Mercy," the pirate begged.

But the main voice that Darrick listened to was his father's, cursing and swearing at him, threatening to beat him to death or bleed him out like a fresh-butchered hog. Darrick drew back his cutlass and swung, aiming to take the pirate's head off.

Without warning, a sword darted out and deflected Darrick's blow, causing the blade to cut into the earth only inches from the pirate's arm-wrapped head. "No," someone said.

Still lost in the memory of beatings he'd gotten at his father's hands, the present overlapping the past, Darrick spun and lifted his sword. Incredibly, someone caught his arm before he could swing and halted the blow.

"Darrick, it's me. It's me, Darrick. Mat." Thick and hoarse with emotion, Mat's voice was little more than a whisper. "It's me, damn it, leave off. We need this man alive."

Head filled with pain, vision still spotty from the pirate's blow, Darrick squinted his eyes and tried to focus. Forced out as he made his way to the present reality, memory of those past events left with reluctance.

"He's not your father, Darrick," Mat said.

Darrick focused on his friend, feeling the emotion drain from him, leaving him weak and shaking. "I know. I know that." But he knew he hadn't, not really. The pirate's blow had almost taken away his senses. He took in a deep breath and struggled to continue clearing his head.

"We need him alive," Mat said. "There's the matter of the king's nephew. This man has information we can use."

"I know." Darrick looked at Mat. "Let me go."

Mat's eyes searched his, but the grip on his swordarm never wavered. "You're sure?"

Looking over his friend's shoulder, Darrick saw the other sailors in his shore crew. Only old Maldrin didn't seem surprised by the bloodthirsty behavior Darrick had exhibited. Not many of the crew knew of the dark fury that sometimes escaped Darrick's control. It hadn't gotten away from him for a long time until tonight.

"I'm sure," Darrick said.

Mat released him. "Those times are past us. You don't ever have to revisit them. Your father didn't follow us from Hillsfar. We left him there those years ago. We left him there, and good riddance, I say."

Nodding, Darrick sheathed the cutlass and turned from them. He swept the horizon with his gaze, conscious of Mat's eyes still on him. The fact that his friend didn't trust him even after he'd said he was all right troubled and angered him.

And he seemed to hear his father's mocking laughter ringing in his ears, pointing out his helplessness and lack of worth. Despite how far he'd pushed himself, even shoving himself up through the Westmarch Navy ranking, he'd never been able to leave that voice behind in Hillsfar.

Darrick took a deep, shuddering breath. "All right, then, we'd best get at it, lads. Maldrin, take a couple men and fetch us up some water, if you please. I want this bonfire wetted so it can't go up by design or by mistake."

"Aye, sir," Maldrin responded, turning immediately and pointing out two men to accompany him. A quick search through the guards' supplies netted them a couple of waterskins. After emptying the waterskins over the pitch blend torch, they set out for the cliff's edge at once to get more water to finish the job.

Turning, Darrick surveyed the big pirate as Mat tied his hands behind his back with a kerchief. "How many of you were on guard here?" Darrick asked.

The man remained silent.

"I'll not trouble myself to ask you again," Darrick warned. "At this point, and take care to fully understand what I'm telling you here, you're a better bargain to me dead than you are alive. I don't look forward to trying to complete the rest of my mission while bringing along a prisoner."

Lon swallowed and tried to look defiant.

"I'd believe him if I were ye," Mat offered, patting the pirate on the cheek. "When he's in a fettle like this, he's more likely to have ye ordered thrown off the mountain than to keep ye alive an' hope ye know some of the answers to whatever questions he might have."

Lying on the ground as he was, Darrick knew it was hard for the pirate to feel in any way in control of the situation. And Mat's words made sense. The pirate just didn't know Mat wouldn't let Darrick act on an impulse like that. Anyway, the loss of control was behind him, and Darrick was in command of himself again.

"So, go on, then," Mat encouraged in that good-natured way of his as he squatted down beside the captive. "Tell us what ye know."

The pirate regarded them both with suspicion. "You'll let me live?"

"Aye," Mat agreed without hesitation. "I'll give ye me word on it, I will, and spit on me palm to seal the deal."

"How do I know I can trust you?" the pirate demanded.

Mat laughed a little. "Well, old son, we've done an' let ye live so far, ain't we?"

Darrick looked down at the man. "How many of you were there here?"

"Just us two," the pirate replied sullenly.

"What time's the changing of the guard?"

Hesitating, the pirate said, "Soon."

"Pity," Mat commented. "If someone happens by in the next few minutes, why, I'll have to slice your throat for ye, I will."

"I thought you said you were going to let me live," the pirate protested.

Mat patted the man's cheek again. "Only if we don't have nasty surprises along the way."

The pirate licked his lips. "New guards won't be until dawn. I just told you that so maybe you'd leave and Raithen wouldn't be so vexed at me for not lighting the torch."

"Well," Mat admitted, "it was a sound plan on your part. I'd probably have tried the same thing. But we're here on some matter of consequence, ye see."

"Sure," the pirate said, nodding. Mat's behavior, as always in most circumstances, was so gentle and understanding that it was confounding.

Immediate relief went through Darrick. Changing of the guard during the middle of the night wasn't something he would have suspected, but the confirmation let him know they still had a few hours to get the king's nephew back before the morning light filled the land.

"What about the king's nephew?" Mat asked. "He's just a boy, an' I wouldn't want to hear that anything untoward has happened to him."

"The boy's alive."

"Where?" Darrick asked.

"Cap'n Raithen has him," the pirate said, wiping blood from his lip. "He's keepin' him aboard *Barracuda.*"

"And where, then, can we find *Barracuda*?" Darrick asked.

"She's in the harbor. Cap'n Raithen, he don't let *Barracuda* go nowheres unless he's aboard her."

"Good." Darrick turned east, noting that Maldrin and his crew had returned with waterskins they'd filled from the river using the rope they left behind. "Get this man up and on his feet, Mat. I'll want him gagged proper."

"Aye, sir." Mat yanked the pirate to his feet and took another kerchief from a pocket to make the gag.

Stepping close to the pirate, Darrick felt bad when the man winced and tried to move away from him, held in place only because Mat blocked him from behind. With his face only inches from the pirate's, Darrick spoke softly. "And let's be having an understanding, you and me."

When the silence between them stretched out, the pirate looked at Mat, who offered no support. Then the prisoner looked back at Darrick and nodded hopefully.

"Good," Darrick said, showing him a wintry smile. "If you try to warn your mates, which could be something you'd be interested in because you might actually be inclined favorably toward some of them, I'll slit your throat for you calm as a man gutting a fish. Nod your head if you understand."

The pirate nodded.

"I've no love of pirates," Darrick said. "There's ways for an honest man to make a living without preying on his neighbors. I've killed plenty of pirates in the Great Sea and in the Gulf of Westmarch. One more won't bump up the score overmuch, but I'd feel better about it myself. Are we clear here?"

Again, the pirate nodded, and crocodile tears showed in his eyes.

"Crystal, sir," Mat added energetically as he clapped the pirate on the shoulder. "Why, I don't think we'll be having any problems with this man at all after your kind explanation regardin' the matter."

"Good. Bring him along, but keep him close to hand." Turning, Darrick started east, following the ridgeline of the Hawk's Beak Mountains that would take them down toward Tauruk's Port.

FIVE

✳

Standing near the dead woman's body in the inn room in Tauruk's Port, Raithen watched as Pettit reached into a pocket under his vest and took out a piece of paper.

"That's what brung me up here to see ye, cap'n," the first mate said. "Valdir sent this along just now as quick as he could after them priests found the door buried down in them ruins."

Raithen crossed the room and took the paper. Unfolding it, he leaned toward the fireplace and the lantern that sat on the mantel.

Valdir was the current spy the pirate captain had assigned to Cholik's excavation team. Raithen kept them rotated out with each new arrival of slaves. The men assigned didn't care for it, and the fact that they didn't become sickly and emaciated as the others did would draw attention from the mercenaries who remained loyal to Cholik's gold.

The paper held a drawing of a series of elliptical lines, centered one within the other, and a different line running through them.

"What is this?" Raithen asked.

Leaning, Pettit spat again, missing the cuspidor this time. He rubbed strings of spittle from his chin. "That there's a symbol what Valdir saw on that door. It's a huge door, cap'n, near to three times as tall as a man, the way Valdir puts it."

"You spoke to him?"

Pettit nodded. "Went in to talk to some of the mercenaries we're doin' business with. Ye know, to kinda keep them on our side. Took 'em a few bottles of brandy we got off that last Westmarch merchant ship we took down."

Raithen knew that wasn't the only reason Pettit had gone to see the men. Since the pirates had all the women in port, a fact that Cholik and his priests didn't much care for, the mercenaries they'd hired had to negotiate prices for the women's services with Pettit.

Being avaricious was one of the reasons Raithen had taken Pettit on as first mate. Pettit's own knowledge that his loyalty ensured not only his career but also his life kept him in place. It helped that Raithen knew Pettit never saw himself as being a captain and that his only claim to power would be serving a captain who appreciated the cruel and conniving ways he had.

"When did the priests find the door?" Raithen asked. If Cholik had known, why hadn't the priest been there? Raithen still didn't know why Cholik and his minions crawled through the detritus of the two cities like ants, but their obvious zeal for whatever they looked for had gotten him excited.

"Only just," Pettit replied. "As it turned out, cap'n, I was in them tunnels when Valdir fetched up with the news of their findin'."

Raithen's nimble mind leapt. He turned his eyes back to the crude drawing. "Where is that bastard Cholik?" They had spies on the priest as well.

"He joined the diggers."

"Cholik's there now?" Raithen's interest grew more intense.

"Aye, cap'n. An' once word of this discovery reached him, Cholik wasted no time in harin' off down there."

"And we don't have any idea what's behind this door?" Of course, Cholik didn't know about the king's nephew Raithen and his pirates were holding for ransom, either. Both sides had their secrets, only Raithen knew Cholik was hiding them.

"None, cap'n, but Valdir will be lettin' us know as soon as he's in the knowin' of it."

"If he can." Any time the priests found something that they thought would be important, they got all the slaves out of the area till the recovery was complete.

"Aye, but if'n any one man can do it, cap'n, Valdir can."

Folding the note then putting it in his pocket, Raithen nodded. "I'd rather have someone down there with the priests. Get a crew assembled. Cover it as a provisions resupply for the slaves."

"It's hardly time for that again."

"Cholik won't know. He works those slaves till they drop, then heaves them into that great, bloody abyss down there."

"Aye, cap'n. I'll get to it then."

"What of our guest aboard *Barracuda*?"

Pettit shrugged. "Oh, he's in fine keepin', cap'n. Fit as a fiddle, he is. Alive, he's worth a lot, but now, dead, cap'n?" The first mate shook his scruffy head. "Why, he's just a step removed from fertilizer, isn't he?"

With care, Raithen touched the wound on his neck beneath the kerchief. Pain rattled through his skull, and he winced at it. "That boy is the king's nephew, Pettit. Westmarch's king prides himself on his knowledge and that of his get. Priests train those children for the most part, and they concern themselves with history, things better left forgotten, I say." *Except for the occasional treasure map or account of where a ship laden with treasure went down in inhospitable seas.*

"Aye, cap'n. Worthless learnin', most of it. If'n ye're askin' me own opinion."

Raithen wasn't, but he didn't belabor the point. "What do you think the chances are that the boy we took from that last Westmarch ship knows a considerable amount about history and things a priest might be interested in? Maybe even knows about this?" He patted the breast pocket where he'd stored the paper with the symbol.

Understanding dawned in Pettit's rheumy eyes. He scratched his bearded chin and grinned, revealing the few straggling teeth stained by beetle-juice. "Me, cap'n? Why, I'd say there was considerable chances, I would."

"I'm going to talk to the boy." Raithen took up his plumed hat from the trunk at the foot of the bed and clapped it onto his head.

"Ye might have to wake him," Pettit said. "An' he ain't none too sociable. Little rapscallion liked to tore ol' Bull's ear off when he went in to feed him this e'ening."

"What do you mean?"

"Ol' Bull, he up and walks into the hold where we're a-keepin' the boy like it was nothin'. That young'un, he come out of the rafters where'd he'd been a-hidin' and dropped down on ol' Bull. Walloped ol' Bull a few good licks with a two-by-four he'd pried loose from the wall of the hold. If'n ol' Bull's head hadn't been as thick as it was, why he'd have been damn near knocked to death, he would. As it was, that boy nearly got his arse offa *Barracuda* for certain."

"Is the boy hurt?" Raithen asked.

Pettit waved the possibility away. "Nah. Mighta picked him up a couple of knots on his head fer his troubles, but nothin' what's gonna stay with him more'n a day or two."

"I don't want that boy hurt, Pettit." Raithen made his voice harsh.

Pettit cringed a little and scratched at the back of his neck. "I ain't gonna let any o' the crew hurt him."

"If that boy gets hurt before I'm done with him," Raithen said, stepping over the dead woman sprawled on the floor, "I'm going to hold you responsible. And I'll take it out of your arse."

"I understand, cap'n. An' trust me, ye got no worries there."

"Get that supply crew together, but no one moves until I say."

"It'll be as ye say, cap'n."

"I'm going to speak with that boy. Maybe he knows something about this symbol."

"If I may suggest, cap'n, while ye're there, just mind ye keep a sharp watch on yer ears. That boy's a quick one, he is."

Buyard Cholik stared at the huge door that fronted the wall. In all the years of knowing about Kabraxis and of knowing the fate of Ransim buried beneath Tauruk's Port, he'd never known how he would feel once he stood before the door that hid the demon's secret. Even months of planning and work, of coming down to the subterranean depths on occasion to check on the work and inspire fear or reprisal in the acolytes who labored under his design, had left him unprepared.

Although he had expected to feel proud and exuberant about his discovery, Cholik had forgotten about the fear that now filled him. Quavers, like the tremor of an earthquake hidden deep within a land, ran through his body. He wanted to shriek and call on Archangel Yaerius, who first brought the tenets of Zakarum to men. But he did not. Cholik knew he had long passed the line of forgiveness that would be offered by any who followed the ways of Light.

And what good would forgiveness do a dying old man? The priest taunted himself with that question as he had for the past few months and stiffened his resolve. Death was only another few years into the future for him, nothing worthwhile left during that distance.

"Master," Brother Altharin whispered, "are you all right?" He stood to Cholik's right, two steps back as respect and the older priest's tolerance dictated.

Letting his irritation burn away the traces that were left from his own anger and resentment at his approaching mortality, Cholik said, "Of course, I am all right. Why would I not be?"

"You were so quiet," Altharin said.

"Contemplation and meditation," Cholik said, "are the two key abilities for any priest to possess in order that he may understand the great mysteries left to us by the Light. You would do well to remember that, Altharin."

"Of course, master." Altharin's willingness to accept rebuke and toil at a relentless pace had made him the natural candidate for being in charge of the excavation.

Cholik studied the massive door. *Or should I think of it as a gate?* The secret texts he'd read had suggested that Kabraxis's door guarded another place as well as the hidden things the demon lord had left behind.

The slaves continued to labor, loading carts with broken rock with their bare hands by lantern light and torchlight. Their chains clinked and clanked against the hard stone ground. Other slaves worked with pickaxes, standing on the stone surrounding the door or atop frail scaffolding that quivered with every swing. The slaves spoke in fearful tones to one another, but they also hurried to finish uncovering the door. Cholik thought that was because they believed that they would be able to rest. If something behind the great door didn't kill them, the old priest thought, perhaps for a time they would rest.

"So much of the door is uncovered," Cholik said. "Why was I not called earlier?"

"Master," Altharin said, "there was no indication that we were so close to finding the door. We came upon another hard section of the dig, the wall that you see before you, which hid the door. I only thought that it was another section of cavern wall. So many times the path that you chose for us has caused us to punch through walls of the existing catacombs."

The city's builders had constructed Ransim to take advantage of the natural caverns in the area above the Dyre River, Cholik remembered from the texts. The caves had provided warehouse area for the goods they trafficked in, natural cisterns of groundwater they could use in event of a siege—which had happened several times during the city's history—and as protection from the elements because harsh storms often raced down from the summits of the Hawk's Beak Mountains. Tauruk's Port, founded after the destruction of Ransim, hadn't benefited from access to the caverns.

"When we started to attack this wall," Altharin continued, "it fell out in large sections. That's why so much rubble remains before the door."

Cholik watched the slaves loading huge sections of broken stone into the carts, then pushing the carts up to the dump sites. Other slaves filled large buckets with smaller debris and filled more carts. The ironbound wheels creaked on dry axles and grated against the floor.

"The work to uncover the door went quickly," Altharin said. "As soon as I knew we had found it, I sent for you."

Cholik strode toward the door, drawing on the remaining dregs of his strength. His legs felt like lead, and his heart hammered against his ribs. He'd pushed himself too far. He knew that. The confrontation with Raithen and the spell he'd summoned to destroy the rats had shoved him past his limits. His breath felt tight in his chest. Using magic no longer came easy to the aged and infirm sometimes. Spellwork had its own demands and often left those too weak to handle the energies warped and broken. And he'd come into the spells late in life after wasting so many years in the Zakarum Church.

The ground inclined toward the door, and Cholik's steps hastened of their own accord. Slaves noticed him coming and cleared the way, yelling at one another to get out of the way.

Hammers rose and fell as more slaves put additional scaffolding into place, climbing higher up against the door. In their haste, part of the scaffolding fell, swinging like a pendulum from a fixed point, and four men fell with it. A lantern shattered against the stone floor and spilled a pool of oil that caught fire.

One of the fallen men screamed in pain, clasping a shattered leg. The torch-light revealed the gleam of white bone protruding through his shin.

"Get that fire put out," Altharin ordered.

A slave threw a bucket of water over the fire but only succeeded in splashing it toward the huge door, spreading the flames into little pockets.

One of the mercenaries stepped forward and cut the ragged shirt from a slave with quick flicks of his dagger. He dipped the shirt into another bucket of water, then plopped the soaked garment on top of the fire. Sizzling, the fire died.

Cholik strode forward through the fire, unwilling to show any fear of it. He summoned a small shield to protect him from the fire and walked through it unscathed. The act created the effect he wanted, drawing the slaves' attention from their fear of the door and replacing it with their fear of him.

The door was a threat, but a toothless one. Cholik had proven on several occasions that he had no compunctions about killing them and having their bodies thrown into the abyss. Gathering himself, standing now despite the weakness that filled him only because he refused to let himself falter, he turned to the slaves.

All their frantic whispering stopped except for the groaning man nursing the broken leg. Even he hid his face in the crook of his arm, whimpering and no longer crying out.

Knowing he needed more strength to face whatever lay on the other side of Kabraxis's door, Cholik spoke words of power, summoning the darkness to him that he had feared decades ago, only begun to dabble in a few years ago, and had grown strong in of late.

The old priest held up his right hand, fingers splayed. As he spoke the words, forbidden words to those of the Zakarum Church, he felt the power leech into him, biting through his flesh and sinking into his bones with razored talons. If the spell did not work, he was certain he would fall and risk becoming comatose until his body recovered.

A purple nimbus flared around his hand. A bolt shot out and touched the slave with the broken leg. When the purple light spread over him and invisible hands grabbed him, the man screamed.

Cholik continued speaking, feeling stronger as the spell bound the man to him. His words came faster and more certain. The invisible hands spread-eagled the slave on the ground, then lifted him up, dangling him in the air.

"No!" the man screamed. "Please! I beg you! I will work! I will work!"

Once, the man's fear and his pleading might have touched Cholik. Those things did not touch Cholik intimately, for the old priest could never remember a time when he'd placed the needs of another above his own. But there had been times he'd gone with the Zakarum Church missionaries in the past to heal the sick and tend to wounded men. The recent trouble between Westmarch and Tristram had been rife with those incidents.

"Nooooo!" the man screamed.

The other slaves drew back. Some of them called to the afflicted man.

Cholik spoke again, then closed his fist. The purple nimbus turned dark, like the bruised flesh of a plum, and sped along the length of the beam that held the slave.

When the darkness touched the slave, his body contorted. Horrible crunching echoed in the cavern as the man's arms and legs shattered their sockets. He screamed anew, and despite the agony that must have been coursing through him, he remained alert and conscious.

A few of the priests who had left Westmarch with Cholik but who had not yet abdicated the ways of the Zakarum Church knelt and pressed their faces against the cavern floor. The teachings of the church held only tenets of healing and hope, of salvation. Only the Hand of Zakarum, the order of warriors consecrated by the church, and the Twelve Grand Inquisitors, who sought out and combated demonic activity within the populace of the church, used the blessings Yaerius and Akarat had given to those who had first chosen to follow.

Buyard Cholik was neither of those things. The priests who had put their faith in him had known that, had believed that he could make them more than what they were, but only now saw what they could become. Cholik, feeding off the slave's fear and life as they came back to him through the conduit of the spell, was aware that some of his followers regarded him with fear while others looked at him hungrily.

Altharin was one of those horrified.

Bracing himself, not knowing for sure what to expect, Cholik spoke the final word of the spell.

The slave screamed in anguish, but the scream stopped in the middle. The spell ripped the man apart. The explosion of blood painted the frightened faces of the nearby men crimson and extinguished two torches as well as the residual pools of flame from the shattered lantern.

A moment more, and the desiccated remains of the slave plopped against the cavern floor.

Even though he'd expected something, Cholik hadn't expected the sudden rush of euphoria that filled him. Pain echoed within him as well, sweet misery as the vampiric spell worked the restorative effects. The lethargy that had descended upon him after using the spells earlier lifted. Even some of the arthritic pains that had started to blossom in his joints faded. Part of the stolen life energy went to him, to borrow and use as he saw fit, but the spell transferred some of it to the demon worlds as well. Spellcraft designed and given by the demons always benefited them.

Cholik stood straighter as the magical nimbus around him lightened from near black to purple again. Then the hellish light drew back inside him. Refreshed, senses thrumming, the old priest regarded his audience. What he'd done here tonight would trigger reaction in the slaves, the mercenaries, Raithen's pirates, and even the priests. Some, Cholik knew, would not be there come morning.

They would be afraid of him and of what he might do.

The realization made Cholik feel good, powerful. Even when he was a young priest of the Zakarum Church and holding a position in Westmarch, only the truly repentant and those without hope who wished to believe in something had clung to his words. But the men in the cavern watched him as canaries watched a hawk.

Turning from the dead slave, Cholik walked toward the door again. His feet moved with comfort and confidence. Even his own fears seemed pushed farther back in his mind.

"Altharin," Cholik called.

"Yes, master," Altharin responded in a quiet voice.

"Have the slaves get back to work."

"Yes, master." Altharin gave the orders.

Trained survivalists themselves, knowing they offered no blood allegiance, the mercenaries showed the greatest haste in getting the slaves back to work. Slaves secured the fallen scaffolding, and work began again. Pickaxes tore at the cavern wall covering the gray and green door. Sledges pounded huge sections of rock into pieces small enough for men to carry to the waiting carts. The steady thump and crack of the mining tools created a martial cadence that echoed within the cavern.

Mastering his impatience, Cholik watched the progress of the slaves. As the slaves worked, whole sheets of rock fell, crashing against the floor or piles of debris that were already there. The mercenaries stayed among the slaves, lashing out with their whips and leaving marks and cuts against sweat-soaked skin. At times, the mercenaries even aided in shoving the laden carts into motion.

The work went faster. In moments, one of the door's hinges came into view. Only a short time after that, further work revealed another hinge. Cholik studied them, growing more excited.

The hinges were large, gnarled works of metal and amber as Cholik had been expecting from the texts he'd read. The metal was there because man had made it, worked by smiths to hold back and constrain, but the amber was in place because it held the essence of the past trapped within the stirred golden depths.

When enough debris was removed to make a path to the door, Cholik walked forward. The energy he'd taken from the slave wouldn't last long, according to the materials he had read. Once depleted, he would be left in worse condition than he had been in unless he reached his rooms and the potions that he kept there to renew himself.

As he neared the door, Cholik sensed the power that was contained within. The powerful presence surged in his brain, drawing him on and repelling him at the same time. Reaching into his robe, he removed the carved box made from a flawless black pearl.

He held the box in his hands, felt it cold as ice against his palms. Finding the box had required years of work. The secret texts concerning it and Kabraxis's door had been hidden deep in the stacks kept in the Westmarch church. Keeping the box secret had required murder and treachery. Not even Altharin knew of it.

"Master," Altharin said.

"Back," Cholik demanded. "And take your rabble with you."

"Yes, master." Altharin moved back, whispering to the men.

Gazing into the polished surface of the black pearl box, Cholik remained aware of the mass exodus from him and the gate. The old priest breathed deeply. During the years the box had been in his possession, while he'd researched and learned where Ransim had been hidden and developed the courage for such an undertaking and desperation strong enough to allow him to deal with the demon he'd have to confront to take what he wanted, he'd never been able to open the box. What the contents of the box were remained to be seen.

Breathing out, concentrating on the box and the door, Cholik spoke the first Word. His throat ached with the pain of it, for it was not meant for the human tongue. As the Word left his lips, deafening thunder cannonaded in the cavern, and a wind rose up, though no wind should have existed within the stone walls.

The elliptical design on the dark gray-green surface of the door turned deep black. A humming noise echoed through the cavern over the thunder and the gusting wind.

Closing his left hand over the black pearl box, Cholik strode forward, feeling the chill of the metal. He spoke the second Word, harder to master than the first.

The amber pieces in the huge hinges lit with unholy yellow light. They looked like the fires trapped in a wolf's eyes reflecting torchlight at night.

The wind strengthened in intensity, picking up powdery-fine particles that stung flesh when they hit. Prayers echoed within the cavern, all of them to the holy Light, not demons. It was almost enough to make Cholik smile, except that a small part of him was just as afraid as they were.

At the third Word, the black pearl box opened. A gossamer sphere, glowing three different colors of green, lifted from the box. The sphere rolled in front of Cholik's eyes. According to the materials he'd read, the sphere was death to touch.

And if he faltered now, the sphere would consume him, leaving only smoking ash in its wake. Cholik spoke the fourth Word.

The sphere started growing, swelling in size like the eels some fishermen took from the Great Ocean. Prized as an exotic delicacy, the flesh of the eels brought a narcotic bliss when prepared with proper care, but it brought death on occasion even when served by a master. Cholik had never eaten of the eels, but he knew how the men and women who did must have felt.

For a moment, Cholik was certain he had killed himself.

Then the glowing green sphere flew away from him and slammed into Kabraxis's door. Amplified to titanic proportions, the *boom!* of magic contacting the door manifested itself as a physical presence that knocked rock from the edges of the door and slammed stalactites from the cavern ceiling.

The stalactites crashed down among the huddled slaves, mercenaries, and fallen Zakarum priests. Cholik somehow retained his own footing while everyone around him toppled. Glancing over his shoulder, the priest saw three men screaming in agony but heard no sound. He felt as though spun cotton filled his head. One of the mercenaries carried on a brief, macabre dance with a stalactite that had transfixed him, then fell over. He spasmed as his life drained away.

In the silent stillness that had descended upon the cavern, Cholik spoke the fifth and final Word. The elliptical design ignited on the top, outside ring. From its starting point, a blood-red bead traced the ellipses, making them all glow as it hopped from one completed ring to another. Then it darted to the line that ran through them all, moving faster and faster.

When it reached the end of the design, the bead burst in scarlet glory.

The massive gray-green doors opened, and sound returned to the cavern in a rush. The door shoveled the remaining debris from in front of it.

Cholik watched in disbelieving horror as death poured through the open door from some forgotten corner of the Burning Hells.

Six

Darrick peered down at Tauruk's Port, cursing the clouded moon that had proven beneficial only a short time before. Even nestled in the lower reaches of the Hawk's Beak Mountains, the darkness that filled the city made it hard to discern details.

The Dyre River ran mostly east and west, flowing through the canyon time had cut through the mountains. The ruins of the city lay on the north bank of the river. The widest part of the city fronted the river, taking advantage of the natural harbor.

"In its day," Mat said in a low voice, "Tauruk's Port must have done all right by itself. Deep harbor like that, on a river that covers a lot of miles, an' wide enough to sail upstream, those people who lived here must have enjoyed the good life."

"Well, they ain't here no more," Maldrin pointed out.

"Wonder why that is?" Mat asked.

"Somebody up an' come along and stomped their city down around their damned ears," the first mate said. "Thought a bright one like yerself woulda seen that without the likes of me needin' to say it."

Mat took no insult. "Wonder who did the stomping?"

Ignoring the familiar bickering of the two men, which at times was tiresome and at other times proved enjoyable, Darrick took a small spyglass from the bag at his waist. It was one of the few personal possessions he had. A craftsman in Kurast had built the spyglass, but Darrick had purchased it from a merchant in Westmarch. The brass body made the spyglass almost indestructible, and clever design rendered it collapsible. He extended the spyglass and studied the city closer.

Three ships sat in the harbor. All of them held lights from lanterns carried by pirates on watch.

Darrick followed the sparse line of pirates and lanterns ashore, focusing at last on a large building that had suffered partial destruction. The building sat under a thick shelf of rock that looked as if it had been displaced by whatever had destroyed the city.

"Got themselves a hole made up," Maldrin said.

Darrick nodded.

"Prolly got it filled with women and wine," the first mate went on. "By the Light, lad, I know we're here for the king's nephew an' all, but I don't like the idea of leavin' them women here. Prolly got 'em all from the ships they looted and scuppered. Wasn't no way to get a proper body count on them what got killed, on account of the sharks."

Darrick gritted his teeth, trying not to think of the abuse the women must have endured at the coarse hands of the pirates. "I know. If there's a way, Maldrin, we'll be after having them women free of all this, too."

"There's a good lad," Maldrin said. "I know this crew ye picked, Darrick. They're good men. Ever last one of them. They wouldn't be above dyin' to be heroes."

"We're not here to die," Darrick said. "We're here to kill pirates."

"An' play hell with 'em if'n we get the chance." Mat's grin glimmered in the darkness. "They don't look as though they're takin' the business of guard duty too serious down here in the ruins."

"They've got all them spotters along the river," Maldrin agreed. "If we'd tried bringin' *Lonesome Star* upriver, why, we'd be sure to be caught. They ain't been thinkin' about a small force of determined men."

"A small force is still a small force," Darrick said. "But while that allows us to move around quick and quiet, we're not going to be much for standing and fighting. A dozen men we are, and that won't take long for killing if we go at this thing wrong and unlucky." Moving the spyglass on, he marked the boundaries of the ruined city in his mind. Then he returned his attention to the docks.

Two small docks floated in the water, buoyed on watertight barrels. From the wreckage thrust up farther east of the floating docks, Darrick believed that more permanent docks had once existed there. The broken striations of the land above the river indicated that chunks had cracked off in the past. The permanent docks probably resided in the harbor deep enough that they posed no threats to shallow-drawing ships.

Two block-and-tackle rigs hung from the lip of the riverbank thirty feet above the decks of the three cogs. Stacks of crates and hogshead barrels occupied space beside the block-and-tackles. A handful of men guarded the stores, but they were occupied in a game of dice, all of them hunkered down to watch the outcome of every roll. Every now and again a cheer reached Darrick's ears. They had two lanterns between them, placed at opposite ends of the gaming area.

"Which one of 'em do ye think is *Barracuda*?" Maldrin asked. "That's the ship that pirate said the boy was on, right?"

"Aye," Darrick replied, "and I'm wagering that *Barracuda* is the center ship."

"The one with all the guards," Mat said.

"Aye." Darrick collapsed the spyglass and put it back into his waist pouch, capping both ends. Glass ground as well as the lenses he had in the spyglass was hard to come by out of Kurast.

"Are ye plannin', then, Darrick?" Mat asked.

"As I ever am," Darrick agreed.

Looking more sober, Mat asked, "This ain't after bein' as much of a bit of a lark as we'd have hoped, is it, then?"

"No," Darrick agreed. "But I still think we can get her done." He rose from the hunkered position. "Me and you first, then, Mat. Quick and quiet as we can. Maldrin, can you still move silent, or have you got too broad abeam from Cook's pastries?"

Lonesome Star had a new baker, and the young man's culinary skills were the stuff of legend within the Westmarch Navy. Captain Tollifer had called in some markers to arrange to have the baker assigned to their ship. Every sailor aboard *Lonesome Star* had developed a sweet tooth, but Maldrin had been the first to realize the baker actually wanted to learn how to sail and had capitalized on giving him time at the steering wheel in exchange for pastries.

"I may have put on a pound or three in the last month or two," Maldrin admitted, "but I'll never get so old or so fat that I can't keep up with ye young pups. If'n I do, I'll tie a rope around me neck and dive off the fo'c'sle."

"Then follow along," Darrick invited. "We'll see if we can't take over that stockpile."

"Whatever for?" Maldrin grumped.

Darrick started down the grade, staying along the edge of the river. The block-and-tackles and the guards were nearly two hundred yards away. Brush and small trees grew along the high riverbank. Raithen's pirates had been lazy about clearing more land than necessary.

"Unless I misread those barrels," Darrick said, "they contain whale oil and whiskey."

"Be better if they contained some of them wizard's potions that explode," Maldrin said.

"We work with what we get," Darrick said, "and we'll be glad about it." He called for Tomas.

"Aye," Tomas said, drawing up out of the dark shadows.

"Once we give the signal," Darrick said, "bring the rest of the men in a hurry. We'll be boarding the middle ship to look for the king's nephew. When we find him, I'll be having him off that ship soon as we're able. Make use of one of those block-and-tackles. Understand?"

"Aye," Tomas replied. "We'll fetch him up."

"I'll be wanting him in one piece, Tomas," Darrick threatened, "or it'll be you explaining to the king how his nephew got himself hurt or dead."

Tomas nodded. "A babe in arms, Darrick, that's how we'll be treatin' the boy. As safe as his own mother would have him."

Darrick clapped Tomas on the shoulder and grinned. "I knew I was asking the right man about the job."

"Just ye be careful down there, an' don't go gettin' too brave until we get down there with ye."

Darrick nodded, then started down the mountainside toward the riverbank. Mat and Maldrin followed him, as silent as falling snow in the winter.

Raithen followed the steps cut into the riverbank overlooking the boats. When the steps had first been cut from the stone of the mountains, they'd doubtless been of an even keel. Now, after the damage that had been done to the city, they canted to one side, making the descent a tricky one. Since Raithen's crew had been holed up at Tauruk's Port, more than one drunken pirate had ended up in the water below, and two of them had been swept away in the current and likely drowned by the time they reached the Gulf of Westmarch.

He carried a lantern to light the way, and the golden glow played over the striations in the mountainside. In the day, the stone shone blue and slate gray, different levels marked by a deepening of color till the rock looked almost charcoal gray before disappearing beneath the river's edge. The fog maintained a soft presence around him, but he saw the three cogs through it without problem.

Pirates assigned to guard duty squared their shoulders and looked alert as he passed. They deferred to him with politeness he'd beaten into some of them.

A sudden shrill of rope through pulleys alerted him to activity above.

"Look alive, ye great bastards," a rough voice called down. "I've got ye a load of victuals, I have."

"Send it on down," a man called on the cog to Raithen's right. "Been waitin' on it a dog's age. Feel like my stomach's been wrappin' itself around me backbone."

Pressing himself against the mountainside, Raithen watched as a short, squat barrel was let go. The pulleys slowed the barrel's descent, proving that the load was light. The scent of salted pork passed within inches of Raithen.

"Got you a bottle of wine in there, too," the man called.

"An' ye damn near hit Cap'n Raithen with it, ye lummox," the guard only a few feet from the pirate captain yelled out.

A muttered curse followed. "Excuse me, cap'n," the man said in a contrite voice. "Didn't know it was ye."

Raithen held the lantern up so the man could plainly see his features. "Hurry up."

"Aye, sir. Right away, sir." The pirate raised his voice. "Ye lads heave off with that barrel. We need another, I'll fetch it up later."

The pirates aboard the first cog threw off the lines, and they were hauled back up the block-and-tackle.

As soon as the way was clear, Raithen walked to the first of the small temporary docks floating on the black water. He climbed the cargo net tossed over the side of the cog and stepped to the cog's deck.

"Evenin', cap'n," a scar-faced pirate greeted. A half-dozen other pirates did the same but didn't slow in their efforts to take the food from the barrel.

Raithen nodded at the man, feeling the pain in his wounded throat. When the ships were in port, he made certain the men stayed out of ships' stores. All of the cogs stayed fully loaded at all times, in case they had to flee out to deep water. His other ships lay a few days away, anchored off the north coastline in a bay that could be treacherous to an understaffed ship.

Planks spanned the distance between the ships. The river current was gentle enough that the cogs didn't fight the tether while they lay at anchorage. On board *Barracuda,* the ship kept between the other two, he saw Bull sitting in the prow puffing on a pipe.

"Cap'n," Bull acknowledged, taking the pipe from between his teeth. He was a big man, seemingly assembled from masts. A scarf tied around his head bound his wounded ear, but bloodstains were visible down the sides of his neck.

"How's the boy, Bull?" Raithen asked.

"Why, he's fine, cap'n," Bull replied. "Any reason he shouldn't be?"

"I heard about your ear."

"This little thing?" Bull touched his wounded ear and grinned. "Why, it ain't nothing for ye to be worryin' over, cap'n."

"I'm not worrying over it," Raithen said. "I figure any pirate who gets taken in by a boy isn't worth the salt I pay him to crew my ship."

Bull's face darkened, but Raithen knew it was out of embarrassment. "It's just that he's such an innocent-lookin' thing, cap'n. Didn't figure him for no shenanigans like this. An' that two-by-four? Why, he like to took me plumb by surprise. I'm right tempted to keep him fer myself if'n the king don't ransom him back. I'm tellin' ye true, cap'n, we've done a lot worse than take on somebody like this boy for crew."

"I'll keep that in mind," Raithen said.

"Aye, sir. I weren't offerin' outta nothin' but respect for ye and that mean-spirited little lad down in the hold."

"I want to see him."

"Cap'n, I swear to ye, I ain't done nothin' to him."

"I know, Bull," Raithen said. "My reasons are my own."

"Aye, sir." Bull took a massive key ring from his waist sash, then knocked the contents of his pipe into the river. No fires except the watch's lanterns were allowed down in the hold, and those were taken there seldom.

Bull walked into the small cargo hold. Raithen followed, inhaling the familiar stink. When he'd been with the Westmarch Navy, ships were not allowed to stink so. Sailors had been kept busy cleaning them out, dosing them with salt water and vinegar to kill any fungus or mold that tried to leach into the wood.

The boy was kept in the small brig in the stern of the cog.

After unlocking the brig door, Bull shoved his big head in, then pulled it out just as quickly. He reached up and caught a board aimed at his face, then tugged on it.

The boy flopped onto the ship's deck, landing hard on his belly and face. Quick as a fish taken out of water, the boy tried to get to his feet. Bull pinned him to the ship's deck with one massive boot.

Incredibly, the boy revealed a huge knowledge of vituperative name-calling.

"Like I said, cap'n," Bull said with a grin, "this 'un here, why, he'd make for a fine pirate, he would."

"Captain?" the boy squalled. Even trapped under Bull's foot, he craned his head around and tried to gaze up. "You're the captain of this pigsty? Why, if I was you, I'd sew a bag for my head and only leave myself one eyehole out of embarrassment."

In the first real amusement he'd felt that night, Raithen glanced down at the boy. "He's not afraid, Bull?"

"Afraid?" the boy squealed. "I'm afraid I'm going to die of boredom. You've had me for five days now. Three of them spent here in this ship. When I get back to my da and he speaks with his brother, the king, why, I'll come back here and help wallop you myself." He clenched his fists and beat the deck. "Let me up, and give me a sword. I'll fight you. By the Light, I'll give you the fight of your life."

Truly taken aback by the boy's demeanor, Raithen studied him. The boy was lean and muscular, starting to lose his baby fat. Raithen guessed he was eleven or twelve, possibly even as much as thirteen. A thick shock of dark hair crowned the boy's head, and the lantern light revealed that he had gray or green eyes.

"Do you even know where you're at, boy?" Raithen asked.

"When the king's navy pays you off or tracks you down," the boy said, "I'll know where you are. Don't you think that I won't."

Squatting down, holding the lantern close to the boy's face, Raithen shook the dagger sheathed along his arm free again. He rammed the point into the wooden deck only an inch from the boy's nose.

"The last person to threaten me tonight," Raithen said in a hoarse voice, "died only minutes ago. I won't mind killing another."

The boy's eyes focused on the knife. He swallowed hard but remained silent.

"I'll have your name, boy," Raithen said.

"Lhex," the boy whispered. "My name is Lhex."

"And you are the king's nephew?"

"Yes."

Raithen turned the knife blade, catching the lantern light and splintering it. "How many sons does your father have?"

"Five. Counting me."

"Will he miss one of them?"

Lhex swallowed again. "Yes."

"Good." Raithen raised the lantern, getting it out of the boy's eyes and letting him see the smile on his face. "This doesn't have to go hard for you, boy. But I mean to have the information I came here for tonight."

"I don't know anything."

"We'll see." Raithen stood. "Get him up, Bull. I'll talk to him in the brig."

Bending down, keeping his foot in place, Bull caught the boy's shirt in one massive hand and lifted him. Without apparent effort, he carried the boy back into the small brig. With exaggerated gentleness, Bull placed the boy against the far wall, then stood by him.

"You can leave, Bull," Raithen said.

"Cap'n," Bull protested, "maybe ye ain't yet figured out exactly what this little snot is capable of."

"I can handle a small boy," Raithen said, hanging the lantern on a hook on the wall. He took the key from Bull and sent the pirate on his way with a look. Gripping the bars of the door with one hand, Raithen closed the door. The clang of metal on metal sounded loud in the enclosed space.

Lhex started to get to his feet.

"Don't stand," Raithen warned. "If you insist on standing, I'll use this dagger and nail you to the wall behind you by one hand."

Freezing halfway to his feet, Lhex looked at Raithen. The look was one of childhood innocence and daring, trying to ascertain if the pirate captain had meant what he'd said.

Raithen maintained his icy stare, knowing he'd carry out the action he'd threatened.

Evidently, Lhex decided he would, too. Grimacing, the boy sat, but he did so with stubbornness, keeping his knees drawn up and placing his back securely against the wall behind him.

"You must think you're something," Lhex snarled. "Menacing a kid like that. What'd you do for breakfast? Kick a puppy?"

"Actually," Raithen said, "I had one beheaded and rendered out to serve you for breakfast chops. They tell me it fried up like chicken for your noonday meal."

Horror flirted with Lhex's eyes. He remained silent, watching Raithen.

"Where did you get such an attitude, boy?" the pirate captain asked.

"My parents blame each other," Lhex said. "I think I get it from them both."

"Do you think you're going to get out of here alive?"

"Either way," the boy said, "I'm not getting out of here scared. I've done that till I'm sick of it. I threw up the first three days."

"You're a most unusual boy," Raithen said. "I wish I'd gotten to know you sooner."

"Looking for a friend?" Lhex asked. "I only ask because I know most of these pirates are afraid of you. They're not here because they like you."

"Fear is a far better tool for command than friendship," Raithen responded. "Fear is instant, and it is obeyed without question."

"I'd rather have people like me."

Raithen smiled. "I'd wager to say that Bull doesn't like you."

"Some people I can live without."

"Wise lad," Raithen said. He paused, feeling the cog shift slightly in the river current.

The boy shifted with the ship automatically, just like a sailor.

"How long have you been at sea, Lhex?" Raithen asked.

The boy shrugged. "Since Lut Gholein."

"You were there?"

"The ship came from Lut Gholein," Lhex said, narrowing his eyes and watching Raithen with a thoughtful expression. "If you didn't know that, how did you find the ship?"

Raithen ignored the question. The information had come from Buyard Cholik's spies within Westmarch. "What were you doing in Lut Gholein?"

Lhex didn't answer.

"Don't trifle with me," Raithen warned. "I'm in an ill mood as it is."

"Studying," Lhex answered.

That, Raithen decided, sounded promising. "Studying what?"

"My father wanted me to have a good education. As the king's younger brother, he was sent abroad and learned from sages in Lut Gholein. He wanted the same for me."

"How long were you there?"

"Four years," the boy said. "Since I was eight."

"And what did you study?"

"Everything. Poetry. Literature. Marketing. Forecasting profits, though the whole thing with chicken gizzards was quite disgusting and not any better than just guessing."

"What about history?" Raithen asked. "Did you study history?"

"Of course I did. What kind of education would you get if you didn't study history?"

Raithen dug in his blouse for the paper Pettit had given him. "I want you to look at this paper. Tell me what it means."

Interest flickered in the boy's eyes as he regarded the paper. "I can't see it from here."

Hesitant, Raithen took the lantern from the wall. "If you try anything, boy, I'll have you crippled. If your father persuades the king to ransom you back, you'll have to hope the healers can make you whole again, or you'll drag yourself around like a circus freak."

"I won't try anything," Lhex said. "Bring the paper here. I've stared at walls for days."

Until you worked the bed support loose and attacked Bull, Raithen thought. He stepped forward, respecting the boy's skills and focus. Most boys Lhex's age would have been sniveling wrecks by now. Instead, the king's nephew had busied himself with planning escape, conserving energy, and eating to keep himself healthy and strong.

Lhex took the paper Raithen offered. His quick eyes darted over the paper. Hesitantly, he traced the design with his forefinger.

"Where did you get this?" Lhex asked in a quiet voice.

The cog shifted in the river, and water slapped against the hull, echoing throughout the ship. Raithen rode out the change in the ship without much thought. "It doesn't matter. Do you know what it is?"

"Yes," the boy said. "This is some kind of demon script. That symbol belongs to Kabraxis, the demon who supposedly constructed the Black Road."

Raithen drew back and scoffed. "There are no such things as demons, boy."

"My teachers taught me to have an open mind. Maybe demons aren't here now, but that doesn't mean that they were never here."

Raithen peered at the paper, trying to make sense of it. "Can you read it?"

Lhex made a rude noise. "Do you know anyone who can read demon script?"

"No," Raithen said. "But I've known some who sold parchments they said were treasure maps to demon hoards." He'd bought and sold a few of those himself as his belief in such creatures had risen and fallen.

"You don't believe in demons?" the boy asked.

"No," Raithen said. "They're only good for stories best told in taverns or over a slow campfire when there's nothing else to do." Still, the boy's words had intrigued him. *The priest is here hunting a demon?* He couldn't believe it. "What else can you tell me about this design?"

*   *   *

A trail scarred the mountainside, running parallel to the Dyre River. Darrick was certain Raithen's pirate crew used it when changing the guard. He stayed off it, choosing the slower path through the brush.

Mat and Maldrin followed him, staying to the path he chose.

As they neared the riverbank's edge overlooking the three pirate vessels, wisps of silver fog threaded through the brush. Tobacco smoke itched Darrick's nose. Though Captain Tollifer didn't allow smoking on *Lonesome Star*, Darrick had been around a number of men who smoked in ports they patrolled and traded with. He'd never acquired the habit himself and thought it was repugnant. And it reminded him of his father's pipe.

The brush and treeline ended twenty yards short of the area the pirates had been using to shift their stolen goods. Shadows painted the stacks of crates and barrels, giving him more cover to take advantage of.

One of the pirates walked away from the group of five who played dice. "That ale's gettin' the best of me. Hold my place. I'll be back."

"As long as ye have money," one of the other pirates said, "we'll stand ye to a place in this game. This is yer unlucky night and our lucky one."

"Just be glad Cap'n Raithen's been keepin' us headed toward fat purses," the pirate said. He walked around to the side of the crates where Darrick hid in the brush.

Darrick thought the man was going to relieve himself over the side of the riverbank and was surprised to see him dig in the bag at his side frantically once he was out of sight of the others. Pale moonlight touched the dice that tumbled out into the man's waiting palm.

The pirate grinned and closed his fist over the dice. Then he started to relieve himself.

Moving with catlike grace, Darrick crept up behind the pirate. Picking up a stone loose on the ground, Darrick fisted it and stepped behind the pirate, who was humming a shanty tune as he finished. Darrick recognized the tune as "Amergo and the Dolphin Girl," a bawdy favorite of a number of sailors.

Darrick swung the stone, felt the thud of rock meeting flesh, and wrapped an arm around the unconscious pirate to guide him to the ground. Leaving the fallen pirate out of sight from the others, Darrick slid to the riverbank's edge. He peered down, seeing that all three cogs did lie at anchorage beneath the overhang as he'd thought.

He drew back, put his shoulders to the crate behind him, slid his cutlass free, and waved to Maldrin and Mat. They crossed, staying low.

"Hey, Timar," one of the pirates called, "ye comin' back tonight?"

"Told ye he had too much to drink," another pirate said. "Probably start cheatin' any minute now."

"If'n I see them loaded dice of his one more time," another pirate said, "I swear I'm gonna cut his nose off."

Darrick glanced up the slight rise of land toward the ruins of Tauruk's Port. No one came down the trail that wound through the wreckage.

"Four men left," Darrick whispered. "Once one of them makes a noise, there'll be no more hiding here for us."

Mat nodded.

Maldrin slitted his eyes and ran a thumb across the knife in his fist. "Better they not have a chance to make noise, then."

"Agreed," Darrick whispered. "Maldrin, hold the steps. They'll come from below as soon as we announce ourselves. And we will be announcing ourselves. Mat, you and I are going to see about setting the ships on fire below."

Mat raised his eyebrows.

"Barrels of whale oil," Darrick said. "Shouldn't be that hard to get them over the edge of the riverbank. They'll fall straight to the ships below. Get them on the decks of the one port of *Barracuda*, and I'll target the one star-board of her."

Smiling, Mat nodded. "They'll be busy tryin' to save their ships."

"Aye," Darrick said. "We'll use the confusion to get aboard *Barracuda* and see to the king's nephew."

"Be lucky if'n ye don't get yerselves killed outright," Maldrin groused. "An' me with ye."

Darrick smiled, feeling cocky as he always did when he was in the thick of a potentially disastrous situation. "If we live, you owe me a beer back at Rik's Tavern in Westmarch."

"I owe ye?" Maldrin looked as though he couldn't believe it. "An' how is it ye're a-gonna buy me one?"

Shrugging, Darrick said, "If I get us all killed, I'll stand you to your first cool drink in the Burning Hells."

"No," Maldrin protested. "That's not fair."

"Speak up first next time, and you can set the terms," Darrick said.

"Timar!" one of the pirates bellowed.

"He's probably fallen in," another pirate said. "I'll go look for him."

Darrick rose slowly, looking over the stack of crates as one of the pirates peeled off from the game. He held his cutlass in his hand, signaling Mat and Maldrin to stand down. If fortune was going to favor them with one more victim before they set to, so be it.

When the man stepped around the crates, Darrick grabbed him, clapped a hand over the pirate's mouth, and slit his throat with the cutlass. Darrick held the man as he bled out. A look of horror filled Mat's face.

Darrick looked away from the accusation he found in his friend's eyes. Mat could kill to save a friend or a shipmate in the heat of battle, but killing as Darrick had just done was beyond him. To Darrick, there was no remorse or guilt involved. Pirates deserved death, whether by his hands or by the hangman's noose in Westmarch.

As the pirate's corpse shuddered a final time, Darrick released it and stepped away. Blood coated his left arm and warmed him against the chill wind. Knowing they were working on borrowed time, Darrick caught the edge of the crates in front of him and hauled himself around them. He lifted his knees and drove his feet hard against the ground, sprinting toward the three men still occupied with the dice game.

One of the men glanced up, attracted by the flurry of motion coming toward them. He opened his mouth to yell a warning.

SEVEN

"Kabraxis is the demon who created the Black Road," Lhex said.

"What is the Black Road?" Raithen asked.

The boy shrugged, bathed in the golden light of the lantern the pirate captain held. "It's all just legend. Old stories of demons. There's talk that Kabraxis was just an elaborate lie."

"But you said if a demon was involved," Raithen said, "it was all truth once."

"I said it was based on something that was supposed to be the truth," Lhex replied. "But so many stories have been told since the Vizjerei started *supposedly* summoning demons from other worlds. Some of the stories are based on incidents that might have or might not have involved demons, but many are total fabrications. Or a story has been fractured, retold, and made more current. Old wives' tales. Harsus, the toad-faced demon of Kurast—if he even existed—has become four different demons in the local histories. The man who taught me history told me there are sages at work now trying to piece together different stories, examining them for common links that bind them and make only one demon exist where two had stood before."

"Why would they bother with something like that?"

"Because there were supposed to be other demons loose in the world according to all those simpleminded myths," Lhex said. "My teacher believed that men spent so much time trying to name the demons in mythology the better to hunt them down instead of waiting for them to act. To pursue their quarry, the demon hunters need to know how many demons were in our world and where to find them. Sages research those things." The boy snorted. "Personally, I think demons were all named so that a *wise and wizened* sage could recommend employing demon hunters. Of course, that sage would get a cut of the gold paid to rid a place or a city or a kingdom of a demon. It was a racket. A well-thought-out scary story to tell superstitious people and separate them from their gold."

"Kabraxis," Raithen reminded, growing impatient.

"In the beginning years," Lhex said, "when the Vizjerei first began experimenting with demon summoning, Kabraxis was supposed to be one of those demons summoned over and over again."

"Why?"

"Because Kabraxis operated the mystical bridges that stretched from the demon worlds to our world more easily than many did."

"The Black Road is a bridge to the Burning Hells?" Raithen asked.

"Possibly. I told you this was all a story. Nothing more." Lhex tapped the drawing of the elliptical lines threaded through by the solitary one. "This drawing represents the power Kabraxis had to walk between the Burning Hells and this world."

"If the Black Road isn't the bridge between this world and the Burning Hells," Raithen asked, "what else could it be?"

"Some have said it was the path to enlightenment." Lhex rubbed his face as if bored, then smothered a yawn.

"What enlightenment?" Raithen asked.

"Power," Lhex said. "Is there anything else that the legends would offer?"

"What kind of power?"

Lhex frowned at him, faking a yawn and leaning back comfortably against the wall behind them. "I'm tired, and I grow weary of telling you bedtime stories."

"If you want," Raithen suggested, "I can have Bull come back and tuck you in."

"Maybe I'll get his other ear," Lhex suggested.

"You're an evil child," Raithen said. "I can imagine why your father shipped you away to school."

"I'm willful," Lhex corrected. "There is a difference."

"Not enough of one," Raithen warned. "I've got gold enough that I can do without your ransom, boy. Making the king pay is only retribution for past indignities I've suffered at his hands."

"You know the king?" Lhex's eyebrows darted up.

"What power can Kabraxis offer?" the pirate captain demanded.

The river current shifted *Barracuda* again. She floated high, then slithered sideways a moment before settling in. The rigging slapped against the masts and yardarms above.

"They say Kabraxis offers immortality and influence," Lhex replied. "Plus, for those brave enough, and I can't imagine there being many, there is access to the Burning Hells."

"Influence over what?"

"People," Lhex said. "When Kabraxis last walked this world—according to the myths I've read in the philosophy studies I did—he chose a prophet to represent him. A man named Kreghn, who was a sage of philosophy, wrote about the teachings of Kabraxis. And I tell you, that was a very ponderous tome. It bored my arse off."

"The demon's teachings? And it wasn't a banned book?"

"Of course it was," Lhex answered. "But when Kabraxis first walked this world then, no one knew he was a demon. That's the story we've all been told, of course, and there's no proof of it. But Kabraxis was better thought of than some of the demons of legend."

"Why?"

"Because Kabraxis wasn't as bloodthirsty as some of the other demons. He bided his time, getting more and more followers to embrace the tenets he handed down through Kreghn. He taught his followers about the Three Selves. Have you heard of that concept?"

Raithen shook his head. His mind buzzed steadily, gaining speed as he tried to figure out what Buyard Cholik was doing seeking out remnants of such a creature.

"The Three Selves," Lhex said, "consist of the Outer Self, the way a person portrays himself or herself to others; the Inner Self, the way a person portrays himself or herself to himself or herself; and the Shadow Self. The Shadow Self is the true nature of a man or woman, the part of himself or herself that he or she most fears—the dark part every person struggles hardest to hide. Kukulach teaches us that most people are too afraid of themselves to face that truth."

"And people believed that?"

"The existence of the Three Selves is known," Lhex said. "Even after Kabraxis was supposedly banished from this world, other sages and scholars carried on the work Kreghn began."

"What work?"

"The study of the Three Selves." Lhex grimaced as if displeased at Raithen's listening skills. "The legend of Kabraxis first developed the theory, but other scholars—such as Kukulach—have made our understanding of it whole. It just sounds better couched in terms that led the superstitious to believe this was one of the bits of wisdom we needed to save from the demons. Fairy tales and mechanisms to define social order, that's all they were."

"Even so," Raithen said, "there's no power in that."

"The followers of Kabraxis reveled in the exposure of their Shadow Selves," the boy said. "Four times a year, during the solstices and the equinoxes, Kabraxis's worshippers came together and partied, reveling in the darkness that dwelt within them. Every sin known to man was allowed in Kabraxis's name during the three days of celebration."

"And afterward?" Raithen asked.

"They were forgiven their sins and washed again in the symbolic blood of Kabraxis."

"That belief sounds stupid."

"I told you that. That's why it's a myth."

"How did Kabraxis get here?" Raithen asked.

"During the Mage Clan Wars. There was some rumor that one of Kreghn's disciples had managed to open a portal to Kabraxis again, but that was never confirmed."

Has Cholik confirmed it? Raithen wondered. *And did that trail lead here, to the massive door that is located beneath the ruins of Tauruk's Port?*

"How was Kabraxis banished from this world?" Raithen asked.

"According to legend, by Vizjerei warriors and wizards of the Spirit Clan," Lhex replied, "and by those who stood with them. They eradicated the temples to Kabraxis in Viz-jun and other places. Only wreckage of buildings and broken altars remain where the demon's temples once stood."

Raithen considered that. "If a man could contact Kabraxis—"

"And offer the demon a path back into this world?" Lhex asked.

"Aye. What could such a man expect?"

"Wouldn't the promise of immortality be enough? I mean, if you believed in such nonsense."

Raithen thought of Buyard Cholik's body bent with old age and approaching infirmity. "Aye, maybe it would at that."

"Where did you find that?" Lhex asked.

Before Raithen could respond, the door opened, and Bull stepped inside.

"Cap'n Raithen," the big pirate said, holding a lantern high. Concern stretched his features tight. "We're under attack."

Only a few steps short of the pirate about to scream out, Darrick leapt into the air. The other two pirates who had been playing dice reached for their weapons as Darrick's feet slammed into the pirate's head.

Caught by surprise and by all of Darrick's weight, almost too drunk to stand, the pirate flew over the steep side of the riverbank. He didn't even scream. The hard thump told Darrick that the pirate had struck the wooden deck of the ship below instead of the river.

"What the hell was that?" a pirate called out from below.

Darrick landed on the bare stone ground, bruising his hip. He clutched his cutlass and swiped at the nearest pirate's legs, slashing both thighs. Blood stained the man's light-colored breeches.

"Help!" the stricken pirate yelled. "Ahoy the ship! Damn it, but he's cut me deep!" He stumbled backward, trying to pull his sword free of its sash but forgetting to release the ale bottle he already held.

Pushing himself up and drawing the cutlass back again, Darrick drove the pirate backward, close to the riverbank's edge. He whipped the cutlass around and chopped into the pirate's neck, cleaving his throat in a bloody spray. The cutlass blade lodged against the man's spine. Lifting his foot, Darrick shoved the dying man over the riverbank. He turned, listening to the splash as the pirate hit the water only a moment later, and saw Mat engaging the final pirate on guard at the supply station.

Mat's cutlass sparked as he pressed his opponent's guard. He penetrated the pirate's guard easily, hesitating about drawing blood.

Cursing beneath his breath, knowing that they had precious little time to rescue the boy and that they didn't know for sure if he was aboard the ship waiting below, Darrick stepped forward and brought his cutlass down in a hand-and-a-half stroke that split the man's skull. A cutlass wasn't a fancy weapon; it was meant to hack and cleave because shipboard battles on vessels riding the waves tended to be messy things guided mostly by desperation and strength and luck.

Blood from the dead man splashed over Mat and onto Darrick.

Mat looked appalled as the pirate dropped. Darrick knew his friend didn't approve of the blow dealt from behind or while the pirate had already been engaging one opponent. Mat believed in fighting fairly whenever possible.

"Get the barrels," Darrick urged, yanking his sword from the dead man's head.

"He didn't even see you comin'," Mat protested, looking down at the dead man.

"The barrels," Darrick repeated.

"He was too drunk to fight," Mat said. "He couldn't have defended himself."

"We're not here to fight," Darrick said, grabbing Mat's bloody shirtfront. "We're here to save a twelve-year-old boy. Now, *move!*" He shoved Mat at the oil barrels. "There's plenty of fair fights left down there if you're wanting for them."

Mat stumbled toward the oil barrels.

Thrusting his cutlass into his waist sash, Darrick listened to the hue and cry taken up from the ships below. He glanced at the top of the stone steps carved into the side of the overhang.

Maldrin had taken up a position at the top of the steps. The first mate held a war hammer with a metal-shod haft in both hands. The hammer took both hands to wield, but the squared head promised crushed skulls, broken bones, or shattered weapons.

" 'Ware arrows, Maldrin," Darrick called.

A sour grin twisted the first mate's mouth. " 'Ware yer own arse there, skipper. Ain't me gonna be goin' after that there boy."

Darrick kicked a barrel over onto its side. The thick liquid inside glugged. Working with haste, he got behind the barrel and used his hands to roll it toward the riverbank's edge. The downward slope favored the rolling barrel.

After he got it started, he knew he couldn't have easily stopped the barrel's momentum. Giving the barrel a final shove, he watched it roll over the edge and disappear. He stopped at the edge, teetering for a moment, and gazed down, spotting the falling barrel just as it smashed against the ship's deck below. Wisps of fog slid over the deck, but silvery patches showed through where the whale oil reflected the lantern lights of the pirate guards on watch.

Another smash caught Darrick's attention. Glancing to the side, he saw that Mat had succeeded in landing an oil barrel on the other cog. Pirates ran out onto the deck and lost their footing, skidding across the wooden surface.

"Oil!" a pirate cried out. "They've done an' rolled a barrel of oil onto us!"

Hustling back to the stacked barrels, Darrick kicked over two more containers and started them rolling for the riverbank. The thunderous clatter of the wooden barrels slamming against the stone surface echoed around him. He took up one of the lanterns the men on guard had carried.

Mat joined him, grabbing another lantern. "Them men down there, Darrick, they ain't going to have many places to run once we up and do this."

"No," Darrick agreed, looking into his friend's troubled face, "and we aren't going to have much running room, either, once we have the boy. I don't want to have to look over my shoulder for those ships, Mat."

Nodding grimly, Mat turned and sprinted for the riverbank.

Darrick paused only long enough to see the rest of the crew from *Lonesome Star* racing from the mountainside. "Help's coming, Maldrin," he shouted as he ran for the river.

"I got what I got here," Maldrin growled.

At the edge of the river, Darrick marked his spot, judged the rise and fall of the cog on the river current, and threw the lantern. Protected by the glass, the flame remained alive and burning brightly in the lantern. It flew, twisting end over end till it smashed against the ship's deck in the center of the spreading oil pool.

For a moment, the wick sputtered and almost drowned in the oil. Then the flames rose up across the oil like an arthritic old hound rising for one last hunt. Blue and yellow flames twisted into a roiling mass as they fed on the wind as well as the oil.

"Fire!" a pirate yelled.

A flurry of action filled the ship's deck as the pirates gathered from belowdecks. Only a skeleton crew remained aboard.

"Save those ships!" another pirate roared. "Cap'n Raithen will kill ye if'n these ships go down!"

Darrick hoped all the ships burned down to the waterline. If they did, he knew there was a chance Captain Tollifer would be able to sail *Lonesome Star* to Westmarch and return with more ships and warriors in time to catch Raithen and his crew crossing overland to wherever the pirate captain had left his main flotilla.

Glancing to the ship Mat had dropped the barrel on, Darrick saw that it had caught fire as well. Evidently Mat's barrel had caught the wheelhouse, too, giving the flames the reach they needed to get into the sails. Fire blazed along the main mast, threading up through the rigging in a rush.

"Mat," Darrick called.

Mat looked at him.

"Are you ready?" Darrick asked.

Looking only a little unsure of himself, Mat nodded. "As I ever was."

"Going to be me and you down there," Darrick said. "I need you to stand with me." He hurried toward the middle of the riverbank, aiming himself at the middle ship, stretching out his stride.

"I'll be there for you," Mat answered.

Without pausing, Darrick took a final step at the edge of the riverbank over-hang, hurling himself toward the cog's railing, hoping he could make the distance. If he fell to the ship's deck, he was certain to break something. Escape would be out of the question.

Even as Darrick's hands reached for the rigging, fingers outspread to hook into the ropes, the riverbank overhang shattered, shrugging off a section of heavy rock that dropped toward the burning ships and the whole one.

"Under attack from whom?" Raithen demanded, turning toward the door. Automatically, he started walking toward the door. His head was so filled with the sheer impossibility of the attack that he didn't recognize the rustle of clothing for what it was until it was too late. He turned, knowing Lhex had chosen that moment to make his move.

"Don't know," Bull said. "They done went an' set fire to the cogs on either side of us."

Fire? Raithen thought, and there wasn't a more fearsome announcement that could be made aboard a ship. Even if a vessel were holed, a crew might be able to pump the hold dry and keep her afloat till they reached port, but an unchecked fire quickly took away the island of wood and canvas a sailing man depended on.

As close to Bull as he was and with the announcement so new, Raithen's and the big man's attention was on each other, not the boy. Lhex was up behind Raithen in a twinkling. As the pirate captain turned to grab the boy, the young captive bent low, stepped in hard against Raithen to knock him against Bull, and was through the door before anyone could stop him.

"Damn it," Raithen swore, watching the boy speed through the darkness in the hold and run for the stairs leading up to the deck. "Get him, Bull. But I'll want him alive when you bring him back."

"Aye, cap'n." Bull took off at once, closing the distance swiftly with his long stride.

Raithen followed the pirate, his left hand tight on his sword hilt. Already he could see the bright light of a large fire through the cargo hold above them. Gray tendrils of smoke mixed with the fog clinging to the river.

He'd been right. Someone had trailed them for a time through the Gulf of Westmarch. But was it other pirates, or was it the king's navy? Were there only a few men out there, or was there a small armada choking down the river?

The ladder to the main deck quivered and shook in Raithen's hands as Bull climbed it. He was at the bigger man's heels and had just reached the top when the riverbank's overhang cracked and sheared off thirty feet above them. He gazed upward in disbelief as sections of the overhang plummeted down like catapult loads.

A huge granite block dropped onto *Barracuda*'s prow. The impact cracked timbers and tore sections of railing free. *Barracuda* rocked as if she'd been seized in a fierce gale.

A lantern tumbled loose from the hand of a pirate who had been knocked from his feet. Skidding across the wooden deck, the lantern swapped ends several times before disappearing over the ship's side.

Gaining the deck, keeping his knees bent to ride out the violent tossing of *Barracuda* fighting her mooring ropes, Raithen looked at the other two ships. Both cogs were fast on their way to becoming pyres. Flames already twisted through the rigging of the port ship, and the starboard ship wasn't far behind.

Who the hell has done this?

Ahead of him, the boy had almost used up all his running room. He stood with his back to the edge of the swaying ship's deck. The look he gave the black water around the ship indicated that he was in no hurry to try his luck with a swim.

Bull closed on the boy, yelling filth at him, ordering him to stay put.

Raithen yelled at his crew, ordering them to break out buckets and attempt to save both burning cogs. If their hiding place had been discovered, he wanted all of the ships so he could haul away as much as he could.

Kegs and crates floated in the river around *Barracuda*, but some of them sank only a moment later. Feeling the fat-assed way the cog sat in the river, Raithen knew she was taking on water. The impact that had struck the prow must have ruptured the ship as well. At least part of the damage was below the waterline.

Surveying the cracked riverbank overhang high overhead, Raithen knew the destruction wasn't a natural occurrence. Something had happened to cause it. His mind immediately flew to Buyard Cholik. The ruins the priests poked through were underground. The pirate captain had a fleeting thought, wondering if the old priest had survived his own greed.

Then movement in the rigging caught Raithen's eye, and he knew someone was up there. He turned, lifting his sword.

EIGHT

Steadying himself in the rigging of the pirate ship *Barracuda*, Darrick reached for a ratline just as Mat landed beside him. Despite the sudden explosion that had taken out the line of supplies perched on the cliff's edge, he'd landed aboard the pirate vessel. His hands still ached from grabbing the coarse hemp rope.

"You made it," Darrick said, cutting the ratline free.

"Barely," Mat agreed. "An' where is that fabulous luck of mine ye were braggin' about earlier? That damned cliffside blew up."

"But not us with it," Darrick argued. The brief glance he had of the two burning cogs gave him a chance to feel proud of their handiwork. He checked the stone steps and saw Maldrin pushing himself to his feet. The explosion had knocked the first mate from his feet.

"There's the boy," Mat said.

Darrick scanned the deck below and saw the small figure chased into the broken prow by the huge man who followed him. He had little doubt that the boy was the king's nephew. There couldn't be many boys on the pirate vessels.

"Darrick!"

Looking up, Darrick saw Tomas standing on the cliffside near the surviving block-and-tackle rig. The other had gone down with the explosion that had restructured the riverbank.

Tomas waved.

"Get it down here," Darrick ordered. He took hold of the ratline and swung himself from the rigging. Even with the ship foundering in the river—taking on water, he judged—he arced out past the big man cornering the small boy. Reaching the end of his swing, he started back, aiming himself at the big man.

"Bull!" a pirate behind the big man yelled in warning.

The big man glanced around instead of up, though, never seeing Darrick until it was too late.

Bending his knees a little to absorb the shock better, Darrick drove both feet into the big man, catching him across the shoulders. Even then, Darrick felt his knees strain with the impact, and for a moment he didn't think the man was going to budge and was going to smash up against him like a wave shredding over a reef.

But the big man tore free of the deck, sprawling forward, unable to stop himself.

Hurting and winded from the impact, Darrick released the ratline and dropped to the deck only a few feet from the boy. Scrambling to his feet immediately, Darrick drew his cutlass.

"Get him," a tall man in black chain mail ordered.

Darrick got set in time to meet two pirates who rushed him. He slapped their weapons aside with the flat of the cutlass, then stepped in, turned, and elbowed one of the pirates in the face. The man's nose broke with a savage snap. It wasn't the honorable thing to do, but Darrick knew he wasn't up against honorable opponents. The pirates would shove a blade into his back as quickly as he'd do it to them.

The pirate with the broken nose staggered to one side, blood smearing his face. But he didn't go down.

Still in motion, Darrick plucked a dagger from his boot, spun, and shoved it between the pirate's ribs, ripping it through the man's chest and planting it in the heart beneath. He kept moving, getting his cutlass up to parry the other pirate's clumsy attack and riposting.

Mat landed on the ship's deck only a heartbeat later.

"Get the boy," Darrick ordered. Then he raised his voice. "Tomas!"

"Aye, skipper," Tomas called from above. "On its way."

Darrick defended against the pirate's attempt to skewer him, aware that the mountain of a man was getting to his feet as well. From the corner of his eye, Darrick saw the block-and-tackle lower, a small cargo net at the end of it.

"Lhex," Mat said, holding up his empty hands and offering no threat. "Be easy, boy. Me friend *an'* I, why, we're in the king's navy, come here to see you to home safe. If you'll allow us."

The cargo net hit the bucking ship's deck in a loose sprawl of hemp.

"Yes," the boy said.

"Good." Mat smiled at him, reaching for the cargo netting and dragging it toward the boy. "Then let's be away." He raised his voice. "Darrick."

"In a minute," Darrick replied, bracing himself for the coming battle. He flicked the pirate's sword aside with his cutlass, then nipped in with a low blow, ducked and caught the pirate under the arm with his shoulder, and used his strength to lever the man over the ship's side.

"Get over here," the man in black chain mail ordered pirates on the starboard vessel.

Darrick turned to confront the big man, noticing the bandage that covered the side of his head. When he parried the man's blade, testing his strength, Darrick found the man uncommonly strong.

The big man grinned, filled with confidence.

Ducking beneath the big man's blow, Darrick stepped to one side and drove a foot into the side of his opponent's knee. Something popped, but the big man somehow remained on his feet, turning again with a sword cut that would have taken Darrick's head from his shoulders if it had struck.

Moving as swiftly as a striking serpent, Darrick kicked the man in the groin. When the man bent over in pain, Darrick performed a spinning back kick that caught the big man on the wounded side of his head. He howled in agony and went down, holding his head.

The man in black chain mail stepped forward, raising his blade into the *en garde* position. He set to without a word, his sword flashing before him with considerable skill. "I am Raithen, captain of this ship. And you're one breath away from being a dead man."

Without warning, the swordfight took on a deadly earnestness. As skilled as he was, Darrick was hard pressed to keep the pirate captain's blade from finding his throat, eyes, or groin. Nothing was off-limits for the man's sword. Dead, blind, or unmanned, it appeared Captain Raithen would take Darrick any way he could get him.

Still howling in furious pain, the big man rose from the ship's deck and rushed at Darrick. The scarf over the man's head had turned dark with fresh blood. Darrick knew he hadn't caused the wound, only aggravated a fresh one.

"Bull!" Raithen commanded. "No! Stay back!"

Enraged and hurting, the big man didn't hear his captain or ignored him. He ran at Darrick, sweeping his big sword behind him, preparing a blow that completely lacked finesse. Bull interfered with his captain's attack, causing Raithen to draw back before he overexposed himself.

Giving ground before the big man, Darrick noticed that Mat had the boy secure and safe in the cargo net. "Tomas, pull them up."

"Darrick," Mat called.

Shadows spun with wild abandon across the ship's deck as nearby lanterns shifted with the ship's rise and fall on the river current. The crews aboard the other two cogs were fighting losing battles; the flames were going to claim them both within minutes. The heat rolled over Darrick as Tomas and his crew started pulling on the ropes, hauling the cargo net up to the cliffside.

"Darrick!" Mat called, concern thick in his voice.

"Stay with the boy," Darrick ordered. "I want him clear of this." He threw himself back from the big man's blow, sliding across the ship's deck in a rolling rush, coming once more to his feet as Bull bore down on him.

Aware that the cargo netting was quickly rising and that the crew on the other cog had succeeded in spanning the distance between the ships with an oak plank, Darrick took two running steps forward, guessing the distance between himself and Bull. He leapt forward, tucking his chin into his chest, and hurled himself into a front flip just as the big man started his blow.

Upside down, in the middle of the flip, Darrick watched as Bull's cutlass blade passed within inches of him. The pirate's blow pulled Darrick off-balance, causing him to bend over slightly. Darrick landed on his feet on Bull's shoulders and back, got his balance between heartbeats to manage a standing position, and leapt up.

Keeping one hand on his cutlass, stretching his arm as far as he could, Darrick focused on the cargo net being hauled up above him. He tried to curl his fingers in the cargo net, missed by inches.

Then Mat caught him, closing a powerful hand around his wrist, refusing to let him fall even as gravity pulled at him. "I've got ye, Darrick."

Hanging by his arm, Darrick watched as Raithen shook his hand. Something metallic glinted in the pirate captain's hand as he drew his arm back to throw. When the pirate's arm snapped forward, Darrick spotted the slender form of the throwing knife hurtling at him with unerring accuracy. Torchlight splintered along the razor-sharp length. Moving before he had time to think, knowing he couldn't dodge, Darrick swung the cutlass.

Metal rang as the cutlass blade knocked the throwing knife away. Darrick's breath locked at the back of his throat.

"Damn, Darrick," Mat said, "I've never seen the like."

"It's your luck," Darrick said, looking down into the angry face of the pirate captain who was powerless to stop them. Feeling cocky and damn fortunate to be alive, Darrick saluted Raithen with his sword blade. "Another time."

Raithen turned from him, yelling orders to his crew, getting them organized.

Spinning under the cargo net as it continued up, Darrick saw the stone steps where Maldrin encountered a pirate. With a short series of sweeps with the war hammer, the first mate knocked the pirate clear of the steps and sent him plunging down into the river harbor.

Then hands grabbed onto the cargo netting and pulled it to the cliffside.

Darrick caught the cliff edge and hauled himself up as Mat sliced through the cargo net with his sword, spilling himself and the king's nephew out onto the cracked stone surface.

The boy pushed himself to his feet. Blood oozed from cuts on his forehead, his nose, and the lobe of one ear as he took in all the destruction of the cliffside. He swung his head to face Darrick. "Did you and your men do this?"

"No," Darrick said, scanning the ruins. All of them seemed to have changed and shifted. The building they had noticed being used by the pirates had disappeared under a pile of rubble.

The boy pushed away from Mat, who had been checking him over to make certain he was not badly wounded. Cold wind poured down through the Hawk's Beak Mountains, ruffling the boy's hair.

"What have they done?" the boy asked in a dry voice. "Kabraxis is only a myth. The gate to the Burning Hells is only a myth." He looked up at Darrick. "Isn't it?"

Darrick had no answer for the boy.

A horde of demonic flying insects flew out of the yawning mouth of the demon's door toward Buyard Cholik.

Lifting his arms, speaking over the dreadful moaning of the insects' wings, and trying not to give in to the stark fear that nearly overwhelmed him, the old priest spoke the words of a protection spell. He didn't know if it would have an effect on the creatures, but he knew he couldn't hope to run in the shape he was in.

The insects passed Cholik by. A streaming mass of turquoise and bottle-green carapaces and wings illuminated by the torches and lanterns used to light the work area cut through the still air of the cavern. Reaching the front line of slaves, the insects shot into the victims like arrows, burying deeply into their bodies, ripping through clothing to get at the flesh beneath.

The slaves screamed, but their agony was scarcely heard over the drone of insect wings.

Curious and appalled, hoping they would prove to be enough of a sacrifice to a demon, Cholik watched as the slaves jerked up from their hiding places. The insects writhed within the slaves' flesh, looking like dozens of growths and abscesses. Insane with pain and the horror of their situation, the slaves tried to run. Most didn't take more than three or four steps before their bodies burst open and they dropped to the cavern floor. Several torches fell with them, leaving individual fires burning in a line back toward the entrance.

In seconds, more than half of the slaves, mercenaries, and priests lay dead, their bones picked clean by the demonic insects, bloody white skeletons gleaming in the torchlight. While the demonic insects stripped victims of their flesh, it looked as if a blood mist had dawned in the air. Abandoning the dead, the insects flew up to the cavern roof and took refuge among the stalactites. Their buzzing quieted only somewhat as they became spectators to the next events.

Buyard Cholik stared into the dark recesses of the open door ahead of him. Fear settled bone-deep into him, but it wasn't fear of what lay ahead of him. True, there was some fear of the unknown. But the greatest fear he had was that the power he found on the other side of that door wouldn't be enough to take away all the damage that the sands of time had wrought.

Or, possibly, that the power on the other side of the door would find him lacking or wouldn't want him.

Being rejected by a demon after stepping away from the Zakarum Church was horrible to contemplate.

"Master," Altharin whispered. Somehow the man had escaped the destruction that had stricken most of the people around Cholik. "Master, we should go."

"Then go," Cholik said without looking at the man.

"This is an evil place," Altharin said.

"Of course it is." Cholik pulled his robes around himself, took a final breath, and marched toward the door to meet his fate.

Even at the open doorway, all Cholik could see was the unending darkness stretching before him. He paused for an instant at the threshold, tempted to call out. Would a demon answer if he spoke? He didn't know. The texts he'd read that had given him the information to come this far had not suggested anything past this point.

Somewhere ahead, if the texts were right, Kabraxis waited for the man who would free him into the world again.

A cold breeze whipped out of the yawning space before the old priest. Perhaps he would have turned around then, but the cold only reminded Cholik of the chill awaiting him in a grave. It was better to die suddenly tonight than to have to live with all his hopes shattered and stillborn.

But even better than that would be to live with the success of his efforts.

He stepped forward and entered the dark room. Immediately, the steady drone of the insects hidden against the cavern roof dimmed. He knew it wasn't because he'd simply entered another cavern in the cave systems beneath Ransim and beneath Tauruk's Port. The noise dimmed because in that one step he moved a long way from the cavern.

The chill burned into Cholik's flesh, but his fear and his determination to stave off death drove him on. With the lighted cavern behind him, he could see the narrow walls of the tunnel on either side of him as he passed but still nothing of what lay ahead.

You are a man, a deep voice boomed inside the priest's head.

Surprised, Cholik almost faltered. "Yes," he said.

Only a weak man. And you seek to face a demon? The voice sounded amused.

"Humans have slain demons," Cholik said, continuing forward through the narrow tunnel.

Not slain them, the deep voice insisted. *Merely succeeded in binding demons from your world. But only for a time. Diablo has returned. Others were never forced away. Still others remain in hiding, not even known of.*

"You were forced away," Cholik said.

Do you taunt me, human?

"No," Cholik said, gathering all his courage. The ancient texts hadn't suggested anything about what would transpire on this side of the door, but he knew from other readings that demons despised fear. It was a tool, like a blacksmith's hammer, that was used to bend and shape the human lives they controlled. Meeting a demon meant controlling the fear.

Don't lie to yourself, human. You fear me.

"As I would fear falling from a high cliff," Cholik agreed. "Yet to climb, a man must face the fear of falling and overcome it."

And have you overcome your fear?

Cholik licked his lips. All the aches and pains of his advanced years settled into him again, letting him know the spell he'd worked to strip the life energy from the slave was being undone. "I have more to fear from living my life trapped in a failing shell of a body than I do of dying suddenly."

I am a demon, Buyard Cholik. Don't you know that you risk dying for centuries?

Cholik stumbled a little in the darkness. He hadn't thought about that. In the years he'd studied Kabraxis and the Black Road, he'd only pursued knowledge. After winning Raithen over to his side to supply him with slaves and provide transport, he had thought only of digging the ruins of Ransim out to discover the door.

Cholik made his voice strong. "You seek a way out of your prison, Lord Kabraxis. I can be that way."

You? As frail and weak and near to death as you are? The demon laughed, and the hollow booming noise trapped in the tunnel sounded caustic and vibrated through Cholik's body.

"You can make me whole and strong again," Cholik said. "You can return my youth to me. I've read that you have that power. You need a man young in years to help you regain the power that you once had in my world." He paused. "You can make me that man."

Do you believe that?

"Yes." And Buyard Cholik believed in the demon's power as much as he'd believed in anything the Zakarum Church had taught him. If one was false, then it all was false. But if it was true—

Then come, Buyard Cholik, once priest of the Zakarum Church and friend to no demon. Come and let us see what can be made of you.

Nervous fear and anticipation welled up inside the old priest. Sickness coiled inside his stomach, and for a moment he thought he was going to throw up. He centered himself, using all the techniques he'd learned while serving the church, and forced his tired, aching body forward.

A star dawned in the darkness before him, spreading gossamer silver light in all directions. The stone walls on either side melted away, revealing only the darkness of the night. He was not enclosed; he stood on a trail suspended over the longest drop he had ever seen. Visibility ended below the path he walked on, and only then did he realize that he was no longer standing on a stone floor but on a swaying bridge of human bones.

Arm bones, leg bones, and ribs made up the bridge, intermixed with the occasional skull that was complete or damaged. Cholik slowed, feeling the bridge shift dizzyingly beneath him. A skull slid out of place ahead, then bumped and rattled and rolled down the bridge, finally striking a hip bone and bouncing over the bridge's side.

Cholik watched the skull fall, the broken jaw hanging askew as if it were screaming. The skull fell for a long time, tumbling end over end, finally disappearing from the reach of the silver star that waited at the end of the bridge. Only then did Cholik realize the bones were not mortared together; they lay crisscrossed, interlocking to provide support for anyone who crossed the bridge.

Would you go back, Buyard Cholik?

Before he could stop himself, Cholik glanced back along the bridge. Some distance behind him, how far he couldn't tell, the rectangular doorway that opened back into the cavern under the ruins of Ransim gaped. The torches and lanterns flickered inside the cavern, and the stripped skeletons lay on the uneven floor. Thoughts of returning to the apparent safety of the cavern wound through Cholik's mind.

An explosion shook the bridge, and Cholik watched in dismay as a section of crossed bones blew high above the bridge. The displaced bones fell through the darkness like leaves, drifting and spinning.

The gap left in the bridge was too far for Cholik to leap. The old priest realized he was trapped on the bridge.

Let that be your first lesson, the demon said. *I will be your strength when you have no strength of your own.*

Knowing he was doomed, Cholik turned and glanced back up the bone bridge. The silver star glowed brighter, revealing more of the path. The bridge of bones continued to lead up, but it zigzagged back and forth. What seemed to be trees occupied the elbows of the zigzags.

Cholik hesitated, trying to muster more strength but knowing that his body had none left to give.

Come, Buyard Cholik, the demon taunted. *You made your choice when you stepped through that doorway. You only had the illusion of being able to change your mind along the way.*

Cholik felt as though a great hand squeezed his chest, squeezing the breath from him. Was it his heart, then? Was it finally going to fail him? Or was this Zakarum's vengeance for abandoning the church?

Of course, Kabraxis said, *you could throw yourself from the bridge.*

Cholik was tempted, but only for a moment. The temptation came not out of fear but out of rebellion. But that was just a momentary spark. The fear in him of death was a raging bonfire. He lifted a foot and went on.

As he neared the first of the trees, he saw that they bore fruit. When he was closer, he saw the fruits on the tree were tiny human heads. The small faces were filled with fear. Their lips moved in pleading that only then became audible to him. Although he couldn't understand their words, Cholik understood their agony. The sound was an undercurrent, a rush of pain and despair that was somehow horribly melodic.

Tormented voices, Kabraxis said. *Isn't it the sweetest sound you've ever heard?*

Cholik kept walking, finding another bend and another tree and another chorus of hopelessness and hurt. His breath burned inside his chest and he felt as if iron bands constricted his chest.

He faltered.

Come, Buyard Cholik. It's only a little farther. Would you die there and become one of the fruits on the tree?

Pain blurred the old priest's vision, but he lifted his head after the next turn and saw that the bridge remained straight to a small island that floated in the middle of the darkness. The silver star hung behind the shoulder of a massive humanoid shape sitting on a stone throne.

Gasping, no longer able to do more than sip air, knowing he was only inches from death, Cholik made the final ascent and stopped in front of the massive figure on the throne. Unable to stand in front of the demon, the old priest dropped to his hands and knees on the abrasive black rock that made up the island. He coughed, weakly; the coppery taste of blood filled his mouth, and he saw the scarlet threads spray onto the black rock. He watched in stunned horror as the rock absorbed the blood, drinking it in till the rock was once more dry.

Look at me.

Wracked by pain, certain of his death, Cholik lifted his head. "You had best work quickly, Lord Kabraxis."

Even seated, the demon was taller than Cholik standing up. The old priest guessed that Kabraxis was twice as tall as a man, perhaps even as much as fifteen feet tall. The demon's massively broad body was black flesh, marbled with blue fire that burned and ran through him. His face was horrid, crafted of hard planes and rudimentary features: two inverted triangle eyes, no nose but black pits that were nostrils, and a lipless gash of a mouth filled with yellowed fangs. Writhing, poisonous vipers sprouted from his head, all of them beautiful, cool crystal colors of a rainbow.

Do you know of the Black Road? the demon asked, leaning close. All the taunting had left his voice.

"Yes," Cholik gasped.

Are you prepared to face what lies on the Black Road?

"Yes."

Then do so. Kabraxis reached forward, taking Cholik's head between his huge three-fingered hands. The demon's talons bit into the old priest's head, driving into his skull.

Cholik's senses swam. His eyes teared as he stared into the demon's monstrous visage and tasted Kabraxis's foul breath. Before he knew he was doing it, Cholik screamed.

The demon only laughed, then breathed fire over him.

Ninе

Glaring out into the harbor of Tauruk's Port, Raithen knew two of the three cogs were lost. The flames ran up the masts, too well established in the rigging and the sails to be beaten back.

He strode *Barracuda*'s deck with grim determination. "Get off that ship," he yelled to the pirates who had feared him more than they had feared the fire and had fought to save it. The effort to raise his voice hurt his wounded throat.

The pirates obeyed at once, showing no remorse at abandoning the vessel. If losing a few of the pirates would have meant saving the ship, Raithen would have done it, but losing the ship and more men was unacceptable.

Raithen leapt onto the plank that led to the narrow shoreline below the overhanging cliff. Rocks and boulders littered the narrow strip of stone that provided a walkway to the steps cut into the cliffside. Dead pirates sprawled across the steps as well, victims of the Westmarch Navy rescue crew who had taken the boy from him. Other pirates had fallen into the river and been swept away. The old man with the war hammer had become death incarnate while holding the steps. Westmarch archers among the rescue group had wreaked havoc among the pirates for a long minute or two until the pirates had no longer tried to storm the steps to the clifftop.

Raithen knew that the Westmarch sailors had gone, taking the boy with them. The pirate captain walked to the burning cog downstream from *Barracuda*, stopped in front of the mooring rope that held the ship in place, and cut it with one mighty blow from the ax he'd carried from *Barracuda*.

With the thick mooring rope severed, the burning cog slid out into the river, caught in the current, and floated away. It wasn't a vessel anymore; it was a pyre.

"On board *Barracuda*," Raithen ordered his men. "Prepare poles, and let's keep that damn burning tub from her." He crossed to the cog upstream from *Barracuda*, waited until pirates lined the cog's railing, then chopped through the hawser line.

The river carried the burning cog into *Barracuda*. The pirates strove to keep the burning ship from the vessel Raithen hoped to salvage. *Barracuda*'s hull might be split or merely leaking, but he planned on saving her. Without the cog, it would be a long walk back to the rendezvous point where he kept the main ships of his pirate fleet.

Raithen cursed his pirates, finally giving up, returning to *Barracuda* himself, and taking up a pole. He felt the blaze's heat against his face, but he yelled at his pirates. Slowly, propelled by the poles, the burning ship bumped and butted around *Barracuda*.

The pirates started cheering.

Angry, Raithen grabbed the two men nearest him in quick succession and heaved them over *Barracuda*'s railing. The other pirates pulled back at once, knowing they'd all feel their captain's wrath if they stayed near him. Bull was one of the first to step out of reach, knocking over three men in his haste.

Raithen drew his sword, and it gleamed. He faced his men. "You damn stupid louts. We just lost two of our ships, our hidden port, and cargo we aren't going to be able to freight out of here—and you stand there cheering like you done something?"

Smoke stained the pirates' faces, and no few of them bore burns and injuries from the brief battle with the Westmarch sailors.

"I want a crew here to pump this vessel out and see to the repairs," Raithen yelled. "We'll sail at dawn. Those damned Westmarch sailors can't get the river's mouth closed by then. Bull, bring the rest of the men with me."

"Where to, cap'n?" Bull asked.

"We're going to find that damned priest," Raithen said. "If he can persuade me to let him, I'll suffer him to live and take him out of here, too. For a price." He touched his wounded throat. "If not, I'll see him dead before I quit this port, and I'll rob whatever treasures he's scavenged from that buried city as well."

"But, Cap'n Raithen," one of the pirates said, "that explosion what took out the cliffside and flattened the ruins came from the priests' digs. I come from there when them buildings fell on us. Them priests were probably all killed."

"Then we'll be robbing dead men if we can find them," Raithen said. "I've no problem with that." He turned and walked toward the cliffside. As he climbed the crooked stone steps, he shoved debris and dead men from his path. At the least, he intended to get his vengeance on Buyard Cholik—unless the old priest had been killed in the mysterious blast.

* * *

"I won't go! I won't go, I tell you!"

Darrick Lang watched the young boy struggle and fight against Mat and one of the other sailors who pulled him toward the Hawk's Beak Mountains, escape, and *Lonesome Star* in the Gulf of Westmarch.

"Please!" the boy yelled. "Please! You've got to listen to me!"

Frustrated, Darrick waved Mat and the other sailor to halt. They were far enough up the mountainside that he had a clear view of the harbor and the city ruins. The second burning cog was passing beside them out on the river far below. A straggling line of pirates still extricated themselves from the ruins and made their way toward the cliffside harbor, but the line of lanterns and torches streaming up the stone steps announced that the pirates weren't ready to abandon the port yet.

"Listen to you about what?" Darrick asked.

"The demon," the boy said. His breath came in ragged gasps because they had pushed him hard after getting him to the top of the cliff. He was too big to carry and run, so Darrick had grabbed the boy's clothing and pushed and pulled him up the mountainside till he couldn't run anymore.

"What demon?" Mat asked, dropping to one knee to face the boy squarely.

After all those years with his younger brothers and sisters in the burgeoning Hu-Ring household, Darrick knew Mat had far more patience with children than he did.

"We don't need any talk of damn demons," Maldrin snarled. The old mate was covered in blood, but little of it was his own. Despite the battle he'd fought while holding the top of the stone steps until archers among the group could kill or chase away pirates eager to die, he still had stamina. Every hand aboard *Lonesome Star* believed that the crusty old mate could walk any sailor who shipped with him to death, then lace up his boots and walk another league or more. "We've been blessed with no bad luck thus far, an' I wouldn't have it any other way."

"The pirate captain," Lhex said. "He showed me a sign of Kabraxis."

"An' this Kabraxis," Mat said, "he'd be the demon you're referrin' to, would he?"

"Yes," Lhex said, turning and gazing back toward the ruins of Tauruk's Port. "The door to Kabraxis's Lair must be somewhere in that. I heard the pirates talking about the priests who were digging there."

"What sign?" Mat persisted.

"Captain Raithen showed me Kabraxis's sign," Lhex said.

"And how is it, then," Darrick asked in a sharp manner, "that you'd be knowing so much about demons?"

Lhex rolled his eyes at Darrick, showing obvious disapproval. "I was sent to Lut Gholein to be priest-trained. I've spent four years in school there. Some of our main philosophy books deal with the thematic struggle between man and his demons. They aren't supposed to be real. But what if they are? What if Kabraxis is somewhere lost in the ruins of this city?"

The wind came down out of the peaks of Hawk's Beak Mountains and chilled Darrick. Sweat from his exertions matted his hair, but it lifted as he gazed at the ruins of the city. Pirates boiled along the top of the cliff overhanging the Dyre River, their lanterns and torches cutting through the stirring fog and reflecting in the river below.

"We've naught to do with demons, boy," Darrick said. "Our orders are to see you safe and home, and I mean to do that."

"We're talking of a demon here, captain," Lhex insisted.

"I'm no captain," Darrick said.

"These men follow you."

"Aye, but I'm no captain. My own captain has ordered me to bring you back, and I'm going to do that."

"And if the pirates find a demon?" Lhex asked.

"They're welcome to any foul demons they might find, says I," Maldrin offered. "Honest men don't have nothin' to do with demons."

"No," the boy said earnestly, "but demons steal the souls of honest men. And Kabraxis was one of the worst while he walked through these lands."

"Ye ain't gettin' me to believe in demons," Tomas said, his face dark with suspicion. "Stories, that's all them legends are. Just meant to give a man a laugh an' maybe a sense of unease now an' again."

"Kabraxis," Lhex said, "was also called the Thief of Hope. People died wearing his chains, chains that they wove themselves because they believed he offered them redemption from sin, wealth, privilege, and everything else mortals have ever put stock in."

Darrick nodded to the carnage left of the city. "If Kabraxis is responsible for that, I'd say the pirates and the priests aren't going to find him any too thankful to be woke up."

"Not woke up," Lhex said. "Returned to this world. The Prime Evils helped work to seal him from this place because Kabraxis grew too powerful here."

"He was no threat to them three, I'll warrant," Maldrin declared. "Else I'd have heard tell of him, 'cause that woulda been one damned bloody battle."

The wind ruffled the boy's hair, and lightning seared the sky, painting his features the pale color of bone. "Diablo and his brothers feared Kabraxis. He's a patient demon, one who works quietly and takes his time. If Kabraxis has a way into this world, we have to know. We have to be ready for him."

"My job is to get you back to Westmarch and to the king," Darrick said.

"You'll have to carry me," Lhex said. "I won't go willingly."

"Skipper," Maldrin said, "beggin' yer pardon, but tryin' to negotiate them cliffs while carryin' a bellerin' young 'un ain't gonna make for good or safe travelin'."

Darrick already knew that. He took a deep breath, smelling the approaching storm on the wind, and hardened his voice. "Better I should leave you here and tell the king I didn't get to you in time."

The boy's dark eyes regarded Darrick for only a moment. "You won't do that. You can't."

Darrick scowled fiercely, hoping to scare the boy.

"And if you take me back without checking on the demon," Lhex threatened, "I'll tell the king that you had the chance to find out more and you didn't. After the troubles in Tristram, I don't think my uncle will take kindly to a sailor derelict in his duty to find out as much as he could." The boy raised his eyebrows. "Do you?"

Darrick held his tongue for a moment, willing the boy to back down. But even if Lhex did, Darrick knew the truth of the boy's words would weigh on him. The king *would* want to know. And despite the possibility of seeing a demon, which filled him with fear, Darrick was curious.

"No," Darrick said. "I don't think the king would take kindly to such a sailor at all." He raised his voice. "Maldrin."

"Aye, skipper."

"Can you and Mat and a couple others manage getting the waif back to the longboat on your own?" Darrick stared at the boy. "If he agrees to be his most peaceable?"

"I can do that," Maldrin said grudgingly. "If it comes to it, I'll tie him up an' lower him by a rope down the mountainside." He glared at the boy for a moment, then turned his attention back to Darrick. "I don't know that I agree that ye a-harin' off right this minute is all that bright."

"I've never been overly accused of brightness," Darrick said, but it was only bravado that he didn't feel.

"I ain't gonna be left behind," Mat said, shaking his head. "No, if it's to be demon huntin' in the offin', ye got to count me in, Darrick."

Darrick looked at his oldest and best friend in the world. "Aye. I will, and glad to have you, but we're not about to have a good time of it."

Mat smiled. "It'll be an adventure we can tell our grandkids about whilst we dandle 'em on our knees in our dotage, me an' ye."

"I should go with you," Lhex interrupted.

Darrick looked at the boy. "No. You've pushed this as far as needs be. You leave the matter with us now. The king wouldn't be happy to hear that his nephew wasn't amenable to being rescued by men who laid down their lives for him, either. Understand?"

Reluctantly, the boy nodded.

"Now, you did yourself a good turn back on the pirate ship by getting yourself free," Darrick said. "I expect the same behavior while you're with these men I'm asking to guard you with their lives. Have we got a bargain?"

"But I can identify the demon—" the boy said.

"Boy," Darrick said, "I believe I'll know a demon should I see one."

The coming storm continued to gather strength as Darrick led the group of sailors back into the ruins of the city. The moon disappeared often behind the dark, threatening masses of storm clouds, leaving the world cluttered with black silk, then appeared again to draw harsh, long shadows against the silvered grounds. The alabaster columns and stones of the city blazed with an inner fire whenever moonlight touched them.

The sailors moved in silence, unencumbered by armor the way militiamen would be. The king's army corps seldom went anywhere without the rattle and clangor of chain mail or plate. Those things were death to a man fighting on a ship if he somehow ended up in the water.

Finding the entrance to the underground cavern in the ruins turned out to be easy. Darrick held his group back, then followed the last of Raithen's pirates down into the cleared path that led into the bowels of the earth beneath the remains of Tauruk's Port.

None of them spoke over the droning buzz that filled the cavern farther down. The dank earth blocked the wind, but it kept the wintry chill locked around Darrick. The cold made his body ache worse. The long climb up the cliff as well as the battles he'd fought had stripped him of energy, leaving him running on sheer adrenaline. He looked forward to his hammock aboard *Lonesome Star* and the few days' journey it would take to reach Westmarch.

Fog or a dusty haze filled the cavern. The haze looked golden in the dim light of the lanterns Raithen's pirates carried.

Gradually, the tunnel Darrick followed widened, and he saw the great door set into the stone wall on the other side of the immense cavern. The tunnel went no farther.

Raithen and his pirates stopped before entering the main cavern area, and their position blocked Darrick's view of what lay ahead. Several of the pirates seemed in favor of turning and fleeing, but Raithen held them firm with his harsh voice and the threat of his sword.

Hunkering down behind a slab of rock that had slid free during the excavation, Darrick stared into the cavern. Mat joined him, his breath rasping softly.

"What's wrong?" Darrick whispered.

"It's this damn dust," Mat whispered back. "Must not have settled from the explosion earlier. It's tightenin' me lungs up a mite."

Taking the sleeve of his torn shirt in one hand, Darrick ripped it off and handed it to Mat. "Tie this around your face," he told his friend. "It'll keep the dust out."

Mat accepted the garment remnant gratefully and tied it around his face.

Darrick tore the other sleeve off and tied it around his own face. It was a pity because the shirt had been a favorite of his, though it was no comparison to the Kurastian silk shirts he had in his sea chest aboard *Lonesome Star*. Still, growing up hard and without as he had, he treasured things and generally took good care of the ones he had.

Slowly and tentatively, Raithen led his pirates down into the cavern.

"Darrick, look!" Mat pointed, indicating the skeletons that lay in the cavern area. A few looked old, but most of them appeared to have been just stripped clean. Ragged clothing, torn but not aged, swaddled the skeletons.

"I see them," Darrick said, and the hair at the back of his neck lifted. He wasn't one for magic, and he knew he was looking at sure proof that magic had been recently worked. *We shouldn't be here,* he told himself. *If I had any sense, I'd leave now before any of us are hurt.* In fact, he was just about to give the order when a man in black and scarlet robes stepped through the immense doorway in the far wall.

The man in scarlet and black looked as if he was in his early forties. His black hair held gray at the temples, and his face was lean and strong. A shimmering aura flowed around him.

"Captain Raithen," the man in scarlet and black greeted, but his words held little warmth.

The droning buzz increased in intensity.

"Cholik," Raithen said.

"Why aren't you with the ships?" Cholik asked. He crossed the cavern floor, oblivious to the carnage of freshly dead men scattered around him.

"We were attacked," Raithen said. "Westmarch sailors set fire to my ships and stole the boy we held for ransom."

"You were followed?" Cholik's anger cut through the droning noise that filled the cavern.

"Who is that man?" Mat whispered.

Darrick shook his head. "I don't know. And I don't see a demon around here, either. Let's go. It's not going to take that Cholik guy long to figure out what Raithen and his pirates are doing here." He turned and signaled to the other men, getting them ready to withdraw.

"Maybe it wasn't me who got followed," Raithen argued. "Maybe one of those men you buy information from in Westmarch got caught doing something and sold you out."

"No," Cholik said. He stopped out of sword's reach from the pirate captain. "The people who do business with me would be afraid to do something like that. If your ships were attacked, it was through your own gross ineptitude."

"Maybe we should just skip all this faultfinding," Raithen suggested.

"And then what should we do, captain?" Cholik regarded the pirate captain with contempt and cold amusement. "Get to the part where you and your murderous crew kill me and try to take whatever it is that you've imagined I've found here?"

Raithen grinned without humor. "Not a very pretty way to put it, but that's about it."

Cholik drew his robes in with imperial grace. "No. That won't be done this night."

Striding forward, Raithen said, "I don't know what kind of night you had planned for yourself, Cholik, but I aim to get what I came for. My men and I have spent blood for you, and the way we figure it, we haven't gotten much in return."

"Your greed is going to get you killed," Cholik threatened.

Raithen brandished his sword. "It'll get you killed first."

A massive shape stepped through the door in the stone wall. Darrick stared at the demon, taking in the writhing snake hair, the barbaric features, the huge three-fingered hands, and the black skin slashed through with pale blue.

Tеп

Raithen and his pirates drew back from the demon, filled with fear as the nightmare from the Burning Hells strode into the cavern. Men yelled in terror and retreated quickly.

"Okay," Mat whispered, fear shining in his eyes, "we can tell the boy an' his uncle the king that the demon exists. Let's be away from here."

"Wait," Darrick said, mastering the thrumming fear that filled him at the sight of the demon. He peered over the stone slab they hid behind.

"For what?" Mat gave him a disbelieving look. He made the sign of the Light in the air before him unconsciously, like the child he'd been when they'd attended church in Hillsfar.

"Do you know how many men have seen a demon?" Darrick asked.

"An' them livin' to tell about it? Damned few. An' ye want to know why, Darrick? 'Cause they were killed by the demons they was gawkin' at instead of runnin' as any sane man should do."

"Captain Raithen," the demon said, and his voice rolled like thunder inside the cavern. "I am Kabraxis, called the Enlightener. There is no need for disharmony between yourself and Buyard Cholik. You can continue to work together."

"For you?" Raithen asked. His voice held fear and awe, but he stood before the demon with his sword in his fist.

"No," the demon replied. "Through me, you can find the true path to your future." He strode forward, stepping in front of the priest. "I can help you. I can bring you peace."

"Peace I can find in the bottom of a cup of ale," Raithen said, "but I'll not resort to serving demon scum."

Darrick thought the reply would have sounded better if the pirate captain's voice hadn't been shaking, but he didn't doubt that he would have had trouble controlling his own voice if he'd spoken to the demon.

"Then you can die," Kabraxis said, waving a hand in an intricate pattern before him.

"Archers!" Raithen yelled. "Feather that hell-spawned beast!"

The pirates were stunned by the presence of the demon and slow to react. Only a few of them nocked and released arrows. The dozen or so arrows that hit the demon glanced off, leaving no sign that they had ever touched him.

"Darrick," Mat pleaded desperately, "the others have already gone."

Glancing over his shoulder, Darrick saw that it was true. The other sailors who had accompanied them were already beating a hasty retreat.

Mat pulled at Darrick's shoulder. "C'mon. There's naught we can do here. Gettin' ourselves safe an' to home, that's our job now."

Darrick nodded, getting up from behind the stone slab just as waves of shimmering force shot out from the demon's hand.

Kabraxis spoke words Darrick felt certain no human tongue could master. The droning inside the cavern increased, and what looked at first like fireflies dropped from the stalactites above. Flashing through the torchlit cavern, the fireflies slammed into Raithen's pirates but stayed clear of the pirate captain.

Frozen with horror, Darrick watched as the insects reduced the pirates they struck to stacks of bloody bones. No sooner did the freshly flensed corpses strike the stony ground than they lurched back to their feet and took up arms against the few pirates who had survived the initial assault.

The sound of men screaming, cursing, and dying filled the cavern.

Kabraxis walked toward the survivors. "If you would live, my children, come to me. Give yourselves to me. I can make you whole again. I can teach you to dream and be more than you ever thought you could be. Come to me."

A handful of pirates rushed to the demon and supplicated themselves before Kabraxis. Gently, the demon touched their foreheads, leaving a bloody mark tattooed into their flesh, but they were saved from the insects and the skeletons.

Even Raithen went forward.

The light in the cavern dimmed as the men abandoned or lost their lanterns and torches. Darrick struggled to see clearly.

Raithen kept his sword at hand as he walked toward the demon. There was no way out of the cavern. Skeletons of his men blocked the path back to the tunnel. And even if he got past them, there were the carnivorous insects to deal with.

But Raithen wasn't a man to surrender. As soon as he was close enough, one hand extended in obeisance for the demon to take, he struck with the sword, plunging it deep into the demon's abdomen. Jewels gleamed in the hilt and the blade, and Darrick knew the sword possessed some magic. He thought just for a moment that it was a lucky thing he'd not crossed blades with the man aboard *Barracuda*. Even a small wound from an enchanted weapon could wreak havoc with a man if the blade held poison.

Raithen's blade held fire. As soon as the sword plunged into the demon's body, flames lashed out from the wound, scorching the flesh.

Kabraxis howled in pain and staggered back, clutching at the wound in his stomach. Not to be denied, Raithen stepped after the creature, twisting his sword cruelly to open the demon's stomach further.

"You'll die, demon," Raithen snarled, but Darrick heard the panic in the man's voice. Perhaps the pirate captain thought he'd had no choice but to attack, but once committed, he had no choice but to continue.

Demons died on men's blades and by spells learned by human mages, Darrick knew, but demons could be reborn, and it took a hell of a lot to kill them. Most of the time, humans only succeeded in banishing demons from the human planes for a time, and even centuries were nothing to the demons. They always returned to prey on men again.

Raithen attacked again, plunging his sword deep into the demon's stomach. Fire belched forth again, but Kabraxis showed only signs of discomfort, not distress. Flinging out one giant hand, the demon wrapped all three fingers around Raithen's head before he could escape.

Kabraxis spoke again, and an inferno whirled to life in his hand fitted over Raithen's head and shoulders. The pirate captain never managed to scream as his body went stiff. When the demon released the pirate captain, flames had consumed Raithen's upper body, leaving a charred and blackened husk where a powerfully built man had once stood. Orange coals still gleamed in Raithen's body, and smoke rose from the smoldering burns. The pirate captain's mouth was open in a silent scream that would never be heard.

"Darrick," Mat whispered hoarsely, tugging on his friend's arm again.

Bone rasped against rock behind Darrick, alerting him to other dangers waiting in the shadows around him. He glanced up, spotting the skeleton behind Mat that lifted its short sword and aimed at Mat's back.

Darrick fisted Mat's shirt with one hand as he stood and lifted his cutlass. Yanking Mat from the skeleton, Darrick parried the short sword then snap-kicked the skeleton's skull. The undead thing's lower jaw tore loose, and broken teeth flew in all directions. The skeleton staggered back and tried to lift the sword again.

Mat swung his sword at the skeleton. The heavy blade caught the skeleton's neck and snapped the skull off.

"Get those men," the demon roared farther down in the main cavern.

"Go," Darrick yelled, pushing Mat before him. They ran together, avoiding the slow-moving skeletons that had been roused by the demon's unholy magic. Darrick had fought skeletons before, and a man could usually outrun one if he outpaced them. However, if a pack of skeletons came upon a man, they wore him down in numbers, taking hellish beatings before they were finally too damaged to continue.

The droning buzz of the insects filled the cavern behind them, then the tunnel as they zipped into that. Other skeletons rose before Darrick and Mat as they ran through the tunnels beneath the dead city. Some of the skeletons had drying blood covering the white ivory of bone, but others wore tatters of clothing that had gone out of fashion a hundred years ago. Tauruk's Port had been home to innumerable dead, and they were all coming back at the demon's call.

Darrick ran, driving his feet hard, breath whistling against the back of his throat, ignoring the pain and fatigue that filled him, fueling himself with the primordial fear that thrilled through him. "Run!" he yelled to Mat. "Run, damn it, or they'll take you!"

And if they do, it will be my fault. The thought haunted Darrick, echoed inside his skull faster even than his feet drummed the stone floor of the tunnel. *I shouldn't have come here. I shouldn't have let the boy talk me into this. And I should have had Mat clear of this.*

"They're goin' to catch us," Mat wheezed, glancing back.

"Don't look back," Darrick ordered. "Keep your eyes facing front. If you trip, you'll never get back up again in time." Still, he couldn't resist ignoring his own advice and looking over his shoulder.

The skeletons pounded after them, weapons upraised to attack. Their bony feet slapped the stone floor with hollow clacks. As Darrick watched, toes snapped off the skeletons' feet, bouncing crazily through the tunnel. But the insects buzzed by them, the drone growing louder in Darrick's ears.

They easily avoided most of the skeletons that stepped out of the shadows in front of them. The undead creatures were slow, and there was room enough, but a few of them had to be physically countered. Darrick used his sword, unable to utilize the weapon with much skill while running at full tilt, but it allowed him to turn aside swords and spears the skeletons wielded. But each contact cost him precious inches that were damned hard to replace.

How far is it to the river? Darrick tried to remember and couldn't. Now, it suddenly seemed like forever.

The buzzing grew louder, thunderous.

"They're goin' to get us," Mat said.

"No," Darrick said, forcing the words out and knowing he couldn't spare the breath it took. "No, damn it. I didn't bring you here to die, Mat. You keep running."

Suddenly, the mouth of the tunnel was before them, around a turn that Darrick had thought would be their last. Jagged streaks of white-hot lightning seared the sky and clawed away long strips of night for a moment. Hope spurred them both on. He saw it in Mat's face and took heart in it himself. Fewer skeletons darted out of the shadows at them now.

"Just a little farther," Darrick said.

"An' then that long run to the river, ye mean." Mat gasped for breath. He was always the better runner of them, always more agile and quick, almost as at home as Caron in the ship's rigging.

Darrick wondered if his friend was holding back, not running at full speed. The thought angered him. Mat should have left with the other sailors, who were long gone from the tunnels.

Miraculously, they reached the final incline to the mouth of the tunnel leading into the ruins of Tauruk's Port. The carnivorous insects stayed so close now that Darrick saw their pale green coloring out of the corner of his eye as he ran.

Outside the tunnel's mouth, as he emerged into a sudden squall of wind and rain, a stray piece of stone slithered out from under Mat's foot. With a startled yelp, he fell sliding and flailing through the clutter and debris that had tumbled from the ruins.

"Mat!" Darrick watched in horror, stopping his own headlong pace with difficulty. The rain was almost blinding, stinging his face and arms. The storm wasn't a normal one, and he wondered how much the demon's arrival in the cavern below had affected the weather. The ground had already turned mushy underfoot from all the rain in the last several minutes.

"Don't ye stop!" Mat yelled, trying desperately to get up. He spat rainwater from his mouth, the sleeve Darrick had given him to mask out the dust below hanging around his neck. "Don't ye dare stop on account of me, Darrick Lang! I'll not have your death on me head!"

"And I'm not about to let you die alone," Darrick replied, coming to a halt and taking a two-handed grip on the cutlass. The rain cascaded down his body. He was already drenched. The cold water ran into his mouth, carrying a rancid taste he'd never experienced before. Or maybe it was his own fear he tasted.

Then the insects were on them. Mat was to his feet but could only start to run as the cloud of insects closed in for the kill.

Darrick swiped at the insects with his sword, knowing it was ineffectual. The keen blade sliced through two of the fat-bodied demonic bugs, leaving smears of green blood across the steel that washed away almost immediately in the pouring rain. In the next instant, the insects vanished in liquid pops of emerald fire that left a sulfuric stench behind.

Staring, Darrick watched as the rest of the insects lost their corporeal existence in the same fashion. They continued flying at him, the haze of green flames getting so thick it became a wall of color.

"Those foul creatures, they have trouble existin' on this plane," Mat said in awe.

Darrick didn't know. Of the two of them, Mat had more use for the stories of mages and legendary things. But the insects continued their assault, dying by the droves only inches from their intended victims. The cloud thinned out, and the color died down in the space of a drawn breath.

That was when Darrick saw the first of the skeletons race through the tunnel mouth, war ax uplifted. Darrick dodged the ax blow and kicked out, tripping the skeleton. The skeleton fell and slid across the mounds of muddy debris like a stone skipping across a pond, then smashed against the side of a building.

"Go!" Darrick yelled, grabbing Mat and getting him started again.

They ran, sprinting toward the river again. And the skeletons poured after them, soundless as ghosts except for the thud of feet against the rain-drenched land.

Having no reason to hide anymore, certain that any pirates who might remain between them and the river wouldn't stick around long enough to engage them, Darrick fled through the center of the disheveled city. The ragged lightning that tore at the purple sky made the terrain uncertain and tricky. But the thing that got them in the end was that they were human and fatigued. Darrick and Mat slowed, their hearts and lungs and legs no longer able to keep up with the demand. The inexorable rush of the skeletons did not waver, did not slow.

Darrick glanced over his shoulder and saw only death behind them. Black spots swam in his vision, and every drawn breath felt empty of air, as if it was all motion and nothing of substance. The rain-filled wind made it hard to breathe and slashed at his face.

Mat slowed, and they were only a hundred yards or less from the river's edge. If they could make the edge, Darrick thought, and throw themselves into the water—somehow survive the plunge without smashing up against the stone bottom of the riverbed—perhaps they had a chance. The river was deep, and skeletons couldn't swim because they had no flesh to help them remain buoyant.

Darrick ran, throwing down his cutlass, only then recognizing that it was dead weight and was slowing him. Survival didn't lie in fighting; it lay in flight. He ran another ten yards, somehow stretched into another twenty, and kept lifting his knees, driving his numbed feet against the ground even though he didn't trust his footing.

And then, all at once it seemed, they were at the edge. Mat was at his side, face pale from being winded and hurting for far too long. Then, just when Darrick felt certain he could almost throw himself into the air and trust his momentum to carry him over the edge and into the Dyre River beyond, some-thing grabbed his foot. He fell. Senses swimming already, he nearly blacked out from his chin's impact against the ground.

"Get up, Darrick!" Mat yelled, grabbing his arm.

Instinctively, driven by fear, Darrick kicked out, freeing himself from the skeleton that had leapt at him and caught up his foot. The rest of them came on, tightly together like a rat pack.

Mat dragged Darrick to the edge, only just avoiding the outstretched hands and fingers of the skeletons. Without pause, Mat flung Darrick over the edge, then readied himself to jump.

Darrick saw all of that as he began the long fall to the whitecapped river so far below. And he saw the skeleton that leapt and caught Mat before he could get clear of the cliff.

"No!" Darrick shouted, instinctively reaching for Mat although he knew he was too far away to do anything.

But the skeleton's rush succeeded in knocking Mat over the cliff. They fell, embraced in death, and bounced from the cliffside no more than ten feet from the river's surface.

Bone crunched, and the sound reached Darrick's ears just before he plunged into the icy river. In just moments since the storm had started, the river current had picked up. What had once been a steady flow out toward the Gulf of Westmarch now became a torrent. He kicked out, his arms and legs feeling like lead, certain that he'd never break the river's surface before he filled his lungs with water.

Lightning flashed across the sky, bringing the sky sandwiched between the cliffsides out in bold relief for a moment. The intensity was almost blinding.

Mat! Darrick looked around in the water, trying desperately to find his friend. His lungs burned as he swam, pushing himself toward the surface. Then he was through, his vision wavering, and he sucked in a great draught of air.

The river's surface was lathered with whitecaps that washed over him. The fog was thicker now, swirling through the canyon between the mountains. Darrick shook the water from his eyes, searching frantically for Mat. The skeleton had gone in with Mat. Had it dragged him down?

Thunder split the night. A moment later, projectiles started plummeting into the river. Tracking the movement, Darrick saw the skeletons hurling themselves from the cliffside. They smashed into the water nearly thirty feet upriver from him, and that was when he realized how much he had moved since he'd entered the water.

He watched the surface for a moment, wondering if the skeletons had been given an ability to swim. He'd never heard of such a thing, but he'd never seen a demon before tonight, either.

Mat!

Something bumped against Darrick's leg. His immediate gut reaction was to push back from it and get away. Then one of Mat's arms floated through the water by him.

"Mat!" Darrick yelled, grabbing for the arm and pulling the other man up. Lightning seared the sky again as he held Mat's back against his chest and fought to keep both their heads above water. The waves slapped him constantly in the face. A moment later, a skeleton's head popped up in the river, letting Darrick know it still had hold of Mat's leg.

Darrick kicked at the undead thing as the river current caught them more securely in its grasp. The cliffsides holding the river on course swept by at greater speed and Mat's weight combined with the weight of the skeleton was enough to keep Darrick under most of the time. He only came up behind Mat's back for a quick gulp or two of air, then submerged again to keep up the fight to keep Mat's head out of the water. *By the Light, please give me the strength to do this!*

Twice, as the current roiled and changed, Mat was nearly torn from Darrick's grip. The water was cold enough to numb his hands, and the exhaustion he felt turned him weak.

"Mat!" he screamed in his friend's ear, then went down again. He managed to call out to Mat twice more as they raced down the river but didn't get any reaction. Mat remained dead weight in his arms.

Lightning strobed the sky again, and this time Darrick thought he spotted blood on his elbow. It wasn't his blood, and he knew it had to have come from Mat. But when the next wave hit him and he resurfaced, the blood wasn't there, and he couldn't be sure if it ever was.

"Darrick!"

Maldrin's voice came out of the night without warning.

Darrick tried to turn his head, but the effort sent him plunging below the waterline again. He kicked the water fiercely, keeping Mat elevated. When he rose again, thunder boomed.

"—rick!" Maldrin squalled again in his huge voice that could reach the top of the rigging or empty a tavern of sailors that crewed aboard *Lonesome Star*.

"Here!" Darrick yelled, spluttering, spitting water. "Here, Maldrin!" He sank, then fought his way up again. Each time was getting harder. The skeleton remained clinging to Mat's leg, and twice Darrick had to kick free of its embrace. "Hang on, Mat. Please hang on. It's only a little longer now. Maldrin's—" The current took him down again, and this time he spotted light from a lantern on his port side.

"—see them!" Maldrin roared. "Hold this damn boat, lads!"

Darrick came up again, seeing a thick black shadow rising up from behind him, then lightning split the sky and reflected from the dark water, illuminating Maldrin's homely features for a moment.

"I got ye, skipper!" Maldrin yelled above the storm. "I got ye. Just ye come back on ahead to ol' Maldrin, an' let me take some of that weight from ye."

For a moment, Darrick feared that the mate was going to miss him. Then he felt Maldrin take hold of his hair—the easiest part of a drowning victim to grab hold of—and would have screamed with agony if he hadn't been choking on water. Then, incredibly, Maldrin pulled him back toward the longboat they'd arrived in.

"Give a hand!" Maldrin yelled.

Tomas reached down and hooked his hands under Mat's arms, then leaned back and started pulling him into the longboat. "I've got him, Darrick. Let him go."

Freed from Mat's weight, Darrick's arms slid away limply. If it hadn't been for Maldrin holding him, he was sure he would have been swept away by the current. He fought to help Maldrin pull him on board, catching a glimpse of the boy, Lhex, wrapped in a blanket that was already soaked through from the rain.

"We waited for ye, skipper," Maldrin said as he pulled. "Held steady to our course 'cause we knew ye'd be here. Hadn't ever been a time ye didn't make it, no matter how bollixed up things looked like they was a-gettin'." He slapped

Darrick on the shoulder. "An' ye done us proud again. We'll have stories to tell after this 'un. I'll swear to ye on that."

"Something's holdin' him," Tomas said, fighting to bring Mat onto the longboat.

"Skeleton," Darrick said. "It's holding on to his leg."

Without warning, the undead thing erupted from the water, lunging at Tomas with an open mouth like a hungry wolf. Galvanized by his fear, Tomas yanked back, pulling Mat into the longboat with him.

Calmly, as if he were reaching for a dish at a tavern, Maldrin picked up his war hammer and smashed the skeleton's skull. Going limp, the undead creature released its hold and disappeared into the whitecapped water.

Darrick's chest heaved as he sucked in huge lungfuls of air. "River's full of skeletons. They followed us in. They can't swim, but they're in the water. If they find the boat anchor—"

The longboat suddenly shuddered and swung sideways, no longer pointed into the current so that it could ride out the gorged river easier. It bucked like a mustang, throwing all the sailors aboard it around as if they were ragdolls.

"Something's got hold of the rope!" one of the sailors yelled.

Shoving the other sailors aside, Maldrin raked a knife from his boot and sawed through the anchor rope as skeletal hands grabbed the longboat's gunwales. The boat leapt into the river, cutting across the whitecaps like a thing possessed.

"Man those oars!" Maldrin bawled, grabbing one from the middle of the longboat himself. "Get this damn boat squared away afore we all go down with it!"

Struggling against the exhaustion that filled him as well as the longboat being tossed like a child's toy on the rushing river, Darrick pushed himself up and crawled over to Mat Hu-Ring. "Mat!" he called.

Lightning flashed, and thunder filled the river canyon through the Hawk's Beak Mountains.

"Mat." Tenderly, Darrick rolled Mat's head over, sickened at once by how lax and loose it was on his neck.

Mat's face kept rolling, coming around to face Darrick. The wide dark eyes stared sightlessly up, capturing the next reflection of the wicked lightning in them. The right side of Mat's head was covered with blood, and white pieces of bone stuck out from the dark hair.

"He's dead," Tomas said as he pulled on his oar. "I'm sorry, Darrick. I know ye two was close."

No! Darrick couldn't believe it—*wouldn't* believe it. Mat couldn't be dead. Not handsome and witty and funny Mat. Not Mat who could always be counted on to say the right things to the girls in the dives in the port cities they visited on their rounds. Not Mat who had helped nurse him back to health those times Darrick's punishment from his father laid him up for days in the loft above the butcher's barn.

"No," Darrick said. But his denial was weak even in his ears. He stared at the corpse of his friend.

"Like as not he went sudden." Maldrin spoke quietly behind Darrick. "He musta hit his head on a rock. Or maybe that skeleton he was fightin' with done for him."

Darrick remembered the way Mat had struck the cliffside on the long fall from the canyon ridge.

"I knew he was dead as soon as I touched him," Maldrin said. "There wasn't nothin' ye could do, Darrick. Every man that took this assignment from Cap'n Tollifer knew what our chances was goin' in. Just bad luck. That's all it was."

Darrick sat in the middle of the longboat, feeling the rain beat down on him, hearing the thunder crash in the heavens above him. His eyes burned, but he didn't let himself cry. He'd never let himself cry. His father had taught him that crying only made things hurt worse.

"Did you see the demon?" the boy asked, touching Darrick's arm.

Darrick didn't answer. In that brief moment of learning of Mat's death, he hadn't even thought of Kabraxis.

"Was the demon there?" Lhex asked again. "I'm sorry for your friend, but I have to know."

"Aye," Darrick answered through his constricted throat. "Aye, the demon was there right enough. He caused this. Might as well have killed Mat himself. Him and that priest."

Several of the sailors touched their good luck charms at the mention of the demon. They pulled at their oars in response to Maldrin's shouted orders, but it was primarily to direct the craft. The swollen river propelled the longboat swiftly.

Upriver, lantern lights burned aboard the single cog fighting the mooring tether as the river rushed against it. Captain Raithen's crew waited there, Darrick guessed. They didn't know the captain wasn't coming.

Giving in to the overwhelming emotion and exhaustion that filled him, Darrick stretched out over Mat's body, as if he were going to protect him from the gale winds and the rain, the way Mat used to do for him when he was racked with fever while getting well from one of his father's beatings. Darrick smelled the blood on Mat, and it reminded him of the blood that had been ever present in his father's shop.

Before Darrick knew it, he fell into the waiting blackness, and he never wanted to return.

Eleven

Darrick lay in his hammock aboard *Lonesome Star,* his hands folded behind his head, and tried not to think of the dreams that had plagued him the last two nights. In those dreams, Mat was still alive, but Darrick still lived with his parents in the butcher's shop in Hillsfar. Since he had left, Darrick had never gone back.

Over the years since his departure from the town, Mat had gone back to visit with his family on special occasions, arriving there by merchant ship and signing on as a cargo guard while on leave from the Westmarch Navy. Darrick had always suspected that Mat hadn't visited his home or his family as much as he had wanted to. But Mat had believed there would be plenty of time. That was Mat's nature: he never hurried about anything, took each thing in its time and place.

Now, Mat would never go home again.

Darrick seized the pain that filled him before it could escape his control. That control was rock-solid. He'd built it carefully, through beating after beating, through bald cruel things his father had said, till that control was just as strong and as sure as a blacksmith's anvil.

He shifted his head, feeling the ache in his back, neck, and shoulders from all the climbing he'd done the night before last. Turning his head, he gazed out the porthole at the glittering blue-green water of the Gulf of Westmarch. Judging from the way the light hit the ocean, it was noon—almost time.

Lying in the hammock, sipping his breaths, stilling himself and controlling the pain that threatened to overflow even the boundaries he'd put up, he waited. He tried counting his heartbeats, feeling them echo in his head, but waiting was hard when he measured the time. It was better to go numb and let nothing touch him.

Then the deck pipe played, blasting shrill and somehow sweet over the constant wave splash of the ocean, calling the ship's crew together.

Darrick closed his eyes and worked on imagining nothing, remembering nothing. But the sour scent of the moldy hay in the loft above the pens where his father kept the animals waiting to be slain and bled out filled his nose. Before Darrick knew it, a brief glimpse of Mat Hu-Ring, nine years old in clothing that was too big for him, flipped down from the rooftop and landed inside the loft. Mat had climbed the chimney of the smokehouse attached to the barn behind the butcher's shop and made his way across the roof until he was able to enter the loft.

Hey, Mat said, digging in the pockets of the loose shirt he wore and producing cheese and apples. *I didn't see you around yesterday. I thought I'd find you up here.*

In his shame, his body covered with bruises, Darrick had tried to act mad at Mat and make him go away. But it was hard to be convincing when he had to be so quiet. Getting loud enough to attract his father's attention—and let his father know someone else was aware of his punishment—was out of the question. After Mat had spread the apples and cheese out, adding a wilted flower to make it more of a feast and a joke, Darrick hadn't been able to keep up the pretense, and even embarrassment hadn't curbed his hunger.

If his father had ever once found out about Mat's visits during those times, Darrick knew he would never have seen Mat again.

Darrick opened his eyes and stared up at the unmarked ceiling. Just as he would never see him again now. Darrick reached for the cold numbness that he used to cover himself when things became too much. It slipped on like armor, each piece fitting the others perfectly. No weakness remained within him.

The shrill pipe played again.

Without warning, the door to the officers' quarters opened.

Darrick didn't look. Whoever it was could go away, and would if he knew what was good for him.

"Mr. Lang," a strong, imperious voice spoke.

Hurriedly, reflexes overcoming even the pain of loss and the walls he'd erected, Darrick twisted in the hammock, fell out of it expertly even though the ship broke through oncoming waves at the moment, and landed on his feet at attention. "Aye, sir," Darrick answered quickly.

Captain Tollifer stood at the entranceway. He was a tall, solid man in his late forties. Gray touched the lamb-chop whiskers he wore surrounding a painfully clean-shaven face. The captain had his hair pulled back in a proper queue and wore his best Westmarch Navy uniform, green with gold piping. He carried a tricorn hat in his hand. His boots shone like fresh-polished ebony.

"Mr. Lang," the captain said, "have you had occasion to have your hearing checked of late?"

"It's been a while, sir," Darrick said, standing stiffly at attention.

"Then may I suggest that when we reach port in Westmarch the day after tomorrow, the Light willing, you report to a doctor of such things and find out."

"Of course, sir," Darrick said. "I will, sir."

"I only mention this, Mr. Lang," Captain Tollifer said, "because I clearly heard the pipe blow all hands on deck."

"Aye, sir. As did I."

Tollifer raised an inquisitive eyebrow.

"I thought I might be excused from this, sir," Darrick said.

"It's a funeral for one of the men in my command," Tollifer said. "A man who died bravely in the performance of his duties. No one is excused from one of those."

"Begging the captain's pardon," Darrick said, "I thought I might be excused because Mat Hu-Ring was my friend." *I was the one who got him killed.*

"A friend's place is beside his friend."

Darrick kept his voice cold and detached, glad that he felt the same way inside. "There's nothing left that I can do for him. That body out there isn't Mat Hu-Ring."

"You can stand for him, Mr. Lang," the captain said, "in front of his peers and his friends. I think Mr. Hu-Ring would expect that of you. Just as he would expect me to have this talk with you."

"Aye, sir."

"Then I'll expect you to clean yourself up properly," Captain Tollifer said, "and get yourself topside in relatively short order."

"Aye, sir." Even with all his respect for the captain and fear of his position, Darrick barely restrained the scathing rebuttal that came to mind. His grief for Mat was his own, not property of the Westmarch Navy.

The captain turned to go, then stopped at the door and spoke, looking at Darrick earnestly. "I've lost friends before, Mr. Lang. It's never easy. We perform the funerals so that we may begin letting go in a proper fashion. It isn't to forget them but only to remind ourselves that some closure is given in death and to help us mark an eternal place for them in our hearts. A few good men are born into this world who should never be forgotten. Mr. Hu-Ring was one of those, and I feel privileged to have served with him and known him. I won't be saying that in the address topside because you know I stand on policy and procedure aboard my ship, but I wanted you to know that."

"Thank you, sir," Darrick said.

The captain placed his hat on his head. "I'll give you a reasonable amount of time to get ready, Mr. Lang. Please be prompt."

"Aye, sir." Darrick watched the captain go, feeling the pain boiling over inside him, turning to anger that drew to it like a lodestone all the old rage he'd kept bottled up for so long. He closed his eyes, trembling, then released his pent-up breath and sealed the emotions away.

When he opened his eyes, he told himself he felt nothing. He was an automaton. If he felt nothing, he couldn't be hurt. His father had taught him that.

Mechanically, ignoring even the aches and pains that filled him from that night, Darrick went to the foot of his hammock and opened his sea chest. Since the night at Tauruk's Port, he hadn't been returned to active duty. None of the crew had except Maldrin, who couldn't be expected to lie abed on a ship when there was so much to do.

Darrick chose a clean uniform, shaved quickly with the straight razor without nicking himself too badly, and dressed. There were three other junior officers aboard *Lonesome Star*; he was senior among them.

Striding out on deck, pulling on the white gloves that were demanded at ceremonial occasions, Darrick looked past the faces of the men as they stared at him. He was neutral, untouchable. They would see nothing on him today because there was nothing to see. He returned their crisp salutes proficiently.

The noonday sun hung high above *Lonesome Star*. Light struck the sea, glittering in the blue-green troughs between the white rollers like a spray of gemstones. The rigging and canvas sheets above creaked and snapped in the wind as the ship plunged toward Westmarch, carrying the news of the pirate chieftain's death as well as the unbelievable return of a demon to the world of man. The men aboard *Lonesome Star* had talked of little else since the rescue crew's return to the ship, and Darrick knew all of Westmarch would soon be buzzing with the news as well. The impossible had happened.

Darrick took his place beside the three other junior officers at the forefront of the sailors. All three of the officers were much younger than he, one of them still in his teens and already knowing command because his father had purchased a commission for him.

A momentary flicker of resentment touched Darrick's heart as they stood beside Mat's flag-covered body on the plank balanced on the starboard railing. None of the other officers deserved those positions; they had not been true sailing men like Mat. Darrick had chosen to follow his own career and become an officer when offered, but Mat never had. Captain Tollifer had never seen fit to extend a commission to Mat, though Darrick had never understood why. As a rule, such a promotion wasn't done much, and hardly ever was it done aboard the same ship. But Captain Tollifer had done just such a thing.

The officers standing beside Darrick had never known a bosun's lash for failing to carry out a captain's orders or for failing to carry them out to their full extent. Darrick had, and he'd borne those injuries and insults with the same stoic resolve his father had trained him to have. Darrick hadn't been afraid to take command in the field even when under orders. In the beginning, such behavior had earned him floggings under hard captains who refused to acknowledge his reinterpretation of their commands, but under Captain Tollifer, Darrick had come into his own.

Mat had never been interested in becoming an officer. He'd enjoyed the hard life of a sailor.

During their years aboard the ships of the Westmarch Navy, Darrick had often thought that he had been taking care of Mat, looking out for his friend. But looking at the sheet-draped body in front of him, Darrick knew that Mat had never been that interested in the sea.

What would you have done? Where would you have gone if I had not pulled you here? The questions hung in Darrick's mind like gulls riding a favorable wind. He pushed them away. He wouldn't allow himself to be touched by pain or confusion.

Andregai played the pipes, standing at Captain Tollifer's side on the stern castle. The wind whipped the captain's great military cloak around him. The boy—Lhex, the king's nephew—stood at the captain's side. When the pipes finished playing and the last echoing sad note faded away, the captain delivered the ship's eulogy, speaking with quiet dignity of Mat Hu-Ring's service and devotion to the Westmarch Navy and that he gave his life while rescuing the king's nephew. Despite the scattering of facts, the address was formal, almost impersonal.

Darrick listened to the drone of words, the call of gulls sailing after *Lonesome Star* and hoping for a trail of scraps to be left behind on the water. *Slain while rescuing the king's nephew. That's not how it was. Mat was killed while on a fool's errand, and for worrying about me. I got him killed.*

Darrick looked at the ship's crew around him. Despite the action two nights ago, Mat had been the only one killed. Maybe some of the crew believed, as Maldrin said he did, that it was all just bad luck, but Darrick knew that some of them believed it was he who had killed Mat by staying too long in the cavern.

When Captain Tollifer finished speaking, the pipes played again and the mournful sound filled the ship's deck. Maldrin, clad in sailor's dress whites that were worn only on inspection days or while at anchorage in Westmarch, stepped up on the other side of Mat's flag-covered body on the plank. Five more sailors joined him.

The pipes blew again, a going-away tune that always wished the listeners a safe trip. It was known in every maritime province Darrick had ever visited.

When the pipes finished, Maldrin looked to Darrick, a question in his old gray eyes.

Darrick steeled himself and gave an imperceptible nod.

"All right, then, lads," Maldrin whispered. "Easy as ye does it, an' with all the respect ye can muster." The mate grabbed the plank and started it up, tilting it on its axis, and the other five men—two on one side with him and three on the other—lifted together. Maldrin kept a firm grip on the Westmarch flag. Maybe they covered the dead given to the sea, but the flags were not abandoned.

As one, Darrick and the other officers turned to the starboard side, followed a half-second later by the sailors, all of them standing at rigid attention.

"For every man who dies for Westmarch," the captain spoke, "let him know that Westmarch lives for him."

The other officers and the crew repeated the rote saying.

Darrick said nothing. He watched in stony silence and kept himself dwindled down to a small ember. Nothing touched him as Mat's shroud-wrapped body slid from under the Westmarch flag and plummeted down the ship's side to the rolling waves. The ballast rocks wrapped into the foot of the shroud to weight the body dragged it down into the blue-green sea. For a time, the white of the funeral shroud kept Mat's body visible.

Then even that disappeared before the ship sailed on and left it behind.

The pipes blew the disassembly, and the men drifted away.

Darrick walked to the railing, easily riding the rise and fall of the ship that had once made him so sick in the beginning. He peered out at the ocean, but he didn't see it. The stink of the blood and the soured hay in his father's barn filled his nose and took his mind away from the ship and the sea. His heart hurt with the roughened leather strokes his father had used to punish him until only the feel of his fists against Darrick's body would satisfy him.

He made himself feel nothing at all, not even the wind that pushed into his face and ruffled his hair. He had lived much of his life numb. It had been his mistake to retreat from that.

That night, having not eaten at all during the day because it would have meant taking mess with the other men and dealing with all the unasked questions each had, Darrick went down to the galley. Cook usually left a pot of chowder hanging over a low fire during the dogwatches.

Darrick helped himself to the chowder, catching the young kitchen apprentice half dozing at the long table where the crew supped in shifts. Darrick filled a tin plate with the thick chowder. The young kitchen apprentice fidgeted, then got to wiping the table as if he'd been doing that all along.

Without speaking, ignoring the young man's embarrassment and concern that his laxness at his duties might be reported, Darrick carved a thick hunk of black bread from one of the loaves Cook had prepared, then poured himself a mug of green tea. Tea in one hand, thick hunk of bread soaking in the chowder in the tin plate, Darrick headed back up to the deck.

He stood amidships, listening to the rustle and crackle of the canvas overhead. With the knowledge they carried and the fact that they were in clear waters, Captain Tollifer had kept the sails up, taking advantage of the favorable winds. *Lonesome Star* sloshed through the moon-kissed rollers that covered the ocean's surface. Occasional light flickers passed by in the water that weren't just reflections of the ship's lanterns posted as running lights.

Standing on the heaving deck on practiced legs, Darrick ate, managing the teacup and the tin plate in one hand—plate on the cup—and eating with his other hand. He let the black bread marinate in the chowder to soften it up, otherwise he'd have had to chew it for what seemed like forever to break it down. The chowder was made from shrimp and fish stock, mixed with spices from the eastern lands, and had thick chunks of potatoes. It was almost hot enough to burn the tongue even after being dipped on bread and cooled by the night winds.

Darrick didn't let himself think of the nights he and Mat had shared dogwatches together, with Mat telling wildly improbable stories he'd either heard somewhere or made up then and there and swore it was gospel. It had all been fun to Mat, something to keep them awake during the long, dead hours and to keep Darrick from ever thinking back to the things that had happened in Hillsfar.

"I'm sorry about your friend," a quiet voice said.

Distanced as he was from his emotions, Darrick wasn't even surprised to recognize Lhex's voice behind him. He kept gazing out to sea, chewing on the latest lump of black bread and chowder he'd put into his mouth.

"I said—" the boy began again in a slightly louder voice.

"I heard you," Darrick interrupted.

An uncomfortable silence stretched between them. Darrick never once turned to face the boy.

"I wanted to talk to you about the demon," Lhex said.

"No," Darrick replied.

"I am the king's nephew." The boy's tone hardened somewhat.

"And yet you are not the king, are you?"

"I understand how you're feeling."

"Good. Then you'll understand if I trouble you for my own peace while I'm standing watch."

The boy was silent for a long enough time that Darrick had thought he'd gone away. Darrick thought there might have been some trouble with the captain in the morning over his rudeness, but he didn't care.

"What are those lighted patches in the water?" Lhex asked.

Irritated and not even wanting to feel that because long years of experience had shown him that even the smallest emotion could snowball into the feelings of entrapment that put him out of control, Darrick turned to the boy. "What the hell are you still doing up, boy?"

"I couldn't sleep." The boy stood on the deck in bare feet and a sleeping gown he must have borrowed from the captain.

"Then go find a new way of amusing yourself. I'll not have it done at my expense."

Lhex wrapped his arms around himself, obviously chilled in the cool night air. "I can't. You're the only one who saw the demon."

The only one alive, Darrick thought, but he stopped himself before he could think too far. "There were other men in that cavern."

"None of them stayed long enough to see the things you saw."

"You don't know things I saw."

"I was there when you talked with the captain. Everything you know is important."

"And what matter would it be of yours?" Darrick demanded.

"I've been priest-trained for the Zakarum Church and guided my whole life by the Light. In two more years, I'll test for becoming a full priest."

"You're no more than a boy now," Darrick chided, "and you'll be little more than a boy then. You should spend your time worrying about boy things."

"No," Lhex said. "Fighting demons is to be my calling, Darrick Lang. Don't you have a calling?"

"I work to keep a meal between my belly and my spine," Darrick said, "to stay alive, and to sleep in warm places."

"Yet you're an officer, and you've come up through the ranks, which is both an admirable and a hard thing to do. A man without a calling, without passion, could not have done something like that."

Darrick grimaced. Evidently Lhex's identity as the king's nephew had drawn considerable depth in Captain Tollifer's eyes.

"I'm going to be a good priest," the boy declared. "And to fight demons, I know I have to learn about demons."

"None of this has anything to do with me," Darrick said. "Once Captain Tollifer hands my report to the king, my part in this is finished."

Lhex eyed him boldly. "Is it?"

"Aye, it is."

"You didn't strike me as the kind of man who'd let a friend's death go unavenged."

"And who, then, am I supposed to blame for Mat's death?" Darrick demanded.

"Your friend died by Kabraxis's hand," Lhex said.

"But not till you made us go there after I told you all I wanted to do was leave," Darrick said in a harsh voice. "Not till I waited too long to get out of that cavern, then couldn't outrun the skeletons that pursued us." He shook his head. "No. If anybody's to blame for Mat's death, it's you and me."

A serious look filled the boy's face. "If you want to blame me, Darrick Lang, then feel free to blame me."

Vulnerable, feeling his emotions shudder and almost slip from his control, Darrick looked at the boy, amazed at the way he could stand up to him in the dark night. "I do blame you," Darrick told him.

Lhex looked away.

"If you choose to fight demons," Darrick went on, giving in to the cruelty that ran within him, "you'll have a short life. At least you won't need a lot of planning."

"The demons must be fought," the boy whispered.

"Not by the likes of me," Darrick said. "A king with an army, or several kings with armies, that's what it would take. Not a sailor."

"You lived after seeing the demon," Lhex said. "There must be a reason for that."

"I was lucky," Darrick said. "Most men meeting demons don't have such luck."

"Warriors and priests fight demons," Lhex said. "The legends tell us that without those heroes, Diablo and his brothers would still be able to walk through this world."

"You were there when I gave Captain Tollifer my report," Darrick said. The boy hadn't shown any reluctance to throw his weight around with the captain, either, and Tollifer had reluctantly allowed him to sit in during the debriefing the morning before. "You know everything I know."

"There are seers who could examine you. Sometimes when great magic is worked around an individual, traces of it remain within that individual."

"I'll not be poked and prodded," Darrick argued. He pointed to the patches of light gliding through the sea. "You asked what those were."

Lhex turned his attention to the ocean, but his expression revealed that he'd rather be following his own tack in the conversation.

"Some of those," Darrick said, "are fire-tail sharks, named so because they glow in such a manner. The light attracts nocturnal feeders and brings them within striking distance of the sharks. Other light patches are Rose of Moon jellyfish that can paralyze a man unlucky enough to swim into reach of their barbed tentacles. If you want to learn about the sea, there's much I can teach you. But if you want to talk about demons, I'll have no more of it. I've learned more than I ever care to know about them."

The wind changed directions slightly, causing the great canvas sheets overhead to luff a little, then to snap full again as the crew managed the change.

Darrick tasted his chowder but found it had grown cold.

"Kabraxis is responsible for your friend's death," Lhex said quietly. "You're not going to be able to forget that. You're still part of this. I have seen the signs."

Darrick pushed his breath out, feeling trapped and scared and angry at the same time. He felt exactly the way he had when he had been in his father's shop when his father had chosen to be displeased with him again. Working hard to distance himself, he waited until he had control back, then whirled to face the boy, intending—even if he was the king's nephew—to vent some of his anger.

But when Darrick turned, the deck behind him was empty. In the moonlight, the deck looked silver white, striped by the shadows of the masts and rigging. Frustrated, Darrick turned back and flung his plate and teacup over the ship's side.

A Rose of Moon jellyfish caught the tin plate in its tentacles. Lightning flickered against the metal as the barbs tried to bite into it.

Crossing to the starboard railing, Darrick leaned on it heavily. In his mind's eye, he saw the skeleton dive at Mat, sweeping him from the cliff's edge, then witnessed again the bone-breaking thump against the wall of stone. A cold sweat covered Darrick's body as memory of those days in his father's shop stole over him. He would not go back there—not physically, and not in his mind.

TWELVE

Darrick sat at a back table in Cross-Eyed Sal's, a tavern only a couple of blocks back from Dock Street and the Mercantile Quarter. The tavern was a dive, one of the places surly sailors of meager means or ill luck ended up before they signed ship's articles and went back to sea. It was a place where the lanterns were kept dim of an evening so the wenches there looked better if they weren't seen as well, and the food couldn't be inspected closely.

Money came into Westmarch through the piers, in the fat purses of merchants buying goods and selling goods, and in the modest coin pouches of sailors and longshoremen. The money spilled over to the shops scattered along the docks and piers first, and most of it stopped there. Little of it slopped over into the businesses crowded in back of the shops and tradesmen's workplaces and the finer inns and even not-so-fine inns.

Cross-Eyed Sal's featured a sun-faded sign out front that showed a buxom red-haired woman served up on a steaming oyster shell with only her tresses maintaining her modesty. The tavern was located in part of the decaying layer that occupied the stretch of older buildings that had been built higher up on the hillside fronting the harbor. Over the years as Westmarch and the harbor had existed and grown, nearly all of the buildings nestled down by the sea had been torn down and rebuilt.

Only a few older buildings remained as landmarks that had been shored up by expert artisans. But behind those businesses that seined up most of the gold lay the insular layer of merchants and tavern owners who barely made their monthly bills and the king's taxes so they could stay open. The only thing that kept them going was the desperate times endured by out-of-work sailors and longshoremen.

Cross-Eyed Sal's had a rare crowd and was filled near to capacity. The sailors remained separate from the longshoremen because of the long-standing feud between the two groups. Sailors looked down on longshoremen for not having the guts to go to sea, and longshoremen looked down on sailors for not being a true part of the community. Both groups, however, stayed well away from the mercenaries who had shown up in the last few days.

Lonesome Star had returned to Westmarch nine days ago and still awaited new orders. Darrick drank alone at the table. During his leave from the ship, he'd remained solitary. Most of the men aboard *Lonesome Star* had hung around him because of Mat. Blessed with his good humor and countless stories, Mat had never lacked for company, friendship, or a full mug of ale at any gathering.

None of the crew had made an attempt to spend much time with Darrick. Besides the captain's frowning disapproval of an officer's fraternization with crew, Darrick had never proven himself to be good company all the time. And with Mat dead now, Darrick wanted no company at all.

During the past nine days, Darrick had slept aboard the ship rather than in the arms of any of the many willing women, and he'd marked time in one dive after another much like Cross-Eyed Sal's. Normally, Mat would have dragged Darrick into any number of festive inns or gotten them invitations to events hosted by the lesser politicos in Westmarch. Somehow, Mat had managed to meet several wives and courtesans of those men while investigating Westmarch's museums, art galleries, and churches—interests that Darrick had not shared. Darrick had even found the parties annoying.

Darrick found the bottom of his mulled wine again and looked around for the tavern wench who had been serving him. She stood three tables away, in the crook of a big mercenary's arm. Her laughter seemed obscene to Darrick, and his anger rose before he could throttle it.

"Girl," he called impatiently, thumping the tin tankard against the scarred tabletop.

The wench extricated herself from the mercenary's grasp, giggling and pushing against him in a manner meant to free herself and be seductive at the same time. She made her way across the packed room and took Darrick's tankard.

The group of mercenaries scowled at Darrick and talked among themselves in low voices.

Darrick ignored them and leaned back against the wall behind him. He'd been in bars like this before countless times, and he'd seen hundreds of men like the mercenaries. Normally he was among ship's crew, for it was Captain Tollifer's standing order that no crewman drink alone. But since they'd been in port this time, Darrick had only drunk alone, making his way back to the ship each morning before daybreak any time he didn't have an early watch.

The wench brought back Darrick's filled tankard. He paid her, adding a modest tip that drew no favoring glance. Normally Mat would have parted generously with his money, endearing himself to the serving wenches. Tonight, Darrick didn't care. All he wanted was a full tankard till he took his leave.

He returned his attention to the cold food on the wooden serving platter before him. The meal consisted of stringy meat and scorched potatoes, covered with flecks of thin gravy that looked no more appetizing than hound saliva. The tavern could get away with such weak fare because the city was burgeoning with mercenaries feeding at the king's coffers. Darrick took a bit of meat and chewed it, watching as the big mercenary got up from his table, flanked by two of his friends.

Under the table, Darrick pulled his cutlass across his lap. He'd made a practice of eating with his left hand, leaving his right hand free.

"Hey there, swabbie," the big mercenary growled, pulling out the chair across the table from Darrick and seating himself uninvited. The way he pronounced the term let Darrick know the man had meant the address as an insult.

Although the longshoremen rode the sailors about being visitors to the city and not truly of it, the mercenaries were even less so. Mercenaries touted themselves as brave warriors, men used to fighting, and when any sailor made the same claim, the mercenaries tried to downplay the bravery of the sailors.

Darrick waited, knowing the encounter wasn't going to end well and actually welcoming it all the same. He didn't know if there was a single man in the room who would stand with him, and he didn't care.

"You shouldn't go interrupting a young girl what's going about her business the way that young wench was," the mercenary said. He was young and blond, broad-faced and gap-toothed, a man who had gotten by on sheer size a lot of the time. The scars on his face and arms spoke up for a past history of violence as well. He wore cheap leather armor and carried a short sword with a wire-wrapped hilt at his side.

The other two mercenaries were about the same age, though they showed less experience. Darrick guessed that they were following their companion. Both of them looked a little uneasy about the confrontation.

Darrick sipped from the tankard. A warm glow filled his belly, and he knew only part of it was from the wine. "This is my table," he said, "and I'm not inviting company."

"You looked lonely," the big man said.

"Have your eyesight checked," Darrick suggested.

The big man scowled. "You're not an overly friendly sort."

"No," Darrick agreed. "Now, you've got the right of that."

The big man leaned forward, thumping his massive elbows on the table and resting his square shelf of a chin over his interlaced fingers. "I don't like you."

Darrick gripped his cutlass beneath the tabletop and leaned back, letting the wall behind him brace his shoulders. The flickering candle flame on a nearby table drew hollows on the big man's face.

"Syrnon," one of the other men said, pulling at his friend's sleeve. "This man has officer's braid on his collar."

Syrnon's big blue eyes narrowed as he glanced at Darrick's neckline. An oak leaf cluster was pinned to Darrick's collar, two garnets denoting his rank. Putting it on had gotten to be such a habit he'd forgotten about it.

"You an officer on one of the king's ships?" Syrnon asked.

"Aye," Darrick taunted. "You going to let fear of the king's reprisal for attacking a ship's officer in his navy cow you?"

"Syrnon," the other man said. "We'd be better off taking our leave of this man."

Maybe the man would have left then. He wasn't too drunk to forget about listening to reason, and Westmarch dungeons weren't rumored to be hospitable.

"Go," Darrick said softly, giving in to the black mood that filled him, "and don't forget to tuck your tail between your legs as you do." In the past, Mat had always sensed when Darrick's black moods had settled on him, and Mat had always found a way to cajole him out of the mood or get them into areas where that self-destructive bent wouldn't completely manifest itself.

But Mat wasn't there tonight, and hadn't been around for nine long days.

Howling with rage, Syrnon stood and reached across the table, intending to grab Darrick's shirt. Darrick leaned forward and head-butted the big mercenary in the face, breaking his nose. Blood gushed from Syrnon's nostrils as he stumbled back.

The other two mercenaries tried to stand.

Darrick swung his cutlass, catching one of the men alongside the temple with the flat of the blade and knocking him out. Before the unconscious man had time to drop, Darrick swung on the other man. The mercenary fumbled for the sword sheathed at his waist. Before his opponent could get his weapon clear, Darrick kicked him in the chest, driving the mercenary from his feet and back onto a nearby table. The mercenary took the whole table down with him, and four angry warriors rose to their feet, cursing the man who had landed upon the table, and they cursed Darrick as well.

Syrnon pulled his short sword and drew it back, causing nearby men to duck and dodge way. Curses and harsh oaths followed his movement.

Vaulting to the table, Darrick leapt over Syrnon's sword blow, flipped forward—feeling his senses spin for a moment from all he'd had to drink—and landed on his feet behind the big mercenary. Syrnon spun, his face a mask of crimson from his broken nose, and spat blood as he cursed Darrick. The big mercenary swung his short sword at Darrick's head.

Darrick parried the man's attack with the cutlass. Steel rang against steel inside the tavern. Holding the man's blade trapped, Darrick balled his left fist and slammed it into Syrnon's head. Flesh split along the mercenary's cheek. Darrick hit his opponent twice more and felt immense satisfaction with his efforts. Syrnon was bigger than him, as much bigger as his father had been in the back of the butcher's shop. Only Darrick was no longer a frightened boy too small and too unskilled to defend himself. He hit Syrnon one more time, driving the big man backward.

Syrnon's face showed abuse. His right eye promising to swell shut, a split lip and a split ear joined the split over his cheekbone.

Darrick's hand throbbed from the impacts, but he barely took notice of it. The darkness within him was loose now, in a way he'd never seen it. The emotion rattled inside him, growing stronger. Syrnon flailed out unexpectedly, catching Darrick in the face with a hard-knuckled hand. Darrick's head popped backward, and his senses reeled for a moment as the coppery taste of blood filled his mouth and the sour stench of straw filled his nose.

Nobody thinks you look like me, boy! The voice of Orvan Lang crescendoed through Darrick's head. *Why is it, do you think, that a boy don't look like his father? Everybody's tongue's wagging. And me, I love your mother, damn me for a fool.*

Parrying the mercenary's desperate attack again, Darrick stepped forward once more. His sword skill was known throughout the Westmarch Navy by any who had faced him or stood at his side when he'd fought pirates or smugglers.

For a time after he and Mat had arrived in Westmarch from Hillsfar, Darrick had trained with a fencing master, exchanging work and willingness for training. For six years, Darrick had repaired and sanded the fencing room floor and walls and chopped wood, and in turn began the training of others while pursuing a career in the Westmarch Navy.

That training had kept Darrick balanced for a time, until Master Coro's death in a duel with a duke over a woman's honor. Darrick had tracked the two assassins down, as well as the duke, and killed them all. He'd also gotten the attention of the commodore of the Westmarch Navy, who had known about the duel and the assassination. Master Coro also trained several of the ship's officers and practiced with captains. As a result, Darrick and Mat had been assigned berths on their first ship.

After Master Coro was no longer around, the tightfisted control aboard the navy ship had granted Darrick a kind of peace, providing a structured environment. Mat had helped.

Now, with this battle at hand, Darrick felt right. Losing Mat and then waiting for days to be given some kind of meaningful assignment had grated on his nerves. *Lonesome Star,* once a home and a haven, was now a reminder that Mat was gone. Guilt mortared every plank aboard the ship, and Darrick longed for action of any kind.

Darrick played with the mercenary, and the darkness stirred inside his soul. Several times during the years that had passed since he'd escaped Hillsfar, he had thought about going back and seeing his father—especially when Mat had returned to visit his family. Darrick felt no pull toward his mother; she had allowed the beatings his father had given him to go on because she had her own life to live, and being married to one of the town's successful butchers had accommodated her lifestyle.

Darrick had chosen to keep the darkness inside him walled up and put away.

There was no stopping it now, though. Darrick beat back the big mercenary's defenses, chasing the man steadily backward. Syrnon called out for help, but even the other mercenaries appeared loath to step into the fray.

A whistle shrilled in warning.

Part of Darrick knew the whistle signaled the arrival of the king's Peacekeepers. All of the Peacekeepers were tough men and women dedicated to keeping the king's peace inside the city walls.

The mercenaries and few sailors inside the tavern gave way at once. Anyone who didn't recognize a Peacekeeper's authority spent a night in the dungeon.

Caught up in the black emotions that had taken hold of him, Darrick didn't hesitate. He kept advancing, beating the big mercenary back till there was nowhere to run. With a final riposte, Darrick stripped the man of his weapon, knocking it away with a practiced twist of his wrist.

The mercenary flattened against the wall, standing on his toes, with Darrick's cutlass at his throat. "Please," he whispered in a dry croak.

Darrick held the man there. There didn't seem to be enough air in the room. He heard the whistle blasts behind him, one of them closing in.

"Put the sword away," a woman's calm voice ordered him. "Put it away now."

Darrick turned, bringing his cutlass around, intending to back the woman off. But when he attempted to parry the staff she held, she reversed the weapon and thumped it into his chest.

A wild electrical surge rushed through Darrick, and he fell.

Morning sunlight streamed through the bars of the small window above the bunk chained to a stone wall. Darrick blinked his eyes open and stared at the sunlight. He hadn't been taken to the dungeon proper. He was grateful for that, though much surprised.

Feeling as though his head were going to explode, Darrick sat up. The bunk creaked beneath him and pulled at the two chains on the wall. He rested his feet on the floor and gazed out through the bars that made up the fourth wall of the small holding cell that was an eight-foot by eight-foot by eight-foot box. Sour straw filled the thin mattress that almost covered the bunk. The material covering the mattress showed stains where past guests had relieved themselves and thrown up on it.

Darrick's stomach whirled and revolted, threatening to empty. He lurched toward the slop bucket in the forward corner of the holding cell. Sickness coiled through him, venting itself in violent heaves, leaving him barely enough strength to hang on to the bars.

A man's barking laughter ignited in the shadows that filled the building.

Resting on his haunches, not certain if the sickness was completely purged, Darrick glared across the space between his cell and the one on the other side.

A shaggy-haired man dressed in warrior's leathers sat cross-legged on the bunk inside that cell. Brass armbands marked him for an out-of-town mercenary, as did the tribal tattoos on his face and arms.

"So how are you feeling this morning?" the man asked.

Darrick ignored him.

The man stood up from the bunk and crossed to the bars of his own cell. Gripping the bars, he said, "What is it about you, sailor, that's got everybody in here in such an uproar?"

Lowering his head back to the foul-smelling bucket, Darrick let go again.

"They brought you in here last night," the shaggy-haired warrior continued, "and you was fighting them all. A madman, some thought. And one of the Peacekeepers gave you another taste of the shock staff she carried."

A shock staff, Darrick thought, realizing why his head hurt so much and his muscles all felt tight. He felt as if he'd been keelhauled and heaved up against the barnacle-covered hull. Several of the Peacekeepers carried mystically charged gems mounted in staffs that provided debilitating jolts to incapacitate prisoners.

"One of the guards suggested they cave your head in and be done with it," the warrior said. "But another guard said you was some kind of hero. That you'd seen the demon everybody in Westmarch is so afraid of these days."

Darrick clung to the bars and took shallow breaths.

"Is that true?" the warrior asked. "Because all I saw last night was a drunk."

The ratchet of a heavy key turning in a latch filled the holding area, drawing curses from men and women held in other cells. A door creaked open.

Darrick leaned back against the wall to one side of the bars so he could peer out into the narrow aisle.

A jailer clad in a Peacekeeper's uniform with sergeant's stripes appeared first. Dressed in his long cloak, Captain Tollifer followed him.

Despite the sickness raging in his belly, Darrick rose to his feet as years of training took over. He saluted, hoping his stomach wouldn't choose that moment to purge again.

"Captain," Darrick croaked.

The jailer, a square-built man with lamb-chop whiskers and a balding head, turned to Darrick. "Ah, here he is, captain. I knew we were close."

Captain Tollifer eyed Darrick with steel in his gaze. "Mr. Lang, this is disappointing."

"Aye, sir," Darrick responded. "I feel badly about this, sir."

"As well you should," Captain Tollifer said. "And you'll feel even worse for the next few days. I should not ever have to get an officer from my ship from a situation such as this."

"No, sir," Darrick agreed, though in truth he was surprised to learn that he really cared little at all.

"I don't know what's put you in such dire straits as you find yourself now," the captain went on, "though I know Mr. Hu-Ring's death plays a large part in your present predicament."

"Begging the captain's pardon," Darrick said, "but Mat's death has nothing to do with this." He would not bear that.

"Then perhaps, Mr. Lang," the captain continued in frosty tones, "you can present some other excuse for the sorry condition I currently find you in."

Darrick stood on trembling knees facing the ship's captain. "No, sir."

"Then let's allow me to stumble through this gross aberration in what I've come to expect from you on my own," Captain Tollifer said.

"Aye, sir." Unable to hold himself back anymore, Darrick turned and threw up into the bucket.

"And know this, Mr. Lang," the captain said. "I'll not suffer such behavior on a regular basis."

"No, sir," Darrick said, so weak now he couldn't get up from his knees.

"Very well, jailer," the captain said. "I'll have him out of there now."

Darrick threw up again.

"Maybe in a few more minutes," the jailer suggested. "I've got a pot of tea on up front if you'll join me. Give the young man another few minutes to himself; maybe he'll be more hospitable company."

Embarrassed but with anger eating away at his control, Darrick listened to the two men walking away. Mat would have at least joined him in the cell, laughing it up at his expense but not deserting him.

Darrick threw up again and saw the skeleton take Mat from the harbor cliff

one more time. Only this time as they fell, Darrick could see the demon standing over them, laughing as they headed for the dark river below.

"You can't take him yet," the healer protested. "I've got at least three more
stitches needed to piece this wound over his eye together."

Darrick sat stoically on the small stool in the healer's surgery and stared
with his good eye at Maldrin standing in the narrow, shadow-lined doorway.
Other men passed by outside, all of them wounded, ill, or diseased.
Somewhere down the hallway, a woman screamed in labor, swearing that she
was birthing a demon.

The first mate didn't look happy. He met Darrick's gaze for just a moment,
then looked away.

Darrick thought maybe Maldrin was just angry, but he believed there was
some embarrassment there as well. This wasn't the first time of late that
Maldrin had been forced to come searching for him.

Darrick glanced at the healer's surgery, seeing the shelves filled with bottles
of potions and powders; jars of leaves, dried berries, and bark; and bags that
contained rocks and stones with curative properties.

The healer was located off Dock Street and was an older man whom many
sailors and longshoremen used for injuries. The strong odors of all the salves and
medicants the thin man used on the people he gave care to filled the air.

Fixing another piece of thin catgut on the curved needle he held, the healer
leaned in and pierced the flesh over Darrick's right eye. Darrick never moved,
never even flinched or closed his eye.

"Are you sure you wouldn't like something for the pain?" the healer asked.

"I'm sure." Darrick stepped away from the pain, placing it in the same part
of his mind that he'd built all those years ago to handle the hell his father had
put him through. That special place in his mind could hold a whole lot more
than the discomfort the healer handed out. Darrick looked up at Maldrin.
"Does the captain know?"

Maldrin sighed. "That ye got into another fight an' tore up yet another tavern? Aye, he knows, skipper. Caron is over there now, seein' about the dam-
ages an' such ye'll owe. Seein' as how much damage ye been payin' for lately,
I don't know how ye've had the wherewithal to drink."

"I didn't start this fight," Darrick said, but the protest was dulled by weeks
of using it.

"So says ye," Maldrin agreed. "But the captain, he's heard from near to a
dozen other men that ye wouldn't walk away when the chance presented
itself."

Darrick's voice hardened. "I don't walk away, Maldrin. And I damn sure
don't run from trouble."

"Ye should."

"Have you ever known me to retreat from a fight?" Darrick knew he was
trying to put everything he'd done that night into some kind of perspective

for himself. His struggles to find something right about the violence that he constantly got himself into during shore leave had only escalated.

"A fight," Maldrin said, folding his big arms over his broad, thick chest. "No. I've never seen ye back down from action we took together. But ye got to learn when to cut yer losses. The things them men say in them places ye hang out, why, that ain't nothin' to be a-fightin' over. Ye know as well as I that a sailin' man picks his battles. But ye—by the blessed Light, skipper— ye're just fightin' to be fightin'."

Darrick closed his good eye. The other was swollen shut and filled with blood. The sailor he'd fought in Gargan's Greased Eel had fought with an enchanted weapon and snapped into action quicker than Darrick had thought.

"How many fights have ye had in the last two months, skipper?" Maldrin asked in a softer voice.

Darrick hesitated. "I don't know."

"Seventeen," Maldrin said. "Seventeen fights. All of 'em partly instigated by yer own self."

Darrick felt the newest suture pull as the healer tied it.

"The Light must be favorin' ye is all that I can tell," Maldrin said, "for they ain't nobody what's been killed yet. An' ye're still alive to tell of it yer own self."

"I've been careful," Darrick said, and regretted trying to make an excuse at once.

"A man bein' careful, skipper," Maldrin said, "why, he'd never get in them fixes ye been into. Hell's bells, most of the trouble ye're in, a man what's got a thought in his damned head would think maybe he should ought not be in them places."

Darrick silently agreed. But the portent of trouble in those places had been exactly what had drawn him there. He wasn't thinking when he was fighting, and he wasn't in danger of thinking on things too long or too often when he was drinking and waiting for someone to pick a fight with.

The healer prepared another stitch.

"What about the captain?" Darrick asked.

"Skipper," Maldrin said in a quiet voice, "Cap'n Tollifer appreciates every-thin' ye done. An' he ain't about to forget it. But he's a prideful man, too, an' him havin' to deal with one of his own always fightin' while in port during these edgy times, why, it ain't settin' well with him at all. An' ye damn sure don't need me tellin' ye this."

Darrick agreed.

The healer started in with the needle again.

"Ye need help, skipper," Maldrin said. "Cap'n knows it. I know it. Crew knows it. Ye're the only one what seems convinced ye don't."

Taking a towel from his knee, the healer blotted blood from Darrick's eye, poured fresh salt water over the wound, and started putting in the final stitch.

"Ye ain't the only man what's lost a friend," Maldrin croaked.

"I didn't say I was."

"An' me," Maldrin went on as if he hadn't heard Darrick, "I'm near to losin' two. I don't want to see you leave *Lonesome Star,* skipper. Not if'n there's a way I can help."

"I'm not worth losing any sleep over, Maldrin," Darrick said in a flat voice. The thing that scared him most was that he felt that way, but he knew it was only his father's words. They were never far from his mind. He'd found he could escape his father's fists, but he'd never been able to escape the man's harsh words. Only Mat had made him feel differently. None of the other friendships he'd made helped, nor did remembering any of the women he'd been with over the years. Not even Maldrin could reach him.

But he knew why. Everything Darrick touched would eventually turn to dung. His father had told him that, and it was turning out true. He'd lost Mat, and now he was losing *Lonesome Star* and his career in the Westmarch Navy.

"Mayhap ye ain't," Maldrin said. "Mayhap ye ain't."

Darrick ran, heart pounding so hard that the infection in his week-old eye wound thundered painfully. His breath came in short gasps as he held his cutlass at his side and dashed through the alleys around the Mercantile Quarter. Reaching Dock Street, he turned his stride toward Fleet Street, the thoroughfare that went through the Military District where the Westmarch Navy harbor was.

He saw the navy frigates in the distance, tall masts thrust up into the low-lying fog that hugged the gulf coastline. A few ships sailed out over the curve of the world, following a favorable breeze away from Westmarch.

So far, Raithen's pirates had presented no real threat to the city and may even have disbanded, but other pirates had gathered, preying on the busy shipping lanes as Westmarch brought in more and more goods to support the navy, army, and mercenaries. With almost two and a half months gone and no sighting of Kabraxis, the king was beginning to doubt the reports *Lonesome Star* had brought back. Even now, the main problems in Westmarch had become the restlessness of the mercenaries at not having a goal or any real action to occupy them and the dwindling food stores that the city had not yet been able to replace since the action against Tristram.

Darrick cursed the fog that covered the city in steel gray. He'd woken in an alley, not knowing if he'd gone to sleep there or if he'd been thrown there from one of the nearby taverns. He hadn't awakened until after cock's crow, and *Lonesome Star* was due to sail that morning.

He damned himself for a fool, knowing he should have stayed aboard ship. But he hadn't been able to. No one aboard, including the captain and Maldrin, talked with him anymore. He had become an embarrassment, something his father had always told him he was.

Out of breath, he made the final turn toward Spinnaker Bridge, one of the last checkpoints where nonnaval personnel were turned back from entering the Military District. He fumbled inside his stained blouse for his papers.

Four guards stepped up to block his way. They were hard-faced men with weapons that showed obvious care. One of them held up a hand.

Darrick stopped, breathing hard, his injured eye throbbing painfully. "Ship's Officer Second Grade Lang," he gasped.

The leader of the guards looked at Darrick doubtfully but took the papers Darrick offered. He scanned them, noting the captain's seal embossed upon the pages.

"Says here you sail with *Lonesome Star*," the guard said, offering the papers back.

"Aye," Darrick said, raking the sea with his good eye. He didn't recognize any of the ships sailing out into the gulf as his. Maybe he was in luck.

"*Lonesome Star* sailed hours ago," the guardsman said.

Darrick's heart plummeted through his knees. "No," he whispered.

"By rights with you missing your ship like you have," the guardsman said, "I ought to run you in and let the commodore deal with you. But from the looks of you, I'd say getting beaten up and robbed will stand as a good excuse. I'll make an entry of it in my log. Should stand you in good stead if you're called before a naval inquest."

You'd be doing me no favors, Darrick thought. Any man caught missing from his ship for no good reason was hung for dereliction of duty. He turned and gazed out to sea, watching the gulls hunting through the water for scraps carried out by the tide. The cries of the birds sounded mournful and hollow, filtering over the crash of the surf against the shore.

If Captain Tollifer had sailed without him, Darrick knew there no longer remained a berth for him aboard *Lonesome Star*. His career in the Westmarch Navy was over, and he had no idea what lay ahead of him.

He wanted nothing more than to die, but he couldn't do that—he wouldn't do that—because it would mean that his father would win even after all these years. He walled himself off from his pain and loss, and he turned away from the sea, following the street back into Westmarch. He had no money. The possibility of missing meals didn't bother him, but he knew he'd want to drink again that night. By the Light, he wanted to drink right now.

Thirteen

✸

"Master."

Buyard Cholik looked up from the comfortable sofa that took up one long wall of the coach he traveled in. Drawn by six horses on three axles, the coach had all the amenities of home. Built-in shelves held his priestly supplies, clothing, and personal belongings. Lamps screwed into the walls and fluted for smoke discharge through the sides of the coach provided light to read by. Since leaving the ruins of Tauruk's Port and Ransim almost three months ago, almost all of his time had been spent reading the arcane texts Kabraxis had provided him and practicing the sorcery the demon had been teaching him.

"What is it?" Cholik asked.

The man speaking stood outside on the platform attached to the bottom of the coach. Cholik made no move to open one of the shuttered windows so that he might see the man. Since Kabraxis had changed him, altering his mind and his body—in addition to removing decades from his age—Cholik felt close to none of the men who had survived the demon's arrival and the attack of Raithen's pirates. Several of them were new, gathered from the small towns the caravan had passed through on its way to its eventual destination.

"We are approaching Bramwell, master," the man said. "I thought you might want to know."

"Yes," Cholik replied. He could tell by the level ride of the coach that the long, winding, uphill trek they'd been making for hours had passed.

Cholik marked his place in the book he'd been reading with a thin braid of human tongues that had turned leathery over the years. Sometimes, with the proper spell in place, the tongues read aloud from profane passages. The book was writ in blood upon paper made from human skin and bound in children's teeth. Most of the other books Kabraxis had provided over the past months were crafted in things that Cholik in his past life as a priest of the Zakarum Church would have believed to be even more horrendous.

The bookmarker made of tongues whispered a sibilant protest at being put away, inciting a small amount of guilt in Cholik as he felt certain Kabraxis had spelled them to do. Nearly all of his days were spent reading, yet it never seemed enough.

Moving with the grace of a man barely entering his middle years, Cholik opened the coach's door, stepped out onto the platform, then climbed the small hand-carved ladder that led up to the coach's peaked, thatched roof. A small ledge was rather like a widow's walk on some of the more affluent houses in Westmarch where merchanter captains' wives walked to see if their husbands arrived safely back from sea.

The coach had been one of the first things Cholik had purchased with the gold and jewels he and his converted priests had carted out of the caverns with Kabraxis's blessing. In its past life, the coach had belonged to a merchant prince who specialized in overland trading. Only two days before Cholik had bought the coach, the merchant prince had suffered debilitating losses and a mysterious illness that had killed him in a matter of hours. Faced with certain bankruptcy, the executor of the prince's goods had sold the coach to Cholik's emissaries.

Standing on the small widow's walk, aware of the immense forest around him, Cholik looked over the half-dozen wagons that preceded the coach. Another half-dozen wagons, all loaded down with the things that Kabraxis had ordered salvaged from Tauruk's Port, trailed behind Cholik's coach.

A winding road cut through the heart of the forest. Cholik couldn't remember the forest's name at the moment, but he had never seen it before. His travels from Westmarch had always been by ship, and he'd never been to Bramwell as young as he now was.

At the end of the winding road lay the city of Bramwell, a suburb north-northwest of Westmarch. Centuries ago, situated among the highlands as it was, the city had occupied a position of prominence that competed with Westmarch. Bramwell had been far enough away from Westmarch that its economy was its own. Farmers and fishermen lived in the tiny city, descendants of families that had lived there for generations, sailing the same ships and plowing the same lands as their ancestors had. In the old days, Bramwell's sailors had hunted whales and sold the oil. Now, the whaling fleets had become a handful of diehard families who stubbornly got by in a hardscrabble existence more with pride and a deep reluctance to change than out of necessity.

Almost ancient, Bramwell was constructed of buildings two and three stories tall from stones cut and carried down from the mountains. Peaked roofs crafted with thatching dyed a dozen different shades of green mimicked the forest surrounding the city on three sides. The fourth side fronted the Gulf of Westmarch, where a breakwater had been built of rock dug from the mountains to protect the harbor from the harsh seasons of the sea.

From atop the coach and atop the mountains, Cholik surveyed the city that would be his home during the first of Kabraxis's conquests. An empire, Cholik told himself as he gazed out onto the unsuspecting city, would begin there. He rode on the platform, rocking back and forth as the heavy-duty springs of the coach compensated for the road's failings, watching as the city drew closer.

Hours later, Cholik stood beside the Sweetwater River that fed Bramwell. The river ran deep and true between broad, stone-covered banks. The waterway also provided more harbor space for smaller craft that plied the city's trade farther inland and graced the lands with a plenitude of wells and irrigation for the farms that made checkerboards outside the city proper.

At the eastern end of the city where the loggers and craftsmen gathered and where shops and markets had sprung up years ago, Cholik halted the caravan in the campgrounds that were open to all who hoped to trade with the Bramwell population.

Children had gathered around the coach and the wagons immediately, hoping for a traveling minstrel show. Cholik didn't disappoint them, offering the troupe of entertainers he'd hired as the caravan had journeyed north from Tauruk's Port. They'd taken the overland route, a long and arduous event compared with travel by sea, but they had avoided the Westmarch Navy as well. Cholik doubted that anyone who had once known him would recognize him since his youth had been returned, but he hadn't wanted to take the chance, and Kabraxis had been patient.

The entertainers gamboled and clowned, performing physical feats that seemed astounding and combining witty poems and snippets of exchanges that had the gathering audience roaring with laughter. The juggling and acrobatics, while pipes and drums played in the background, drew amazed comments from the families.

Cholik stood inside the coach and watched through a covered window. The festive atmosphere didn't fit with how he'd been trained to think of religious practices. New converts to the Zakarum Church weren't entertained and wooed in such a manner, although some of the smaller churches did.

"Still disapproving, are you?" a deep voice asked.

Recognizing Kabraxis's voice, Cholik stood and turned. He knew the demon hadn't entered the coach in the conventional means, but he didn't know from where Kabraxis had traveled before stepping into the coach.

"Old habits are hard to break," Cholik said.

"Like changing your religious beliefs?" Kabraxis asked.

"No."

Kabraxis stood before Cholik wearing a dead man's body. Upon his decision to go among the humans and look for a city to establish as a beachhead to begin their campaign, Kabraxis had killed a merchant, sacrificing the man's soul to unforgiving darkness. Once the mortal remains of the man were nothing more than an empty shell, Kabraxis had labored for three days and nights with the blackest arcane spells available, finally managing to fit himself into the corpse.

Although Cholik had never witnessed something like that, Kabraxis had assured him that it was sometimes done, though not without danger. When the host body was taken over a month ago, it had been that of a young man who had not yet seen thirty. Now the man looked much older than Cholik, like a man in his twilight years. The flesh was baggy and loose, wrinkled and crisscrossed by hair-fine scars that marred his features. His black hair had gone colorless gray, his eyes from brown to pale ash.

"Are you all right?" Cholik asked.

The old man smiled, but it was with an expression Cholik recognized as Kabraxis's. "I've put many harsh demands on this body. But its use is almost at an end." He stepped past Cholik and peered out the window.

"What are you doing here?" Cholik asked.

"I came to watch you observe the festivities of the people coming to see you," Kabraxis said. "I knew that this many people around you, and so many of them happy and needing diversion, would prove unnerving for you. Life goes much easier for you if you can maintain a somber vigilance over it."

"These people will know us as entertainers," Cholik said, "not as conduits to a new religion that will help them with their lives."

"Oh," Kabraxis said, "I'll help them with their lives. In fact, I wanted to have a word with you about how this evening's meeting will go."

Excitement flared within Cholik. After two months of being on the road, of planning to found a church and build a power base that would eventually seek to draw its constituency from the Zakarum Church, it felt good to know that they were about to start.

"Bramwell is the place, then?"

"Yes," Kabraxis said. "There is old power located within this town. Power that I can tap into that will shape your destiny and my conquest. Tonight, you will lay the first stone in the church we have discussed for the past month. But it won't be of stone and mortar as you think. Rather, it will be of believers."

The comment left Cholik cold. He wanted an edifice, a building that would dwarf the Zakarum Church in Westmarch. "We will need a church."

"We will have a church," Kabraxis said. "But having a church anchors you in one spot. Although I've tried to teach you this, you've still not learned. But a belief—Buyard Cholik, First Chosen of the Black Road—a belief transcends all physical boundaries and leaves its mark on the ages. That's what we want."

Cholik said nothing, but visions of a grand church continued to dance in his head.

"I've given you an extended life," Kabraxis said. "Few humans will ever achieve the years that you've lived so far without the effects of my gift. Would you want to spend all the coming years in one place, looking only over the triumphs you've already wrought?"

"You are the one who has spoken of the need for patience."

"I still speak of patience," Kabraxis insisted, "but you will not be the tree of my religion, Buyard Cholik. I don't need a tree. I need a bee. A bee that flits from one place to another to collect our believers." He smiled and patted Cholik on the shoulder. "But come. We start here in Bramwell with these people."

"What do you want me to do?" Cholik asked.

"Tonight," Kabraxis said, "we will show these people the power of the Black Road. We will show them that anything they may dream possible can happen."

*   *   *

Cholik walked out of the coach and toward the gathering area. He wore his best robe, but it was of a modest style that wouldn't turn away those who were poor.

At least three hundred people ringed the clearing where the caravan had stopped. Other wagons, some of them loaded with straw, apples, and livestock, formed another ring outside Cholik's. Still more wagons, empty of any goods, made seating areas beneath the spreading trees.

"Ah," one man whispered, "here comes the speechmaker. The fun and games are over now, I'll warrant."

"If he starts lecturing me on how to live my life and how much I should tithe to whatever religion he's shilling for," another man whispered, "I'm leaving. I've spent two hours watching performers that I didn't have time to lose and will never get back."

"I've got a field that needs tending."

"And the cows are going to be expecting an early morning milking."

Aware that he was losing part of the audience the performers had brought in for him, knowing not to make any attempt to speak to them of anything smacking of responsibility or donations, Cholik walked to the center of the clearing and brought out the metal bucket containing black ash that Kabraxis had made and presented to him. Speaking a single word of power that the audience couldn't hear, he threw out the ashes.

The ashes roiled from the bucket in a dense black cloud that paused in midair. The long stream of ash twisted like a snake on a hot road as it floated on the mild breeze wafting through the clearing. Abruptly, the ash thinned and shot forward, creating whorls and loops that dropped over the ground. In places, the lines of ash crossed over other lines, but the lines didn't touch. Instead, the loops and whorls stayed ten feet away, creating enough distance that a man might walk under.

The sight of the thin line of ash hanging in the air caught the attention of the audience. Perhaps a mage might be able to do something like that, but not a typical priest. Enough curiosity was created that most people wanted to see what Cholik would do next.

When the line of ash ended its run, it glowed with deep violet fire, competing just for a moment with the deepening twilight darkening the eastern sky and the embers of the sunset west over the Gulf of Westmarch.

Cholik faced the audience, his eyes meeting theirs. "I bring you power," he said. "A path that will carry you to the dreams you've always had but were denied by misfortune and outdated dogma."

An undercurrent of conversation started around the clearing. Several voices rose in anger. The populace of Bramwell clung to their belief in Zakarum.

"There is another way to the Light," Cholik said. "That path lies along the Way of Dreams. Dien-Ap-Sten, Prophet of the Light, created this path for his children, so that they might have their needs met and their secret wishes answered."

"I've never heard of yer prophet," a crusty old fisherman in the front shouted back. "An' ain't none of us come here to hear the way of the Light maligned."

"I will not malign the way of the Light," Cholik responded. "I came here to show you a clearer way into the beneficence of the Light."

"The Zakarum Church already does that," a grizzled old man in a patched priest's robe stated. "We don't need a pretender here digging into our vaults."

"I didn't come here looking for your gold," Cholik said. "I didn't come here to take." He was conscious of Kabraxis watching him from inside the coach. "In fact, I will not allow the gathering of a single copper coin this night or any other that we may camp in your city."

"The Duke of Bramwell will have something to say to you if you try staying," an elderly farmer said. "The duke don't put up with much in the way of grifters and thieves."

Cholik pushed aside his stung pride. That chore was made even harder by the knowledge that he could have blasted the life from the man with one of the spells he'd learned from Kabraxis. After he'd become one of Zakarum's priests and even while he was wearing the robe of a novice, no one had dared challenge him in such a manner.

Crossing the clearing, Cholik stopped in front of a large family with a young boy so crippled and wasted by disease that he looked like a stumbling corpse.

The father stepped up in front of Cholik protectively. The man gripped the knife sheathed at his waist.

"Good sir," Cholik said, "I see that your son is afflicted."

The farmer gazed around self-consciously. "By the fever that come through Bramwell eight years ago. My boy ain't the only one that was hurt by it."

"He hasn't been right since the fever."

Nervously, the farmer shook his head. "None of them has. Most died within a week of getting it."

"What would you give to have one more healthy son to help you work your farm?" Cholik asked.

"I ain't going to have my boy hurt or made fun of," the farmer warned.

"I will do neither," Cholik promised. "Please trust me."

Confusion filled the man's face. He looked at the short, stocky woman who had to be the mother of the nine children who sat in their wagon.

"Boy," Cholik said, addressing the young boy, "would you stay a burden to your family?"

"Hey," the farmer protested. "He ain't no burden, and I'll fight the man that says he is."

Cholik waited. As an ordained priest of the Zakarum Church, he'd have had the father penalized at once for daring to speak to him in such a manner.

Wait, Kabraxis whispered in Cholik's mind.

Cholik waited, knowing the audience's full attention was upon him. It would be decided here, he told himself, whether the audience stayed or went.

Something lit the boy's eyes. His head, looking bulbous on his thin shoulders and narrow chest, swiveled toward his father. Reaching up with an arthritic hand with fingers that had to have been painful to him all the time and could barely be expected to enable him to feed himself, the boy tugged on his father's arm.

"Father," the boy said, "let me go with the priest."

The farmer started to shake his head. "Effirn, I don't know if this is right for you. I don't want you to get your hopes up. The healers at the Zakarum Church haven't been able to cure you."

"I know," the boy said. "But I believe in this man. Let me try."

The farmer glanced at his wife. She nodded, tears flashing diamondlike in her eyes. Looking up at Cholik, the farmer said, "I hold you accountable for what happens to my son, priest."

"You may," Cholik said politely, "but I assure you the healing that young Effirn will shortly enjoy shall be the blessing of Dien-Ap-Sten. I am not skilled enough to answer this boy's wish to be healed and whole." He glanced at the boy and offered his hand.

The boy tried to stand, but his withered legs wouldn't hold him. He folded his hand with its twisted and crooked fingers inside Cholik's hand.

Cholik marveled at the weakness of the boy. It was hard to remember when he'd been so weak himself, but it had been only scant months ago. He helped the boy to his feet. Around the clearing almost every voice was stilled.

"Come, boy," Cholik said. "Place your faith in me."

"I do," Effirn replied.

Together, they walked across the clearing. Not quite to the nearest end of the long rope of black ash that still sparked with violent fire, the boy's legs gave out. Cholik caught Effirn before he could fall, overcoming his own discomfort at handling the disease-ridden child.

Cholik knew that every eye in the clearing was upon him and the child. Doubt touched Cholik as he gazed up at the tall trees around the clearing. If the boy died along the path of the Black Road, perhaps he could hold the townspeople off long enough to get away. If he didn't get away, he was certain he'd be swinging by a noose from one of those branches overhead. He'd heard about the justice meted out by the people of Bramwell to bandits and murderers among their community.

And Cholik intended to help them suckle a serpent to their breasts.

At the beginning of the black ash trail, Cholik helped the boy stand on his own two feet.

"What do I do?" Effirn whispered.

"Walk," Cholik told him. "Follow the trail, and think about nothing but being healed."

The boy took a deep, shuddering breath, obviously rethinking his decision to follow a path so obviously filled with magic. Then, tentatively, the boy released his grip on Cholik's hands. His first steps were trembling, tottering things that had Cholik's breath catching at the back of his throat.

With agonizing slowness, the boy walked. Then his steps came a little smoother, although the swaying gait he managed threatened to tear him from the path.

No sound was made in the clearing as the audience watched the crippled boy make his way around the black ash trail. His feet kicked violet sparks from the black ash with every step he took, but it didn't take long for the steps to start coming more sure, then faster. The boy's shoulders straightened, and his carriage became more erect. His thin legs, then his arms, then his body swelled with increased muscle mass. No longer did his head look bulbous atop his skeletal frame.

And when the black ash trail rose up in the air to pass over a past section, the boy stepped up into the air after it. Before, even omitting the impossibility of following such a thin line of ash into the air, the boy would not have been able to meet the challenge of the climb.

Conversations buzzed around Cholik, and he gloried in the amazement the audience had for what was taking place. While serving at the Zakarum Church, he would never have been allowed to take credit for such a spell. He turned to face the audience, moving so that he faced them all.

"This is the power of the Way of Dreams," Cholik crowed, "and of the generous and giving prophet I choose to serve. May Dien-Ap-Sten's name and works be praised. Join me in praising his name, brothers and sisters." He raised his arms. "Glory to Dien-Ap-Sten!"

Only a few followed his example at first, but others joined. Within a moment, the tumultuous shout rose above the clearing, drowning out the commonplace noise that droned from the city downriver.

Buyard Cholik!

The voiceless address exploded in Cholik's mind with such harshness that he momentarily went blind with the pain and was nauseated.

Beware, Kabraxis said. *The spell is becoming unraveled.*

Gathering himself, Cholik glanced back at the maze created by the line he'd cast, watching as the starting point of the line suddenly burst into violet sparks and burned rapidly. The small fire raced along the length of the line of ash. As the fire moved, it consumed the ash, leaving nothing behind.

The fire raced for the boy.

If the fire reaches the boy, Kabraxis warned, *he will be destroyed.*

Cholik walked to the other end of the line of ash, watching as the fire swept toward the boy. He thought furiously, knowing he couldn't show any fear to the cheering audience.

If we lose these people now, Kabraxis said, *we might not get them back. If a miracle occurs, we will win believers, but if a disaster happens, we could be lost. It will be years before we can come back here, and maybe even longer before these people will forget what happened tonight to let us attempt to win them over again.*

"Effirn," Cholik called.

The boy looked up at him, taking his eyes from the path for a moment. His steps never faltered. "Look at me!" he cried gleefully. "Look at me. I'm walking."

"Yes, Effirn," Cholik said, "and everyone here is proud of you and grateful to Dien-Ap-Sten, as is proper. However, there is something I need to know." Glancing back at the relentless purple fire pursuing the boy, he saw that it was only two curves back from Effirn. The end of the ash trail was still thirty feet from the boy.

"What?" Effirn asked.

"Can you run?"

The boy's face worked in confusion. "I don't know. I've never tried."

The violet fire gained another ten feet on him.

"Try now," Cholik suggested. He held his arms out. "Run to me, Effirn. Quickly, boy. Fast as you can."

Tentatively, Effirn started running, trying out his new muscles and abilities. He ran, and the violet fire burning up the ash trail chased him, still gaining, but by inches now rather than feet.

"Come on, Effirn," Cholik cheered. "Show your da how fast you've become now that Dien-Ap-Sten has shown you grace."

Effirn ran, laughing the whole way. The conversation of the audience picked up intensity. The boy reached the trail's end, sweeping down the final curve to the ground, and was in Cholik's arms just as the violet blaze hit the end of the trail and vanished in a puff of bruised embers.

Feeling as though he'd just escaped death again, Cholik held the boy to him for a moment, surprised at how big Effirn had gotten. He felt the boy's arms and legs tight against him.

"Thank you, thank you, thank you," Effirn gasped, hugging Cholik with strong arms and legs.

Embarrassed and flushed with excitement at the same time, Cholik hugged the boy back. Effirn's health meant nothing but success for him in Bramwell, but Cholik didn't understand how the demon had worked the magic.

Healing is simple enough, Kabraxis said in Cholik's mind. *Causing hurt and pain are separate issues, and much harder if it's going to be lasting. In order to learn how to injure someone, the magic is designed so that first a person learns to heal.*

Cholik had never been taught that.

There are a number of things you haven't been taught, Kabraxis said. *But you have time left to you. I will teach you. Turn, Buyard Cholik, and greet your new parishioners.*

Easing the boy's grip from him, Cholik turned to face the parents. No one thought to challenge him about why the ash trail had burned away.

Released, wanting to show off his newfound strength, the boy raced across the clearing. His brothers and sisters cheered him on, and his father caught him up and pulled him into a fierce hug before handing him off to his mother. She held her son to her, tears washing unashamedly down her face.

Cholik watched the mother and son, amazed at the way the scene touched him.

You're surprised by how good you feel at having had a hand in healing the boy? Kabraxis asked.

"Yes," Cholik whispered, knowing no one around him could hear him but that the demon could.

It shouldn't. To know the Darkness, a being must also know the Light. You lived your life cloistered in Westmarch. The only people you met were those who wanted your position.

Or those whose positions I coveted, Cholik realized.

And the Zakarum Church never allowed you to be so personal in the healing properties they doled out, the demon said.

"No."

The Light is afraid to give many people powers like I have given you, Kabraxis said. *People who have powers like this get noticed by regular people. In short order, they become heroes or talked-about people. In only a little more time, the tales that are told about them allow them to take on lofty mantles. The stewards of the Light are jealous of that.*

"But demons aren't?" Cholik asked.

Kabraxis laughed, and the grating, thunderous noise echoing inside Cholik's head was almost painful. *Demons aren't as jealous as the stewards of Light would have you believe. Nor are they as controlling as the stewards of Light. I ask you, who always has the most rules? The most limitations?*

Cholik didn't answer.

Why do you think the stewards of Light offer so many rules? Kabraxis asked. *To keep the balance in their favor, of course. But demons, we believe in letting all who support the Darkness have power. Some have more power than others. But they earn it. Just as you have earned that which I'm giving you the day you faced your own fear of dying and sought out the buried gateway to me.*

"I had no choice," Cholik said.

Humans always have choices. That's how the stewards of Light seek to confuse you. You have choices, but you can't choose most of them because the stewards of Light have decreed them as wrong. As an enlightened student of the Light, you're supposed to know that those choices are wrong. So where does that really leave you? How many choices do you really have?

Cholik silently agreed.

Go to these people, Buyard Cholik. You'll find converts among them now. Once they have discovered that you have the power to make changes that will let them attain their goals and desires, they will flock to you. Next, we must begin the church, and we must find disciples among these people who will help you spread word of me. For now, give the gift of health to those who are sick among these before you. They will talk. By morning, there won't be anyone in this city who hasn't heard of you.

Glorying in the newfound respect and prestige he'd gained by healing the boy, Cholik went forward. His body sang with the buzzing thrill of the power Kabraxis channeled through him. The power drew him to the weak and infirm in the crowd.

Laying hands on the people in the crowd as he came to them, Cholik healed fevers and infections, took away warts and arthritis, straightened a leg that had grown crooked after being set and healing, brought senses back to an elderly grandmother who had been addled for years according to the son who cared for her.

"I would like to settle in Bramwell," Cholik said as the Gulf of Westmarch drank down the sun and twilight turned to night around them.

The crowd cheered in response to his announcement.

"But I will need a church built," Cholik continued. "Once a permanent church is built, the miracles wrought by Dien-Ap-Sten will continue to grow. Come to me that I may introduce you to the prophet I choose to serve."

For a night, Buyard Cholik was closer to lasting renown than he'd ever been in his life. It was a heady feeling, one that he promised himself he would get to know more intimately.

Nothing would stop him.

FOURTEEN

"Are you a sailor?" the pretty serving wench asked.

Darrick looked up at her from the bowl of thick potatoes and meat stew and didn't let the brief pang of loss her words brought touch him. "No," he replied, because he hadn't been a sailor for months.

The serving girl was a raven-haired beauty scarcely more than twenty years old if she was that. Her black skirt was short and high, revealing a lot of her long, beautiful legs. She wore her hair pulled back, tied at the neck.

"Why do you ask?" Darrick held her eyes for a moment, then she looked away.

"Only because your rolling gait as you entered the door reminded me of a sailor's," the wench said. "My father was a sailor. Born to the sea and lost to the sea, as is the usual course for many sailors."

"What is your name?" Darrick asked.

"Dahni," she said, and smiled.

"It's been nice meeting you, Dahni."

For a moment, the wench gazed around the table, trying to find something to do. But she'd already refilled his tankard, and his bowl remained more than half full. "If you need anything," she offered, "let me know."

"I will." Darrick kept his smile in place. He'd learned in the months since losing his berth aboard *Lonesome Star* that smiling politely and answering questions but asking none ended conversations more quickly. If people thought he was willing to be friendly, they didn't find his lack of conversation as threatening or challenging. They just thought he was inept or shy and generally left him alone. The ruse had kept him from a number of fights lately, and the lack of fighting had kept him from the jails and fines that often left him destitute and on the street again.

Tilting his head, he glanced briefly at the four men playing dice at the table next to his. Three of them were fishermen, he knew that from their clothing, but the fourth man was dressed a little better, like someone who was putting on his best and hoping to impress. It came off as someone down on his luck and getting desperate. That appearance, Darrick knew, was an illusion.

He ate hungrily, trying not to act as if he hadn't eaten since yesterday. Or perhaps it was the day before. He was no longer certain of time passing. However few meals he'd had, he'd always managed to make enough money to drink. Drinking was the only way to keep distanced from the fears and nightmares that plagued him. Almost every night, he dreamed of the cliffside in Tauruk's Port, dreamed that he almost saved Mat from the skeleton's clutches, from the awful thump against the cliffside that had broken Mat's skull.

The tavern was a dive, another in a long string of them. They all looked alike to him. When he finished with his work, wherever he was, he ate a meal, drank until he could hardly walk, then hired a room or bedded down in a stable if the money hadn't been enough to provide drink and a proper bed.

The clientele was mostly fishermen, hard-faced men with callused hands and scars from nets, hooks, fish, the weather, and years of disappointment that ran bone-deep. They talked of tomorrows that sounded much better than the morning would bring, and what they would do if someday they escaped the need to climb aboard a boat every day and pray the Light was generous.

Merchants sat among the fishermen and other townspeople, discussing shipments and fortunes and the lack of protection in the northern part of the Great Ocean since Westmarch was keeping its navy so close to home these days still. There still had been no sign of the demon whom the Westmarch sailors had seen at Tauruk's Port, and many of the merchants and sailors north of Westmarch believed that the pirates had made up the story to lure the king into pulling his navy back.

Dissent grew among the northern ports and cities because they depended on Westmarch to help defend them. With the Westmarch Navy out of the way, men turned to piracy when they couldn't make the sea pay any other way. Although most pirates weren't acting together, their combined raiding had hurt the economies of several independent ports and even cities farther inland. Westmarch diplomacy, once a feared and treasured and expansive thing, had become weak and ineffective. Northern cities no longer curried favor with Westmarch as much.

Darrick sopped a biscuit through the stew and popped it into his mouth. The stew was thick and oily, seasoned with grease and spices that made it cloying and hot, a meal that finished off a hardworking man's day. Over the last months, he'd lost weight, but his fighting ability had stayed sharp. For the most part, he stayed away from the docks for fear that someone might recognize him. Although the Westmarch Navy and guardsmen hadn't made a strong effort to find him, or other sailors who had intentionally jumped ship, he remained leery of possible apprehension. Some days death seemed preferable to living, but he couldn't make that step. He hadn't died as he'd grown up under his father's fierce hands, and he didn't intend to die willingly now.

But it was hard to live willingly.

He glanced across the room, watching Dahni as she talked and flirted with a young man. Part of him longed for the companionship of a woman, but it was only a small part. Women talked, and they dug at the things that bothered a man, most of them wanting only to help, but Darrick didn't want to deal with that.

The big man sitting at the end of the bar crossed the floor to Darrick. The man was tall and broad, with a nose flattened and misshapen from fights. Scars, some freshly pink and webbed with tiny scabs, covered his knuckles and the heels of his palms. An old knife scar showed at his throat.

Uninvited, he sat across from Darrick, his truncheon lying across his knees. "You're working," the man said.

Darrick kept his right hand in his lap where his cutlass was. He gazed at the man. "I'm here with a friend."

To his right, the gambler who had hired Darrick for an evening's protection after they had come in on the trade caravan together praised the Light for yet another good turn. He was an older man, thin and white-haired. During an attack by bandits only yesterday, Darrick had learned that the man could handle himself and carried a number of small knives secreted on his person.

"Your friend's awfully lucky tonight," the big man said.

"He's due," Darrick said in a level voice.

The big man eyed Darrick levelly. "It's my job to keep the peace in the tavern."

Darrick nodded.

"If I catch your friend cheating, I'm throwing you both out."

Darrick nodded again, and he hoped the gambler didn't cheat or was good at it. The man had gamed with others on the caravan as they had wound their way back from Aranoch and trading with a port city that supplied the Amazon Islands.

"And you might have a care when you step out of here tonight," the bouncer warned, nodding at the gambler. "You got a demon's fog that's rolled up outside that won't burn off till morning. This town isn't well lighted, and some folks that gamble with your friend might not take kindly to losing."

"Thank you," Darrick said.

"Don't thank me," the bouncer said. "I just don't want either of you dying in here or anywhere near here." He stood and resumed his position at the end of the bar.

The serving wench returned with a pitcher of wine, a hopeful smile on her face.

Darrick covered his tankard with a hand.

"You've had enough?" she asked.

"For now," he answered. "But I'll take a bottle with me when I leave if you'll have one ready."

She nodded, hesitated, smiled briefly, then turned to walk away. The bracelet at her wrist flashed and caught Darrick's eye.

"Wait," Darrick whispered, his voice suddenly hoarse.

"Yes?" she asked hopefully.

Darrick pointed at her wrist. "What is that bracelet you wear?"

"A charm," Dahni replied. "It represents Dien-Ap-Sten, the Prophet of the Way of Dreams."

The bracelet was constructed of interlinked ovals separated by carved amber and rough iron so that none of the ovals touched another. The sight of it sparked memory in Darrick's mind. "Where did you get it?"

"From a trader who liked me," Dahni answered. It was a cheap attempt to make him jealous.

"Who is Dien-Ap-Sten?" That name didn't ring a bell in Darrick's memory.

"He's a prophet of luck and destiny," Dahni said. "They're building a church down in Bramwell. The man who gave me this told me that anyone who had the courage and the need to walk the Way of Dreams would get whatever his or her heart desires." She smiled at him. "Don't you think that's a bit far-fetched?"

"Aye," Darrick agreed, but the story troubled him. Bramwell wasn't far from Westmarch, and that was a place he'd promised himself he wouldn't be any time too soon.

"Have you ever been there?" Dahni asked.

"Aye, but it was a long time ago."

"Have you ever thought of returning there?"

"No."

The serving wench pouted. "Pity." She shook her wrist, making the bracelet spin and catch the lantern light. "I should like to go there someday and see that church for myself. They say that when it is finished, it will be a work of art, the most beautiful thing that has ever been built."

"It's probably worth seeing, then," Darrick said.

Dahni leaned on the table, exposing the tops of her breasts for his inspection. "A lot of things are worth seeing. But I know I won't get to see them as long as I stay in this town. Perhaps you should think about returning to Bramwell soon."

"Perhaps," Darrick said, trying not to offer any offense.

One of the fishermen called Dahni away, raising his voice impatiently. She gave Darrick a last, lingering look, then turned in a swirl of her short skirt and walked away.

At the next table, the gambler had another bit of good fortune, praising the Light while the other men grumbled.

Pushing thoughts of the strange bracelet from his mind, Darrick returned his attention to his meal. Swearing off wine for the rest of the gambler's turn at the gaming table meant the nightmares would be waiting on Darrick when he returned to his rented room. But the caravan would be in town for another day before the merchants finished their trading. He could drink until he was sure he wouldn't be able to dream.

Fog rolled through the streets and made the night's shadows seem darker and deeper as Darrick followed the gambler from the tavern two hours later. He tried to remember the man's name but wasn't surprised to find that he couldn't. Life was simpler when he didn't try to remember everything or everyone. On the different caravans he hired onto as a sellsword, there were people in charge, and they had a direction in which they wanted to go. Darrick went along with that.

"I had a good night at the table tonight," the gambler confessed as they walked through the street. "As soon as I get back to my room, I'll pay you what we agreed on."

"Aye," Darrick said, though he couldn't remember what amount they had agreed on. Usually it was a percentage against a small advance because a true gambler could never guarantee that he would win, and those who could were cheats and would guarantee a fight afterward.

Darrick gazed around at the street. As the tavern bouncer had said, the town had poor lighting. Only a few lamps, staggered haphazardly and primarily centered near the more successful taverns and inns as well as the small dock lit the way. The heavy fog left a wet gleam on the cobblestones. He looked for a sign, some way of knowing where he'd ended on this journey, not really surprised that he didn't know where he was, and not truly caring, either. Many of the towns he'd been to in the last few months had tended to blur into each other.

The sound of the gambler's in-drawn breath warned Darrick that something was wrong. He jerked his head around to the alley they'd just passed. Three men bolted from the alley, hurling themselves at Darrick and the gambler. Their blades gleamed even in the fog-dulled moonlight.

Darrick drew his cutlass, dropping the jug of wine he carried under one arm. By the time the ceramic jug shattered across the poorly fit cobblestones, he had his cutlass in hand and parried a blow aimed to take off his head. Fatigued as he was, with the wine working within him, it was all Darrick could do to stay alive. He stumbled over the uneven street, never seeing the fourth man step out behind him until it was too late.

The fourth man swung a weighted shark's billy that caught Darrick over his left ear and dropped him to his knees. Almost unconscious from the blow, he smashed his face against the cobblestones, and the sharp pain brought him back around. He fought to get to his knees. From there, he felt certain that he could make it to his feet. After that, perhaps he'd even be able to fight. Or at least earn the money the gambler had paid to protect him.

"Damn!" one of the thieves shouted. "He cut me with a hide-out knife."

"Watch out," another man said.

"It's okay. I got him. I got him. He won't be sticking anybody else ever again."

Warm liquid poured down the side of Darrick's neck. His vision blurred, but he saw two men taking the gambler's purse.

"Stop!" Darrick ordered, finding his cutlass loose on the cobblestones and picking it up. He lurched toward them, lifting the blade and following it toward one of the men. Before he reached his intended target, the other man whirled around and drove a hobnailed boot into Darrick's jaw. Pain blinded him as he fell again.

Struggling against the blackness that waited to take him, Darrick pushed his feet, trying in vain to find purchase that would allow him to stand. He watched in helpless frustration as the men vanished back into the shadows of the alley.

Using the cutlass as a crutch to keep his feet, Darrick made his way to the gambler. Darrick peered through his tearing eyes, listening to the thundering pain inside his head, and stared at the gambler.

A bone-hilted knife jutted from the gambler's chest. A crimson flower blossomed around the blade where it was sunk into flesh to the cross-guard.

The man's face was filled with fear. "Help me, Darrick. Please. For the Light's sake, I can't stop the bleeding."

How can he remember my name when I can't remember his? Darrick wondered. Then he saw all the blood streaming between the man's hands, threading through his fingers.

"It's okay," Darrick said, kneeling beside the stricken gambler. He knew it wasn't going to be okay. While serving aboard *Lonesome Star*, he'd seen too many fatal wounds not to know that this one was fatal as well.

"I'm dying," the gambler said.

"No," Darrick croaked, pressing his hands over the gambler's hands in an attempt to stem the tide of his life's blood. Turning his head, Darrick shouted over his shoulder. "Help! I need help here! I've got an injured man!"

"You were supposed to be there," the gambler accused. "You were supposed to look out for this kind of thing for me. That's what I paid you for." He coughed, and bright blood flecked his lips.

From the blood on the gambler's lips, Darrick knew the knife had penetrated one of his lungs as well. He pressed his hands against the gambler's chest, willing the blood to stop.

But it didn't.

Darrick heard footsteps slap against the cobblestones just as the gambler gave a final convulsive shiver. The gambler's breath locked in his throat, and his eyes stared sightlessly upward.

"No," Darrick croaked in disbelief. The man couldn't be dead; he'd been hired to protect him, still had a meal he'd paid for from his advance in his belly.

A strong hand gripped Darrick's shoulder. He tried to fight it off, then gazed up into the eyes of the tavern bouncer.

"By the merciful Light," the bouncer swore. "Did you see who did it?"

Darrick shook his head. Even if he saw the men responsible for the gambler's murder, he doubted that he could identify them.

"Some bodyguard," a woman's voice said from somewhere behind Darrick.

Looking at the dead gambler, Darrick had to agree. *Some bodyguard.* His senses fled, making his aching head too heavy to hold upright. He fell forward and didn't even know if he hit the street.

The silver peal of the bells in the three towers called the citizens of Bramwell to worship at the Church of Dien-Ap-Sten. Most were already inside the warren of buildings that had been erected over the last year since the caravan's arrival in the city. Foundations for still more buildings had been laid, and as soon as they were completed, they would be added to the central cathedral. Beautiful statuary, crafted by some of the best artisans in Bramwell as well as other artists in Westmarch, Lut Gholein, and Kurast and beyond the Sea of Light, sat at the top of the buildings.

Buyard Cholik, called Master Sayes now, stood on one of the rooftop gardens that decorated the church. Staring down at the intersection near the church, he watched as wagons carrying families and friends arrived. In the beginning, he remembered, the poorer families were the first to begin worship at the church. They'd come for the healing and in hopes of having a lifelong dream of riches or comfort answered.

And they came wishing to be chosen that day to walk on the Way of Dreams. Only a few were allowed to walk the Way of Dreams, generally only those afflicted with physical deformities or mental problems. People with arthritis and poorly mended broken limbs were nearly always admitted. Kabraxis achieved those miracles of healing with no difficulty. Every now and again, the demon rewarded someone with riches, but there was always a hidden cost none of the population could know about. As the Church of Dien-Ap-Sten had grown, so had the secrets it kept.

The church had been built high on a hill overlooking the city of Bramwell proper. Quarried from some of the best limestone in the area, which was generally shipped off to other cities while plain stone was used for the local buildings, the church gleamed in the morning light like bone laid clean from under the kiss of a knife. No one in the city could look southeast toward Westmarch and not see the church first.

The forest had been cleared on two sides of the church to accommodate the wagons and coaches that arrived during the twice-a-week services. All the believers in Bramwell came to both services, knowing the way would be made clear to the Way of Dreams where the miracles could take place.

Special, decorated boats tied up in front of the church at the newly built pilings. Boatmen in the service of the church brought captains and sailors from the ships that anchored out in the harbor. Word of the Church of Dien-Ap-Sten had started spreading across all of Westmarch, and it brought the curious as well as those seeking salvation.

High in their towers, the three bells rang again. They would ring only once more before the service began. Cholik glanced down in front of the church and saw that, as usual, only a few would be late to the service.

Cholik paced through the rooftop garden. Fruit trees and flowering plants, bushes, and vines occupied the rooftop, leaving a winding trail over the large building. Pausing beside a strawberry plant, Cholik stripped two succulent fruits from it, then popped them into his mouth. The berries tasted clean and fresh. No matter how many he took, there were always more.

"Did you ever think it would be this big?" Kabraxis asked.

Turning, the taste of the berries still sweet in his mouth, Cholik faced the demon.

Kabraxis stood beside a trellis of tomato vines. The fruits were bright cherry red, and more tiny yellow flowers bloomed on the vines, promising an even greater harvest to come. An illusion spell, made strong by binding it to the limestone of the building, kept him from being seen by anyone below. The spell had been crafted so intricately that he didn't even leave a shadow to see for anyone not meant to see him.

"I had hopes," Cholik answered diplomatically.

Kabraxis smiled, and the effect on his demonic face was obscene. "You're a greedy man. I like that."

Cholik took no offense. One of the things he enjoyed about the relationship with the demon was that he had to offer no apologies for the way he felt. In the Zakarum Church, his temperament always had to be in line with accepted church doctrine.

"We're going to outgrow this town soon," Cholik said.

"You're thinking of leaving?" Kabraxis sounded as though he couldn't believe it.

"Possibly. It has been in my thoughts."

"You?" Kabraxis scoffed. "Who thought only of the building of this church?"

Cholik shrugged. "We can build other churches."

"But this one is so big and so grand."

"And the next one can be bigger and more grand."

"Where would you build another church?"

Cholik hesitated, but to know the demon was to speak his mind. "Westmarch."

"You would challenge the Zakarum Church?"

Cholik answered fiercely, "Yes. There are priests there whom I would see humbled and driven from the city. Or sacrificed. If that is done, and this church is positioned to look as though it can save all of Westmarch from great evil, we could convert the whole country."

"You would kill those people?"

"Only a few of them. Enough to scare the others. The survivors will serve the church. Dead men can't fear us and properly worship us."

Kabraxis laughed. "Ah, but you're a willing pupil, Buyard Cholik. Such bloodthirstiness is so refreshing to find in a human. Usually you are all so limited by your own personal desires and motivations. You want revenge on this person who wronged you or that person who has been fortunate enough to have more than you. Petty things."

A curious pride moved through Cholik. Over the year and some months of their acquaintance, he had changed. He hadn't been lured over to the Darkness as so many priests he'd known had feared for those they sought to save. Rather, he'd reached inside himself and brought it all forward.

The Zakarum Church taught that man was of two minds as well, constantly fighting an inner war between the Light and the Darkness.

"But my plan to move into Westmarch is a good one?" Cholik asked. He knew he was currying the demon's favor, but Kabraxis liked to give it.

"Yes," the demon answered, "but it is not yet time. Already, this church has earned enmity from the Zakarum Church. Gaining the king's permission to build a church within the city would be hard. The tenets between the king and the church are too tight. And you forget: Westmarch still seeks the demon that was seen with the pirates. If we move too quickly, we will draw more suspicion."

"It has been more than a year," Cholik protested.

"The king and the people have not forgotten," Kabraxis said. "Diablo has left his mark upon them after the subterfuge he ran at Tristram. We must first win their trust, then betray them."

"How?"

"I have a plan."

Cholik waited. One thing he'd learned that Kabraxis didn't like was being questioned too closely.

"In time," Kabraxis said. "We have to raise an army of believers before then, warriors who will go and kill anyone who stands in their way to bringing the truth to the world."

"An army to oppose Westmarch?"

"An army to oppose the Zakarum Church," Kabraxis said.

"There are not enough people in all of Bramwell." The thought staggered Cholik. Images of battlefields painted red with the blood of men flashed through his mind. And he knew those images were probably much less horrific than the actual battles would be.

"We will raise the army from within Westmarch," Kabraxis said.

"How?"

"We will turn the king against the Zakarum Church," the demon replied. "And once we make him see how unholy the Zakarum Church has become, he will create that army."

"And the Zakarum Church will be razed to the ground." Warmth surged through Cholik as he entertained the idea of it.

"Yes."

"How will you turn the king?" Cholik asked.

Kabraxis gestured toward the church. "In time, Buyard Cholik. Everything will be revealed to you in time. Diablo returned to this world only a short time ago by corrupting the Soulstone that bound him. He unleashed his power in Tristram, taking over King Leoric's son, Prince Albrecht. As you will remember, for you were privy to the machinations of the Zakarum Church at the time, Tristram and Westmarch almost warred. The human adventurers who fought Diablo thought they destroyed him, but Diablo used one of his enemies as the new vessel in which to get around these lands. As we plan for conquest and success, so Diablo plans. But demons must be cunning and crafty, as we are being now. If we grow too quickly, we will attract the attention of the Prime Evils, and I'm unwilling to deal with them at the moment. For now, though, you have a service to give. I promise you a miracle today that will bring even more converts."

Cholik nodded, stilling the questions that flooded into his brain. "Of course. By your leave."

"Go with Dien-Ap-Sten's blessings," Kabraxis said, intoning the words that they had made legendary throughout Bramwell and beyond. "May the Way of Dreams take you where you want to go."

Fifteen

The service passed with liquid ease.

Standing in the shadowed balcony that overlooked the parishioners, Buyard Cholik watched as the crowd fidgeted and waited through the singing and the addresses of the young priests speaking of Dien-Ap-Sten's desires for each and every man, woman, and child in the world of men to rise and succeed to their just rewards. The young priests stood on the small stage below Cholik's balcony. Mostly, though, the young priests' messages intoned the virtues of serving the Prophet of the Light and sharing profits with the church so that more good work could be done.

But they were all truly waiting on the Call to the Way of Dreams.

After the last of the priests finished his message and the final songs were sung, songs that Kabraxis had written himself, which echoed of drumbeats like a hammering heart and melodic pipes that sounded like blood rushing through a man's ears, a dozen acolytes stepped up from the pit in front of the small stage with lighted torches in their hands.

The drums hammered, creating an eerie crescendo that resounded among the rafters of the high-vaulted ceiling. Cymbals crashed as the pipes played.

Frenzy built within the crowd. There still, Cholik saw, were not enough seats in the church. They'd just opened the upper floor of the church three weeks ago, and the membership had more than filled the cathedral again. Many of the worshippers were from other cities up and down the coastline, and a number of them were from Westmarch. They made pilgrimages from the other cities by hired caravan or by paying ship's passage.

Some ships' captains and caravan masters made small fortunes out of operating twice-weekly round-trips to Bramwell. Many people were willing to pay passage for the chance to walk the Way of Dreams, for health reasons or in hopes of gaining their heart's desire.

Once Cholik had discovered the startup of the lucrative business, he'd sent word to the captains and caravan masters that they would be expected to bring offerings in the way of building materials for the church with each trip. Only two ships had gone down and one caravan was destroyed by a horde of skeletons and zombies before the tribute asked of them started getting delivered on a regular basis. More caravans were starting up from Lut Gholein and other countries to the east.

The crowd shouted, "Way of Dreams! Way of Dreams!" Their manner would not have been permitted in the Zakarum Church, and they bordered on the fringe of becoming an unruly crowd.

Guards Cholik had chosen from the warriors who believed in Dien-Ap-Sten lined the cathedral walls and stood in small raised towers in the midst of the congregation. For the most part, the guards carried cudgels that bore the elliptical rings that were Kabraxis's sign cleverly worked into the wire-bound hilt. Other guards carried crossbows that had been magically enchanted by mystic gems. The guards dressed in black chain mail with stylized silver icons of the elliptical rings on their chests. All of them were hard men, warriors who had ventured down the Black Road, as the Way of Dreams was called by initiates, and had been imbued with greater strength and speed than normal men.

The dozen acolytes touched their torches to different spots on the wall that held the stage and Cholik's balcony. Cholik watched as the flames leapt up the whale-oil-fed channels and came straight up to him.

The flames, aided by a ward that was laid upon the wall, raced around Cholik and lifted the balcony and the design from the wall, exposing the flaming face of the cowled snake that had been designed by black stones intermixed with white. The flames danced along the black stones and lit in the pits of the snake's eyes.

The audience quieted waiting expectantly to see what would occur. But Cholik sensed the violence in the room that was on the cusp of breaking out. The guards moved at their posts, reminding everyone they were there.

"I am Master Sayes," Cholik said into the sudden silence that filled the cathedral. "I am the Wayfinder, designated so by the hand of Dien-Ap-Sten, Prophet of the Light."

Polite applause followed Cholik's words as it was supposed to, but the expectant air never left the room. Believers though they were, the people waited like jackals at a feast, knowing that as soon as the larger predators left the area, they would have what was left.

Cholik scattered powder around him that ignited in great gouts of green, red, violet, and blue flames that stopped short of the closest parishioners. The scents of honeysuckle, cinnamon, and lavender filled the cathedral. He spoke, unleashing the spell that held the gateway to the wall.

In response to the spell, the flaming cowled snake's head lunged from the wall, hanging out over the crowd and opening its mouth. Cholik rode the balcony that stood out over the snake's eyes. The snake's mouth was the entrance to the Black Road, leading to the gateway where a black marble trail wound over and under and through itself, winding around to bring the traveler back to the snake's mouth bearing the gifts Kabraxis had seen fit to bestow.

"May the Way of Dreams take you where you want to go," Cholik said.

"May the Way of Dreams take you where you want to go," the audience roared back.

Beneath the hood of his robe, Cholik smiled. It felt so right to be in charge of all this, to be so powerful. "Now," he said, knowing they hung on his every word, "who among you is worthy?"

It was a challenge, and Cholik knew it, reveled in the knowledge.

The group went wild, screaming and yelling, announcing their needs and wants and desires. The crowd became a living, feral thing, on the brink of lashing out at itself. People had died within the church, victims of their friends and neighbors and strangers over the past year, and the limestone floor had drunk down their blood, putting down crystal roots into the ground beneath that Kabraxis had one day shown Cholik. The roots looked like cones of weeping blood rubies, never quite solid and seeming to ooze into the earth more with every drop that was received.

Undulating, taking Cholik with it, the fiery snake head reached out over the crowd, over the first tier of people, then over the second. People held their ill and diseased children above them, calling out to Dien-Ap-Sten to bless them with a cure. The wealthier people among the audience hired tall warriors to hold them on their shoulders, putting them that much closer to the entrance to the Black Road.

The snake's tongue flicked out, a black ribbon of translucent obsidian that was as fluid as water, and the choice was made.

Cholik gazed at the child who had been held up by his father, seeing that it wasn't one child but two somehow grown together. The children possessed only two arms and two legs attached to two heads and a body and a half. They looked no more than three years of age.

"An abomination," a man in the audience cried out.

"It should never have been allowed to live," another man said.

"Demon born," still another said.

The dozen acolytes with the torches raced forward, aided by the guards till they reached the chosen one.

There has to be some mistake, Cholik thought as he stared at the afflicted children knitted together of their own flesh and bone. He couldn't help feeling that Kabraxis had betrayed him, though he could think of no reason the demon would do that.

Children so severely deformed usually died during childbirth, as did the women who bore them. Their fathers put the children who didn't die to death, or it was done by the priests. Cholik had executed such children himself, then buried them in consecrated earth in the Zakarum Church. Other deformed children's bodies were sold to mages, sages, and black marketers who trafficked in demonic goods.

The acolytes surrounded the father and the conjoined children, filling the area with light. The chain mail–clad guards shoved the crowd back from the father, making more room.

Cholik looked at the man and had to force himself to speak. "Will your sons follow the Black Road, then?"

Tears ran down the father's face. "My sons can't walk, Wayfinder Sayes."

"They must," Cholik said, thinking that was perhaps the way to break the moment. Some who wanted to walk the Black Road gave in to their own fears at the last minute and did not go. The chance to walk the Black Road was never offered again.

Unbidden, the snake's obsidian tongue flicked out and coiled around the twin boys. Without apparent effort, the snake pulled the boys into its fanged mouth. They screamed as they approached the curtain of flames that hugged the huge head.

Standing on the platform over the ridge of the snake's heavy brow and peering through the fire, Cholik only saw the two boys disappear beneath him and couldn't see them anymore. He waited, uncertain what would happen, afraid that he was about to lose all that he had invested in.

Meridor stood at her mother's side, watching as the massive stone snake licked her little brothers into its huge, gaping maw. Mikel and Dannis passed so close to the flames that light the snake's face—she knew they didn't actually have faces because her father told her that, and her older brothers made fun of her when she mentioned it—that she felt certain they were going to be cooked.

Her uncle Ramais always told stories about children getting cooked and eaten by demons. And sometimes those children were baked into pies. She always tried to figure out how a child pie would look, but whenever she asked her mother, her mother would always tell her she needed to stay away from her uncle and his terrible stories. But Uncle Ramais was a sailor for the Westmarch Navy and always had the best stories. She was old enough that she knew she couldn't believe all of her uncle's stories, but it was still fun making believe that she did.

Meridor really didn't want her younger brothers baked or broiled or burned in any manner. At nine years of age and the youngest girl in a household of eight children, she was the one who watched and cleaned Mikel and Dannis the most. Some days she got tired of them because they were always cranky and uncomfortable. Da said it was because each of her brothers was a tight fit living in one body. Sometimes Meridor wondered if Mikel's and Dannis's other arms and legs were somehow tucked up into the body they shared.

But even though they were troublesome and cranky, she didn't want them eaten.

She watched, staring at the stone snake head as it gulped her brothers down. Since no one was listening to her, she prayed the way she'd been taught to in the small Zakarum Church. She felt guilty because her da had told her that the new prophet was the only chance her brothers had of living. They were getting sicker these days, and they were more aware that they weren't like anybody else and couldn't walk or move the way they wanted to. She thought it must be pretty horrible. They couldn't be happy with each other or anyone else.

"Way of Dreams! Way of Dreams!" the people around her yelled, shaking their fists in the air.

The yelling always made Meridor uncomfortable. The people always sounded so angry and so frightened. Da had always told her that the people weren't that way; it was just that they were all so hopeful. Meridor couldn't understand why anyone would want to walk down into the stone snake's belly. But that was where the Way of Dreams was, and the Way of Dreams—according to Da—could accomplish all kinds of miracles. She had seen a few of them over the past year, but they hadn't mattered much. No one she knew had ever been chosen by Dien-Ap-Sten.

On some evenings, when the family gathered around their modest table, everyone talked about what they would wish for if they had the chance to walk the Way of Dreams. Meridor hadn't added much to the conversation at those times because she didn't know what she wanted to be when she grew up.

Lying on the snake's tongue, Meridor's brothers wailed and screamed. She saw their tiny faces, tears glittering like diamonds on their cheeks as they screamed and wept.

Meridor looked up at her mother. "Ma."

"Shhh," her mother responded, knotting her fists in the fancy dress she'd made to go to the Church of the Prophet of the Light. She'd never worn anything like that to the Zakarum Church, and she'd always said that being poor wasn't a bad thing in the eyes of the church. But Da and Ma both insisted that everybody be freshly bathed and clean both nights a week that they went to the new church.

Scared and nervous, Meridor fell silent and didn't talk. She watched as Mikel and Dannis rolled in the snake's mouth toward the Way of Dreams housed in its gullet. Over the months of their visits to the church, she had seen people walk into the snake's mouth, then walk back out again, healed and whole. But how could even Dien-Ap-Sten heal her brothers?

The snake's mouth closed. Above it on the platform over the snake's fiery eyes, Master Sayes led the church in prayer. The screams of the two little boys echoed through the cathedral. Knotting her fists and pressing them against her chin as she listened to the horrid screams, Meridor backed away and bumped into the man standing beside her.

She turned at once to apologize because many adults in the church were short-tempered with children. Children got chosen a lot by Dien-Ap-Sten for healing and miracles, and most of the adults didn't feel they deserved it.

"I'm sorry," Meridor said, looking up. She froze when she saw the monstrous face above her.

The man was tall and big, but that was somewhat hidden beneath the simple woolen traveling cloak he wore. His clothing was old and patched, showing signs of hard usage and covered over with road dust and grit. The frayed kerchief at his neck was tied by a sailor's knot that Uncle Ramais had showed her. The man stood like a shadow carved out of the crowd.

But the most horrible thing about him was his face. It was blackened from burning, the skin crisp and ridged as it had pulled together from the heat. Fine, thin cracks showed in the burned areas, and flecks of blood ran down his face like sweat. Most of the damage was on the left side of his face and looked like an eclipse of the moon. There had been one of those the night Mikel and Dannis had been born.

"It's all right, girl," the man said in a hoarse voice.

"Does it hurt?" Meridor asked. Then she clapped a hand over her mouth when she remembered that many adults didn't like being asked questions, especially about things they probably didn't want to talk about.

A small smile formed on the man's cracked and blistered mouth. New blood flecks appeared on his burned cheek, and pain shone in his eyes. "All the time," he answered.

"Are you here hoping to get healed?" Meridor asked, since he seemed to be open to questions.

"No." The man shook his head, and the movement caused the hood of his traveling cloak to shift, baring his head a little and revealing the gnarled stubble of burned hair that poked through the blackened skin.

"Then why are you here?"

"I came to see this Way of Dreams that I had heard so much about."

"It's been here a long time. Have you been here before?"

"No."

"Why not?"

The burned man glanced down at her. "You're a curious child."

"Yes. I'm sorry. It's none of my business."

"No, it's not." The man stared at the stone snake as the drums boomed, the cymbals clashed, and the pipes continued their writhing melodies. "Those were your brothers?"

"Yes. Mikel and Dannis. They're conjoined." Meridor stumbled over the word a little. It just didn't sound right. Even after all the years of having to tell other people about her brothers, she still couldn't say it right all the time.

"Do you believe they're abominations?"

"No." Meridor sighed. "They're just unhappy and in pain."

The boys' screams tore through the cathedral again. Atop the stone snake, Master Sayes showed no sign of stopping the ritual.

"They sound like they're in pain now."

"Yes." Meridor worried about her brothers as she always did when they were out of her sight. She spent so much time taking care of them, how could she not be worried?

"You've seen others healed?" the burned man asked.

"Yes. Lots." Meridor watched the undulations of the stone snake. Were Mikel and Dannis walking the Way of Dreams now? Or were they just trapped inside the snake while truly terrible things happened to them?

"What have you seen?" the man asked.

"I've seen the crippled made whole, the blind made to see, and all kinds of diseases healed."

"I was told that Dien-Ap-Sten usually picks children to heal."

Meridor nodded.

"A lot of adults don't like that," the burned man said. "I heard them talking in the taverns in town and on the ship that brought me here."

Meridor nodded again. She had seen people get into fights in Bramwell while discussing such things. She was determined not to argue or point out that there were a lot of sick kids in the city.

"Why do you think Dien-Ap-Sten picks children most of the time?" the burned man asked.

"I don't know."

The burned man grinned as he watched the stone snake. Blood wept from his upper lip and threaded through his white teeth and over the blistered flesh of his pink lips. "Because they are impressionable and because they can believe more than an adult, girl. Show an adult a miracle, and he or she will reach for logical conclusions for why it happened. But the heart of a child . . . by the Light, you can win the heart of a child forever."

Meridor didn't completely understand what the man was talking about, but she didn't let it bother her. She'd already discovered that there were things about adults that she didn't understand, and things about adults that she wasn't meant to understand, and things that she understood but wasn't supposed to act as if she understood.

Abruptly, Master Sayes ordered silence in the cathedral. The musical instruments stopped playing at once, and the hoarse shouts of the crowd died away.

Once when she had been there, Meridor remembered, a group of rowdy men hadn't stopped making noise as Master Sayes had ordered. They'd been drunk and argumentative, and they had said bad things about the church. Master Sayes's warriors had forced their way through the crowd, sought them out, and killed them. Some said that they had killed two innocent men as well, but people stopped talking about that by the next meeting.

Silence echoed in the massive cathedral and made Meridor feel smaller than ever. She clasped her hands and fretted over Mikel and Dannis. Would the Way of Dreams simply tear off one of their heads, killing one of them to make a whole child out of what was left? That was a truly horrible thought, and Meridor wished it would leave her mind. But it would have been even worse, she supposed, if Dien-Ap-Sten had asked her da or ma to decide which child lived and which child died.

Then the power filled the cathedral.

Meridor recognized it from the other times she had experienced it. It vibrated through her body, shaking even the teeth in her head, and it made her all mixed up and somehow excited inside.

The burned man lifted his arm, the one with the hand that was completely blackened by whatever had cooked him. Crimson threads crisscrossed the cooked flesh as he worked his fingers. Flesh split open over one knuckle, revealing the pink flesh and the white bone beneath.

But as Meridor watched, the hand started to heal. Scabs formed over the breaks, then flaked away to reveal whole flesh again. However, the new flesh was still crisp, burned black. She glanced up at the burned man and saw that even the cracks in his face had healed somewhat.

Taking down his hand, the burned man gazed at it as if surprised. "By the Light," he whispered.

"Dien-Ap-Sten can heal you," Meridor said. It felt good to offer the man hope. Da always said hope was the best thing a man could wish for when dealing with fate and bad luck. "You should start coming to church here. Perhaps one day the snake will pick you."

The burned man smiled and shook his head beneath the hood of his traveling cloak. "I would not be allowed to seek healing here, girl." Crimson leaked down his cracked face again. "In fact, I'm surprised that I wasn't killed outright when I tried to enter this building."

That sounded strange. Meridor had never heard anyone speak like that.

With a sigh that sounded like a bellows blast she'd heard at the blacksmith's shop, the snake's huge lower jaw dropped open. Smoke and embers belched from the snake's belly.

Meridor stood on her tiptoes, waiting anxiously. When Mikel and Dannis had entered the snake, she'd never thought that she might not see them again. Or even that she might not see one of them again.

A boy stepped through the opening of the snake's mouth on two good legs. He gazed out at the crowd fearfully, trying in vain to hide.

Dannis! Meridor's heart leapt with happiness, but it plunged in the next moment when she realized that Mikel, little Mikel who loved her sock puppet shows, was gone. Before her first tears had time to leave her eyes or do more than blur her vision, she saw her other little brother step out from behind Dannis. *Mikel! They both live! And they are both whole!*

Da whooped with joy, and Ma cried out, praising Dien-Ap-Sten for all to hear. The crowd burst loose with their joy and excitement, but Meridor couldn't help thinking that it was because having Mikel and Dannis returned meant that another would soon be selected to journey down the Way of Dreams.

Da rushed forward and took her brothers from the fiery maw of the stone snake. Even as he pulled them into an embrace, joined by Ma, movement at Meridor's side drew her attention to the burned man.

She watched as everything seemed to slow down, and she could hear her heartbeat thunder in her ears. The burned man whipped his traveling cloak back to reveal the hand crossbow he held there. The curved bow rested on a frame no longer than Meridor's forearm. He brought the small weapon up in his good hand, extended it, and squeezed the trigger. The quarrel leapt from the crossbow's grooved track and sped across the cathedral.

Tracking the quarrel's flight, Meridor saw the fletched shaft take Master Sayes high in the chest and knock him backward. The Wayfinder plunged from the snake's neck, disappearing from sight. Screams split the cathedral as Meridor's senses sped up again.

"Someone has killed Master Sayes!" a man's voice yelled.

"Find him!" another yelled. "Find that damned assassin!"

"It came from over there!" a man yelled.

In disbelief, Meridor stood frozen as cathedral guards and robed acolytes plunged into the crowd brandishing weapons and torches. She turned to look for the burned man, only to find him gone. He'd taken his leave during the confusion, probably brushing by people who were only now realizing what he had done.

Altough the cathedral guards worked quickly, there were too many people inside the building to organize a pursuit. But one man fleeing through people determined to get out of the way of the menacing guards moved rapidly. She never saw him escape.

One of the acolytes stopped beside Meridor. The acolyte held his torch high and shoved people away, revealing the abandoned hand crossbow on the floor.

"Here!" the acolyte yelled. "The weapon is here."

Guards rushed over to join him.

"Who saw this man?" a burly guard demanded.

"It was a man," a woman in the nearby crowd said. "A stranger. He was talking to that girl." She pointed at Meridor.

The guard fixed Meridor with his harsh gaze. "You know the man who did this, girl?"

Meridor tried to speak but couldn't.

Da strode forward to protect her, she knew that he did, but one of the guards swung his sword hilt into her da's stomach and dropped him to his knees. The guard grabbed the back of her da's head by the hair and yanked his head back, baring his throat for the knife that he held.

"Talk, girl," the guard said.

Meridor knew the men were afraid as well as angry. Perhaps Dien-Ap-Sten would take vengeance against them for allowing something terrible to happen to Master Sayes.

"Do you know the man who did this?" the burly guard repeated.

Shaking her head, Meridor said, "No. I only talked to him."

"But you got a good look at him?"

"Yes. He had a burned face. He was scared to come in here. He said Dien-Ap-Sten might know him, but he came anyway."

"Why?"

"I don't know."

Another guard rushed up to the burly one. "Master Sayes lives," the guard reported.

"Thank Dien-Ap-Sten," the burly guard said. "I would not have wanted to go where the Way of Dreams would have taken me if Master Sayes had died." He gave a description of the assassin, adding that a man with a burned face should be easy enough to find. Then he turned his attention back to Meridor, keeping a painful grip on her arm. "Come along, girl. You're coming with me. We're going to talk to Master Sayes."

Meridor tried to escape. The last thing she wanted to do was talk to Master Sayes. But she couldn't escape the grip the guard had on her arm as he dragged her through the crowd.

Sixteen

"I'm tellin' ye, I've seen it with me own two eyes, I have," old Sahyir said, looking mightily offended. He was sixty if he was a day, lean and whipcord tough, with a cottony white beard and his hair pulled back into a ponytail. Shell earrings hung from both ears. Scars showed on his face and hands and arms. He wore tarred breeches and a shirt to stand against the spray that carried across the still-primitive harbor.

Darrick sat on a crate that was part of the cargo he'd been hired to help transport from the caravel out in the bay to the warehouse on the shoreline of Seeker's Point. It was the first good paying work he'd had in three days, and he'd begun to think he was going to have to crew out on a ship to keep meals coming and a roof over his head. Shipping out wasn't something he looked forward to. The sea held too many memories. He reached into the worn leather bag he carried and took out a piece of cheddar cheese and two apples.

"I have trouble believing the part about the stone snake gulping people down, I do," Darrick admitted. He used his small belt knife to cut wedges from the half-circle of cheese and to cut the apples into quarters, expertly slicing the cores away. He gave Sahyir one of the cheese wedges and one of the sliced apples. Tossing the apple cores over the side of the barge attracted the small perch that lived along the harbor and fed on refuse from the ships, warehouses, and street sewers. They kissed the top of the water with hungry mouths.

"I seen it, Darrick," the old man insisted. "Seen a man that couldn't use his legs pull himself into that snake's gullet, an' then come up an' walk outta there on his own two legs again. Healthy as a horse, he was. It was right something to see."

Darrick chewed a piece of cheese as he shook his head. "Healers can do that. Potions can do that. I've even seen enchanted weapons that could help a man heal faster. There is nothing special about healing. The Zakarum Church does it from time to time."

"But those all come for a price," Sahyir argued. "Healers an' potions an' enchanted weapons, why, they're all well an' good for a man what's got the gold or the strength to get 'em. And churches? Don't get me started. Churches dote on them that put big donations in the coffers, or them what's got the king's favor. Churches keep an eye on the hands what feed 'em, I says. But I ask ye, what about the common, ordinary folk like ye and me? Who's gonna take care of us?"

Gazing across the sea, feeling the wind rush through his hair and against his face, the chill of it biting into his flesh in spite of his own tarred clothing, Darrick looked at the small village that clung tenaciously to the rocky land of the cove. "We take care of ourselves," he said. "Just like we always have." He and the old man had been friends for months, sharing an easy companionship.

Seeker's Point was a small town just south of the barbarian tribes' territories. In the past, the village had been a supply fort for traders, whalers, and seal hunters who had trekked through the frozen north. Little more than a hundred years ago, a merchant house had posted an army there meant to chase off the marauding barbarian pirates who hunted the area without fear of the Westmarch Navy. A bounty had been placed on the heads of the barbarians, and for a time the mercenary army had collected from the trading house.

Then some of the barbarian tribes had united and laid siege to the village. The trading house hadn't been able to resupply or ship the mercenaries out. During the course of one winter, the mercenaries and all those who had lived with them had been killed to the last person. It had taken more than forty years for a few fur traders to reestablish themselves in the area, and only then because they traded favorably with the barbarians and brought them goods they couldn't get on their own with any dependability.

Houses and buildings dotted the steep mountains that surrounded the cove. Pockets of unimproved land and forest stood tall and proud between some of the houses and buildings. The village slowly eroded those patches, though, taking the timber for buildings and for heat, but baring several of those places only revealed the jagged, gap-toothed, rocky soil beneath. Nothing could be built in those places.

"Why didn't you stay in Bramwell?" Darrick asked. He bit into the apple, finding it sweet and tart.

Sahyir waved the thought away. "Why, even before they up an' had all this religious business success, Bramwell wasn't for the likes of me."

"Why?"

Snorting, Sahyir said, "Why, it's too busy there is why. A man gets to wanderin' around them streets—all in a tizzy and a bother—an' he's like to meet hisself comin' and goin'."

Despite the melancholy mood that usually stayed with him, Darrick smiled. Bramwell was a lot larger than Seeker's Point, but it paled in comparison with Westmarch. "You've never been to Westmarch, have you?"

"Once," Sahyir answered. "Only once. I made a mistake of signing on with a cargo freighter needin' a hand. I was a young strappin' pup like yerself, thought I wasn't afeard of nothin'. So I signed on. Got to Westmarch harbor and looked out over that hell-spawned place. We was at anchorage for six days, we was. An' never once durin' that time did I leave that ship."

"You didn't? Why?"

"Because I figured I'd never find my way back to the ship I was on."

Darrick laughed.

Sahyir scowled at him and looked put out. "'Tweren't funny, ye bilge rat. There's men what went ashore there that didn't come back."

"I meant no offense," Darrick said. "It's just that after making that trip down to Westmarch and through the bad weather that usually marks the gulf, I can't imagine anyone not leaving the ship when they had a chance."

"Only far enough to buy a wineskin from the local tavern and get a change of victuals from time to time," Sahyir said. "But the only reason I brought up Bramwell today was because I was talkin' to a man I met last night, an' I thought ye might be interested in what he had to say."

Darrick watched the other barges plying the harbor. Today was a busy day for Seeker's Point. Longshoremen usually had two jobs in the village because there wasn't enough work handling cargo to provide for a family. Even men who didn't take on crafts and artisan work hunted or fished or trapped when finances ran low. Sometimes they migrated for a time to other cities farther south along the coast like Bramwell.

"Interested in what?" Darrick asked.

"Them symbols I see ye a-drawin' and a-sketchin' now an' again." Sahyir brought up a water flask and handed it to Darrick.

Darrick drank, tasting the metallic flavor of the water. There were a few mines in the area as well, but none of them was profitable enough to cause a merchant to invest in developing and risk losing everything to the barbarians.

"I know ye don't like talkin' about them symbols," Sahyir said, "an' I apologize for talkin' about 'em when it ain't no business of me own. But I see ye a-frettin' an' a-worryin' about 'em, an' I know it troubles ye some."

During the time he had known the old man, Darrick had never mentioned where he'd learned about the elliptical design with the line that threaded through it. He'd tried to put all that in the past. A year ago, when the gambler had died while under his protection, Darrick had lost himself to work and drink, barely getting by. Guilt ate at him over losing Mat and the gambler. And the phantasm of his father back in the barn in Hillsfar had lived with him every day.

Darrick didn't even remember arriving in Seeker's Point, had been so drunk that the ship's captain had thrown him off the ship and refused to let him back on. Sahyir had found Darrick at the water's edge, sick and feverish. The old man had gotten help from a couple of friends and taken Darrick back to his shanty up in the hills overlooking the village. He'd cared for Darrick, nursing him back to health during the course of a month. It had been a time, the old man had said, when he'd been certain on more than one occasion he was going to lose Darrick to the sickness or to the guilt that haunted him.

Even now, Darrick didn't know how much of his story he'd told Sahyir, but the old man had told him that he'd drawn the symbol constantly. Darrick couldn't remember doing that, but Sahyir had produced scraps of paper with the design on it that Darrick had been forced to assume were in his own hand.

Sahyir appeared uncomfortable.

"It's all right, then," Darrick said. "Those symbols aren't anything."

Scratching his beard with his callused fingers, Sahyir said, "That's not what the man said that I talked to last night."

"What did he say?" Darrick asked. The barge had nearly reached the shore now, and the men pulling the oars rested more, letting the incoming tide carry them along as they jockeyed around the other barges and ships in the choked harbor.

"He was mighty interested in that there symbol," the old man said. "That's why I was a-tellin' ye about the Church of the Prophet of the Light this mornin'."

Darrick thought about it for a moment. "I don't understand."

"I was worried some about tellin' ye that I'd done a bit of nosin' about in yer business," Sahyir said. "We been friends for a time now, but I know ye ain't up an' told me everythin' there is to know about that there symbol or yer own ties to it."

Guilt flickered through Darrick. "That was something I tried to put behind me, Sahyir. It wasn't because I was trying to hide anything from you."

The old man's eyes fixed him. "We all hide somethin', young pup. It's just the way men are an' women are, an' folks in general is. We all got weak spots we don't want nobody pokin' around in."

I got my best friend killed, Darrick thought, *and if I told you that, would you still be my friend?* He didn't believe that Sahyir could, and that hurt him. The old man was salt of the earth; he stood by his friends and even stood by a stranger who couldn't take care of himself.

"Whatever it is about this symbol that draws ye," Sahyir said, "is yer business. I just wanted to tell ye about this man 'cause he's only gonna be in town a few days."

"He doesn't live here?"

"If he had," Sahyir said with a grin, "I'd probably have talked to him before, now, wouldn't I?"

Darrick smiled. It seemed there wasn't anyone in Seeker's Point who didn't know Sahyir. "Probably," Darrick said. "Who is this man?"

"A sage," Sahyir replied, "to hear him tell it."

"Do you believe him?"

"Aye, I do. If'n I didn't, an' didn't think maybe he could do ye some good, why, we'd never be having this talk, now, would we?"

Darrick nodded.

"Accordin' to what I got from him last night," Sahyir said, "he's gonna be at the Blue Lantern tonight."

"What does he know about me?"

"Nothin'." Sahyir shrugged. "Me, young pup? Why, I done forgot more secrets than I ever been told."

"This man knows what this symbol represents?"

"He knows somewhat of it. He seemed more concerned learnin' what I knew of it. 'Course, I couldn't tell him nothin' 'cause I don't know nothin'. But I figured maybe ye could learn from each other."

Darrick thought about the possibility as the barge closed on the shoreline. "Why were you telling me about the Church of the Prophet of the Light?"

"Because this symbol ye're thinkin' about so much? That sage thinks maybe it's tied into all that what's going on down in Bramwell. And the Church of the Prophet of the Light. He thinks maybe it's evil."

The old man's words filled Darrick's stomach with cold dread. He had no doubt that the symbol denoted evil, but he no longer knew if he wanted any part of it. Still, he didn't want to let Mat's death go unavenged.

"If this sage is so interested in what's going on down in Bramwell, what is he doing here?" Darrick asked.

"Because of Shonna's Logs. He came here to read Shonna's Logs."

Buyard Cholik lay supine on a bed in the back room of the Church of the Prophet of the Light and knew that he was dying. His breath rattled and heaved in his chest, and his lungs filled with his own blood. Try as he might, he could not see the face of the man—or woman—who had so gravely wounded him.

In the beginning, the pain from the arrow embedded in his chest had felt as if a red-hot poker had been shoved into him. When the pain had begun to subside, he'd mistakenly believed it was because he hadn't been as badly hurt as he'd at first feared. Then he'd realized that he wasn't getting better; the pain was going away because he was dying. Death closing in on him robbed him of his senses.

He silently damned the Zakarum Church and the Light he'd grown to love and fear as a child. Wherever they were, he was certain that they were laughing at him now. Here he was, his youth returned to him, stricken down by an unknown assassin. He damned the Light for abandoning him to old age when it could have killed him young before fear of getting infirm and senile had settled in, and he damned it for letting him be weak enough to allow his fear to force him to seek a bargain with Kabraxis. The Light had driven him into the demon's arms, and he'd been betrayed again.

You haven't been betrayed, Buyard Cholik, Kabraxis's calm voice told him. *Do you think I would let you die?*

Cholik had believed the demon would let him die. After all, there were plenty of other priests and even acolytes who could step into the brief void that Cholik felt he would leave in his passing.

You will not die, Kabraxis said. *We still have business to do together, you and I. Clear the room that I may enter. I don't have enough power to maintain an illusion to mask myself and heal you at the same time.*

Cholik drew a wheezing breath. Fear rushed through him, winding hard and coarse as a dry-mouthed lizard's tongue. He had less room to breathe now than he had during his last breath. His lungs were filling up with his blood, but there was hardly any pain.

Hurry. If you would live, Buyard Cholik, hurry.

Coughing, gasping, Cholik forced open his heavy eyelids. The tall ceiling of his private rooms remained blurred and indistinct. Blackness ate at the edges of his vision, steadily creeping inward, and he knew if it continued it would consume him.

Do it now!

Priests attended Cholik, putting compresses on the wound in his chest. The crossbow quarrel jutted out, the shaft and feathers speckled with his blood. Acolytes stood in the background while mercenaries guarded the doorway. The room was decorated with the finest silks and hand-carved furniture. An embroidered rug from the Kurast markets covered the center of the stone floor.

Cholik opened his mouth to speak and only made a hoarse croaking noise. His breath sprayed fine crimson droplets.

"What is it, Master Sayes?" the priest beside Cholik's bed asked.

"Out," Cholik gasped. "Get out! Now!" The effort to speak nearly drained him.

"But, master," the priest protested. "Your wounds—"

"Out, I said." Cholik tried to rise and was surprised that he somehow found the strength.

I am with you, Kabraxis said, and Cholik felt a little stronger.

The priests and acolytes drew back as if watching the dead return to life. Perplexity and maybe a little relief showed on the faces of the mercenaries. A dead employer meant possibly some blame in the matter, and definitely no more gold.

"Go," Cholik wheezed. "*Now. Now,* damn you all, or I'll see to it that you're lost in one of the hell pits that surround the Black Road."

The priests turned and ordered the acolytes and the mercenaries from the room. They closed the massive oaken double doors, shutting him off from the hallway.

Standing beside the bed where he'd lain hovering between life and death, Cholik gripped a small stand that held a delicate glass vase that had been blown in the hands of a master. Flowers and butterflies hung trapped in death inside the glass walls of the vase, preserved by some small magic that had not allowed them to burn while the molten glass had been formed and cooled.

The secret door hidden at the back of the chamber opened, turning on hinges so that the section of wall twisted to reveal the large tunnel behind it. The church was honeycombed with such tunnels to make it easier for the demon to get around inside the buildings. Even as tall as the ceiling was, the demon's horns almost scraped it.

"Hurry," Cholik gasped. The room blurred further still, then abruptly seemed to spin around him. Only a moment of dizziness touched him, but he saw the rug on the floor coming up at him and knew he was falling although there was no sensation of doing so.

Before Cholik hit the floor, Kabraxis caught him in his huge, three-fingered hands.

"You will not die," the demon said, but his words took on more the aspect of a command. "We are not done yet, you and I."

Even though the demon was in his face, Cholik barely heard the words. His hearing was failing him now. His heart had slowed within his chest, no longer able to struggle against his blood-filled lungs. He tried to take a breath, but there was no room. Panic set in, but it was only a distant drumbeat at his temples, no longer able to touch him.

"No," Kabraxis stated, gripping Cholik by the shoulders.

A bolt of fire coursed through Cholik's body. It ignited at the base of his spine, then raced up to the bottom of his skull and exploded behind his eyes. He went blind for a moment, but it was white light instead of darkness that filled his vision. He felt the pain of the quarrel as it was ripped from his chest. The agony almost pushed him over the edge of consciousness.

"Breathe," Kabraxis said.

Cholik couldn't. He thought perhaps he didn't remember how or that he lacked the strength. Either way, no air entered his lungs. The world outside his body no longer mattered; everything felt cottony and distant.

Then renewed pain forked through his chest, following the path the quarrel had made and spiking into his lungs. Gripped by the pain, Cholik instinctively took a breath. Air filled his lungs—now empty of blood—and with each heaving breath he took, the incredible iron bands of pain released their hold on him.

Kabraxis guided him to the edge of the bed. Cholik only then realized that his blood smeared the bed coverings. He gasped, drinking down air as the room steadied around him. Anger settled into him then, and he glanced up at the demon.

"Did you know about the assassin?" Cholik demanded. He imagined that Kabraxis had let the assassin shoot him only to remind Cholik how much he was needed.

"No." Kabraxis crossed his arms over his huge chest. Muscles rippled in his forearms and shoulders.

"How could you not know? We built this place. You have wards everywhere around the grounds."

"I was also making your miracle happen at the time of your attack," Kabraxis said. "I made two whole boys from the conjoined twins, and that was no easy feat. People will be talking about that for years. While I was still working on that, your assassin struck."

"You couldn't save me from that arrow?" Assessing the demon's abilities and powers had been out of Cholik's reach. Did the Black Road consume Kabraxis so much that it left him weak? That knowledge might be important. But it was also frightening to realize that the demon was limited and fallible after Cholik had tied his destiny to Kabraxis.

"I trusted the mercenaries hired with the gold that I have made available to you to save you from something like this," Kabraxis answered.

"Don't make that mistake again," Cholik snapped.

Deliberately, Kabraxis twisted the bloody quarrel in his hands. Lines in his harsh face deepened. "Never make the mistake of assuming you are my equal, Buyard Cholik. Familiarity breeds contempt, but it also pushes you toward sudden death."

Watching the demon, Cholik realized that Kabraxis could just as easily thrust the bolt through his chest again. Only this time the demon could pierce his heart. He swallowed, hardly able to get around the thick lump in his throat. "Of course. Forgive me. I forgot myself in the heat of the moment."

Kabraxis nodded, dipping his horns, almost scratching the ceiling.

"Did the guards catch the assassin?" Cholik asked.

"No."

"They failed even in that? They could not protect me, and they could not get vengeance on the person who nearly killed me?"

Disinterested, the demon dropped the quarrel to the floor. "Punish the guards as you see fit, but realize that something else has come of this."

"What?"

Kabraxis faced Cholik. "Hundreds of people saw you killed today. They were certain of it. There was much weeping and wailing among them."

The thought that the crowd had lamented his apparent death filled Cholik with smugness. He liked the way the people of Bramwell curried favor with him when he passed through the city's streets, and he liked the desperate envy he saw in their eyes regarding his place in the worship of their new prophet. They acknowledged the power that he wielded, each in his or her own way.

"Those people thought the Way of Dreams was going to be denied to them as a result of your murder," Kabraxis said. "Now, however, they're going to believe that you're something much more than human, made whole again by Dien-Ap-Sten. Talk will go out past Bramwell even more, and the miracles that were seen here will grow in the telling."

Cholik thought about that. Although he would not have chosen the action, he knew that what the demon said was true. His fame, and that of Dien-Ap-Sten, would grow because of the murder attempt. Ships and caravans would carry the stories of the conjoined twins and his near assassination across the sea and the land. The stories, as they always did, would become larger than life as each person told another.

"More people will come, Buyard Cholik," Kabraxis said. "And they will want to be made to believe. We must be prepared for them."

Striding to the window, Cholik looked out at Bramwell. The city was already bursting at the seams as a result of the church's success. Ships filled the harbor, and tent camps had sprung up in the forests around Bramwell.

"An army of believers lies outside the walls of this church waiting to get in," Kabraxis said. "This church is too small to deal with them all."

"The city," Cholik said, understanding. "The city will be too small to hold them all after this."

"Soon," Kabraxis agreed, "that will be true."

Turning to face the demon, Cholik said, "You didn't think it would happen this quickly."

Kabraxis gazed at him. "I knew. I prepared. Now, you must prepare."

"How?"

"You must bring another to me whom I may remake as I have remade you."

Jealousy flamed through Cholik. Sharing his power and his prestige wasn't acceptable.

"You won't be sharing," Kabraxis said. "Instead, you will take on greater power by acquiring this person and bending him to our power."

"What person?"

"Lord Darkulan."

Cholik considered that. Lord Darkulan ruled Bramwell and had a close relationship with the King of Westmarch. During the problem with Tristram, Lord Darkulan had been one of the king's most trusted advisors.

"Lord Darkulan has let people know he's suspicious of the church," Cholik countered. "In fact, there was talk for a time of outlawing the church. He would have done it if the people hadn't stood so firmly against that, and if the opportunity for taxing the caravans and ships bringing the people from other lands hadn't come up."

"Lord Darkulan's concern has been understandable. He's been afraid that we would win the allegiance of his people." Kabraxis smiled. "We have. After today, that is a foregone conclusion."

"Why are you so sure?"

"Because Lord Darkulan was in the audience today."

SEVENTEEN

A chill stole over Cholik at Kabraxis's announcement about Lord Darkulan's presence in the church. The man had never come there before.

"Lord Darkulan entered the church disguised," Kabraxis went on. "No one knew he was here except for his bodyguards and me. And now you."

"He may have hired the assassin," Cholik said, feeling his anger rise. He gazed down at his chest, seeing the crimson-stained robe and the hole where the quarrel had penetrated. Only unblemished flesh showed beneath now.

"No."

"Why are you so certain?"

"Because the assassin strove alone to murder you," Kabraxis said. "If Lord Darkulan had organized the murder, he would have ordered three or four crossbowmen into the church. You would have been dead before you hit the floor."

Cholik's mouth went dry. A thought occurred to him, one that he didn't want to investigate, but he was drawn to it as surely as a moth was drawn to the candle flame. "If they had killed me, would you have been able to return me to life?"

"If I'd had to do that, Buyard Cholik, you would not have recognized the true chill of death. But neither would you have known again the fiery passion of life."

An undead thing, Cholik realized. The thought almost made him sick. Images of lurching zombies and skeletons with ivory grins came to him. As a priest for the Zakarum Church, he'd been called on to clear graveyards and buildings of undead things that had once been humans and animals. And he had nearly been damned with coming back as one of them. His stomach twisted in rebellion, and sour bile painted the back of his mouth.

"You would not have been merely animated as those things were," Kabraxis said. "I would have gifted you with true unlife. Your thoughts would have remained your own."

"And my desires?"

"Your desires and mine are closely aligned at this time. There would have been little you would have missed."

Cholik didn't believe it. Demons lived their lives differently from men, with different dreams and passions. Still, he couldn't help wondering if he would have been less—or more?

"Perhaps," Kabraxis said, "when you are more ready, you'll be given the chance to find out. For now, you've learned to hang on to your life as it is."

"Then why was Lord Darkulan here?" Cholik asked.

The demon smiled, baring his fangs. "Lord Darkulan has a favored mistress dying of a slow-acting poison that was given to her by Lady Darkulan only yesterday."

"Why?"

"Why? To kill her, of course. It seems that Lady Darkulan is a jealous woman and only discovered three days ago that her husband was seeing this other woman."

"Wives have killed their husbands' mistresses before," Cholik said. Even past royal courts of Westmarch had stories about such events.

"Yes," Kabraxis replied, "but it appears that Lord Darkulan's mistress of the last three months is also the daughter of the leader of the Bramwell merchants' guild. If the daughter should die, the merchant will wreak havoc with Bramwell's trade agreements and use his influence in the Westmarch royal courts to have his daughter's murderess brought to justice."

"Hodgewell means to have Lady Darkulan brought up on charges?" Cholik couldn't believe it. He knew the merchant Kabraxis was talking about.

Ammin Hodgewell was a spiteful, vengeful man who had stood against the Church of the Prophet of the Light since its inception.

"Hodgewell means to have her hanged on the Block of Justice. He's working now to bring charges against Lady Darkulan."

"Lord Darkulan knows this?"

"Yes."

"Why doesn't he enlist the aid of an apothecary?"

"He has," Kabraxis said. "Several of them, in fact, since it was discovered yesterday that his mistress is doomed to a lingering illness. None of the apothecaries or healers can save her. She has only one salvation left to her."

"The Way of Dreams," Cholik breathed. The implications of the impending murder swirled in his mind, banishing all thoughts of his near death.

"Yes," Kabraxis said. "You understand."

Cholik glanced at the demon, hardly daring to hope. "If Lord Darkulan comes to us for aid and we are able to save his mistress from the poison, save his wife from being hanged, and keep the peace in Bramwell—"

"We will claim him on the Black Road," the demon said. "Then Lord Darkulan will be ours now and forever. He will be our springboard into Westmarch and the destiny that lies before us."

Cholik shook his head. "Lord Darkulan is no young man to give into his passions with a woman of Merchantman Hodgewell's standing."

"He had no choice," Kabraxis said. "The young woman's desire for him became overwhelming. And Lord Darkulan's desires for her became strong as well."

Understanding flooded Cholik, and he gazed at the demon in wonder. "You. *You* did this."

"Of course."

"What about the poison that Lady Darkulan used? I can't believe that all of Lord Darkulan's healers and apothecaries couldn't find an antidote."

"I gave it to Lady Darkulan," Kabraxis admitted, "even as I consoled her over her husband's infidelity. Once she had the poison, she wasted no time in the administration of it."

"How much longer does Hodgewell's daughter have before the poison kills her?" Cholik asked.

"Till tomorrow night."

"And Lord Darkulan knows this?"

"Yes."

"Then today—"

"I believe he meant to come forward today after the service," Kabraxis said. "Your attempted assassination caused his bodyguards to get him clear of the church. Some of the church's guards—as well as the lord's protectors—were killed in that maneuver, which helped cover the real assassin's escape."

"Then Lord Darkulan will still come," Cholik said.

"He must," Kabraxis agreed. "He has no choice. Unless he wishes to see his mistress dead by nightfall tomorrow and witness his wife's hanging shortly after that."

"Lord Darkulan might take his wife and try to run."

Kabraxis grinned. "And leave his riches and power behind? For the love of a woman he betrayed? A woman who can no longer love him back in the same manner as before? No. Lord Darkulan would see them both dead before he would willingly abdicate his position here. But even that won't save him. If all of this comes to light and the women die—"

"Especially when the people believe he could have saved them both by turning to the Church of the Prophet of the Light as they have all done with their own problems," Cholik said, halfway stunned by the devious simplicity of Kabraxis's scheme, "Lord Darkulan will fall out of favor with the populace."

"You do see," Kabraxis said.

Cholik stared at the demon. "Why didn't you tell me any of this?"

"I did," Kabraxis explained. "As soon as you needed to know."

Part of Cholik's upbringing in the Zakarum Church whispered into the back of his mind. *Demons can influence men, but only if those men are willing to listen.* At any point, Kabraxis's multitiered scheme might have come apart. The mistress might not have fallen for the lord. The lord might not have betrayed his lady or might have broken the relationship off and confessed his indiscretions. And the lady might have taken a lover out of vengeance rather than poison the woman who took her husband.

If the plan had not worked, Cholik would never have known, and the demon's pride would have been intact.

"I humbled them all," Kabraxis said, "and I have brought these lands under our control. And we will have some of the most powerful people here as our allies. Lord Darkulan will be thankful for the salvation of his mistress, just as Merchantman Hodgewell will be grateful for the salvation of his daughter."

Cholik examined the plan. It was bold and cunning and duplicitous— exactly what he would have expected from a demon. "We have it all," he said, looking back at Kabraxis.

"Yes," the demon replied. "And we will have more."

Someone knocked on the chamber doors.

"What?" Cholik said with some annoyance.

"Master Sayes," the priest called from the other side, "I only wanted to know that you were all right."

"Go to them," Kabraxis said. "We will talk again later." He retreated to the back of the room and passed through the secret door.

Cholik strode to the door and flung it open. The priests, acolytes, and mercenaries stepped back. One of the mercenaries held a small girl before him, one hand clapped over her mouth as she struggled to get free.

"Master," the head priest said, "I beg your forgiveness. Only my worry over you prompted me to interrupt you."

"I am fine," Cholik said, knowing the priest would continue to excuse himself out of his own fear.

"But the arrow went so deep," the priest said. "I saw it for myself."

"I was healed by the grace of Dien-Ap-Sten." Cholik pulled his robe open, revealing the unmarked flesh beneath the bloody clothing. "Great is the power of the Prophet of the Light."

"Great is the power of the Prophet of the Light," the priests replied at once. "May Dien-Ap-Sten's mercies be eternal."

Cholik pulled his robe back around himself. He looked at the struggling girl in the mercenary's hands. "What is this child doing here?"

"She is the sister to the boys that Dien-Ap-Sten made whole today," the mercenary said. "She also saw the assassin."

"This child did, and yet you and your men did not?" Cholik's voice held the unforgiving edge of bared steel.

"She stood beside him when he loosed his shaft at you, Master Sayes," the mercenary replied. He looked uncomfortable.

Cholik stepped toward the man. The priests and the other mercenaries moved back, as if expecting Cholik to summon down a lightning bolt to reduce the mercenary leader to ash. The thought, Cholik had to admit, was tempting. He looked away from the quaking mercenary and at the girl. The resemblance between the girl and the conjoined twins was striking.

Tears leaked from the girl's eyes as she shuddered and cried. Her fear had turned her pale.

"Release her," Cholik said.

Reluctantly, the mercenary removed his big, callused hand from the girl's mouth. She drew in a deep, quaking breath. Tears continued to trickle down her face as she glanced around, seeking some way to escape.

"Are you all right, child?" Cholik asked in a soft voice.

"I want my da," the girl said. "I want my ma. I didn't do anything."

"Did you see the man who shot me?" Cholik asked.

"Yes." Her tear-filled eyes gazed up at Cholik. "Please, Master Sayes. I didn't do anything. I would have screamed, but he was too fast. He shot you before I could think. I didn't think he was going to do it. I wouldn't hurt you. You saved my brothers. Mikel and Dannis. You saved them. I wouldn't hurt you."

Cholik put a comforting hand on the girl's shoulder. He felt her shudder and cringe at his touch. "Easy, child. I only need to know about the man who tried to kill me. I won't hurt you, either."

She looked at him. "Promise?"

The girl's innocence touched Cholik. Promises were easy to give to the young; they wanted to believe.

"I promise," Cholik said.

The girl looked around, as if making sure the hard-faced mercenaries had heard Master Sayes's promise as well.

"They will not touch you," Cholik said. "Describe the man who shot me."

She gazed at him in big-eyed wonderment. "I thought he killed you."

"He can't," Cholik said. "I'm one of the chosen of Dien-Ap-Sten. No mortal man may take my life as long as I stay in the prophet's favor."

The girl sipped air again, becoming almost calm. "He was burned. Nearly all of his face was burned. His hands and arms were burned."

The description meant nothing to Cholik. "Is there anything else you noticed about him?"

"No." The girl hesitated.

"What is it?" Cholik asked.

"I think he was afraid that you would know him if you saw him," the girl said. "He said that he was surprised that he was let into the building."

"I've never seen a man burned so badly as you say who still lived."

"Maybe he didn't live," the girl said.

"What makes you say that?"

"I don't know. I just don't see how anyone could live after being burned so bad, is all."

Pursued by a dead man? Cholik turned the thought over in his mind for a short time.

Come, Kabraxis said in his mind. *We have things to do. The assassin is gone.*

Cholik reached into the pocket of his robe and took out a few silver coins. The amount was enough to feed a family in Bramwell for months. Once, perhaps, the money might have meant something to him. Now, it was only a bargaining tool. He placed the silver coins in the girl's hand and folded her fingers over them.

"Take this, girl," Cholik said, "as a token of my appreciation." He glanced up at the nearest mercenary. "See that she gets back to her family."

The mercenary nodded and led the little girl away. She never once looked back.

Despite the fact that more than a year had passed since he'd found Kabraxis's gateway under the remains of Tauruk's Port and Ransim, Cholik's mind wandered back to the labyrinth and the chamber where he'd released the demon back into the human world. One man had escaped that night, a Westmarch sailor who had even evaded the skeletons and zombies Kabraxis had raised to kill everyone there.

Cholik felt that no one in Bramwell would have dared attack him in the church. And if the man were burned as badly as the girl described, someone would have come forward to identify him and hope to earn a reward from Dien-Ap-Sten or himself.

So it had been an outsider. Someone not even the populace of the city had known about. Yet it had to be someone who had known Cholik from before.

Where had the man who had escaped from Tauruk's Port gone? If this was him, and it made no sense for it to be anyone else, why had he waited so long before he'd stepped forward? And why approach Cholik now at all?

It was unsettling. Especially when Cholik thought about how near the quarrel had come to piercing his heart. Thoughts churning, Cholik reentered his private chamber to plan and scheme with the demon he had freed. Whatever chance the assassin had had was now gone. Cholik would never be caught unprepared again. He consoled himself with that.

Back and shoulders on fire from all the lifting he'd done during the day, Darrick entered the Blue Lantern. Pipe smoke and the closing night filled the tavern with darkness. Men swapping stories and telling lies filled the tavern with noise. To the west, near where the mouth of the Gulf of Westmarch met the Frozen Sea, the sunset settled into the water, looking like dying red embers scattered from a stirred campfire.

A cold north wind followed Darrick into the tavern. The weather had changed in the last hour, just as the ships' captains and mates had been thinking it would. Come morning, Sahyir had told Darrick, there might even be a layer of ice covering the harbor. It wouldn't be enough to lock the ships in, but that time wasn't far off, either.

Men looked up as Darrick walked through the small building. Some of the men knew him, and some were from the ships out in the harbor. All of their eyes were wary. Seeker's Point wasn't a big village, but the numbers swelled when ships were in the harbor. And if a man wanted trouble in the village, the Blue Lantern was where he came.

There was no table space in the tavern. Three men Darrick knew slightly offered their tables with their friends. Darrick thanked them but declined, passing on through the tables till he spotted the man Sahyir had talked about earlier that day.

The man was in his middle years, gray showing in his square-cut beard. He was broad-shouldered and a little overweight, a solid man who had seen an active life. His clothing was second-hand, worn but comfortable-looking, and warm enough against the cool winds blowing in from the north. He wore round-lensed spectacles, and Darrick could still count on the fingers of both hands how many times he'd seen such devices.

A platter of bread and meat sat to the sage's left. He wrote with his right hand, pausing every now and again to dip his quill into an inkwell beside the book he worked in. A whale-oil lantern near the book provided him more light to work by.

Darrick stopped only a short distance from the table, uncertain what he should say.

Abruptly, the sage looked up, peering over his spectacles. "Darrick?"

Startled, Darrick said nothing.

"Your friend Sahyir named you," the sage said. "He told me when he talked to me last night that you might be stopping by."

"Aye," Darrick said. "Though I must confess I don't truly know what I'm doing here."

"If you've seen that symbol as Sahyir seems inclined to believe that you have," the sage said, "it's probably marked you." He gestured to the book before him. "The Light knows that the pursuit of knowledge about it has marked me. Much to my own detriment, according to some of my mentors and peers."

"You've seen the demon?" Darrick asked.

Renewed interest flickered in the sage's deep green eyes. "You have?"

Darrick paused, feeling that he'd admitted more than he should have.

An irritable look filled the sage's face. "Damnation, son. If you're going to talk, then sit. I've been working hard for days here, and weeks and months before that in other places. Looking up gets hellaciously tiresome for me." He pointed at a chair across from him with the quill, then closed his book and put it aside.

Still feeling uncertain, Darrick pulled out the chair and sat. Out of habit, he laid his sheathed cutlass across his thighs.

The sage laced his fingers together and rested both elbows on the tabletop. "Have you eaten tonight?"

"No." Unloading imported goods from the ship and then loading exported goods had filled the day. Darrick had only eaten what he'd carried along in the food bag, which had been empty for hours.

"Would you like to eat?"

"Aye."

The sage gestured to one of the serving wenches. The young woman went to get the order immediately.

"Sahyir told me you were a sailor," the sage said.

"Aye."

"Tell me where you saw the demon," the sage suggested.

Darrick held himself in check. "I never said that I saw such a thing, now, did I?"

A frown deepened the wrinkles over the sage's eyes. "Are you always this churlish?"

"Sir," Darrick stated evenly, "I don't even know your name."

"Taramis," the sage replied. "Taramis Volken."

"And what is it that you do, Taramis Volken?" Darrick asked.

"I gather wisdom," the man replied. "Especially that pertaining to demons."

"Why?"

"Because I don't like them, and usually the things that I learn can be used against them."

The serving wench returned with a platter of goat's meat and shrimp and fish, backed by fresh bread and portions of melon that had shipped up that day. She offered mulled wine.

The temptation was there only for a moment for Darrick. For the last year he had tried to bury his life and his pain in wine and spirits. It hadn't worked, and only old Sahyir had seen fit to save him from himself. But as the old man had told him, saving himself was a day-to-day job, and only one man could do that.

"Tea," Darrick said. "Please."

The wench nodded and returned with a tall tankard of unsweetened tea.

"So," Taramis said, "about your demon—"

"Not my demon," Darrick said.

A fleeting smile touched the sage's lips. "As you will. Where did you see the demon?"

Darrick ignored the question. He dipped his finger into the gravy on his plate and drew out the ellipses with the single line threading through them. He even drew the symbol so that the line went under and over the appropriate ellipses.

The sage studied the gravy symbol. "Do you know what this is?"

"No."

"Or whom it belongs to?"

Darrick shook his head.

"Where did you see this?" the sage asked.

"No," Darrick replied. "You'll get nothing from me until I'm convinced I'm getting something from you."

The sage reached into the worn lizard-hide traveler's pack in the chair beside him. Thoughtfully, he took out a pipe and a bag. After shoving the bowl full of tobacco, he set his pipe ablaze with the lantern. He smoked in silence, a hazy wreath forming around his head. He never blinked as he stared at Darrick.

Fresh-shaved that morning, Darrick hadn't seen a more fiercely demanding gaze since the mirror then. Even the Westmarch ships' officers paled by comparison. But he ate, savoring the hot food. By the working standards he was accustomed to in Seeker's Point, the meal was an extravagance. The cargo handling he'd done for the day might have to feed him for two weeks in order to keep him from hunting meager game in the forest with winter soon to be breathing down their necks.

Taramis reached back into his traveler's pack and took out another book. Flipping through the tome, he stopped at a page, laid the book on the table, spun it around, and pushed it across the table toward Darrick. The sage moved the lantern so it shone on the pages more directly.

"The demon that you saw," Taramis said. "Did it look anything like this?"

Darrick glanced at the page. The illustration was done by hand and in great detail.

The picture was the demon he'd seen at Tauruk's Port, the one who had summoned the undead creatures responsible for Mat Hu-Ring's death.

Not entirely responsible, Darrick told himself, feeling his appetite ebb. He owned the majority of that responsibility. He kept eating mechanically, knowing it would be days or weeks before he had the chance to eat so well again.

"What do you know about the symbol?" Darrick asked, not answering the sage's question.

"You're a hard sell, aren't you, boy?" Taramis asked.

Darrick broke a piece of bread and slathered honey butter onto it. He started eating while Taramis tried to wait him out.

Finally giving up, Taramis replied, "That symbol is the one that was longest associated with a demon called Kabraxis. He is supposed to be the guardian of the Twisted Path of Dreams and Shadows."

"The Way of Dreams?" Darrick asked, remembering the stories Sahyir had been telling about Bramwell that morning.

"Interesting, isn't it?" the sage asked.

"Sahyir told me he'd gone to church in Bramwell," Darrick said. "There's a new church there called the Church of the Prophet of the Light. They also mention the Way of Dreams there."

Taramis nodded. "They worship a prophet there named Dien-Ap-Sten."

"Not Kabraxis?"

"It would be pretty stupid for a demon to be going around telling people to call him by his rightful name, now, wouldn't it?" Taramis grinned. "I mean, the whole bit of anonymity would be right out the window if that was the case. Most people wouldn't worship a demon by choice, although there are some."

Darrick waved a hand over his platter. "I appreciate this fine meal you went and bought me, I really do. But I have to tell you, if this story hasn't picked up some by the time I finish, I'm out of here."

"Patience isn't one of your virtues, is it?"

"No." Darrick felt no shame in admitting such.

"Kabraxis is an old and powerful demon," Taramis said. "He's been around, in one form or another, since the beginning of recorded history. He's been known by dozens, possibly hundreds, of names."

Darrick pointed to the gravy-rendered symbol on the tabletop. "And this is his symbol?"

Taramis puffed on his pipe. The coals in the pipe bowl glowed orange. "I believe this is the demon's primary symbol. Did you see this in Bramwell?"

"I've not been to Bramwell in years," Darrick answered. It had been too close to Westmarch.

"Then where did you see the demon?" The sage's interest was intense.

"I never said I did," Darrick reminded.

"Your friend told me—"

"He told you that I knew about this symbol."

"That's all you've ever told him?"

Darrick sipped his tea and ignored the question. He pointedly returned his attention to his meal. The plate steadily emptied.

"Do you know the meaning of the symbol?" Taramis asked.

"No."

"It's supposed to represent the layers of man. The facets of a man that a demon may prey on."

"I don't understand," Darrick said.

The sage seemed surprised. "You've had no priest's training?"

"No."

"And yet you know of Kabraxis's most potent symbol without training?"

Darrick said nothing as he used his knife to spear a potato chunk.

Taramis sighed. "All right, then. You intrigue me, and that's the only reason I'm going to continue, because I will not tolerate being treated in such a cavalier manner." He tapped the ellipses. "These are the layers of man as divined by Kabraxis, Banisher of the Light."

"Why is he called Banisher of the Light?" Darrick asked. He glanced around them, making sure none of the sailors or longshoremen was taking much interest in their conversation. In some communities, the discussion of demons was enough to get a man strung up or, at the least, tested by a dunking chair or a red-hot poker.

"Because Kabraxis's main objective in the world of man is to eclipse and replace Zakarum. Kabraxis worked during the Sin War to keep Zakarum from being brought forth by the Archangel Yaerius through his disciple Akarat."

"What of the Archangel Inarius?" Darrick asked, remembering the old stories he'd been told of the Sin War. "It was Inarius who first built a Cathedral of Light in this world."

"Inarius grew overconfident and destroyed Mephisto's temple, and Inarius was enslaved and returned with the Seraph to Hell to be tortured for all time. Kabraxis aided in Inarius's downfall by winning them over to the demon's side."

"I don't remember that," Darrick said.

"The war was primarily between Mephisto and Inarius," Taramis said. "Only a sage or someone who has had priest training would know of Kabraxis's part in the Sin War. The Banisher of Light is a conniving demon. Kabraxis works in the shadows, stretching their boundaries till they cover the Light. Most men who have worshipped him over all those years have never known his true name."

"But you believe he is in Bramwell?" Darrick asked.

"At the Church of the Prophet of the Light." The sage nodded. "Yes. And there he is known as Dien-Ap-Sten."

Darrick tapped the symbol. "What of this?"

"Again," Taramis said, "those ellipses represent the layers of man as Kabraxis perceives them. It is through those layers that he is able to reach into a man's soul, twist it, bend it, and finally possess it. He is not by nature a confrontational demon as are Diablo, Mephisto, and Baal."

Darrick shook his head. "You can't go about just dropping the names of all those demons like that. They aren't real. They can't be all real."

"The Prime Evils are real."

A chill threaded through Darrick, but even after everything he'd seen—even after everything he'd lost after seeing the demon in Tauruk's Port—he struggled to believe that the worlds of the demons, the Burning Hells, were real and not just stories.

"Have you seen the Church of the Prophet of the Light?"

"No."

"It is huge," Taramis said. "In less than a year, the Church of the Prophet of the Light has become one of the most prominent structures in Bramwell."

"Bramwell isn't a big city," Darrick said. "Mainly fishermen and farmers live there. Westmarch barely keeps a garrison of guards there, and it's mostly a show of support because no invading army would attack Westmarch through Bramwell. The roads are too harsh and uncertain."

"Kabraxis takes generations to build his power," Taramis said. "That's why even the unholy trinity of brothers learned to fear him. Where they waged war and fought with human armies with their own demonic ones, Kabraxis won believers to him."

"Through the layers of man."

"Yes." The sage tapped the outermost ellipse. "First is the fear mankind has of demons. People who fear Kabraxis will acknowledge his leadership, but they will break away at the first chance." He tapped the next ellipse. "Next comes greed. Through the Church of the Prophet of the Light, Kabraxis and the high priest known as Master Sayes, also called the Wayfinder have granted gifts to their worshippers. Good fortune in business, money, an unexpected inheritance. Then he moves closer to the heart." He tapped the next ellipse. "Covetousness. Do you secretly want your neighbor's wife? His land? Worship Kabraxis, and it will be yours in time."

"Only if the man you want those things from doesn't worship Kabraxis as well."

"Not true." Taramis paused to relight his pipe. "Kabraxis weighs and judges those who serve him. If one man—more powerful in the community than another—will better serve Kabraxis's purposes, the Banisher of the Light rewards the more powerful man."

"What of the worshipper who loses whatever the other man wants?"

The sage waved the question away. "Simple enough. Kabraxis tells everyone that the man who lost his lands or his wife or his family wasn't strong in his faith. That he played Kabraxis—or, in this case, Dien-Ap-Sten—falsely and deserved what he got."

Sour bile rumbled in Darrick's stomach. Every word the sage spoke had the ring of truth in it.

Taramis moved to the next ellipse. "From that point, Kabraxis seeks out those people with greater fears. Sickness in your family? Come to the church to be healed. Your father is becoming senile? Come to the church, and have clarity returned to him."

"Kabraxis can do these things?"

"Yes," Taramis said. "And more. Demons have many powers. In their own way, they offer salvation to those who serve them. You've heard of the gifts

Diablo, Baal, and Mephisto have given their own champions in the past. Enchanted armor, mystical weapons, great power to raise armies of dead. The Prime Evils rule through fear and destruction, always aiming for subjugation."

"Kabraxis has no interest in that?"

"Of course he does," Taramis said. "He's a demon, after all. Even archangels want those who worship them to fear them just a little bit. Otherwise, why would they choose such fearsome forms and act the way they do?"

Darrick considered the question and supposed it was true. Still, all this talk of demons was foreign to him, something he didn't even want to invest in. Yet he felt he had no choice.

"Archangels for the Light threaten man with being tortured by demons for the rest of his eternal life, and they promise dire vengeance for any who worship and aid the demons." Taramis shook his head. "Archangels are warriors, just as demons are."

"But they have a more generous view of how man is supposed to fit into this world with them."

"That," the sage said, "depends on your belief, doesn't it?"

Darrick sat quietly.

"There are some who believe this world should be cleansed of demons and angels, that there should be no Light or Darkness, and men should find their own way in life."

"What do you believe?" Darrick asked.

"I believe in the Light," Taramis replied. "That's why I hunt demons and expose them for what they are. I've killed eight lesser demons in the last twenty years. Not all of them are the likes of the Prime Evils."

Darrick knew that, but he'd only seen the one demon, and it had been a truly horrifying creature. "What are you going to do to Kabraxis?"

"Kill him if I can," the sage stated. "If not, I mean to see him exposed for what he is, his priest slain, and his church razed to the ground."

The man's words drew Darrick in, and he took comfort in them. Taramis made doing such an incredible thing sound possible.

"You've lost someone to the demon," Taramis whispered.

Darrick drew back.

"Don't bother to deny it," the sage said. "I see the truth in your eyes. You wear your pain like a chevron for anyone who has been through the same thing." He paused, his eyes sliding from Darrick's for a moment. "I lost my family to a demon. Twenty-three years ago. I was a priest. Such a thing wasn't supposed to happen to me. But a demon's hand took my wife and my three children from me."

The lantern light flickered on the table.

"I was young then and full of my studies as a Vizjerei mage. I taught in one of the outlying schools in my homelands. A stranger came to our door. We lived in back of the school, just my family and I. This man told us that he had no place to sleep and had eaten nothing for two days. Fool that I was and full of my new position, I let him in. During the night, he killed my family. Only I lived, though most thought I would not." He pulled back the sleeves of his shirt, revealing the long, wicked scars across his flesh. "I have more scars over the rest of my body." He tilted his head back, revealing the thick scar that curved around half of his neck and across his throat. "The priests who saved me had to piece me back together. All of the healers told me later that I should have died. The Light knows I wanted to."

"But you lived," Darrick whispered, drawn into the horror of the story.

"Yes." Taramis knocked ash from his pipe and put it away. "For a time, I resented my life. Then I came to realize that it was a more focused one. The demon that had killed my family would go on to kill other families. I resolved to get well, mentally and physically. And I did. It took me three years to heal and nine years to track down the demon that took my family from me. I had killed two other demons by that time and revealed four others."

"And now you hunt Kabraxis?"

"Yes. When the Church of the Prophet of the Light first came into being, I became suspicious. So I began researching it and found enough similarities between the healing and the changes wrought within the worshippers to lead me in the direction of Kabraxis."

"Then why come here?" Darrick asked.

"Because," the sage said, "Kabraxis was once here. For a time, the barbarian tribes worshipped him when they warred against the people of the southern lands. During that time he was known as Iceclaw the Merciless. He succeeded in uniting some of the more powerful barbarian tribes, creating a great horde that landed between the Twin Seas, the Great Ocean, and the Frozen Sea."

Darrick considered the implications. The stories about the barbarian horde went so far back that they were considered only tales to frighten children with. The barbarians had been depicted as cannibalistic warriors who filed their teeth and filled their bellies from the bodies of women and children. "Until Hauklin came with his great sword, Stormfury, and slew Iceclaw during a battle that took six days."

Taramis grinned. "You've heard the stories."

"Aye," Darrick replied. "But that doesn't answer why you're here."

"Because Stormfury is still here," the sage answered. "I came for the sword because it is the only thing that can slay Kabraxis."

"It didn't slay him the first time," Darrick pointed out.

"The texts I read said that Kabraxis fled before the devastating might of Stormfury. Only in the stories of men was the demon reported dead. But I believe the sword has the power to kill Kabraxis. If you can track him back into the Burning Hells with it."

"If you knew all of this, why did you bother to talk to me?"

The sage's eyes searched Darrick. "Because I am one man, Darrick Lang, and I'm not as young as I used to be."

"You know my name?"

"Of course." Taramis waved at the books before him. "I am a learned man. I heard the stories of the discovery of the demon at Tauruk's Port more than a year ago while I was down in Westmarch. And I heard of the young navy officer who lost his best friend while carrying out a mission given him by the king's nephew."

"Then why go through all this subterfuge?"

"So that I could convince you of my cause," Taramis said softly, "and perhaps your destiny."

"What destiny?" Darrick immediately felt trapped.

"You're tied to this thing somehow," the sage said. "You lost blood to Kabraxis, so perhaps that's it. Or maybe there is something more that binds you to the demon."

"I want nothing more to do with that demon," Darrick said. But even as he said it, he felt uncertain, and with that uncertainty came a harsh wave of fear.

"Really? Then how is it you've ended up here? Where the weapon that will cut Kabraxis down is?"

"I've been drunk most of the past year," Darrick said. "I lost my post in the Westmarch Navy. Drunk and destitute most of the time, I only drifted from town to town, finding enough work to keep myself alive and away from Westmarch. I didn't know I was here till I woke up damn near freezing to death. I knew nothing of that sword until you told me just now. I haven't been following a demon's trail."

"No?" Taramis glanced at the elliptical symbol drawn in gravy on the table-top. "Then what are you doing here now? Unless you've only come for a free meal."

"I don't know," Darrick admitted.

"You already knew who that symbol belonged to before you spoke to me," Taramis said. "Now that you know the demon is in Bramwell, hiding behind the mystical auguries of the Church of the Prophet of the Light, can you truly walk away from this? From any of this?"

Unbidden, the memory of Mat plunging over the cliffside to his doom trickled through Darrick's mind in slow motion again. The pain, once blinded and muffled by drink for the past year, twisted within him again as if it were new and fresh. Anger raged within him, but somehow he managed to keep it under control.

"The Light has guided you here, Darrick," the sage said in his quiet voice. "It has guided you here to this place and at this time, and made it possible for us to meet, because you have a stake in this. Because you can make a difference. My question is whether you're ready to take up the battle that awaits you."

Darrick hesitated, knowing that either answer he gave—and, perhaps, even giving no answer at all—would doom him.

"You believe the sword can kill Kabraxis?" Darrick asked in a hoarse whisper.

"Yes," Taramis answered. "But only here in the final layer." He tapped the elliptical symbol again. "Two layers yet remain that we've not spoken of. The outermost is where Kabraxis takes initiates to forge them into something more than mere men. Here they must face the fears of a demon world, walk the Twisted Path of Dreams and Shadows. The Black Road."

"The Black Road?" Darrick asked.

"As Kabraxis calls it. He's had several names for it during his campaigns here in the world of men, but its true and proper name is the Twisted Path of Dreams and Shadows. Once facing the demonic world, Kabraxis's chosen must give themselves to him, mind and body and soul, for now and forever. Many fail, and they are cast into the Burning Hells to die and die again for all eternity."

"How are the men changed?"

"They become faster and stronger than normal men," the sage replied. "Harder to kill. And some of them are given an understanding of demonic magic."

"You make getting to Kabraxis sound impossible."

"Not with Stormfury," Taramis said. "And I'm not without magic of my own."

"What if I chose not to go?"

"Then I would go alone." The sage smiled. "But you can't deny this, can you, Darrick? This has become too much a part of you. Perhaps a year ago you would have been able to turn your back on me and walk away. But not now. You've tried to live around what happened to your friend and what happened to you. It's nearly destroyed you." He paused. "Now you must find the strength to live through this."

Darrick looked at the elliptical drawing. "What lies in the final layer?"

Hesitating, Taramis shook his head. "I don't know. The texts that I've read regarding Kabraxis have no answer. It has been referred to as the layer of the greatest fear, but I have no idea what that is."

"It might be good to know what is there."

"Perhaps we can find out together," the sage suggested.

Darrick locked eyes with the man, wishing he were strong enough to say no, that he wouldn't go. But he couldn't do that because he was tired of trying to live half a life and avoid the guilt. He should have died with Mat. Perhaps the only way to escape was to die now.

"Aye," Darrick whispered. "I'll go with you."

Eighteen

Buyard Cholik stood on the platform above the snake's head and awaited the arrival of his guest. Anticipation filled Cholik as he surveyed the empty pews around him. That morning, he had been enthused to see the large room overflowing with people. Every day the service was larger than the day before. There was no longer seating for all those in attendance. Even building as quickly as they were able, the construction crews weren't able to keep pace with the growth.

Yet tonight there was only one person in attendance, and Cholik's elation soared even higher. He remained silent as Lord Darkulan paused at the great central entrance.

Around the lord, a score of armored guards held lanterns and bared weapons. The lantern light glinted from scale mail and keen-edged steel. Voices whispered, and in their barely heard words Cholik detected fear and hostility.

Lord Darkulan was a young man of thirty. His regal bearing showed the regimen he used to stay in shape as a warrior as well as a leader of men. An open-faced helmet with fierce curved horns framed his lean, hawklike features. A mustache followed the sneering curve up his mouth. He wore a dark green cloak that blended with his black breeches and tunic over a dark green shirt. Although it was hidden, Cholik was certain the lord wore mystical chain mail armor beneath the tunic.

Impatiently, Lord Darkulan waved to one of his warriors.

The man nodded and stepped into the main area of the cathedral. His metal-shod boots clanked as he crossed the stone floor into the cathedral proper.

Cholik raised his voice, knowing from the way the room was constructed that it would be easily heard. "Lord Darkulan, this meeting time was set aside for you. No one else may enter this part of the church."

The warriors swung their lanterns in Cholik's direction. Some of the lanterns had bull's-eye construction and lit on Cholik directly.

Cholik squinted against the blinding light but did not raise his hand to shield his eyes.

"These are only my personal bodyguards," Lord Darkulan responded. "They will offer you no harm. In fact, after the episode today, I thought you would appreciate their presence."

"No," Cholik said. "You requested this meeting, and I acceded to it. We will keep it like that."

"And if I insist?" Lord Darkulan asked.

Cholik spoke words of power and thrust his hands straight out. Flames leapt from his fingertips and ignited the oil-filled channels around the snake's head. Alive once more, the snake's head leapt from the stone wall toward the guard.

Unnerved, the guard threw himself backward. His metal-shod boots scraped sparks from the stone floor as he hurried to rejoin the other guards. The warriors clustered around Lord Darkulan, trying to draw him back to safety. Lanterns swirled like a cloud of fireflies in the main entrance.

"Would you have your mistress die?" Cholik asked as he rode the swaying snake's head. "Would you have your lady hung by the neck? Would you have your own good name dragged through the mud and dung of this city? Especially when I can change all that?"

Lord Darkulan cursed his men and fought them off him. Reluctantly, the warriors stepped away from him. Their leaders talked quickly to their lord, trying to get him to listen to their reason.

The lord paused at the mouth of the entrance and stared at Cholik atop the stone snake's head. Below Cholik, fire clung to the snake's jaws, and he knew it must be a horrific sight in the middle of the dark cathedral.

"They said you were killed this morning," Lord Darkulan said.

Cholik spread his arms, enjoying the role he played. "Do I look like a dead man, Lord Darkulan?"

"More like he's a zombie," one of the guards muttered.

"I'm no zombie," Cholik said. "Come closer, Lord Darkulan, that you may hear my heartbeat. Perhaps, should you truly not believe, I'll let you bleed me. Zombies and dead things don't bleed as the living do."

"Why can't my men accompany me?" Lord Darkulan asked.

"Because if I am to save the people in your life whom you wish saved—if I am to save *you*, Lord Darkulan—you must trust me." Cholik waited, trying not to act as though he had as much depending on the lord's decision as he did. He wondered if Kabraxis were watching, then realized that wasn't the proper question. The proper question was from where the demon watched.

Lord Darkulan took a lantern from one of his men, steeled himself for a moment, then strode into the cathedral. "How is it that you know so much about my business and the affairs of state?" he demanded.

"I am the Wayfinder," Cholik declared. "Chosen of Dien-Ap-Sten himself. How could I not know?"

"A few among those who counsel me suggest that somehow you and this church are behind the troubles that plague me."

"Do you believe that, Lord Darkulan?" Cholik asked.

The lord hesitated. "I don't know."

"This morning you saw me dead, slain by a quarrel from the hand of a treacherous assassin. Yet here I stand. I am whole and alive and ready to help you in your hour of need, my lord. Or perhaps I should turn from you as you have turned from Dien-Ap-Sten and this church since we first began our sojourn among you." Cholik paused. "I could do that, you know. There are some among my own counsel who believe the assassin who tried to kill me today was hired by you and that you are jealous of my own rise to power within your community."

"Those are lies," Lord Darkulan responded. "I have never been one to skulk around."

"And does Lady Darkulan still feel that is a fair assessment of you?" Cholik asked softly.

Lord Darkulan's hand dropped to the hilt of his saber. His voice turned gruff and hard. "Don't press your luck, priest."

"I stared death in the eye today, Lord Darkulan. Your threats won't carry much weight with me. I know that I walk hand-in-hand with Dien-Ap-Sten."

"I could have you driven from this church," Lord Darkulan said angrily.

"There are more citizens and visitors here who wouldn't allow that to happen than you have army or navy to get it done."

"You don't know—"

"No," Cholik interrupted, causing the stone snake's head to rear up above the lord. "You don't know what you're dealing with."

The snake opened its fanged jaws and spewed fire against the stone floor in front of the guards and drove them back.

"You need me," Cholik told Lord Darkulan. "And you need the salvation that Dien-Ap-Sten can offer. If your mistress is saved, your wife will be saved. If both women are saved, your power will be saved."

"Letting you stay here was a mistake," Lord Darkulan said. "I should have had you banished from the city."

"After the first night of miracles here," Cholik said, "you wouldn't have been able to do that. Dien-Ap-Sten and the Way of Dreams bring power to people. Wealth and privilege. Both are for the taking. Health for the sick and infirm and dying." He silently commanded the snake's head to the ground where it lay prone.

Lord Darkulan stepped backward, but the flame still roiled where it had struck the stone floor. He was separated from his men, but Cholik was also grimly aware that some of the guards had bows, and even knives could be thrown that distance.

"You did the only thing you could in coming here tonight," Cholik said. He walked down the platform circling the stone snake's neck.

The snake lay quiet and still, but the fiery eyes darted and watched. Its tongue, smoldering and steaming, flicked out rapidly, scenting the air. Deep orange embers swirled through the still air inside the dark cathedral, turning to black ash shortly before reaching the ceiling. Waves of heat rolled off the stone snake.

Cholik stopped in front of the snake, knowing the animated creature outlined him, making him seem like a dark shadow in front of a dreadful beast.

"Perhaps you think you have sealed your doom by coming here tonight, Lord Darkulan," Cholik said softly.

The lord said nothing. Fear etched deep shadows into his face despite the light given off by his lantern and the snake.

"I assure you," Cholik said, "that the opposite is true: you have sealed your future." He gestured at the snake, feeling the furnace blast of heat as the creature opened its jaws. "Walk with me, Lord Darkulan. Give your worries and fears over to Dien-Ap-Sten that he may make them go away."

Lord Darkulan stood his ground.

"You were here today," Cholik said. "You witnessed the miracle that Dien-Ap-Sten performed on the Black Road by separating the two boys locked in each other's flesh. Have you ever seen such a thing done before?"

"No," the lord replied in a quaking voice.

"Have you even heard of such a thing?"

"Never."

"With Dien-Ap-Sten at his side," Cholik promised, "a man who ventures down the Way of Dreams may do anything." He held out his hand. "Come with me that I may show you even more miracles."

Hesitation showed on Lord Darkulan's face.

"By morning," Cholik said, "it will be too late. The poison will have claimed the life of your mistress. Her father will demand the life of your wife in return."

"How am I supposed to save them by going with you?"

"On the Way of Dreams," Cholik said, "all things are made possible. Come."

Trying not to show his fear, Lord Darkulan stepped forward and allowed Cholik to take his arm and guide him.

"Be brave, Lord Darkulan," Cholik advised. "You are going to see wonders seldom seen by human eyes. Step into the snake's mouth, and all your fear will be taken from you if you but believe."

Lord Darkulan followed a half-step behind Cholik. They stepped over the stone snake's sharp teeth and followed the black, smoldering ribbon of tongue down into the snake's throat, where it became a black road that wound down into a long hallway.

"Where are we?" Lord Darkulan asked.

"On the Way of Dreams," Cholik replied. "We're going to find your destiny. It takes a strong man to follow the teachings of Dien-Ap-Sten. You will become an even stronger man."

The hallway widened and changed a number of times, but the Black Road remained constant beneath Cholik's feet. He'd talked to several parishioners who had ventured along the Black Road to be healed or receive a blessing, and all of them had described the path differently. Some had said they'd journeyed down familiar hallways, while others were taken through places they'd never seen and hoped they would never see.

A green sun dawned in the hallway before them, and suddenly they were no longer in a hallway. Now the Black Road clung to a cliffside. The path they followed was so high that clouds obscured the view below. Still, the harsh mountain range towered above. Ice glinted on the peaks only a little farther up.

Lord Darkulan stopped. "I want to go back."

"You can't," Cholik replied. "Look." He turned and pointed back along the way they had come.

Flames clung to the Black Road, twisting and curling three times the height of a man.

"The only way open to you is forward," Cholik said.

"I've made a mistake," Lord Darkulan announced.

"This was not the first," Cholik replied.

Spinning abruptly, Lord Darkulan raised his sword, bringing it to within inches of Cholik's unprotected throat. "You will let me out of here now, or I'll have your head from your shoulders!"

Secure in the knowledge that Kabraxis watched over him, Cholik grasped the sword. The sharp edges cut into the flesh of his hand. Blood trickled down the blade and dripped to the Black Road, giving birth to fist-sized fires at their feet.

"No," Cholik said, "you won't." Power coursed through him, turning the sword red-hot in a heartbeat.

Screaming in pain, Lord Darkulan released his weapon and stumbled back. He held his burned hand in disbelief.

Cholik ignored the sizzling pain of his own burning hand, ignored the stink of scorched flesh and the smoke that curled up. Much worse things had happened to him during the trips down the Black Road that Kabraxis had led him on. He could still occasionally feel the demon's talons rooting around inside his brain, scraping against his skull.

Swiveling, Cholik flung the lord's sword over the cliff's edge. He held out his burned and bleeding hand for inspection.

"You're insane," Lord Darkulan said in disbelief.

"No," Cholik stated calmly. "I believe in Dien-Ap-Sten and the power of the Way of Dreams." He held his hand up. Even as he watched, the cuts knitted together, and the burns healed and went away. In less than a moment, his hand was completely healed. "You can believe, too. Hold out your hand, and accept what I am telling you."

Trembling, afraid, and hurting, Lord Darkulan held his hand up.

"Believe," Cholik said softly. "Believe, and you will be given the power to heal yourself and end your misery."

Lord Darkulan concentrated. Sweat popped out on his brow. "I can't," he whispered hoarsely. "Please, I beg you. Make the pain go away."

"I can't," Cholik said. "That is for you to do. Just come to Dien-Ap-Sten willingly. Only a little faith is needed. Trust that."

Slowly, then, Lord Darkulan's hand began to heal. The burns scabbed over, and only a moment or two after that, smooth flesh remained where the horrible burns had been.

"I've done it." Lord Darkulan gazed at his uninjured hand in disbelief. His fingers still trembled.

"Yes," Cholik said. "But the worst is yet to come."

Without warning, the ledge broke away, dropping them into the abyss over the clouds.

Lord Darkulan screamed.

Cholik controlled his own fear. He was on the Black Road now. The warriors and priests who had become part of his inner circle had all experienced much worse than this. All of those men who had reached this point had to relive a horrific nightmare that was their deepest secret.

The bottom of the long fall through the cottony clouds wasn't the bone-breaking stop against jagged rocks that Cholik had expected. Instead, he landed light as a feather in the midst of a moon-dappled bog under a clear night sky.

Lord Darkulan plummeted into the bog, disappearing with a huge splash that threw black mud in all directions.

Cholik grew worried after a time that something had gone wrong. Initiates had died along the way of the Black Road, but generally Kabraxis was selective about who was brought into the inner circle.

"He's fine," the demon said. "Give him a moment more. I found this place and this event in a tight secret place that he seldom goes to these days. Pay attention."

Cholik waited, amazed that he could stand on the bog's surface tension.

Then Lord Darkulan shoved an arm up through the bog, clapped it onto a semi-submerged tree trunk that had fallen a long time ago. Mud covered his head and face, stripping away the regal look and leaving only the frightened man behind.

Lord Darkulan reached toward Cholik. "Help me! Hurry!"

"What is he afraid of?" Cholik asked Kabraxis. Neither of them made a move toward the struggling lord. "The bog is not so deep that he will drown."

"He fears the past," the demon said. "And he should."

Fearfully, Lord Darkulan gazed over his shoulder at the swamp. Naked and dead trees stood out from the loose mud. Dead brush with ashy, curling leaving lined the shore. Skeletons of small creatures, some of them recently dead so that patches of fur clung to them, lay partially submerged in the swamp and on the shore. Dead birds clung upside down by their claws from naked tree branches. Frog corpses floated in the bog.

Lord Darkulan screamed, then was pulled under the bog by something strong and fierce. Bubbles erupted from the mud.

"Is he going to die here?" Cholik asked.

"He will," Kabraxis answered, "if I don't save him. He can't fight this nightmare. It's too strong for him."

The man's arm shot out of the bog again, found the tree trunk, and succeeded in pulling himself out of the muck. When he appeared, a skeleton clung to his back.

Years of submersion in the bog had turned the dead woman's skin to leather, and it sank in tightly to her skull. Once, Cholik knew, she might have been pretty, but there was no way to know that now. The soft blue dress that might once have hidden womanly curves now clung to the emaciated form of the horror that rode Lord Darkulan's back. The dead woman bent close to him, teeth showing through her ruined flesh. She licked out a dead, leathery tongue that caught his ear, then drew it back between her broken teeth. When she bit down, crushing the earlobe like a grape, crimson sprayed.

Lord Darkulan screamed in pain and flailed, trying desperately to shove the dead woman from him and haul himself onto the tree trunk.

"Help me!" the lord called out.

"Who is the woman?" Cholik asked.

"Once," Kabraxis said, "she was his lover. It was during the early years before his marriage. She was a common girl named Azyka, a shopkeeper's daughter. Before the marriage, she told Lord Darkulan she was going to have his child. Knowing he couldn't allow that, Lord Darkulan killed her and left her body in this bog outside Bramwell."

"The girl was never found?" Cholik asked.

"No."

Cholik watched the horrified lord fighting to maintain his grip on the moss-encrusted tree trunk. The dead woman's weight steadily bore him under. Cholik was not amazed by Kabraxis's story. As a priest of the Zakarum Church, he was no stranger to the special privileges invoked by royalty. In Westmarch's history, several murders had been forgotten about and the murderers absolved by special dispensation from the church.

"Help me!" Lord Darkulan screamed.

Kabraxis strode forward. His large feet left only small ripples on the bog water and never once became wet. "Lord Darkulan," the demon called.

The lord glanced up, seeing the demon for the first time. For a moment, Lord Darkulan froze, but the dead woman chewing his ear into ragged, bloody bits caught his attention again. He fought against her, losing his grip on the tree trunk and plunging into the bog up to his chin. The dead woman's hair floated on the bog water.

"Lord Darkulan," the demon said. "I am Dien-Ap-Sten. I am your salvation."

"You're no salvation," Lord Darkulan cried. "You're a demon."

"And you're a drowning man," Kabraxis stated. "Accept me or die."

"I'll not be tricked by one of your illusions—"

The dead woman reached up behind Lord Darkulan and knotted her skeletal fingers in his hair. When she yanked, Lord Darkulan vanished beneath the black muck of the bog.

Kabraxis stood patiently waiting.

For a moment, Cholik believed it was done and that the lord had died in the bog with the specter of the girl he had murdered so long ago. The chill of the swamp blew through Cholik, and he wrapped his arms around himself. As many times as he had ventured down the Black Road, he had never gotten used to the experience. Each time was unique, each fear different.

Lord Darkulan's hand broke the surface, and Kabraxis's hand was there to catch it. Effortlessly, the demon hauled the lord from the muck and the mire with the dead woman still riding him.

"Live or die," Kabraxis offered calmly. "The choice is yours."

Lord Darkulan hesitated only a moment. "Live. May the Light forgive me, I want to live."

A cruel smile carved Kabraxis's horrendous face. "*I* forgive you," the demon mocked. He continued pulling the muddy, bloody lord from the swamp. The dead woman still clung to Lord Darkulan's back, biting his mangled ear and scratching his face with the claws of her free hand.

Kabraxis backhanded the dead woman from Lord Darkulan's back. When he finished hauling the man up, Cholik found that they all once more stood on the solid ground of the Black Road twisting through the high mountains. The swamp was nowhere to be seen.

Lord Darkulan gave in to his fear, shaking and shivering before the demon's wrath. "Don't kill me," the lord pleaded.

"I won't kill you," Kabraxis said, pushing the man to his knees before him, humbling him. "I am going to give you your life."

Shuddering, Lord Darkulan stayed still before the demon.

"You are weak." Kabraxis spoke in deep tones. "I will be your strength." The demon wrapped one of his large hands around Lord Darkulan's head. "You are unguided. I will be your design." The fingers elongated into sharp spikes. "By your own hand and childish desires of flesh, you are unmade. I will make you a man and a leader of men." With a quick snap of his wrist, the demon drove his spiked fingers through Lord Darkulan's skull. Blood leaked down his face, threading through the mud that clung to his features. "Mind, body, and soul, you are *mine*!"

Lightning flashed through the dark sky above the mountains, followed immediately by the rumbling roar of thunder that shattered all other sounds. The Black Road trembled beneath Cholik's feet, and for a dreadful moment he thought the whole mountain range was going to fall.

Then the lightning and the thunder faded, and Kabraxis withdrew his spiked fingers from Lord Darkulan's skull.

"Rise," the demon ordered, "and begin the new life that I have given you."

Lord Darkulan rose, and as he did the mud and fatigue and blood vanished from him. He stood straight and tall, clear-eyed and calm. "I hear and obey."

"Only one thing yet remains," Kabraxis said. "You must bear my mark that I may keep watch over you."

Without hesitation, Lord Darkulan stripped away his tunic, chain mail shirt, and blouse beneath to bare his chest. "Here," he offered. "Over my heart that I may keep you close to me."

Kabraxis placed his palm over Lord Darkulan's chest. When he removed his hand, the tattoo that was the demon's mark marred the lord's flesh.

"You are in my service," the demon said.

"Till the end of my days," Lord Darkulan said.

"Go then, Lord Darkulan, and know that you have the power to heal your mistress and prevent your wife's hanging. Draw a bit of your blood, mix it in wine, and have her drink it to cure her."

Lord Darkulan agreed and offered his undying loyalty to the demon once more, then followed the Black Road back out of the stone snake's mouth. At the other end of the Black Road, Cholik once more saw the interior of the great cathedral.

"So now you have him," Cholik said, watching as Lord Darkulan rejoined his guards.

"We have him," Kabraxis agreed.

Surprised that the demon didn't sound more satisfied, Cholik looked at him. "Is something wrong?"

"There is a man I have learned of," the demon said. "Taramis Volken. He's a demon hunter, and he has picked up my trail."

"How?"

"It doesn't matter. After tonight, he will no longer be a concern to me. But after the burned man attempted to kill you today, which I did not see coming, I think you should tighten security around the church." Kabraxis paused. "Lord Darkulan should be more than willing to aid you with that."

"There's no way to tighten security completely in the church," Cholik objected. "We admit too many people, and many of them we can't identify, to screen everyone."

"Do it better," Kabraxis snapped.

"Of course," Cholik said, bowing his head and watching as the demon vanished from sight. Cholik's thoughts rushed, scrambling over one another in his head. Who was this demon hunter Kabraxis feared? In their year and more together, Cholik had never seen the demon concerned about anything. The matter was puzzling and more than a little unsettling, even after Kabraxis's assurances that the matter was taken care of.

And how was it that Kabraxis had taken care of the man who hunted him?

Nineteen

Although he'd ridden horses a few times while working with overland trade caravans, Darrick had never grown used to their lurching gait. Even a ship's deck riding the crests of a storm-tossed sea felt more certain than the beast beneath him as it picked its way down the forested hillside.

Luckily, the animal followed Taramis Volken's mount along the narrow trail and required no real guidance from him. He only wished he could sleep in the saddle as some of the other men accompanying them seemed able to do.

Last night at the Blue Lantern tavern, Darrick would not have guessed that Taramis headed the small army of men encamped outside Seeker's Point. But after witnessing their professionalism and dedication to their quest, he understood how they could have escaped notice.

All of the warriors rode in single file along the trail. Two riderless horses testified to the fact that scouts ranged on foot ahead of the group. The men rode with hardly any noise, their gear carefully padded so that nothing clinked or clanked. They were hard-eyed men, like wolves that hunted in a pack. The wintry wind and the leaden, overcast sky of morning further brought that appearance out.

Darrick straightened in the saddle, trying to find a comfortable position. Since leaving the Blue Lantern last evening, he'd ridden all night. A few times he'd dozed in the saddle, exhaustion finally overcoming his fear of falling off the horse, but that had been reawakened after only a moment or two when he woke and found himself sliding.

A birdcall sounded in the quiet of the forest.

Darrick's sharp ears picked the sound out, recognizing that it was false only because he'd heard the same cry earlier. The call came from one of the two scouts ahead. During the night, they'd used owl calls to communicate, but this morning they emulated a small ruby-throated wren that sailors sometimes took on board sailing ships to raise.

One of the scouts stepped from the forest and loped alongside Taramis Volken's mount, matching the long-limbed animal with ease. The scout and the sage talked briefly, then the scout disappeared again.

Taramis appeared unconcerned, so Darrick tried to relax. His muscles were stiff and sore from hauling cargo the day before and the long ride during the night. More than anything, he wanted off the horse, and he wished he'd stayed in Seeker's Point. He had no business among these men. They all seemed to be veteran warriors, and the few words that Darrick had overheard them say alluded to past battles with demons, though none of them was as powerful as Kabraxis.

Darrick pushed his breath out, watching it fog briefly in the chill of morning. He couldn't imagine why Taramis had asked him to come along when there were already so many warriors.

A little farther on, the trail they followed led out into a cleared space. Among a littering of tree stumps sat a small house with a thatched roof. The land to the south of the house had been cleared for gardening. The current crop appeared to be onions and carrots, but there were stands where vine crops had grown during the summer. In back of the garden was a door set into a small hill that Darrick believed would lead to a root cellar. A well occupied the space between the garden and the small barn.

An old man and a young boy came out of the barn. They looked enough alike that Darrick believed they were family, probably grandfather and grandson.

The old man carried a pitchfork and a milking pail. He handed the pail to the boy and waved him back into the barn. The old man was bald and had a long gray beard. He wore deerskin outer garments, but the neck of a purple blouse showed under the jacket.

"May the Light bless you," the old man said, holding the pitchfork in both hands. A little fear showed in his eyes, but the confident manner in which he wielded the pitchfork told Darrick that the old man was prepared for trouble.

"And may the Light bless you," Taramis said, reining his horse in at a respectful distance from the old man. "My name is Taramis Volken, and if I got your directions right, you'd be Ellig Barrows."

"Aye," the old man said, keeping his stance open. His bright blue eyes roved over the warriors and Darrick. "And if you're who you says you are, I've heard of you."

"I am," Taramis said, swinging down from his horse with easy grace. "I've got papers that prove it right enough." He reached inside his blouse. "They bear the king's mark."

The old man held up a hand. A light sapphire glow enveloped Taramis. For a moment a ruby glow surrounded the sage and kept the sapphire glow from him. Then the ruby light faded and vanished entirely.

"Sorry," Taramis apologized. "Wooten told me you'd be a cautious man."

"You're no demon," Ellig Barrows said.

"No," Taramis agreed. "May the Light blind them and bind them and burn them forever." He spat.

"I bid you welcome to my home," Ellig said. "If you and your men have not eaten, I'll have a simple breakfast out soon enough if you'll have it."

"We wouldn't want to impose," Taramis said.

"It's not imposition," the old man assured him. "As you can tell from the trail you followed up, we seldom have company here."

"I need you to know something further," Taramis said.

Ellig regarded him. "You've come for the sword. I knew that from the reading I took of you. Come on inside the house, and we'll talk. Then we'll see if you get it or not."

Taramis waved to his men to dismount, and Darrick dismounted with them. The wind whistled through the trees overhead.

Cholik found Kabraxis in one of the rooftop gardens. The demon faced north, his arms folded over his broad chest. The illusion spell he maintained over the garden prevented anyone in the street below from seeing him.

Pausing, Cholik peered over the roof's side, spotting the steady stream of worshippers pouring into the building.

"You sent for me?" Cholik asked, coming to a halt behind the demon. Kabraxis had, of course, because Cholik wouldn't have heard the demon's voice in his head while he was preparing for the morning service otherwise.

"Yes," Kabraxis said. "In dealing with the man I'd learned of, I found out something else interesting."

"Taramis Volken?" Cholik asked. He remembered the demon hunter's name from the previous night's conversation.

"Yes. But there is another man that I recognize with Taramis Volken's group. I wanted you to look at him as well."

"Of course."

Kabraxis turned and crossed the rooftop to one of the small pools in the garden. Passing a hand over the pool, the demon stepped back. "Look."

Moving forward, Cholik knelt and gazed into the pool. Ripples passed over the water's surface, then settled out again. For a moment, Cholik only saw the reflected blue of the sky.

Then the image formed, showing a small house tucked away under the embrace of tall fir, maple, and oak trees. Warriors sat outside the small house, all of them rough-looking and hard traveled. Cholik knew at once that there were too many of them to live at the house. They were visitors, then, but he didn't recognize the house.

"Do you see him?" Kabraxis demanded.

"I see many men," Cholik replied.

"Here." Kabraxis gestured impatiently.

The pool rippled and clouded for a moment, then cleared once more and focused on a wan young man with reddish hair pulled back into a queue. Seated at the base of a big oak tree, a cutlass across his knees, the young man appeared to sleep with his back to the tree. A ragged scar marred one of his eyebrows.

"Do you recognize him?" Kabraxis asked.

"Yes," Cholik replied, recognizing the man now. "He was at Tauruk's Port."

"And now he is with Taramis Volken," Kabraxis mused.

"They know each other?"

"Not that I was aware of. For all I know, Taramis Volken and this man, Darrick Lang, met each other in Seeker's Point last evening."

"You have spies watching the demon hunter?" Cholik asked.

"When I am not watching the man myself, of course. Taramis Volken is a dangerous human, and the quest he's on pertains to us. If he is given what he seeks at this farmer's house, his next move will be to come for us."

"What is it he seeks?"

"Stormfury," Kabraxis replied.

"The mystic sword that turned the barbarian horde hundreds of years ago?" Cholik asked. His nimble mind searched for the reasons Kabraxis would be interested in the sword and why he would think that the demon hunter would turn his sights on them.

"The same." A grimace twisted the demon's hideous face.

Cholik thought then that Kabraxis was afraid of the sword and what it might do, but he also knew he dared not mention that. Desperately, he tried to eradicate the errant thought from his mind before the demon sensed it.

"The sword can be a problem," Kabraxis said, "but I have minions that are even now closing in on Taramis Volken and his band. They won't escape, and if the sword is there, my minions will retrieve it."

Cholik thought and worked to couch his words carefully. "How is the sword a problem?"

"It is a powerful weapon," Kabraxis said. "A blacksmith imbued with the power of the Light forged the sword hundreds of years ago to use against the barbarian horde and the dark force they worshipped."

Understanding dawned in Cholik. "They worshipped you. You were Iceclaw."

"Yes. And the humans used the sword to drive me from this world then."

"Can it be used against you again?" Cholik asked.

"I am more powerful now than I was then," Kabraxis said. "Still, I will see to it that the sword is destroyed forever and always after this day." The demon paused. "But the presence of this other man troubles me."

"Why?"

"I have cast auguries to show the portents of the things we have done concerning Lord Darkulan," Kabraxis said. "This man keeps turning up in them."

Cholik considered that. Spies he had placed inside the lord's keep had relayed that Darkulan's mistress was already better and on her way back to a full recovery. Lord Darkulan had visited her immediately after leaving the church last evening.

"When did you see this man again after Tauruk's Port?" Cholik asked.

"Only moments ago," Kabraxis said. "When I summoned the lezanti and set them upon the hunt for Taramis Volken and his warriors. I had to scry upon the group to set the lezanti upon the scent."

A shudder passed through Cholik when he considered the lezanti. He'd always believed the creatures to be truly the stuff of legends and myth.

According to the tales he'd been told, the lezanti were created by the blending of a human female's corpse, a freshly slain wolf, and a lizard, creating a fast and ferocious chimera that possessed super-animal cunning, a partially upright physique, and an ability to take a lot of damage and grow limb replacements after amputation.

"If you've only just now seen this man," Cholik said, "how do you know he was the one you saw in your auguries?"

"Do you distrust my abilities, Buyard Cholik?" the demon demanded.

"No," Cholik replied quickly, not wanting Kabraxis to vent the cold rage that filled him. "I just wondered how you kept him separate from Taramis Volken or another of the warriors with him."

"Because I can," the demon replied. "Just as I robbed time of your years and returned your youth to you."

Cholik stared into the pool, looking into the young man's relaxed face. He wondered how the young man had gotten there, more than a year after the events at Tauruk's Port.

"I am concerned because of the magic that was used to open the gateway," Kabraxis said. "When demons come from the Burning Hells, so, too, come the seeds of their potential downfall. It is a balance that is kept between the Light and the Darkness. But by the same hand, no champion of the Light may burst forth without a weakness that can be exploited. It's up to the champion which propensity—strength or weakness—wins out. And it is up to the demon whether he stands against the power that would banish him from this plane again."

"And you think such power has been assigned to this man because he was there the night you came through the gateway back into our world?" Cholik asked.

"No. This man doesn't have such power. And there is a great affinity for darkness in his soul." The demon smiled. "In fact, were we able to get him here and persuade him properly, I think he could be turned to serve me. There is weakness in him as well as strength. I feel it would be no problem to exploit that weakness."

"Then why the concern?"

"The juxtaposition of all the variables," Kabraxis said. "Taramis Volken's discovery of Stormfury is bad enough, but for this man to appear here so soon after the burned man attempted to kill you, I have to consider how threatening our situation can get. The balance between Light and Dark has always been maintained, and somewhere out there is a threat I have to recognize."

Staring into the pool of water as the view shifted and pulled back, Cholik watched the sleek forms of the lezanti cluster along the ridgeline around the small house. The lezanti stood hunchbacked and broad-shouldered on two clawed feet and legs that bent backward like a horse's rear legs. Lizard's skin hugged the body and shifted colors as quickly as a chameleon's, allowing them to blend into their surroundings with astonishing ease. Tufts of fur spread over their shoulders, crowned their heads around their small triangular ears, and covered their flanks where a hairless lizard's tail flicked and twisted. Their jaws were filled with large fangs.

The church bells rang, signaling the beginning of the morning service.

Cholik stood, waiting for the order to dismiss and return to the church. "This situation is under your control," he said. "The lezanti will leave no one alive."

"Perhaps," Kabraxis said. He gestured toward the pool.

In the image trapped in the water, the lezanti began stealthily closing in on the warriors and the little house in the forest. Hypnotized, remembering the violence the demon-formed creatures were reputed to be capable of, Cholik watched while the cathedral below them continued to fill.

Darrick sat under the spreading oak tree a short distance from the house and held the deep wooden plate he'd been given in his hands. He wished the house had been bigger or that there had been fewer men. The dark chimney smoke pouring into the air let him know there was a fire inside. He wasn't truly cold, but a chance to sit by the fire for a few moments to break the chill that covered him would have been welcome.

The generosity Ellig Barrows showed his unexpected guests was amazing. It was one thing for the old man to have been willing to care for such a large group, but it was even more surprising that he was able to. Breakfast consisted of simple fare: eggs, stringy venison chops, potato mush, thick brown gravy, and fat wedges of bread. But it was all warm and welcome.

As it turned out, both of Taramis's scouts had taken deer in the forest and dressed them out to replace the meat they ate from the old man's larder. There was no replacing the bread, though, and Darrick guessed that the old man's wife would be busy for several days baking to replace what they'd consumed that morning.

Darrick sopped up the last of the gravy and eggs with his remaining piece of bread and drank from his waterskin. Setting the plate to one side for the moment, he enjoyed the sensation of being full and off the horse. He pulled a blanket from his pack and wrapped it around his shoulders.

Winter was coming, marching down from the harsh northlands. Soon enough, mornings would be filled with frost and cold that made a man's bones ache. Darrick kept to himself, watching the other warriors break up into small groups and talk among themselves. As they ate, the warriors also relieved the guards posted in the forest, making sure everyone was fed and rested.

Ellig Barrows and Taramis Volken talked on the covered porch in front of the house. Each man seemed intent on taking the measure of the other. Taramis wore orange-colored robes with silver designs worked into them. During his travels, Darrick had heard descriptions of the Vizjerei robes, but he had never seen them before. The enchanted robes offered protection from spells and demonic creatures.

Darrick knew that Taramis sought to persuade the old man to give him Stormfury, the sword from the old legend. Although he'd seen a number of things in his life as a sailor for Westmarch even before he'd seen the demon at Tauruk's Port, Darrick had never seen anything as legendary as the sword. His mind played with the idea of it, what it might look like and what powers it might hold. But again and again, his thoughts insisted on coming back to why Taramis would believe he belonged with them on this quest.

"Darrick," Taramis called a few minutes later.

Rousing from near slumber, regretting the need to move when he'd finally gotten comfortable against the tree, Darrick glanced at the sage.

"Come with us," Taramis requested, standing and following the old man across the yard.

Reluctantly, Darrick got to his feet and carried the plate to the porch, where it was taken by the old man's grandson. Darrick followed Taramis and Ellig Barrows into the root cellar built into the hillside.

The old man took a lantern from the root cellar's wall inside, lit it with a coal he'd carried from the house, and followed the short flight of earthen stairs down into the small root cellar.

Darrick hesitated in the doorway. The cloying smell of dank earth, potatoes, onions, and spices filled his nostrils. He didn't like the darkness of the cellar or the closed-in feeling he got from the racks of foods canned in jars or the wine bottles. For a house in the middle of nowhere along the Frozen Sea coast, Ellig Barrows and his family had a large larder.

"Come on," Taramis said, following the old man to the back of the cellar.

Darrick crossed the uneven floor dug from the earth and covered with small rock. The cellar's ceiling was so low his head scraped a couple of times, and he kept hunkered down.

A huge stone surface blocked the other end of the cellar. The lantern Ellig Barrows carried clanked against the stone as he stood next to it.

"I was given care of the sword," the old man said, turning to face Taramis, "along with the power to do so by my grandfather, as he was given the power to care for it by his grandfather. I teach this responsibility and power to my own grandson now. For hundreds of years, Stormfury has been in the possession of my family, awaiting the time when the demon would rise again and it would be needed."

"The sword has been needed before now," Taramis said gravely. "But Kabraxis is a cunning demon and doesn't ever use the same name twice. If it were not for Darrick's encounter with the demon in Tauruk's Port more than a year ago, we would not know which one we faced now."

"Iceclaw was a fierce and evil beast," the old man said. "The old stories tell of all the murder and carnage he wrought while he was in our world."

"There were two other times Kabraxis was in the world," Taramis said. "Both times before, Diablo and his brothers sought him out and returned him to the Burning Hells. Only the sword now offers a chance against the demon."

"You know why the sword has never been taken from my family before," Ellig Barrows said. The lantern light deepened the hollows of his eye sockets, making him look like a man days dead.

Darrick shivered at the thought.

"The sword has never allowed itself to be taken," Taramis said.

"Two kings have died trying to take this sword," the old man said.

Darrick hadn't known that. He glanced at Taramis, studying the sage's appearance in the lantern's pale yellow glow.

"They died," the sage said, "because they didn't understand the sword's true nature."

"So you say," Ellig Barrows replied. "There are mysteries about the sword that I don't know. That my grandfather before me didn't know, and his grandfather before him. Yet you come to my house and tell me you know more than all of them."

"Show me the sword," Taramis said, "and you can see for yourself."

"We have been responsible for the sword for so long. It has not been an easy burden to bear."

"It shouldn't have been," Taramis agreed. He faced the old man. "Please."

Sighing, the old man turned to the wall. "You take your own lives in your hands," he warned. His fingers inscribed arcane symbols in the air. As soon as each one was completed, it glowed briefly, then sank into the wall.

Darrick glanced at Taramis, wanting to ask why he instead of one of the other warriors had been brought on this part of their search. Even as he started to open his mouth, the root cellar wall shimmered and turned opaque.

Ellig Barrows raised the lantern, and the light shone into the room on the other side of the opaque stone wall. Eldritch energy sparkled inside the wall, illuminated by the lantern light.

Beyond the wall, wreathed in the shadows of the hidden room, a dead man lay in a niche cut into the hillside. His snow-white beard trailed down to his chest, and he wore animal hides over crude chain mail. A visored helm hid part of the shrunken features that bound the dead man's head. His arms crossed over his chest, and his withered hands—the yellow ivory of his knuckles showing through—gripped the hilt of a long sword.

Twenty

✦

In the hidden room in Ellig Barrows's root cellar, Darrick studied the sword Taramis Volken had come all this way to get and found the weapon was in no way like anything he'd imagined since the sage had told him of it. The sword appeared plain and unadorned, hammered from steel with a craftsman's skill but lacking the touch of an artist. The blade was an infantryman's weapon, not something that would invoke fear in demons.

"You're disappointed?" Ellig Barrows asked, looking at Darrick.

Darrick hesitated, not wanting to offend. "I had just expected something more."

"A jeweled weapon, perhaps?" the old man asked. "Something every bandit you met would want and try to steal? A weapon so unique and striking-looking that everyone would mark its passage and know it for what it was?"

"I hadn't thought of it like that," Darrick admitted. But he also wondered if someone had stolen the real sword a long time ago and left the barbaric piece in its stead. He immediately felt guilty for that, because it would have meant the old man's life had been spent doing useless guard duty.

Ellig Barrows stepped through the opaque wall. "The smith who forged this weapon did think of those things. Perhaps Stormfury isn't an elegant weapon, but you'll never find a truer one. Of course, you'll only know that if you're able to take it."

Taramis followed the old man through the wall.

After a moment, Darrick stepped through the mystical wall as well. A cold sensation gripped him as he passed through, and it felt as if he were walking through the thickest forest growth, having to fight his way through.

"The sword is protected from interlopers," Ellig Barrows said. "No man may touch it or take it if Kabraxis is not within this world."

"And if any try?" Darrick asked.

"The sword can't be taken," the old man said.

"What of the kings who died?"

"One slew members of my family," Ellig Barrows said. "He and all his warriors died less than a day later. The Light is not evil as the demons are, but it is vengeful against those who transgress against it. Another tried to drag Hauklin's body from its resting place. He rose that time and slew them all."

Standing in the crypt carved from the root cellar, Darrick felt afraid. Although the caverns under Tauruk's Port were larger and the huge doorway had seemed more threatening, the dead man lying with the sword clasped in his hands seemed just as deadly. Darrick would have gladly left the crypt and been satisfied never to see anything more of a magical nature.

He glanced at Taramis. "Why did you want me here?"

"Because you are tied to this," the sage said. "You have been since you witnessed Kabraxis's arrival on this plane." He looked at the dead man. "I think that you are the one who can take Hauklin's sword to use against the demon."

"Why not you?" Darrick demanded. For a moment he wondered if the sage was only using him, willing to risk his life in the effort to recover the sword.

Taramis turned and reached for the sword. His hand halted, quivering, in the air several inches from the weapon. The effort he made to reach the weapon corded muscle along his arm. Pain showed on his features. Finally, in disappointed disgust, he drew his arm back.

"I can't take it," the sage said. "I am not the one." He turned to Darrick. "But I believe that you are."

"Why?"

"Because the Light and the Darkness balance each other," Taramis said. "Any time power is passed into this world from the Light or the Darkness, a balance must be made. Demons come into this world, and a means of defeating them is also created. If the Light tries to upset the balance by introducing an object of power that can be used against the Darkness, the powers of Darkness intercede to make the balance whole again. Ultimately, the true threat to the balance, whether the Light or the Darkness has the greater power in our world, is left up to us. The people. Just as when the Prime Evils appeared in this world during the time that came to be known as the Dark Exile, the Angel Tyreal gathered the magi, warriors, and scholars in the East and formed the Brotherhood of the Horadrim. Those people would never have come together with such power if the demons had not been loosed in our world. If Tyreal had tried to do this before the Prime Evils had arrived here, Darkness would have found a means to strike a balance."

"That doesn't explain why you think I can pick up that sword," Darrick said. He made no move to try.

"I heard the stories about you when I arrived in Westmarch," Taramis said. "And I began looking for you. But by the time I'd arrived, you'd vanished. I caught up with your ship, but no one knew where you were. I couldn't tell many that I was searching for you, because that might have alerted Kabraxis's minions, and your life could have become forfeit." He paused, locking his gaze with Darrick's. "As for the sword, perhaps I'm wrong. If I am, it will prevent you from taking it. You have nothing to lose."

Darrick glanced at Ellig Barrows.

"Over the years before the sword was hidden away," the old man said, "many tried to take it just as Taramis has. If there was no true evil in their hearts, they were only prevented from removing the sword."

Darrick looked at the corpse and the plain sword it held. "Has Hauklin's sword ever been taken?"

"Never," Ellig Barrows said. "Not once from his hand. Not even I can remove it. I have only been made their protector. As my grandson shall be after me."

"Try," Taramis urged. "If you can't take up the sword, then I've come on a fool's quest and uncovered secrets best left hidden."

"Yes," Ellig Barrows said. "No one has ever come for the sword in my lifetime. I had begun to think the world had forgotten about it. Or that the demon Kabraxis had been permanently banished from this world."

Taramis put his hand on Darrick's shoulder. "But the demon is back," the sage said. "We know that, don't we? The demon is back, and the sword should come free."

"But am I the one?" Darrick asked in a hoarse voice.

"You must be," Taramis said. "I can think of no other. Your friend died in that place. There has to be a reason you were spared. It's the balance, Darrick. The needs of the Light must always be balanced against the power of the Darkness."

Darrick gazed at the sword. The stink of the barn behind his father's butcher shop returned to him. *You'll never amount to anything!* his father had shouted. *You're dumb, and you're stupid, and you're going to die dumb and stupid!* Days and weeks and years of that rolled through Darrick's head. Pain tingled through his body again, reminding him of the whippings he'd endured and somehow survived. His father's voice had often haunted him during the past year, and he'd tried to drown it in wine and spirits, in hard work and bleak disappointment.

And in the guilt over Mat Hu-Ring's death.

Hadn't that been punishment enough? Darrick stared at the simple sword clasped in the dead man's hands.

"And if I can't take the sword?" Darrick asked in a ragged voice.

"Then I will search out the true secret," Taramis said. "Or I will find another way to battle Kabraxis and his accursed Church of the Prophet of the Light."

But the sage believed in him, and Darrick knew that. It was almost too much to bear.

Pushing away his own fears, going numb and dead inside the way he had when he'd faced his father in that small barn in Hillsfar, Darrick stepped toward the dead man. He reached for the sword.

Inches from the blade's hilt, his hand froze, and he found he was unable to go any farther.

"I can't," Darrick said, refusing to give in, wanting desperately to be able to pick up the sword and prove his worth even if only to himself.

"Try," Taramis said.

Darrick watched his hand shake with the effort he was making. It felt as if he were pushing against a stone wall. Pain welled up inside him, but it had nothing to do with the sword.

You're stupid, boy, and you're lazy. Not worth the time or the trouble or the food to keep you.

Darrick fought the barrier, willing his hand to pass through. He pressed his whole body against it now, feeling it support most of his weight.

"Ease off," Taramis said.

"No," Darrick said.

"C'mon, lad," Ellig Barrows said. "It's not meant to be."

Darrick strained for the sword, wanting even another fraction of an inch if he could get it. It felt as if his finger bones were going to pass through the flesh. Pain raced up his arm, and he clenched his teeth against it.

I should have knocked you in the head the day you were born, boy. That way you wouldn't have lived to be such a disgrace.

Darrick reached, in agony now.

"Give it up," Taramis said.

"No!" Darrick said in a loud voice.

The sage reached for him, gripping him by the shoulder and trying to pull him away.

"You're going to get hurt, lad," Ellig Barrows said. "You can't force this thing."

Pain dimmed Darrick's hearing. Images of Mat falling from the cliffside spun through his brain again. Guilt filled Darrick, echoed by the worthlessness he felt from his father's oft-repeated words. For a moment, he thought the pain was going to destroy him, melt him down where he stood. He was locked in the pursuit of the sword, didn't think he could pull back if he wanted to.

And where would he go from here after failing this? He had no answers.

Then a calm, cool voice holding just a hint of mocking amusement filled his head. *Take up the sword, skipper.*

"Mat?" Darrick said aloud. He was so surprised at hearing Mat's voice that he didn't even realize at first that he had fallen across the corpse, bruising his knees against the earthen floor. Instinctively, his hand curled around the sword's hilt, but he glanced around the shadows of the crypt looking for Mat Hu-Ring.

Only Taramis and Ellig Barrows stood there.

"By the Light," the old man whispered. "He has taken the sword."

Taramis smiled in triumph. "As I told you he would."

Darrick gazed down at the dead man so close to him. The corpse felt unnaturally cold.

"Take the sword, Darrick," the sage urged.

Slowly, disbelieving, not knowing if he'd truly heard Mat's voice or it had been part of some spell that opened the ward protecting the sword or a delusion of his own, Darrick pulled the sword away from the dead warrior. Despite its length and unfamiliar style, the sword felt comfortable in Darrick's hand. He stood, holding it out before him.

Something in the scarred and dark metal caught the light of Ellig Barrows's lantern, glinting dulled silver.

Tentatively, Taramis reached for the sword, but his hand stopped inches away. "I still cannot touch the sword."

The old man tried to touch the weapon as well but with the same results. "Nor can I. None in my family has ever been able to touch the sword. Whenever we moved it, we had to move Hauklin's body as well." A note of sadness sounded in the old man's voice.

For the first time, Darrick realized that taking the sword would leave the old man and his grandson with nothing to care for or protect. Darrick gazed at the old man. "I'm sorry," he whispered.

Ellig Barrows nodded. "All of us who have defended the sword have prayed that this day would come, this day when we would be free of our burden, but to see it actually happen—" Words failed him.

"Taramis!" one of the men shouted from outside.

Even as the sage started for the magical door, the sound of inhuman and monstrous yips and growls cascaded into the root cellar.

Darrick followed the sage, bolting through the racks of foodstuffs and wines, trailed by Ellig Barrows with the lantern. The weak gray daylight pouring through the root cellar door marked the entrance.

The noise of men fighting, their curses and yells, as well as the growls and howls of the creatures they fought, pummeled Darrick's ears as he raced up the earthen steps. He was on Taramis's heels as they burst from the root cellar.

The clearing around the house, which had moments ago been peaceful and restful, was now filled with battle. Taramis's warriors formed a quick skirmish line against the bloodthirsty beasts that raged against them from the forest.

"Lezanti," Taramis breathed. "By the Light, Kabraxis has found us out."

Darrick recognized the demon-forged beasts, but only from tales he'd been told aboard ship. Even in all of his travels, he'd never before encountered the creatures.

The lezanti stood a little less than five feet tall. They were human-shaped, but they possessed the reverse-hinged knees of a wolf and the thick hide of a lizard. The head was lizard-shaped as well, bearing an elongated snout filled with serrated teeth and flat, flaring nostrils. The eyes were close-set under a hank of wooly hair and surprisingly human. The hands and feet were oversized, filled with huge claws. Lizards' tails, barbed on the ends, swung around behind them.

"Archers!" Taramis cried hoarsely as he stood his ground and began weaving his hands through the air, inscribing symbols that flared to flaming life.

Four warriors took up longbows, stood behind swordsmen, and drew back shafts. They had two arrows away each, dropping the lezanti in their tracks, before the first wave of the creatures reached them. Then the swordsmen held them back with their shields, staggered by the lezantis' speed, strength, and weight. The clang of flesh meeting steel boomed in the clearing.

"Darrick," Taramis said, his hands still moving, "hold the door to the house. There are women and children inside. Hurry."

Darrick ran, trusting the line of warriors to protect his back as he made for the small house.

Taramis unleashed a wave of shimmering force that hit the center of the lezanti pack, scattering them and showering them with flame. Several of the smoldering bodies hung in the trees or landed with bone-breaking thumps against the ground. Only a few of them tried to get up. The archers calmly nocked more shafts and fired again, as cool as any crew Darrick had ever seen. The clothyard shafts drilled into the eyes and throats of their foes, putting them down. But the odds were not in the favor of the warriors. They numbered twenty-six men, including Darrick, and there had to be at least eighty of the lezantis.

We're going to die, Darrick thought, but he never once considered running. Hauklin's mystical sword felt calm and certain in his hand despite the unaccustomed length.

A scrabbling sound alerted Darrick. He swung around in time to see the lezanti on the roof of the house leap at him, its claws reaching for him.

Darrick ducked beneath the creature's attack, set himself as it thudded against the ground. Not dazed even for a moment, the lezanti came up snarling and snapping. The elongated snout shot at Darrick's head. He parried the head with the sword, then drove a boot into the lezanti's stomach, doubling it over.

Still moving, Darrick stepped to the side and brought the sword down in a hand-and-a-half grip that powered the blade into the creature's side. To his surprise, the sword sliced through the lezanti, dropping it to the ground in halves. The body parts quivered and jerked, then lay still. Blue energy crackled along the sword's length, and the lezanti's blood dried and flaked away, leaving the steel clean of it again.

Men cursed and fought out in the clearing, striving to hold back the merciless horde of creatures. Two men were down, Darrick saw, and others were wounded. Taramis unleashed another bolt of mystical energy, and two of the lezantis were covered in ice, frozen in place, shattering beneath the blades of the warriors who took advantage of their weakness.

Racing into the house, Darrick surveyed the small room filled with carvings and a few books. Ellig Barrows's wife, as gray-haired and gaunt as the old man was, stood in the center of the room with her hands over her chest.

Darrick glanced around at the wide windows in the front wall of the room as well as one of the side walls. There was too much open space; he could never hope to guard the old man's family there.

The grandson tugged at a heavy rug that covered the floor. "Help me!" he cried. "There is a hiding place beneath."

Understanding, Darrick grabbed the rug in one hand and yanked, baring the trapdoor beneath the material. Many of the homes along the border where the barbarian tribes often crossed over and raided were constructed with security holes. Families could lock themselves beneath the houses and live for days on the food and water stored there.

The boy's clever fingers found the hidden latch, and the trapdoor popped up.

Darrick slid the sword under the trapdoor's edge and levered it up, revealing the ladder beneath.

The boy took a lantern from the floor and reached for the old woman. "Come on, Grandmother."

"Ellig," the old woman whispered.

"He would want you to be safe," Darrick told her. "Whatever may come of this."

Reluctantly, the old woman allowed her grandson to lead her into the hiding place.

Darrick waited until they were both inside, then closed the trapdoor and dragged the rug back over it. Glass shattered behind him. He rose with the sword in his hand as the lezanti howled in through the broken window and threw itself at him.

There was little room to work with inside the house. Darrick reversed the sword in his right hand, gripping it so that it ran down his arm to his elbow and beyond. He kept his left hand back but ready, allowing his body to follow the line of the sword.

The lezanti reached for him. Darrick swung the sword, not allowing it to drift out beyond his body, keeping it in nice and tight as he'd been trained by Maldrin, who had been one of the best Darrick had ever seen at dirty infighting.

Darrick slapped the lezanti's claws to one side with the blade, then whipped his body back the other way, reversing the sword still along his arm, and slashed the creature across the face. The lezanti stumbled back, one hand to its ruined eye and crying out in pain. Darrick stepped in, keeping the sword close, and slashed at the creature's face again. Before it could retreat, he cut the head from its shoulders.

Even as the decapitated head rolled across the hardwood floor, another lezanti crashed through the door, and a third came through the window overlooking the well and the barn.

Breath rasping in his throat but feeling calm and centered, Darrick parried the spear the first creature wielded with surprising skill, caught the spear haft under his left arm, and caught it in his left hand. Holding the spear-carrying lezanti back by holding on to the spear, Darrick wheeled, dropped his sword, turned his hand over, caught the weapon in a regular grip before it fell, and chopped an arm from the other lezanti.

The spear-carrying lezanti shoved forward, trying to drive Darrick backward over a cushioned bench. Darrick pushed the spear out so that the point dug into the wall behind him and halted the lezanti. Releasing the spear, he stepped forward, knowing the one-armed lezanti was closing in on him from behind again. He sliced the lezanti in front of him, shearing its head and one shoulder away, amazed at the sharpness of the sword. With the sword still in motion, he reversed his grip and drove the blade through the chest of the lezanti behind him.

Energy crackled along the blade again. Before Darrick could kick the lezanti free of the sword, blue flames erupted from where the blade pierced the creature's chest and consumed it in a flash. Ash drifted to the ground before Darrick's stunned eyes.

Before he could recover, another lezanti hurled itself through the broken window on the house's side. Darrick succeeded in escaping the fist full of claws the lezanti threw at him but caught the brunt of the creature's charge. He flew backward, stumbling back through the door, unable to get his balance, and landed on the porch. He flipped to his feet as the lezanti charged again. Ducking this time, Darrick slashed the blade across the creature's thighs, chopping both legs off. The lezanti's torso hurtled by overhead and landed in the dirt in front of the porch.

"They're after the sword, Darrick!" Taramis called. "Run!"

Even as he realized what the sage said was true, Darrick knew he couldn't run. After losing Mat at Tauruk's Port, and himself for most of the past year, he couldn't run anymore.

"No," Darrick said, rising to his feet. "No more running." He took a fresh grip on the sword, feeling renewed strength flow through him. For the moment, all uncertainty drained away from him.

Several of the lezanti tore past the sprawling bodies of the warriors who had fought them. Nearly half of Taramis's group lay on the ground. Most of them, Darrick felt certain, wouldn't rise again.

Darrick waited on the charging creatures, lifting the sword high in both hands. Seven of them came at him, getting in one another's way. Energy flickered along the sword's blade. He slashed at his foes as they came into reach, cutting into them, then stepping through the gap that was filled with the swirling ash the mystical flames left behind. Three had died in that attack, but the other four came around again.

Regrouping, moving the sword around in his hands as if he'd trained with it all his life, Darrick cut at them, taking off a head, two arms, and a leg, then thrusting into two more creatures and reducing them to swirling ash as well. He stepped over to the creatures he had maimed, piercing their hearts with the enchanted blade and watching them burst into pyres that left the ground scorched.

Rallied by Darrick's show of power against the lezantis, the warriors drew up their steel and their courage, and attacked their foes with renewed vigor. The price was high, for men dropped where they stood, but the lezanti died faster. Taramis's and Ellig Barrows's spells took their toll among the demon-forged creatures as well, burning them, freezing them, twisting them into obscene grotesqueries.

Darrick continued battling, drawn by the bloodlust that fired him. It felt good to be so certain and sure of himself, of what he was doing, of what he needed to do. He hacked and slashed and thrust, cleaving through the lezantis that seemed drawn to him.

From the corner of his eye, he saw the lezanti rush toward Ellig Barrows from the side, giving the old man no warning. Knowing he'd never reach the old man in time to prevent the creature's attack, Darrick reversed his grip on the sword and threw it like a spear without thinking about what he was doing, as if it were something he'd done several times.

The sword flashed across the distance and embedded itself in the lezanti's chest. The blade halted the creature, then quivered in its chest as the eldritch scarlet energies gathered again. With a sudden fiery flash, the lezanti crisped to ash. The sword dropped point-first to the ground and stuck.

Out of reflex, Darrick thrust his hand out for the blade. The weapon quivered again, then yanked free of the earth and flew back to his hand.

"How did you know to do that?" Taramis asked.

Shocked himself, Darrick shook his head. "I didn't. It just—happened."

"By the Light," Ellig Barrows said, "you were the one destined for Hauklin's sword."

But Darrick remembered Mat's voice in his head. If Mat hadn't been there, somehow, Darrick felt certain that he'd never have been able to pick up the weapon. He turned and gazed across the battleground, not believing the carnage that he'd somehow survived almost completely unmarked.

"Come on," Taramis said, walking to help his men. "We can't stay here. Somehow Kabraxis has discovered us. We've got to leave as soon as we're able."

"And then what?" Darrick asked, sheathing the sword in his belt and catching the bag of medicants the sage tossed his way.

"Then we make for Bramwell," Taramis replied over the moans of the wounded warriors. "Kabraxis knows we have Stormfury now, and I've never been one to hide. Besides, now that we have the sword, the demon has every reason to fear us."

Even though he knew the sage's words were meant to be reassuring, and even though the power contained in the sword inspired a lot of confidence, Darrick knew the quest could still take them all to their deaths. The warriors who had fallen today and wouldn't get back up were grim reminders of that. He opened the medicants bag and tried to help those who still lived.

But confusion dwelt in his thoughts as well. *If I was the one meant for Hauklin's sword, then why couldn't I pick it up immediately? And where did Mat's voice come from?* He felt those questions were important but had no clue what the answers were. Grimly, he set to work, trying desperately not to think too far ahead.

Twenty-one

✳

Perched high on a northern hill overlooking Bramwell and the Church of the Prophet of the Light to the south, Darrick scanned the imposing edifice with the spyglass he'd managed to hang on to even over the worst of the past year. A quarter-mile distant, the church was lighted, festooned with lanterns and torches as worshippers continued their pilgrimage into the structure.

Farther out into the harbor, several ships remained lighted as well. Along with the influx of worshippers wanting to try their luck at getting to walk along the Way of Dreams, smugglers had also seen opportunities to reap financial gain by supplying the populace with black market goods. Guards stayed with the ships during all watches, and it still wasn't unusual for some of them to be attacked and raided by pirates. Thieves picked the pockets of worshippers and robbed them in the alleys.

Bramwell was fast becoming one of the most dangerous port cities on the Gulf of Westmarch.

Darrick lowered the spyglass and rubbed his aching eyes. It had taken the group almost three weeks to reach Bramwell as they journeyed down from the north. It seemed that winter had followed on their heels, blowing in on cold gusts.

Seven men had died at Ellig Barrows's home, and two more had been permanently crippled during the attack of the lezantis and couldn't continue. Seventeen men remained of Taramis Volken's original group of demon hunters.

Seventeen, Darrick mused as the cold air cut through the forest around him, *against hundreds and maybe thousands that Kabraxis has inside the church.* The odds were overwhelming, and their chances of success seemed nonexistent. *Even an army wouldn't stand a chance.*

And yet Darrick couldn't turn away. There was no fear left in him, and no anticipation, either. For the last three weeks, his father's voice had been inside his head—during his waking moments as well as his sleep—telling him how worthless he was. His dreams had been nightmares, looping segments of events that had transpired in the small barn behind the butcher's shop. Worst of all had been the memories of Mat Hu-Ring bringing him food and medicines, being there to let Darrick know he wasn't alone—yet all the while he had been trapped. Until he had made his escape.

Brush stirred behind Darrick. He shifted slightly, his hand dropping to the hilt of the long sword across his thighs. The blade was naked and ready as he faded into the long shadows of the approaching night.

A dim sunset, a thin slice of ocher and amber, like grapes smeared through pale ale, hung in the west. The last dregs of the day managed to cast a silvery sheen over the harbor, making the ships and boats look like two-dimensional black cutouts on the water. The light barely threaded through the city and seemed not to touch the Church of the Prophet of the Light.

Darrick released his breath slowly so it wouldn't be heard, emptying his lungs completely so he could draw in a full breath if he needed to go into action. The demon hunters had camped within the forest high in the mountains for the last two days and not been disturbed. In the higher reaches where they were, where the cold could reach them, game had been chased up from the foothills by the tent city that had sprung up outside Bramwell and was plentiful.

Maybe it was only a deer, Darrick thought. Then he dismissed the possibility. The sound he'd heard had been too calm, too measured.

"Darrick," Rhambal called.

"Aye," Darrick said in a low voice.

Tracking the sound of Darrick's voice, Rhambal crept closer. The warrior was a big man but moved as quietly as a woodlands creature through the forest. A square-cut beard framed his broad face, and he had a cut across his nose and beneath his left eye from a lezanti claw that hadn't quite healed during the past three weeks. Exposure to the harsh weather and not being able truly to rest had slowed the healing. Several of the other warriors bore such marks as well.

"I've come to get you," Rhambal said.

"I'd prefer to stay out here," Darrick said.

The big man hesitated.

Despite the fact that Darrick was the only one among them who could carry Hauklin's enchanted blade, Darrick's lack of interest in getting to know the other warriors had made him suspect to them. If it hadn't been for Taramis Volken's leadership, Darrick thought the warriors would have abandoned him or forced him to leave.

Of course, without Taramis Volken, the quest to break into the Church of the Prophet of the Light would have been abandoned. Only Taramis's charisma and his own unflinching courage kept them moving forward.

"Taramis has returned from the town," Rhambal said. "He wants everyone to gather and talk. He thinks he has a way into the church for us."

Darrick had known that the demon hunter had returned. He'd watched Taramis come up the mountainside less than an hour before.

"When do we go?" Darrick asked.

"Tonight."

The answer didn't surprise Darrick.

"And I for one am ready to do this thing," Rhambal said. "Crossing all this distance from the north and haunted by nightmares the way we've been, I'm ready to get shut of it all one way or another."

Darrick didn't reply. The nightmares had been a constant in all their lives.

Even though Ellig Barrows and Taramis had carefully constructed a warding around the group that prevented Kabraxis's scrying on them, they all knew their lives were forfeit if they were caught. The demon had identified them. Several times during the last few weeks, they'd barely escaped patrols of warriors as well as herds of demonic-forged creatures that hunted them.

The group hadn't been able to escape the nightmares, though. Taramis had said that he was certain the night terrors were inspired by an insidious spell that they hadn't been able to escape. Not a warrior among the group avoided them, and the three weeks of sleepless nights and private hells had taken their toll. A few of the warriors had even suggested that the nightmares were a curse, that they'd never be free of them.

Palat Shires, one of the oldest warriors among them, had tried to leave the group, unable to bear whatever it was that had haunted him. Darrick had heard whispers that Palat had once been a pirate, and as vicious a killer as any might fear to meet, till Taramis had exorcised the lesser demon that had crawled into Palat's mind from the enchanted weapon he carried and almost driven him insane with bloodlust. Still, even though he knew it had been the demon's possession of him that had caused him to do such horrible things, Palat had never been truly able to forgive himself for the murders and maiming he had committed. But he had sworn himself to Taramis's cause.

Three days after he'd left the group, Palat had returned. All knew from his haggard look that he had failed to escape the nightmares. Two days later, in the still hours near dawn, Palat had slashed his wrists and tried to kill himself. Only one of the other warriors, unable to sleep, had prevented Palat's death. Taramis had healed the old warrior as much as he could, then they'd holed up for four days to weather out a rain squall and let Palat regain his lost strength.

"Come on," Rhambal said. "There's stew still in a pot back there, and Taramis brought up loaves of bread and honeyed butter. There's even a sack of apple cakes because he was in such a generous mood." A wide grin split the warrior's face, but it didn't get past the fatigue that showed there.

"What about a sentry?" Darrick asked.

"We've been here two nights before this," Rhambal said. "Hasn't anyone come close to us in all that time. There's no reason to think it's going to happen in the next hour."

"We're leaving in the next hour?"

Rhambal nodded and squinted toward the dimming of the day. "As soon as true night hits and before the moon comes into full. Only a fool or a desperate man would be out in the chill of this night."

Reluctantly, because it meant being around the warriors and seeing the damage the harsh journey and the sleepless nights had wrought on them, Darrick stood and crept through the forest, heading higher up the mountainside. The heavy timber blocked most of the north wind that ravaged the mountain.

The campsite was located in a westward-facing cul-de-sac of rock near the peak of the mountain. The cul-de-sac was a small box of stone that stood up from the scrub brush and wind-bent pine trees.

The campfire was that in name only. No flames leapt up around piles of wood to warm the warriors gathered there. Only a heap of orange-glowing coals sheathed amid white and gray ash took the barest hint of the chill away. A pot of rabbit stew sat in the coals and occasionally bubbled.

The warriors sat around the campfire, but it was more because there was so little room in the cul-de-sac than out of any vain hope that the coals might stave off the cold. The horses stood at the back of the canyon, their breaths feathering the air with gray plumes, their long coats frosted over. The animals filled the cul-de-sac with the scent of wet horse and ate the long grass that the warriors had harvested for them earlier.

Taramis sat nearest the campfire, his legs crossed under him. The dim orange glow of the coals stripped the shadows from his face and made him look feverish. His eyes met Darrick's, and he nodded in greeting.

Holding his hands out over the coals, the sage said, "I can't guarantee you the success of our foray this night, but I will tell you that it is warmer down in Bramwell than it is up on this mountain."

The warriors laughed, but it was more out of politeness than real humor.

Rhambal took a seat beside Darrick, then picked up two tin cups from their meager store of utensils by the campfire. The big warrior dipped both cups into the stew they'd made from vegetables and leaves they could find and three unwary hares caught just before sunset. After pulling the cups back from the stewpot, Rhambal dragged a large finger along their sides to clean them, then popped his finger into his mouth.

Despite his fatigue and the feeling of ill ease that clung to him, Darrick accepted the cup of stew with a thankful nod. The warmth of the stew carried through the tin cup to his hands. He held it for a time, just soaking up the warmth, then started to drink it before it cooled too much. The bits of rabbit meat in the stew were tough and stringy.

"I've found a way into the church," Taramis announced.

"A place as big as that," Palat grumbled, "it should be as full of holes as my socks." He held up one of the socks that he'd been drying on a stick near the campfire. The garment was filled with holes.

"It is full of holes," Taramis agreed. "A year ago, Master Sayes arrived in Bramwell and began the Church of the Black Road from the back of a caravan. That sprawl of buildings that makes up the church now was built in sections, but it was built well. There are secret passages honeycombing the church, used by Master Sayes and his acolytes, as well as the guards. But the church is well protected."

"What about the sewers?" Rhambal asked. "We'd talked about getting into the building through the sewers."

"Mercenaries guard the sewer entrances," Taramis answered. "They also guard the underground supply routes into the building."

"Then where's this way you're talking about?" Palat asked.

Taramis took a small, charred stick from the teeth of the dying coals. "They built the church too fast, too grand, and they didn't allow for the late-spring flooding. All the building along the shore, including new wells to feed the pools and water reservoirs inside the church, created problems."

The sage drew a pair of irregular lines to represent the river, then a large rectangle beside it. He added another small square that thrust out over the river.

"Where the church hangs out over the river here," Taramis continued, "offering grand parapets where worshippers can wait to get into the next service and look out over the city as well as be impressed by the size of the church, the river has eroded the bank and undermined the plaza supports, weakening them considerably."

Accepting the chunk of bread smothered in honey butter that Rhambal offered, Darrick listened to Taramis and ate mechanically. His mind was full of the plan that the sage sketched in the dirt, prying and prodding at the details as they were revealed.

"One of the problems they had in constructing that parapet that was more vanity than anything else," Taramis continued, "was that the pilings for the parapet had to be laid so that they missed one of the old sewer systems the church had outgrown. Though the church's exterior may look polished and complete, the land underneath hasn't improved much beyond the quagmire it was that persuaded the local populace not to build there."

"So what are you thinking?" Palat asked.

Taramis gazed at the drawing barely lit by the low orange glow of the coals. "I'm thinking that with a little luck and the theft of one of those boats out there, we'll have a way into the church tonight as well as a diversion."

"Tonight?" Rhambal asked.

The sage nodded and looked up, meeting the gaze of every man in front of him. "The men I talked to down in Bramwell's taverns this afternoon said that the church services go on for hours even after nightfall."

"That's something you don't always see," Corrigor said. "Usually a man working the field or a fishing boat, he's looking for a warm, dry place to curl up after the sun sets. He's not wanting a church service."

"Most church services," Taramis said, "aren't giving away healing or luck that brings a man love or wealth or power."

"True," Corrigor said.

"So we go tonight," Taramis said. "Unless there's someone among us who would rather wait another night." He looked at Darrick as he said that.

Darrick shook his head, and the other men all answered the same. Everyone was tired of waiting.

"We rested up last night," Rhambal said. "If I rest any more, I'm just going to get antsy."

"Good." Taramis smiled grimly, without mirth and with perhaps a hint of fear. Despite the sage's commitment to hunting demons and the loss of his family, he was still human enough to be afraid of what they were going to attempt.

Then, in a calm and measured tone, Taramis told them the plan.

A light fog shrouded the river, but lanterns and torches along the banks and aboard the ships at anchorage in front of the warehouses and taverns burned away patches of the moist, cottony gray vapor. Men's voices carried over the sound of the wind in the rigging and the loose furls of sailcloth. Other men sang or called out dirty limericks and jokes.

Stone bridges crossed the river in two places, and both of them were filled with people walking from one bank to the other in search of food or drink. Some of the people were tourists, whiling away the time till the church let out and the next service began. Others were thieves, merchants, and guardsmen. The prostitutes were the loudest, yelling offers to the sailors and fishermen aboard their boats.

Darrick followed Taramis along the shore toward the cargo ship that the sage had selected as their target. *Blue Zephyr* was a squat, ugly cargo ship that held the rancid stench of whale oil. Not a sailor worth his salt would want to crew aboard her because she was such a stinkpot, Darrick knew, but she could guarantee a small crew a decent profit for their efforts.

Three men remained on board the small cargo ship. The captain and the rest of the crew had gone into the taverns along Dock Street. But careful observation of the crew revealed that they also had a bottle on board the ship and gathered in the stern to drink it.

The thieves and smugglers in Bramwell wouldn't want *Blue Zephyr's* cargo, Darrick knew. The barrels of whale oil were too heavy to steal easily or escape with from the harbor.

Without breaking his stride, Taramis reached the bottom of the gangplank leading up to the cargo ship. The sage started up the gangplank without pause. Darrick trailed after him, heart beating rapidly in his chest as his boots thudded against the boarding ramp.

The three sailors gathered in the cargo ship's stern turned at once. One of the men grabbed a lantern sitting on the plotting table and shined it toward them.

"Who goes there?" the sailor with the lantern asked.

The other two sailors filled their hands with swords and took up defensive positions.

"Orloff," Taramis said, walking toward the men without hesitation.

Darrick split off from the sage, surveying the rigging and deciding in the space of a drawn breath which canvases to use and how best to free them. Only four other men among the sage's warriors had any real experience aboard masted ships, and they all had considerably less than he did.

"I don't know no Orloff," the sailor with the lantern said. "Mayhap ye got the wrong ship there, mate."

"I've got the right ship," Taramis assured the man. He closed on them, walking with a confident gait. "Captain Rihard asked me to drop by with this package." He held up a leather-covered bottle. "Said it would be something to warm you up against the night's chill."

"I don't know no Cap'n Rihard," the sailor said. "Ye got the wrong ship. Ye'd best be shovin' off."

But by that time, Taramis was among them. He sketched an eldritch symbol in the air. The symbol flared to emerald-green life and flickered out of existence.

Before the last of the color died away, a shimmering wall of force exploded toward the three sailors and knocked them all over the stern railing, scattering them like leaves before a fierce gust. The sailor carrying the lantern hung on to it, arcing out over the river and falling like a comet from the heavens till he disappeared into the water with a loud splash.

At the same time, signaled by the spell Taramis had used, Rhambal set fire to the oil-soaked exterior of one of the larger warehouses on the south side of the river to create a diversion. Flames blossomed up the side of the warehouse, alerting dozens of people living in the surrounding neighborhood. In seconds, even as the three sailors were knocked from *Blue Zephyr*'s stern, the hue and cry about the fire filled the streets and the banks on both sides of the river.

When the sailors surfaced, they didn't gain much support for their troubles. Palat joined Taramis in the stern, an arrow to bowstring and the fletchings pulled back to his ear. The sailors got the message and swam for the riverbank.

"Get those sails down," Darrick ordered. Now that they were into the action, with little chance of turning back, his blood sang in his veins. A part of him came back alive after a year of trying to deaden it. He remembered times past when he and Mat had scrambled aboard a ship to prepare for battle or respond to a surprise attack.

The four warriors with sailing experience split up. One went to the stern to take the wheel, and the others scrambled up the rigging.

Darrick climbed the rigging like a monkey, all the moves coming back to him even though it had been months since he'd last climbed in a sailing ship. Hauklin's mystic sword banged against his back as he climbed. The cutlass had been short enough that he'd kept it sheathed at his side, but the long sword felt more natural slung across his shoulder.

As he climbed the rigging and reached the furled sails, he slashed through the neatly tied ropes with his belt knife. His sailor's soul resented the loss of the rope, always a prized commodity of a ship at sea, but he knew they'd have no further use of it. Thinking like that made him remember what Taramis had in store for the cargo vessel, and that made Darrick even sadder. The small ship wasn't much, but she was seaworthy and had a purpose.

At the top of the mast, all the sails cut loose below him, Darrick gazed down at the deck. The remaining eleven warriors—Rhambal would join them in a moment—busied themselves with bringing small casks of whale oil up from the hold. *Blue Zephyr* had shipped with small kegs of oil as well as the large kegs, otherwise they'd have needed a block-and-tackle to get them on deck.

Darrick slipped down through the rigging, dropping hand-over-hand to the deck. "Lash those sails in place. Hurry." He scanned the river anchorage.

The three sailors Taramis had knocked over the cargo ship's side had reached the riverbank, calling out to other sailors and city guards. For the most part they were ignored. The fire at the warehouse was more important because if it spread, the city might be in danger.

Watching the flames blaze, stretching long tongues into the sky above the warehouse, while he tied the sails fast, Darrick knew he couldn't have given the order to fire the building as Taramis had. The people who owned the warehouse had done nothing wrong, nor had the people who stored their goods there.

It had been a necessary evil, the sage had told them all. None of the warriors had exhibited any problems with the plan.

"Darrick," Taramis called from the ship's stern. He'd taken off his outer coat, revealing the orange Vizjerei robes with the silver mystic symbols.

"Aye," Darrick called back.

"Are the sails ready?"

"Aye," Darrick replied, finishing the last lashing and glancing around at the other warriors working on the canvas. They had been slower at it than he had, but it was all done. "You're clear." He glanced at the other men again. "Stand ready, boys. This is going to be a quick bit of work if we can pull it off."

Taramis spoke, and the words he used sounded like growls. No human throat was meant to use the phrases, and Darrick was certain that the sage's spell was from some of the earliest magic that had been brought into the world by the demons among the Vizjerei. Some mages and sorcerers believed that spellcraft was purer when used in the old language it had first been taught in.

A wavering reflection of the warehouse fire spread over the choppy surface of the river. Other glowing dots spread along the banks reflected on the river, too. More were in a straight line under the second bridge that lay between the cargo ship and the church. Hoarse shouts drifted, trapped and held close to the water as sound always was. A bucket brigade had started near the warehouse.

Despite his readiness, Darrick was almost knocked from his feet as Taramis's spell summoned a wild wind from the west. The canvas popped and crackled overhead as the sails filled. Her sails filled with the magically summoned wind, and the ship started forward, cutting through the river against the current.

Twenty-two

✹

Propelled by the sudden onslaught of wind, *Blue Zephyr* nosed down into the river. The sudden action caught three of the warriors unprepared, and they fell onto the deck. The oil kegs overturned and rolled, creating a brief hazard till the ship's keel came up. One of the warriors almost rolled through the open space in the railing where the boarding ramp had fallen away, but he managed to stop himself just short of it.

"Hold what you've got!" Darrick cried out over the roaring wind to the other warriors manning the sails. He strained to hang on to the ropes, keeping the sail full into the wind. Little work was necessary on the part of the ship-trained men, though. Taramis's wind caught the cargo vessel squarely and sped her across the river.

Other nearby ships rocked at anchor, and small sailcraft that had been used to ferry goods across the river were blown down, their sails lying in the water.

"Wheel!" Darrick yelled, watching as *Blue Zephyr* closed with frightening quickness on a low barge.

"Aye," Farranan called back.

"Hard to starboard, damn it, or we're going to end up amidships," Darrick ordered.

"Hard to starboard," Farranan replied.

Immediately, the cargo ship came about. The port-side hull rubbed along the low-slung barge, coming up out of the river slightly and cracking timbers. Darrick hoped most of the cracking timbers belonged to the barge.

Hanging on to the ropes tied to the sail, he watched as the corner of the barge went under the cargo ship, the prow of the boat and the other corner coming clear of the water. Boxes and crates and longshoremen spilled into the water. Two lanterns dropped into the river as well, both of them extinguishing as soon as the water touched the flames.

Then the cargo ship was past the barge, running free through the channel in the middle of the river. The others ships were packed so close together that there wasn't much space to navigate between them. Darrick saw the surprised faces of several sailors peering over taller ships down at the small cargo vessel.

"Break that oil open," Taramis ordered.

The warriors broke the oil kegs open with hand axes, spilling the dark liquid across the prow deck. The whale oil ran thick and slow, like blood from a man almost bled out.

When the cargo ship passed under the bridge that marked the boundary of the last harbor area, Darrick glanced up in time to see Rhambal throw himself over the side of the bridge. The warrior made a desperate grab for the rigging as it passed, caught hold of it and slammed back into the web of rope, then tossed himself into the nearest sail and slid down to the deck. He landed hard and on his back.

"Are you all right?" Darrick asked, offering a hand as the wind roared around them and the ship's deck pitched.

"Nothing wounded but my pride," Rhambal said, taking Darrick's hand. The warrior clambered to his feet and winced. "And maybe my arse." He looked back at the blazing warehouse. "Now, that'll be enough of a diversion."

"It's already lasted long enough," Darrick replied, gazing at the thick, syrupy liquid that covered the prow.

"Provided we get over into the pilings that Taramis was talking about," Rhambal said.

"We'll get there," Darrick said. He raised his voice. "Hard to port."

"Hard to port!" Farranan shouted from the stern.

Darrick felt *Blue Zephyr* lunge in response, cutting back toward the northern riverbank where the imposing monolith of the Church of the Prophet of the Light stood. The parapet stood out over the river less than three hundred yards away, and the distance was closing fast. Two pillars of square-cut blocks held the parapet twenty feet up from the river surface, allowing for the rising current during the flood season.

On both sides of the river, torches and lanterns trailed *Blue Zephyr*'s passage, marking the passage of the city guards. Church guards filled the parapet as the cargo ship sailed within a hundred yards of the overhang. Several of them had crossbows, and the air filled with quarrels.

"Take cover!" Palat squalled, ducking down and behind the cargo hold amidships. Quarrels slapped into the deck around him.

Darrick heard the missiles whistle by his head within inches of striking him. He pulled himself behind the center mast, trusting the magical winds that Taramis had stirred up to drive *Blue Zephyr* into the pilings. Overhead, more quarrels ripped through the canvas sails.

"Hold the wheel!" Darrick commanded, gazing back at the stern.

Farranan had ducked down, trying desperately to take cover. The weak grip he kept on the wheel allowed the ship to glide back toward the center of the river channel.

Throwing himself from the mast, Darrick charged toward the ship's stern. His back and shoulders tightened up as he ran across the heaving deck, expecting to feel the unforgiving bite of a steel arrowhead at any moment. Grabbing the stairwell railing, he hurled himself up the short flight of steps, almost stumbling over Farranan in his haste.

Taramis stood at the railing. "Get back from the prow!" he yelled.

Darrick grabbed the wheel and pulled hard to port, bringing the cargo ship back on course. The winds continued unabated, whipping the rigging and tearing the canvas where the quarrels had ripped through. The wheel jerked in Darrick's hands as the rudder fought the river current and the mystical winds.

After inscribing a glowing seven-pointed symbol in the air, Taramis spoke a single word. Activated by the magic, the symbol spun the length of the deck and ignited the whale oil spilled over the prow. The dark liquid went up in a liquid *whoosh!* of twisting yellow and lavender flames.

A wall of heat washed back over Darrick, causing him to squint against it. Panic filled him for a moment when he realized he could no longer see the parapet because of the whirling mass of flames and flying embers. Leaping into the rigging and catching the first sail, the fire climbed the forward mast like a lumbering bear cub, testing each new resting place, then diving upward again.

He looked up, thinking for one insane moment that he could chart by the stars.

Instead, he spotted the tall bell tower atop the tallest part of the Church of the Prophet of the Light. He aimed the ship by the bell tower, figuring out where it was in relation to the parapet.

"Hold what you have," Taramis said.

Darrick nodded grimly.

Quarrels continued to fall onto the ship, sinking deep into the wood. Another caromed from the ship's wheel in Darrick's hands and bit into his left side. For a moment he thought his ribs had caught fire, then he glanced down and saw the quarrel lodged there.

Sickness twisted Darrick's stomach as he thought the shaft had penetrated his stomach or chest. Then he noticed that it had taken him low, skimming across his ribs with bruising force but not biting into muscle or an organ. The quarrel would probably have gone on through if it hadn't been for his traveling cloak.

Steeling himself, Darrick reached down and pulled the quarrel through his own flesh and tossed it over the side. His fingers gleamed crimson with his own blood.

"Look out!" Palat yelled.

For one frozen moment, Darrick saw the thick pilings supporting the parapet before him. *We're too high*, he thought, realizing the cargo ship came up higher on the structure than they'd guessed. *The impact is going to turn us away.*

But he had forgotten about the sheer, unstoppable tonnage the wild winds drove before them. As cargo ships went, not many were loaded more compactly or more heavily than oil freighters. *Blue Zephyr* was loaded to the top with driving weight and powered by a whirling storm.

The ship slammed into the pilings, driving from their moorings against the riverbed, collapsing the parapet in a sudden stream of rubble, driving a wall of water up and into the swirling winds so that a sudden monsoon rained down. *Blue Zephyr*'s starboard side took a beating as rock fell from above.

Shudders ran the length of the ship, feeling like monstrous blows from a blacksmith's hammer. *Blue Zephyr* was the anvil, and just as unrelenting and uncompromising. Rock and rubble bounced from the deck, which was canted hard to starboard as it scraped along the exposed riverbank.

The church's guards fell amid the rubble as well. Darrick watched them fall, some of them dropping into the foaming river current on the starboard side of the ship and others bouncing across the deck, caught up in an avalanche of stone and mortar. Two of the guards fell into the flaming canvas on the forward mast. They screamed and dove from the rigging, candle flames burning brightly till they plunged into the river.

Releasing the wheel, knowing he could no longer attempt to hold it in place without risking dire injury, Darrick stepped back and seized the railing. He held on as the ship battled the wind and the riverbank. Pulling himself along the railing, he reached up for a ratline running to stern, caught it, and forced his way to the port side.

Blue Zephyr ground to a halt on rock.

Darrick heard the rock scraping along the ship's hull, giant's teeth worrying at a bone. He winced as he realized the amount of damage they'd done to the vessel and the countless hours of work it would take to get her seaworthy again. He gazed over the deck, wondering if, after all they'd risked, they'd accomplished what they set out to do.

Shadows clung to the fallen debris and the dark mud of the riverbank. Darrick searched the riverbed but didn't see the threatened sewer system Taramis's research had turned up. Still, despite the grimness of their situation, no real fear touched Darrick. All he felt was an anxiety and a hope that the desperate madness of guilt of the last year would soon be over. Kabraxis's church guards wouldn't let them live after the assault.

Taramis joined Darrick at the railing. The sage spoke a word and pointed to the torch he held. Flames instantly wreathed the torch, and light glared down over the ship's side.

"That torch is going to light us up for the crossbowmen," Farranan said as he stood at the railing.

"We can't stay here," Rhambal said.

Blue Zephyr continued to rub and buck against the exposed limestone of the riverbed.

"The ship's not going to be here for long, either," Darrick said. For the first time he noticed the quiet that was left after the storm winds had died away. "The current's going to dislodge us, sweep us away."

Thrusting the torch out, Taramis scanned the riverbank. More rock dropped from the broken parapet.

"They've got a boat in the water," Palat warned.

Looking over the stern railing, Darrick saw a guard ship streaking for them. Lanterns lighted Lord Darkulan's flag in the stern and on the prow, marking the vessel for all to see.

"The torch is too weak," Taramis said. "But it's got to be down there." He waved the torch, reaching down as far as he could, but it was futile. The light simply wouldn't reach the riverbank properly.

Draw the sword, Mat Hu-Ring said into Darrick's mind.

"Mat?" Darrick whispered. The guilt returned full blast, disrupting the peace he thought he'd have when it became apparent there would be no escape. Accepting his own death was far easier than accepting Mat's.

Draw the sword, Mat repeated, sounding far away.

Turning, knowing he wasn't going to find his friend standing somewhere behind him the way it sounded, Darrick looked at the warriors assembling in the stern, looking toward Taramis to call their next move.

The sword, ye damned fool! Mat said. *Draw the bloody great sword. It'll help ye an' them with ye.*

Darrick reached over his right shoulder, feeling the pain along his left side where the quarrel had gone through, and gripped the hilt of Hauklin's sword. A tingle ran through his hand, and the sword seemed to spring into his grip. He held the weapon before him, a huge gray bar of sharpened steel bearing battle scars.

Taramis and the other warriors holding lanterns and torches they'd gotten from the whale-oil freighter tried to penetrate the shadows covering the riverbank.

"Maybe if someone goes down there," Rhambal suggested.

"A man going down there ain't gonna be with the ship if it leaves," Palat said. "We might need to stick with this old scow if we're going to make it out of here."

"Be better off trying our luck in the streets," Rhambal said. "Even if we made it out into the harbor without being closed in, they'd run us down. We don't have a seasoned crew working the sails and ropes."

Call out the sword's name, Mat ordered.

"Mat," Darrick whispered, hurting inside as if he'd just witnessed his friend's death. He wasn't imagining Mat's voice. It was real. It was real, and it was inside his head.

Call out the sword's name, ye great lumberin' lummox, Mat ordered.

"What are you doing here?" Darrick asked.

Same as ye, Mat replied, *only I'm a damn sight better'n ye at it. Now, call on the sword's power before ye get swept off them rocks an' back into the arms of them guards. We got a ways to go tonight.*

"How do I call on the sword?" Darrick asked.

Yell out its name.

"What is the sword's name?" In all the confusion, Darrick suddenly couldn't remember.

Stormfury, Mat replied.

"Are you alive?" Darrick said.

We ain't got time to go into that now. We're hard up against it now, an' there's still Kabraxis to contend with.

The freighter scraped rock again, shifting more violently than ever. For a moment, Darrick thought the vessel had torn free.

"Stormfury," Darrick said, holding the hilt in both hands and not knowing what to expect. The unaccustomed tingle flared through his hands again.

In an eyeblink, a cold blue light ran the length of the sword blade. As lacking as it was in heat, though, the light was bright but colored so that it didn't hurt the eyes.

The magical light given off by the blade cut through the darkness swaddling the riverbank with ease. Blue highlights reflected on the river water pouring into the broken section of the eight-foot sewer system that ran under the church. The ship's collision with the riverbank had sheared away the parapet and the mud, revealing the sewer tunnel and cracking it open.

"There it is," Taramis said.

Darrick whispered, "Mat."

There was no answer, only the whistling sound of the normal breeze moving through the rigging.

The whale-oil freighter bucked again, sliding four or five feet backward and almost coming free of the rocks.

"We're losing the ship," Taramis said. "Move! Now!" He stepped over the railing and threw himself at the riverbank, leading the way.

Go! Mat whispered in Darrick's mind, sounding farther away than ever.

Trapped, wanting to know more about how Mat was able to talk to him, thinking perhaps his friend was actually alive somewhere, Darrick climbed the railing and stepped over as the freighter shifted once more, turning slightly as the river current caught it. Another good shove like that by the current, and Darrick knew the ship would twist free. Stepping off the ship, he threw himself forward.

Darrick landed in the mud, sinking his boots up past the ankles, losing his footing and sliding out of control, ending up facedown in the cold muck. The river current washed over him, drenching him and chilling him to the bone. In contrast, the wound in his side burned as if he'd been jabbed with a red-hot poker.

The other warriors leapt after him, landing in the mud for the most part, but the last few landed in the river and were nearly washed away in the current before the others helped them. For a moment as they gathered themselves, *Blue Zephyr* acted as a defensive wall. Quarrels thunked into the ship's side from the guard ship that closed on them.

In the space of the next drawn breath, the burning ship twisted once more and was gone, following the river current. The ship full of guards managed to avoid the bigger ship, but the wash left by its passing and their efforts to get out of the way caught them and nearly capsized them. Then the freighter was by them, plunging downriver toward the ships lying at anchor, promising all manner of destruction before morning saw Bramwell again.

"Damnation," Palat swore. "We're like to burn this unfortunate town down around its ears while we're trying to save it tonight."

"If it happens," Taramis said, "the people here would be better served if it were humans doing the rebuilding instead of demons."

Slipping and sliding, Darrick followed the sage into the sewer tunnel. He only noted then that his sword had dimmed, leaving Taramis's torch and the lanterns and torches carried by the other warriors.

The sewer was halfway submerged from the problems Taramis had found out about during his foray through Bramwell's taverns. The collision with the freighter had broken through the wall as Taramis had planned, but the extent of the damage was greater than what Darrick would have believed possible. Water poured through cracks in the mortared brick wall wide enough to fit the fingers of a man's hand, sluicing in to join the waist-high deluge that rapidly deepened. Moss and slime grew on the sewer walls, and muck clung to the stone floor beneath the rancid-smelling water.

Taramis halted in the middle of the wide sewer, glancing to the left and the right.

"Which way?" Palat asked, raking an arm over his face to clear the water and mud. Smears streaked his features.

"To the left," Taramis said, and turned in that direction.

To the right, Mat said in Darrick's ear. *If ye go to the left, ye will be caught.*

Taramis waded through the rising water.

Tell them!

Hesitant, not truly trusting that Mat was speaking to him, knowing that he could have gone insane and never noticed it until now, Darrick said, "You're going the wrong way."

Taramis halted in water that was now chest deep. He peered at Darrick. "How do you know?" the sage asked.

Darrick didn't answer.

Tell him, Mat said. *Tell him about me.*

Shouts outside the sewer system echoed inside the tunnel, carried flat and hard across the water. Torchlight neared the break, and Darrick knew it wouldn't be long before the guards attacked them.

"Because Mat is telling me which way to go," Darrick said.

"Mat who?" Taramis demanded suspiciously. "Your friend who was killed at Tauruk's Port?"

"Aye," Darrick replied, knowing he wouldn't have believed his story if he'd been the one it was being told to. He could scarcely believe it now.

"How?" Taramis asked.

"I don't know," Darrick admitted. "But it was him who got me to activate the sword's power and show us the way into this sewer."

The warriors gathered around Taramis, all of them wet and bedraggled, all of their faces filled with doubt and dark suspicion.

"What do you think?" Palat asked Taramis, taking a half-step in front of the sage to separate him further from Darrick.

Aware of the big warrior's cautionary measure, Darrick remained silent and understood. He would have thought he was mad as well if he hadn't been the one hearing Mat's voice.

Taramis held his torch higher. The flames licked at the stones overhead, charring the moss and lichens that grew there. "Every time a demon is loosed into the world of men," he quoted, "the balance must be kept. A way will be made, and only human choice can rid the world of the demon again." He smiled, but there was no mirth in the expression. "Are you certain of this, Darrick?"

"Aye."

Rhambal pointed his lantern at the wall. "We've got no choice about moving. Those damned guards are going to be on top of us in no time. And most of them are honest men, men just getting paid for enforcing the peace. I don't want to hang around and fight them if I can help it."

Taramis nodded. "To the right, then." He led the way, pushing his torch before him.

The sewer channel gradually headed up. Darrick felt the incline more because the inrushing water flooded around him and made him more buoyant, which made walking up the hill harder than it should have been. Gradually, though, the water level dropped, and Taramis's torchlight reflected in hundreds of eyes before them.

"Rats," Rhambal said, then swore.

The rats occupied the sides of the sewer, shifting and slithering against one another, islands and clots of rat flesh. Their hairless tails flipped and wriggled as they moved constantly.

The rising water lapped over the sides of the sewer tunnel, lifting small groups of tightly clustered rats free of their temporary retreat. Riding the crest of the water as it ebbed and flowed, the rats fixated on the warriors in the tunnel.

And in the next moment, they attacked.

Buyard Cholik rode the stone snake's head back to the wall as guards circulated through the crowd. The confluence of whispered voices created a din in the cathedral that made it impossible to talk.

Someone attacked the church.

The thought pounded through Cholik's mind. He didn't know who could dare such a thing. During the last month, the relationship with Lord Darkulan had become even better. Ties and agreements were beginning to be made to erect a church in Westmarch. The Zakarum Church was fighting politically to disallow the Church of the Prophet of the Light entrance to the capitol city, but

Cholik knew it was only a matter of time before even that resistance went away. Through Lord Darkulan and his own observers, many of whom Cholik had entertained in the church during the last month with Lord Darkulan's help, the king had learned how much wealth the hopeful pilgrims brought to Bramwell.

But even beyond the basic wealth that the church could bring to Westmarch, there was no doubt about the miracles. Or about the man who made them happen. With more people coming to the church, Cholik had begun doing more services. He now conducted six from dawn until after dusk. A normal man, Cholik knew, a simply human man, would have dropped in his tracks from the demands, but he had reveled in them, meeting them and surpassing them. Kabraxis had given Cholik his strength, shoring him up and keeping him going.

More miracles had been worked, all of them received by those fortunate enough to be chosen to journey along the Way of Dreams. During the past months, the size and number of the miracles had increased along with the number of services. Health had been restored. Crooked limbs had been straightened. Wealth had been given. Love had been granted. Husbands and sons who had gone missing in battles had emerged from the gaping, flaming jaws of the stone snake, called from wherever they had been to the path of the Black Road. Those survivors had no memories of where they had been until the moment they stepped from the snake's mouth into the cathedral.

And three times, youth had been restored to aging parishioners.

That had all of the coastal cities along the Gulf of Westmarch talking as the story was carried by ship from port to port. Caravans picked up the stories in the port cities and carried them to the east, to Lut Gholein and possibly across the Twin Seas to Kurast and beyond.

Giving the youth back to the three men was the most difficult, Cholik knew, and required great sacrifice. Kabraxis made the sacrifice, but the demon didn't pay the price himself. Instead, Kabraxis took children from the city during the nights and sacrificed them on the Black Road, robbing them of their years so he could reward the parishioners he'd chosen with extended years. All three of those parishioners were men who could help the Church of the Prophet of the Light grow and earn the favor of the king. One of them, in fact, had been one of the king's own observers, a man—Lord Darkulan insisted—who was like a father to the king.

It was a time of miracles. Everyone in Bramwell spoke of the Church of the Prophet of the Light that way. Health, wealth, love, and a return to youth— there was nothing more a man could hope for in life.

But someone had dared attack the church.

Deep anger resonated inside Cholik as he gazed out over the filled cathedral. One of the lesser priests Cholik had groomed stepped forward into the lighted area below.

"Brothers and sisters," the priest said, "beloved of Dien-Ap-Sten, join me now in prayer to our magnificent prophet. Wayfinder Sayes goes to speak on your behalf to our prophet and ask that only a few more miracles be granted before we take leave of this service."

His words, amplified by the specially constructed stage, rolled over the church audience and quieted the whispering that had resulted from the news about the attack on the church.

Threaten to take away their chances at a miracle for themselves, Cholik mused, *and you get the attention of every person in the room.*

The priest guided the assembly in prayers to Dien-Ap-Sten, singing of the prophet's greatness, goodness, and generousness.

Once the snake's head was again locked into place on the wall and had become immobile, the flames died away, and that section of the cathedral darkened. Many worshippers screamed out Dien-Ap-Sten's name then, begging that the prophet return and grant more miracles.

Cholik stepped from the platform on the snake's back onto the third-floor balcony. A guard hidden in the shadows pulled the heavy drapes back and opened the door for him. Two crossbowmen stood behind the drapes at all times, relieved every hour during the times of service.

Stepping through the door into the hallway beyond, Cholik found a dozen members of his personal guard waiting for him. No one used this hallway except him, and it led to the secret passageways that had been honeycombed throughout the church. They held lanterns to light the darkened hallway.

"What is going on?" Cholik demanded, stopping among them.

"The church has been attacked, Wayfinder," Captain Rhellik reported. He was a hard-faced man, used to commanding mercenaries and waging small, hard-won wars or tracking bandits.

"I knew that," Cholik spat. "Who has dared attack my church?"

Rhellik shook his head. "I've not yet learned, Wayfinder. From what I've been told, a ship smashed into the courtyard south of the church that overhung the river."

"An accident?"

"No, Wayfinder. The attack on the parapet was deliberate."

"Why attack the courtyard there? What could they possibly hope to gain?"

"I don't know, Wayfinder."

Cholik believed the mercenary captain. When Rhellik had been brought to the church almost a year ago, he'd been dying a paraplegic, paralyzed from the neck down by a horse stepping on him during a battle with bandits while traveling from Lut Gholein. His men had bound him to a litter and brought him almost two hundred miles for healing.

At first, Cholik had seen no value in the mercenary captain, but Kabraxis had insisted that they watch him. For weeks, Rhellik had stayed at every service, fed by his men and bathed in the river, and he had sung praises to Dien-Ap-Sten as best as he was able with his failing voice. Then, one day, the snake's head had lifted him from the crowd and gulped him down. A few minutes after that, the mercenary captain had walked back from the Way of Dreams, hale and hearty, and he had pledged his service forever to the prophet Dien-Ap-Sten and his Wayfinder.

"It doesn't make any sense," Cholik said, starting down the hallway.

"No, Wayfinder," Rhellik agreed. He raised the lantern he carried in one hand to light their way. He carried his vicious curved sword in the other hand.

"None of these people has been identified?"

"No."

"How large is the force that attacked the church?" Cholik demanded.

"No more than a couple dozen warriors," Rhellik said. "The city guards tried to turn them."

"The boat had to sail upriver to crash into that parapet." Cholik turned and followed the passageway to his right, going up the short flight of steps. He knew every hallway in the church. His robes swished as he hurried. "It couldn't have been going fast. Why didn't the city guards stop it?"

"The ship was driven by magic, Wayfinder. They had no chance to stop it."

"And we don't know who these people are?"

"I regret to say, Wayfinder, that we don't. As soon as that changes, I'll let you know."

Only a little farther on, Cholik reached the hidden door that opened into one of the main hallways on the fourth floor. He released the lock and stepped out into the hallway.

No one was in the hallway. No visitors were allowed up from the first and second floors where seating was made available in the cathedral. And none of the staff who lived there was in those rooms because they were all attending the service. The south fourth-floor wing was reserved for acolytes who had been with the church for six months or longer. It was surprising how quickly those small rooms had filled.

Cholik turned to the left and walked toward the balcony that overlooked the parapet courtyard at the river's edge below.

"Wayfinder," Rhellik said uncomfortably.

"What?" Cholik snapped.

"Perhaps it would be better if you allowed us to protect you."

"Protect me?"

"By taking you to one of the lower rooms where we can better defend you."

"You want to hide me away?" Cholik asked in exasperation. "At a time when my church is attacked, you expect me to hide away like some coward?"

"I'm sorry, Wayfinder, but it would be the safest course of action."

The mercenary's words weighed heavily on Cholik's thoughts. He had sought out Kabraxis with his mind, but the demon was nowhere to be found. The situation irritated and frightened him. As big as the church was, there was nowhere for him to go if he'd been targeted by assassins.

"No," Cholik said. "I am guarded by Dien-Ap-Sten's love for me. That will be my buckler and my shield."

"Yes, Wayfinder. I apologize for doubting."

"Doubters do not stay in the grace of the Prophet of the Light for long, captain. I would have you remember that."

"Of course, Wayfinder."

Cholik strode up the final flight of steps to the balcony. The night wind whipped over him. There was no sign of the mystical winds of which Rhellik had spoken. But Cholik's eyes settled on the burning ship loose on the river current.

Flames roiled across the entire length of the ship, twisting and shifting and racing toward the heavens. Swirls of orange and red embers leapt up from the topmost parts of the masts and rigging, dying in their suicidal race to reach the night sky. In the next moment, the ship rammed into one of the vessels anchored in the river harbor, catching the other ship broadside.

A shower of embers and flying debris from the sails blew over the line of ships beyond the two that remained locked together. Torches and lanterns marked the sailors running to deal with the fire and save the ships. As tightly packed as they were, the fire would spread rapidly if it remained unchecked.

Cholik glanced upriver, spotting the guards at the base of the river where the hanging courtyard had been torn away. He watched in confused speculation as the guards leapt from their craft and waded through the water. Only when their lanterns and torches neared the opening in the sewer did he spot it.

"They're inside the sewers," Cholik said.

Rhellik nodded. "I have already sent a runner to take some of my men there to intercept them. We have maps of the sewer systems." His mouth tightened into a grim line. "We shall protect you, Wayfinder. You need have no fear."

"I have no fear," Cholik said, turning to address the mercenary captain. "I am chosen of Dien-Ap-Sten. I am the Wayfinder of the Way of Dreams where all miracles take place. The men who have broken into my church are dead men, whether they know it or not. If they don't die at the hands of the guards or at my own hands, then they will die at the hands of Dien-Ap-Sten. Although generous to his believers, Dien-Ap-Sten is merciless against those who would strike against him."

The guards funneled into the breached sewer tunnel. Their lantern light and torchlight made the opening glow cherry red like a wound gone bad with poisonous infection.

"Pass the word along to your men, captain," Cholik said. "I want them to watch for the burned man who attacked me last month."

"Yes, Wayfinder. I only pray that no worshipper comes here this night with such an affliction in hopes of being healed. Such a person would find only death waiting."

Cholik stared across the black river. Clusters of lights stood on either bank.

More lights raced along the two bridges that connected the north and south sections of the city.

When the attackers were caught, and Cholik had every reason to believe that they would be, they would be put to death. He'd have their heads mounted on pikes at the main entrance through the church walls, and he would say that Dien-Ap-Sten had commanded that it be so, to show the enemies of the Church of the Prophet of the Light that the prophet could be fierce and unforgiving as well. It would temper the faith of those who believed, and it would be a grand story that would bring more people in to see the church and the religion.

Buyard Cholik.

Surprised by the demon's voice in his head, Cholik started. "Yes, Dien-Ap-Sten."

The mercenary captain signaled his men, waving them back away from Cholik, taking two steps himself. He touched the back of his sword hand to the tattoo that had been placed over his heart when he had sworn loyalty to the church. A rote prayer to the prophet tumbled from his lips, praying for a safe and enlightening journey that the wisdom and power of Dien-Ap-Sten be spread even farther.

Return to the services, Kabraxis said. *I will not have those disrupted. I will not be shown as weak or wanting.* The demon sounded far away.

"Who has attacked the church?" Cholik asked.

Taramis Volken and his band of demon hunters, Kabraxis said.

A worm of fear crawled through Cholik's heart. Although he had not talked to Kabraxis of the demon hunter, Cholik had read about the man. Taramis Volken had been a powerful force against demons for years. Once he had read and heard some of the stories about the man, Cholik remembered reading about him from the archives in the Zakarum Church. Taramis Volken was viewed as an inflexible man, one who would not quit. The demon hunter had proven that over the last few weeks. Ever since recovering Stormfury, Hauklin's sword, the group had vanished.

They've only been hidden, Kabraxis said. *Now they are once more in my grasp.*

But before he could stop himself, Cholik wondered if they were somehow in Taramis Volken's grasp instead. All his training in the Zakarum Church had taught him that demons didn't enter the human world without affecting the balance between Light and Darkness. Taramis Volken had proven himself to be the champion of Light on several occasions.

Taramis Volken will die in those sewers, Kabraxis growled inside Cholik's mind. *Doubt me, and you will pay, Buyard Cholik, even if you are my chosen one.*

"I don't doubt you, Dien-Ap-Sten," Cholik said.

Then go. I will deal with Taramis Volken.

"As you wish, my prophet." Cholik touched his head in benediction, then turned with a swirl of his robe.

"Wayfinder," Rhellik said, looking up, "returning to the cathedral might not be the safest thing you can do."

"It is the safest place to be," Cholik said, "when you go there with Dien-Ap-Sten's blessing." *And not going there could be the most dangerous.* But he amended that even as he thought it.

The most dangerous place to be was in the sewers beneath the Church of the Prophet of the Light.

Twenty-three
※

Hairless tails flicking, sharp teeth snapping, the rat packs poured toward Darrick, Taramis Volken, and the demon hunters. The pale yellow light of the warriors' lanterns and torches played over the wriggling rat bodies as they raced along the ledges and the uneven walls and swam through the murky water of the sewer mixing with the river encroaching through the break in the tunnel behind them.

For a moment, ice-cold terror thudded through Darrick's veins as he thought about being covered over in a mass of furry bodies and dragged under the water. The other warriors cursed and called out to the Light as they spread out and took up defensive positions.

Rhambal stood tall and massive at the head of the group. With a backward swipe of his shield, the warrior knocked a dozen of the leaping rats from the air. The thuds of their bodies slamming against the shield echoed in the sewer tunnel.

"Stand," Taramis ordered his warriors. "Hold them from me for only a moment more."

Rats leapt from the walls, landing on the armored helms and shoulders of the warriors. Their claws scratched against the plate and chain mail, demanding blood.

Darrick swiped at one of the foul creatures and halved it from nose to tail with Hauklin's sharp blade. The rat's blood sprayed across him, blinding him in one eye for a moment. By the time he'd wiped the blood from his face and cleared his vision, three more rats landed on him, staggering him with their sudden weight. The rats started up toward his face at once, the flickering torch-light dancing across their fangs. Cursing, Darrick knocked the rats from him. They plopped into the water and disappeared for a moment before they bobbed back to the surface.

Despite their best efforts, the warriors gave ground before the onslaught of rats. Blades and hammers flashed through the air, coming dangerously close to hitting their comrades. Blood mixed in with the dark sewer water and the white froth of the river rushing into the tunnel.

The undertow created by the pull of the river and the push of the sewer almost dislodged Darrick's tenuous stance atop the muck-lined stone floor. Darrick whipped the sword around, amazed at how easily and fluidly the weapon moved. Dead rats and pieces of dead rats flew around him, but still many managed to reach him. Their fangs cut his arms and legs where they were left uncovered by the chain mail shirt he wore.

Working quickly, Taramis inscribed magical symbols in the air. Green fire followed his fingertips, and the finished symbols glowed brightly. With another gesture, the sage sent the symbols spinning forward.

The symbols exploded in the air only a few feet away, and white light stabbed out. The light shafts speared through the rats and dropped them in their tracks, shredding the flesh from their bones till only skeletons remained.

For a moment, Darrick believed the danger had passed. The bites stung, but none of them was bad enough to slow him. Infection, however, was a concern, but only if they lived through the attack on the church.

"Taramis," Palat said, supporting one of the warriors and keeping a hand pressed over his neck. "One of the rats tore Clavyn's throat and cut the jugular vein. If we don't get the bleeding stopped, he's going to die."

Wading through the rising water to examine the warrior, Taramis shook his head. "There's nothing I can do," he whispered hoarsely. They'd not been able to find healing potions along the way and lacked gold to buy it, besides.

Palat's face turned wintry hard as the blood continued seeping between his fingers. "I'm not going to let him die, damn it," the grizzled old warrior said. "I didn't come all this way just to watch my friends die."

Shaking his head, Taramis said, "There's nothing you can do."

Horror touched Darrick, sliding past the defenses he tried to erect. If Clavyn died a quick death, they'd have to leave his body there—for the rats. And if the warrior died slowly, he'd have to die alone, because they couldn't afford to stay with him.

Since arriving in the tunnel, Darrick had stepped back into that safe place he'd first created to endure his father's beatings and harsh words. He refused to let Clavyn's death touch him.

No, Mat whispered. *He doesn't have to die, Darrick. Use the sword. Use Hauklin's sword.*

"How?" Darrick asked. Inside the tunnel, his voice cut through the splashing echoes of the water swirling into the walls on either side of him.

The hilt, Mat replied. *The hilt must be pressed to Clavyn's flesh.*

Desperate, not wanting to see the man die in such an ignoble fashion, Darrick moved forward. As he did, the sword's blade glowed fierce blue again.

Palat stepped forward, standing between Darrick and the wounded warrior. "No," Palat said. "I'll not have you ending his life."

"I'm not going to kill him," Darrick said. "I'm going to try to save him."

Still, the big warrior refused to move.

In that moment, Darrick knew that he'd never been one of them and would never be one of them. They had traveled together and eaten together and fought together, but he was apart from them. Only his ability to take Hauklin's sword had bound them to him. Anger stirred in him.

Darrick, Mat said. *Don't give in to this. You're not alone.*

But Darrick knew that wasn't true. He'd been alone all his life. At the end, even Mat had left him.

No, Mat argued. *The way ye're feelin' isn't real, Darrick. It's the demon. It's Kabraxis. He's down here with us. He's aware of us. Even now, there are warriors coming to intercept yer group. But Kabraxis's thoughts are within ye's. I'm tryin' to keep him from ye, but he's sortin' out yer weaknesses. Don't let the demon turn ye from these men. They need ye.*

A fierce headache dawned between Darrick's temples, then throbbed with an insane beat that almost dropped him to his knees in the cold water. Black spots swam in his vision.

Use the sword, Darrick, Mat insisted. *It can save all of ye.*

"What can I do?" Darrick asked.

Believe, Mat answered.

Struggling, Darrick tried to find the key to make the magic work. It would be better if there were a magic word or something else. All he could remember was how the sword had acted and felt at Ellig Barrows's house, and how the sword had behaved when it lit the riverbank to reveal the tunnel they'd clambered through only moments before. It wasn't belief, Darrick knew, but it was something he knew to be true.

The sword shivered and glowed blue again. Calm warmth filled the tunnel and soaked into Darrick's flesh and bones as a humming sound filled the air. In stunned amazement, he watched as the blood stopped slipping between Palat's fingers.

Hesitantly, Palat removed his hand from Clavyn's neck, revealing the jagged wound that had severed the warrior's jugular. As they watched, the flesh knitted, turning back into seamless flesh with only a small scar left behind.

The humming and the warmth continued, and Darrick watched as even the wounds he'd endured healed, including the rip along his ribcage made by the arrow earlier. In less than a minute, the warriors were all healed.

"Blessed by the Light," Rhambal said, a childlike grin on his broad face. "We've been blessed by the Light."

"Or saved to be killed later," Palat growled, "if you're going to stand there flapping your lips."

Darrick reached for Mat, wanting to hear his voice.

Stay strong, Mat said. *The worst is yet to come. This is only the calm before the storm.*

"Damn," Palat swore, pointing back the way they'd come. "The guards are nearly upon us."

Head buzzing, still filled with the headache, Darrick gazed back along the tunnel.

Flickering light filled the darkness behind them, proof that the guard ship had arrived. Splashing echoed around Darrick and signaled the guards' approach.

"Forward," Taramis ordered, lifting his lantern and moving farther up the sewer.

The group started forward, fighting the water and the sewer's slick stone bottom. The darkness ahead of them retreated before the torches and the lanterns. Darting through the shadows and the water, a few rats shrilled and squeaked at their approach but made no move to attack.

Something thudded into Darrick's side, drawing his attention. He looked down, barely able to spot the short piece of ivory bone that slid through the water. At first, he thought the bone was some sore of creature with a hard carapace, then he saw that it was a leg bone from one of the rats Taramis had slain with his spell.

"Hey," Rhambal called out, reaching down and snatching a small rat's skull from the water. "These are the bones of the rats."

Before the big warrior could say any more, the skull leapt from his hand and snapped at his face, causing him to draw back. He swept his armored fist at it, but the skull was gone, dropping back into the water.

"Hold," Taramis said, taking a lantern from one of the nearby warriors and raising it. The light chased the darkness, splintering the shadows and reflecting from the tossed and uneven planes of the water.

Revealed by the lantern light, hundreds of bones slid through the water, flashing greenish white under the light.

"It's the demon's doing," Palat snarled. "The demon knows we're down here."

In the next instant, a frightening figure surged from beneath the water. The line of warriors closest to it stepped back.

Formed of the rats' bones, the creature stood eight feet tall, built square and broad-chested as an ape. It stood on bowed legs that were whitely visible through the murky water. Instead of two arms, the bone creature possessed four, all longer than the legs. When it closed its hands, horns formed of ribs and rats' teeth stuck out of the creature's fists, rendering them into morning stars for all intents and purposes. The horns looked sharp-edged, constructed for slashing as well as stabbing. Small bones, some of them jagged pieces of bone, formed the demon's face the creature wore.

"That's a bone golem," Taramis said. "Your weapons won't do it much harm."

The bone golem's mouth, created by splintered bones so tightly interwoven they gave the semblance of mobility, grinned, then opened as the creature spoke in a harsh howl that sounded like a midnight wind tearing through a graveyard. "Come to your deaths, fools."

Taramis gestured with his free hand, inscribing a mystic symbol. Immediately, the symbol became a pumpkin-sized fireball that streaked for the incredible bone creature.

Striking the bone golem in the chest, the impact of the fireball knocked the creature back on its heels for a moment. Flames wreathed the demon-made thing, crawling through the gaps in the bones till it seemed to be burning on the inside as well. Steam welled out of the bone golem but didn't appear to do any further damage.

Opening its mouth again, the bone golem howled once more, and this time flames spat into the air as well. The ululating wail echoed the length of the sewer, so loud it was deafening. Several of the warriors put their hands to their ears, their mouths open as they screamed in pain.

Darrick never heard the warriors' screams over the spine-chilling roar. But he heard Mat's voice.

It's up to ye, Darrick, Mat said calmly. *The bone golem will kill them if it gets the chance. Only Hauklin's enchanted blade can damage the creature.*

"I'm no hero," Darrick whispered as he looked at the creature.

Perhaps not, Mat said, *but there's no place to run.*

Glancing back over his shoulder, Darrick saw the line of church guards filling the sewer behind them. Retreat only offered the inevitable battle with the guards and the promise of even more waiting for them out in the harbor.

The warriors drew back beside Darrick, obviously preferring their chances against human foes instead of the bone golem. Darrick stared at the creature, pushing himself through and past his fear. There was no way out except through the bone golem.

He stepped forward, falling into a defensive position as the creature closed on him. One of the spiked fists slashed at him. Ducking beneath the blow, Darrick set himself and cut upward. Catching the bone golem's arm with the edge of his blade, Darrick tried to cut through the elbow joint. The blow missed by a couple of inches and skidded along the creature's arm.

Sensing his opponent's movement more than he saw it, Darrick dodged backward, narrowly avoiding the balled left fist that streaked for his head. The bone blades jutting from the fist slashed through the chest of his traveling leathers, then splashed into the waist-high water swirling around them.

Before the bone golem could draw its arm back, Darrick swung the enchanted blade again. This time the sword sheared through the arm, splintering it into a thousand bone shards and scattering them through the water. The bone golem threw a right fist at Darrick's face that would have carved the face from his skull if it had landed.

Desperately, Darrick threw himself backward. The razor edges of the fist slashed across his chest again, cutting through his traveling leathers but scoring on the flesh beneath this time as well. Fear rattled through Darrick, almost causing him to give up hope, but Hauklin's sword felt steady and true in his hands. He parried the bone golem's next blow, turning the huge fist from its target, stepping back as the creature followed the bony hammer into the water and bent double. Spinning, Darrick landed a blow against the bone golem's ribcage beneath the stub of its bottom left arm. Broken bone shards flew in all directions, but the creature remained whole.

Still moving, somehow keeping his footing in the water and in the muck, Darrick retreated, slashing and parrying with Hauklin's sword. Crimson stained the front of his traveling leathers as he bled. While pulling back, he tripped and fell.

The bone golem swiped at Darrick at once, aiming a fist at his face.

Then Rhambal was there, blocking the blow with his shield. The razor-sharp spikes that festooned the bone golem's fist tore through the warrior's shield less than a foot from Darrick's face. Getting his feet under him again, Darrick saw the bone golem's spike pierce Rhambal's shield and into the arm that held it. Blood spurted as the bone golem drew its fist free.

In obvious agony, Rhambal stepped back, then faltered and fell to his knees, clutching his wounded arm to his chest and leaving his head exposed.

Guilt hammered Darrick, more painful than the cuts across his chest. *It's my fault*, he told himself. *If I hadn't been able to free Hauklin's sword, they would have never come here.*

No, Mat said. *They would have come, Darrick. Even without ye an' that sword. It's the demon working inside ye. It's puttin' them thoughts there. Fillin' ye with bad thoughts an' makin' ye weak. Ye can make a difference in this, an' that's what I come back for. Now move!*

The bone golem wasted no time in setting itself and attacking the new prey it found before it. Gripping the enchanted sword in both hands, Darrick stepped forward and swung. When the blade met the bone golem's arm, the weapon shattered the limb.

Roaring with rage, the bone golem turned its attention back to Darrick, flailing after him with its two remaining arms. Darrick fended one of the blows off, then avoided the other, throwing himself into the air and flipping over the arm.

Taramis and Palat dashed forward, caught Rhambal under the arms, and dragged him back from the bone golem's reach.

Landing on his feet, Darrick blocked another sweeping roundhouse blow, feeling the impact vibrate through his wrists and arms. He almost lost his grip on the sword but clung to it tightly. Running at the wall on the left, knowing if he stopped the bone golem would swarm over him, Darrick threw himself into the air and struck the wall with his water-filled boots. Water splashed out of his boots on impact.

You're a blight on me, boy, his father's voice thundered inside his head. *An embarrassment to me. By the Light, I hate the sight of your ugly face. It ain't no face that ever belonged to me. And that red hair of yours, you'll never find it in my family. Nor in your ma's, I'll warrant.*

The words tumbled through Darrick's mind, splitting his concentration as he cushioned the impact against the wall by bending his knees and falling forward.

Don't listen to him, Mat said. *It's only the damned demon talkin' to ye. He's lookin' for yer weak spots, he is. An' yer personal business, why, it's no business of his.*

But Darrick knew that the words didn't just come from the demon. They came from that small stable in back of his father's butcher shop, and they came from years of abuse and cold hatred that he hadn't understood as a child. Even as a young man, Darrick had been powerless to defend himself against his father's harsh words. Maybe his father had learned not to be so quick with his hands when Darrick had started fighting back, but Darrick had never learned to protect himself from his father's verbal assaults and his mother's neglect.

Darrick fell forward on the wall, his forward momentum allowing him to make contact for just an instant before gravity pulled him toward the water-filled tunnel. From the corner of his eye, he saw the bone golem throwing another punch. By the time it reached the wall where he'd landed, he had pushed off with one hand—the other gripping Hauklin's sword—and flipped back toward the tunnel behind his attacker.

The bone golem's fist crunched into the wall, splitting stone and breaking loose mortar that held it together.

Darrick forced his father's words from his mind, stilled his shaking hand, and squared himself as he took a full breath of the fetid air around him. Taking a two-handed grip on the magical blade, watching the bone golem start turning to face him, Darrick saw Taramis and his warriors on the other side of the creature. Beyond them, the church guards awaited an opportunity. Crossbowmen fired their weapons, but the quarrels caught on the shields of the men at the rear of the warrior group.

Do it! Mat roared in Darrick's head.

The sword blazed blue again, a true and cold blue like that found in the sea before the deep turned black. Swinging, not holding anything back, Darrick felt the enchanted weapon shatter through the bone golem's ribcage and grate to a stop embedded in the creature's spine.

The bone golem howled with pain, but its macabre voice carried laughter as well, rolling gales of it. "Now you're going to die, insect."

"No," Darrick said, feeling the power tingling through the sword. "Go back to hell, demon."

Eldritch blue flames leapt down the length of the sword and curled around the bone golem's spine as it reached for Darrick. The fire grew, enveloping the bone golem and burning away whatever magic bound the skeletal remains of the dead rats together. Flaming bones toppled into the sewer water, hissing when they struck.

For a moment, everyone—including Darrick—stood frozen in disbelief.

Run! Mat yelled.

Turning, Darrick ran, raising his knees high to clear the water level. The sword continued to glow, chasing back the shadows that filled the tunnel. Taramis and the demon hunters came after Darrick.

Less than fifty yards farther on, the tunnel ended at a T juncture. Without hesitation, the sword pulled Darrick to the right. He ran on, filmed by the condensation filling the tunnel as well as perspiration pouring from every pore. His breath burned the back of his throat, and he was convinced the stench of the place was soaking into him.

Only a short distance farther on, the tunnel ended without warning. Sometime in distant years past, the sewer had collapsed. The sword's bright blade illuminated the pile of rubble that blocked the passageway. Cloaked in the shadows and the collapse of broken rock, rats prowled the rubbish heap. Hundreds of them scampered and crept along the broken rock.

Above the rubble, a rounded dome of fallen earth peeked through. No longer shored up by the stones, the earth had collapsed inward over the years but had not completely fallen. There was no way to guess how many feet of earth and rock separated the tunnel from the surface.

"Dead end," Palat growled. "That damned sword has played us false this time, Taramis. Those guards will be down on us in another moment, and there's no place for us to run."

Taramis turned to Darrick. "What is the meaning of this?"

"I don't know," Darrick admitted.

TWENTY-FOUR

In the distance, the splash of the closing guards running through the sewer grew steadily louder in Darrick's ears. At least in this part of the tunnel, the water level was a few inches below knee-high, and the current was weak, little more than a steady flow.

Darrick felt betrayed. The voice that he'd thought had been Mat's had only been another demon-spawned trick. Staring at the sword, he knew it had been bait for an insidious trap.

No, Mat said. *This is where ye're supposed to be. Just hold yer water, I say, an' things will be revealed to ye.*

"What things?" Darrick demanded.

Taramis and the other warriors turned to watch him, and the splashing of the approaching church guards grew louder, more immediate.

There were three of us in that cavern when Kabraxis stepped through into our world, Mat answered. *The magicks that Buyard Cholik unleashed when he opened that gateway to the Burning Hells marked all of us. Them doubts in yer head, Darrick, that's just Kabraxis playing on yer fears. Just hold the course.*

"Three?" Darrick repeated. "There weren't three of us." Unless Buyard Cholik was being counted.

There was another, Mat insisted. *We all lost somethin' that night, Darrick, an' now we must stand together to get it back. Demons never enter this world without sowing the seeds of their own destruction. It's up to men to figure out what they are. Me? I been lost for a long time, an' it wasn't until ye found Hauklin's sword that I come back to meself and ye.*

Darrick shook his head, doubting all of it.

You're worthless, boy, his father's voice said. *Hardly worth the time to kill you. Maybe I'll just wait until you get a little bigger, put a little more meat on your bones, then I'll dress you out and tell everybody you up and ran away.*

The old fear vibrated through Darrick. In the shadows he thought he could almost see his father's face.

"Darrick," Taramis called.

Even though he heard the man clearly, Darrick found he couldn't respond. He was trapped by the memory and by the old fear. The stink of the stables behind the butcher's shop filled his nostrils, making the images of the men before him and the sewer tunnel around him seem dreamlike.

C'mon, Darrick! Mat called. *Pay attention, damn ye! This is the hold that Kabraxis has found over ye. Me, why, that foul demon up an' lost me out in the ghost ways, an' maybe I'd be there still if ye hadn't found Hauklin's blade the way ye done.*

Darrick felt the sword in his fist, but he blamed it for leading them into the dead end. Maybe Mat still believed the sword was a talisman of power, something to stand tall against the demons, but Darrick didn't. It was a cursed thing, like other weapons he'd talked about. Palat had owned a cursed weapon; he knew what he was talking about when he denounced Hauklin's sword.

It's the demon, Darrick, Mat said. *Be strong.*

"I can't," Darrick whispered hollowly. He watched the torchlights of the approaching guards gather at the far end of the tunnel.

"You can't what?" Taramis asked him.

"I can't believe," Darrick said. All his life he'd trained himself not to believe. He didn't believe that his father had hated him. He didn't believe that it was his father's fault that he was beaten. He'd trained himself to believe that life was one day after another at the butcher's shop and that a good day was one when a beating didn't cripple him up.

But ye escaped that, Mat said.

"I ran," Darrick whispered, "but I couldn't outrun what was meant to be."

Ye have.

"No," Darrick said, gazing at the guard.

"They're waiting," Palat said. "They figure there's too many of us for them to take without losing more than a few of their own. They're going to hold up, get more archers in here, then take us down."

Taramis stepped toward Darrick. "Are you all right?"

Darrick didn't answer. Helplessness filled him, and he struggled to push it away. The feeling settled over his chest and shoulders, making it hard for him to breathe. For this past year, he'd put his life into a bottle, into the bottom of a glass, into the cheap wine in every lowdown tavern he'd wandered through. Then he'd made the mistake of trying to sober himself up and believe there was more than futility in his life.

More than the bad luck and the feeling of being unwanted that had haunted him all his life.

Worthless, his father's voice spat.

And why had he saved himself? To die at the end of a collapsed sewer like a rat? Darrick wanted to laugh, but he wanted to cry as well.

Darrick, Mat called.

"No, Mat," Darrick said. "I've come far enough. It's time to end it."

Moving closer, holding the lantern he held up to Darrick's face, Taramis stared into his eyes. "Darrick."

"We've come here to die," Darrick said, telling Mat as well as Taramis.

"We didn't come here to die," Taramis said. "We've come here to expose the demon for what he is. Once the people here who worship him know what he is, they will turn from him and be free."

The malaise that possessed Darrick was so strong that the sage's words barely registered on him.

It's the demon, Mat said.

"Are you talking to your friend?" Taramis asked.

"Mat's dead," Darrick said in a hoarse whisper. "I saw him die. I got him killed."

"Is he here with us?" Taramis asked.

Darrick shook his head, but the movement felt distant from him, as if it were someone else's body. "No. He's dead."

"But he's talking to you," the sage said.

"It's a lie," Darrick answered.

It's not a lie, ye bloody great fool! Mat exploded. *Damn ye, ye thick-headed mullet. Ye was always the hardest to convince of somethin' ye couldn't see, couldn't touch for yerself. But if ye don't listen to me now, Darrick Lang, I'm gonna be travelin' the ghost ways forever. I'll never know no rest, never be at peace. Would ye wish that on me?*

"No," Darrick said.

"What is he saying?" Taramis asked. "Have we come to the right place?"

"It's a trick," Darrick said. "Mat says that the demon is in my head, trying to weaken me. And he's telling me he's not the demon."

"Do you believe him?" Taramis asked.

"I believe the demon is in my head," Darrick said. "I've somehow betrayed you all, Taramis. I apologize."

"No," Taramis said. "The sword is true. It came to you."

"It was a demon's trick."

The sage shook his head. "No demon, not even Kabraxis, could have power over Hauklin's sword."

But Darrick remembered how the sword had resisted him, how it hadn't come free at first down in that hidden tomb.

The sword couldn't be freed at first, Mat said. *It couldn't. It had to wait on me. It took us both, ye see. That's why I was wanderin' the ghost ways, stuck between hither an' thither. That's me part of this. An' the third man, why, he's yer way out, he is.*

"The third man is the way out," Darrick repeated dully.

Taramis studied him, moving the lantern in front of Darrick's eyes.

Despite the irritation he felt at having the light so close to his eyes, Darrick found that he couldn't move.

You ain't my son, his father roared in his mind. *Folks look at you, and they wouldn't blame me if I killed your mother. But she's bewitched me. I can't even raise a hand to her.*

Pain exploded along Darrick's cheek, but it was pain from the memory, not something that was happening at present. The boy he'd been had landed in a heap on a pile of dung-covered straw. And his father had closed in and beaten him, causing Darrick to spend days lying in the stable with fever and a broken arm.

"Why didn't I die then?" Darrick asked. Everything would have been so much easier, so much simpler.

Mat would still have been alive, still living in Hillsfar with his family.

I chose not to be there, Mat said. *I chose to go with me friend. An' if ye hadn't given me reason to get out of Hillsfar, I'd have gotten out of there on me own. Hillsfar wasn't that big a place for the likes of ye and me. Me da knew that, just like he knew about me leavin' for ye.*

"I killed you," Darrick said.

An' if it wasn't for ye, how many times over dead would I have been by now? Before we ended up at Tauruk's Port?

In his mind, Darrick saw Mat slam into the cliff wall again, the skeleton hanging to him like a leech.

How many times did them captains we crewed with tell us that the life of a Westmarch Navy sailor wasn't worth havin'? Long hours, short pay, an' an even shorter life was it come to that, as it most likely would. The only things what made it all worthwhile was yer shipmates an' what few tavern wenches would roll their eyes at ye like ye was some kind of big damn hero.

Darrick remembered those speeches and those times. Mat had always made the best of it, always got the prettiest wenches, always had the most friends.

An' I'd be knowin' if me luck holds true in the hereafter, Mat said, *were I ever to*

get finished with this last bit of business we signed on for. Take up the sword, Darrick,
an' stand ready. The third man is comin'.

Part of the malaise lifted from Darrick. Only then did he realize that
Taramis had gripped the front of his shirt in both fists and was shaking him.

"Darrick," the sage said. "Darrick."

"I hear you." Darrick heard the thunk of quarrels meeting the metal shields
that the other warriors held up as well. Evidently the church guards had
grown braver and decided to pick some of them off if they could. At the
moment, the warriors were able to keep the shields overlapping so that none
of the fletched missiles got through.

"What third man?" Taramis demanded.

"I don't know."

"Is there a way out of this?"

"I don't know."

Desperation creased the sage's face. "Use the sword."

"I don't know how."

Ye're waitin', Mat said.

"We're waiting," Darrick repeated dully. He'd dwindled so close inside
himself that nothing mattered. His father's voice was muted, somewhere in
the background. Maybe Mat had found a way to keep it quiet, but if he
believed that, then Mat couldn't be the demon, and Darrick was pretty certain
that the demon inside his head was Mat, too.

"There's other guards coming," Palat announced.

Without warning, stone shifted against stone.

Taramis glanced over Darrick's shoulder. "Look," the sage said. "Perhaps
your friend was right."

Numbly, Darrick turned and spotted the rectangular hole that opened in
the sewer ceiling above the pile of rubble. Peering closer, he realized it wasn't
a door that had opened but rather a large section of rock that had been lifted
up and out of the way. Light shone on the rubble and the water below.

A man shoved his head through the rectangle. "Darrick Lang," he called.

Shifting his lantern, Taramis brought the man into view.

Staring into the burned wreckage of the man's face, Darrick didn't believe
for a moment that help had arrived.

"Darrick Lang," the burned man called again.

"He knows you," Taramis said at Darrick's side. "Who is he?"

Shaking his head, unable to recognize the burned man's features in the
shifting of light and shadows, Darrick said, "I don't know."

Ye know him, Mat said. *That's Cap'n Raithen. From the pirates what was at*
Tauruk's Port. Ye fought him aboard the pirate ship.

Amazed, knowing somehow Mat was speaking the truth, Darrick recognized the man. "But he died."

"He looks like he did," Taramis agreed in a quiet voice, "but he's offering us
a way out of certain death. He's certainly mastered close escapes."

"This way," Raithen said. "If you would live, hurry. That damned demon has sent more people into the tunnel after you, and now that they've seen me open this one, they're likely to check up with the maps and figure out how I got here."

"Come on," Taramis said, taking Darrick by the arm.

"It's a trick," Darrick argued.

No, Mat said. *We're joined, the three of us. Joined in this endeavor.*

"We stay here, and we'll die like fish in a barrel," Taramis said. He shoved Darrick into reluctant movement.

As they neared the debris pile, the rats scattered, and quarrels struck the stones and sometimes the rats, but luckily the warriors all got through.

Raithen shoved his hand down toward Darrick. "Give me the sword," the pirate captain said. "I'll help you up."

Before Darrick could move the sword, Raithen reached down for it. As soon as the man's fingers touched the sword, they hissed.

Raithen yelped and yanked his hand back. Fresh steam rose from his burned fingers as he retreated into the tunnel above the sewer. He cursed and broke two more rocks free, enlarging the space so the demon hunters could more easily gain entrance.

Taramis went through first, clambering into the smaller tunnel above them. Dully, Darrick followed, taking care to watch the enchanted sword.

After introducing himself, Taramis offered his hand.

The pirate captain remained out of arm's reach and ignored the hand. His gaze focused on Darrick. "Has your dead friend been in touch with you?" the pirate captain demanded.

Darrick looked at him, unwilling to answer. If anything, Darrick was ready to put Hauklin's sword through the pirate captain's heart.

A cold smile framed Raithen's lips. Cracks opened in the burned flesh, and blood beaded his mouth. "You don't have to answer," the pirate captain said. "There was no other way you'd be here if it weren't for your meddling friend."

Meddlin' friend, is it, then? Mat demanded. *Why, if I could put me hands on ye, or take a good length of steel up to do battle, I'd have the head off yer shoulders for that, ye mangy swab.*

"He's still with us, I see," Raithen said.

Surprised, Darrick asked, "You can hear him?"

"Whenever he's around, aye. He prattles on constantly. I just thank the Light that I've only listened to him these past few weeks." Raithen's gaze dropped to the sword in Darrick's hand. "He told me you'd come bearing Hauklin's mighty blade. Is that it?"

"Aye," Darrick replied.

The other warriors clambered into the small tunnel and milled around. Taramis issued quiet orders, getting men on either side of the opening in the bottom of the new tunnel.

"And that will kill Kabraxis?" Raithen demanded.

"So I've been told," Darrick replied. "Or at least drive the demon from this world back to the Burning Hells."

Spitting blood onto the tunnel floor, Raithen said, "I'd rather we gutted him and threw him to the sharks, then watched them carry him away a bite at a time."

"The church guards are coming," Palat said. "We'd best be on our way."

"Running through this tunnel with them on our heels?" Raithen asked. He grimaced, and the bloody froth at his mouth made him look demented.

He is demented, Mat said. *What Kabraxis did to him has nearly taken his sanity.*

"What are you doing here?" Darrick demanded of Raithen.

The pirate captain smiled, and more blood flecked his lips. "The same as you, I expect. I came to be free of the demon. Although, after hearing of your friend's death and knowing what's happened to me, I'd have to say that you appear to have gotten better treatment than any of us."

Darrick didn't say anything.

Splashing sounded in the sewer below.

"Those church guards aren't going to wait for you two to finish palavering," Palat said.

Raithen stepped back and pulled a barrel from the wall beside the opening. As he yanked on the heavy barrel, the skin covering his hands split and bled. Crimson stained the barrel as Darrick and Palat lent hands, pushing the barrel toward the opening in the floor. Yanking the lid from the barrel, the pirate captain revealed the dark oil inside.

"Pour," Raithen commanded.

Together, they poured the contents of the barrel into the sewer water and over the rocks below. Rats scampered from beneath the dark liquid, and the guards held their positions warily.

Two crossbow quarrels flew through the opening in the floor. One of them splintered through the side of the barrel, and the other sliced through Raithen's right calf. Cursing with the pain, Raithen reached back to the wall and yanked a torch from the sconce there. He tossed the torch through the hole in the floor and onto the pile of debris below.

Peering cautiously over the side of the hole, Darrick watched as the oil caught fire. Flames spread over the pile of rubble, chasing the rats from their hiding places and onto the guards and into the water. The oil floating on top of the water caught fire as well. Carried by the slow current of the sewer, flames floated toward the guards, forcing them to retreat.

"That will buy us some time," Raithen said. He turned to the left and hurried along the tunnel.

"Where are you taking us?" Taramis asked.

"To the demon," Raithen said. "That's where we've got to go." He ran down the tunnel, pausing only long enough to take another torch from a sconce farther on.

The passageway was smaller than the sewer below, only wide enough for three warriors to jog abreast. Drawn by the urgency that vibrated within him, Darrick took the lead position among the demon hunters, joined quickly by Taramis and Palat.

"Who is that man?" Taramis asked, eyes locked on the fleeing figure ahead of them.

"Raithen," Darrick replied. "He is—"

Was, Mat assured him.

"—*was*," Darrick amended, "a pirate captain in the Gulf of Westmarch. A year ago, Raithen worked with Buyard Cholik."

"The Zakarum priest who opened the gateway for Kabraxis?"

"Aye."

"What happened to him?"

"He was killed by the demon in Tauruk's Port," Darrick said, knowing how strange it sounded as they watched the burned madman racing before them.

"He's not dead enough to my way of thinking," Palat said.

At the same time Raithen was killed, Mat said, *Kabraxis also cast the spell to raise the zombies an' skeletons to pursue us. The magic pervaded Raithen's corpse afterward, causin' him to rise again. After ye freed the sword, I was drawn here to him. I found I could talk to him as I talk to ye. The three of us are bound, Darrick, an' in our bindin', we present the way to end Kabraxis's reign here.*

"He's dead," Darrick explained, giving the details that Mat had given him.

"The prophecy of Hauklin," Taramis said.

"What prophecy?" Darrick asked. They trailed after Raithen, following the pirate captain around a bend in the tunnel.

"It was said that Hauklin's sword would never be taken from his tomb except to unite the Three," the sage said.

"What three?" Darrick asked.

Twenty-five
✳

"One lost in death, one lost in life, and one lost in himself," Taramis said. "One trapped in the past, one trapped in the present, and one trapped in the future."

A cold chill of dread filled Darrick.

"Your friend Mat must be the one who is trapped in death, unreleased by his death in the past. Raithen has to be the one trapped in life, unable to die and doomed to live out the way he is through the present." He gazed at Darrick. "That leaves you."

"Why didn't you mention this earlier?" Darrick asked.

"Because not all prophecies are true," the sage answered. "All weapons and artifacts have stories that are told about them, but not all of those stories are true. When you drew the sword from Hauklin's body, I thought the prophecy was false."

Taramis's words hammered Darrick.

Aye, Mat said inside his head, *ye've been the one lost in yerself. But them sad times is behind ye. Just like Hillsfar an' that stable behind yer father's butcher shop. Just ye keep that in yer head, an' ye're gonna be all right. I'll not desert ye.*

"The prophecy goes on," Taramis said. "One will lift the sword, one will provide the way, and one will face the demon." The sage stared at Darrick. "You couldn't lift the sword at first because your friend wasn't with you then. You couldn't lift the sword till you heard Mat's voice."

Darrick knew it was true, and in a way it made sense with all the events that had transpired since.

"And he shows us the way," Taramis said, pointing at Raithen still running before them. "That leaves you to face the demon."

"Beside the sage," Palat snorted derisively.

Darrick's face flamed in embarrassment, knowing the warrior didn't believe him strong enough or brave enough to confront the demon even with Hauklin's enchanted sword. And truth to tell, he didn't feel strong enough or brave enough himself.

Worthless, his father's voice said.

Cringing inside, Darrick desperately wanted out of the course of action left before him. He was no hero. At best, he would have made a decent Westmarch naval officer; perhaps—but only perhaps—he might have made a decent ship's captain.

But a hero?

No. Darrick couldn't accept that. But if he left, if he walked away from this confrontation to save himself, what would be left of him? Cold realization flooded him, and his footing nearly faltered. If he backed away from the coming battle, he knew he would be everything his father had ever accused him of being.

And if he did that, he would be as trapped between life and death as Mat or Raithen.

There's salvation in this for us all, Mat said.

Even if I become a martyr? Darrick wondered.

"We got men behind us," Clavyn called from the rear of the warriors.

"It's the guards," Raithen said. "I told you they'd find us. This tunnel is one of the newer ones. They use it to bring supplies into the church. Secret passageways and tunnels honeycomb these buildings. Over the last few weeks, I've ferreted out most of them."

"Where are you taking us?" Taramis asked.

"To the central cathedral," Raithen answered. "If you want to face Kabraxis, you'll find him and Cholik there."

Only a few feet farther on, the pirate captain came to a halt under a slanted section of ceiling. The door was as slanted as the ceiling, fitting into it.

"Guards sometimes wait here," Raithen said. "But they're not here now. They went below to help trap you in the sewer, not knowing the way the tunnel overlapped the sewer as I did." He pulled himself up and peered through a slit.

Darrick joined the man, keeping his sword naked in his fist. Taramis stood on the other side of him.

Gazing out through the slit, Darrick saw Buyard Cholik standing on a platform on top of a huge stone snake with a flaming face. As Darrick watched, the snake bobbed and weaved above the expectant audience. The way the audience beseeched and cried out to the snake and the man atop it left a sick knot in Darrick's stomach. He knew a few of the worshippers might know they prostrated themselves before evil, but most of them didn't. They were innocents, praying for miracles and never knowing they were being preyed on by a hell-spawned demon.

"There are hundreds, maybe thousands of people out there," Palat said in wonderment as he crowded up to the viewing slit as well. "If we step out into that, we're going to be outnumbered."

"The crowd will also give us a means of escaping," Taramis said. "The church guards won't be able to seal off all the exits and keep the crowd under control. Once we kill Buyard Cholik, there should be confusion enough to cover our retreat. After that, we'll spread the truth about Kabraxis through the city."

"You can't kill Buyard Cholik," Raithen said.

Darrick looked at the pirate captain. Aware of the pounding boots echoing down the tunnel, Darrick knew they didn't have much time.

"What do you mean?" Taramis asked.

"I tried to kill the bastard," Raithen said. "Weeks ago. I was part of the audience. I slipped a handheld crossbow past his guards and put a quarrel through his heart. I know I did. Yet a few hours later, Buyard Cholik gave another of his services. My attempt to assassinate him only made his fame grow even stronger."

It was Kabraxis, Mat said. *The demon saved him. But even the demon can't save him from Hauklin's blade.*

"We can't stay here," Palat said. "And retreat is out of the question."

Darrick swept his eyes over the demon hunters, marveling again at the small group of men who had been brave enough to walk into the church against such insurmountable odds. If he'd been asked to do such a thing, instead of being chosen by an enchanted sword and accompanied by the ghost of his dead friend, he doubted he would have accompanied them. He had no choice about being there, but they did.

Ye had a choice, Mat said. *Ye could have walked away from this.*

The sour smell of the hay in the stable behind his father's butcher shop swirled around Darrick. He could almost feel the heat of the day press against him, trapped by the small crawlspace among the rafters where the hay was kept. And where he'd lain while waiting to die or be killed the next time his father beat him.

No, Darrick told himself. There had been no choice.

Worthless, his father's voice snarled.

Steeling himself, drinking in air to keep his muscles loose and ready and energized, Darrick tried to ignore the voice.

"What's above us?" Darrick asked.

The thunder of the approaching guards' boots sounded closer, louder.

"Steps," Raithen said, "but they're counterweighted. Once I release the lock, the steps will rise."

Darrick looked at Taramis, who glanced at his men.

"If we stay here," Palat said, "we'll die. But out there, even with that stone snake moving around, we've got a chance."

Taramis nodded. "Agreed."

All the warriors readied their weapons.

"We make the attempt on Cholik," Taramis said, "then we get out of here if we can. We hope the demon will reveal himself. If not, we plan again." He glanced at Darrick. "Hauklin's sword is our best chance to get Kabraxis to come out of hiding."

"Aye," Darrick said, taking a two-handed grip on the sword hilt. He gazed out at the cathedral again, noting how the circular area beneath the shifting stone snake resembled an arena. The flames around the snake's snout blazed. Atop the serpent's neck, Buyard Cholik rode the platform with calm assurance.

"Do it," Taramis ordered Raithen.

The pirate captain reached beneath his robe and brought out a handheld crossbow. Along his burn-blackened hands, thick, crusty scabs cracked open and leaked blood. A madman's grin fitted itself to his bloody lips as he reached for a small lever overhead. He gazed at Darrick. "Don't fail me, sailor. I crossed blades with you before, aboard *Barracuda*. Be as good now as you were then. And be everything your little dead friend said you could be."

Before Darrick could respond, Raithen tripped the lever. In response, the hidden doorway built into the steps swung upward as light as a feather. Light from the cathedral invaded the small tunnel.

Taramis led the way out, his orange robes swirling.

Stepping out of the hiding place after the sage, Darrick was almost overwhelmed by the cacophony of sound that filled even the huge cathedral. Thousands of voices were lifted in praise of Dien-Ap-Sten, the Prophet of the Light.

Church guards occupied a raised area to the right. All of them spotted the secret door opening. One of the bowmen lifted his weapon and drew an arrow back to his ear. Before the guard could properly aim his shaft, Raithen extended his hand with the crossbow in it and squeezed the trigger. The small bolt left Raithen's weapon and pierced the guard's Adam's apple, nailing it to the back of his throat. The guard toppled from the raised area into the crowd, inciting a small riot and starting a wave of hoarse shouting and screaming.

The guards erupted from the checkpoint, and the demon hunters ran to meet them. Steel rang on steel, and Darrick was in the thick of them.

On the platform attached behind the stone snake's head, Buyard Cholik brought the beast to a standstill even as the great, flaming mouth opened and disgorged a small boy who was swept up in the arms of his father.

Stand ready, Mat said into Darrick's mind. *What ye've been facin' so far is about to turn worse.*

"We can't hold this position," Palat said. Blood streaked his face, but not all of it was his own. "We need to run."

Runnin' ain't the answer, Mat said. *Ye have the power, Darrick. We have the power. Me an' Raithen, why, we done brung ye this far, but the rest of it is up to ye.*

"Worshippers of Dien-Ap-Sten," Buyard Cholik's voice thundered. "You see before you infidels, people who would see this great church torn down and stripped of its ability to house and hold the Prophet of the Light and the Way of Dreams."

Howls of fear and rage filled the cathedral.

Darrick battled for his life. Outnumbered as they were at the moment, he knew it was only going to get worse. He parried and riposted, turning a blade aside, then following through behind the point as it sank through the heart of a mercenary. Placing his foot against the dead man's chest, Darrick kicked him backward into three others who rushed to take his spot.

Hands moving with grace and speed, Taramis inscribed mystic symbols in the air. At a shouted phrase, the symbols flew toward the cathedral's peaked roof.

A black cloud formed near the high ceiling as Darrick blocked another blade. Holding the weapon trapped, Darrick stepped up and delivered an elbow and a backfist blow to a church guard who had hard pressed Rhambal, who was having trouble due to his wounded arm. The guard dropped in front of Rhambal.

"Thanks," the warrior gasped. His face looked pasty white beneath his helm.

But even though Darrick had dealt with the one opponent, others stepped up immediately to take his place. And the man Darrick had engaged had slipped his weapon free. The guard slashed at Darrick's face as the dark cloud overhead roiled and flashed. Darrick trapped the man's blade again, set himself, twisted, and drove a foot into the man's head, knocking him from his feet and back into a knot of worshippers.

Breathing hard, feeling the chill in the air now, Darrick swept the cathedral with his desperate gaze. Even now, some of the worshippers pulled belt knives and were on their way to join the fight.

They're innocents, Mat said inside Darrick's head. *Not all of 'em are evil. They're just drawn to it.*

"Where's the demon?" Darrick asked.

Inside the snake, Mat said. *Where the Black Road is. Kabraxis has returned to his place of power. He knows you have Hauklin's sword, he does.*

Darrick blocked, blocked again, parried, and riposted, putting his point through a man's throat. Scarlet bubbled at the guard's throat as he stumbled backward, dropped his sword, and wrapped both hands around his neck in an effort to stem the blood flow.

The cloud Taramis created suddenly unleashed a wintry keening. Freezing storm winds whipped up and tore through the cathedral, twisting the flames wreathing the snake's snout into a flickering frenzy. Frost formed on the great stone creature but quickly melted away as the snake belched fire. Steam shimmered around it.

Cocking its head, the snake focused on the group of demon hunters. Baleful flames danced in the snake's eyes.

Buyard Cholik is the first, Mat said. *He must die, Darrick, for he holds Kabraxis anchored to this world.*

A blizzard suddenly filled the cathedral, whipping fat snowflakes over the central area as well as the worshippers. The whirling blanket of whiteness made it hard to see, and naked skin burned at the snowflakes' touch like acid.

The stone snake struck, flashing forward, fire wreathing its exposed fangs.

"Look out!" Palat yelled, knocking Rhambal from the snake's path.

The demon hunters cleared the area, but not all of the guards got free. Three of the guards were smashed to bloody pulp by the impact. Despite the stone that shattered across the cathedral floor and the chunks that skittered through the pews, the snake wasn't harmed at all.

Gathering his courage, overcoming the doubts that assailed him, Darrick ran toward the snake. Curling in on itself, bloody pieces of the three guards still caught in its fangs, the snake pursued Darrick. Conscious of the unnatural beast closing on him, Darrick cut to the right and hit the ground rolling, sliding up under the snake's own body.

Reaching up, Darrick caught hold of the carved scales with his free hand. The snake head pummeled the cathedral floor, tearing flagstones loose and shattering others. Darrick pushed himself up, clinging to the carved scales along the stone serpent's underside, pulling himself to his feet. He leapt, landing on the snake's snout. Hissing, gurgling flames, the snake opened its mouth, and a forked tongue made of flames stabbed out at him.

The flames singed Darrick's hair as he ran up the snake's snout. Aided by the unnatural beast opening its mouth, Darrick hurled himself into the air toward the platform where Buyard Cholik stood.

Suddenly understanding Darrick's desperate move, Cholik lifted his hands to work his magic. But it was too late. Before the spell was complete, Darrick grabbed the man's robe. Cholik's only saving grace was that Darrick hadn't managed to land on the platform with him.

Knowing that he'd missed the platform in his desperate lunge, Darrick flailed with his free hand and caught Cholik's robe skirts. When his weight hit the end of his arm, Darrick pulled Cholik from his feet, slamming the man against the iron railing and breaking his concentration. Holding on to the robe with one hand, swaying wildly, knowing the snake was curling again, trying to dislodge him and cause him to fall so it could get at him, Darrick flexed his arm, bending his elbow and pulling himself closer to Cholik.

The blizzard swirled around them with blinding intensity. Cold burning his face and exposed skin, buffeted by the storm winds that Taramis had raised with his magic, Darrick drew back his sword, flipped his hand on the hilt, and threw it like a spear.

Hauklin's enchanted blade sailed true even in the terrible wind. It pierced Buyard Cholik's heart, causing the man to stumble backward, tripping over the robe that Darrick held so tightly to.

"No," Cholik said, clutching the sword that had transfixed him. His hands burst into blue flame as they gripped the sword, but he seemed powerless to let go just as he was powerless to pull the blade from his chest.

Taking advantage of Cholik's inability to fight against him, Darrick caught the edge of the platform in his other hand, then pulled himself up. Cholik stepped backward, freed from Darrick's grip, and fell over the platform's edge.

The sword! Mat yelled in Darrick's head. *Kabraxis is still ahead of ye!*

Clinging to the platform mounted behind the snake's bobbing head, watching the movement around him with his peripheral vision, Darrick held fast to the platform with his left hand and stretched his right out for the sword. He willed it to come back to him just as he had that day at Ellig Barrows's house.

Even as Cholik's corpse fell toward the cracked stone floor below, Darrick felt the power binding him to the sword. He watched as the enchanted blade pulled free of the dead man. Hauklin's sword was in the air, streaking toward Darrick as the snake suddenly popped its head up, flinging him high into the air and knocking the sword away.

Whirling, almost colliding with the cathedral ceiling because he was thrown so high, Darrick flailed and tried to get control of his body. Horrified, he watched as the snake lowered its head below him and opened its massive jaws. Flames roiled in the snake's throat, promising a fiery death if it caught him.

Get the sword! Mat yelled. *If ye don't have the sword, ye ain't got nothin'!*

Darrick focused on the sword, but he couldn't clear his mind of the snake below as he reached the apex of his flight and started back down. Even if the snake somehow missed him, he felt certain that he wouldn't survive the fall.

The sword! Mat cried. *The sword will protect ye if ye have it. An' I can help ye through the sword's magic.*

Darrick pushed thoughts of death from him. If he died, it would only put an end to the pain he'd lived in for the last year, and from all the pain he'd borne in those years before that.

He concentrated on Hauklin's sword, strengthening the bond he felt between the weapon and himself. Cholik's corpse plummeted toward the waiting stone floor beside the yawning snake's mouth. But the enchanted blade pulled free of the dead man and flew toward Darrick's waiting hand.

Hold to the sword, Mat said. *Hold to the sword that I may help ye.*

Unable to change directions in the air, Darrick fell, dropping like a stone into the waiting snake's mouth. Flames wrapped him, and for an instant he thought he was going to be incinerated. Unbelievable heat surrounded him and stole his senses away.

Stand easy, Mat warned. His voice, even though Darrick was certain it came from within his head, also sounded distant and small. *This is going to be the worst of it, Darrick, an' there ain't no way around it.*

Darrick couldn't believe he wasn't dead. The fall alone against the stone mouth of the snake should have killed him, but the addition of the flames had taken away all chance of his survival.

Yet—

He lived. He knew it from the way he felt, from the ragged and tortured breath he took and the way he hurt all over.

Ye can't lie there, Mat said, and his voice was thin and distant. *This here's the Black Road. The Twisted Path of Shadows. Kabraxis rules supreme here. At least, he believes he does. He'll kill ye if ye lie there. Get up—*

"Get up," a harsh voice grated. "Get up, you worthless bastard."

Darrick recognized the voice as his father's. His eyes snapped open, and he saw the familiar stable area behind his father's butcher shop. He found himself lying on the sour hay that lined the hayloft.

"You didn't think I'd catch you back up here sleeping, did you?" his father demanded.

Instinctively, Darrick curled into a ball, trying to protect himself. His body hurt from the beating he'd remembered getting the day before. Or maybe it was the same day, only earlier. Sometimes after a beating Darrick had lost track of time. He suffered blackout periods as well as lost time.

"Get up, damn you." His father kicked him, driving the wind from his lungs and perhaps breaking yet another rib.

Fearfully, Darrick got to his feet before his father. Something dangled from Darrick's hand, but when he looked he could see nothing. Perhaps he had another broken arm, but this one felt different from the last.

He thought he heard Mat Hu-Ring's voice, but he knew Mat would never come around when his father was in one of his moods. Even Mat's father wouldn't come around during those times.

"Get up, I said," his father roared. He was a big man with a broad belly and shoulders as wide as an ax handle. His hands were big and tough from hard work and long hours and countless tavern fights. A curly mop of brown hair matched the curly beard he wore to mid-chest.

"I can't be here," Darrick said, dazed. "I was a sailor. There was a church."

"Stupid, worthless bastard," his father roared, grabbing him by the arm and shaking him. "Who'd make a sailor out of the likes of you?" His father laughed derisively. "You've been having another one of those dreams you cling to so much when you hide out up here."

Face burning in shame, Darrick looked down at himself. He was a boy, no more than eight or nine. No threat at all to his father. Yet his father treated him like the fiercest opponent he'd ever encountered.

His father slapped him, causing his head to ring with pain.

"Don't you look away from me when I'm talking, boy," his father commanded. "Maybe I haven't taught you anything else, but you'll know to respect your betters."

Tears ran down Darrick's cheeks. He felt them hot on his cheeks, and he tasted their salt when they reached his quivering lips.

"Look at you, you sniveling coward," his father roared, and raised his hand again. "You don't have sense enough to come out of the rain."

Darrick took the blow on the back of his head, watched the world spin around him for a moment, and remembered how only last week he'd watched his father beat three caravan guards in a fight in the muddy street outside the Lame Goose Tavern. As a butcher, his father was passable, but as a fighter, there were few who could compare.

"Have you fed the livestock like I told you to, boy?" his father demanded.

Peering over the edge of the hayloft, afraid he knew what the answer was, Darrick saw that all the feed bins and water troughs were empty. "No," he said.

"That's right," his father agreed. "You haven't. I ask so little of you because I know that's all I have the right to expect from an idiot like you. But you'd think you'd have enough sense to feed and water livestock."

Darrick cringed inside. He knew there was no winning when his father was in one of his moods. If he had fed the livestock, his father would have found fault with it, would have insisted it was too much or too little. Darrick's stomach lurched as if he were on a storm-tossed sea.

But how could he know what that felt like? Other than one of the stories he sometimes overheard outside the taverns his father frequented in the evening. His father always tried to leave Darrick at home, but his mother was seldom there in the evenings, and Darrick had been too afraid to sit at home alone.

So Darrick had secretly followed his father from tavern to tavern, having an easy time not being seen because his father had been deep in his cups. As mean as his father could be, he was also the most permanent point of Darrick's life because his mother was never around.

. . . not there . . .

Darrick breathed shallowly, certain he'd heard Mat Hu-Ring's voice. But that couldn't be, could it? Mat was dead. He'd died . . . died . . .

Died where?

Darrick couldn't remember. In fact, he didn't want to remember. Mat had died somewhere far from his family, and it was Darrick's fault.

Ye're on the Black Road, Mat said. *These are demon's tricks. Don't give in . . .*

Mat's voice faded away again.

The weight hung at the end of Darrick's arm.

"What is this, boy?" His father yanked Darrick around, displaying the rope and the knotted noose at the end of it. "Is this something you were playing with?"

Darrick didn't speak. He couldn't. Only a few days ago, using the tricks he'd learned from Mat, who had learned them from his uncle the sailor, Darrick had made the rope from scraps of rope left by farmers who brought their animals to his father's shop to be butchered.

For days Darrick had thought about hanging himself and putting an end to everything.

"You couldn't do it, could you, boy?" his father demanded. He coiled the rope up, shaking the noose out.

Darrick cried and shook. His nose clogged up, and he knew he sounded horrible. If he tried to speak, his father would only make fun of him and slap him to make him speak better, not stopping till Darrick was unconscious or nearly so. He knew he'd taste blood for days from the split lips and the torn places inside his cheeks.

Only this time, his father had something different in mind. His father threw the rope over the rafter support on the other side of the hayloft, then caught the noose when it came back down.

"I wondered how long it might be before you got the gumption to try something like this," his father said. He peered over the side of the hayloft and lowered the noose a little. "Do you want to just hang yourself, boy, or do you want to snap your neck when you fall?"

Darrick couldn't answer.

It didn't happen like that, Mat said. *I found the rope. Not yer da. I took the rope away from ye that day, an' I made ye promise that ye'd never do somethin' like that.*

Darrick thought he almost remembered, then the memory slipped away from him.

His father fitted the noose over his neck and grinned. His breath stank of sour wine. "I think snapping your neck is a coward's way out. I'm not going to let no bastard son of mine be afraid of dying. You're going to meet it like a man."

It's the demon! Mat yelled, but his voice tore apart as if he were shouting through a strong wind. *'Ware, Darrick! Yer life can still be forfeit in there, an' if the demon takes it on the Black Road, it's his to keep forever!*

Darrick knew he should be afraid, but he wasn't. Dying would be easy. Living was the hard part, stumbling through all the fears and mistakes and pain. Death—slow or quick—would be welcome relief.

His father cinched the hangman's knot tight under the corner of his jaw. "Time to go," his father growled. "At least when this story goes through the town, they'll say my son went out with the courage of his da."

Darrick stood at the edge of the hayloft. When his father put his big hand against his chest, there was nothing he could do to prevent the fall.

His father pushed.

Arms flailing—*Hang on to the sword,* some part of his mind yelled—he fell. But his neck didn't snap when he hit the end of the rope. His father hadn't let it down enough for that.

Darrick dangled at the end of the rope, the life choking out of him as the hemp bit into his neck. His right arm remained at his side while he gripped the rope with his left and tried to keep his breath.

"Just let go," his father taunted. "You can die easily. It's only minutes away."

He's lying, Mat said. *Damn ye, Darrick, look at the truth! This never happened! We'd have never gone to sea if this had happened!*

Darrick stared up at his father. The man had knelt down on the side of the hayloft, his face split in a wide grin, his eyes on fire with anticipation.

Look past him! Mat cried. *Look at the shadow on the wall behind him!*

Through dying vision growing black around the edges, Darrick saw his father's shadow on the wall behind him. Only it wasn't his father's. Whatever cast the shadow on the wall there wasn't human. Then Darrick remembered the cathedral in Bramwell, the stone serpent with the flaming maw.

Without warning, Darrick suddenly realized he was full-grown, dangling from the strangling rope thrown over the rafter.

"You're too late," the demon said. His form changed, shifting from that of Darrick's father to his own true nature. "You're going to die here, and I'm going to have your soul. Perhaps you've killed Buyard Cholik, but I'll use you to anchor me to this world."

Anger flamed through Darrick. He fanned it and hung on to it, letting it give him strength. He swept the sword up, slashing through the rope that held him, and dropped to the straw-covered ground below.

Only it wasn't the straw-covered ground of the stable behind the butcher's shop anymore. Now it was a thin black ribbon that hung out over nothingness.

Kabraxis dropped to the Black Road in front of Darrick. Without a word, the demon rushed at Darrick, claws flaring, fangs bared.

With the noose still around his neck, restricting his airways and causing spots before his eyes, Darrick fought. The sword was a live thing in his hands, moving inhumanly quick, but it was only enough to keep his inhuman opponent from killing him.

Kabraxis flicked his tail at Darrick, but Darrick swept the sword out, intercepting the appendage and cutting it off. The demon roared with rage and swung both his arms in a scissoring move. "You can't beat me, you worthless human."

Ducking beneath the blows, Darrick threw himself forward, sliding between the tall demon's legs, slipping on the blood from the amputated tail.

Then he was up again, racing toward the demon's back. Darrick leapt, putting aside all thoughts of failing or being afraid of the unending drops on either side of the Black Road, and hurled himself at the demon's back.

Kabraxis tried to brush Darrick from his back but froze when Darrick wrapped one hand around the demon's head and slid Hauklin's blade under the demon's neck against his throat.

"Wait," Kabraxis said. "If you kill me, you're going to pay a price. You're not pure the way Hauklin was. You carry fears inside you that will forever taint you. You'll carry something of me that will haunt you. There is a price."

Darrick froze for only a moment. "I'll . . . pay . . . it . . ." he whispered hoarsely. And he pulled the enchanted blade across the demon's throat, metal grating on bone as lightning filled the darkness around them.

A frantic burst of light filled Darrick's vision, blinding him.

When he opened his eyes again, he stood in the center of the cathedral. Snow covered the floor around him. He had Kabraxis's head in his hand, gripping it by one of the horns.

The stone serpent was still animated, hovering above Buyard Cholik's corpse.

Taramis and the other demon hunters faced an onslaught of church guards, and four of the warriors were down, dead, or severely wounded.

The stone serpent coiled, then struck at Darrick.

"No," Darrick said, feeling the unnatural power that filled him. He struck Hauklin's blade down into the stones of the snow-covered floor.

Cold blue lightning bolts crashed through the cathedral roof and smashed into the stone snake, tearing it into a twisted serpentine pile of bricks and mortar. The flames in its mouth and eyes flickered and died.

Everyone in the cathedral froze as Darrick turned on them.

Lifting the demon's head, Darrick yelled, "It's over! The demon is dead! The false prophet is dead!"

The church guards put down their weapons and backed away. Taramis and his warriors, bloody but unbent, turned guardedly to look at Darrick.

"Go home," Darrick told the worshippers. "It's over."

He told them that, but he knew it wasn't true. There was still the price to be paid, and he was only now beginning to understand what it was.

EPILOGUE

Cold, distant morning sun split the eastern sky, threading the white clouds with violent reds and purples like a fertilized egg that had been cracked too close to term and held blood in the yolk. Despite the cold blowing down out of the mountains, the sun's rays chased the night's shadows away from Bramwell and out into the sea.

Darrick Lang stood atop the garden-covered roof of the Church of the Prophet of the Light as he had all through the long night. He wore his heavy cloak, but the wind cut through it and left him near frozen; still, he wouldn't walk away. His father's voice had rung in his head for hours and had only started to dim a short time ago. Darrick didn't hear Mat's voice at all and didn't know if Mat had continued on through the ghost roads or if he had died yet again during the final confrontation. It was hard not knowing.

Some of Buyard Cholik's mercenaries had threatened to put up a fight, but since their employer had been killed, not many of them had the heart for it. Palat had spat blood and told them they were all mad because they'd lost easy jobs, and if they wanted to lose more than that, all they had to do was step up. None of the mercenaries had. During the confusion, Raithen had disappeared.

Taramis had kept his group together, fearing retaliation on the part of the stunned crowd. At first, it had looked as if the audience would turn on the demon slayers despite the fact that Darrick had held Kabraxis's head and showed them the lie they had been told. They had been there to witness and receive miracles and had seen all that torn away instead. Some of them had sat in the pews for hours, in faint hope that the Prophet of the Light and the Wayfinder would return for those who truly believed.

Footsteps scraped the rooftop.

Darrick turned, Hauklin's mystic sword still bared in his fist. Although he had worked with Taramis and the other demon hunters and had slain both Buyard Cholik and Kabraxis, Darrick knew they still didn't trust him. His path was not theirs; he wouldn't ride off into the new dawn or find a ship out in the harbor to make war against another demon.

Another demon. A bitter laugh rose to Darrick's lips, but he let it die. He wasn't over the last demon yet. Nor was he over the demons his father had instilled within him.

Taramis Volken walked through the gardens. The sage still carried the signs of battle—blood, some of it his and some belonging to others, and soot—on his orange robes. Shadows clung to his face despite the dawn, and he looked older somehow in the clean light.

"I wondered if you would still be up here," the sage said.

"No, you didn't," Darrick said. "You've had Rhambal watching the passageway from the rooftop."

Taramis hesitated only a moment. "You're right, of course."

Darrick said nothing.

Walking over to the roof's edge, the sage looked down. The breeze ruffled his orange robes. "Many of the worshippers aren't leaving."

Reluctantly, Darrick joined the older man at the roof's edge and peered down as well. The streets in front of the church were choked with people despite the city guard's best efforts to move them along. Smoke billowed from a half-dozen burning buildings.

"They haven't stopped believing," Taramis said.

"Because Cholik and Kabraxis gave them what they wanted," Darrick said.

"Some of them," Taramis corrected. "And the price was high. But it was enough to keep the others here, hoping that they would be picked out next for fortune's favor." He looked up at Darrick. "What the demon did was a terrible thing."

Darrick remained silent. The north wind wasn't any colder than the sage's words.

"The city guard is fighting with roving bands of worshippers in the city," Taramis said. "Many of them are protesting the night's events. They say that Cholik and the Prophet Dien-Ap-Sten were slain by Lord Darkulan out of jealousy and that there never was a demon."

"The demon is gone," Darrick said. "Not believing Kabraxis wasn't a demon isn't going to bring him back."

"No, but they want revenge against the city for the guilt and confusion and anger they feel. If Bramwell is lucky, only a few buildings and a few lives will be lost before the guard gets the situation under control."

Darrick reflected on his own dark anger. The emotion was residue from what his father had done to him. He knew that now, but he also knew that residue was indelible and would be with him forever.

"They say," Taramis said, "that when a man faces a demon, that man comes to know himself in ways he was never shown before. You faced Kabraxis, Darrick, more closely than any man I've ever known before."

"You've fought and killed demons," Darrick countered.

Taramis leaned against the roof ledge and crossed his hands over his chest. "I've never followed them into the Burning Hells to do it as you did."

"Would you have?"

"If I'd had to, yes." No trace of hesitation sounded in the sage's voice. "But I have to ask myself why you did."

"I didn't choose that path," Darrick pointed out. "The snake swallowed me."

"The snake swallowed you because Kabraxis thought he could beat you on the Black Road. And he thought he could beat Stormfury. My question to you is, why did the demon think that?"

For a long while, Darrick held the silence between them, but he realized that the sage wasn't going to go anywhere. "Because of the guilt I carry," he finally said.

"Over your friend Mat?"

"And more," Darrick admitted. Then, before he could stop himself, he told the sage the story of his father and of the beatings he'd received in the butcher's shop in Hillsfar. "It took me a long time to figure out that my mother had been unfaithful to my father and that I didn't know who my true father was. I still don't."

"Have you ever wanted to know?"

"Sometimes," Darrick admitted. "But the Light only knows what trouble that would bring if I did find out. I've had trouble enough."

"Kabraxis thought he could weaken you by confronting you with your father's anger."

"He would have done it," Darrick said, "were it not for Mat. Always during those times after the beatings, Mat stood by me. And he stood by me again on the Black Road."

"By helping you through Kabraxis's subterfuge."

"Aye." Darrick gazed at the sage. "But the winning wasn't all mine, you see."

Taramis looked at him.

"I defeated Kabraxis in the Burning Hells," Darrick said, "but I brought a part of it back with me." With a quick move, he thrust Stormfury into one of the nearby garden beds. Such treatment to a weapon was unthinkable because the moisture would make it rust. But he knew the mystical sword would suffer no damage. He left the sword quivering there and held out his hand. "The damned demon tainted me somehow."

Darrick's hand shimmered, then began to change, losing its humanness and twisting into a demonic appendage.

"By the Light," Taramis whispered.

"I destroyed Buyard Cholik and Kabraxis's way into our world," Darrick said, "but I became that way." Long talons jutted from his fingers now covered in hairy, green and black skin.

"When did this happen?"

"While I was on the Black Road," Darrick said. "I'll tell you another thing, too. Kabraxis isn't dead. I don't know if he'll ever have another body that will survive in our world, but he's still alive in the Burning Hells. Every now and again, I can hear him whispering to me, mocking me. He's waiting, you see, for me to give up and die or to lose control of myself by getting drunk or not caring if I live or die." He reached for Hauklin's sword, closed his hand around it, and watched as the hand became human again.

"Hauklin's sword grounds you," Taramis said.

"Aye," Darrick said. "And it keeps me human."

"Kabraxis cursed you."

Darrick sheathed the sword at his side. "Kabraxis's gateway from the Burning Hells no longer lies under the ruins of the city on the Dyre River. His gateway is now me."

"And if you should be killed by another?"

Darrick shook his head. "I don't know. If my body were completely destroyed, maybe Kabraxis wouldn't be able to make his way into this world again." He smiled, but it was cold and devoid of humor, holding only bitterness. "By revealing this to you, I feel as though I've put my life at risk."

Taramis didn't say anything for a time. "There are some who would be tempted to put you to death rather than risk the demon's return."

"And you?"

"Doing such a thing would make me no better than the monsters I hunt," the sage replied. "No, you have nothing to fear from me. But should Kabraxis gain the upper hand within you, I'll hunt you down and kill you."

"Fair enough," Darrick agreed. He knew he could expect no less.

"You will need to keep Hauklin's sword with you," Taramis said. "I'll explain the matter to Ellig Barrows, but chances are that he and his family will be glad to be shut of it."

Darrick nodded.

"What will you do?" Taramis asked. "Where will you go?"

"I don't know."

"You could ride with us."

"We both know my place isn't with you," Darrick replied. "Although it would probably prove easier for you to keep your eye on me."

A wry grin fitted Taramis's face. "True."

"There is something more I received from the demon's death," Darrick said. He strode close to the sage. "You're wounded. Show it to me."

Hesitantly, Taramis pulled his robe away and revealed the deep wound in his side. Someone had clumsily bandaged it, but the blood still seeped through.

Darrick clapped a hand over the sage's side, causing him to wince. Power flowed through Darrick, and for the time it took to work, he heard Kabraxis's whispers more loudly in the back of his mind. He took his hand away. "Check the wound."

In disbelief, Taramis pulled the bandage away and inspected his side. "It's healed."

"Aye," Darrick said. "As are the wounds that I suffered last night. But such healing comes with a price. While I do it, Kabraxis has greater access to me. Only Hauklin's sword keeps me sane and human."

"You've healed me more quickly and better than any healer or potion I've ever used," Taramis said. "You could be a great asset."

"But to whom?" Darrick asked. "And at what cost? Perhaps Kabraxis has given me this power so that I will continue to use it and grow closer and closer to him."

"Then what will you do?"

"I don't know," Darrick answered. "I know I need to get away from here. I need the sea again for a time, Taramis. Something to clear my head. I need to find good, honest work again, a sailor's life, so I won't have so much time to think."

"Believe in the Light," Taramis said. "The Light always shows you the way even in the darkest times."

Hours later, with the sun now in the west out over the ocean and a ship's passage secured, Darrick stood on the Bramwell docks. Taramis and the other demon hunters joined him, agreeing to take at least this much of the voyage together.

The docks were congested, people milling around like cattle being herded onto cargo ships. The waves pressed the ships up against the dock pilings, causing sonorous booms to echo over the dockyards.

Without warning, a woman's shrill scream punctuated the noise.

Halfway up the gangplank leading onto the ship he'd booked passage on, Darrick turned and looked back.

Men hauled a young girl from the water, her body torn and shattered in her long dress.

An older woman, probably her mother, knelt beside the little girl as the sailors stretched her out on the docks. "Please," the woman begged. "Can someone help my little girl? Is there a healer here?"

"A healer wouldn't do that one any good," a gruff sailor beside Darrick said. "That little girl had the ill luck to fall between the ship an' the pilin's as she was boardin'. Smashed her up inside. Ain't nobody gonna be able to do anything about that. She's dead, just waitin' for it to come callin'."

Darrick looked at the frail girl, her body busted up from the impact, drenched and in horrible pain.

"Darrick," Taramis said.

For a frozen moment, Darrick remained on the boardwalk. What if the little girl's accident was no accident? What if it was a temptation arranged by Kabraxis to use the healing power again? What if someone in the crowd, a traveling Vizjerei or another wizard, recognized that Darrick's power wasn't given by the Light but from a demon spawn from the Burning Hells?

Then Darrick was moving, vaulting from the gangplank and back to the shore. He shoved people from his path, feeling the old anger and intemperance surging within him. A moment more, and he was at the little girl's side.

Her mother looked up at him, her face stained with frightened and helpless tears. "Can you help her? Please, can you help her?"

The little girl was no more than six or seven, hardly older than one of Mat's sisters the last time Darrick had seen her.

"Ain't no good," a man nearby whispered. "Seen people all squashed up like this before. That little girl's as good as dead, she is."

Without a word, Darrick placed his hands on the girl's body, feeling the broken bones shifting within her. *Please,* he thought, ignoring Kabraxis's harsh whispers fouling the back of his mind. He wouldn't let the demon's words come forward, wouldn't allow himself to understand them.

Power flowed through Darrick's hands, pouring into the little girl. A long moment passed, then her body arched suddenly, and she stopped breathing. During that still moment, Darrick felt certain that Kabraxis had somehow betrayed him, had somehow made him cause the girl's death instead of preventing it.

Then the girl opened her eyes, the clearest blue eyes Darrick thought he'd ever seen. She called for her mother and reached for her. The woman took up her child and hugged her to her breast fiercely.

"A healer," someone whispered.

"That's not just a healer," someone else said. "He brought her back from the dead, he did. That little girl weren't nothin' more than a corpse, an' he done brung her back like it was nothin'."

Darrick pushed himself to his feet, suddenly ringed in by people who were curious and suspicious of him. He put his hand on his sword, barely resisting the impulse to draw the weapon and clear the path from him. In the back of his mind, he heard the demon laugh.

Taramis was suddenly at Darrick's side, as were Rhambal and Palat. "Come on," the sage urged.

"It's the Prophet of the Light," someone else said. "He's returned."

"No," another said. "Those are the people who killed the Wayfinder and destroyed the Way of Dreams. Hang them!"

"We've got to go," Taramis said.

Was this what Kabraxis wanted? Darrick wondered. Would his death at the hands of a lynch mob allow the demon to step back into the world of men? Darrick didn't know.

The mother rose to his defense, holding her child to her. "Don't you men dare touch him. He brought my little Jenna back to me. If he is the one who killed the Wayfinder, then he had to have done it for good cause, says I. This man is a miracle worker, a chosen one of the Light."

"The Wayfinder was leading you to demons," Taramis said. "If he had not killed the servant of the false Prophet of the Light, all of you would have been doomed to the Burning Hells."

Darrick felt sickened. He was no hero, and he was no saint. He forced himself to release his tight hold on Stormfury.

Grudgingly, the lynch mob mentality gave way, surrendering to the people who were looking for something to make sense out of all they had been through with the Church of the Prophet of the Light.

In amazement, Darrick watched as people came forward with wounded friends and family, beseeching him to heal them. He turned to Taramis. "What do I do?"

The sage gazed at him. "The choice is yours. You can board that ship and tend to your own needs as best you can, or you can stay here in this moment and tend the needs of others."

Darrick looked out over the huge crowd. "But there are so many."

Already two dozen litters with men and women lying near death were spread across the docks. People called out to him, begging him to aid their fallen family and comrades.

"But the power I have," Darrick said, "it isn't from the Light."

"No," Taramis agreed. "Listen to me, though. How do you know that in this moment the Light hasn't had a design in placing you exactly in the position you find yourself in now?"

"I'm tainted with the demon."

"You also possess a demon's great power, and you can do a lot of good with it if you choose."

"And what if in using that power I also lose myself?" Darrick asked.

"Life is about balance," Taramis said. "Balance between the Light and the Dark. I would not be able to champion the will of the Light so strongly, so willingly, had I not been exposed to the Darkness that waits to devour us in the Burning Hells. Just as steel must be tempered, Darrick, so must a man. You've come a long way. Your present is balanced between your past and the dreams you might have. You stand between the Light and the Dark as Kabraxis's gateway, but it is your choice to remain open or closed. Your choice to hide the power or to use it. You can fear it or embrace it. Either way, it has already changed your life forever."

Quietly, thoughts racing inside his head, the demon whispering somewhere at the back, Darrick looked at the crowd that waited so expectantly. Then, taking a deep breath, he went forward to meet his future, his head high, no one's unloved bastard child anymore but a man of compassion and conviction. He went to the wounded and the dying, and he healed them, listening to the demon scream at the back of his mind.

Kingdom of Shadow

Richard A. Knaak

for Chris Metzen and Marco Palmieri

Oпе

❈

The horrific scream came from the direction of the river.

Kentril Dumon cursed as he shouted orders to the others. He had warned his men to avoid the waterways as much as possible, but in the dense, steamy jungles of Kehjistan, it sometimes became difficult to keep track of the myriad wanderings of the rivers and streams. Some of the other mercenaries also had a tendency to forget orders when cool water lay just yards away.

The fool who had screamed had just learned the danger of growing complacent—not that he would likely live long enough to appreciate that lesson.

The slim, sunburnt captain battled his way through the lush foliage, following the pleading call. Ahead of him, he saw Gorst, his second, the giant, shirtless fighter ripping through the vines and branches as if they had no substance at all. While most of the other mercenaries, natives of cooler, highland regions in the Western Kingdoms, suffered badly from the heat, bronzed Gorst ever took all in stride. The scraggy mop of hair, dark black compared with Kentril's own light brown, made the giant look like a fleeing lion as he disappeared toward the river.

Following his friend's trail, Captain Dumon made better time. The screaming continued, bringing back graphic memories of the other three men the party had lost since entering the vast jungle that covered most of this land. The second had died a most horrible death, snared in the web of a horde of monstrous spiders, his body so injected with poison that it had become bloated and distorted. Kentril had ordered torches used against the web and its hungry denizens, carefully burning out the creatures. It had not saved his man, but it had avenged the death somewhat.

The third hapless fighter had never been found. He had simply vanished during an arduous trek through an area filled with soft soil that pulled one's boots down with each step. Having nearly sunken to his knees at one point, the weary captain suspected he knew the fate of the lost soldier. The mud could be quick and efficient in its work.

And as he considered the death of the very first mercenary lost to Kehjistan's fearsome jungles, Kentril stepped out into a scene almost identical to that disaster.

A huge, serpentine form rose well above the riverbank, long reptilian orbs narrowed at the small figures below who sought in vain to pry free the struggling form in its tremendous maw. Even with its jaws clamped tight on the frantic mercenary whose screams had alerted Kentril and the others, it somehow managed to hiss furiously at the humans. A lance stuck out of its side, but the strike had evidently been a shallow one, for the behemoth appeared in no way even annoyed by it.

Someone loosed an arrow toward the head, likely aiming for the terrible eyes, but the shaft flew high, bouncing off the scaly hide. The tentacle beast— the name their esteemed employer, Quov Tsin, had used for such horrors— swung its prey around and around, giving Kentril at last a glimpse of whom it had seized.

Hargo. Of course, it would be Hargo. The bearded idiot had been much a disappointment on this journey, having shirked many of his duties since their arrival on this side of the Twin Seas. Still, even Hargo deserved no such fate as this, whatever his shortcomings.

"Get rope ready!" Kentril shouted at his men. The creatures had twin curved horns toward the backs of their heads, the one place on their snakelike bodies that the mercenaries might be able to use to their advantage. "Keep him from returning to deep water!"

As the others followed his instructions, Captain Dumon counted them. Sixteen, including himself and the unfortunate Hargo. That accounted for everyone—except Quov Tsin.

Where was the damned Vizjerei this time? He had a very annoying habit of wandering ahead of the band he had hired, leaving the mercenaries to guess half the time what he wanted of them. Kentril regretted ever taking this offer, but the talk of treasure had been so insistent, so beguiling . . .

He shook such thoughts from his head. Hargo still had a slim chance for life. The tentacle beast could have easily bitten him in two, but they just as often preferred to drag their prey under and let the water do their work for them. Made their meals soft and manageable, too, so the cursed sorcerer had said with scholarly indifference.

The men had the ropes ready. Kentril ordered them in place. Others still harassed the gargantuan serpent, making it forget that it could have long finished this encounter just by backing away. If the mercenaries could rely on its simple animal mind a little longer—

Gorst had a line set to toss. He did not wait for Kentril to give the order, already understanding what the captain wanted. The giant threw the loop with unerring accuracy, snagging the rope on the right horn.

"Oskal! Try to throw Hargo a line! Benjin! Get that rope on the other horn! You two—give Gorst a hand with that now!"

Stout Oskal tossed his rope toward the weakening, blood-soaked figure in the behemoth's maw. Hargo tried in vain to grab it, but it fell short. The tentacle beast hissed again and tried to retreat, only to have the line held by Gorst and the other two men keep it from getting very far.

"Benjin! The other horn, damn you!"

"Tell 'im to quit wigglin', and I will, captain!"

Oskal threw the rope again, and this time Hargo managed to grab it. With what strength he had, he looped it around him.

The entire tableau reminded Kentril of some macabre game. Again he cursed himself for accepting this contract, and he cursed Quov Tsin for having offered it in the first place.

Where *was* the foul sorcerer? Why had he not come running with the rest? Could he be dead?

The captain doubted his luck could be that good. Whatever the Vizjerei's present circumstances, they would have no effect on the desperate situation here. Everything rested on Kentril's already burdened shoulders.

A few of the fighters continued to try to wound the serpentine monster in any way they could. Unfortunately, the tough hide of the tentacle beast prevented those with lances and swords from doing any harm, and the two archers still at work had to watch out for fear of slaying the very man they hoped to save.

A rope caught the left horn. Captain Dumon fought back the swell of hope he felt; it had been one thing to catch the monster, but now they had to bring it in.

"Everyone who can, grab onto the lines! Bring that thing onto shore! It'll be more clumsy, more vulnerable on land!"

He joined with the others, pulling on the line Benjin had tossed. The tentacle beast hissed loudly, and although it clearly understood at some level the danger it faced, it still did not release its captive. Kentril could generally admire such tenacity in any living creature, but not when the life of one of his men was also at stake.

"Pull!" the captain shouted, sweat from the effort making his brown shirt cling to his body. His leather boots—his fine leather boots that he had bought with the pay from his last contract—sank into the muddy ground near the river. Despite four men on each rope, it took all they could give just to inch the aquatic horror onto the shore.

Yet inch it they did, and as the bulk of the beast came onto land, the mercenaries' efforts redoubled. A little more, and surely they could then free their comrade.

With the target much closer, one of the archers took aim.

"Hold your—" was all Kentril got out before the shaft buried itself in the left eye.

The serpentine monster reared back in agony. It opened its mouth, but not enough to enable the gravely-injured Hargo to fall free, even with two men pulling from the ground. Despite having no appreciable limbs, the tentacle beast writhed back and forth so much that it began dragging all of its adversaries toward the dark waters.

One of the men behind Gorst slipped, sending another there also falling. The imbalance threw the rest of the mercenaries off. Benjin lost his grip, nearly stumbling into his captain in the process.

One orb a mass of ichor, the tentacle beast pulled back into the river.

"Hold him! Hold him!" Kentril shouted uselessly. Between the two ropes snaring the horns remained only five men. Gorst, his huge form a mass of taut muscle, made up for the fact that he had only one other mercenary with him, but in the end even his prodigious strength proved ineffective.

The back half of the gigantic reptile vanished under the water.

They had lost the battle; the captain knew that. In no way could they regain enough momentum to turn the tide.

And Hargo, somehow madly clinging onto life and consciousness, obviously knew that as well as Kentril Dumon did. His face a bloody mess, he shouted out hoarse pleas to all.

Kentril would not let this man go the same way the first one had. "Benjin! Grab the line again!"

"It's too late, captain! There's nothin'—"

"Grab hold of it, I said!"

The moment the other fighter had obeyed, Kentril ran over to the nearest archer. The bowman stood transfixed, watching the unfolding fate of his unfortunate companion with a slack jaw and skin as pale as bone.

"Your bow! Give it to me!"

"Captain?"

"The bow, damn you!" Kentril ripped it out of the uncomprehending archer's hands. Captain Dumon had trained long and hard with the bow himself, and among his motley crew he could still count himself as the second or third best shot.

For what he intended now, Kentril prayed he would have the eye of the best.

Without hesitation, the wiry commander raised the bow, sighting his target as he did. Hargo stared back at him, and the pleas suddenly faltered. A look in the dying man's eyes begged the captain to fire quickly.

Kentril did.

The wooden bolt caught Hargo in the upper chest, burying itself deep.

Hargo slumped in the beast's jaws, dead instantly.

The act caught the other mercenaries completely by surprise. Gorst lost his grip. The others belatedly released theirs, not wanting to be pulled in by accident.

In sullen silence, the survivors watched as the wounded monster sank swiftly into the river, still hissing its rage and pain even as its head vanished below the surface. Hargo's arms briefly floated above the innocent-looking water—then suddenly, they, too, disappeared below.

Letting the bow drop, Kentril turned and started away from the area.

The other fighters nervously gathered their things and followed, keeping much closer to one another. They had grown complacent after the third death, and now one of them had paid for that. Kentril blamed himself most of all, for, as company captain, he should have kept a better watch on his men. Only once before had he ever been forced to resort to slaying one of his own in order to alleviate suffering, and that had been on a good, solid battlefield, not in some insufferable madhouse of a jungle. That first man had been lying on the ground with a belly wound so massive that Captain Dumon had been amazed any life lingered. It had been a simple thing then to put the mortally wounded soldier to rest.

This . . . this had felt barbaric.

"Kentril," came Gorst's quiet voice. For someone so massive, the tanned giant could speak very softly when he chose. "Kentril. Hargo—"

"Quiet, Gorst."

"Kentril—"

"Enough." Of all those under his command through the past ten years, only Gorst ever called him by his first name. Captain Dumon had never offered that choice; the simplistic titan had just decided to do so. Perhaps that had been why they had become the best of friends, the only true friends among all those who had fought under Kentril for money.

Now only fifteen men remained. Fewer with whom to divide the supposed treasure the Vizjerei had offered, but fewer also to defend the party in case of trouble. Kentril would have dearly loved to have brought more, but he had been able to find no more takers of the offer. The seventeen hardened fighters accompanying him and Gorst had been all who would accept this arduous journey. The coins Quov Tsin had given him had barely paid them enough as it was.

And speaking of Tsin—*where* was he?

"Tsin, damn you!" the scarred captain shouted to the jungle. "Unless you've been eaten, I want you to show yourself right now!"

No answer.

Peering through the dense jungle, Kentril searched for the diminutive spellcaster, but nowhere did he see Quov Tsin's bald head.

"Tsin! Show yourself, or I'll have the men start dumping your precious equipment into the river! Then you can go and talk to the beasts if you want to do any more of your incessant calculations!" Since the beginning of this trek, the Vizjerei had demanded pause after pause in order to set up instruments, draw patterns, and cast minor spells—all supposedly to guide them to their destination. Tsin seemed to know where he headed, but up until now none of the others, not even Kentril, could have said the same.

A high-pitched, rather nasal voice called from the distance. Neither he nor Gorst could make out the words, but both readily recognized their employer's condescending tones.

"That way," the giant said, pointing ahead and slightly to the right of the party.

Knowing that the sorcerer had not only survived but had utterly ignored Hargo's fate ignited a fire within Kentril. Even as he proceeded, his hand slipped to the hilt of his sword. Just because the Vizjerei had purchased their services did not mean in any way that he could be forgiven for not lending his dubious talent with magic to the desperate hope of rescuing the ill-fated mercenary.

Yes, Kentril would have more than words with Quov Tsin . . .

"Where are you?" he called out.

"Here, of course!" snapped Tsin from somewhere behind the thick foliage. "Do hurry now! We've wasted so much valuable time!"

Wasted it? Captain Dumon's fury grew. *Wasted it?* As a hired fighter and treasure hunter, he knew that his livelihood meant risking death every day, but Kentril had always prided himself on knowing the value of life nonetheless. It had always been those with the gold, those who offered riches, who least appreciated the cost the mercenary captain and his men suffered.

He drew the sword slowly from the scabbard. With each passing day, this trek had begun to seem more and more like a wild chase. Kentril had had enough. It was time to break the contract.

"That's not good," Gorst murmured. "You should put it back, Kentril."

"Just mind your place." No one, not even Gorst, would deter him.

"Kentril—"

At that moment, the object of the slim captain's ire burst through the jungle foliage. To Kentril, who stood just over six feet in height, Gorst had always seemed an astonishing sight, but as tall as the giant appeared in comparison with his commander, so, too, did Dumon loom over the Vizjerei.

Legend had always made the race of sorcerers seem more than men, tall, hooded figures clad in rune-covered, red-orange cloaks called *Turinnash*, or "spirit mantles." The small silver runes covering much of the voluminous garment supposedly protected the mage from lesser magical threats and even, to a limited degree, some demonic powers. The Vizjerei wore the Turinnash proudly, almost like a badge of office, a mark of superiority. However, although Quov Tsin, too, had such a cloak, on his barely five-foot frame it did little to enhance any image of mystical power. The slight, wrinkled figure with the long gray beard reminded Kentril of nothing more than his elderly grandfather—without any of the sympathetic nature of the latter.

Tsin's slanted, silver-gray eyes peered over his aquiline nose in obvious disdain. The diminutive mage had no patience whatsoever and clearly did not see that his own life hung by a thread. Of course, as a Vizjerei, he not only had spells with which to likely defend himself, but the staff he held in his right hand also carried protective magicks designed for countless circumstances.

One quick strike, though, Kentril thought to himself. *One quick strike, and I can put an end to this sanctimonious little toad . . .*

"It's about time!" snapped the mercenary's employer. He shook one end of the staff in the captain's face. "What took you so long? You know I'm running out of time!"

More than you think, you babbling cur . . . "While you were wandering off, Master Tsin, I was trying to save a man from one of those water serpents. We could've used your help."

"Yes, well, enough of this babble!" Quov Tsin returned, his gaze slipping back to the jungle behind him. Likely he had not even heard what Kentril had just said. "Come! Come quickly! You must see!"

As the Vizjerei turned away, Captain Dumon's hand rose, the sword at the ready.

Gorst put his own hand on his friend's arm. "Let's go see, Kentril."

The giant casually stepped in front of the captain, effectively coming between Kentril and Tsin's unprotected back. The first two moved on, Kentril reluctantly following them.

He could wait a few moments longer.

First Quov Tsin, then Gorst, vanished among the plants. Kentril soon found himself needing to hack his way through, but he took some pleasure in imagining each dismembered branch or vine as the spellcaster's neck.

Then, without any warning, the jungle gave way. The early evening sun lit up the landscape before him as it had not done in two weeks. Kentril found himself staring at a series of high, jagged peaks, the beginnings of the vast chain running up and down the length of Kehjistan and heading even farther east for as far as the eye could see.

And in the distance, just above the eastern base of a particularly tall and ugly peak at the very southern tip of this particular chain, lay the weatherworn, jumbled remains of a once mighty city. The fragments of a great stone wall encircling the entire eastern side could still be made out. A few hardy structures maintained precarious stances within the city itself. One, possibly the home of the lost kingdom's ruler, stood perched atop a vast ledge, no doubt having once enabled the master of the realm to gaze down upon his entire domain.

Although the jungle had surrendered in part to this region, lush plants still covered much of the landscape and had, over time, invaded the ruins themselves. What they had not already covered, the elements had battered well. Erosion had ripped away part of the northern section of the wall and taken with it a good portion of the city. Farther in, a sizable chunk of the mountain had collapsed onto the interior of the city.

Kentril could not imagine that there would be much left intact anywhere inside. Time had taken its toll on this ancient place.

"That should assuage your anger a bit, Captain Dumon," Quov Tsin suddenly remarked, eyes fixed on the sight before them. "Quite a bit."

"What do you mean?" Lowering his sword, Kentril eyed the ruins with some discomfort. He felt as if he had just intruded upon a place where even ghosts moved with trepidation. "Is that it? Is that—"

" 'The Light among Lights'? The most pure of realms in all the history of the world, built upon the very slope of the towering mountain called Nymyr? Aye, captain, there it stands—and, for our needs, just in time, if my calculations hold true!"

Gasps came from behind Kentril. The other men had finally caught up, just in time to hear the sorcerer's words. They all knew the legends of the realm called the Light among Lights by the ancients, a place fabled to be the one kingdom where the darkness of Hell had feared to intrude. They all knew of its story, even as far away as the Western Kingdoms.

Here had been a city revered by those who followed the light. Here had stood a marvel, ruled by regal and kind lords who had guided the souls of all toward Heaven.

Here had been a kingdom so pure, stories had it that it had at last risen whole above the mortal plane, its inhabitants transcending mortal limitations, rising to join the angels.

"You see a sight worthy of the loss of your men, captain," the Vizjerei whispered, extending one bony hand toward the ruins. "For now you are one of the few fortunate ever to cast your eyes upon one of the wonders of the past—fabulous, lost *Ureh!*"

Two

She had alabaster skin devoid of even the slightest imperfection, long chestnut-red hair that fell well below her perfectly rounded shoulders, and eyes of the deepest emerald green. If not for the eastern cast of her facial features, he might have taken her for one of the tempestuous maidens of his own highland home.

She was beautiful, everything a weary, war-bitten adventurer like Kentril had dreamed of each night during the innocence of his youth—and still did to this very day.

A pity she had been dead for several hundred years.

Fingering the ancient brooch he had almost literally stumbled upon, Kentril surreptitiously studied his nearby companions. They continued their back-breaking labor in complete ignorance of his find, searching among the crumbled, foliage-enshrouded ruins for anything of value. So far, the treasure hunt had been an utter failure as far as Kentril had been concerned. Here they worked, fifteen men strong, in the midst of the remains of one of the most fabled cities of all, and the sum total for three days of hard effort had been a small sack of rusted, bent, and mostly broken items of dubious value. The intricately detailed brooch represented the greatest find yet, and even it would not pay for more than a fraction of their arduous journey to this bug-infested necropolis.

No one looked his way. Deciding that he had earned at least this one token, Kentril slipped the artifact into his belt pouch. As leader of the mercenaries, he would have been entitled to an extra share of all treasure anyway, so the scarred commander felt no qualms about what he did.

"Kentril?"

The captain bit back his startlement. Turning, he faced the one who had so stealthily approached him. Somehow, Gorst could always manage to move in silence when he chose to, despite his oxlike appearance.

Running one hand through his hair, Kentril tried to pretend that he had done nothing wrong. "Gorst! I thought you'd been helping our esteemed employer with his tools and calculating devices! What brings you here?"

"The magic man . . . he wants to see you, Kentril." Gorst had a smile on his round face. Magic fascinated him as it did many small children, and while so far the Vizjerei sorcerer had shown little in the way of spells, the brutish mercenary seemed to enjoy the incomprehensible and enigmatic devices and objects Quov Tsin had brought with him.

"Tell him I'll be along in a little bit."

"He wants to see you now," the bronzed figure returned, his tone that of one who could not understand why someone would not want to rush over immediately to find out what the Vizjerei desired. Gorst clearly believed that some wondrous spectacle of sorcery had to be imminent and any delay by his friend in returning to Tsin would only mean prolonging the waiting.

Knowing the futility of holding off and realizing suddenly that he had reason to talk to the Vizjerei, Captain Dumon shrugged. "All right. We'll go see the magic man."

As he started past Gorst, the giant abruptly asked, "Can I see it, Kentril?"

"See what?"

"What you found."

Kentril almost denied having found anything, but Gorst knew him better than anyone. With a slight grimace, he carefully withdrew the brooch and held it in his palm so that only the other mercenary could see he had anything at all.

Gorst gave him a wide grin. "Pretty."

"Listen—" Kentril began.

But the massive fighter had already started past him, leaving the captain to feel foolish about his attempted subterfuge. He never knew completely what Gorst thought, but it seemed that to his friend the matter of the brooch had been satisfied, and now they needed to move on. Gorst's "magic man" awaited them, obviously a far more interesting subject to the mercenary leader's companion than any picture of a centuries-dead female.

They found Tsin impatiently scurrying around a display of stones, alchemaic devices, and other tools of his disreputable trade. Every now and then, the balding sorcerer would scribble notes on a parchment atop the makeshift desk his hired crew had put together early on. He seemed especially interested this day in peering through an eyeglass pointed at the very tip of Nymyr, then consulting a tattered scroll. As they approached, Kentril heard him chuckle with glee, then resort to the scroll again.

The Vizjerei reached for a device that most resembled to the mercenary a sextant, save that the sorcerer had clearly made some changes in the design. As his bony fingers touched the object, Quov Tsin noticed the pair.

"Ah! Dumon! About time! And has your latest day's labor born any more fruit than the previous?"

"No . . . it's just as you said. So far, we've found little more than junk." Kentril chose not to mention the brooch. With his luck, Tsin would have found some relevance in the artifact and therefore confiscated it.

"No matter, no matter! I let you and your band search mostly to keep you out of my way until the final readings could be made. Of course, had you found anything, that would have been a plus, but in the long run, I am not bothered by the lack of success."

Perhaps the sorcerer had not been, but the mercenaries certainly grumbled. Kentril had promised his companions much based on the words of the Vizjerei, and the failure would hang more around his neck than even Tsin's.

"Listen, sorcerer," he muttered. "You paid us enough to get this madness underway, but you also made promises of a lot more. Myself, I could go home right now and be happy just to be out of this place, but the others expect much. You said that we'd find treasure—ample amounts of it—in this ancient ruin, but so far we've—"

"Yes, yes, yes! I've explained it all before! It is just not the proper time! Soon, though, soon!"

Kentril looked to Gorst, who shrugged. Turning his gaze back to the slight mage, Captain Dumon snarled, "You've told me some wild things, Vizjerei, and they keep getting wilder the longer this goes on! Why don't you explain once more to Gorst and me what you've got in mind, eh? And make it clear for once."

"That would be a waste of my time," the diminutive sorcerer grated. Seeing Kentril's expression darken further, he sighed in exasperation. "Very well, but this is the last I'll speak of it! You already know the legends of the piousness of those who lived in the city, so I'll not bother with retelling that. I'll go straight to the time of troubles—will that do?"

Propping himself against a large chunk of rubble once forming part of the great wall, Kentril folded his arms, then nodded. "Go from there. That's when your story starts getting a little too fantastic for my tastes."

"The mercenary's a critic." Nonetheless, Quov Tsin paused in his tasks and began the tale that Captain Dumon suspected he could hear a hundred times and still not completely fathom. "It began during a time . . . a time known to those of us versed in the arts and the battle between light and darkness . . . a time known as the *Sin War*."

Hardened as he had become over the years, Kentril could not help but shudder whenever the short Vizjerei muttered those last two words. Until he had met Tsin, he had never even heard such legends, but something about the mythic war of which his employer spoke filled the mercenary's head with visions of diabolic demons seeking to guide the mortal world down the path of corruption, leading all to Hell.

The Sin War had not been fought as normal wars, for it had been fought by

Heaven and Hell themselves. True, the archangels and demons stood opposing one another like two armies, but the battles most often took place behind the scenes, behind the eyes of mortals. The supposed war had also stretched hundreds of years—for what were years to immortal beings? Kingdoms had risen and fallen, fiends such as Bartuc, the Warlord of Blood, had come to power, then been defeated—and still the war had pressed on.

And early on in this struggle, wondrous Ureh had become a central battleground.

"All knew of Ureh's greatness in those days," the bald sorcerer went on. "A fount of light, the guiding force of good in those troubled days—which, of course, meant that it drew the attention not only of the archangels but of the lords of Hell themselves, the *Prime Evils.*"

The Prime Evils. Whatever land one had been born in, whether in the jungles of Kehjistan or the cooler, rockier realms of the Western Kingdoms, all knew of the Prime Evils, the three brothers who ruled Hell. Mephisto, Lord of Hatred, master of undead. Baal, Lord of Destruction, bringer of chaos.

Diablo.

Diablo, perhaps the most feared, the ultimate manifestation of terror, the nightmare not only of children but of veteran warriors who had already seen the horrors men themselves could produce. Diablo it had been who had gazed most at bright Ureh from his monstrous domain, who had most been offended by its glorious existence. Order could be brought forth from the chaos created by Baal, and the hatred of Mephisto could be mastered by any man with strength, but to have no fear of fear itself—such a thing Diablo could not believe and would not stand.

"The lands around Ureh grew darker with each passing year, Captain Dumon. Creatures twisted by evil or born not of this world harried those who would journey to and from the city walls. Sinister magicks insinuated themselves where they could, barely driven back by the sorcerers of the kingdom."

And with each defeat by the peoples of Ureh, the Vizjerei added, Diablo grew more determined. He would bring down the wondrous city and make its inhabitants the slaves of Hell. All would see that no power on the mortal plane could withstand the most foul of the Prime Evils.

"It came to the point when no one dared travel to the city and few could escape it. It is said that then the lord of the realm, the just and kind Juris Khan, gathered his greatest priests and mages and decreed that they would do what they had to in order to save their people once and for all. Legend has it that Juris Khan had been granted a vision by an archangel, one who had declared to him that the powers above had seen the trials of their most honored followers and had felt moved to grant them the greatest of havens, so long as the humans put it upon themselves to reach it." Quov Tsin had an almost enraptured expression on his wizened face. "He offered the people of Ureh the very safety of Heaven itself."

Gorst grunted, his way of expressing his outright awe at these words.

Kentril held his peace, but he had trouble imagining such an offer. The archangel had opened the very gates of Heaven to the mortals of Ureh, opened to them a place where not even all three Prime Evils combined could have made the slightest incursion. All the people of Ureh had to do was find their way there.

"Some gesture," the mercenary captain interjected, not without some sarcasm. " 'Here we are, but you can find your own good way to get to us.' "

"You asked for the story, Dumon—do you want it or not? I've far more important things to do than entertain you."

"Go ahead, sorcerer. I'll try to keep my awe reined in."

With a disdainful sniff, Tsin said, "The archangel came twice more in Juris Khan's dreams, each time with the same promise and each time with some clues as to how this miracle could come to be . . ."

Guided by his visions, Lord Khan urged the sorcerers and priests to efforts such as none had ever conjectured before. The archangel had left what hints he could of what needed to be done, but the restrictions by which he existed forbade him from granting the mortals any more than that. Still, with the faith of Heaven behind them, Ureh dedicated its efforts to achieving this wondrous task. They knew what they had been offered, and they knew what fate likely would befall them if they failed.

"What little we know of that period comes from Gregus Mazi, the only inhabitant of Ureh to be found afterward. One of the circle of mages involved in the casting of the great spell, it is assumed by most scholars that at the last moment he must've faltered in his faith, for when the sorcerers and priests finally opened the way to Heaven—how is never said—Gregus Mazi was not taken with the rest."

"Hardly seems fair."

"From him," Quov Tsin went on, utterly ignoring Kentril, "we know that a tremendous red light enshrouded Ureh at that point, covering everything up to and including the very walls surrounding it. As Gregus—still heart-stricken at being left behind—watched, a second city seemed to rise above the first, an exact if ethereal twin of Ureh . . ."

Before the wide, unblinking eyes of the unfortunate sorcerer, the vast, phantasmal display hovered above its mortal shell. Even from where he stood, Gregus Mazi could see torchlight, could even see a few figures standing upon the ghostly battlements. To him, it had been as if the soul of Ureh had left the mortal plane, for when he glanced at the abandoned buildings around him, they had already begun to crumble and collapse, as if all they had been had been sucked from their very substance, leaving only swiftly decaying skeletons.

And as the lone figure looked up once more, he saw the shimmering city grow more insubstantial. The crimson aura flared, growing almost as bright as the sun that had set but moments before. Gregus Mazi had shielded his eyes for just a second—and in that second the glorious vision of a floating Ureh had faded away.

"Gregus Mazi was left a broken man, Captain Dumon. He was found by followers of Rathma, the necromancers of the deep jungle, and they cared for him until his mind had healed enough. He left them, then, an obsession already growing in his heart. He would join his family and friends yet. The sorcerer traveled all over the world in search of what he needed, for although he had been a part of the spellwork that had enabled the people of Ureh to ascend to Heaven, he had not known all of it."

"Get to the point, Tsin, the point of our being here at all."

"Cretin." With a scowl, the robed figure continued. "Twelve years after Ureh, Gregus Mazi returned to his abandoned homeland. In his wake he left scrolls and books, all indications of his studies. He left notes here and there, most of which I've tracked down. Twelve years after Ureh, Gregus Mazi came to the ruins . . . and simply vanished."

Kentril rubbed his mustache. He had a very real answer for the ancient sorcerer's fate. "An animal ate him, or he had an accident."

"I might have thought the same, my dear captain, if I had not early on in my efforts procured this."

Quov Tsin reached into a massive pouch where he kept his most valued notes and withdrew an old scroll. He held it out to Kentril, who reluctantly took it.

Captain Dumon unrolled it as gently as he could. The parchment was fragile and the script written on it badly faded, but with effort he could make it out. "This was written by a man from Westmarch!"

"Yes . . . the mercenary captain who journeyed with Gregus Mazi. I found it both ironic and perhaps telling that you approached me when I sent news of my offer to those who might be interested. I see it as fate that we two follow the tracks of my predecessor and this man."

"This man" proved to be one Humbart Wessel, a veteran fighter with a thankfully plain manner of writing. Kentril puzzled through the passages, at first finding nothing.

"Toward the bottom," Tsin offered.

The slim mercenary read over that part of the aged scroll, which Humbart Wessel had clearly written years after the fact.

On the seventh day, near dusk, the passage began, *Master Mazi again approached the edge of the ruins. Says I to him, that this quest's seen no good end and we should go, but he says he's certain this time. The shadow will touch at just the right angle. It has to.*

Master Mazi promised much gold to us and another offer none there'd take, however worthy any might think themselves. Fly up to Heaven . . . older now, I still wouldn't have taken it.

The shadow came like he said, Nymyr's hand reaching out for old Ureh. We watched, certain as before that we'd been on a fool's quest.

Aah, what fools we were to believe that!

I recall the shadow. I recall the shimmering. How the ruins suddenly looked alive again. How the lights glowed inside! Swear I still will that I heard the voices of folk, but couldn't see any!

"I'm coming . . ." Those were Master Mazi's last words, but not to us, though. I remember them still, and I remember how we thought we saw the glitter of the gold that he'd told us about again and again—but not one man would enter. Not one man would follow. Master Mazi went it alone.

We camped there, hearing the voices, hearing some of them call to us, it seemed. None of us would go, though. Tomorrow, I says to the others, tomorrow when Master Mazi comes out and shows all's well, we'll go in and get our fill. One night, it won't matter.

And in the morning, all we saw were ruins. No lights. No voices.

No Master Mazi.

Lord Hyram, I writ this down like I agreed and it goes to the Zakarum—

Captain Dumon turned the scroll over, looking for more.

"You'll see nothing. What little was left beyond this passage speaks of other matters and was of no concern to me. Only this page."

"A few scribbled lines by an old warrior? This brought us all the way here?" Kentril felt like tossing the parchment back into Tsin's ugly face.

"Cretin," Quov Tsin repeated. "You see words but cannot read past them. Don't you trust one of your own?" He waved a gnarled hand. "Never mind! That was just to show the one point. Gregus Mazi found a way to the Ureh of old, the Ureh he had lost twelve years before—and we can do the very same!"

Kentril recalled the line about gold, the selfsame gold that had lured him into this foolishness in the first place. However, he also recalled how Humbart Wessel and his men had been too frightened to go after it once the opportunity had finally presented itself. "I've no desire to go to Heaven just yet, sorcerer."

The diminutive Tsin snorted. "Nor have I! Gregus Mazi was welcome to that path, but I seek earthier rewards. Once they had ascended, the people of Ureh would not need the items they had collected in their mortal lives. Any valuables, books of spells, talismans . . . those would have been left behind."

"Then why haven't we found anything?"

"The clues are in the manuscript of Humbart Wessel! For these living mortals to ascend, Juris Khan and his sorcerers had to cast a spell like no other. They had to bridge the gap between this plane and that of Heaven. In doing so, they created a place in between—in the form of this shadow Ureh that Gregus found again years later!"

Captain Dumon tried desperately to follow the mage's reasoning. The gold that he had been promised existed not in these ruins but rather in the floating vision described by the previous mercenary leader, the ghostly city.

He glanced at the rubble, all that remained of physical Ureh. "But how can we possibly reach such a place, even if it does exist? You said it isn't part of our world, but in between ours and—and—"

"And Heaven, yes," finished the Vizjerei. He returned to his devices, peering through one. "It took Gregus Mazi more than a decade to do it, but because of him, my own calculations took but three years once I had the proper information. I know exactly when it will all occur!"

"It's coming back again?"

Tsin's eyes widened, and he gave Kentril an incredulous look. "Of course! Have you not been paying attention to anything I have said?"

"But—"

"I have told you more than enough now, Captain Dumon, and I really must return to my work! Try not to bother me again unless it is absolutely necessary, is that understood?"

Gritting his teeth, Kentril straightened. "You summoned me, Vizjerei."

"Did I? Oh, yes, of course. That's what I wanted to tell you. It is tomorrow evening."

More and more the slim captain began to wonder if he and Quov Tsin actually spoke the same language. "*What's* tomorrow evening, sorcerer?"

"What we were just speaking of, cretin! The shadow comes tomorrow evening, an hour before night!" Tsin glanced again at his notes. "Make that an hour and a quarter to be safe."

"An hour and a quarter . . ." the captain murmured, dumbstruck.

"Exactly so! Run along now!" The bald Vizjerei became enmeshed in his work once more. Watching him, Kentril realized that the slight figure had already completely forgotten the presence of the two fighters. The only thing that mattered to Quov Tsin, the only thing that *existed* for him, was lost, legendary Ureh.

Kentril retreated from the vicinity of the wizened mage, thoughts racing. Now he knew that he had indeed followed a madman. All the talk of gold in the past had made the captain assume that Tsin actually meant that the wealth of the city had been secreted in some cache whose whereabouts could be ascertained only by the direction of the shadows at some point of the day. He had never truly understood that the Vizjerei had literally hunted a ghost realm, a place not of this world.

I've brought us here to chase phantoms . . .

But what if Tsin were right? What if the legend of the city had any grain of truth? Heaven had no need of gold. Perhaps, as the sorcerer had claimed, it had all been left behind, there for the taking.

Yet, Humbart Wessel had been offered the opportunity, and not one man of his had risked the shadowed kingdom.

Kentril Dumon's hand slipped to his belt pouch, removing from it the elegant brooch he had discovered. For the woman it depicted, he would gladly have journeyed into Ureh, but, failing that, some bit of valuable jewelry from her household or that of another wealthy citizen of the fabled realm would satisfy him just as much.

It was not as if any of the owners would still need them.

*   *   *

Zayl watched the band of mercenaries from his position atop the crumbling guard tower with much trepidation. The men below moved about the ruins like a small but determined swarm of ants. They went through every crevice, searched under every boulder, and even though they obviously met with meager success, they pushed on.

Pale of skin and with a studious expression more suited to a clerk in a shipping house than to a well-trained and well-versed necromancer, Zayl had observed the newcomers since their arrival. None of his readings had predicted the coming of these intruders, and at such a critical juncture Zayl felt this no mere coincidence.

Ureh had always been treated most gingerly by the followers of Rathma, who had sensed in it some delicately held balance among the various planes of existence. Zayl knew the legends as well as anyone and knew a little of the true history behind them. Ureh had always drawn him, much to the displeasure and dismay of his mentors. They believed him enchanted by the notion of the astonishing spells utilized and the power one might wield if one learned how to recreate them. After all, the sorcerers of the ancient land had blurred the lines between life and death far more than any necromancer could have ever dreamed. In fact, if the legends spoke true, then the people of Ureh had bypassed death altogether, which went against everything in the teachings of Rathma.

Zayl, however, did not desire to relearn the secrets of those mages—not that he had bothered to tell his teachers that fact. No, the plain-faced necromancer who now watched the mercenaries through almond-shaped eyes of gray desired something entirely different.

Zayl sought to commune with the archangels themselves—and the power behind them.

"Like rats hunting for garbage," mocked a high-pitched voice from his side.

Without looking at the speaker, the necromancer replied, "I was thinking more of ants."

"Rats is what they are, I say . . . and I should know, for didn't they gnaw off my legs and arms, then burrow through my chest for good measure? This bunch has the same look to 'em as those beasts did!"

"They should not be here at this time. They should have stayed away. That would have been common sense."

Zayl's companion laughed, a hollow sound. "I didn't have enough sense even though I knew better!"

"You had no choice. Once so touched by Ureh, you had to come back eventually." The hooded necromancer peered beyond the mercenaries, surveying the region from which their apparent captain had just come. "There is a sorcerer with them. He has not stepped out into the open since he came here, but I can sense him."

"Smells that awful, does he? Wish I still had a nose."

"I sense his power . . . and I know he senses mine, although he may not realize the source." Zayl slipped back a little, then rose. The grave robbers would not be able to see him from their much lower vantage points. "Neither he nor his paid underlings must interfere."

"What do you plan to do?"

The black-clad form did not answer. Instead, he reached for a small array of objects previously positioned by his side. Into a pouch he kept handy at his belt went a dagger carved from ivory, two candles nearly burned down to wax puddles, a small vial containing a thick, crimson liquid—and the human skull, minus jaw, that had been the centerpiece of the display.

"Gently now," mocked the skull. "We're quite a height up! I wouldn't want to be repeating that fall again!"

"Quiet, Humbart." Zayl placed the macabre artifact in the pouch, then strung the latter shut. Finished with his task, he took one last look at the treasure hunters below and pondered their fates.

One way or another, they could not be permitted to be here tomorrow evening—for their sakes as well as his own.

THREE

"Cap'n Dumon . . ."

Kentril rolled over in his sleep, trying to find comfort on the rocky ground beneath his blanket. Only Quov Tsin had a tent, the mercenaries more accustomed to dealing with the elements. Yet the area around the ruins of Ureh seemed the most disturbing, most awkward of places to try to rest even for such hardened fighters. Throughout the camp, the captain's tossing and turning were duplicated by every man save Gorst, who most believed could slumber peacefully on a bed of thorns.

"Cap'n Dumon . . ."

"Mmm? Wha—?" Kentril stirred, pushing himself slowly up on one elbow. "Who's there?"

The nearly full moon shone with such brightness that it took little time for his eyes to adjust to the night. Kentril looked around, noted the snoring forms around the low fires. From the sorcerer's tent, the snoring sounded particularly loud.

"Damned place . . ." The mercenary lowered his head again. He would be glad when they abandoned the ruins. Not even the field of battle left him so on edge.

"Cap'n Dumon . . ."

Kentril rolled off his blanket, hand already on the hilt of the dagger he always wore on his belt. The hair on the back of his neck stiffened, and a cold chill washed over the mercenary leader as he focused on a figure only a few feet to his right, a figure who had not been standing there a second before.

Of itself, that discovery might not have bothered the captain, for he himself could move with the utmost stealth. However, what did unnerve him so very much, even to the point where the dagger nearly fell from his shaking fingers, had to do with the fact that the one who faced him could be none other than the hapless *Hargo*.

Faced might have been an inappropriate and unfortunate choice of terms, for Hargo no longer had a good portion of his. The right side of his head had been ripped away, exposing skull and rotting muscle. One eye had been completely lost, a deep red and black crater all that remained. The mercenary's bedraggled beard framed a mouth curled open to reveal death's grin, and the eye that did remain stared almost accusingly at Kentril.

The rest of Hargo had fared no better. The right arm had been gnawed away just below the shoulder and the chest and stomach torn wide open, revealing ribs, guts, and more. Only tatters of clothes still existed, emphasizing even more the horrific fate of the man.

"Cap'n Dumon . . ." rasped the monstrous visitor.

Now the dagger did slip, Kentril's fingers limp. He glanced around, but no one else had been disturbed by this monstrous vision. The others all slumbered away.

"Har-Hargo?" he finally managed.

"Cap'n Dumon . . ." The corpse shambled forward a couple of steps, water from the river still dripping from the half-devoured form. *"You shouldn't be here . . ."*

As far as Kentril had suddenly become concerned, he should have been back in Westmarch, drinking himself into a stupor at his favorite tavern. Anywhere in the world but where he now stood.

"You gotta leave, cap'n," Hargo continued, ignorant of the fact that his own throat had a gaping hole in the side and therefore should not have let him even speak. *"There's death in this place. It got me, and it'll get you all . . . all of you . . ."*

As he warned Kentril, the ravaged figure raised the one good arm he had left, pointing at his captain. The moon accented the pale, deathly sheen of Hargo's corpse and the rot already taking place even on the otherwise untouched appendage.

"What do you mean?" Dumon managed. "What do you mean?"

But Hargo only repeated his warning. *"It'll kill you all. Just like me, cap'n . . . Take you all dead just like me . . ."*

And with that, the corpse raised his face to the moonlit heaven and let out a blood-chilling cry full of regret and fear.

A brave man, Kentril still broke. He fell to his knees, his hands over his ears in a pathetic attempt to keep the heart-jolting sound out. Tears streamed from his eyes, and he looked earthward, no longer able to face the ghastly sight before him.

The cry came to an abrupt halt.

Still holding his ears, the mercenary captain dared to glance up—

—and awoke.

"Aaah!" Kentril scrambled from his bedroll, tossing aside his blanket and stumbling to his feet. Only as he straightened did he realize that all around him his men acted in similar fashion, shouts of dismay and wild looks abounding. Two men had swords free and now swung them madly about, risking injuring their fellows. One hardy fighter sat still, eyes wide and unblinking, body shivering.

From more than one Kentril heard whispered or shouted a single name . . . the name of *Hargo*.

"I saw 'im!" gasped Oskal. "Standin' before me as big as life!"

"Nuthin' live about him!" snarled another. "Death himself couldn'ta looked worse!"

"It was a warning!" Benjin declared. "He wants us out of here now!" The fighter reached down for his bedroll. "Well, I'm all for that!"

Seeing his men in disarray brought Captain Dumon back to his senses. Whatever fearful message Hargo might or might not have delivered, common sense still dictated certain cautions.

"Hold it right there!" the fair-haired officer shouted. "No one goes anywhere!"

"But cap'n," protested Oskal. "You saw him, too! I can see it plain in your face!"

"Maybe so, but that's no reason to go fleeing into the jungle, the better to end up like Hargo did, eh?"

This bit of truth struck all of them. Oskal dropped his blanket, eyes briefly shifting to the murky landscape to the south. Benjin shivered.

"What do you say, Gorst?" Kentril's second appeared the most calm of the band, although even he had a perturbed expression on his generally cheerful countenance. Still, it did Captain Dumon some good to see that Gorst had not fallen prey to the panic of the others.

"Better here," grunted the massive figure. "Not out there."

"You hear that? Even Gorst wouldn't venture back into the jungle right now! Any of you think you'd survive better?"

He had them back under control now. No one wanted to reenter that hellish place, at least not in the dark. Even the almost full moon would do little to illuminate the many dangers of the jungle.

Kentril nodded. "We'll decide better come morning. Now, sheathe those weapons! Put some order back into this camp, and build up those fires!"

They moved to obey, especially in regard to the last command. Kentril noted them beginning to relax as the familiarity of the routine took hold. He felt certain that the nightmare would soon fade some in the veterans' minds.

Men in their line of work often suffered bad dreams. Kentril himself still experienced nightmares of his first campaign, when his commander and nearly all those in the squad had been slaughtered before his very eyes. Only luck had saved him then, but the memories of that terrible time remained clear.

Yet this horrific dream stood out even from those recurring torments, for Kentril had not suffered it alone. Everyone had experienced it at the same time, in the same way. He had no doubt that if he questioned each man, they would all describe the details in more or less the exact manner.

A harsh, cutting sound suddenly brought back vestiges of the fearful vision. Kentril had his hand on the hilt of his dagger before he realized that what he had just heard had been, in reality, the sound of *snoring*.

Quov Tsin's snoring.

The Vizjerei had slept through not only the dream but the panic ensuing afterward. In utter disbelief, Captain Dumon started toward the tent, only to pause at the last moment. What good would it do to look upon the sleeping sorcerer or, for that matter, to wake him? Tsin would only sputter denigrating words at the captain, then demand to know why he had been disturbed.

Kentril backed away. He could imagine the Vizjerei's wrinkled face tightening into an expression of deep contempt once the spellcaster heard the reason. Big, brave mercenaries frightened by a nightmare? Quov Tsin would laugh at such fear, mock Dumon and his men.

No, Kentril would let sleeping sorcerers lie. Tomorrow, however, he would inform their employer that the mercenaries had no intention of waiting for the gold of Ureh to come falling from the sky. Tomorrow morning, Kentril's band would be leaving.

After all, how much gold could dead men spend?

Just into the jungle and well out of sight of the camp, the damp, shambling form of Hargo paused. Branches and leaves stirred up by the night wind fluttered through the ghastly form, unhindered by the rotting flesh and gnawed bone. The lone eye stared sightlessly ahead, and the mouth hung open, revealing a blackened tongue and gums.

From atop a tall, gnarled tree, Zayl looked down upon the ghoulish shade. In his hand the pale necromancer held a tiny talisman shaped like a dragon around which had been wrapped a piece of torn material.

"Your mission is done," he quietly informed the ghost. "Rest easy now, friend."

Hargo turned his gaze up toward the necromancer—and faded away.

"Not the most talkative fellow," remarked the skull from the branch upon which Zayl had propped it. "Me, I think death needs to have a little life to spice it up, eh?"

"Be quiet, Humbart." The slim necromancer slipped the bit of fabric off the talisman, putting the latter then within the confines of his cloak. The cloth he studied for a moment.

"You think them boys'll get the point?"

"I should hope so. I went through much trouble for this." And, indeed, Zayl had. He had smelled the death of the one mercenary even from his vantage point near the ruins. That had enabled him to track the death to its point of origin, and there Zayl had searched the area around the river for some time for any vestiges of the late, lamented Hargo. The necromancer had been rewarded with this scrap of garment, but only after dodging the hungry senses of the very beast that had taken the man.

A bit of flesh, a few drops of blood . . . those would have served Zayl better, but the cloth had come from the body of the dead, had been worn for so long close to his skin that it had contained link enough to its wearer for the summoning. Zayl had wanted only to touch the sleeping minds of the other mercenaries, use their dead comrade to scare them into leaving Ureh before it became too late. Hargo's shade had performed his task to perfection. The necromancer felt certain that the fighters would flee the area come the first hints of sun.

He had not even bothered to try the spell on the Vizjerei. Not only would it have been a waste of time, but the sorcerer's defensive spells, active even during his sleep, might have warned of Zayl's presence. That could not be condoned.

"He will have to leave if they do," the ebony-clad figure muttered to himself. "He will have to." Living mostly alone, necromancers had a habit of talking much to themselves. Even after finding Humbart Wessel's remains two years before and animating the skull, Zayl had been unable to break his old habit.

Humbart did not care whether the other spoke to himself or to the skull; he answered as he felt, which meant often. "That was a mighty fine piece of work, that was," he interjected. "And maybe that'll send the sorcerer packing, too—but only if the fighters do leave, you know."

"Of course, they will leave. After an omen such as that, experienced by all, they would be fools otherwise."

"But come the morning, my not-so-worldly friend, the sweet murmurs of gold can easily outshout the rasping warnings of a nightmare! Think you I came back for the lovely weather and the playful serpents of the river? Ha! Mark me, Zayl! If they don't leave at daybreak, they won't be leaving at all!" The jawless skull chuckled.

Letting the scrap fall to the jungle floor, the necromancer nodded solemnly. "Let us pray you are wrong, Humbart."

The men readied themselves, lining up for inspection by their captain. Looks of unease still branded the visages of many, unease combined with growing uncertainty. They had all come far, risked their lives for promised gold and jewels. To go back now would mean to go back empty-handed.

But at least they would be able to go back. No one desired Hargo's fate.

Kentril stood determined to lead his men out of here. The others might waver in their decisions, but he knew a true harbinger of danger when he saw it. As he finished his inspection, his hand grazed the pouch in which he carried the brooch. At least he had that more soothing memory to bring back with him.

Quov Tsin exited his tent just as Kentril steeled himself for the confrontation. The short sorcerer blinked as he stepped out into the sunshine, then noticed the officer coming toward him.

"Today is the day, Dumon! The secrets, the riches of Ureh, today they shall be open to us!"

"Tsin—we're leaving."

The silver-gray eyes narrowed even more than normal. "What's that you say?"

"We're leaving. We won't stay in this cursed place." The captain chose not to tell his employer just why.

"Don't be absurd! One, two more days, and you'll be able to leave here all of you as rich as kings!"

This brought a couple of murmurs from the men, who had been watching the two from the distance. Captain Dumon silently cursed. Here he was trying to save all their lives, and already the hint of gold had staked a claim in the hearts of some. How quickly some could forget.

"We're leaving. That's all there is to it."

"You've been paid—"

"Only enough to get you here. We've no more obligation to you, Vizjerei, and you've nothing you could possibly give us."

The sorcerer opened his mouth to speak, then abruptly shut it. Kentril, expecting the usual tirades, found himself slightly disconcerted. Still, perhaps he had convinced Tsin of the uselessness of arguing.

"If that is your choice, so be it." The diminutive figure suddenly turned back to his tent. "If you will excuse yourselves, I've much work to do."

As he watched Quov Tsin vanish again, Kentril frowned. He had successfully faced the sorcerer. His pact with the Vizjerei had been severed. The captain and his men could leave right now if they so chose.

So why did his own feet move with such sluggishness?

We will be leaving! he silently roared at himself. Turning to the others, Kentril shouted, "Get your packs ready! I want us on the path back home within the next few minutes! Understood?"

Under his stern gaze and commanding tone, the mercenaries hurried to break camp. As he gathered his own things, Captain Dumon glanced now and then toward the tent of his soon-to-be former employer. Never once, though, did the Vizjerei poke his bald head out. Kentril wondered whether the sorcerer might be sulking or had simply begun his preparations for the supposed spectacle. It bothered him slightly to leave Tsin alone here, but if the Vizjerei chose to stay even with everyone else abandoning Ureh, the captain would not waste any more time on him. The men came first.

In short order, the mercenaries stood prepared to march. Gorst grinned at Kentril, who opened his mouth to give the order to move out.

A rumble from the south froze the words on his very lips.

He looked over his shoulder to see dark clouds rolling toward them from the direction of the jungle. Black as pitch, the thick, angry clouds roared over the landscape at a phenomenal pace. The wind picked up nearby, growing to near hurricane proportions in the space of a few breaths. Lightning played across the sky. A dust storm arose, turning the camp into chaos.

"Find shelter!" Kentril looked around quickly, saw that, other than the crumbling city, there stood nothing around that could protect him and his men from what would surely be a titanic assault by the elements. With much reluctance, he waved for the others to follow him.

At a section of the outer wall that had some years past collapsed, the mercenary band slipped into ruined Ureh, paying no more mind to the once fabulous architecture than they had during their earlier treasure forays. Kentril quickly spotted a rounded building three stories in height and judged it to be among the most stable in the vicinity. He led the rest there, and the fighters huddled inside, waiting for the blast to come.

An ocean of rain swamped the area almost as soon as the mercenaries found cover. Jagged bolts shot dangerously close to their location. Rumbles of thunder shook the building as if an army of catapults assaulted it. Dust and bits of masonry dropped from the ceiling.

Seated near the entrance, Kentril fought to turn his mind from the horrendous storm. The thunder and lightning once more brought back the memories of earlier battles and comrades lost. In desperation, he finally slipped the brooch out, holding it hidden in one hand while he stared at the perfect face and dreamed.

One hour passed. Two. Three. Still the dire storm did not let up. Unable to make a fire, the mercenaries sat in small groups, some trying to slumber, others talking among themselves.

More time passed—and then Gorst, blinking, suddenly asked a question that Kentril realized he himself should have asked long, long ago. "Where's the magic man?"

In all their haste, the motley band had not even bothered to think about the Vizjerei. As little as he cared for the man, Kentril could not leave the sorcerer out there. Thrusting the brooch back into its pouch, he surveyed the others, then decided that it remained up to him to find out the truth.

Rising, he looked at his second. "Gorst. You keep the others under control. I'll be back as soon as possible."

The torrential rain showed no sign of letting up as he stood in the doorway. Swearing at his own burdensome sense of decency, Captain Dumon raced out into the storm.

The wind nearly buffeted him back inside. Despite such terrible resistance, though, he struggled through the ruins, finding some meager protection along the way.

At the gap in the outer wall, the captain paused. A bolt of lightning struck the rocky ground just ahead, pelting him with bits of stone and clay. As the earthy shower ended, Kentril took a deep breath and stepped from the relative safety of Ureh.

Squinting through drenched eyes, he searched for the sorcerer's tent.

There it stood, seemingly unaffected whatsoever by the rampaging elements. The flimsy tent looked remarkably untouched, as if not even the slightest wind blew nor a single drop of rain had alighted onto it. Despite his own lamentable situation, Kentril paused again and stared, disbelieving.

Another bolt struck near. Common sense revived, Kentril charged toward the tent, fighting the storm with as much ferocity as he would have any other foe. Twice he slipped, but each time the captain leapt back to his feet. As Kentril reached Quov Tsin's abode, he shouted out the sorcerer's name, but no one answered.

Lightning ravaged the area. Rain and rock assaulting him, Kentril Dumon finally threw himself into the tent—

"And what exactly do you think you're doing?"

Bent over a scroll and seemingly unaffected by the storm raging around him, the wrinkled Vizjerei eyed Kentril as if he had just grown a second head.

"I came . . . to see if you're all right," the soldier lamely replied. Tsin looked as if he had just risen from a long, refreshing nap, while Kentril felt as if he had just swum the entire length of one of the dank jungle rivers.

"Such concern! And why shouldn't I be?"

"Well, the storm—"

The sorcerer's brow furrowed slightly. "What storm?"

"The huge one raging out—" The mercenary captain stopped. In the tent, he could no longer hear the roar of thunder, the howl of the wind. Even the heavy rain left not the slightest patter on the fabric.

"If there's a storm out there," Quov Tsin remarked dryly, "shouldn't you be wet?"

Kentril glanced down and saw that no moisture covered his boots, his pants. He stared at hands devoid of rain, and when he reached up to touch his head, only a few droplets of sweat gave any hint of dampness.

"I was soaked to the bone!"

"The humidity here can be very harsh at times, especially in the jungle, but you look fairly well to me, Dumon."

"But outside—" The captain whirled toward the entrance, thrusting aside the tent flaps so that both could witness the horrific weather beyond.

A sunlit day greeted Kentril's dumbstruck eyes.

"Did you come all the way back here because of this mythical storm, Dumon?" the dwarfish spellcaster asked, his expression guarded.

"We never left camp, Tsin . . . it started just after we'd packed up!"

"So, then, where are the others?"

"Taking . . . protection . . . in the ruins . . ." Even as he said it, Kentril felt his embarrassment growing. More than a dozen veteran fighters now huddled inside a building, for the past several hours trying to shield themselves from—a cloudless sky?

But it *had* stormed . . .

Yet when he looked around for any sign of the deluge, Kentril saw nothing. The rocky ground appeared parched, not a single droplet to be seen. The wind blew strong, but only at a fraction of the velocity that he recalled from earlier. Even his own body betrayed his beliefs, for how to explain the relative dryness of his clothes, his very skin?

"Hmmph."

Captain Dumon turned to find Quov Tsin drawn up to his full height. The sorcerer had his arms crossed, his expression one of growing bemusement.

"Dipping into the rum rations before leaving, Dumon? I'd thought better of you in at least that regard."

"I'm not drunk."

The robed figure waved off his protest. "That's neither here nor there now, captain. We've a more important matter to discuss. Since you and yours have decided to be here after all, we should make plans. The hour approaches rapidly . . ."

"The hour—" Realizing what Tsin referred to, Kentril made a quick calculation. With the time his men had already lost, they would not get very far. Even if they had started off as planned, the mercenaries would have barely made what he considered a safe place to camp by sundown.

Yet if they stayed one more night here, they might be able to go back with something to show for their misfortunes.

But did they want to stay even one more night in a place where the dead invaded one's dreams and monstrous rain storms appeared and vanished in the blink of an eye?

Before Kentril could come to any conclusion of his own, Tsin made it for him. "Now, run along and gather your men, Dumon," the sorcerer ordered. "I've a few outside calculations to make. Come back in a couple of hours, and I'll inform you of what must be done. We must time this right, after all . . ."

With that, Quov Tsin turned his back on the tall fighter, once more becoming engrossed in his curious tasks. Still at a loss, Kentril blinked, then reluctantly stepped outside. He took one last look around for any sign of the storm, then started back to Ureh, hoping all the while that by deciding to stay a little longer he had not made a terrible mistake.

Only when Kentril had already reached the broken wall did it occur to him that the Vizjerei might have been too calm, too relaxed, when told about the tempest. Only then did he wonder if perhaps the sorcerer had known more about it than he had revealed, if perhaps the timeliness of the storm, not to mention its abrupt end, had been no coincidence.

But Tsin had never shown such power . . . unless everything the fighters had experienced had been nothing more than illusion. Still, even that would have required great skill, for not one of Captain Dumon's men had seen through it.

A shout came from the building in which he had left Gorst and the others. The huge, shirtless mercenary waved at Kentril, grinning as usual. He seemed not at all bothered by the peculiar finish to the rain.

The captain decided to say nothing about his concerns . . . for now. At the very least, he and the others still had a chance of coming out of this with some profit. Surely, then, one more night in the vicinity of Ureh would not matter.

They could always leave tomorrow . . .

Kentril's quick talk of the possibility of yet garnering some profit from their venture rapidly eradicated any apprehensions caused by the unsettling weather. They all understood, as he did, that a late start into the jungle would not be a good thing, but they understood even more that by waiting the one night, they might leave with their packs filled with treasure. The fears of the previous eve became more and more simply a bad dream, replaced gradually by visions of gold and jewels.

And so, just before the appointed hour, the captain positioned his men as requested and turned to the sorcerer, who had made still more last-minute calculations. The shadow of the mountain Nymyr had already stretched forth its fingers over much of fallen Ureh, but Tsin had informed him again that only when it touched the entire city in just a certain way would they all be rewarded for their waiting.

Finally lifting his head from the scrolls, the Vizjerei announced, "It is time."

Like a plague of black ants, the shadow spread faster and faster. A sense of unease once more enveloped Kentril, but he held his position. Soon, very soon . . .

"*Basara Ty Komi . . .*" chanted Quov Tsin. "*Basara Yn Alli!*"

Kentril's body tingled, as if some powerful force had spread over him. He glanced at the others and saw that they, too, felt it. To their credit, however, none moved from his location.

Together, the party formed a crude, five-sided form, with the sorcerer in the very middle. Both the pattern and the unintelligible words spoken by Tsin had been gleaned from the works of Gregus Mazi, and with them the ancient spellcaster had supposedly reopened the corridor by which he had finally joined the other blessed inhabitants of the city. None now desired to take that same path to its ultimate conclusion, but if enough earthly belongings lay scattered along the trail, so to speak, every man would feel very, very blessed indeed.

"*Gazara! Wendo Ty Ureh! Magri! Magri!*"

The air felt charged with what could only be described as pure magical energy. Clouds began to form over the shadowed kingdom, dark ones that did not remind Kentril so much of Heaven as of that other realm. Still, if the words had worked once, they surely would work again . . .

Arms stretched toward the ruins, Quov Tsin shouted, "*Lucin Ahn! Lucin—*"

"In the name of the Balance," someone broke in, "I charge you to cease this effort before you cause great calamity!"

Tsin faltered. The mercenaries turned as one, some reaching for blades. Kentril bit back the yelp he had been about to make and glared at the fool who had interrupted at such a crucial moment.

A slim figure clad completely in black eyed them all with the arrogance reserved for those who did not just believe themselves superior in all ways but *knew* it to be truth. Plain of face and younger than the captain by more than a few years, the intruder would not have disturbed Kentril if not for two things. One had to do with the slanted eyes, so unearthly a gray color that they seized the attention of all who looked into them. Yet almost immediately those same eyes repelled, for in them Kentril sensed his own mortality, not something any mercenary desired to come to know.

The second had to do with the garments he wore, for while many folk favored black, the dark robe and cloak of the stranger had upon them tiny patterns, markings of which Captain Dumon had some past knowledge. Each symbol represented an aspect of the afterlife, including those shunned by most.

As the intruder marched toward him, Kentril also caught glimpses of a dagger at the other's belt, one unlike those the mercenaries carried. This dagger had been carved, not forged, and even from where he stood, Kentril could guess that it had been made from the purest ivory.

The man was a necromancer, the most feared of spellcasters . . .

"Take good sense and leave here now!" the black-clad figure cried out. "Only death awaits in those troubled ruins!"

Oskal started to retreat, but a look from the captain put him in his place again.

"*Ques Ty Norgu!*" replied Quov Tsin with a sneer. Ignoring the warnings of the necromancer, he gestured a final time at the remains of the once proud city. "*Protasi! Ureh! Protast!*"

The sky rumbled. The wind swirled and roared, changing direction each second. Kentril saw the necromancer fall to one knee, a hand touching the ivory dagger. Despite the gathering clouds, the shadow that had been enshrouding the fabled realm seemed, if anything, stronger, more distinct.

Lightning flashed . . . lightning from places in the heavens where no clouds yet floated.

"*Ureh!*" screamed the wrinkled Vizjerei. "*Ureh Aproxos!*"

Three bolts shot forth, striking one another simultaneously over the ruins. The men cringed, and one or two even let out gasps.

And when the lightning ceased and the rumbling faded, Kentril stared at last at what Quov Tsin had wrought, stared at the culmination of the weeks of sweat, even of blood. He eyed Ureh, the legendary city, the *Light among Lights*, and finally blurted, "*Well?*"

The ruins had not changed.

FOUR

✳

"I don't understand!" Tsin fairly shrieked. "I don't understand!"

Ureh remained untouched, the same crumbling skeleton that the party had first come across. The clouds, the lightning, the wind—all had died or faded away. Only the immense shadow cast by Nymyr still lay claim to the ancient kingdom, and with each passing second it tightened its grip, sinking Ureh deeper and deeper into darkness.

"Him!" The Vizjerei poked a gnarled finger at the necromancer. "It was him! He caused it all to go astray! He interrupted at the time most crucial!"

"My interruption," responded the studious-looking figure, "did nothing, I regret to say." Despite his dire warnings and his clear attempt to get the others to flee, to Kentril even he seemed a bit disappointed by the lack of any fantastic change in Ureh. "I am as mystified as you."

With no apparent reason remaining for them to stay in position, the mercenaries swarmed around the necromancer. Even Gorst, who found the Vizjerei sorcerer fascinating, studied the other spellcaster with little enthusiasm. All knew how the necromancers trafficked with the dead, blurred the lines between the mortal world and the afterlife.

His own sword drawn, Captain Dumon confronted the arrogant intruder. "Who are you? How long've you been spying on us?"

"My name is Zayl." He stared down the length of Kentril's blade as if unconcerned. "This is my home."

"That doesn't answer my second question . . ." The mercenary leader hesitated, his mind suddenly racing. Necromancers toyed with the dead. Could that mean—

Suddenly certain he knew the truth, Kentril put the tip of his blade just under Zayl's jaw. "It was you! You sent Hargo's ghost into our dreams, didn't you? You sent that warning to get us to leave!"

At this, the other fighters grew incensed. Tsin, standing slightly back, cocked his head, studying his rival spellcaster with more interest.

"I did what had to be done . . . at least, I thought so at the time."

"So!" announced Tsin. "You, too, felt certain that the path opened by Gregus Mazi could be reopened this day! I thought so!"

Kentril heard a slight chuckle, but one that did not seem to come from the direction of any of his men. Zayl's hand slipped momentarily to a large, bulging pouch at his side, which looked as if it contained a melon or some similarly shaped object. When the necromancer noted the captain's interest, he casually pulled his hand away.

"I had my confidence in that fact," Zayl reluctantly agreed. "As unfounded, it seems, as all your research."

"So there's no gold?" Benjin asked mournfully.

Kentril scowled at the other mercenary. "Shut up. As for you"—he tapped Zayl's throat with the sword tip—"I think you know even more than you're saying."

"Undoubtedly true, captain," added Quov Tsin. "It would be best if you kept this creature under guard, even bound, perhaps. Yes, that would be the right course, I think."

For once Kentril found himself in utter agreement with his employer. Everyone knew that necromancers could not be trusted. Zayl might already have a poison or potion just up his sleeve.

In the course of their brief conversation, the shadow of the mountain had continued to stretch forth, so much so that now it even began to blanket the party. A chill wind arose as the shadow settled on them, one that made some of the mercenaries shake. Zayl's cloak began to flutter wildly, and Kentril had to tighten the collar of his shirt.

"Nymyr has a cold touch," the necromancer commented. "If you plan to stay near Ureh, you had best be better dressed."

"What's the point?" Oskal muttered. "Buncha rocks and empty tombs! All this way for nothin' . . ."

"We're gonna need more than cloaks," agreed another fighter. "This gets any darker, we'll even need torches!"

Indeed, the mountain had caused the area to turn almost as black as night, truly a contrast when one saw the sun shining but a few yards farther. Ureh lay in such darkness that one could barely even make out distinct shapes in the city, and the longer the band stood where it was, the more the shadow covering them thickened to the same murkiness.

"Let's withdraw to the camp," Kentril suggested. "And that includes you, too, Master Zayl."

The pale necromancer bowed slightly and, under guard by four of the captain's men, started off. Gorst quickly helped Quov Tsin with his scrolls and talismans, following after the Vizjerei like an obedient puppy. Kentril himself stood his ground until everyone else had departed, then took one last sweeping survey of the vicinity in order to make certain that nothing had been left behind.

His gaze froze as it fell upon the ruins.

A glimmer of *light* flickered in one of the distant towers.

He blinked, thinking the sight simply a momentary trick of his imagination—only then to see *two* lights, the second far to the right in another part of the city.

And as every nerve tingled, and every hair on his neck stood on end, Captain Kentril Dumon watched a dead city blossom with illumination. Light after flickering light burst to life, transforming fabled Ureh before his very eyes.

"Tsin!" he shouted, gaze still fixed on the fantastic display. *"Tsin!"*

Now more visible, the ruined city also proved not so ruined anymore. The gaping hole in the wall had vanished, and what had been a crumbling watchtower again stood proud sentinel. From the top of the battlements, Kentril almost swore he even saw banners fluttering in the ever-increasing wind.

"It's true . . ." muttered a very familiar voice to his side. Kentril glanced down to see the wizened Vizjerei, the latter's expression akin to that of a child who had just received the greatest toy, staring at the wondrous sight. "It's true . . ."

Around Captain Dumon, the rest of the party quickly gathered, many of the veteran mercenaries gazing slack-jawed at Ureh. Even the necromancer Zayl watched the city with something akin to astonishment. That no one at the moment guarded the black-clad spellcaster did not bother Kentril in the least, for clearly Zayl had no intention of flight. As it had done with the rest, the miracle before them had ensnared the necromancer.

"The legends spoke truth," Zayl whispered. "You were right, Humbart."

"What are we waiting for?" Tsin suddenly demanded. "This is why we came so far! Why we struggled so long! Dumon! Your men were promised gold and more! Well? There it is for the taking!"

This finally stirred the mercenaries. "He's right!" laughed Benjin. "Gold! A city full of gold!"

Even Kentril found the lure of treasure enough to push back the anxiety he felt. Ureh had been a kingdom said to be among the wealthiest in the history of the world. Tales had been told of other hunters who had come seeking its riches, but none of those tales had ever left any belief that the searches had been successful. That meant that enough might be found to make each man here as wealthy as any king or sultan . . .

"You cannot be serious," Zayl interjected. "Ureh's riches are for Ureh alone. You rob the dead."

"They're not dead, remember?" Kentril pointed out. "They departed . . . and if that's the case, anything they left behind they surely didn't want. That means that Tsin's right. It's ours."

The necromancer looked as if he wanted to argue further but clearly had little with which to counter the captain's claim. He finally nodded, albeit with much reluctance.

Turning to the Vizjerei, Kentril asked, "Those lights. Does that mean any trouble?"

"Nonsense! The story clearly indicates that the people left the mortal plane in the space of but a few minutes. If we see Ureh as they abandoned it, surely many lamps and torches were left lit. Beyond the mortal plane, time is but a word. Why, we may even find food left in bowls and good ale for your men! What do you say to that?"

The other fighters cheered at this possible bonus. Something about the sorcerer's logic briefly troubled Captain Dumon, but, unable to decide just what, the mercenary officer shrugged off the slight concern. Even he could not help feeling much enthusiasm.

"All right!" he cried to the others. "Get what each of you needs! Bring rope and torches with you, too—I'm not going to trust those lights alone! Don't forget sacks! Hurry!"

With far more eagerness than before, Kentril's men went into action. Quov Tsin also prepared himself, retrieving his magical staff and placing about his neck three amulets he had been carrying in a pouch at his belt. Despite their many disagreements, the captain planned to search alongside Tsin once they entered Ureh. Kentril felt certain that wherever the Vizjerei sought his magical artifacts and tomes they would also find great riches.

To everyone's surprise, when the small troop reassembled, the necromancer stood waiting for them. In their eagerness to ready themselves, the mercenaries had more or less forgotten to guard him, but it seemed that Zayl, too, continued to be drawn by the possible offerings of the magical kingdom. Once more he had one hand on the bulging pouch, but as Kentril approached him, the slim figure let the cloak cover it.

"I will be going with you," he stated firmly.

Kentril did not like that notion, but, to his surprise, Tsin readily agreed.

"Of course you will," the Vizjerei declared. "Your knowledge and expertise will prove most invaluable. You'll come with Captain Dumon and myself, naturally."

Zayl executed his slight bow, his face impassive. "Of course."

While none of the mercenaries protested the necromancer's presence, they kept their distance from him as the band, torches already lit, headed toward Ureh. With the outer wall no longer visibly damaged, Kentril, under Zayl's guidance, led them toward the main gate. Although the fear existed that with the city seemingly whole the gate might also be blocked, they came around to the entrance to discover it open and the drawbridge down as well.

"Almost as if we're invited in," commented Kentril.

Quov Tsin snorted. "Then, by all means, let us not stand around here gaping!"

Weapons drawn and torches held ahead, the group entered.

To the naked eye, it might have seemed as if the inhabitants had just stepped out or even simply gone to sleep. Buildings that on previous visits had been crushed in or at least cracking stood tall and new. Rows of high oil lanterns that had previously been rusted, crumbling wrecks now brightly illuminated the avenues. Other lights boldly shone from towers and structures deeper in the city. Even the very street upon which the band walked looked as if it had been freshly swept.

Yet not one sound did they hear. No words, no laughter, no crying, not even the calls of birds or insects.

Reborn Ureh itself might seem, but the stillness within reminded all of the stunning fates of the inhabitants.

A short distance in, the main avenue split off into three directions. Kentril studied each in turn before saying, "Gorst! Take four men down the right for about a hundred paces, no more. Albord! You, Benjin, and four more check the left. The rest of you, come with Tsin and me. No one goes farther than I said, and we all meet back here as soon as possible."

He did not include Zayl in any of the groups, especially his own, but the necromancer followed him regardless. Kentril took the point, Oskal and another man flanking him just a step behind. Eyes darting from one side of the street to the other, the captain kept careful count of each step as they proceeded.

Building after building they passed. Light gleamed in some of them, but each time one of the party investigated, they found no sign of any life.

"Check those doors," Kentril commanded Oskal, pointing to what looked to be a business on the left. Lit within more than any of the previous structures, it drew the captain's attention like a moth to the proverbial flame.

Guarded by another mercenary, Oskal tried one of the doors. It swung open with little effort. Leaning in, the veteran surveyed the interior for a moment, then, in a relaxed voice, called back, "A potter's shop, cap'n! Stacks of fancy pieces on the walls. There's one even sittin' on the wheel lookin' freshly shaped." An avaricious look spread over his ugly features. "Think we should check to see if he left any coin in the till?"

"Leave it. It'll still be there when we get around to it—if you even want such meager coin once we've gone through this entire place!"

The mercenaries laughed at this suggestion, and even Tsin cracked a rare smile, but Zayl remained almost devoid of emotion. Kentril noticed that his hand touched the large pouch again.

"What is that you've got in there, necromancer?"

"A keepsake, nothing more."

"I think it's more than—"

A shriek filled the air, echoing time and again through the empty avenues of Ureh.

"That sounds like one of ours!" gasped Oskal.

The captain had already begun to turn back. "It is! Run, you fools!"

The cry did not repeat, but now came the sounds of cursing men, the clatter of arms, and what very briefly might have been the low, sinister rumble of some animal.

Gorst and the rest joined Kentril's men at the original intersection. No one spoke, each breath now saved only for action.

They came across tall, gangly Albord, a white-haired fighter from an area north of Captain Dumon's own, shouting at four other mercenaries, all of whom had hunted looks in their eyes. Near Albord's feet, a torn and ravaged form lay sprawled near the right side of the avenue. It took Kentril a moment to realize by process of elimination that the mangled, bloody mess had once been Benjin.

"What happened?" the captain demanded.

"Something came out, tore him apart, and moved so quick none of us saw it much at all!"

"Was a cat!" insisted another man. His expression turned dumbfounded. "A huge, hellish cat . . ."

"All I saw was a blur!" insisted Albord.

"No blur rips open a man's guts like that!"

Kentril looked to Tsin. "Well?"

The sorcerer raised his staff, drawing a circle in the air. He stared upward for a moment, then said, "Whatever it was, it's not around here anymore, Dumon."

"Can you be certain?" asked Zayl. "Not all things are so easily detected by magic."

"Do you sense anything, cretin?"

Zayl pulled free the ivory dagger Kentril had earlier seen. Before the eyes of the startled mercenaries, he pricked a finger with the tip. As a few droplets of blood coursed down the blade, the necromancer muttered silent words.

The dagger flared bright, then faded to normal again.

"I sense nothing," the pale figure reported. "But that does not mean that there is nothing."

Swearing, Kentril turned to Albord. "Which way did it head after it killed Benjin?"

"Toward that building there on the left . . . I think."

"Nah!" interrupted a fellow mercenary. "It turned and went farther up into the dark!"

"You're daft!" came the one who had identified it as a cat. "It whirled around and darted back the way it came! That's how I saw it fer what it was!"

The rest of the party looked at Albord's group as if all of them had gone mad. One of Gorst's men spat on the building next to which he stood, snarling, "I'm beginnin' to wonder if maybe they killed 'im themselves, eh, captain?"

It would not have been the first time that mercenaries had murdered one another over treasure, but Captain Dumon did not see that as the case this time. Still, it made sense to question those involved further. "Where were each of you when Benjin bought it?"

"Spread out like you've always taught us, captain," Albord replied. "Jodas there, me next to him, Benjin right there where Toko,"—he indicated the man who had accused him of murder—"is—"

And at that moment, a flash of black burst out of the doorway next to Toko, catching him across the chest.

The fighter screamed in much the same way as Benjin had as curled claws a foot in length tore through padded leather and flesh, revealing to his horrified companions wet, red ribs and ravaged organs. Toko actually managed to look down at his horrendous wound before death claimed him and he toppled forward.

A beast that, yes, could vaguely be described as a cat emerged from the building, hissing at the humans. Yet no cat stood seven feet in height and had eyes red and without pupils. In the light of the lamps, its fur looked jagged, almost sharp, and fire black. The hell cat roared once, a blood-curdling sound, and revealed not one but *two* sets of long, feline teeth.

"Pincer pattern!" called Kentril. "Pincer pattern!"

The familiar tone of their captain giving commands brought the rest of the soldiers back to the moment at hand. They quickly formed themselves as he had ordered, working to cut off the monstrous beast's escape.

Barbed tail swishing back and forth, the cat stepped toward its foes. The eyes went from man to man, studying each.

"What's that thing doin'?"

"Maybe it's deciding who to eat next?"

"Silence in the ranks!" Kentril demanded. The beast paused in its study of the others to take special care in viewing him. Captain Dumon met the inhuman gaze and, despite his inner fears, matched it.

At last, it proved to be the creature who looked away first. It slowly backed up, almost as if intending to return to the building from whence it had come.

That could not be allowed. Kentril knew better than to follow any foe back into his lair. Worse, if the cat escaped, it would likely catch them again later, when their guards were down. "Albord! Oskal! You and—"

With another horrific cry, the cat suddenly crouched, then leapt for him.

Kentril had no time to recover. Claws flared from the paws of the monster, the same razor-sharp sickles that had ripped to bloody gobbets two of his men. He saw his own terrible death coming and knew that his reactions would be too slow even to delay the dire event.

Then a form as much a shadow as the beast met the cat in midair. Although smaller, the second hit with such force that both fell directly to the street.

A flash of white appeared at the end of the new figure's limb. Not a claw or talon, as Kentril first believed, but rather a dagger—a dagger made of ivory.

Zayl had sacrificed himself to save the captain.

Never had Kentril seen such agility and speed in any man. Despite still wearing his voluminous cloak, the necromancer danced around the savage claws of the cat. The hellish creature snapped at Zayl, tasting only air. The pale spellcaster leapt atop his gargantuan foe and this time struck true with the ivory dagger.

A flash of emerald-green light flared where the peculiar blade bit in, and although Zayl clearly managed only a shallow wound, the cat howled as if pierced through the heart. It writhed wildly, finally sending the necromancer tumbling to the side.

Kentril dove in, determined that no man should die for his sorry sake. As he attacked, Oskal, Jodas, and two others joined in while another fighter dragged Zayl to momentary safety.

The cat swiped at the necromancer, howling when the claws missed. Kentril thrust, managing only to catch its unwanted attention again.

As one paw reached with lightning swiftness for their leader, Oskal and Jodas attacked from opposing sides. The beast's head turned toward the latter, who stumbled back as quickly as he could. On the other side, Oskal, still undetected, jabbed as hard as possible into the unprotected flank.

His sword went in a foot and more. The cat shrieked, turning upon the mercenary. Withdrawing his blade, Oskal fled from the reach of either the jaws or the curved claws.

The retreat proved a fatal mistake.

With the full force of a footman's mace, the barbed tail swung down hard on the unwary fighter.

The weaponlike appendage crushed the back of the mercenary's skull with an audible crack. Blood splattered the two men nearest Oskal. Eyes still wide, the already dead soldier fell forward, his sword clattering to the ground.

Enraged, Kentril charged again, thrusting with all his might at the cat's throat. The beast turned to meet him, but something distracted it again from the other side. Caught between two directions, the monstrous feline hesitated.

With as much force as he could muster, Captain Dumon drove the full length of his sword into the thick, muscular throat.

The hellish cat pulled back, taking Kentril's weapon with it. Hacking, its life clearly flowing from the great wound, the badly injured beast spat and swiped at everything in sight. Albord barely missed having his head taken from his body. The mercenaries retreated a step, hoping that death would come quick.

But even with such a wound, the cat did not forget Kentril. Still lithe, still quick, it focused on the cause of its agony, the unblinking eyes locked on Kentril's own. In those crimson orbs, the captain saw clearly his death coming.

Then Gorst acted, the barbarian giving a howl worthy of the cat and leaping atop from behind. The monstrous creature tried to twist backward to get the shirtless giant. However, Gorst wrapped his arms around the neck and used the hilt of Kentril's sword as a grip. Not only did he keep his foe from reaching him, but with his prodigious strength he worked the already deep blade around, further tearing at the cat's dripping wound.

At last, the murderous beast stumbled, then fell. It tried to rise but failed. Even then, Gorst held on tight. His muscles strained, seeming almost ready to tear apart, but still he held his position. The barbed tail flew at him once, twice, but, positioned where he was, Gorst remained beyond its limited reach.

"Let's finish it!" Kentril demanded.

Zayl alongside them, the rest of the mercenaries closed in, everyone still avoiding the tail. Seizing Oskal's sword, Kentril joined the others in stabbing the cat time after time. For what seemed an hour but in truth was only a minute, maybe two, they tried to put an end to the murderous creature.

Then, when Kentril had just begun to believe that nothing could completely slay the monster, the cat exhaled once . . . and fell motionless.

Still untrusting, the survivors watched with blades ready as Gorst dismounted. When the hellish beast made no move for Captain Dumon's second, they knew at last that they had slain it.

"Are you well?" asked a much-too-calm voice.

Kentril turned to see Zayl, the necromancer, looking untouched both physically and mentally by the disastrous event. At another time, that might have irritated the mercenary, but Zayl had saved his life, and Kentril would never forget that.

"Thank you, Master Zayl. I would've surely been dead if not for your quick reaction."

This brought a brief ghost of a smile. "I am simply Zayl. One born to the jungle finds it necessary to learn to react even quicker than the animals, captain—or one gets eaten at an early age."

Not certain whether the necromancer had just made a jest or not, Kentril nodded politely, then turned toward the only one in the party who had done nothing to avert the tragedy.

"Tsin! Damn you, Tsin! Where was all your vaunted power? I thought you Vizjerei had all sorts of magical spells! Three men are dead!"

Yet again, the diminutive sorcerer managed somehow to look down his nose at the much taller fighter. "And I stood ready in case there existed more than one of these beasts—or did you think your little troop capable of fending off a second at the same time?"

"Captain," Albord cut in. "Captain, let's leave this place. No gold's worth this."

"Leave?" snarled another fighter. "I ain't going back without something!"

"How about your head still on your shoulders, eh?"

Kentril whirled on his men. "Quiet, all of you!"

"Leaving would probably be a wise choice," suggested Zayl.

Tsin waved the wooden staff at the necromancer. "Nonsense! So much awaits us in this city! Likely the animal already lived here before the change, and we just never ran across it. And since no other came to its defense, I dare say it lived alone after all. There should be nothing else to fear here. Nothing!"

And at that moment, music began to play.

"Where's that from?" blurted Jodas.

"Sounds like it's comin' from everywhere!" replied one of his comrades.

Indeed, the music seemed to close in on the band from all sides. A simple yet haunting tune, not entirely unmerry, played on what sounded like a single flute. Kentril felt two urges at once, one to dance to the tune and the other to run away as fast as he could.

A man's light laughter briefly joined the music.

To Kentril's far right, a figure moved . . . a human figure.

Albord pointed down the street. "Captain, there's folk over by that old inn!"

"Horse and rider comin' this way!" shouted another mercenary.

"That old man! He wasn't there before!"

All around the party, figures that had not been visible moments before now walked, rode, or simply stood nearby. They wore free-flowing garments of all shades, and Kentril identified the old, young, strong, and infirm all in the space of one sweeping glance.

And through each one he could see the buildings beyond . . .

"Not all the riches in the world are enough for this, Tsin!" The captain summoned the men toward him. "We head to the front gate together! No one strays, no one tries to turn off to search for a few trinkets, understand?"

None of the fighters argued. To ransack an abandoned city was one thing, but to be trapped in a city of *ghosts* . . .

"No!" spat the Vizjerei. "We're so close!" Nevertheless, he did not wait behind when the mercenaries and Zayl started off.

Thinking of the necromancer, Kentril asked, "Zayl! You deal with the likes of these. Any suggestions?"

"Your command is the most prudent course, captain."

"Can you do anything about the ghosts?"

The pale figure's brow furrowed. "I can ward them off, I believe, but something about them leaves me uneasy. It would be best if we could escape Ureh without any confrontation."

This warning from the necromancer did not ease Kentril's concerns in the least. If even Zayl found Ureh's ghosts unsettling, then the sooner the band made it through the gates, the better.

So far, though, the phantasmal figures had done nothing, did not even seem to notice the intruders. And while the flute continued to play, its song growing stronger with each passing moment, it, too, had caused the fleeing group no actual harm.

"There's the gate!" Albord shouted. "There's the—"

He got no further. As one, the mercenaries froze, the blood draining from their faces as they beheld the way to safety . . . a way open to them no more.

Yes, there indeed stood the gate, but not as they had left it. Now the drawbridge stood high, and the gate itself had been bolted shut. Worse, a throng had assembled before it, a throng of pale, spectral forms with drawn faces and hollow eyes, the ghostly inhabitants of the shadow-enshrouded kingdom. The hollow eyes turned as one toward the treasure hunters, stared at Kentril and his companions with dreadful intensity.

Above the music, the light laughter of a man continued.

Five

Zayl held up the ivory dagger, at the same time muttering something under his breath. The dagger flared bright, and for a moment, the unearthly horde seemed to back away. Then, as if galvanized by some unseen force, they surged forward, moving in determined silence toward the small party.

"That should have worked," muttered the necromancer in an almost clinical tone. "They are ghosts, nothing more . . . I think."

The horrific throng seemed to swell further with each second. They did not stretch forth grasping hands toward the fighters, did not in any visible way show menace, but they kept coming, more and more of them. Their eyes never strayed from Kentril's band, never gave any indication but that they sought to reach those before them.

No one wanted to know what would happen when they did.

One of the mercenaries finally broke, turning and fleeing back the way the group had just come. Captain Dumon swore, yet he could think of no other course of action. Waving his sword high over his head, he ordered the rest back as well.

Weapons clutched tightly—although what use against fleshless horrors blades might be no one could say—the treasure hunters retreated into Ureh in quick fashion. Even Zayl and the Vizjerei ran, Quov Tsin remarkably quick for one of his size and age. Behind them, seeming barely to move yet somehow more than keeping pace, the legion of pale figures followed.

"At the next street, turn left!" Kentril called to the others. If memory served him, that way led to one of the watchtowers. If they could gain entrance to it, then they could use it to climb over the wall. Two of the men still alive carried rope, certainly enough for them to reach the ground outside.

But as they approached the intersection, movement from down the very path Kentril had chosen made the mercenaries pause.

More of Ureh's forgotten inhabitants approached from there, their faces as hollow and wanting as those behind.

"They're comin' from ahead, too!" shouted Albord, pointing.

True enough, more filled the street before them. Kentril glanced right. Only in that direction did no ghastly horde yet confront the party. Only to the right did any hope of escape remain.

Beside him, Zayl murmured, "What other choice do we have?"

With a wave of his hand, Kentril led the way. At every moment, he expected them to be cut off, but, despite his concerns, their path remained clear as they went along.

Not so any of the side avenues. When two of the mercenaries broke away from the rest and tried to take one, spectral figures materialized from the shadows barely inches from the startled men. The fearful pair quickly returned to the group. Curiously, although the new ghosts also gave pursuit, they, like those already behind, neared the fleeing party but never actually came within reach.

The necromancer said it first. "We are being led, captain. We are going exactly where they want us."

Kentril knew what he meant. Even the slightest indication of variance in the party's route summoned forth scores of additional silent, horrific shades, but none that ever actually caught any of their prey. No, so long as the mercenaries continued on the path designated, the ghosts only kept pace.

But what, the captain wondered, awaited the intruders at the end?

Past tall stonework shops they fled. Past narrow, elegant homes with domed roofs and walled entrances the band ran. In many, lamps and torches flickered, and now and then voices could be heard, but the few times Kentril managed a glance into one of the structures, he saw no sign of life.

And throughout their perilous flight, the flute continued to play the same, never-ending tune. The jovial laugh of the unseen man would now and then join in, seeming to mock the efforts of the harried company.

Then the weary mercenaries found the path ahead cut off by more of the ghastly throng. At first, Kentril did not understand why, but then he saw the narrow alley to the left, a dark, uninviting place that went on seemingly forever. The captain quickly surveyed the rest of his surroundings for some other recourse, but only the alley offered any chance.

"That way!" he shouted, pointing with the sword and hoping that he had not just made a terrible mistake.

No unblinking, ghoulish forms materialized to block their way. One by one, the men slipped into the narrow passage. Kentril kept the sword ahead of him at all times, aware of the foolishness of the act but feeling some slight comfort despite that knowledge.

"They're still behind us, cap'n!" shouted the last in line.

"Keep following me! There has to be an end to this! There has to be—"

As if reacting to his very words, the alley abruptly gave way to a vast, open plaza. Kentril paused just beyond the end of the alley, staring at what he could not recall having seen at all during the first few days' scavenging.

"We couldn't have missed this . . ." he whispered. "We couldn't have . . ."

"By the dragon!" gasped Zayl, now behind him. When Kentril glanced at the necromancer, he saw that Zayl's mouth hung open in outright awe, a sight in some manner nearly as startling as what lay before them.

A massive hill—in actuality a huge outcropping of Nymyr itself—rose up in the very midst of Ureh. The hill itself Captain Dumon did recall, of course, and even then he had wondered why the inhabitants would have chosen to build their kingdom to encompass a several-hundred-foot-tall mound of pure, black rock. Yet not only had they chosen to include it in their plans, but some-one had successfully carved out an entire stairway leading up to the very top.

And there, looming over all else, stood what had so ensnared the eyes of all. A magnificent stone edifice with three spiral towers and a high wall of its own overlooked not only Ureh but the countryside far beyond. In shape it reminded Kentril more of the castles from back home, tall, jagged, cold. Fierce winged figures guarded the gate through which any had to pass even to reach the outer grounds. Where the black hill upon which it stood melted perfectly into the shadow cast by the mountain, a faint aura seemed to surround the peculiar white marble from which the keep had evidently been built.

Kentril blinked twice, but the hint of light surrounding the regal structure remained. A bad feeling rumbled to life in his stomach.

"The palace of Juris Khan!" whispered Zayl. "But it vanished with him—"

"Juris Khan's palace?" Quov Tsin barged through the stunned group, bat-tering larger, more able fighters with only the staff. He stepped to the front and surveyed it as best he could from his low position. More than a hint of avarice tinged his voice as he muttered, "Yesss . . . what better place to look? What better place to look?"

Kentril suddenly recalled the pursuing phantoms. He glanced over his shoulder, expecting to see them even now emerging from the alley, only to find his party seemingly abandoned by their terrifying companions.

"They have ended the hunt," declared the necromancer, expression guarded. "They have led us to where we must go."

Captain Dumon examined again the high, twisting stairway leading up to the huge, barred gate and the murky, winged forms atop the wall who seemed to stare down at the newcomers. "We go up there?"

"At the moment," Zayl remarked, "it would seem better than returning to our friends. Do not doubt that if we turn back, they will come again . . . and this time, they may do more than follow."

"Of course we should go up!" Tsin nearly spat. He jabbed the staff in the direction of the fabled palace. "In there, Juris Khan's master spellwork was completed by the combined efforts of his priests and wizards! In there, the greatest of the magebooks will be found—and much gold, of course!"

Only the Vizjerei seemed at all interested in the pursuit of power and treas-ure. Kentril and his surviving men had lost their lust for riches, at least for the moment. Not a soldier there wanted more than to be far from the shadowed kingdom, even if it meant leaving without the smallest coin.

But no choice had been given them. They had been led to this stairway, and the mercenary captain knew that it had indeed not been by accident.

"Up we go," he growled. "Keep those torches well lit."

As they reluctantly began the climb, Kentril noticed that something else had changed with the vanishing of their unearthly pursuers. No longer did he hear the unnerving music or even the laughter. Ureh had fallen as silent as death.

Up they slowly struggled, the stairway so steep, so awkward, that Kentril wondered how anyone could have made the journey often. Here and there, parts of steps had given way, making the trek even more troublesome. The torches helped little to guide them, the flames seeming to be dulled somehow by the intense shade. Kentril had seen pitch-black nights brighter than this day. Why, he wondered, had he not noticed how dark it had been on the previous excursions into the ruins? Why did it seem so different now?

Up and up the band climbed. The stairway seemed twice as long as it should have been. After what felt like a thousand steps, Kentril noted the ragged breathing—his own included—and called for a brief rest. Even Tsin, who so desired to reach the palace, did not argue.

Zayl, looking far less worn than the rest, sat down a few paces above, hand once more on the bulging pouch. Eyes closed, he sniffed the air, as if seeking something.

The necromancer opened his eyes quickly when Kentril approached him. Once more, the hand slipped away, and the cloak obscured the pouch. "Captain Dumon."

"A word with you, Zayl?"

"I am at your service."

Squatting down near the spellcaster, Kentril commented, "You evidently know a lot about this place. You know more even than old Tsin, and he's been obsessed with this region all his life."

"He has been obsessed all *his* life, but I have lived near it all *mine,* captain."

"A point well taken, Zayl. How much *do* you know? When you saw this"—Captain Dumon indicated the palace—"you reacted with some surprise, but not nearly as much as me. This *wasn't* here, necromancer! This hill, yes, but this palace of marble, *it* wasn't!"

"And in a realm with ties to Heaven itself, this surprises you?"

Kentril snorted. "For an earthly Heaven, Ureh's shown me only blood."

Zayl's left eyebrow arched. "You have a very sharp sense, Captain Dumon, and an innate knowledge of the world I suspect would surprise even me."

"I ask you again, necromancer, what do you know about this palace?"

"Only that, as the *Vizjerei* indicated"—the pale figure pronounced the one word with something akin to disgust—"it was the place where the spell unfolded, where the path to Heaven was opened. It does not surprise me to find that the home of Juris Khan would not follow mortal dictates even now. It was touched by forces beyond our ken, and even a few centuries would not lessen their effect upon it."

The words did Kentril little good. He tried a different tack. "I want to know what's in that pouch."

"As I said, a keepsake."

"And for what reason are you keeping it? It seems very precious to you."

Zayl stood, his face unemotional. In a louder voice, he asked, "Is it not time we pushed on, captain? We have a bit of a climb still."

"He's right, Dumon," muttered Tsin from farther down. "Time is wasting."

Zayl started up without another word. Kentril gritted his teeth, then reluctantly nodded to the others to continue the climb. The time would come when the spellcaster told him the truth, the captain swore to himself . . . provided that they survived this madness, of course.

Curiously, from that point on, the remainder of the trek went much swifter. The walled domain of the great and long-absent Juris Khan grew larger and larger with each passing step. Before very long, the high gates finally beckoned to the climbers.

"Ugly beasts," Albord grunted, eyeing the two winged gargoyles. Up close, they had manlike bodies but with leonine tendencies and beaked faces reminiscent of vultures. Their paws ended in curved talons like those of eagles or hawks. Wide, inhuman orbs glared down at any who stood directly before the barred entrance.

"This is the home of the most pious of the pious?" Kentril remarked.

"Gargoyles are often considered the guardians against Hell," Zayl explained. "These obviously impress upon the visitor that only the good of heart will cross into the palace."

"Does that mean we got to wait out here, cap'n?" someone in the rear called.

"We all go in, or none of us goes in." Kentril studied the barred gateway. "If we get in at all."

In answer, Zayl reached forward to check. At the slightest touch of his hand, the massive door swung wide open.

"Shall we enter?" he politely asked the mercenaries.

The captain fought down a shiver. In opening, the ancient gate had been perfectly silent, as if freshly oiled.

Zayl took a step forward, then, when nothing happened, he continued on to the palace grounds. Emboldened by the necromancer's success, Captain Dumon followed him, then signaled his men to come one by one.

Albord crossed next, to be followed by Jodas and the rest. The more nothing happened to the first through, the easier the minds of those following became. One man even jested with the gargoyles, insisting that they reminded him of a former wife. For the first time since the city had awakened, the mood became somewhat relaxed.

Tsin stood back, watching each mercenary enter. When the last had passed through the gate, he tightened his grip on the staff and strode forward with all the arrogance of a conqueror.

From above the entrance, the gargoyles suddenly howled to life.

Wings outspread, the beaked creatures reared up, stony orbs glaring at the Vizjerei. Talons stretched forth. Tsin immediately retreated.

The gargoyles instantly returned to their still positions.

"The guardians are wise-eyed," murmured Zayl from behind Kentril.

Ignoring him, the captain stepped to the gate, looking over each gargoyle in turn. Had he not seen it himself, he would have thought someone had made the incident up over a few mugs of strong ale. Reaching up with his sword, he tapped lightly on one figure, hearing only the sound of metal against solid rock.

"Stand aside, Dumon," the sorcerer abruptly commanded. "I shall deal with these noisy dogs."

Quov Tsin had the tip of his magical staff pointed at the gargoyle to his left. Even as he spoke, his other hand gestured over the wooden rod, causing some of the many runes inscribed in it to glow ominously.

Zayl joined Kentril. "That might not be wise, Captain Dumon."

The mercenary officer had to agree. "Don't do it, Tsin. You'll only make matters worse!"

"This from the man who so demanded my magical aid earlier?" the Vizjerei scoffed. "These beasts will not keep me out!"

Kentril quickly jumped through the entranceway, blocking Tsin. The Vizjerei stepped back but did not lower the staff.

"Get next to me," ordered the captain. "Stay close, and we might be able to avoid unnecessary trouble."

"What do you intend?"

"Just do as I said, Tsin!"

As Kentril started to moved back to the gate, Zayl confronted him. "If you insist upon this, you will need someone other than the Vizjerei to watch the second gargoyle." He held the ivory dagger steady. "I will assist you."

"I don't need any—" the wrinkled spellcaster began.

"Quiet, Tsin!" Sorcerer or not, Captain Dumon had finally had more than enough of his employer. Zayl had been able to step where Tsin could not, and that said much about both men.

With the diminutive figure between them, Kentril and the necromancer moved sideways toward the gate. The gargoyles stood fixed, simple statues of rock. No hint of their previous awakening could be seen.

Placing one foot within the palace grounds, Kentril exhaled slightly. His idea appeared to be working; with the sorcerer hidden between the two taller men, the magical guardians seemed caught unaware.

"Just a step or two more—"

As Tsin's robed form began to cross the threshold, the gargoyle before Kentril leapt to life, wings suddenly flapping, monstrous eyes glaring, and stony mouth opened in a wild, ear-splitting roar.

Behind him, Kentril heard a second, identical cry, proof enough that Zayl also faced a newly revived beast.

The beaked head came forward, snapping at an area just to the left side of the fighter. The captain's sword clanged hard against the marble maw, but the gargoyle at least withdrew. From the necromancer, Kentril heard words of some unfamiliar tongue, then a brief flash of light at the corner of his vision startled him.

The first gargoyle used his surprise to attack again, and again it tried to reach around the mercenary. *It wants Tsin!* Kentril realized. *It's trying to avoid fighting me! It wants only him!*

Fearsome talons swept by his shoulder, snatching at the small sorcerer. The Vizjerei batted at them with the staff, sparks flashing whenever the wooden rod touched stone.

"Tsin!" Kentril shouted. "Now's your chance! Jump—"

At that moment, the flute music began again, seeming to come from everywhere at once. Kentril clamped his mouth shut, wondering what the return of the haunting melody portended.

The music had a startling effect on the gargoyles. The one before the leader of the mercenaries paused in mid-attack, then peered up at the sky. It squawked once, then quickly repositioned itself as the party had first seen it. As Kentril watched, all semblance of life swiftly vanished, the guardian once more simply a sentinel of stone.

"Incredible . . ." he heard Zayl remark. Twisting, Kentril saw that the necromancer's monstrous foe had also returned to its original state.

There could be no question but that the music had given them this reprieve, and the captain intended to make good use of that sudden luck. "Move it, Tsin!"

The Vizjerei needed no encouragement. Already he had one foot on the inner yard of the ancient palace, and by the time Kentril and Zayl turned to follow, Quov Tsin stood waiting for them some distance inside.

And still the music played . . .

"It comes from inside," insisted the Vizjerei, now very eager to enter. "Follow me!"

A chuckle escaped from the vicinity of Zayl. "Brave man, indeed, I say, to go where he's clearly not wanted!"

Kentril glanced at the necromancer, but Zayl acted as if he had not spoken, and the captain had to admit that the voice had not sounded like his. Nor had it sounded like any of the men under Kentril's command.

No one else seemed to have noticed the voice, though. Albord and the others awaited his orders. Tsin already had a good start on the rest of the party, and for some reason, Kentril did not want the Vizjerei getting too far away. Something told him that he should keep an eye on the short, arrogant figure. The gargoyles had been placed at the entrance for a reason, and they had reacted only to Tsin—not Zayl, as one might have expected. That did not bode well.

Guided by the flute, the party reached the entrance, a high, arched opening with two bronze doors upon which had been sculpted sword-wielding archangels. Curiously, the images looked badly battered while everything else appeared untouched.

With the tip of his staff, Quov Tsin pushed at one of the doors. Like the gate, it swung open in silence. With all the confidence of one returning to his *own* home, the Vizjerei marched inside.

Marble columns three stories tall flanked a magnificent hall illuminated by a massive chandelier that the captain estimated held more than a hundred lit candles. The floor consisted entirely of skillfully crafted mosaic patterns of fanciful animals such as dragons and chimaera—something of a contrast to the archangels, Kentril thought. Between the two series of columns, portraits of imposing figures in robes of state no doubt gave homage to those who had ruled Ureh over the centuries.

At the end of the corridor, another set of doors awaited them. Making their way past the staring visages of lords long dead, the party paused there, everyone quite aware that the music seemed now to be coming from within. Once again, archangels with swords adorned the entrance, and once again, the figures had been battered hard. Tsin reached for the doors, but this time they would not open for him. When Zayl, too, tried, he met with no better success.

Kentril stepped up next to the two spellcasters. "Maybe there's a lock or a—"

He had been about to touch one of the ruined images when suddenly *both* doors swung wide open. The trio backed away as a rush of cold air swept out from the darkened chamber before them.

At first, they saw nothing, but then the music drew their gazes to the very back of the room, where they could faintly make out a dim lamp . . . and, seated next to it in a high-backed chair, an elderly man in robes of white.

He leaned forward, as if not noticing their coming. Kentril's eyes adjusted enough to see that a slim, hooded figure sat upon the floor before the elder, a figure with a flute held up to where the lips would have been.

"More ghosts . . ." Albord muttered.

Although he had spoken only in whispers, the two within reacted as if the chandelier had suddenly fallen whole from the ceiling, loudly smashing to fragments on the marble floor. The hooded form ceased playing, then rose and slipped into the darkness with one graceful movement. The robed patriarch glanced up and, to everyone's surprise, *greeted* them as if having waited all this time for their arrival.

"You have come at last, friends," he announced in a soft voice that yet seemed to carry the strength of an army in it.

Never one to stand on ceremony save where it concerned his own magnificence, the Vizjerei tapped the staff once on the floor and declared, "I am Quov Tsin! Sorcerer of the Innermost Circle, Brother of the High Initiate, Master of—"

"I know who you are," the elder responded solemnly. He looked at Kentril and the others, and even though a vast distance stretched between them, the captain felt as if he stood immediately in front of the former, every thought and emotion revealed. "I know who all of you are, my friends."

Zayl pushed ahead of the sorcerer. He wore an intense expression that surprised most of those around him, especially Kentril. All had come to assume that the necromancer had such utter control over his emotions that nothing, not even a ghostly kingdom, could draw much reaction from him. Even the expression he had worn when first seeing the looming palace could not match his present eagerness.

"And am I right, honored sir, am I right in thinking I know you as well?"

This the white-robed figure found almost amusing. He leaned on one arm of the chair, his chin resting on the palm of his hand. "And do you?"

"Are you not—are you not the great *Juris Khan*?"

A frown escaped their host. "Yes . . . yes, I am Juris Khan."

"Saints above!" whispered one mercenary.

"Another ghost!" snapped another.

Kentril silenced the mercenaries with a swift wave of his hand. He looked to Tsin for confirmation, and although the sorcerer did not respond directly, the Vizjerei's covetous expression said it all.

Incredible as it seemed, they had found Juris Khan, he who had been the guiding light of a kingdom considered the most holy of all . . . and a man who should have been as dead as the horrific phantoms that had herded them to this place.

Herded them?

"He did it," Kentril informed the others, advancing on the seated form. "He had them force us here. He's the one who trapped us so that our only path could be to his palace."

If he expected the lord of Ureh to deny the charges, Juris Khan much surprised him. Instead, the regal figure rose quietly from his seat and, arms folded into the voluminous sleeves of his robes, bent his head in what appeared remorse. "Yes. I am responsible. It is through my means that you were forced to come to me . . . but that is because I could not leave here to come to you."

"What sort of nonsense—" But Captain Dumon got no further, for as he finished speaking, Khan reached down, seized his robe, and raised it just enough to reveal his feet.

Or where they would have been.

Just above the ankles, the lord of Ureh's feet melded perfectly into the front legs of the chair, so much so that one could not tell where the man ended and the wood began.

Juris Khan lowered the robe and, in a most sincere tone, said, "I hope you will forgive me."

Even Tsin found this too extraordinary to ignore. "But what does this mean? What about the path to Heaven? The legends say that—"

"Legends say many things," Zayl interrupted. "And most of them are found false in the end."

"Ours being the falsest of all," murmured a voice from the darkness to their left.

Juris Khan reached his hand forward to that darkness, smiling at the one within. "They are what they seem. It is safe to come forth."

And from the shadows, the flute player emerged, hooded no more. For the first time, Kentril saw that the flowing garment had hidden a woman, a young and very beautiful woman with smooth skin like alabaster, eyes that gleamed like emeralds even in the faint light of the lamp and his men's torches, cascading red hair even more vivid than that of the women of his homeland, and an eastern cast to her features that spoke true of her birth in this faraway realm.

"My friends . . . my daughter, Atanna."

Atanna. A name that buried itself there and then in the veteran fighter's heart. Atanna, the most beautiful of beautiful women Captain Kentril Dumon had ever beheld. Atanna, an angel among mortals . . .

Atanna . . . the face from the brooch.

Six

"It was betrayal," Juris Khan told them as Atanna passed to each a goblet filled with wine. "Betrayal from one whom all trusted most."

"Gregus Mazi," his daughter interjected, seating herself on the floor near Kentril. Her eyes met the captain's, and for a moment, a brief light seemed to shine in those almond-shaped, emerald orbs, but then the subject at hand doused that light. "Gregus Mazi . . . my father once called him *brother of brothers.*"

"He sat at my left hand, as the good priest Tobio sat at my right." The white-haired lord leaned back, the head of his own goblet cupped in his palms. "To them I gave the glorious task of translating the visions to reality. To them I gave the blessed task to lead us to the sanctuary of Heaven."

The mercenaries and the two spellcasters sat on the floor before the imprisoned monarch, fruit and wine brought to each of them by the graceful and beauteous Atanna. After so much bloodshed, so much fear, the entire party gratefully accepted Lord Khan's hospitality. Besides, many questions needed to be answered, and who better than the legendary ruler of the holy kingdom himself?

Juris Khan fit very much the mold of a leader. Standing, he had been as tall as Kentril and almost as broad. For one of advanced years, Khan had a youthful appearance and personality and little sign of frailty. Although his features had become weathered, his strong jaw, regal nose, and piercing green eyes still gave him a commanding countenance. Even his long silvering hair did not age the ruler so much as mark his years of wisdom.

Thinking over his host's words, Kentril frowned into his wine. "But the legends say that Mazi was left behind by accident, that he spent years trying to join you . . ."

Juris Khan sighed. "Legends tend to be more fiction than fact, my friend."

"So you didn't make it to Heaven?" asked Tsin, already having downed most of his drink. "The spell failed?" To the captain, the Vizjerei appeared more disappointed in the fact that the magic had not worked than in the fates of the hapless citizenry of Ureh.

"No. We found ourselves trapped in limbo, trapped in a timeless passage between the earthly plane and our glorious destination . . . and all because of one man's evil."

"Gregus Mazi," Atanna repeated, her eyes downcast.

A tremendous desire to comfort her arose in Captain Dumon, but he fought down the urge. "What did he do?"

"When the time came for the final casting," the fatherly monarch explained, "Tobio realized that the words did not read right. Their meaning had been reversed, an invitation not to journey to Heaven . . . but to be thrust down into the pits of Hell!"

Kentril glanced at Zayl, who had been listening as intently as any. The necromancer nodded to him. "In many forms of spellwork, to reverse subtlely the meanings of single words is to reverse the effect. A spell of healing can be made to wound further or even to slay."

"Gregus sought to do more than slay us," murmured Juris Khan. "He sought to damn our very souls . . . and nearly succeeded."

The captain thought of the woman next to him cast down into the realm of Diablo and shuddered. Had he been able to, Kentril would have taken the foul Gregus Mazi by the neck and twisted tight until with his eyes the sorcerer would have been able to look down upon his own heels.

"He would have succeeded," Atanna added, blushing slightly under Captain Dumon's gaze, "if not for my father and Tobio."

"We tried to respeak the already spoken incantation, reverse what had been reversed, and so, instead of Heaven, instead of Hell, we ended up in the middle of a vast nothingness, that timeless realm from which we could not escape."

Snorting, Quov Tsin commented, "You should have recast the spell from there! It would've been a simple matter for any well-trained group of Vizjerei, much less—"

"Not so simple, my friend, when the priests and mages were all slain by the selfsame spell." A cold look spread over the generally kind features of the ruler of Ureh. "Gregus planned thoroughly. A single line altered also drained swiftly the life of each chanting the spell except for Tobio and myself. Our superior strength and knowledge saved us but left us weak. Worse, without the others, we lacked the power to recast it."

If not able to recast the spell, Juris Khan and the head priest were at least able to expel Gregus Mazi in his moment of triumph. The battle cost Tobio his life, but by sending the traitorous sorcerer away, they prevented him from fulfilling his horrific plan to send Ureh to the realm of the Prime Evils.

And so the kingdom and its people had floated in the midst of nothingness, time forever locked—until there came a moment when suddenly the world materialized around them again, the world in deep shadow.

"No one who had lived his life in Ureh would have failed to recognize immediately grand Nymyr and the shade it always cast upon our fair kingdom. With the belief that our curse had abruptly ended, more than twoscore of my people rushed through the front gate without thinking. All they wanted was to feel the sun, feel the soft wind . . ." Khan leaned back, more pale than even the necromancer. "And what they were repaid with was death most horrible."

Out into the sun they had raced and therein sealed their fates. The moment the light touched them, they *burned*. Like chips of mountain ice tossed into a smith's well-heated forge, the hapless inhabitants of Ureh literally melted away, their screams echoing long after they had been reduced to puddles that themselves evaporated in seconds. Some at the edge managed to cross back into the shadow of the mountain, but in doing so they only worsened their agony, for that which had been touched a breath too long still burned away. In the end, those who had managed to halt in time became forced to slay the shrieking, suffering, half-eaten victims.

Atanna poured Kentril more wine, giving him a soft smile. However, at the same time, tears coursed down her cheeks. She took up her own untouched goblet and added to her father's shocking tale. "We had underestimated Gregus Mazi's monstrosity. That vile serpent had left us no longer a true part of the mortal world. Worse, we began to fear that once the shadow vanished and sunlight touched our home, we would all suffer as the first had."

But what would initially be seen as a miracle visited the terrified citizens that next morning, for, as the first glimpse of sunlight came over the horizon . . . the world began to fade away.

Once more, the nothing of limbo welcomed back the city and its people.

Although shocked, all agreed that until a solution could be found, exile remained much preferable to the ghastly deaths some had suffered. All looked to their blessed leader, Juris Khan, certain that he would yet discover a way to freedom. Many even took the escape from the burning sunlight as a sign that Heaven had not forsaken them. Somehow, Ureh would either return to the mortal plane safely or continue on its intended journey to the holy realm.

"And I determined after much study," Atanna's father revealed, "that a way did exist at least to anchor us without danger in the real world, for I had also determined that we would be returning there again at some point. With the aid of my precious daughter"—he smiled lovingly at the young, crimson-tressed woman—"skilled in her own way, I worked hard to fashion two unique and mystical gems."

Juris Khan handed Atanna his goblet and then, before the eyes of his guests, drew with one finger a fiery circle in the air. In the midst of that blazing ring, a pair of images alternated, a pale crystal as glittering as sun-touched ice and its raven-black twin. Never before had there been two such perfect gemstones, and Captain Dumon and his remaining men both admired and coveted them from the first moment.

"The Key to Shadow," Khan uttered, indicating the black one. "The Key to Light," he added, showing again the icy one. "One placed below Ureh, in the deepest of caverns, the other atop Nymyr, there to catch the first rays of day. Together to tie the shadow now over us, keep it in place at *all* times so that we may stay here while we seek our final escape."

And so, when it came to pass that Ureh did again appear on the mortal plane—just as Juris Khan had predicted—the plan was put into motion. Volunteers were asked for, brave men, ten in all. Five were sent to the depths below, there to find the most dark of the dark places, where shadow had its strongest ties. The other five set out to reach the top of Nymyr, to position the other gem at a place their lord had determined would be the prime location. In addition to the Key to Light, the second group also carried a specially designed pair of tongs so as to avoid the threat of sun. Hopes rose to their fullest as the two parties started out, for truly it seemed that the prayers of the people had been answered.

Unfortunately, no one had counted on the return of Gregus Mazi.

It could only be assumed that he had suspected or even detected the presence of those he had so long ago betrayed. When Ureh reformed in the shadows the next time, the corrupt sorcerer already stood waiting just beyond its borders. He discovered the attempt to save the kingdom and quickly followed those who climbed the mountain. There, with words of power, he shattered the very top of the peak with a bolt of lightning, slaying the five.

That part of his wicked work done, Gregus Mazi then secretly made his way into the palace of his former master. There he caught Khan by surprise.

"I had scarce time to look up before I realized that he had struck. When I moved to confront him, I found that I and the chair had become one, and we, in turn, had become a part of the palace itself. 'I leave you to sit and contemplate your failures forever, my lord,' the foul beast jested to me. 'And now I go to seal your beloved kingdom's fate by seizing the second gem deep below and destroying it as I have the first.'"

The robed figure ran a hand through his silvering hair. A tear slipped from one eye. "Understand, my friends, that I loved Gregus as I would've my own son. There had been a time when I had thought—" He glanced briefly at Atanna, who reddened. Next to her, Kentril experienced an unwarranted pang of jealousy. "But that is nothing. What matters is that he intended to leave me there, unable to pursue, while he went to destroy the final hopes of all those who had depended on me."

Yet Gregus Mazi had underestimated his former master. Weakened, yes. Trapped, surely so. But Khan had another source of strength. He had the people and his love for them. Khan drew from that now, drew from all Ureh. When he struck at the mocking Gregus Mazi, he did so with the raw force of thousands, not a single being.

"I admit it," the weary monarch muttered, eyes closing briefly in remembrance and regret. "I struck with anger, struck with hatred, struck sinfully . . . but I also struck with gladness and determination. Gregus had no chance."

There had been no body of the traitor to bury or burn; only a few wisps of smoke marked the final moment of he who had cursed the Light among Lights. Unfortunately, although the monster had paid, he had succeeded in again cursing Juris Khan's beloved kingdom to its horrific exile. Without the crystal in place atop Nymyr, Ureh had no permanent hold in the real world. When dawn broke the next morning, the entire city once more found itself cast into limbo, this time with no hope.

"I could not remake the crystals, you see," Khan revealed. "For their formation required elements no longer available to me. Worse, I was now trapped in this chamber, unable to free myself no matter how I tried, depending ever on my loving daughter to care for me."

But even confined as he was, Juris Khan did not give up. He had all books, scrolls, and talismans to be found brought to him. He researched spell after spell, hoping that when his kingdom returned to the mortal plane, some aid might be found. On those rare occasions Ureh did reappear, he used scrying stones to seek out any possible help that might have wandered near.

And so he had this time discovered the presence of Kentril Dumon and the others, already within the very walls of the city.

"You cannot imagine my delight at finding you! Brave explorers in the heart of my own realm! I knew that I could not pass up this chance, this one hope. I had to bring you to me!"

Kentril saw in his mind the legions of ghostly figures guiding his group from street to street. "You could've chosen a better manner . . ."

"My father did what he could, captain," Atanna interjected apologetically. "He could not come to you. He had to do it."

"Those were your people?" Zayl asked in a tone that indicated he required no answer. "They are like the dead . . . and yet they are not."

The master of Ureh nodded grimly. "Being trapped between Heaven and the mortal plane has taken its toll. We are not quite alive anymore, not quite dead, either. Atanna and I and those others who serve in the palace suffer less so, for the spells that protect and bind this place have helped us, yet even we will eventually turn as they if someone does not help us soon."

"Someone," the fiery-tressed beauty at Kentril's side murmured, gazing at him.

"But what can we do?" the mercenary leader blurted to her.

The smile she gave him seemed to swallow his heart whole. "You can replace the Key to Light."

"Replace the crystal?" snapped Quov Tsin. "You said it was destroyed!"

Khan nodded politely to the Vizjerei. "So we had thought. So Gregus had thought. But one time in the past, when I sought help from such as you, I found instead that the Key to Light had not been shattered with the mountaintop. Instead, it had been cast far from its intended location, thrown down the other side of the mountain by the force of the blast."

The diminutive sorcerer rubbed his bony chin. "And you've not retrieved it? Surely during night, when all is in shadow—"

"But not *the* shadow. That first time when we once again beheld our homeland, the very eve after the victims of the sun, I sent a small band out to get the lay of the land, discover what might have occurred. Under cover of night, that surely would have been no difficult task. All I sought was some little knowledge, some hope of a nearby settlement." He bared his teeth. "The moment the first stepped beyond where Nymyr's shade would have ended, he, too, *burned* to death."

Atanna placed her hand on Kentril's own, her eyes asking for understanding and assistance. "We're well and truly trapped, captain. Our world ends just beyond the walls of the city. Were I to step one inch farther, I would risk the flesh melting from my bones, my bones incinerating to ash."

Against those eyes, that face, Captain Dumon could not struggle. He slipped his hand on top of hers, then faced Juris Khan. "Can we reach the crystal? Can we get it in place in time?"

Hope lit the elder man's expression. "You will do this for us? You will help us? I promise a king's reward for each if you can do this!"

Jodas nearly choked on his wine. The moods of the other fighters brightened. Here seemed a quest harsh but doable and with much gain to be made. At once, each volunteered, leaving only Zayl and Tsin silent.

"We don't all need to go," Kentril told the others. "Gorst, I need you definitely. Jodas, you can climb well. Brek, Orlif, you come with us also. Albord, you're in charge of the rest."

Some of those to be left behind started to complain, but Khan silenced their concerns by stating, "If this miracle is done for us, all shall share in the reward, I promise."

Kentril asked again about the time factor and where the gem might be found. In response to the first question, Juris Khan assured him that if they left within the hour, there would be time enough. A path cut along the mountain centuries past would serve them well in that respect.

In regard to the second question, the lord of Ureh requested that his daughter retrieve a box. Moments later, when Atanna had returned with the small silver container and given it to him, Khan produced for the captain a small stone of brilliant clarity upon whose top had been etched a single rune.

"This is a piece left from the shaping of the original. The rune spell ties it to the other. Hold it before you, and it'll guide your way."

"You should depart now," his daughter informed them. She touched Kentril's hand again. "Go with my blessing."

Zayl confronted him. "Captain Dumon, I would like to go with you. My skills could be of use, and I know this area well. It would speed matters up some, I believe."

"A sage suggestion," Juris Khan declared. "I thank you."

"Well if he goes, you've no need of me up on that chill mountain," snapped Tsin. "I prefer to wait here."

Their host accepted this decision also. "You would do me a boon by being here, master sorcerer. Perhaps with you to aid me, I can be freed of Gregus's wicked magic. I offer you all the books, scrolls, and other works gathered in my sanctum as a start for your research, and in exchange for my freedom, afterward you may keep any that you wish."

If the talk of gold and riches had stirred the hearts of Kentril's men, the mention of so much magical knowledge did the same for the Vizjerei. "You're—you're *most* generous, my Lord Khan."

"I would give anything to end this nightmare," the elder responded, his gaze turning to Captain Dumon. "Is that not so, Atanna?"

"Anything," she agreed, also looking at Kentril.

The tiny gem glowed bright, an encouraging sign.

Quickly folding his hand so as not to risk losing the small stone, Kentril deposited it in the same pouch in which he also carried the brooch. He had not told Atanna about finding the latter but swore he would return it to her once the Key to Light had been set in its proper place.

Juris Khan had given them explicit instructions about what they needed to do once they had obtained the magical gem. Kentril knew exactly where to place it, not only to make certain that the wind did not blow it off but also so as to catch the very first hint of sun. Only by following the instructions to the letter could he hope to keep Ureh—and Atanna—from vanishing from his life.

The five men struggled their way around the mountain. While the path had been well carved, time had taken its toll. More than once, they had been forced to leap over breaks or climb above rock falls. Orlif had nearly slipped once, but Gorst and Jodas had pulled him back before anything could happen.

Much to the mercenaries' surprise, Zayl proved an excellent guide. He had spoken truth when he said he knew the area well. True, the necromancer had never climbed to the top of Nymyr, but he seemed to have a sense for how the mountain had been shaped.

Torch in hand, Kentril now followed Zayl, which meant that as the fierce, cold wind blew the necromancer's cloak about, the captain had a good look every once in a while at the mysterious pouch. Something about its contents still bothered him; he almost felt that the bag stared back at him. The notion struck Kentril as ludicrous, but still he could not shake off the sensation of being watched.

"There is an outcropping here that we must go over," Zayl informed him.

"Gorst." The brawny fighter, now clad in a simple cloak of his own, slipped ahead with a length of rope. With Kentril's aid, the pair secured the rope, then, one by one, each man worked his way up.

Once over, Kentril called a pause while he checked the tiny stone again.

This time, it flared so bright that he almost expected to see the Key to Light sitting on the ledge before them.

"It must be close," he muttered.

"Yes, we are in luck," replied the pale spellcaster. "Juris Khan thought it had fallen much farther away."

"How long do you reckon we still have?"

Zayl peered up at the night sky. It had taken them several hours to reach this point. The shadow of Nymyr had been swallowed by the dark some time ago. "Just enough, if we find the Key soon. This side of the mountain is not so harsh a climb as that which overlooks Ureh."

They moved on, steeling themselves against the cold night. Kentril retrieved the small stone again, correcting their path.

Minutes later, they literally stumbled over the magical gemstone.

Dirt and rock, possibly from Gregus Mazi's murderous spell, had all but buried the artifact. Only when Kentril turned in a circle, trying to find out why it seemed the party should go no farther, did he kick up a few loose pieces of rock and uncover one glittering edge.

Although the only nearby illumination consisted of their meager torches, the Key to Light still shone like a miniature star. Zayl bent down, digging up the gem. It fit in the cup of his hands, a perfectly shaped crystal.

"Must be worth a fortune," grunted bearded Brek. "What do you think we could get for it, captain?"

"From Ureh, more than you could ever get selling it elsewhere," Kentril retorted, glaring at the mercenary. The thought of betraying Atanna filled him with anger.

Zayl quickly played peacemaker. "No one would think to do anything less than what we intended, captain. Now we must hurry; dawn will be too quick in coming."

With the necromancer carrying the artifact, they began their final ascent. Gorst secured all lines for them and acted as a counterweight now and then when they had to swing from place to place. Kentril actually found the way far more easy than he would have expected; the mountains of his homeland would have caused him much more difficulty. If not for the fact that the people of Ureh had been cursed to remain hidden in the shadow of this very peak, they could have easily rectified their own situation.

At last, they neared the top. As the group paused on a large ledge, Zayl handed the Key to Light over to Kentril.

"Say, cap'n?"

"What is it, Jodas?"

"What happens to the rest of the party if we don't get this thing in the right place? They disappear with the rest?"

Kentril's gaze shifted to Zayl, who shrugged and answered, "It is best we do not find out."

After a few moments' more searching, both Captain Dumon and the necromancer came to the same conclusion regarding the most appropriate location. Unfortunately, that location meant a treacherous climb up a dangerous rise some three hundred feet and more. Although only a small part of the tip of Nymyr, both agreed that based on Khan's calculations it would be best.

"I'll do it alone," Kentril informed the others.

Gorst, however, would not hear it. Although he had remained fairly quiet up until now, Kentril's suggestion stirred him to protest. "You need an anchor. We'll tie the end of a rope around our waists. You fall, I'll catch you, honest."

Knowing better than to try to argue at this point, Kentril agreed to let the giant join in the climb. In truth, it made him feel safer knowing Gorst would be there. They had fought side-by-side in many battles and could always depend on each other's aid. If anyone could be trusted up there, it would have to be Gorst.

Kentril gritted his teeth hard as he began. After a fairly simple journey, even a relatively easy search for the artifact, this last bit threatened to rip victory from their grasp. The wind felt a hundred times more fierce, and nowhere could he get a hold that satisfied him. Out of fear that to stop would mean slipping and falling to his death, Kentril pushed faster and faster, praying he would reach the top before his luck ran out.

With the natural skill he seemed to have for everything, Gorst more than kept pace. Kentril imagined his friend gouging handholds out of the rock face. Likely it would have been better if the much larger mercenary had gone up by himself, but then it would have been his captain who would have protested.

Kentril's fingers finally stretched over the upper edge. He had to rebrace himself when ice caused his initial grip to falter, but after that, he managed to pull himself up with little trouble. Peering around, Kentril studied the immediate area. Large enough for four men to stand, it definitely offered the first place on Nymyr to receive the sun's kiss.

With the agility of a mountain goat, Gorst climbed up after him. Thick hair flying in his face, the other mercenary gave Kentril a big grin.

From his belt pouch, Captain Dumon removed the artifact. He looked the vicinity over, not wanting the Key to Light to fall from its perch the moment the climbers had returned to Ureh.

"There?" suggested Gorst.

There proved to be a tiny outcropping shaped somewhat like a bowl turned on its side. It faced the right direction and fit in with Juris Khan's directions but was not quite large enough for the gem to fit.

Taking his dagger, Kentril began chopping at the spot. He only needed to remove a little of the frozen earth below. Then he could securely place the artifact within and be finished with this chill place.

His dagger slowly bit into the icy ground. Chips of rock-hard dirt flew away—

The tip of the blade scratched at something white. Kentril worked at it, trying to remove the obstacle to his success.

He swore. With his dagger, he had unearthed a bone.

There existed little doubt in his head that this bone had belonged once to one of the five unfortunates who had been murdered by Gregus Mazi. Now fate had let the dead sorcerer again hinder the plans to free Ureh from his curse. Try as he might, Kentril could not dig the bone out, and no other spot atop Nymyr would do.

"Let me try." Gorst took Kentril's place, pulling out his own blade. For many men, the giant's dagger would have almost served as a short sword. Gorst chipped away using his prodigious might, making progress where even his captain could not.

Finally, enough of the bone—likely from the forearm—had been exposed that Gorst seized it in his huge hands and began to pull. The massive fighter grunted with strain, the muscles and veins in his neck throbbing. The frozen ground around the area cracked . . .

The bone came free.

With a startled yell, Gorst fell backward, slipping on the icy mountaintop.

He began to slide toward the edge.

Thrusting the artifact into the newly created hole, Kentril wrapped one arm around the outcropping, then braced himself against it. With his other hand, he seized the rope linking him to Gorst and pulled with all his might.

The other mercenary's head and arms went over the side. However, as the rope went taut, he spun sideways, sending one leg over but giving one hand the chance to reach for a hold.

Gasping, Kentril tugged with all his might, fighting exhaustion, gravity, and Gorst's not inconsiderable weight. The arm that held tight to the outcropping shrieked with pain but held.

Gorst lost his first attempt at finding a grip, nearly skidding off into the air in the process. Only Kentril kept him from doing so, the captain throwing his own weight back to counter as best he could that of the larger mercenary.

On his second attempt, the giant managed to grab hold of a small rocky area. With care, Gorst pulled himself to safety, for once gasping from effort.

"The Key," he called to Kentril.

"Where it should be." Barring another sorcerer blasting away what remained of the mountaintop, it would stay there for some time to come. Juris Khan had also indicated that even on days of rain or snow, the artifact would somehow be able to do its duty.

The Key to Light twinkled suddenly, almost as if stirring to life. For a moment, Kentril wondered what inner magic would cause it to do so, but then it occurred to him that not only did the gemstone look brighter, but he could now see his surroundings in better detail.

He looked over his shoulder.

They had cut this even closer than he had thought.

Dawn had come.

The artifact flared like a sun itself, seeming to take in every bit of illumination around it. Kentril watched it a few seconds more, then hurried as best he could across the icy top of Nymyr.

The light of day encroached upon where Ureh had sat protected. In the distance, the jungle seemed to open its green canopy. Nearer, the rocky landscape leading to the fabled realm took on distinct shapes.

And Ureh?

As the captain watched, sunlight hit the city where Atanna prayed for his success. Sunlight touched where shadow had kept her safe.

And in the end, sunlight failed . . . and under the impenetrable and impossible shade of the mountain, the walled city stood triumphant.

SEVEN

Music touched the returning party, music full of gaiety and life. Not only did flutes play, but so did horns, lutes, and drums. As Kentril and the others entered, they also heard voices raised in merriment and noted light upon light darting about in the city below.

Deep shadow still covered the kingdom, but hopelessness no longer enshrouded the lost realm.

Atanna met them almost immediately. Her eyes became Kentril's world, and her voice as she thanked him stirred again his heart and soul.

"I want you to see something before we go to my father," she immediately said. Taking him by the hand, she led the captain and the others to a high balcony, from which nearly all the city could be seen. Atanna waved her hand across the vision of Ureh, showing Kentril the fruits of his success.

There were people—*live* people—celebrating in the streets.

They were everywhere. Not the pallid specters of before, but breathing folk in flowing, colorful clothes more like those donned by the desert inhabitants of Lut Gholein rather than the more dour and formal eastern wear normally seen in Kehjistan. They laughed, they danced, they sang, all the things of life.

"Nice," Gorst commented, grinning at the festive activity.

Captain Dumon looked at his hostess, ever a wonderful sight in herself. "I don't understand. The people—"

"It happened the moment the sun failed to touch our kingdom. Not only did the shadow hold, but all of Ureh seemed to gain earthly substance. We're still not truly yet a part of the world again, but we are nearer to it than ever before!"

The necromancer leaned close. "Magic is a strange and complicated creature, captain. Perhaps the lord of the realm can better explain this miracle."

Kentril nodded. "We shouldn't keep him and the others waiting any longer."

Atanna did not release his hand, and he made no move to force her. They and the rest hurried through the halls of the palace, halls that, like all else, looked different in ways not noticeable at first.

The chandeliers and oil lamps had become brighter, that much Kentril would have readily sworn. In addition, the sense of death and decay that he had experienced on his first entry had been replaced by one of spirit, of rebirth.

And as there had been people of flesh in the streets, there now stood in the halls figures both solid of body and clad in gleaming metal. Armored from toe to neck in chain and plate and wearing open helmets with broad rims in front that stretched a good hand's width ahead, they saluted the mercenaries and Atanna as the group passed. In some ways, their narrow eyes and pale skin reminded Kentril of Zayl, and he wondered if the necromancer's ancestry held some link to Ureh.

More people crossed their path as they neared Juris Khan's chamber. These wore robes of state with blue or red sashes, and each bowed gracefully as Atanna and the captain headed to the doors. Courtiers also paid homage, men going down on one knee and women curtsying. Brek almost paused to make a play for one of the latter, but Gorst batted him lightly on the back of the head, urging the fighter on.

The doors opened—and what had once been a room plunged in darkness even greater than that of the deepest shadow now glittered in gold and jewels.

The very *walls* had been gilded in gold. Scrollwork lined each segment, and reliefs decorated the centers. To accent figures and designs, gemstones of every color, hue, and transparency had been artfully interjected. Likely it had taken years for those who had crafted this astonishing display to complete their work, but their effort had obviously been worth the difficulties and time.

A full honor guard greeted them as they walked inside, a score of armored figures snapping to attention, their lances pointing to the ceiling. At the far end, where the rich crimson rug that started at the doors finally came to its conclusion, a jubilant Juris Khan awaited the new arrivals. Albord and the rest who had been left behind seemed no less pleased at Kentril's return than the lord of Ureh, and why not? The success of the venture meant that all of them would leave the shadowed kingdom laden with as much treasure as they could carry.

Of Tsin, however, there was no sign. Remembering the talk of the Vizjerei aiding their host in escaping his personal curse, Kentril assumed that the bearded sorcerer had already rushed off to peruse Khan's vast library of magical knowledge. So much the better, as far as the captain felt concerned. Not only would Tsin finally do something of value, but he would also be well out of the way.

"My friends!" the gray-haired monarch gladly called. "My good and trusted friends! You have the gratitude of an entire realm! You have given Ureh a chance to be whole again in a manner we never thought possible!" He indicated the room, the guards, even the courtiers beyond the doors. "Already the fruits of your labors ripen. You bring life to a city! The people celebrate not only their renewal, but those who granted it to them."

"Captain Kentril Dumon," Khan continued, resting his arms on his knees and smiling graciously. "You and your men—and you, too, Master Zayl—are the guests of the palace. It will take a few days to formulate your rewards properly, but in the meantime, whatever you desire in Ureh is yours."

Kentril thought of the festival outside. "Are my men free to leave the palace if they so choose?"

"I think my people would demand it!" Juris Khan looked over the other mercenaries. "There are places for you to sleep in the palace, but there's no need for you to stay here otherwise. Outside, I know that wine, food, and other entertainments are available to you, my friends! If you like, go now with my blessing, and when you finally reach your limit, you are welcome back here!"

The captain nodded permission. That was all the news that Albord and the others needed. With much backslapping and cheerful words, they started out of the chamber, each saluting Kentril as they passed.

"You men can go, too," he informed Jodas and those who had journeyed to the mountain.

They quickly joined their fellows. As Gorst started to leave, though, the captain called him over.

"Keep a bit of an eye on them if you can," he asked of his loyal second. "Make certain that they don't wear out our welcome despite everything, eh?"

Gorst gave him his biggest grin yet. "I'll watch, Kentril. I will."

That left only Zayl, and while Captain Dumon felt more comfortable around the necromancer than he had at first, he still desired his pale companion to find some other interest. Atanna still held Kentril's hand, and he hoped that meant that she would not be averse to advances made by him.

As if reading his thoughts, Zayl suddenly announced, "Great Lord of Ureh, with your permission, I think that I shall see if the Vizjerei might need some of my assistance."

"That would be most appreciated, my friend. One of the guards can direct you."

With a sweeping bow, the necromancer backed away, leaving Kentril with Juris Khan's daughter.

Her father smiled at the pair. "Atanna, I'm sure that the captain hungers. See that he is satiated."

"If that is your order," she replied with a slight inclination of her head.

Atanna led Kentril out, guiding him down a hall he had not traversed previously. Not once did she loosen her hold on him, and not once did the veteran fighter struggle to free his hand. In his mind, she could have led him the length and breadth of the kingdom, and he would have willingly followed.

"You've done so much for us, so much for me," she said as they walked alone. "I don't know how to thank you, captain."

"Kentril. My name's Kentril, my lady."

Under thick lashes, she smiled at him. "Kentril. You must call me Atanna in return, of course."

"It'd be my honor." He frowned. "Is Ureh really safe? Have we really beaten Gregus Mazi's spell?"

The smile faltered a bit. "You have secured us to the world. We cannot go beyond the area the shadow forms, but there is hope now that soon we can. Once my father is free of the other spell, he can proceed with some thoughts he has had, possibilities in which the sorcerer and the necromancer would be of much aid."

"You'd better have someone keep an eye on old Tsin. He's not the most honest of his ilk."

"My father knows how to read people, Kentril. You should realize that."

The corridor suddenly felt much too warm. The captain tried to think of another direction of conversation . . . and finally recalled the brooch.

"My lady—Atanna—I've got to confess that when I saw you with Lord Khan, it wasn't the first time I'd seen your face."

She laughed lightly, a musical sound. "And here I thought that I had entranced you with one single glimpse! I noted that you reacted far more than any of your comrades." Atanna cocked her head. "Tell me, then. How do you know of me?"

"Because of this." He pulled forth the brooch.

Atanna gasped when she saw it. She took it from his hand, running her index finger over the image of herself. "So long! So very long since I saw this! Where did you find it?"

"In the ruins, in the midst of the city—"

"He took it," the crimson-tressed young woman said in a tone so dark it actually made Kentril shiver slightly. "Gregus. He took it."

"But why?"

"Because he desired me, Kentril, desired me heart and soul. When he discovered that Ureh would return once the shadow of Nymyr touched this area in just such a way, he came not only to rectify his foul failure but to try to take me as his prize!"

Without his realizing it, the mercenary captain's hand slipped to the hilt of his sword. Atanna, however, noticed his action and blushed.

"You would be my champion, Kentril? If only you would've been there the first time. I know you wouldn't have let him do to Ureh what he did. I know that you would have slain the beast for us . . . for me."

He wanted to throw his arms around her but managed to hold back. Yet Captain Dumon could not help himself from replying, "I would do anything for you."

Her blushing only increased . . . and made her that much more alluring.

Atanna put the brooch back into his palm. "Take this back as a gift from me. Let it be a sign of my gratitude and . . . and my favor."

He tried to speak, tried to thank her, but before he could, Juris Khan's daughter stepped up on her toes and kissed him.

All else in the world faded to insignificance.

Zayl felt extremely uncomfortable. He had felt so for quite a long time, almost since he and the others had first met Juris Khan. That no one else might have recognized this discomfort gave credit to the necromancer's mental and physical skills. The training through which he had lived his entire life had granted Zayl virtual control over every aspect of his being. Few things could disturb the balance within him.

But something about Ureh and its inhabitants had. On the surface, the necromancer could see nothing capable of doing so. Khan and his people had been thrown into a most dire predicament, the victims of a spell twisted by a corrupted sorcerer. He as much as Captain Dumon had wanted to help them, although while the mercenary's interests had much to do with the beauteous offspring of Ureh's ruler, Zayl's interest had been in returning to balance that which had been madly left awry. Such a travesty as Gregus Mazi had enacted could have threatened the stability of the world itself, for whenever innocents suffered as the citizens of this kingdom had, it strengthened the cause of Hell.

Gregus Mazi . . .

"Here we are, sir," the guard who had accompanied Zayl remarked.

"Thank you. I have no more need of you."

The pale spellcaster entered. As he had requested, he had been led to the library where Juris Khan had kept Ureh's greatest magical tomes, holy works, scrolls, and artifacts. In the days of the kingdom's glory, a hundred scholars of both the mystical and theological paths would have been in the vast room perusing the ceiling-high shelves for the secrets and truths gathered here over the centuries.

Now only one slight figure hunched over a massive, moldering book almost as large as himself. Even as he entered, Zayl could hear Quov Tsin muttering to himself.

"But if the rune here means the sun's power and this segment refers to the Eye of Hest . . ."

The Vizjerei suddenly looked up, then glanced over his shoulder in the direction of the necromancer.

"Master Tsin," Zayl greeted the other spellcaster.

The short, bearded man snorted at the newcomer, then returned his gaze to the book.

"How goes your research?"

Without looking at Zayl, Quov Tsin testily retorted, "It goes slowly when young cretins constantly interrupt it with their blather!"

"Perhaps a combination of efforts would—"

Now the elderly Vizjerei did look at the necromancer again, but with eyes that burned bright with growing fury. "I am a sorcerer of the first magnitude. There is nothing I could learn from you."

"I only meant—"

"Wait! It occurs to me that there is one thing you can do."

Zayl frowned, suspicious. "What?"

With a venomous tone, the Vizjerei replied, "You can leave this library right now and get as far away from me as possible! You taint the very air I breathe."

The necromancer's gray eyes met Tsin's silver-gray ones. Both the Vizjerei and the servants of Rathma shared some common ancestry, but neither spellcaster would have ever acknowledged such a blood relation. As far as both sides were concerned, a gulf almost as wide as that between Heaven and Hell existed, a gulf neither wished to bridge.

"As you desire," the pale mage responded. "I would not want to put too much distress on one of such senior years. It could prove fatal."

With a snarl, Quov Tsin turned away. Zayl did likewise, leaving the library and marching down a deserted hallway.

He had not meant to get into any confrontation with the Vizjerei, no matter how minor. The necromancer had honestly wanted to help, the better to see Juris Khan free.

However, there were spells and research that Zayl could do on his own, paths of which the more materialistic Tsin would have never approved. Those who followed the ways of Rathma often found what other spellcasters carelessly overlooked. How ironic it would be if Zayl discovered quickly what his counterpart so struggled to find. Tsin badly wanted the magical tomes and relics Khan had promised him; it would eat him up inside if Zayl instead garnered the prizes.

"Zayl, boy! I must speak!"

He planted a hand over the bulky pouch at his side, trying to smother the voice that could not be smothered. Even though it had hardly spoken above a whisper, to the necromancer it had resounded like thunder in the empty hall.

"Zayl—"

"Quiet, Humbart!" he whispered. Quickly surveying the area, Zayl noticed the entrance to a balcony. With smooth, silent movements, the slim, pale man darted outside.

Below, the sounds of merriment continued. Zayl exhaled; out here, no one would hear him speaking with the skull.

He pulled what remained of Humbart Wessel out of the pouch, glaring into the empty eye sockets. "More than once you have nearly given away yourself, Humbart, and thereby put me in straits! Trust is not always an easy thing for one of my kind to attain, but it is a fairly easy thing for us to lose. Those who do not understand the truth of Rathma prefer to believe the lies."

"You mean, like raising the dead?"

"What is it you want, Humbart?"

"Gregus Mazi," answered the skull, the eye sockets almost seeming to narrow.

He had captured Zayl's attention. "What about him?"

"You didn't believe that hogwash about old Gregus, did you?" mocked Humbart. "Gregus, who wanted so badly to join his friends in Heaven that he prayed each morning and eve and cried most of the day through?"

Looking down at the torchlit city, the necromancer thought over everything that had been said about the sorcerer. During Juris Khan's revelations, Zayl had more than once pondered inconsistencies with what Humbart Wessel had told him but had also assumed that the lord of Ureh would certainly know Mazi better. "Sorcerers, especially those like the Vizjerei, can be a treacherous, lying bunch. Mazi simply fooled you, Humbart."

"If he fooled me, lad, then I've got two legs, a pair of arms, and all the bones in between still—and covered in a good wrapping of flesh to boot! Old Gregus, he was a torn man, blaming himself for not being good enough and praying for redemption from day one. He was no monster, no corrupted wizard, mark me!"

"But Juris Khan—"

"Either was fooled or lies through his teeth. I'd swear on my grave, and you know that's one oath I'll hold true to."

Now Zayl truly understood his own earlier anxieties. In the past, he had heard from the skull bits and pieces of the events that had taken place outside the shadowed kingdom, when Humbart Wessel and his men had watched Gregus Mazi rush to the ghostly city, arms raised in praise to Heaven and voice calling out thanks for this second opportunity. Every time Humbart had mentioned the spellcaster, it had always been as a man driven to redeem himself, to prove himself worthy.

Not at all the beast that Khan and his daughter had described.

"And what would you suggest?" the necromancer muttered.

"Find out the truth from the source, of course!"

Zayl gaped. "Gregus Mazi?"

It had never occurred to him to try to raise the specter of the dead mage. In the past, it had seemed impossible, for all trace of the man had been thought to have vanished along with the legendary kingdom, but now Zayl stood within that realm himself.

One problem remained, though. According to Juris Khan, Mazi had been utterly destroyed, his corporeal form incinerated. Without skin, hair, blood, or a sample of well-worn clothes, even a skilled necromancer such as Zayl could hope to accomplish little.

He said as much to the skull, which brought back a harsh and sarcastic response from Humbart. "Am I the only one of us who still has a brain in his head? Think, lad! Gregus was born and raised in Ureh. He lived here all his life until the spell that cast the soul of the city and its people into oblivion, and then he still came back again. More to the point, Zayl, Ureh's been frozen in time, almost unchanging. If old Gregus had a place to call his own here, the betting's good that it still stands."

What Humbart said made such sense that Zayl could not believe that he had not thought it. If a piece of clothing or an item often used could be found among the dead mage's belongings, it might prove enough to summon the shade of the man. Then from Gregus Mazi himself the necromancer could learn the truth—and possibly even the key to Ureh's salvation. If Mazi proved to be the evil that Juris Khan claimed him to be, Zayl could wring the secret of his spellwork from him far faster than Tsin could ever hope to do by thumbing through volume after volume of dusty tomes.

"We must find his home."

"Can't likely just ask, though, can we?"

Eyeing again the city below, where the celebrations continued unabated, Zayl allowed himself the slightest of smiles. "Perhaps we can, Humbart . . . perhaps we can."

A few minutes later, the cloaked spellcaster walked among the citizens of Ureh, a tower of black among the colorful locals dancing, cheering, and singing under the light of torches and oil lamps. It seemed odd to need torches and lamps at what should have been the brightest part of the day, but with the deep shadow of Nymyr also their protection from both exile and horrific death, the inhabitants of Ureh certainly seemed unwilling to complain.

Several men insisted on shaking his hand or slapping his back, while more than one enticing female sought to thank him even more personally. Zayl suffered the slaps and accepted politely the kisses on his cheek, but although he could not help being slightly caught up by the mood around him, the necromancer kept his mind on the task ahead.

"Damn, but I wish I had a body to go with this cracked old skull," came Humbart's voice from the pouch. "Ah, to drink some good ale, to find some bad women—"

"Quiet!" While it seemed unlikely that anyone would hear the skull in the midst of all this festivity, Zayl wanted to take no chances.

One of Kentril Dumon's men came swaggering down the street, a young woman on each arm. The bearded mercenary kissed the one clad in a golden outfit more appropriate for a harem, then noticed the necromancer watching him.

"Enjoyin' yourself, spellcaster?" He grinned and, momentarily releasing his companions, extended his arms to include all of Ureh. "The whole blasted kingdom wants ta celebrate us heroes!"

Zayl recalled the dark-haired fighter's name. Putting a slight smile on his own face, he commented, "A change from the usual mercenary's reward, yes, Brek?"

"You can say that!" Brek placed his arm around the second young woman, a sultry beauty with ample curves whose gossamer dress hid little. The fighter let his fingers dangle a scant inch or two over the uppermost of those curved areas as he paused to kiss her on the throat.

The one in gold began giving Zayl admiring glances. Under shaded eyes, she said, "Are you one of the heroes, too?"

"Careful there!" the mercenary jested. "He's a necromancer, ladies! You know, raise the dead and commune with spirits!"

If Brek thought that this would scare the two, he was sorely mistaken. In fact, both eyed Zayl with much more interest, so much, in fact, that he felt like a bound mouse set before two hungry cats.

"You raise the dead?" the first breathed. "And spirits, too?"

"Can you show us?" asked the second.

"Here now, ladies! Don't go givin' him any notions about that!"

Zayl shook his head. "It is not something lightly done, anyway, my ladies. Besides, I would not wish to dampen these festivities. After all, the curse of Gregus Mazi has finally been countered."

The one in gold lost all trace of humor. "A terrible, terrible man!"

"Yes, a traitorous person. Ureh would be well rid of all memory of him. Any images, any writings, they should all be destroyed. Even his sanctum should be razed to the ground, the better to forget his evil . . . that is, unless to do so would endanger the homes of others."

"There'd be little enough to burn," replied the curvaceous woman, "built into the mountain as it is."

"The mountain? He lived in a cave? How monstrous!"

"It was part of an old monastery, built before the city," she offered. "But monstrous of him, yes," the woman quickly added. "Monstrous, indeed."

Brek had heard enough such talk. "Now, girls, why don't we let the spell-caster be on his way? I'm sure he's got himself a rendezvous of his own, don't you, sir?"

Zayl recognized the suggestion to leave. With the smile still in place, he said, "Yes, as a matter of fact, there is someone dying to meet me."

The women laughed lightly at this, but the fighter gave Zayl's jest a sour expression in reply. Bowing slightly, the necromancer bid them goodbye, then walked off as if rejoining the celebration.

"Now I know where they got the expression *gallows humor,*" Humbart muttered from his pouch.

"I merely wanted them to think I had no purpose but amusement tonight."

"With jests like that? Now, me, I would've said—"

"Quiet." Zayl gave the pouch a slight rap as added emphasis.

He now knew where to find the former abode of the mysterious Gregus Mazi, and, once there, he would surely be able to locate some item with which to summon the man's shade. Then, at last, Zayl would find out the truth, find out whose version of facts fit.

Find out why a reborn Ureh would trouble him so.

Brek stumbled into the home of one of his two companions with lust fully on his besotted mind. Even the necromancer's thankfully brief interruption of his pleasuring had not lessened his desires. Not only did both young women seem willing, but they were far, far more attractive than those with whom he usually found himself. It would be good, for a change, not to find the next morning that he had bedded some one-eyed she-demon with skin more leathery than his boots. Brek felt certain he had it in him to more than satisfy both beauties, and even if it turned out he didn't, at least if they satisfied him, it would all be worth it.

Only a dim light far, far back in the building cast any illumination. The mercenary wended his way toward it, only belatedly realizing that he no longer had an arm around either of his intended treats. At some point near the doorway, both had gone missing.

"Here now, ladies!" he called. "Where've you run off to?"

"Over here . . ." called the voice of the one Brek recalled as wearing the striking golden outfit.

If she wanted to be first, then he would not disappoint her. Brek followed the call, reaching out with his hands as he gradually made his way toward the faint light.

"Almost there . . ." murmured the second, the woman whose shape the fighter had found so appealing.

"So you both want a piece of me at once?" He laughed. "That's fine with me!"

"We're glad you think so," said the first, moving into the light.

Brek screamed.

Under scraps of hair, a husk of a face stared empty-eyed at the mercenary. A mouth shaped into a circle and filled at the edges with sharp, needlelike teeth gaped. Any flesh on what had once been a female face had dried away, leaving skin so taut it barely could hold in the skull.

Bony claws stretched forth, seeking him. Vaguely he noted the tattered remains of the golden dress, then the horror of what he faced finally stirred Brek to action. He reached down for his sword, only to find the scabbard empty.

Where had the weapon gone? He slowly recalled how, at an inn, he had showed the women and some other onlookers how he had helped battle the hellish cat. After that, there had been a round of drinks in honor of his heroism, and then—

He had never retrieved the sword from next to his chair.

Brek fearfully backed away, only to collided with someone. He looked over his shoulder and saw, to his horror, another cadaverous yet hungry face, a mummified shell who could only be the other of his feminine companions.

"We'd all like a piece of you," it said.

And as she spoke, Brek became aware that other figures moved in the dim light, figures with similar outlines, figures all around him, reaching, hungering . . .

He managed one last, short cry before they enveloped him.

EIGHT

Captain Dumon had always imagined Heaven as a place of light, a place where darkness could never invade. He would have never thought that Heaven could be a realm where shadow preserved and even the light of dawn could mean death.

Of course, Heaven to him was any place where he could be with Atanna.

He had left her some hours before, but still she had his heart and mind. Kentril had only slept lightly since, yet he felt refreshed, more alive than ever in his entire life.

He peered out of the window of the room given to him, to see the city still alive with torches. Although a part of him yearned for some bit of daylight simply in order to mark the passage of time, the captain knew that could not be. Until the people of Ureh could safely stand in the sun, the shadow had to remain fixed over the kingdom.

Atanna felt certain that her father could remedy the situation now that they had some stability on the mortal plane. However, to accomplish anything, he first had to be free, and only through Quov Tsin could that be possible.

Never before had Kentril looked to the Vizjerei for any true magical assistance. He had desired some, yes, during the battle with the demon cat, but had not actually expected much. Now he prayed that Tsin would prove himself the master he claimed to be.

"Kentril."

Gorst stood at the doorway to his chambers, the massive fighter at attention. Kentril blinked, recalling that each morning he generally received a status report from his second. Of course, with their work for Tsin seemingly at an end, the captain had put all such tasks from his mind. Only Khan's daughter concerned him now.

"Yes, Gorst."

"Three missing, Kentril."

"Missing?"

"Seven came back." He grinned. "Drunk. Three didn't."

Captain Dumon shrugged. "Not too surprising, all things considered. Actually, I'm amazed that so many returned."

"Want me to watch for them?"

"Not unless they go missing for a couple days. We're all being treated like kings here, Gorst. They're just reveling in it, that's all."

The black-maned fighter started to turn away, then commented, "She's prettier than on the brooch, Kentril."

"I know. Gorst . . . any word from Tsin on his efforts?" If any of them had kept some track of the Vizjerei's work, it would have been the huge mercenary.

"The magic man thinks he's got something."

That pleased Kentril. "Good. Where can I find him?"

"With the books." When it became clear that his captain did not understand, Gorst grunted. "I'll show you."

Kentril followed him through a maze of halls until they came to what surely had to be one of the largest collections of writings the mercenary had ever either heard of or seen. While he could read and write after a fashion—not something most of his men could do—Kentril could not imagine himself putting together so many words. Moreover, the words in these tomes and scrolls had not only meaning but *power*. These words had magic.

The shelves rose high, each filled with leather-bound volumes or tightly sealed parchments. No direct system of order could be seen, but as a military man, Captain Dumon assumed that there had to be one. Well-worn ladders stood before every other set of shelves, and tables with stools had been set aside for those making use of Ureh's literary treasures.

As a mercenary, Kentril could also appreciate the value of the many writings stored in this vast chamber. Sorcerers like Quov Tsin often paid hefty prices for such books, and he had himself retrieved one or two for good pay. Still, at the moment, all Kentril saw in the library was the means by which Atanna could be free.

No, he saw something else besides. Seated in the midst of the lamplit chamber, Quov Tsin huddled over books and sheets, scribbling notes with a quill and keeping his index finger on one of the pages of one particularly massive tome.

The Vizjerei did not look up as Kentril neared. Under his breath, Tsin muttered incomprehensible things, and the sorcerer had a look upon his wrinkled features that caused the hardened fighter to pause. He had seen the diminutive Vizjerei obsessed before, but now Tsin resembled a man gone completely mad. His eyes never blinked as he worked, and his gaze went only from the book to the sheet upon which he wrote and back again. A grin that the captain had only seen on corpses stretched far across the slight figure's face, giving Tsin a very unsettling expression.

Kentril cleared his throat.

The stooped figure did not look up, instead scrawling new notes over the already heavily covered parchment.

"Tsin."

With what almost seemed a monumental struggle, the avian face turned his way. *"What is it, Dumon?"*

The venom with which the Vizjerei spoke each syllable left both Kentril and Gorst taken aback. The captain realized that his hand had slipped to the hilt of his sword, and he quickly removed it before Tsin could take any further umbrage.

"I came to see how you were progressing with Lord Khan and the city's—"

"*I could be progressing much faster without constant and inane interruptions by the likes of you, cretin!*" Quov Tsin slammed his fist on the table, sending ink spreading across the bottom of the parchment and over his hand. He seemed not to notice what he had done, more concerned with spitting barbed words at those before him. "*You come clawing and squeaking and questioning, all of you, when here I sit on the verge of discovery! Can your feeble minds not comprehend the magnitude of what I struggle toward?*"

Releasing the quill, the ink-stained hand reached for the sorcerer's staff. Malice filled Tsin's eyes.

Kentril backed up more, nearly colliding with Gorst. "Easy there, Tsin! Are you insane?"

Knuckles white, the Vizjerei clutched the staff. His silver-gray eyes darted from the two men to the rune-covered rod and back again. For a few dangerous seconds, a struggle between choices clearly unfolded . . . and then at last Quov Tsin put the staff to the side and with much effort turned back to his task.

Without looking at the pair, he whispered, "You had better leave."

"Tsin, I think you need some rest . . . and when's the last time you ate any—"

Both of the spellcaster's bony hands tightened. Eyes still downcast, he said again, "*You had better leave.*"

Gorst took Kentril by the shoulder, and the two backed out of the library. They said nothing until several steps down the corridor, where they hoped Tsin could not hear them.

"Was he like that the last time you saw him?" Captain Dumon interrogated his second.

"No . . . not so bad, anyway, Kentril."

"I knew the old mage was ill tempered, but Tsin nearly tried to kill us, you know that, don't you?"

The giant gave him a brooding look. "I know."

"I should go have a talk with Juris Khan. It won't do anyone any good if old Tsin goes violently mad. He might hurt someone."

"Maybe he just needs to take a nap."

Kentril grimaced. "Well, if anyone can make him do it, it'd have to be Khan. You saw how much he listened to me."

"You want me to keep an eye on him?" Gorst asked.

"Only if you keep your distance. Don't do it immediately, though. Let him get lost in his work again for an hour or two first. That might be better."

From somewhere within the palace, a flute began to play. Suddenly, Kentril lost all interest in the damnable Vizjerei's antics. He knew of only one person in Khan's sanctum who played a flute.

"Maybe if I talk to Atanna first, she can better explain it to her father," the captain could not help saying. "That'd probably be the best course of action for me."

The grin returned to Gorst's broad face. "Probably be."

Kentril felt his face flush. He turned to go, but could not help adding at the last, "Just be careful, Gorst."

The grin remained. "You, too."

The flute playing continued, the same haunting melody that he had heard that first fateful time. Captain Dumon followed the music through numerous, winding halls that made it feel to him as if he were repeating his journey to the library. At last, Kentril came not to a balcony or one of the many vast chambers but rather to an open gate leading to, of all things, a vast inner courtyard open to the sky, a courtyard doubling as an extensive garden.

Garden perhaps understated severely the sight. A miniature forest—more a jungle—spread out before the veteran soldier. Exotic trees and plants that seemed like none Kentril had ever encountered, not even on the trek to this distant part of Kehjistan, grew tall and strong. Dark greens, vivid crimsons, bright yellows, and fiery oranges decorated the tableau in arresting fashion. There were hanging vine plants and monstrous flowers, some of the latter larger than his head. One could literally become lost within a garden such as this, of that Kentril had no doubt.

And near the path leading into it, Atanna, seated on a stone bench, played her flute. A billowing, silky dress with a long, thin skirt somehow emphasized rather than hid her slim but curved form. Her long red tresses hung down over the left side of her face, reaching all the way to a most attractive décolletage. She did not notice him at first, but when he started toward her, captivated by the sight of her playing, Atanna suddenly looked up.

Her eyes held such an intensity that they left Kentril at a loss for how to proceed. Atanna, however, took control of the situation by putting down her flute and coming to him.

"Kentril! I hope you slept well."

"Very much. You play beautifully, Atanna."

She gave him a most demure look. "I think not, but my father shares your opinion."

Not certain what to say yet, the captain glanced past her at the garden. "One never knows what to expect next here."

"Do you like it? This is my favorite place. I've spent much of my life here, and much of our exile, too."

"It's . . . unique."

Atanna pulled him toward it. "You must have a closer look!"

Despite the fanciful colors of the flowers and some of the plants, the garden had a rather foreboding look that Kentril did not truly notice until his hostess had led him up to the path running through it. Suddenly the beauty and wonder of it gave way to an uneasiness. Now it reminded him more of the jungle through which he and his men had fought, the same jungle that had claimed four of his party.

"What's the matter?" Juris Khan's daughter asked.

"Nothing." He steeled himself for the walk through. This was not the same stark jungle. This was simply a fanciful garden built for the lord of the realm. What danger could possibly exist within such a confined space?

"I love it here," she murmured. "It takes me away from the world in which I'm trapped, lets me imagine I'm far away, in another land, about to meet a handsome stranger."

Kentril started to say something but decided he could not trust his tongue not to tie itself up. He could scarcely believe himself. Never in his life had any woman left him feeling so befuddled.

Broad-leafed plants brushed their shoulders, and occasional vines, seeming to drop from nowhere, dangled near their heads. The path at their feet had been made to seem quite natural, a covering of soft dirt and sand over what felt like solid stone.

With each step, though, it grew darker and darker, until at last he could see neither the entrance through which they had come nor the exit far ahead. Now he truly felt as if he had stepped back into the jungle.

His companion noticed his sudden anxiety. "You're shivering!"

"It's nothing, my lady."

"You're supposed to call me Atanna," she responded in mock anger. "Or did this mean so little to you?"

She leaned forward and kissed him. His anxieties concerning his surroundings vanished in an instant. Kentril wrapped his arms around her and returned her passion.

Then he felt something on his neck, a slow but steady movement like that of a worm or a caterpillar. Yet whatever crawled upon his skin did so with appendages as sharp as needles.

Unable to withstand it, Captain Dumon pushed Atanna back and quickly reached for the creature. However, as his hand neared, the thing suddenly pulled away, as if perhaps falling off.

"What is it?" Atanna cautiously asked.

"Something landed on me! It felt as if it walked across my neck with tiny swords at the end of each leg!"

Even in the darkness, he could make out her face well enough. Atanna frowned in consideration, but seemed to have no knowledge to offer. "Shall we leave?"

The pain had faded, and Kentril had no desire to look cowardly and foolish before her, especially over some insect. "No, let's go on as we have."

They moved on a few paces, stopping again to kiss. Atanna then buried her head in his chest, saying, "Father still hopes to complete the journey to Heaven."

He stiffened. "Is that still possible?"

"So he believes. I pray he's wrong."

"But why?"

She put her hand on his cheek. "Because I find the mortal world more to my liking."

"Can you talk him out of it?" The gentle caress of her hand against his skin helped Kentril relax again.

"It would help if I knew that we stood an easier and safer chance of making our tentative hold on the mortal plane a permanent one. If I could convince him that for the sake of all, we would be better off once more among men, then I feel that he'd acquiesce. After all, the threat we fled no longer exists."

She wanted to stay, and he wanted her to stay. Yet Juris Khan wished at last to achieve the holy goal offered to him during those dark years of terror. Not surprising, but certainly not wanted by either here.

"Maybe Tsin would know—" Kentril started before recalling the possession the Vizjerei seemed under. He did not want to try to speak with Tsin, at least not until the sorcerer had been persuaded to rest and eat properly.

"Maybe he could convince Father?" Her tone spoke openly of hope. "The old one seems very skilled, if lacking in common courtesy. Do you think he could do it?"

"I don't—" The captain paused. An idea began to formulate, one that would possibly play on old Tsin's personality.

Atanna appeared to sense his shifting mood. "You've thought of something, haven't you?"

"A possible idea. If Tsin remains constant, it could work to our—*your* benefit. I need to think about it a little longer, and it would be good if I didn't talk to him just now."

"I have no intention of parting with you just yet, anyway," the young woman responded. "Not at the moment." Atanna stepped up and kissed him again.

Feeling much better about matters, Captain Dumon responded in kind. If the Vizjerei could be persuaded to see his way, then Tsin, in turn, would likely persuade Khan. All Kentril had to do was play on the spellcaster's greed—

He let out a gasp of pain. Something dug at his back as if trying to reach all the way into his heart. He twisted around, felt what seemed one of the vines, and swiftly grabbed it.

What felt like a thousand pins sank into his fingers and palm.

"Kentril!"

Despite his agony, the mercenary kept his hold, then tugged with all his might.

A peculiar and not at all human squeal coursed through the garden. The entire vine tumbled to the path, a dark, sinewy form more than three times the length of a man.

Throwing the end down, Kentril clutched the hand that had held the plant with his other. It felt as if he had stuck the throbbing appendage into an open fire.

"Atanna! Wh-what was—"

"I've no idea! Your hand! Give me your hand!"

Her soft fingers lightly touched his own. The pain receded. Atanna whispered something, then leaned down and let her lips lightly touch his palm.

Fearful of her suffering from whatever plant poison had gotten him, the captain tried to pull away. With surprising strength, however, Juris Khan's daughter held on.

"Please, Kentril! Rest easy. I know what I'm about."

It seemed that she did, for the more she worked at his injury, the less and less it hurt him. Before long, he could even flex the fingers without feeling so much as a twinge.

"What did you do?" he finally asked.

"I am my father's daughter," was her reply. "I am the daughter of the Most Revered Juris Khan."

Meaning that she shared some of his wondrous skills. Caught up in her glory, he had forgotten that she had such talents.

Now that Atanna had dealt with his injury, he recalled what had attacked him in the first place. Squinting, Kentril searched the dark path for the end of the vine.

His companion found it first. "Were you looking for this?"

"Be careful!"

But she looked unaffected by the vile plant. "This could not be what stung you. This is only a *Hakkara* vine. In some parts of the world, they eat the fleshy bottom part. It has much juice and is claimed to be healthy."

"That spiny thing?" He took it from her, only to find it smooth and soft save for a few tiny bumps. Frustrated, Kentril ran his hands along the length of the vine, finding nothing out of the ordinary.

"You must've been bitten by an insect of some sort. Probably the same one that bothered you before," Atanna suggested. "Sometimes some of the jungle insects used to make their way to the city, despite how the mountain causes the air here to be cooler than they like."

"An insect? In Ureh?"

"And why not? You and your friends are here. Why not an insect that happened to be near? The jungle isn't that far from the edge of our kingdom."

Her words made sense, but did not completely mollify him. He looked around the darkened garden, finally saying, "Let's move on."

Only when the first glimmer of light at the other end materialized did Kentril feel any calmer. As they exited, he looked back with barely concealed distaste. Atanna and others in Ureh might find such a grove peaceful and beautiful, but to the soldier, it now seemed more in tune with the nightmarish curse Gregus Mazi had wrought. Had the timeless exile in limbo somehow changed the plants in ways that Khan's daughter did not notice?

"Now that we've got better light," Atanna suddenly said, "let me see your hand again."

He turned it over for both of them to study—and saw little more than a few healing welts. Kentril could scarcely believe it, having felt as if his entire hand should be a bloody, perforated mess.

Running her finger over the remaining marks, the young woman commented, "In a short time, these, too, will vanish."

"It's amazing. Thank you." He had witnessed magic before, but never had any been performed on him. Kentril felt certain that if Atanna had not used her skills, he would have been much worse at this moment.

"It's only a small thing . . . and I feel bad that you suffered because of me. If I hadn't invited you to walk with me—"

"Such things happen. Don't blame yourself."

She looked up at him with imploring eyes. "Will you still talk to Master Tsin about trying to get Father to change his mind?"

"Of course I will!" How could Atanna think otherwise? The captain did this as much for himself as for her. "Old Tsin's consistent. I explain the matter to his liking, he'll be certain to do what he can to make Lord Khan see it right, too."

"I hope so." She kissed him again. "And thinking of my father, I must go to him now. Since he cannot move from the chair, I play for him to help ease his burdens. Perhaps I can even make a mild suggestion already. He's always more agreeable after my music."

With one final kiss, Atanna left him, her slim form disappearing into the garden. Kentril watched her vanish, but although the garden would have likewise been the appropriate route for him, the mercenary did not enter. Instead, he walked around the perimeter, keeping a cautious distance. By the time Kentril reached where Khan's daughter had been playing, both she and the flute had long left.

Alone, Captain Dumon took one last, measured look at the unsettling grove. At first glance, it seemed no more unusual than any patch of jungle or forest, and as a place specifically sculpted by some master gardener, it should have presented an even less intimidating image than either of the former. Yet, the more he studied it, the more Kentril felt that if he had entered alone, it would have been much more difficult to come out.

From behind him, someone cleared his throat. "Captain?"

"Albord." He hoped that the other mercenary had not noticed him jump ever so slightly. "What is it?"

"Sorry to bother you, but a couple of us were wonderin' when we might get our reward from his lordship so we can get goin' home."

"You're already tired of all the acclamation, Albord?"

The plain-faced, white-haired fighter looked a bit uncomfortable. Kentril forgot that despite his experience and skills, Albord was much younger than most of those in the company. That he had often been left in charge when Gorst could not be spared had said much for his abilities. "It's not that—I had as good a time as any, captain—but a few of us want to head back to Westmarch." He shrugged. "Just feel more comfortable at home than here, sir."

The last thing that Kentril wanted was to leave, but he could understand how the others might feel. Gorst would probably stay; he had no family, no kin. The rest, though, had ties to the Western Kingdoms, even loved ones. That these men served as mercenaries had as much to do with feeding mouths as with becoming rich.

All thought of the garden fading, the captain patted Albord on the shoulder. "I'll see what can be done about the lot of you going home. If I do, can I trust you to bring something back to the families of those lost? If I read our host right, one small sack should have enough to split among the survivors and leave them well off."

"Aye, captain! You know I'll be honest."

Kentril had no doubt about that. He also knew which other men from the survivors would be cut from similar cloth. No one joined Captain Dumon's company who did not first undergo thorough scrutiny. If Kentril sent Albord home with coin for those left behind by Benjin, Hargo, and the others, it would reach them.

Grateful, the younger fighter saluted. He started to step away, then hesitated. "Captain, two men still haven't come back from the city."

"I know. Gorst told me three, actually."

"Simon dragged himself in just a little while ago, but he said Jace was headin' back hours before, and no one's seen a sign of Brek."

Having known far too many men like the pair missing, Kentril shrugged off Albord's concern. "They'll pop up, you'll see. They won't want to miss their share, remember."

"Should I send someone out to look?"

"Not now." The captain became a little impatient. He needed to take some time to think about how best to phrase things so that Tsin would readily see his point of view. Kentril had no more time to waste on drunken mercenaries gone astray. "I told Gorst already that if they don't show up in a couple days, maybe then." Hoping he had not sounded too uncaring, Captain Dumon patted Albord's shoulder again. "Try to relax. Enjoy this! Believe me, Albord, it happens all too little for those like us. The jungle we crossed or that winter near the Gulf of Westmarch, that's our usual payoff."

Albord gave him a plowboy's smile, reminding Kentril of the background of almost every low-paid mercenary ever born. "I suppose I can take the food and women a little longer."

"That's the spirit!" the older fighter proclaimed as he began guiding the other back down the hall. In his mind, Kentril pictured Atanna, his own reason for staying . . . perhaps forever. At least until he had talked the Vizjerei into persuading Juris Khan no longer to seek the righteous path to Heaven, the captain did not want to broach the subject of payment. It was not as if Albord and the others were not being rewarded in other ways.

Besides, Kentril thought, what *harm* could a few more days' waiting do?

Nine

❋

The perpetual shadow over Ureh worked in Zayl's favor as he climbed toward Gregus Mazi's mountain sanctum. Even though the former monastery faced away from much of the city below, enough of a line of sight existed that would have made it quite simple in daylight for anyone to spot the cloaked form wending his way up the half-broken path carved into the rock face.

Zayl could appreciate the location the sorcerer had chosen and wondered why he had never noticed the ruins of it earlier. The spell that had taken a spirit form of Ureh and cast it Heavenward had interesting touches to it that he hoped later to investigate.

Below him, the celebrating continued unabated. Zayl frowned. Did the people require no sleep? True, the realm of limbo did not fall under the same laws as the mortal plane, but surely by now exhaustion should have taken many of the inhabitants.

Huge, ominous forms stood guard as he at last reached what passed for a gateway to the monastery. Once they had been archangels with majestic, blazing swords and massive, outstretched wings, but, like their counterparts on the doors of Khan's palace, these had been heavily damaged. One angel missed an entire wing and the right side of its face; the other had no head at all and only stubs where once the magnificent, plumed appendages had risen.

Zayl crawled over rubble, finding it interesting that Gregus Mazi's abode remained so ruined when all else in Ureh had been restored to new. The necromancer could only assume that the people of the cursed city had taken out their anger at some point on the abode of their absent tormentor. Zayl only hoped that this did not mean that Mazi's sanctum had been ransacked.

He wished again that he knew more about the ways of the realm in which Ureh had been trapped. Khan hinted that a semblance of the passage of time did exist, for had he not talked of researching a method of escape during those centuries of imprisonment? Yet it seemed that no one had needed to eat, for certainly the food could not have lasted so very long.

What remained of the monastery itself did not initially impress Zayl. Thrust out of the very side of the mountain, the unassuming outline indicated only a two-story, block-design structure that could not have held more than two rooms to a level. A single small balcony overlooked all below, and only a low wall pretended to give any protection whatsoever to the place.

Despite some disappointment in what he had found so far, the necromancer continued on. At the base of the building, he found a plain wooden door the likes of which might have decorated a simple country inn. His eyesight far better suited to the dark than most humans, Zayl made out damage on every side of the doorway. Someone had used axes and clubs to batter every inch of the stone frame, almost as if in absolute frustration. Oddly, though, the door itself looked absolutely untouched.

It took only the placing of his hand on the wood to discover why. A complex series of protective spells crisscrossed all over, making the door itself virtually impenetrable not only to physical attack, but even to many forms of magical assault. The stone frame, which had suffered some superficial cracks, also had spells cast over it, but those felt older, as if not laid upon the structure by its last and most infamous tenant. Zayl's estimate of the monastery as a place for a sorcerer to live rose. The monks who had built it had evidently strengthened it through some very powerful prayers if even after all this time most of the wards held.

Looking up, the necromancer found no visible windows. In one place, it appeared as if once there had been a window, but in the past it had been covered over quite thoroughly with stone. Zayl assumed that if he climbed up and investigated it, he would find the former opening as well-shielded as the entrance.

That left only the door as a way inside. The pale spellcaster touched it again, sensing the myriad bindings Gregus Mazi had set into place to ensure the safety of his sanctum. The ancient sorcerer had clearly been very adept at his art.

Zayl pulled Humbart's skull free. "Tell me what you see."

"Besides the door, you mean?"

"You know what I want from you."

He thrust the skull closer to the entrance, letting it survey everything. After a few moments, Humbart said, "There's lines all over, boy. Some good strong magic here and not all by one person. Most of it is, but there's underlying lines that have to be from two, even three. Even some prayer work, too."

One interesting feature concerning the skull that the necromancer had discovered after animating it had been that the spirit of Humbart Wessel could now see the workings of magic in ways no living spellcaster could. Zayl had no references upon which to draw for a reason for this ability and could only assume that the many centuries of having lain near the ruins of Ureh had somehow changed the skull. Over the past few years, the talent had come in quite handy, saving Zayl hours, even days, of painstaking work.

With his other hand, the black-clad figure removed the ivory dagger. Hilt held up, he asked Humbart, "Where do most intersect?"

"Down to the left, boy. Waist level—no!—not there. More to the right—stop!"

Pointing the hilt at the spot the skull had indicated, Zayl muttered under his breath.

The dagger began to glow.

Suddenly, a multicolored pattern reminiscent of a hexagon within a flower burst into existence at the point specified. Still whispering, Zayl thrust the hilt into the exact center, at the same time turning the end of the dagger in a circular motion.

The magical pattern flashed bright, then instantly faded away.

"You've cleared much of it, lad. There's still a little lock picking to do, though."

With Humbart's fleshless head to guide him, Zayl gradually removed the last impediments. Had he been forced to rely on his own skills alone, he doubted that he would have had such quick success. The wards had been skillfully woven together. However, one advantage the necromancer had discovered had been that the most cunning had been set to guard against *demons*, not men. Questioning the skull revealed that the majority of those had been created more recently, which likely pointed to Gregus Mazi as their caster.

"You can walk right in now," Humbart finally announced.

The skull in the crook of one arm and the dagger now held ready for more mundane use, Zayl stepped inside.

A darkened hall greeted him. The necromancer muttered a word, and the blade of the dagger began to glow.

Zayl had thought Mazi's sanctum rather small, but now he saw that he had been sorely mistaken. The empty hall led deep into the mountainside, so deep that he could not even see the end. To his left, a set of winding steps obviously led to the more visible portion of the structure, but Zayl only had interest in where the corridor ahead ended. True, he might have been able to find what he needed in the outer rooms, but the spellcaster's curiosity had been piqued. What secrets had Gregus Mazi left behind?

With the dagger lighting the way, Zayl headed down the hall. The walls had been patiently carved from bedrock, then polished fine. However, the same monks who had no doubt performed the back-breaking work had not then bothered much with adornment. Now and then, the fluttering figure of an armed archangel pointed farther ahead, but other than that, neither the monks nor Mazi had bothered to decorate further.

Zayl paused at the third such image so lovingly carved into the walls, suddenly noticing something about it.

Humbart, still in his arm, grew impatient. "I'm staring at a blank wall inches from where my nose used to be, Zayl, lad. Is there anything more interesting above?"

The cloaked figure raised the skull so that his dead companion could see. "It is untouched."

"And that would mean?"

"Think about it, Humbart. The doors of the palace. The archangels at the gateway leading here. All purposely damaged, as if by those who hated such holy images."

"Aye, and so?"

Moving to the next angel, Zayl saw that it, too, remained in pristine condition. "Why would so corrupted a mage as Gregus Mazi has been claimed to be leave these untouched?"

"Maybe he didn't want to make a mess in his own good home?"

"This means something, Humbart." But what it meant exactly, the necromancer did not know. He pushed on, glancing at some of the other heavenly guides, yet none had more than a slight weathered look to it. No, Mazi had not wreaked any harm on those images within his own abode, and that made no sense to Zayl.

They came at last across the first rooms actually carved into the mountain, rooms the last tenant had clearly not bothered much to use. Little remained of any furnishings. A few very old beds sat lonely in the far corners of some, the wood slowly rotting away. Some had already collapsed.

"Old Gregus never struck me as a sociable sort," Humbart commented quietly. "Looks like that was truth. Can't think he had too many visitors here."

After several more such rooms, Zayl at last came across a set of stone steps leading down. Unable to see the bottom, the necromancer proceeded with even more caution, the dagger ahead of him and a spell upon his lips.

Fortunately, no trap or demon struck. At the end of the stairway, he found a short corridor ending in three closed doors, one in front and the others flanking him. A quick study revealed all to be identical, and when Zayl had the skull look them over, Humbart informed him that none of them had any sort of ward in place.

"I'm reminded of a story about an adventurer," the skull went on while the necromancer considered his choice. "He came across three such doors. Now, he had been told that two doors led to treasure and escape, while the third held certain, horrible death. Well, the lad gave it some thought, listened at the doors, and finally made his choice."

Zayl, just on the point of picking the one to his left, noticed Humbart's sudden silence. "And so what happened?"

"Why, he opened one and got himself eaten alive by a pack of ghouls, of course! As it turns out, none of the doors led to gold or safety, and all of them, in fact, had monstrous, grisly ends waiting for those who—"

"Shut up, Humbart."

Even though the skull had not seen any wards, Zayl did not assume the entranceways were free of risk. Placing his unliving companion back in the pouch, he readied himself for any trap his opening the first door might spring.

A vast chamber full of dust and nothing more greeted him.

"Are you eaten yet?" came Humbart's muffled voice.

The necromancer grimaced. Gregus Mazi might have taken over what had been left of the old monastery, but he had not made use of much of it. Perhaps, Zayl thought, he would have been better off searching through the outer rooms first after all.

Looking at the remaining two doors, he chose the first of the pair. Surely the door faced first by any who came down the steps had to be the one.

Steeling himself again, Zayl pushed it open.

Row upon row of half-rotted tables spread out before him, and a looming archangel with one hand held forward in blessing seemed to reach out from the wall on the far side. Zayl swore under his breath, realizing that he had found where the monks had met for their meals. From the looks of everything, it was yet another chamber not bothered much with by the late Mazi.

With little fanfare, he turned about and headed directly for the one entrance left. Thrusting the glowing dagger before him, Zayl barged in.

An array of glassware and arcane objects greeted him from every direction, even the ceiling.

Zayl paused to drink it all in. Here now, the world of Gregus Mazi began. Here, displayed before the necromancer, was the workplace of a man of intense interest in every aspect of his calling. With one sweep of the illuminated blade, Zayl saw jars filled with herbs of every kind, pickled and preserved creatures the likes of which even the necromancer could not identify, and chemicals by the scores in both powder and liquid form. There were racks of books and scrolls, open parchments with notes, and drawings atop some of the tables, and even artifacts hung by chains from certain parts of the ceiling.

Everything had a polished appearance to it, making it seem as if it had been only yesterday that the sorcerer had been at work here. In point of fact, Zayl realized that for this sanctum, it *had* only been a few days at most. The peculiarities of limbo had once again preserved history.

"Must be very interesting out there . . . I suppose," Humbart called.

Pulling the skull free, the necromancer placed it on the main table next to where Mazi had been making notes. Holding the dagger near, Zayl looked over the writing.

"What is it?"

"Spell patterns. Theoretical outcomes. This Gregus Mazi was a practical thinker." The necromancer frowned. "Not what I would have expected of him."

"Evil can be very clever, if that's what you mean, lad."

Zayl studied the parchment in more detail. "Yes, but all of these notes concern only how to make the ascension to Heaven possible. It is written as if by someone who truly believes in the quest."

Giving the parchment one more glance, the necromancer turned to study the rest of the chamber again. As he held the dagger ahead of him, Zayl saw that the room stretched farther back than he had initially imagined. In the dim light, he could make out more shelves, more jars . . .

"Here now! You're not going to leave me alone, are you?"

"You will be fine, Humbart."

"Says the one with the legs."

Disregarding the skull's protests, Zayl moved farther into Gregus Mazi's sanctum. From container after container, creatures long dead stared back at him with bulbous, unseeing eyes. A black and crimson spider larger than his head floated in a thick, gooey mixture. There were young sand maggots and even a fetish, one of the sinister, cannibalistic denizens of the jungle. Doll-like in appearance, but with a totem mask face, they hid among the trees and thick foliage, seeking to take down the unwary by numbers. Necromancers destroyed them wherever they found the foul creatures, for nothing but evil came from them.

"Zayl, lad? You still alive there?"

"I'm still here, Humbart."

"Aye, and so am I, but it's not like *I've* so much choice in that respect!"

One specimen in particular caught the necromancer's attention. At first, he thought it a square sample of skin, perhaps even from one of the tentacle beasts in the jungle rivers. Yet, as he peered closely at the gray, hand-sized patch, he saw that on each corner were three tiny but very sharp claws and in the center what might have been a mouth of sorts. Slight bits of fur also seemed evident near the edges of the form.

Curious about this oddity, Zayl took the jar down, placing it on the nearest table.

"What's that you've got there, boy? I heard glass clink."

"Nothing to concern yourself with." The necromancer removed the lid, then, after locating a pair of tongs no doubt used just for such a purpose, fished for the specimen. He pulled the bizarre creature free of the soupy liquid, letting residue drip back into the container as he used the dagger to study it up close.

"I don't like to complain, boy, but are you going to investigate every damned jar—"

Zayl glanced over his shoulder at the barely seen skull. "I will not be long—"

A hiss suddenly arose from the container.

The tongs were pulled from his hand as something massive tried to wrap itself over the top half of his body.

"Zayl! Zayl, lad!"

The necromancer could not answer. A dripping, pulsating form with hide like an alligator covered his face, shoulders, and most of one arm. Zayl cried out as what felt like daggers thrust into his back, tearing through his garments as if they were nothing.

Teeth, jagged teeth, tore at his chest.

Belatedly, he realized that he had also lost the dagger. Zayl tried to speak a spell, but could barely breathe, much less talk.

The force of his monstrous attacker sent both tumbling to the floor. The shock of striking the stone surface almost did Zayl in, but he held on, well aware that to give in to unconsciousness would mean certain, grisly death.

The hissing grew louder, more fearsome, and, so it seemed, did the monstrosity seeking to overwhelm him. Now the necromancer could feel it almost covering his body down to his hips. If the creature managed to enshroud him entirely, Zayl knew well that he would be lost.

With all his might, he struggled to push the moist, unsettling form up. As he did, though, the talons tore at his back, ripping through everything. The agony almost caused him to lose his grip.

From without came the muffled, desperate voice of Humbart Wessel. "Zayl! Lad! I can see a light! I think the blade's by your left! Just a few inches left!"

Using his weight, Zayl sent both his attacker and himself sliding in that direction. He felt something near his shoulder, but then the tapestry-like horror shifted, causing the necromancer to move with it.

Humbart shouted something else, but whatever it was became stifled by the thick, suffocating form atop Zayl.

More desperate now, Zayl threw himself again to the left. This time, he felt the hilt of the dagger under his shoulder blade. Half-smothered, in danger of being bitten, he twisted to reach it with his right hand.

The teeth clamped down on his forearm with such ferocity that the necromancer screamed. Nonetheless, Zayl forced himself to continue reaching for the ivory dagger. His fingers touched the blade, and although he knew it would cause him more suffering, the injured spellcaster seized the weapon tightly by the sharp edges.

Blood dripping from the cuts in his fingers, the necromancer brought the dagger up. At the same time, he muttered the quickest, surest spell of which he could think.

A lance of pure bone thrust up from the dagger, flying unhindered through the thick hide of the beast, tearing flesh, and soaring upward until it struck the ceiling hard.

Zayl's horrific foe fluttered back, a strange, keening sound escaping its bizarre mouth. Ichor spilled over the necromancer as it pulled away.

As he dragged himself back, Zayl gave thanks to the dragon, Trag'Oul. The lance represented one of the talons of the mystical leviathan who served as the closest thing the followers of Rathma had for a god. Among the most effective of a necromancer's battle spells, the bone lance had been summoned twice in the past by Zayl, but never under such dire circumstances.

However, despite its terrible injury, the tapestry creature seemed far from dying. Moving with swift, gliding motions, it rose up to the ceiling, then over to a corner. A slight shower of life fluids spilled onto the floor below it.

"Are you all right, lad?"

"I will live. Thank you, Humbart."

The skull made a peculiar noise, like the rushing of air out of pursed lips. "Thank me when you've finished that abominable rug off!"

Zayl nodded. Raising the dagger toward the heavily breathing creature, he muttered another spell. Trag'Oul had helped him once; perhaps the great dragon would grant him one more boon.

A shower of bony projectiles roughly the size of the dagger formed from the air, shooting upward with astonishing swiftness.

The thing near the ceiling had no chance to move. Without mercy, the needle-sharp projectiles ripped through its hard hide. A rain of blood—or whatever equivalent the monster possessed—splattered the necromancer, the sanctum, and one cursing skull.

Now the creature keened, loud and ragged. It tried to flee, but Zayl had summoned the Den'Trag, the Teeth of the Dragon Trag'Oul, and they struck so hard that they pincushioned the struggling form to the wall and ceiling.

The movements of Zayl's adversary grew weaker, sporadic. The flow of life fluids slowed.

At last, the monster stilled.

"Zayl! Zayl!" called Humbart. "Gods! Wipe this slime off of me! I swear, even without a good, working nose, I can smell the stench!"

"Q-quiet, Humbart," the necromancer gasped. Summoning the aid of Trag'Oul twice had taken much out of him. Had he been more prepared, it would have not been so, but the initial assault by the beast had left him weakened even before the first spell.

As he tried to recoup his strength, Zayl eyed the vast array of specimens Gregus Mazi had collected over his life. The monster had been one small, seemingly dead sample among so many others. Did that mean that each of the sorcerer's collected rarities still had some life left in it? If so, Zayl gave thanks that none of the shelves had been disturbed or their contents accidentally sent shattering on the floor. The necromancer doubted that he would have long survived among a room filled with dozens of strange and dire creatures.

When his legs felt strong enough to trust, Zayl returned to where the skull lay. A thick layer of yellowish ichor covered most of what remained of the late Humbart Wessel. Taking the cleanest edge he could find on his cloak, the necromancer proceeded to wipe the skull as well as possible.

"*Pfaugh!* Sometimes I wish you'd left me to rot where you found me, boy!"

"You had already rotted away, Humbart," Zayl pointed out. Putting the skull on a clear part of the table, he looked around. Something on the wall to his right caught his attention. "Aaah."

"What? Not another of those beasts, is it?"

"No." The pale figure walked to what he had noticed. "Just a cloak, Humbart. Just a cloak."

A cloak once worn by Gregus Mazi.

Yet it was not the garment itself that so intrigued Zayl, but rather, what he could find upon it. Under the light of the dagger, he carefully searched.

There! With the utmost caution, the necromancer plucked two hairs from inside the collar region. Even better than clothing, strands of hair granted almost certain success when summoning a man's shade.

"You finally got what you want?"

"Yes. These will help us call the sorcerer forth."

"Fine! It'll be good to see old Gregus after all this time. Hope he's looking better than I am."

Surveying the chamber, Zayl noticed a wide, open area to the side of the entrance. As he neared, he saw that symbols had been etched into the floor there. How more appropriate—and likely helpful—than to summon the ghost of Gregus Mazi using the very focal point from which he had cast many of his own spells?

Muttering under his breath, the necromancer knelt and began to draw new patterns on the floor with the tip of his blade. As the point slowly drifted over the stone surface, it left in its wake the design Zayl wanted.

In the center of the new pattern, he placed the two hairs. Moving carefully so as not to disturb them, Zayl brought his free hand over, then, with the dagger, reopened one of the cuts he had suffered earlier.

The barely sealed cut bled freely. Three drops of crimson fell upon the hair.

A greenish smoke arose wherever the blood touched the follicles.

The necromancer began chanting. He uttered the name of Gregus Mazi, once, twice, and then a third time. Before him, the unsettling smoke swelled, and as it did, it took on a vaguely humanoid shape.

"I summon thee, Gregus Mazi!" Zayl called in the common tongue. "I conjure thee! Knowledge is needed, knowledge only you can supply! Come to me, Gregus Mazi! Let your shade walk the mortal plane a time more! Let it return to this place of your past! By that which was once a very part of your being, I summon you forth!"

Now the smoke stood nearly as tall as a man, and in it there appeared what might have been a figure clad in robes. Zayl returned to chanting words of the Forgotten Language, the words that only spellcasters knew in this day and age.

But just as success seemed near, just as the figure began to solidify, everything went awry. The billowing smoke abruptly dwindled, shrinking and shrinking before the necromancer's startled eyes. All semblance of a humanoid form vanished. The hairs curled, burning away as if tossed into hungry flames.

"No!" Zayl breathed. He stretched a hand toward his two prizes, but before he could touch them, they shriveled, leaving only ash in their wake.

For several seconds, he knelt there, unable to do anything but stare at his failure. Only when Humbart finally spoke did the necromancer stir and rise.

"So . . . what happened there, lad?"

Still eyeing the pattern and the dust that had once been hair, Zayl shook his head. "I don't—"

He stopped, suddenly looking off into the darkness.

"Zayl?"

"I *do* know why it failed now, Humbart," the necromancer responded, still staring at nothing. "It never had a chance to succeed. From the first, it was doomed, and I never realized it!"

"Would you mind speaking in less mystifying statements, lad?" the skull asked somewhat petulantly. "And explain for us mere former mortals?"

Zayl turned, eyes wide with understanding. "It is very simple, Humbart. There is one and one reason alone that would make this and any other summoning of Gregus Mazi a futile gesture: he still *lives!*"

Ten

�֎

If anything, Quov Tsin had grown more unsettling, more unnerving, by the time Captain Dumon next visited him. An empty mug and a small bowl of half-eaten food sat to the side of where he feverishly scribbled notes. His withered features had become more pronounced, as happened only in the dead as the flesh dried away, and he looked even more pale than the necromancer. Now the Vizjerei did not just mumble to himself; he spoke out in a loud, demanding tone.

"Of course, the sign of Broka would be inherently necessary there! Any cretin could see that! Ha!"

Before entering, Kentril questioned Gorst, who leaned against the wall just outside the library. "What sort of state is he in?"

The giant had always been untouched by Tsin's acerbic personality, but now Gorst wore a rare look of concern and uncertainty. "He's bad, Kentril. He drank a little, ate even less. He don't even sleep, I think."

The captain grimaced. Not the mood he had been hoping for, although from the beginning it had been unlikely that the Vizjerei would be any more reasonable than before. Still, Kentril had no choice; he had to try to speak with Tsin now.

"Keep an eye out, all right?"

"You know I will, Kentril."

Straightening, Captain Dumon walked up to the stooped-over sorcerer. Quov Tsin did not look his way, did not even acknowledge that anyone had entered. Taking a quick glance at the spellcaster's efforts, Kentril saw that Tsin had filled more than a dozen large parchment sheets with incomprehensible notes and patterns.

"You're a bigger fool than I thought, Dumon," the Vizjerei abruptly announced in an even more poisonous voice than previously. He still had not looked up at the fighter. *"I went against my better judgment last time in forgiving your interruptions—"*

"Easy, Tsin," Kentril interrupted. "This concerns you greatly."

"Nothing concerns me more than this!"

The mercenary officer nodded sagely. "And that's exactly what I mean. You don't realize just what you might lose."

At last, the diminutive figure looked at him. Bloodshot eyes swept over the captain, Quov Tsin clearly pondering what value the words of the other man might contain. "Explain."

"Knowing you as I do, Tsin, you've got two reasons for doing this. The first is to prove that you actually can. The Vizjerei sorcerers are well known for their reputations as masters of their art, and your reputation exceeds most of your brethren."

"Seek not to mollify me with empty flattery."

Ignoring the dangerous expression on the bearded face, Kentril continued. "The second reason I can appreciate more. We came to Ureh for glory and riches, Tsin. My men and I want gold and jewels—"

"Paltry notions!"

"Aye, but you came for riches of a different sort, didn't you? You came for the accumulated magical knowledge gathered in this kingdom over the many centuries, rare knowledge lost when true Ureh vanished from the mortal plane."

Tsin began tapping on the table with one hand. His gaze briefly shifted to the magical staff, then back to the mercenary, as if measuring options.

Kentril defiantly met the baleful gaze of the Vizjerei. "Lord Khan has offered you all that you can carry off if you succeed, hasn't he? That would mean books and scrolls worth a kingdom each, I imagine."

"More than you can imagine, actually, cretin. If you could understand one iota of what I've discovered here so far, it would leave you astounded!"

"A shame, then, that so much else will be lost again."

The spellcaster blinked. "What's that?"

Resting his knuckles on the table, Captain Dumon leaned forward and in conspiratorial tones whispered, "What could you accomplish if given a year, even two, to further study this collection?"

Avarice gleamed bright in the sorcerer's bloodshot eyes. "I could become the most powerful, most adept, of my kind."

"Juris Khan intends to open the way to Heaven again."

"He lacks the assistance he had the first time," Tsin commented, "but I must admit from listening to him that I think he has some notion of how to get around that. I'd not bet against him that once he is free, he will succeed with his holy dream in short order."

"And with him goes this entire library."

Kentril saw then that he had Quov Tsin. More than the mercenaries, the Vizjerei had known that the riches of the fabled realm would only return when the city once more breathed life. Tsin had not even attempted to inspect the library before the coming of the shadow because he had known that there would be nothing. The Vizjerei had pinned all his hopes on the legend, and now that same legend threatened to take from him much of that for which he had worked so hard.

"So much lost again," the wrinkled spellcaster muttered. "So much lost and for no good reason . . ."

"Of course, you could fail to find a solution to Khan's own curse, but then he might eventually suspect and send you away. If you tried to steal all this—"

Tsin snorted. "Don't even blather on in that direction, Dumon. Even if I would stoop so low, there are wards in this library that only our good host can unravel, or else why do you think I stay in here save when I must heed personal needs?"

"So there's no hope, then."

The robed figure stood straight. "Quite obviously, you *do* have a suggestion, my good captain. Kindly tell me what it is right now."

"A clever mage like yourself could find excellent reasons why it would be to Lord Khan's benefit to make Ureh a permanent part of the real world."

Quov Tsin stared silently at Kentril, so much so that the captain began to question the worth of his notion. What if Tsin could not convince the ruler? What if it only served to make Juris Khan angry at the adventurers? He might demand that all of them be escorted out of the kingdom. The Vizjerei might be skilled, but against a squadron of trained warriors such as now guarded the palace, he would quickly lose.

"You have—the core—of a possibility, I must admit," the sorcerer grumbled, seating himself again. "And, curiously, you may have come at just the right moment."

Now it was Kentril's turn to wonder what the other meant. "What do you mean, 'the right moment'?"

With a sweep of one thin arm, Tsin indicated the mountain of notes he had compiled. "Look there, Captain Dumon, and gaze in wonder! Stare at what only I, Quov Tsin, could have wrought in such short notice. I have done it!"

"Done it? Done—"

"Aaah! I see by your gaping mouth that you've realized what I mean. Yes, Dumon, I think I can release our good host from Gregus Mazi's foul but quite masterful spell!"

Conflicting thoughts rushed through Kentril's mind as he absorbed Tsin's announcement. On the one hand, they would have the gratitude of Ureh's monarch, but on the other hand, that would mean time would be at even more of a premium should Khan decide to go on with his holy mission.

"You've got to convince him to end this quest, Tsin!"

A cunning expression spread across the wrinkled countenance. "Yes, and for something far more worthy than your dalliance with his daughter. It'll take me two more days' work, I suspect, to be positive of my calculations and phrasings, but I am almost completely certain that I walk the right path, so much so that I'll begin the effort to turn his mind to our thinking within hours. First, however, I shall need time to clear my thoughts and prepare myself for an audience with him."

"Should I come with you?"

This brought another snort from the sorcerer. "By all means, no! He sees you, Dumon, and he'll think that this is all for your sake. The lust of one paid fighter does not balance well against the glorious sanctuary of Heaven!"

Nor does the greed of one very ambitious mage, Kentril could not help thinking . . . but Quov Tsin did have a clever tongue when he needed it and knew well how to deal with those of breeding. Surely he would be able to do far better than a base-born mercenary.

"Well? Why do you still stand here, Dumon? Do you want me to succeed or not? Go, so that I can organize everything."

Nodding quickly, Kentril immediately left the Vizjerei to his own devices. He knew that he could trust Tsin to attack this with the same obsessiveness with which he had attacked all that concerned the shadowed kingdom. With the endurance and determination of a predator, the sorcerer would somehow convince Juris Khan.

And then Captain Dumon could press his own suit for Atanna.

"You're still alive," Gorst commented as Kentril left the library. "I think the magic man's beginning to like you."

"Heaven forbid that should ever happen. We came to an understanding, that's all."

"He going to try to keep you from losing her?"

Kentril's brow furrowed.

The giant gave him a Gorst grin. "Only thing'd make you go to him is her. Only thing he's interested in is magic. Ureh vanishes, you both lose."

Even Kentril sometimes let Gorst's barbaric appearance cause him to forget why he had made the ebony-maned fighter his second in command—and his friend. "That sums it up."

"He'll do it, Kentril. He'll convince Juris Khan."

The captain grunted. "You see any sign of Zayl lately?"

"Not for a long time."

Kentril did not trust the necromancer on his own. Someone of Zayl's ilk could bring out the distrust in the most trustful of people. While he harbored no dislike for the easterner and actually found Zayl's presence more tolerable than Tsin's, Kentril worried about the other spellcaster wandering among the locals. Perhaps it was time to make certain that nothing else happened to endanger his hopes.

"I'm going for a walk, Gorst."

"Down into the city?"

"That's right. If Zayl shows up, tell him I want to talk with him."

The decision to hunt for the necromancer did not sit well at all with Kentril. He would have preferred his original plan, which had entailed telling Atanna of his success with Tsin, thereby ensuring some reward from her. Now, instead of the beauteous company of Khan's alluring daughter, he sought that of the dour, formal Zayl.

No one challenged the captain as he left the abode of Juris Khan. In fact, the armored guards stood straighter, and some even saluted him as he passed. Truly their master had given the mercenaries the run of the kingdom.

That made him think about his own men, including the pair who had not so far returned. There had been no reports of unseemly behavior, but Kentril wanted nothing to undo the good will they had gained.

The moment he touched foot at the bottom of the long, winding steps leading down from the palace and entered the city proper, Kentril found himself surrounded by merrymakers. Under the ever-present lamps and torches, women in bright, exotic garments of silk danced to the music of guitars, horns, and drums. Children laughed and ran between celebrating throngs. A table of local men hard at work on flagons of ale waved for the captain to come over, but with a smile and a shake of his head, Kentril excused himself.

There had to be people asleep somewhere in Ureh, but Captain Dumon would be damned if he could find any evidence of that. Several of those out now must have slumbered when he had, or else they surely could not have been up and about at this moment.

Some distance ahead, he spotted Orlif and Simon playing a game of dice with some of the locals. Kentril started toward them, then decided that it was unlikely that they would know where Zayl was. Both men had probably just returned to the city after some recuperation in the palace.

Leaving the duo to their entertainment, the captain wandered deeper into Ureh. Wherever he went, merriment seemed to be in full swing. The citizens of the legendary kingdom celebrated with such exuberance that Kentril found it somewhat difficult to believe that this had been the most revered, the most pious of realms. Still, he supposed that they deserved such harmless pleasure after suffering as they had.

"Are you one of the heroes?" asked a melodious voice.

Turning around, Kentril found himself facing not one but two enticingly clad young women. One wore a fanciful golden outfit that reminded him of the harems an older mercenary had described to him, while the other, blessed with the curves men desire most, smiled under long, dark lashes. Either would have at one time been a prize greater than Kentril could have ever imagined, but now, although he still found them most interesting to look at, they offered nothing he wanted. Atanna held sway over him.

"He must be," said the one with the curves. She smiled. "My name is Zorea."

"And I'm Nefriti," added the one in gold, bouncing prettily.

"My ladies," Kentril returned, bowing.

This action caused both of the women to blush and laugh lightly. "A true gentleman!" exclaimed black-tressed Zorea. She let her fingers caress his right arm. "And so strong!"

"Will you celebrate with us?" asked Nefriti, pursing her full lips as she took his left arm.

"It would honor us to honor you," said her companion. "Ureh wishes to offer you all the reward you deserve."

He carefully and politely pulled away from them. "I thank you for your kind offer, my ladies, but I'm in search of someone at the moment."

Zorea brightened. "One of your friends? I saw two strangers playing dice with some of the men."

"Yes, I saw them. I'm looking for someone else." It occurred to him that Zayl would certainly stand out among the people here. Perhaps this unexpected encounter would turn out to be of some use to him after all. "Maybe you've seen him after all? Tall, pale of skin, with eyes more like yours than mine. He would've been dressed mostly in garments of black."

"We've seen him!" chirped Nefriti. "Haven't we, Zorea?"

"Oh, yes!" she responded, her reaction almost identical to that of her friend. "We even know where he is."

"We'll take you there!"

The captain allowed himself to be guided on by the pair. He would not have thought this celebrating of much interest to the necromancer, but perhaps he had misjudged Zayl.

With great perseverance and more than a little strength, the two women pulled him along through the throngs. Zorea and Nefriti each held a hand—out of fear of becoming separated, so they claimed. The women clearly knew where they were going, expertly turning here and there and moving among the other celebrators with ease.

The crowds gradually began to thin, and as they did, Captain Dumon's suspicions arose. He had believed the women when they said that they knew Zayl's whereabouts, but the situation now resembled one far too familiar to any seasoned fighter in a strange land. The area toward which they headed looked fairly deserted. More than one mercenary had ended his career with a ʻdagger in his back thanks to such charming decoys. A holy city Ureh might be, but Gregus Mazi had already proven that even the most devout of lands had their personal demons.

Before they could lead him any further astray, Kentril stopped in his tracks. "You know, my ladies, I almost feel certain that my friend has left wherever you saw him last and now heads back to the palace to meet me."

"No!" gasped Nefriti. "He's just ahead."

"Not far at all," insisted Zorea, sounding like a twin of the first girl.

Kentril gently but firmly twisted free of both. "I thank the two of you for trying. The people of this kingdom have been most kind."

"No!" insisted Zorea. "This way."

Nefriti nodded. "Yes, this way."

They gripped his arms anew and with such force it brought a slight sound of startlement from the captain. He tried again to pull free, only to discover that the two women had surprisingly powerful holds.

"Let me go!" He managed to get away from Zorea, but Nefriti held on as if she were a leech.

"You must go this way. Please!" she demanded.

Kept in place by the one, Kentril risked being snared again by the second. Not trusting that a third partner—this one probably a male wielding a well-worn knife—might not materialize at any moment, the mercenary dropped any sense of honor and swung at the oncoming Zorea.

He could just as well have struck one of the nearby walls. His fist hit her chin hard, but it proved to be Kentril who suffered from the blow. Every bone in his hand, in his arm, jarred. Pain shot through him, and he almost felt as if he had broken one or more fingers.

Zorea's grasping hands came within inches of him, but at the last Captain Dumon turned to the side, leaving her ripping at only the air. At the same time, he used his free hand to draw his sword as best he could.

Reacting to his weapon, Nefriti flung Kentril back. Caught off guard by her astounding strength, he could not keep himself from colliding with the nearest wall.

As the back of his head struck, the world around Kentril changed. First he saw everything in duplicate, even down to two Zoreas and two Nefritis glaring at him. Then an even more horrific transformation took place.

A nightmare surrounded the captain. Gone suddenly were the sea of torches and the crowds of happy revelers. The magnificent buildings had not only crumbled back to ruin, but they bore a dark stain about them, a sense of foreboding and despair together. Somewhere in the distance, what sounded like the cries of thousands of men, women, and children in agony tore at his ears. Above, a horrific light with no obvious origin spread its monstrous crimson touch over everything.

And everywhere he turned, Kentril Dumon confronted what he could only imagine were the souls of the damned.

They strained for him, hungered for him, pleaded with him, even as they sought to make him one of them. All looked as if a great beast had sucked them dry, leaving only husks who wished to do the same to the fighter. Eyes sunken in, skin dry as dead leaves, they moved as if they had just burst free of their tombs. In tattered clothing, they strained toward Kentril, mouths gaping in anticipation.

"No!" he shouted without thought. "Get away from me!"

The blade free, he swung to and fro, forcing back the tide but finding no immediate escape. A sense of doom filled Kentril as he quickly realized that sooner or later, he would tire enough for them to overwhelm him.

"Captain! Captain Dumon!"

Ignoring the calling of his name, Kentril swung wildly at the fiends. Suddenly, they seemed fewer in number and dwindling more so by the second. Hope resurrected, the captain took a step forward, thinking that perhaps he might yet cut a path to escape.

"Captain Dumon! Look at me! Listen to me!"

Someone seized his shoulders from behind. Tearing free, Kentril spun about, determined that if they now came at him from all sides, he would wreak what havoc he could before they claimed his life and soul.

"Captain, it's Zayl! Zayl!"

Slowly, the necromancer's concerned visage came into focus. Kentril stared at the spellcaster, both fearful and grateful to see the man.

"Zayl! Do something! Don't let them get us!"

"Us?" Zayl looked confused. "Who, captain?"

"*Them*, of cour—"

Kentril stopped dead in his tracks. The horrifying mob had vanished. The cries had ceased. In fact, all Ureh again looked as it should have, the buildings, the people, and the sky all normal. The inhabitants themselves watched the mercenary with expressions mixing concern and sympathy.

However, of the two women who had led him into this he could see no sign.

The necromancer quickly pulled him away from the watching crowd. With Zayl leading, they headed back in the direction of the palace. Neither man said anything until they had gone some distance from the area of the incident.

Guiding Kentril to a narrow side street, Zayl muttered, "Tell me what happened back there, captain. I heard your voice and came running to find you standing there in the midst of everyone, slashing with your sword and screaming as if the hosts of Hell sought your blood."

"Not my blood," murmured the fighter. Kentril glanced at his hand, saw that he still gripped the sword's hilt so tightly his knuckles were white. "My life . . . my eternal soul."

"Tell me about it. Everything. Describe it in detail, if you can."

Taking a deep breath, Captain Dumon did as requested. He told Zayl about the two females and how they had tried to trick him into a deserted area, then how, after a curiously difficult struggle with them, the entire world had gone monstrously mad.

The necromancer listened closely, saying nothing, revealing nothing with his eyes. Yet, despite the silence, Kentril did not feel that Zayl thought the mercenary insane. Rather, the tall, pale figure listened as if he took every single word with the utmost seriousness. That, in turn, enabled Kentril to relax more as he told his tale and thus allowed him to recall even more specifics.

Only when he had finished did Zayl finally question him, and to Kentril's surprise, the necromancer asked first not about the demonic horde, but rather about the two women.

"You described the one wearing a revealing golden outfit much like what might be found in Lut Gholein. You also gave ample detail of her friend's rather generous charms, captain. More than enough detail, in fact, to make me most curious."

"I'm not the first man to fall prey to a woman's honeyed words, Zayl, and they both made it sound credible that they could lead me to where you were."

Kentril's companion nodded. "And I am not trying to insult you. Rather, I would commend your memory. I did meet those two as they claimed, Captain Dumon. I met them when they were celebrating with one of your men, the one called Brek."

"Brek?" Kentril's episode of madness became a secondary concern. One of his soldiers had been in the company of a pair of conniving wenches who had clearly tried to do away with the captain. "As far as I know, he never came back from the city. Neither Gorst nor Albord, both of whom keep track of the others, has seen him since he initially stepped out with the rest."

"A point to be investigated . . . one of many, I think."

"What does that mean?" Kentril cautiously asked.

"Captain Dumon, it was no mistake that I came upon you. I needed to find you in order to discuss a disturbing encounter of my own."

"And what's that?"

The necromancer frowned. "I will not go into my own story now, but I have reason to believe that what we have been told concerning Gregus Mazi might not be the entire truth."

"Entire?" blurted a voice from Zayl's side. "It's all a blessed lie!"

Kentril, in the act of finally sheathing his sword, suddenly drew it anew. "What in the name of Heaven was that?"

"An unruly and far too vocal companion." To the pouch, Zayl added, "I am warning you for the last time, Humbart. Cease these careless interruptions, or I will remove the spell animating you."

"Hmmph . . ." came the reply.

Suddenly, every bizarre and vile rumor that Kentril had heard concerning the mysterious followers of Rathma seemed to come true. He backed away from Zayl, disregarding the fact that the necromancer had only been of aid to him so far.

"Captain, that is not necessary."

"Keep back from me, spellcaster! What is that in there? A familiar?"

Zayl glanced with annoyance at the pouch. "Much too familiar at times. Humbart forgets his place and the danger he presents to me every time he feels the need to voice his opinion."

"Hum—Humbart *Wessel?*"

"What remains of me, lad! Listen! As one old soldier to another—"

"Silence!" The necromancer rapped hard on the side of the pouch. To Kentril, he said, "Captain, I have lived near the ruins of Ureh most of my life. I watched and waited for it to appear as we know it now, but never did the right conjunction of shadow and light bring it back. Yet that does not mean that I did not have any success in my quest in the meantime." He reached into the bag. "One day, I found this."

The empty eye sockets of a battered skull stared unblinking at Kentril. The jaw bone was missing, and some of the upper teeth had been broken. Near the back of the cranium, a great crack indicated a likely blow, either intentional or accidental, he could not say.

"The final remains of Humbart Wessel," Zayl quietly announced. "Soldier, mercenary, adventurer—"

"And the last man to see Gregus Mazi before he vanished into the shadowed city to try to complete his foul plan."

From the direction of the skull, a hollow and exasperated voice retorted, "Old Gregus would've never harmed another soul!"

Kentril barely held onto his sword. He had known that Zayl's kind could raise the spirits of the dead, but a talking skull was just a bit too much even for the hardened soldier. "What're you up to, necromancer? What's your plan?"

With a frustrated sigh, Zayl answered, "My plan is to find out the truth, Captain Dumon, as it relates to the balance of the mortal plane. In attempting that, I went in search of something to use to summon the spirit of Gregus Mazi so that I could perhaps find some way to help break his spells."

"And did you?"

The sound of revelry passed nearby. Quickly putting the skull back into the pouch, Zayl waited until the merriment faded away. Then, beckoning Kentril to look toward Nymyr, he continued, "In the mountainside sanctum once used by the sorcerer, I retrieved that which I could use to call him back. I cast a spell that I have cast a hundred times and more, all without failure." His countenance grew grim. "This time, though, no shade from beyond answered."

The captain found this entirely unimportant. "So you failed at last. One dead man escaped your power."

"He escaped because he was not dead in the first place."

Zayl let his words sink in. Kentril frowned, not certain he understood and, if he did, not certain that he wanted to know such news. "But Juris Khan told us plainly that he and Mazi fought, and after Mazi trapped him, Khan still managed to destroy the villain before any further harm could be done to Ureh."

The shadowy spellcaster nodded sagely. "Yes, Juris Khan did say that."

"Then Gregus Mazi is dead."

"He is not. I know this. The only reason for my failure is his continued life."

Sheathing his sword at last, Kentril turned toward the palace. Sudden fear for Atanna had replaced his uncertainty about his own sanity and even his distrust of the necromancer. "We've got to warn them! There's no telling where Mazi might be."

Zayl, however, clamped a slim but strong hand onto the mercenary's shoulder. Leaning near, he whispered, "There is . . . and I have performed that spell. Gregus Mazi is still in Ureh, captain." His gaze also shifted to the grand structure atop the hill. "And I fear that he is in the palace itself."

Eleven

If Zayl had told Kentril that Diablo himself resided in the palace where Atanna lived, the veteran soldier could not have been more horrified. Gregus Mazi, the man who had cursed a kingdom and lusted after Khan's daughter, not only lived but lurked near enough to do her harm. Never in his life had Kentril wanted so much to slay a person, not even after so many campaigns. During those, he had been performing a duty for which he had been paid, nothing more. Here, though, the task had a personal nature beyond any he had ever confronted.

"Where in the palace?" he demanded of Zayl as the duo worked their way to the hill. "Where?"

"Below it, actually. As for a precise location, that cannot be ascertained. There are forces in play the likes of which I have never come across. Spells I cast that should work to delve deeper are twisted and turned, rendering them useless. If I get closer, perhaps that will change."

"They've got to be warned," Kentril insisted. "They have to know the danger's right below them."

At the base of the ancient steps, the necromancer forced his companion to halt. "Captain Dumon, have you noticed anything amiss in the palace so far?"

"Only that some of my men haven't returned."

"But neither Lord Khan nor his daughter seems at all at risk."

The soldier did not like the way Zayl spoke. "What of that?"

"You have fought in many battles, in many wars. Do you announce to the enemy your intentions, or do you instead try to trick him, to leave him unsuspecting?"

Kentril's eyes narrowed. "Are you trying to tell me we should say nothing to them?"

"Not until we at least discover more—or until we sense some danger to them."

"And what would you suggest, necromancer?"

Zayl glanced around, making certain that no one stood near enough to hear. "We find out what lies beneath first."

A part of Kentril thought Zayl's suggestion foolish, that the right thing to do would be to alert Atanna of Gregus Mazi's return. Another part, though, feared that the corrupted sorcerer would also find out. Surely Mazi watched Khan and his daughter closely to make certain that they did not know of his hidden presence. Alerted, he would most likely strike and strike to destroy.

But the odds were good that the villain also watched his old master's guests. If they simply went in hunt of him, he would surely lay traps designed to kill all.

"We won't tell them just yet," Kentril finally agreed. "But we'll need some sort of distraction that would capture his interest so much that he won't pay any mind to searchers."

"He's got a point there," came Humbart's muffled voice.

Zayl tapped the pouch, then nodded agreement.

They kept silent about their goals as they reentered the palace some time later. Neither had yet thought up a manner by which the attention of the hidden spellcaster might be diverted, but both knew that they could not wait long. Surely Gregus Mazi had some imminent mischief in mind.

Thinking of that, Kentril sought out Albord. He found the younger mercenary just preparing to set out with two others for the city, which fit in directly with the captain's plan. Pulling Albord aside, Kentril whispered, "Don't ask why, but I have orders for you."

Although his body revealed no reaction to his commander's surprising words, the blond fighter's eyes let Kentril know that Albord understood the seriousness. "Aye, captain?"

"I need to cut short the men's celebrations for the time being. I want you three to go down and collect the others you find. I want everyone up here and accounted for. Anyone who can't be found, let me know. Above all else, don't split up, and don't let any of the locals know what you're up to . . . and if anyone offers to help you find someone missing, refuse that help."

This at last brought some reaction. "Just how serious is this, captain?"

Kentril recalled his own encounter, when the city had been transformed into a nightmare straight out of Hell. He had finally come to the conclusion that the two women had used some exotic potion that had not only weakened him but also caused his horrific hallucinations. It had been said that some assassins used such potions on their nails and that only a touch might be needed to affect a victim. "Serious enough. Beware especially of two women, one in gold and both far too eager for your company."

As he sent Albord and the others off, Zayl rejoined him. "What did you tell him?"

"Enough to be wary. It won't look out of the question that I would be checking up on my men, necromancer. Mercenaries have a tendency to wear out their welcome quickly in times of peace, and having them all called in will just seem like a simple, honest precaution."

"Do we tell Master Tsin as well?"

Kentril shrugged. "I don't know. I do want to tell Gorst right away, though, and he's near the sorcerer."

They quickly hurried to the library but found, to their mutual surprise, that it was empty. The table where the Vizjerei had sat for so long still lay all but hidden under a cluttered pile of books and scrolls, but Tsin and the mountain of notes he had made had vanished.

The captain noticed one other thing missing: Gorst. The giant might have simply followed Tsin in order to keep track of him, but the considerable pile of parchment missing coupled with the difficulty the short spellcaster would have had trying to carry all of it around made it obvious that Tsin had commandeered Gorst into helping him with something.

Barely had Kentril and Zayl turned back when from down the corridor Atanna appeared. She saw the two, and her expression, already bright, seemed to the fighter to positively glow.

"Kentril! You've done it! You've done it!"

Utterly ignoring the necromancer, she threw her arms around the captain and kissed him passionately. Kentril momentarily forgot the sinister danger below as he accepted Atanna's gratitude. That he knew not what she thanked him for he did not care.

Gradually, he became aware of a bemused Zayl watching him from behind Lord Khan's daughter. At first annoyed by this intrusion, Kentril finally recalled what he and his companion had been trying to accomplish. With gentle force, Kentril pushed away Atanna, reconciling himself with at least being able to gaze at her up close.

"And for what am I being thanked so well?"

"As if you didn't know!" She almost kissed him again, but noticed his reluctance. A playful smile spreading across her perfect features, she allowed Zayl to join in the conversation. "You might find this of interest, too, sir."

"I suspect I might, my lady."

Atanna graciously accepted his courtesy. "At this moment," she informed both, "the Vizjerei sorcerer Quov Tsin has an audience with my father."

"Already?" interrupted Kentril. He had not thought Tsin would begin trying to persuade Lord Khan for some time yet. Surely the Vizjerei's greed had much to do with this sudden development. Kentril only hoped that by rushing in, old Tsin had not ruined everything.

"The good sorcerer has told Father that he thinks in a day or two he can help remove Gregus's curse! It will take hours of preparation and at least as much spellwork, but he feels certain it will succeed!"

Her eyes widened in hope and anticipation. Kentril prayed that Tsin would not let Juris Khan down, if only for Atanna's sake. "I'm pleased to hear that, but—"

"And more important for some," the red-haired princess added, her gaze especially fixed on Captain Dumon now. "Master Tsin has already accomplished one miracle. He has convinced Father that Ureh should be a part of the world again, that the quest for Heaven is one we should undertake in the manner of any other mortal, through the trials of life itself."

Kentril hesitated to respond, hoping he had correctly understood her. "Juris Khan won't try to recast the spell? He won't try a second time to claim the sanctuary of Heaven?"

"No! Thanks to the Vizjerei, Father now believes that we've a role here. He thinks that we may be needed to help guide the rest of the world toward the proper path. Father even wonders now if this was meant to be from the beginning!"

It all sounded too fantastic to Captain Dumon, but in Atanna's face he read only truth. Lord Khan had changed his mind. Tsin had actually succeeded, and far sooner than Kentril could have ever imagined possible.

"My congratulations on this news, my lady," Zayl politely said.

"Thank you," she replied, giving the necromancer a momentary smile before returning her full attention to Kentril. "Father is so thrilled, he would like to honor you and Master Tsin shortly with a private dinner. You, too, if you wish, Master Zayl."

The pale figure shook his head. "My kind are not known for their social behavior, and besides, I have really done nothing to deserve such recognition. However, I certainly agree that Captain Dumon and the sorcerer should be so honored."

"As you wish." Atanna seemed to forget the necromancer from there on. "Kentril, I hope you'll say yes."

What else could he say? "Of course. The honor's mine."

"Splendid! It's all settled, then. A servant will be at your quarters before long to help you dress."

"Dress?" The mercenary did not like the sound of that.

"Of course," interjected Zayl innocently. "One must always be properly attired for a state dinner, captain."

Before Kentril could protest, Atanna kissed him once more, then hurried away. Both men watched her alluring form swiftly vanish down the hall.

"A unique woman, Captain Dumon."

"Very much."

The necromancer swept closer. "This dinner could also be to our benefit. With Lord Khan and his daughter occupied with you and the Vizjerei, I can try surreptitiously to investigate our likely route to below. There must be some detailed outline of the palace's design and possibly even mention of the caverns Khan hinted of even deeper."

Kentril continued to eye the direction down which Atanna had disappeared. "I still don't like not at least telling her."

"Remember that Gregus Mazi once desired Khan's daughter. He has not touched her so far, but if he realizes she has been alerted, he may decide to steal her away. Her ignorance is her safety."

"All *right*," the captain snapped. He glared at the tall, slim figure beside him. "Just make certain that you don't get caught. That would be hard to explain."

"If I am, I shall make it known to all that I acted on my own. She will have no reason to lose her trust in you, captain."

With a slight bow, Zayl departed. Kentril frowned, still not quite certain about this pact he had made with the necromancer, then headed to his quarters to see what could be done about making himself presentable for this no doubt elegant dinner.

He would have rather been fighting a pitched battle.

A crisp black dress uniform with gold ornamentation had been laid out on his bed, a uniform with long, sleek pants and a jacket with sharp tails. Epaulets decorated the jacket's shoulders, and the stylized image of a crown and sword had been sewn onto the left breast. The gleaming black leather boots rose knee-high, completing a rather dashing image.

Kentril felt foolish in the outfit. He was a soldier, a mercenary. The uniform should have been worn by a commander, a general, not someone of his lowly station. Still, he could not appear at a formal dinner with Lord Khan and Atanna dressed in his tired, oft-mended garments.

That the uniform fit perfectly did not entirely surprise the captain. Atanna would not have bothered to have it set aside for him if she had not known it would serve perfectly. He wondered whether it had once belonged to someone else, or if she had somehow simply conjured it up.

Although he knew the way to his destination, Kentril found two armed guards outside his door waiting to escort him. With much ceremony, they marched down the halls with him, leading the fighter at last to where Khan waited.

"Welcome, my friend!" the fatherly figure called from his chair. "I am so pleased that you've agreed to join us."

Because of the robed monarch's inability to move, a heavy sculpted table had been brought in for the dinner. Decorated with filigree and lovingly carved by some expert hand, it likely cost as much as Kentril made in ten years—if he was lucky. Atop it, a golden cloth had been set, and on top of that, gleaming plates, pristine silverware, and tall, magnificent candelabras.

Three chairs had been placed at the table. Juris Khan himself could not be moved off the dais, but a smaller yet no less richly adorned table had been positioned near him. The larger table had been turned so that the lord of Ureh sat at its head.

Quov Tsin already sat on what would have been the left of their host, but Kentril saw no sign of Atanna. However, as he approached, she suddenly emerged from the side of the room, hand held out toward him.

He stared unashamedly at her, both because he could not see how he had missed her entrance and because nothing else in the richly decorated chamber could match the vision she presented.

Her billowing emerald gown complemented her lush, crimson tresses, which had been artfully draped down over her shoulders and breast. The sleeves stretched all the way to the backs of her hands and even fit over the three lower fingers of each, almost like a partial glove. Other than her hair, her shoulders were bare, and the gown itself plunged just enough to entice but not to flaunt her perfect form shamelessly.

He took the hand she offered and kissed the back. Atanna then took his hand in hers and led him to the table.

"You shall sit there, at the end," she murmured. "I shall be on your left, very near."

Kentril almost went to his appointed place, then recalled how polished officers acted in the presence of ladies of the court. He steered her toward her own chair, then held it out for her. Smiling prettily, Atanna accepted this gracious gesture.

"About time," Tsin muttered as Kentril seated himself. Judging by the empty goblet in front of him, the Vizjerei had already had at least one cup of wine. He had come clad, of course, in the robes that he always wore. As a sorcerer, Tsin was not expected to dress in anything other than the garments of his calling, and, in truth, the rune-inscribed robes did not seem out of place here.

"You look splendid!" Juris Khan informed the captain. "Does he not look splendid, my dear?"

"Yes, Father." Atanna blushed.

"A wise and portentous choice, daughter! Truly, Captain Dumon, the uniform is appropriate for you."

"I thank you, my lord." Kentril did not know what else to say.

"I'm so gratified that both of you could come on such short notice. I owe each of you much already, and it appears I'll owe so much more before very long!"

"We are honored, Lord Khan," Quov Tsin responded, raising his empty glass in salute. A liveried servant appeared from nowhere and filled it from a dark green bottle, which perhaps had been what the Vizjerei had desired all along.

Kentril nodded in appreciation of his host's words, although he did not feel as if he had done so much to deserve the praise. Yes, he had helped set the Key to Light in place, but any strong arm could have done that. More to the point, it would be Tsin who would release Ureh's ruler from Gregus Mazi's curse. Captain Dumon could understand the sorcerer being given his due, but for himself, he felt grateful just to be able to sit near Atanna.

Snapping his fingers, Juris Khan had the first portion of their dinner brought out by several uniformed servants so similar in appearance that Kentril had to study each golden figure in turn in order to ascertain that they were not all identical. The servants treated him with as much honor as they did their master, which only further embarrassed him. He was a hired soldier, a man of rank only because he had survived when so many other brave but poor men had not.

As the dinner went on, the veteran fighter feasted on fruits and vegetables the likes of which he had never seen and thick, well-cooked meats dripping with their own juices. The wine he drank had such full flavor that Kentril had to take care for fear he would imbibe too much. Everything he tasted had been made to perfection. The dinner seemed more a dream than a reality.

Throughout it all, he also feasted on the glorious sight of Atanna, so much so that it was not until late into the meal that a question that had bothered him earlier came again to mind. He stared at what little remained of the contents of his plate, finally asking with the utmost caution, "My lord, where does all the food come from?"

Tsin glanced at him as if having just heard an unruly child interrupt. Juris Khan, however, not only took his question in stride, but made it sound so very wise. "Yes, well you should ask. You wonder, no doubt, because I've indicated that although we were trapped between Heaven and the mortal plane, we were aware of our fate. In some ways, time did indeed pass, but in others, it did not. Even I can't fully explain it, I'm sorry to say. We only knew that years went by in the true world, but we did not age, we did not much sleep, and, most important, we did not *hunger* at all."

"Not at all?" Kentril uttered with some surprise.

"Well, perhaps we did . . . but only for our *salvation*. And as we did not age, so, too, did our food not age. Thus, we are still plentifully stocked and shall be for some time." Atanna's father smiled benevolently at both guests. "And by then, I hope our situation will be already much improved."

Kentril nodded, grateful for the answer but inwardly still embarrassed for having asked it in the first place.

"My lord," piped up the Vizjerei, "during the time you were explaining the obvious to the captain here, some further considerations formulated in my head."

Khan found much interest in this. "Considerations dealing with my condition?"

"Aye. I will definitely have need of your daughter's abilities as well as your own, just as I earlier proposed. You see . . ."

As Tsin began a lengthy and, for the mundane captain, incomprehensible explanation, Kentril gladly returned his attention to his hostess. Atanna noticed him gazing at her again and smiled over the goblet she had just started raising to her lips.

Eyes and mind on the heavenly view before him, Captain Dumon grew careless with the knife and fork he had been using. The blade slipped from the bit of meat he had been carving and jabbed the side of the hand that had been holding the other utensil.

Drops of blood splattered on the dish.

Pain shot through Kentril.

The lavish, brightly lit chamber became a chamber of *horrors* instead.

Blood—fresh blood—seemed to flow over tarnished, scratched walls, and the ceiling, which now existed only as a jagged hole, revealed a sky as turbulent and tortured as the rest of his surroundings. Crimson and black clouds did battle, monstrous bolts of lightning marking where they collided. Swirling maelstroms formed, seeming ready to swallow the bleeding world below.

Bones that looked suspiciously human lay scattered everywhere upon the stained and cracked floor, and something not a rat scurried over one before disappearing into a small fissure running along the side of the room. A fierce wind coursed through, howling as it went. An intense heat that somehow still chilled Kentril to his very soul swept along in its wake.

Moans and cries suddenly assailed his ears. He rose at last from the rotting table, seeing on the broken, dust-ridden plate before him not the freshly cooked meal he had been eating, but instead a moldy, maggot-infested piece of greenish meat.

The moans and cries continued to increase in intensity, so much so that the captain had to cover his ears. He stumbled back, falling against one wall—and only then finding the source of the mournful pleas.

From each of the walls, hundreds of mouths began to cry out for help. Those nearest him seemed to scream the loudest. Pulling away in horror, Kentril stumbled back to the table . . . and into, of all things, a very *annoyed* Quov Tsin.

"What do you think you're doing, cretin? You're making a fool of yourself in front of our host!" The Vizjerei pointed in the direction of the dais.

But when Kentril looked there, he did not see the good and fatherly Juris Khan. The chair remained fixed in place, true, and of all things it looked most untouched by the horrors around, but in it did not sit the lord of Ureh.

Before Captain Dumon's fearful eyes arose—

"Kentril! Speak to me! It's Atanna! Kentril!"

And as if it had all been a dream, the grand chamber immediately became whole and bright and *alive* once more.

Atanna held his bleeding hand tight, her eyes wide and concerned. Staring into those eyes gave the mercenary something on which to focus, to use as an anchor for his suddenly questionable sanity.

"Captain Dumon, are you unwell?"

With great reluctance, Kentril looked to Juris Khan. He breathed a sigh of relief upon seeing the robed, masterful monarch standing tall, absolute concern written over the elderly visage. Gone was the image of—of what? Kentril could not even recall exactly what he had seen, only that it had been like nothing he had ever come across in all his life. The sheer act of trying to remember even the slightest image caused him to shiver.

Khan's daughter brought a goblet to his mouth. "Drink this, my darling."

For her and her alone he drank it. The wine calmed him, pushed away all but the vestiges of his nightmare.

Atanna led him back to his chair. As he sat, Kentril mumbled, "I'm sorry . . . sorry, everyone."

"There is no need for one who is ill to apologize," Khan kindly remarked.

One hand still on the captain's shoulder, Atanna said, "I think I know what happened, Father. We walked in the garden earlier, and something bit him."

"I see. Yes, the jungle insects sometimes make their way here, and some are said to carry disease that causes delusions and more. One must've bitten you, Captain Dumon."

Having fought in many vile lands, where weather and wildlife made a more fearsome foe than the opposing soldiers, Kentril could well believe their conclusions. Yet the monstrous clarity of his hallucination still stuck with the fighter. What within him could dredge up such horrors? As a man who had seen and shed blood, he had dreamt about the dark side of war, but never had his imagination created such a picture.

Still, Atanna's explanation would also give reason for his earlier episode in the city. Had that been the first sign of the sickness? He had assumed that Zorea or the other woman had drugged him, but such a drug should have worn off by now.

Lord Khan seated himself again. "Well, whatever the cause, I am sure that under my daughter's ministrations, you will recover fine. I want you to be able to accept my gifts with full clarity of mind so that I may not force upon you anything you do not wish."

"Gifts?"

"Aye, good captain—although if you accept, you'll be captain no more." The robed figure leaned toward his two guests. "In the struggle against Gregus Mazi, lives were lost. Important ones. Good ones. Good friends. A vacuum thus exists in Ureh, and if we're to become part of the mortal world again, that vacuum must be filled. You two can help in that."

Kentril felt Atanna's fingers tighten on his shoulder, and when he looked up, she gave him an expression of pride and pleasure.

"Master Tsin, you and I've already discussed this in part, so you have some advantage over Captain Dumon. Nonetheless, the decision is no less a significant one for you, and so I state my offer again, with more conciseness this time. All those who wielded and governed the magic arts of my kingdom have perished save my daughter and myself. I ask of you if you will bring honor again to that which Gregus tainted. I ask you to take up the mantle of royal sorcerer, the magical knowledge of my realm yours if you will sit ever at my left hand."

The Vizjerei rose slowly, a satisfied smile across his wrinkled countenance. Kentril could only imagine the spellcaster's pleasure. He had more than gained long-term access to the books and scrolls of the library; for all practical purposes, Juris Khan had given the diminutive figure *everything* the Vizjerei could have wanted.

"My Lord Khan," Quov Tsin graciously replied, "nothing would please me more."

"I am gratified." Now the stately monarch turned toward Kentril, who felt his stomach tie in knots. "Captain Kentril Dumon, through your efforts to help us and the recommendations of one who has come to know you better than I, I've learned of a man of ability, determination, honor, and loyalty. I can think of no better qualities in a soldier—nay, in a leader!" Khan steepled his fingers. "We are an old realm in a new world, one you know much better. There's need for such a man as you to guide us, to protect us from elements that may desire our downfall in this different time. I need you as a commander of my warriors, a protector of my people, a general, as that uniform calls for."

Despite his recent spell, Kentril pushed himself back to his feet. "My gracious Lord Khan—"

But his host politely cut him off. "And in Ureh, you should know that such a rank comes hand in hand with a title. The commander of our defenders is not only a soldier but a *prince* of the land as well."

He left the captain momentarily speechless. Atanna, her hand now on his arm, squeezed tightly.

"And as a member of the nobility, all rights therein are yours. You will be granted an estate, be able to raise servants of your own, marry other members of nobility—"

At the last, Atanna's hand squeezed particularly tightly. When Kentril briefly let his gaze fly to her, he saw the answer for why Juris Khan would especially offer him this wondrous posting. Despite their liaison so far, the soldier had always known inside that he truly had no hope for a lasting love. Atanna was a princess, born and raised to marry someone equal to or higher than her lofty station. Kings, sultans, emperors, and princes could have easily asked for her hand, but not a lowly officer.

Now her father had eradicated that one impediment with a single gesture.

"—and so forth," finished Juris Khan. He smiled as a father would smile at his son . . . perhaps a foreshadowing of events. "What say you, good captain?"

What could Kentril say? Only a fool or a madman could refuse, and despite his recent episodes, he did not feel himself either of those. "I-I am honored to accept, my lord."

"Then all that I've offered is most definitely yours. You and Master Tsin have made me very happy! Master Tsin assures me of complete success in freeing me, and if that holds true, three days hence, as marked by the sun seen beyond our borders, I shall before the entire court officially acknowledge your new stations." Khan nearly fell back into his chair, as if both physically and emotionally exhausted by his grand gesture. "You've the gratitude of all Ureh . . . but the gratitude of my humble self the most."

Atanna returned to her seat, and she blushed even more whenever her eyes and Kentril's met. The talk began to turn again to Quov Tsin's plan to free Lord Khan from his chair, eventually even drawing Atanna in because of her necessary role. Left alone now, Captain Dumon turned to his own thoughts.

And those thoughts concerned his subterfuge. Even after all Juris Khan had granted him, after all Atanna had promised him with her eyes and lips, he had said nothing concerning the possibility that Gregus Mazi still lived and might yet turn his black arts again on them. At this moment, Kentril knew, Zayl crept about the palace, seeking behind the backs of their hosts the plans of its design. True, the pair had only the best of intentions in mind, but still the captain felt as if each second he failed to speak he betrayed Atanna and her father further.

Despite his regrets, though, Kentril chose to say nothing. If Zayl proved to be wrong, no harm would be done. Yet if the necromancer had divined correctly, there would be only him and Kentril to deal with the threat. Khan could do nothing while so impaired, and not for a moment would Captain Dumon even consider letting Atanna face the corrupted spellcaster. Tsin already had too much with which to deal. No, if Gregus Mazi did indeed live, Kentril would have to see to it himself that the corrupted sorcerer paid the ultimate price for his past crimes.

Atanna caught his gaze once more. She smiled and blushed, completely ignorant of the darkening thoughts behind the captain's own smile. No, no matter what happened, Gregus Mazi could not be allowed ever again to touch her . . . not even if it cost Kentril Dumon his own life in the process.

TWELVE

Zayl met him some hours after the dinner, the necromancer's expression giving no sense of success or failure as he slipped into the captain's chambers. Only when Zayl had held up his ivory dagger and turned one complete circle did the pale figure finally announce the results of his search.

"An easier task than I had anticipated. Clearly marked and filed in the library among other papers. In his own abode, our host apparently did not think he had to be cautious about such information."

"No," responded Kentril somewhat bitterly. "He probably believes that he can trust everyone."

Zayl presented to him a tracing of the chart someone had made showing how to reach the caverns beneath and what routes the system of tunnels took. "You can see that it is good we have this. The system is complex, almost maze-like. One could get lost down there and never find the way back."

"Where do you think Mazi might be?"

"That is something I shall try to divine just before we depart, captain. I did not leave the sorcerer's former sanctum empty-handed. I have a few more samples of his hair. I will try to use them to find his location. It may not be exact, but should be enough for me to hazard an expert guess."

Kentril tried not to think of the two of them wandering through the caverns seeking the insidious spellcaster. "Will he be able to detect what you're doing?"

"There is always the chance of that, but I have taken the utmost precaution each time and will do so again. The methods of my kind are much more subtle than those likely learned by such as Mazi or Tsin. That has been in great part for the sake of simple survival, for we know how most others view us. We have even learned by necessity how to move among other practitioners of the magic arts without them ever knowing we were present. You may rest assured, Gregus Mazi will not notice."

The ability to fool Tsin did not impress Kentril as much as Zayl perhaps thought it did, but the time to turn back had long passed. "How long do we have?"

"Such a spell as the Vizjerei must cast will require many hours, even a day, but we must start out as soon as they begin preparations." The necromancer glanced again at the tracing. "Which makes it all the better that we have this. Do not lose it, captain." Zayl stepped back as if preparing to leave, then suddenly asked, "How went the dinner?"

"Well." Now did not seem the time to tell the necromancer all that had happened.

Zayl waited for him to elaborate, but when Kentril remained quiet, the cloaked figure finally departed.

Kentril fell back onto his bed. He had nearly managed to fall asleep when a single tap on the door made him sit up straight, one hand already on the dagger habit caused him to keep at his side. A moment later, Gorst and Albord stepped in, both looking perturbed.

"What is it, Gorst?" Kentril asked, hand relaxing only slightly.

"Albord's got something to say."

The younger mercenary clearly felt ill at ease. "Captain, there's something I don't like."

"What's that?"

"No one's still seen hide nor hair of Brek, and now besides him there's two more missing."

Not what Kentril wanted to hear at any time, but even more so with the coming events. "Who?"

"Simon. Mordecai. I asked the others, and no one knows when they were last seen."

"Everyone else accounted for?"

Gorst nodded. "Kept 'em in. They're a little cranky about it, but it ain't too bad bein' stuck in here, eh, Kentril?"

The captain was certain that his face flushed, but he could hardly worry about that now. Counting Albord, that made only seven men left besides Kentril and Gorst. "Three missing now. I don't like that. Someone resents our being here." Inwardly, he wondered if the disappearances had anything to do with Gregus Mazi. Did the sorcerer work to eliminate his former master's new allies?

"What do we do?" asked Albord.

"We keep this to ourselves. No one leaves the palace until I say so. There's not enough of us to go hunting the others. We'll have to consider the worst, I'm afraid." Kentril rubbed his chin in thought. "Albord, you've got charge of them. I've something in mind I need Gorst for. Can you handle it?"

The younger mercenary snapped to attention. "I'll see it done, captain!"

"Good lad. And if any of the three do return, question them carefully as to their whereabouts. We need to find out all we can."

Not once did he mention saying anything to Lord Khan, and not once did Albord or Gorst suggest it. Whatever choice their captain made they would accept.

Kentril dismissed Albord, but had his second stay. "Gorst, there's something I need you to help with, but since there's a strong element of risk, I'll only accept you as a volunteer. If you don't want to go, I'll understand."

The familiar grin faded. "What is it, Kentril?"

Captain Dumon told him, starting with Zayl's astonishing revelation and what the necromancer and he had decided to do. Gorst listened quietly through it all, the dark, round eyes of the giant never once leaving his commander.

"I'll come," he responded as soon as Kentril had finished.

"Gorst, this could be more dangerous than any battlefield."

The giant smiled. "So?"

Despite some guilt at having included his friend in this possibly suicidal quest, Kentril also felt much relieved. Having Gorst at his back made coming events seem a little more reasonable, a little more normal. This would just be another battle situation, a special mission behind enemy lines. True, the foe wielded sorcery, but they had the talents of Zayl for that. If the necromancer could keep Gregus Mazi at bay, the two fighters would move in to strike the mortal blow. A three-pronged assault on a single enemy, a nearly perfect battle plan.

Kentril snorted at his own naive notion. It all sounded so simple when thought of in such terms, but he doubted that would turn out to be the case once reality hit. One thing he had learned early on in his career, when the battle began in earnest, *all* the magnificent plans for victory went up in smoke.

Waiting for the moment itself proved to be the worst of ordeals. To the captain, each minute felt like an hour, and each hour a day. If not for those interludes when Atanna could break away from the preparations Tsin required, Kentril suspected that he would have gone mad.

Lord Khan's daughter and he spoke little when they were together, and what talk did take place concerned more hints of the future. Half-veiled promises filled the captain's head as the enchantress herself filled his arms.

"Not long now," Atanna whispered more than once, "but so much longer than I want to wait . . ."

Fueled by such honeyed words, Kentril silently swore that when the time came, he would take Gregus Mazi's head himself and present it to Atanna and her father as proof of his worthiness. Surely then Lord Khan would see him as a respected suitor.

And then at long last came the time. A different Atanna met Captain

Dumon as he pretended to be cleaning his gear. She wore a chaste white robe much akin to that of Juris Khan, and her luxurious hair had been tied tightly back in a tail. The solemn expression alone informed Kentril of why she had come dressed so.

"It's to begin?" he asked, his question having double meaning to him.

"Master Tsin says that the forces are in correct alignment and the patterns matched to their purposes. It will still take us hours, but I must be there for all of it. I came to ask for your confidence, your belief in our success."

He kissed her. "You'll succeed—and I'll be there in spirit."

"Thank you." She gave him a hopeful smile, then rushed off.

Kentril's own smile reversed as he understood that his quest had also now begun. Gathering his gear, he waited a few minutes to be safe, then marched out of his chambers to seek Gorst and the necromancer.

The giant met him in the hall, their encounter quite casual in the eyes of any guard seeing them. They spoke of stretching their legs, taking a run to keep their muscles strong, the typical routines of veteran fighters. Acting completely at ease, the pair made their way through the many halls of the palace, finally exiting the building altogether.

Far beyond the protective wall surrounding the palace lay what the necromancer had revealed as the best of entrances to the caverns that honeycombed Nymyr. This had been the very opening that Khan's brave volunteers had utilized to carry the Key to Shadow to its resting place deep below. According to Zayl, the passage through which they would enter the system had no natural origin; someone had carved into the rock until they had met up with one of the natural caverns inside. The necromancer suspected that perhaps the ancient monks had taken up the task, either as a place to hide should the monastery be overwhelmed or possibly as some part of their holy rituals.

Kentril had not cared at the time of explanation about the history of the cave, only that it existed and gave them a direct route to the underworld. However, when he initially saw the craggy mouth, his heart suddenly beat as it had not since his first battle. Only by quickly taking deep breaths was Kentril able to approach without revealing to Gorst his inexplicable fear.

"I don't see Zayl," the captain muttered.

"I am here," replied one of the shadows near the narrow opening.

A section of rocky mountainside suddenly fell away as the cloak of the necromancer dropped, revealing the waiting figure. "I thought it might be best to mask myself in illusion until you arrived."

Gritting his teeth, Kentril pretended not to have been startled by the spellcaster's astounding appearance. "How's it look inside?"

"Carved to let one man pass at a time. Your friend will have to bow his head and may find a few parts a bit tight."

"Don't worry about Gorst. He'll make his own path if necessary."

Turning from the two mercenaries, Zayl led the way inside. As Kentril entered, he experienced a slight sensation of the walls closing in on him, but fortunately, the feeling quickly passed.

Zayl muttered something. A moment later, a peculiar, pale light filled the shaft. In the necromancer's left hand, Kentril saw the ivory dagger gleam.

"This should go on for about five, six hundred yards," Zayl commented. "After that, the caverns should begin to open up."

Gorst was indeed forced to keep his head bent much of the way, but only once did he have to squeeze through in order to continue on. As for Kentril, he might as well have been taking a walk through a darkened hall in the palace. Even the floor had been smoothed, making footing almost perfect.

Their good luck appeared to end almost where the caverns should have opened up before them. Rounding a turn, the trio at first saw not the widening mouth that they had expected but instead, a wall of rubble.

"I had not counted on this," responded the necromancer. "And according to the drawing, there is no other path."

Kentril went up to investigate the wall of rock and dirt, pulling at a few good-sized stones.

The vast pile suddenly rolled toward him, burying his legs up to the tops of his boots in a matter of only seconds. Gorst pulled him back before he could become any more trapped. The trio stepped back quickly and waited for the dust to settle.

"I think . . . I see something," Zayl declared after a brief coughing fit.

Sure enough, the dagger revealed a hole near the top. Borrowing the necromancer's enchanted blade, Kentril quickly but carefully crawled up to investigate. "It opens wide just ahead. If we can crawl through safely for a few yards, we should be clear."

Gorst and Kentril worked to make the opening bigger while Zayl held the light for them. Once that had been accomplished, the necromancer worked his way through, followed by the giant, then Kentril.

And on the other side of the collapse, they at last stood before the true beginning of the cavern complex.

The chamber stretched hundreds of feet up and across. Jagged limestone teeth thrust down from the ceiling, some of them three, four times the size of Gorst. Others burst from the floor of the vast cave, several more than a yard thick and twice that in height.

Water trickled over the walls, carving niches, creating myriad shapes everywhere, and, in the process, revealing bright, glittering crystals embedded in the rock face. In the light of the dagger, the cavern *glistened*.

Kentril looked down, and any wonder over the beauty of the chamber died as he saw what faced them. Roughly twenty yards ahead, the floor dropped off abruptly, a veritable cliff that ended in a chilling, black abyss.

"Down there?" Gorst cheerfully asked.

Zayl nodded as he reached into the confines of his voluminous cloak. Kentril marveled that despite their crawling, the spellcaster looked unsullied.

From the cloak, Zayl suddenly pulled forth a short, almost laughable length of rope. However, as the necromancer began tugging on the ends, it *grew*. Only a foot long in the beginning, under his effort it stretched to twice, then three times more what it had been.

"Gorst," the pale figure called, "help me with this."

Handing the dagger again to Kentril, Zayl gave one end of the small rope to the larger mercenary. As the two pulled, Kentril saw that it stretched even farther.

Five feet, six, eight, and more. Gorst and the necromancer pulled and pulled, and each time they did, the rope gave way. In but the space of a few breaths, the party ended up with a sizable length, more than enough to begin their descent.

Zayl wordlessly took back the dagger. The two soldiers secured the astonishing rope around one of the broader stalagmites, then tested it. The necromancer, meanwhile, leaned over the edge, studying the dark depths.

"If the original drawing is correct, we should have more than enough room on which to land."

The captain did not like the sound of that. "And if it's not?"

"Then we shall find ourselves dangling over a thousand-foot drop."

Fortunately, the calculations of the nameless person who had originally charted the caverns proved to be accurate not only with this initial descent, but with those that followed. Moving with more confidence, the trio journeyed farther and farther down into the system, guided all the while by Zayl's glowing blade.

At last, they came to an area where the passages leveled off. The necromancer paused to consult the tracing, not desiring to head off toward a dead end or a pit. Kentril and Gorst, meanwhile, drew their weapons just in case.

"Are we on the right trail still?" the captain asked of Zayl.

"I believe so. The spell I cast before leaving for the cave did not give me as exact a location as I had hoped, but it did pinpoint matters enough for me to believe we are very near. Be wary."

Slowly they wended their way through a series of twisting passages punctuated on occasion by small and unprepossessing chambers. Only once did they have any cause to halt, that being when Gorst came across a tattered water sack that they all assumed had been left by the party carrying Juris Khan's creation. Zayl inspected it for any clues, but found none.

Then Kentril noticed that the area ahead of them seemed slightly brighter than Zayl's dagger should have been able to make it. He touched the necromancer on the arm, indicating that he should cover the enchanted blade.

Despite the momentary loss of the weapon's light, the passage ahead remained illuminated.

Sword at the ready, the captain proceeded, Zayl and Gorst ready to back him up at the slightest sign of danger. With each step, the glow ahead increased a bit. It never truly grew bright, and even what illumination there was had a dark quality to it, but Kentril could definitely see better the nearer he drew.

And suddenly the party entered a wide, rounded chamber in the midst of which, atop a reworked stalagmite, gleamed the source of the illumination . . . the *Key to Shadow*.

Those who had risked themselves to bring it down here had carefully chipped away at the cavern growth, creating a stone hand of sorts in the very center of whose craggy palm the mighty black crystal pulsated quietly.

Seeing no sign of danger, Kentril moved to investigate better Lord Khan's creation. Dagger thrust forward, Zayl stepped up next to him, also eager to see the magical gemstone.

A face of utter horror suddenly greeted both men from a stalactite just beyond the crystal.

Both mercenaries swore loudly, and even Zayl muttered something under his breath. They stared in disquiet at the figure carved into the growth. A man of limestone and other minerals, he hung as if violently tied to the very stalactite from which he had been sculpted. Arms and legs had been pulled back as far as they could humanly go, seemingly bound together from behind. The expression of agony and dismay had been shaped so exquisitely that Kentril expected the trapped figure to finish his silent cry at any moment. The artisan had managed to touch both the macabre and the human at the same time, making the sculpture even more arresting.

"What is that thing?"

"Some sort of guardian, perhaps. Like the gargoyles and archangels we have seen."

"Why didn't he raise the alarm when we entered?"

The necromancer shrugged.

Kentril stepped up to the horrific sculpture. With great care, he stretched forth his sword and tapped the figure on the chest.

Nothing happened. The eyes shut in pain did not open to condemn him; the mouth did not move to bite the foolish interloper's head off. The statue remained just that, a statue.

Feeling a little foolish, the captain turned back to the others. "Well, if Gregus Mazi isn't around here, we'd better—"

A chill ran up his spine, and he saw both of his companions' gazes suddenly widen—and focus not on Kentril, but rather *behind* him.

Captain Dumon spun around.

The eyes—the eyes that had stayed closed even after his somewhat arrogant inspection—now did indeed glare madly at him.

The already open mouth let loose with a terrible, haunting cry.

All three men covered their ears as the harsh, painful sound overwhelmed all else. Over and over, the sentinel cried, the mad scream echoing throughout the chamber and well beyond.

For more than a minute, the horrific sound continued. Then, finally, the cry gradually lessened, enough so that at last the party could lower their hands.

And that was when they could finally hear the flapping of oncoming wings.

A flock of batlike forms darted into the chamber, shrieking wildly as they attacked. In the uncertain illumination, Kentril saw small, gray, demonic shapes no more than knee-high and looking vaguely like reptilian men. Talons akin to those of predatory birds slashed at the trio whenever one of the creatures passed overhead, and toothy maws sought bites of their flesh.

"*Alae Nefastus!*" shouted the necromancer. "Winged Fiends! Lesser demons but dangerous in quantity!"

And in quantity they had come. Kentril quickly ran one through the torso, watching with grim satisfaction as it fell twitching to the floor. Unfortunately, in its place came six new and very eager ones. Nearby, Gorst battered two with the flat of his ax, only to have another dig deep into his shoulder. The giant shouted in surprise and pain, even his muscular hide no match for the demon's razor-sharp nails.

They filled the chamber, their savage cries almost as terrible as the warning by the sentinel. The captain managed to slay two more yet still felt as if he accomplished nothing. Nevertheless, he continued fighting, the only other recourse not at all attractive.

One of the fiends dove past him, seeking instead Zayl. Opening his vast cloak, the necromancer trapped the small demon within.

A brief, muffled squeal escaped the creature . . . then a pile of brown ash dropped near the spellcaster's boot. Zayl released the cloak and focused on the other attackers.

"They must serve Gregus Mazi!" Kentril called. "That thing that screamed was meant to alert him!"

Zayl did not answer. Instead, the necromancer now shouted incomprehensible words at another group of fluttering terrors. At the same time, he drew a circle in their direction with the tip of the dagger.

The winged imps he had targeted, five in all, suddenly turned away and, to Kentril's surprise, began attacking their fellows. Two unsuspecting fiends perished under shredding talons before others began to assault in great numbers the traitors in their midst. In moments, the five ensorcelled demons had fallen, but not before taking two more with them.

An imp raked the captain across the cheek, splattering Kentril with his own blood. The wound stung so greatly it made his eyes water, yet he managed to catch the offending demon as it flew away, impaling it.

Unfortunately, even another death seemed not to deter the massive flock.

"There're too many!" grunted Gorst.

"Captain Dumon! If you and Gorst can fend them off me for a moment or two longer, I may be able to rid ourselves of this trouble!"

Seeing no other option, Kentril battled his way back to the necromancer, Gorst doing the same from the other side.

As the pair shielded Zayl, the cloaked mage again spoke in the unknown language. With the dagger he draw another glowing image, this one resembling to the mercenary officer an exploding star.

A haze suddenly filled the chamber, a noxious-smelling but otherwise seemingly harmless fog that rapidly spread to every corner, every crack, leaving no place untouched.

Yet if the haze did nothing to the trio save to irritate their nostrils and obscure their vision some, its effect on the winged demons proved anything but harmless. One by one, then by greater and greater numbers, the taloned fiends suddenly lost control. They collided with one another, crashed into the walls, even simply dropped to the floor of the chamber.

Once on the ground, the savage imps shook as if in the throes of madness. Gradually, their hisses and squawks became more feeble. Finally, they began to still, first a few, then more and more.

Soon all lay dead.

"*Zerata!*" called the necromancer.

The haze instantly faded away, leaving no trace.

Zayl suddenly staggered forward and would have dropped if not for Gorst's quick reflexes. The spellcaster leaned against the giant for a few seconds, then seemed to recover.

"Forgive me. The last took much out of me, for I had to say and control it perfectly, otherwise the effect would have been different."

"What do you mean?" Kentril asked.

"We would be lying there with the imps."

Gorst kicked at a few bodies, making certain that none pretended, then took a peek down the passage from which they had come. "Don't hear anything more."

"There were quite a few attacking us." Zayl joined the other mercenary near the passage. "It is quite possible that we destroyed the entire flock."

The giant nodded, then asked, "So where's their master?"

That had been a question on Kentril's mind as well. Were these creatures all that Gregus Mazi had been able to send after them? Why had he not attacked with some spell while the three had been distracted? Even the most basic tactician understood the value of such a maneuver.

Another thing bothered him. Turning back to the Key to Shadow, he stared at the artifact, wondering why Mazi had not simply removed the black crystal and shattered it on the floor. While it was perhaps possible that such a deed would have required far more effort than it appeared, Juris Khan had given every indication that his former friend had been a sorcerer of tremendous skill and cunning. Gregus Mazi should have been able to reduce the crystal to shards . . .

So why had he not destroyed the gemstone?

Any hesitation likely had nothing to do with the Key's monetary value, although Kentril knew of several dukes and other nobles back in the Western Kingdoms who would have paid him enough for the stone for the mercenary to retire in wealth. One could scarcely believe that it had been created from magic, so real did it look. Still, he had heard of few stones so perfect. Each facet seemed almost a mirror. In some, the captain could see himself reflected back. In others, he could make out the vague forms of his companions or even some of the dead imps. Captain Dumon could even make out details of the macabre sentinel's face . . .

Kentril spun around, gaze fixed on the eyes of the horrific figure. Of all the features of the monstrous sculpture, they showed the most precision, the most care.

They were the most human.

"There's no need to worry about looking for Gregus Mazi," Kentril called to the others. He tried to will the eyes to look his way, but they did not move. "I think I've found him."

THIRTEEN

"I think you must be correct, captain," Zayl quietly answered after studying the figure in detail. "Now that I have had a chance to cast a few spells of detection, I can swear that there is life in it."

"But how?" Kentril wanted desperately to know. "How could this be? How can this have happened to Mazi?"

The necromancer did not look at all pleased. "I can only assume that Juris Khan has not been forthcoming in his tales."

"That can't be! Lord Khan would never do anything like this. You know that."

"I am as deeply troubled as you by this discovery . . . and just as confused. I suppose it is quite possible that Lord Khan is also unaware of the true fate of his former friend, and, therefore, one must assume Khan's daughter is unaware also."

"Of course she is!" the captain snapped.

Gorst shook his head. "Can you do anything? Can you make him human again?"

"Alas, I fear not. This is far more complex than the curse upon our host. What I have been able to determine is that Gregus Mazi is more than just sealed to the stalactite. He is, in essence, a very part of the mountain. Such a spell cannot be reversed, I'm afraid."

"But he's still alive, you said," persisted the giant.

Zayl shrugged, to Kentril quite clearly disturbed more than he tried to show. "Yes, otherwise my spell to summon his shade would have worked the first time. If it is any comfort, I suspect that if his mind survived after the transformation, then it has long since fallen into total madness. I daresay he suffers no longer."

"I want to see," demanded a voice. "Take me out so I can get a good look at him."

From the pouch, Zayl produced Humbart Wessel's skull. Gorst looked on with some slight unease but overall more interest. Kentril realized that he had forgotten to tell his second of the necromancer's unique companion.

Holding the skull up high, Zayl let it examine the ghoulish display. Humbart said nothing save to direct the spellcaster to point the empty eye sockets this way or that.

"Aye, 'tis him," he remarked rather sadly. " 'Tis old Gregus come to a more ill end than myself."

"Did you sense anything?" the necromancer asked. "Any hint of who might have done this?"

"This is powerful sorcery, lad. I can't tell. Believe me, I'm sorry. You're right on one thing, though; this can't be changed. There's no way to make him human again."

Kentril tried hard not to think of what it must have been like for the man. Had he suffered much? Had it been as Zayl had suggested, that perhaps Gregus Mazi had been cursed to this form with his mind still functioning? All those centuries trapped like that, unable to move, unable to do anything?

"But why?" the captain finally asked. "Why do this? It looks like more than punishment. You saw what happened, Zayl. He let out a scream that alerted those winged beasts!"

"Yes . . . apparently he is part of some method of warning." The necromancer turned toward the Key to Shadow. "I am wondering if perhaps he did so because we were too near this."

"That makes no sense! We'd be the last ones to want to touch the crystal! Ureh needs that in place, too, or else it won't matter that we set its counterpart atop Nymyr."

Zayl reached for the artifact as if to pick it up, at the same time watching to see how the monstrous figure would react.

The all-too-human eyes suddenly widened, almost glaring at the presumptuous necromancer. However, this time, no scream alerted guardians, perhaps because there might not have been any left.

As Zayl withdrew his hand, they saw the eyes of the sentinel relax, then close again. The mouth remained open in mid-scream.

"He does guard it. Interesting. I recall that when you walked up to him, I shifted position slightly, which would have placed me about as near to the crystal as I was just now. That must have been what caused him to react."

"So what do we do now?" asked Gorst.

Kentril sheathed his blade. "There doesn't seem much at all for us to do. We might as well make our way back. There's no telling how far along Tsin might already be with the spell."

Zayl looked to the ceiling. "I still sense great forces at work, but you are correct. He may be done soon . . . and, as you said, there remains nothing of value for us to do here. We will retire to the palace and discuss this among ourselves in more detail."

"Hold on there!" called Humbart Wessel's skull. "You can't leave him like that."

"Now, Humbart—"

But the skull would not be silenced. "Are you good men or the kind of villain you thought old Gregus to be? Captain Dumon, what would you do if one of your fellows lay trapped and bleeding badly on the field of battle and you couldn't take him with you? Would you leave him for the enemy to do with as they pleased?"

"No, of course not . . ." The veteran officer understood exactly what the ghostly voice meant. You never left a comrade behind to be tortured by the foe. You either let him take his own course of action, or with your sword you did it for him. Kentril had been forced to such action more than once, and while he had never taken any pleasure in it, he had known that he had been doing his duty. "No . . . Humbart's right."

Drawing his weapon again, he approached the ensorcelled Gregus Mazi and, with much trepidation, started tapping at the torso in search of a soft enough spot. Unfortunately, his initial hunt revealed nothing but hardened minerals. The spell had been very thorough.

"Allow me to do it, captain. I think my blade will better serve." Zayl came forward with the ivory dagger, but Kentril stepped in front of him.

"Give the weapon to me, necromancer. I know where best to strike to kill a man quickly and cleanly. This has to be done right."

Bowing to the soldier's experience, the cloaked spellcaster turned over the dagger to Kentril. The captain studied the rune-inscribed blade for a moment, then turned his attention once more to Gregus Mazi.

As he raised the dagger to strike, the eyes of the limestone-encrusted sentinel suddenly opened, focusing upon Kentril with an intensity that made the fighter's hand shake.

On a hunch, he moved the dagger slightly to the side.

The eyes followed the weapon with especially keen interest.

There and then, Captain Dumon realized that the mind of the sorcerer remained intact. Insanity had not granted Gregus Mazi any escape from his tortured existence.

For just a short moment, Kentril hesitated, wondering if perhaps there might be some way yet to free the man, but then the eyes above his own answered that question, pleading for the soldier to do what he must.

"Heaven help you," the captain muttered.

With a prayer on his lips, Kentril thrust the dagger into the chest area with expert precision.

Not one drop of blood emerged from the wound. Instead, a brief gust of hot wind smelling of sulfur burst forth, almost as if Kentril had opened a way to some volcanic realm deep within the mountain. It startled the mercenary so much that he stepped back a pace, withdrawing the blade as he retreated.

He expected another hellish cry such as had brought the imps to attack, but instead only a tremendous sigh emerged from the frozen mouth. In that short-lived sigh, the captain heard more than just a death; he heard Gregus Mazi's relief at being at last released from his terrible prison. The eyes gave him an almost grateful look before quickly glazing over and closing for a final time.

"His curse is ended," whispered Zayl after a time. "He has left this terrible place." The necromancer gently took the dagger back from Kentril. "I suggest we do the same."

"Rest well, Gregus," the skull muttered.

Much subdued, the trio completed their ascension through the caverns in silence. They had gone in search of an evil sorcerer and found a fellow human being in torment. Nothing they had assumed had proven to be fact, and that bothered all of them, Kentril most of all.

Exiting through the shaft by which they had first entered the mountain, the fighters separated from Zayl, who advised that it might not be wise for the three of them to return together.

"I will spend some more time out here, then return as if from the city. We need to meet again later, captain. I feel we both have questions we wish answered."

Kentril nodded, then, with Gorst trailing, headed back to the palace. Although the unsettling events in the caverns remained an important part of his thoughts, Kentril could not help but think more and more about the out-come of Tsin's work as he neared Lord Khan's abode. Had that, too, gone awry? Was nothing to be as he had assumed it would be?

To his further apprehension, he and Gorst discovered the gates—the entire entrance, in fact—utterly unmanned. Worse, as they entered the ancient edi-fice, both quickly noticed that not a sound echoed throughout the vast palace, almost as if the deathly quiet of the abandoned ruins had swept once more over the kingdom. Down an ominously empty hall Kentril and the giant cau-tiously journeyed, searching in vain for some hint of life.

At last, they came across the massive doors to Juris Khan's sanctum. Kentril glanced at his friend, then reached forward . . .

The doors swung open of their own accord, revealing a reverent crowd kneeling before the dais occupied by the robed lord's tall, regal chair.

A chair now empty . . . for Juris Khan stood among his flock, reaching down now and then to touch guard, peasant, and courtier alike upon the back of the head, giving them his blessing. Near his side, Atanna followed, her expression enraptured. Utter silence filled the room, the silence of awe and respect.

Yet it seemed that even the wonder of her father's freedom could not with-stand the pleasure Atanna manifested when she saw Kentril at the door. She immediately touched Lord Khan on the arm, indicating to him who stood at the entrance.

"Kentril Dumon!" the elder monarch called cheerfully. "Let you and your good man come forth and be part of the celebration, for surely you are as much a reason for this glorious moment as the masterful sorcerer!"

He indicated with one hand a very self-satisfied Quov Tsin. The Vizjerei stood far to the left side of the dais, fairly preening as courtiers both male and female moved to pay their humble respects. Tsin caught Kentril's gaze and gave the captain a triumphant look that contained not one iota of humility.

Urged on by Atanna, Captain Dumon strode toward the regal pair. The kneeling throng gave way for him with as much respect as they showed for their master. Never in his life had Kentril felt so awed by the simple fact that others honored him so much. He recalled all that Juris Khan had offered him and for the first time actually believed it could come to pass without trouble.

"My good Kentril!" Lord Khan gave him a strong, comradely hug with one arm while pulling his daughter near with the other. "This is a day of rejoicing as great as when the archangel first presented to me the hope of our salvation. Truly, the rebirth of Ureh as a beacon of light in the world is near at hand."

"I'm very happy for you, my lord."

The weathered yet noble face twisted into an expression of bemusement. "How certain I am of that. But look! Here is another more eager to express our gratitude and able to do so far better than I. If you'll excuse me, my son, I must show myself to the people beyond the palace walls. They must know that the end of our great curse is near at hand!"

Armored guards hurried to flank their master. The gathered throng rose as one behind Lord Khan, following him as he headed out the chamber for the first time. Atanna guided Kentril to the side so that they would not be swept away by the human flood. Gorst, grinning, let the pair be, the giant instead breaking his way through the crowd as he headed toward Quov Tsin.

"All my hopes," she breathed. "All my dreams . . . they come true at last, Kentril . . . and there is no one but you to thank for that!"

"I think you might thank Tsin some. He broke the spell on your father, after all."

Atanna would not hear his protests. "The Vizjerei master provided the mechanics of my father's freedom, but I know that you urged him on, you enabled him to convince my father that we would be served best and would serve best by not seeking the pathway to Heaven again." She leaned up and kissed him. "My thanks for all that."

"I'm just glad it went well."

"That it did, but all the while I worked with them, I couldn't help thinking of you . . . so much so I feared a couple of times that I might accidentally ruin the spell!" Her eyes twinkled as she looked at him. "Much better to see you before me than only as imagination!" A brief frown graced her exquisite visage. "Why, Kentril, you're dusty, and your cheek is bloody! What's happened to you?"

In all the excitement, he had forgotten about his appearance. Kentril had not decided yet what to say about Gregus Mazi, so in the end he could only reply, "As a soldier, I'm used to training. I took a run outside, then a small climb." He shrugged. "I lost my hold once and slid down a few yards."

"How dreadful! You mustn't let that happen again. I won't have it. I won't lose you now!"

Although her reaction caused him to regret his lie, Kentril did not change his story. "I'm sorry to worry you."

But her mood had already begun to lighten. "Never mind. I've just realized that you must come with me to the grand balcony. You've never been there yet. That's where Father's gone now."

"Then we shouldn't bother—"

"No! You must be there!" She pulled him in the direction Juris Khan and his court had gone.

Because of its lofty location, the palace of Ureh's rulers had, of course, many balconies, but none so vast as the grand one upon which they found Atanna's father already standing. Kentril estimated it to be wide enough to hold more than a hundred people. With its gleaming white marble floor and stylishly crafted stone rail, it likely served also as a place where guests congregated during state functions. He even imagined that during the height of Ureh's power, it had acted as a place for elegant outdoor dining.

At the moment, however, it served a more important purpose. To the captain's astonishment, Lord Khan did not face his court, but rather leaned forward over the rail, calling down to the city below.

And evidently they could hear him well despite the distance, for cheers arose at some remark he made, cheers that lasted for quite some time.

Six guards stood in attendance near the white-robed figure, each bearing a torch that the captain assumed somehow enabled those in the city to see their master. Another half dozen soldiers stood watch, making certain that no one attempted something so foolish as to push Juris Khan over the edge. Kentril thought the precaution unnecessary; clearly everyone both nearby and below worshipped the elder leader.

"This is where Harkin Khan made the Speech of the Saints," Atanna told him. "This is where my grandfather, Zular Khan, married my grandmother and presented her to the people. This is where my father spoke the words of the archangel for all to hear."

"How can anyone possibly hear him all the way up here? Or even see him, for that matter?"

"Come look!"

Kentril had no intention of becoming part of the event, but Atanna proved quite determined. She pulled him forward, but far to the right of where Lord Khan continued to speak. As they reached the rail, Kentril noticed a pair of gleaming metal spheres with rounded openings pointed in the direction of the masses below.

"What are those?"

The scarlet-tressed woman pointed out an identical duo on her father's left. "They amplify and project the voice of whoever speaks from where Father stands. At the same time, an image several times larger can be seen clearly by the crowds below. They are very, very old, and the spellwork used to create them has been lost to us, yet still they function."

"Incredible!" Kentril remarked, feeling the word highly inadequate but unable to summon anything stronger.

Suddenly putting her finger to his lips, Atanna whispered, "Hush! You'll want to hear this."

At first, all Captain Dumon heard were more of the same promises of the future that Juris Khan had been announcing to his flock. He spoke of the ending of Ureh's trials, of once more the sun touching their flesh without burning it away. He talked of the new role the Light among Lights would play in the world, guiding it toward goodness and peace . . .

And then he began talking about Kentril.

The veteran mercenary shook his head, hoping that his host would stop. Khan, however, spoke at length about the captain's role—much of that role an exaggeration as far as Kentril could recall. To hear Ureh's ruler describe him, Kentril Dumon was a paladin extraordinary, a defender of the weak and challenger of evil wherever it lurked. The people below began to cheer loudly every time Lord Khan spoke his name, and several of those on the balcony twisted their heads to see this righteous paragon.

Then, to his even greater fear, Atanna's father gestured for Kentril to join him.

He would have refused, but Atanna gave him no choice, guiding him to where Juris Khan awaited. The benevolent lord again placed one arm around the fighter's shoulder, his other extended to his audience in the city.

"Kentril Dumon of Westmarch, officer at large, skilled commander . . . hero of Ureh." More cheering. "Shortly to take up a new mantle . . . general of this holy realm's defenders!"

This brought renewed cheering plus jubilant applause from the court. Kentril wanted nothing more than to melt into the background, but with Atanna tightly attached to his other side, he could not move.

"General Kentril Dumon!" Khan called. "Commander of the Realm, Protector of the Kingdom, Prince of the *Blood*!" The fatherly monarch smiled at Kentril. "And soon . . . I hope . . . member of my own house!"

And the cheers erupted with such fervor that it seemed certain Nymyr would collapse from the sheer vibration. Kentril stood confused for a moment about what the last meant, but then Juris Khan placed the mercenary's hands atop Atanna's and eyed both with much favor.

Only then did the captain realize that his host had just given his blessing for the two to marry.

Atanna kissed him. Still dazzled, he followed her from the balcony, uncertain yet whether it had all been a dream. Hope filled him, true, but so did much uncertainty. Did he really dare to take on all that Ureh offered? General, prince, and royal consort?

"I must return to my father," Atanna whispered quickly. "I'll see you soon." She kissed him, then, with a last lingering glance, hurried back to the grand balcony.

"Well," said a voice near his ear. "My sincerest congratulations, captain—pardon me—my lord."

Kentril turned to find Zayl emerging from a shadowed corner. The necromancer nodded, then looked past him. "Quite a display."

"I never asked for anything—"

"But it is pleasing to receive it, is it not? At the very least, the affections of the glorious Atanna must put a thrill in your heart."

Not certain whether or not the cloaked figure mocked him, Kentril scowled. "What do you want?"

"Only to ask you how you found things when you entered. I became curious, I must admit, and decided to return to the palace earlier than I had said. To my surprise, there were no guards at the entrance, no people in the halls. I heard the noise from this direction and came just in time to hear you named heir to the throne."

"I'm not *heir*," the captain retorted. "I'll be royal consort if I marry her, not—" Kentril hesitated. In some lands, those who married a princess or the equivalent became ruler when the crown was finally passed. Had Juris Khan just made him future ruler of Ureh?

Zayl took one look at Kentril's questioning expression and, with a hint of a smile, replied, "No, I do not know how the line of succession works in Ureh. You may be right . . . or you may not be right. Now, come! We likely have but moments together before she returns to see to your dressing properly for your new roles."

"What do you want to know?"

"Did you say anything about Gregus Mazi?"

Captain Dumon felt insulted. "I keep my word."

"I thought as much, but I had to ask." The necromancer's eyes narrowed to slits. "Tell me as best you can what has happened to you since you entered." When Kentril had related to him everything as detailed as the fighter could, Zayl frowned. "An interesting but uninformative tableau."

"What did you expect me to tell you?"

"I do not know . . . just that I felt that something should have given a hint to our next course of action." The necromancer sighed. "I will return to my quarters and meditate on it. If you should recall some significant moment that you forgot to mention, please come to me at once."

While he doubted very much that he had forgotten anything of value, Kentril promised Zayl that he would do as the spellcaster desired. As Zayl departed, Kentril suddenly thought again of his present condition, realizing that he had stood among the nobles and before the people of Ureh dressed in dusty, worn garments. Although it was already too late to rectify that situation, he could at least present a better image when next anyone, especially Atanna and Juris Khan, saw him. Surely now would be the time to don the regal dress uniform he had worn at the private dinner. At the very least, it would serve him until he could procure other appropriate clothing.

He started for his quarters, only to see down the hall Gorst and Tsin. The Vizjerei seemed quite disturbed by something the giant was saying, and when Tsin noticed Kentril, he glared at the captain as if the latter had just burned down Ureh's treasure trove of magical tomes.

An uneasy feeling coursed through Kentril, and the glance Gorst gave him over his shoulder only strengthened that uneasiness. He picked up his pace, praying that he had read their faces wrong.

"I told him," Gorst said as his commanding officer neared. "I had to."

"By the seven-eyed demon Septumos, Captain Dumon! What were you thinking? Why was I not informed? Is everything this cretin said about the caverns and Gregus Mazi truth? I find it hard to believe—"

"If Gorst told you, then it's true," Kentril replied, cutting off the sorcerer's tirade. He had no time for this. What had the other mercenary been thinking? Gorst usually had a level head. Why would he include Tsin without first discussing it with his captain?

The Vizjerei shook his head in disbelief. "I should have been down there! Gregus Mazi! So many things he could've explained!"

"There wasn't much of anything that he could explain." Kentril eyed Gorst, who did not look at all ashamed. "You did tell him how we found Mazi, didn't you?"

Gorst nodded. "Everything. I had to, after what Master Tsin said."

"And what was that you said, Tsin?"

Drawing himself up, the robed sorcerer muttered, "I still don't know if this brute here has a point, but—"

"*What* did you say that set Gorst off, Tsin?"

For once he had made the Vizjerei uncomfortable. "The one trait that makes this one here more tolerable than the rest of you is his proper respect for all things magical. Because of that, I tolerated his questions about the work involved in casting my great spell. He wanted to hear about the difficulty and how I overcame it. He also—" Tsin broke off as Kentril stepped closer, hand on the hilt of his sword. "I'm coming to it! I told Gorst about the patterns and incantations I'd created to undo the clever binding of the curse and how all proceeded as smoothly as I'd expected it would."

If the bragging did not cease quickly, Captain Dumon suspected he would soon try to throttle the spellcaster regardless of the consequences. "Everything went well. You expected that. Not one hitch. I assumed—"

"Then you assumed wrong, cretin," the bearded figure snapped. "There *was* one point when I feared that all my hard work would come to naught, when something outside my control nearly ruined a carefully prepared work of art!"

Quov Tsin tapped his staff on the floor. "I expected trouble only from the girl, a skilled wielder of power but one far too distracted by daydreams . . ." At this, he frowned hard at Kentril, an obvious hint to the captain being the cause of those distractions. "What I did not expect was someone as well-versed, as well-trained, as our *host* nearly to turn it all into disaster!"

"What did he do?" Kentril asked, suddenly unconcerned with such mundane things as dress uniforms and marrying the daughters of lords.

Tsin snorted. "Like a first-year apprentice, he did the unthinkable! We had come to the threshold, the point where there could be not the slightest fraction of an error. I had the girl drawing together the proper forces, while I, guiding them by words and gesture, worked to reverse that which had turned flesh, wood, and stone to one. Had it been more than simply his legs, the complexity might have been too great even for me, but, fortunately, that was not the case. I—"

"Tsin—"

"All right, all right! He *moved,* cretin! Juris Khan, whose task was to focus his power, his will, from within in order to foment changes to the spell structure of his own body, *moved*!"

The Vizjerei leaned back, as if what he had said explained everything. Kentril, however, knew that there had to be more. Gorst did not overreact.

"He did more'n just move," the giant interjected, now as impatient as his captain with the sorcerer. "Tsin says he almost leapt up, Kentril! Leapt up as if someone lit a fire underneath him. And from how Tsin describes it, I'd say it happened right about the time you put the dagger through Gregus Mazi's *chest."*

Fourteen

Gorst's unsettling suggestion remained with Captain Dumon long after the three had separated. Kentril did not yet know what to make of the notion that somehow Juris Khan had reacted to Mazi's death, but the implications did not bode well. That Tsin had been unable to offer any other idea that sufficiently explained the reaction did not help, either.

Despite that, the Vizjerei had not completely accepted Gorst's concerns that their host hid some secret from them, and neither could Kentril. However, the captain had to admit to himself that a tremendous part of his own reluctance had to do with the honors Lord Khan had bestowed upon him, especially the upcoming marriage to his daughter. As for Quov Tsin, his reasons for reluctance were even more obvious; the vast collection of Ureh's magical library lay open to him for as long as he had the good graces of the elder ruler.

Sleeping on it did little good for Kentril, for even his dreams turned to the troubling development. In truth, he welcomed the unexpected knock on his chamber doors, for the noise stirred him from a dream in which Juris Khan proved to be Gregus Mazi in disguise and Atanna the willing lover of the masked villain.

Although he hoped that it would be Khan's wondrous daughter at the door, Captain Dumon instead found himself facing a rather pensive Albord. Kentril's first fear was that some of the other men had gone missing, but the younger mercenary quickly erased that fear. Unfortunately, in its place he presented one that in some ways disturbed his commander even more.

"Captain, the men want to leave."

"No one goes into the city until I say so."

Albord shook his head. "Captain . . . they want to leave *Ureh*. They want to go home . . . and I think they should be able to."

This time, Kentril could think of no good reason to hold them back. He had a life offered to him here, but the others wanted only to return to the Western Kingdoms. They might have even had their rewards by now if not for his own hesitation.

"All right, give me a few days, and I'll see that our host makes sure each—"

Now Albord looked even more uncomfortable. "Captain, Jodas and Orlif have already talked to him."

Kentril almost seized the white-haired mercenary by the throat, but fought back the impulse before he could betray himself. "When? When did they do it?"

"Just a little while ago. I only found out myself after they came to me. They said they told his lordship that they had to go, and would he be still granting them that which he'd promised."

"And Khan said he would?"

"To listen to them, he hugged each like a brother and promised that every man would have a full sack!"

There existed no doubt in Kentril's mind that the fatherly ruler had done just that, yet another example of graciousness that made it difficult to fathom what tie existed between the saintly monarch and the mysterious Mazi. The captain leaned on a nearby chair, trying to organize his thoughts. What could he do, though, but accept their departure as wisely and kindly as Juris Khan had? After all, by rights, they could do as they pleased now. Their contract to Tsin had ended long ago.

"Can't say as I blame them," he finally responded. "And they're probably safer out of Ureh, at least for now. So how long before you all leave?"

"They want to go when next it's day beyond Nymyr, captain. I'd say that's basically tomorrow." Albord straightened. "I'm not going with them, sir."

"You're not?"

The plowboy face lit up. "Captain, I thought about it a lot after the last time I mentioned leaving. Under you, I've learned more than I ever would've back in my village. I've got family there like everyone else has somewhere, but they knew I might not return for a long time, if ever. I'd like to stay on awhile longer after all." He grinned. "Leastwise, I can always go home sayin' I served under a prince!"

The words brought some relief to Kentril. "You sure you don't want to go with them?"

"My mind's staying made up this time, sir."

"All right. I'll see they're sent off right. They've done well . . . you've *all* done well."

A grin as great as any Gorst had ever given spread across Albord's youthful visage. "Appreciate that, captain—my *lord*. I'll be happy to volunteer to escort them to the outer gates of the kingdom, though."

The task seemed simple and safe enough, even with the yet-unexplained disappearances of the three other men. Kentril still suspected that, like him, each had been lured to a more deserted area, then knifed. The odds were their bodies would never be found. Still, so long as Albord kept in the open where the crowds could see him, he would be safe.

"I'll be glad to give you that pleasure, lad . . . and thanks for the loyalty."

Giving his commanding officer a sharp salute, Albord left. Kentril started back to his bed, but his thoughts would now not leave his men. He could not help wondering if even one of the vanished trio could have been saved if he had let the men go home sooner. To die on the field of battle was one thing for a mercenary, to end up tossed into an alley with a dagger in your spine was another. For that matter, Kentril did not even know if the men had actually been slain; it was possible that they still lived as prisoners or—

Prisoners?

Captain Dumon bolted upright. He knew of one way to tell . . .

Kentril found the necromancer in one of the rooms farthest away from the others, a special request, it appeared, from Zayl himself. The spellcaster did not respond to his quiet knock, but something made the fighter certain that he would find Zayl within. Kentril knocked again, this time quietly calling out the other's name.

"Enter," came the unmistakable hollow voice of Humbart Wessel.

Slipping inside, Kentril discovered the necromancer seated on the floor, his legs folded in, his hands on his knees, and his eyes staring straight at the ivory dagger that hung suspended in the air before him. Zayl's vast cloak lay on the bed. Atop a small wooden table to the side, the skull had been set so it faced the doorway.

"Hallo, lad!" it cheerfully greeted him. "He does this two to three times a day, if he can. Mind completely disappears from this world . . ."

"How long does he stay like this?" whispered the captain.

The necromancer's left hand suddenly moved. At the same time, the dagger dropped toward the floor, only to be caught by the hand.

"As long as need be," Zayl remarked, quickly unfolding his legs, then rising in one smooth action.

The skull chuckled. "Just in case, though, he leaves me pointed at the door. Anyone comes in, I give the alarm."

Zayl gave Humbart a dark look. "And I am still waiting to hear it."

" 'Tis only our good comrade Kentril Dumon, boy! I recognized his voice right away."

"While I have nothing against you, captain, what Humbart fails to remember is that you might not be alone . . . or you might not even be you. There are spells of illusion that can fool almost anyone, even the overconfident dead." The slim, pale man retrieved his cloak. "Now, what is it I can do for you?"

"I came because . . . because an idea occurred to me based on your own experiences."

"And that would pertain to—?"

The captain found his gaze drifting to the skull. "Three of my men have never returned from the city. The rest, by the way, are making plans to leave come the morrow. Before that happens, though, I may need them to plan a rescue."

He had Zayl's full attention now. "A rescue? You have reason to believe that the missing ones still live?"

"That's where you come in. I remembered all of a sudden that you said the reason for your earlier failure had to do with Gregus Mazi actually still being alive. You then used a different spell to locate his general surroundings—"

"And you wish me to attempt to do the same for those of your command now lost." The necromancer frowned in thought. "I can see no reason why it should not work—and perhaps it might yet shed some light on this shadowed land. Yes, captain, I would be glad to try."

"How soon can you start?"

Zayl reached for the skull, placing it in the pouch hidden by his cloak. "I cannot do anything until we find some personal item or, better yet, a hair or clipping from any of the three. Would it be prudent at this time to visit the quarters they used?"

Doubting that anyone would question the company's captain wanting to investigate the missing men's belongings for some clue to their disappearance, Kentril readily nodded. That seemed all the necromancer needed to satisfy himself. With a wave of his hand, he indicated for the captain to lead on.

In that most rare of circumstances for a mercenary, the kindness of their host had enabled each man of the hired company to have rooms of his own. Some, like Kentril, had become so used to cramped quarters or sleeping without a roof at all that they had barely made use of more than the bed. Others, meanwhile, had taken advantage of the situation to the point where the few items they had lay scattered everywhere. Kentril felt certain that they would find something useful in the rooms of all three.

Which made it all the more startling when, upon entering the first set of rooms, they found no trace of habitation at all.

When Kentril had first stepped into his own chambers, he had not been able to imagine anyone else ever having entered them before. From the silky, gold-threaded draperies to the wide, plush, canopied bed, everything in sight had looked absolutely new. Both the bed frame and the elegant furniture had been meticulously carved from the finest oak, a wood that the captain could not recall having seen anywhere in eastern Kehjistan, then stained a dark, rich reddish brown. Besides the bed, the main room in his quarters came equipped with a sturdy bronze-handled cabinet, four chairs, and a pair of tables—the wide one possibly used for dining and the other a small twin near the doorway. The filigreed walls had also been accented by a series of small but detailed tapestries that seemed to outline the early history of Ureh.

Beyond the main room, the smaller of the two lesser chambers gave the occupant a place for personal care, including rarely seen plumbing, a true mark of the wealth wielded by Lord Khan and his predecessors. The remaining room consisted of a pair of leather chairs, a tiny but no less elegant table, and a shelf filled with books. Out of mild curiosity, Captain Dumon had picked over the collection in his own chambers, but he knew that most of his men could not even decipher letters, much less read.

Brek's rooms had been chosen first, and one quick survey of them led the captain to decide quickly that someone else had straightened up after the mercenary's disappearance. Brek had not been the most organized of fighters and certainly not one of the cleanest; there should have been food, empty bottles, and more lying about. Even the bearded warrior's pack, which he would have left in the palace during his sojourns down to the city, had vanished.

"This is most troubling," Zayl quietly remarked.

A quick hunt through the rooms of the other two brought the same unsettling results. All had been arranged as if they had never been occupied by the hardened mercenaries. Even Kentril, who kept his quarters neater than most of his kind, could not match the cleanliness.

He sought out Gorst, whom he found playing cards with Albord and two other men. The fighters rose as he entered the giant's quarters, but Kentril quickly ordered them at ease.

"Who's been in Brek's rooms? Anyone?" When all four shook their heads, he focused on Albord, whose own quarters sat next to those of the missing man. "You've heard nothing through the wall?"

"Not since the last time Brek himself was in there . . ."

Letting them return to their game, Captain Dumon rejoined the necromancer. It did not please Kentril to see that the generally calm Zayl looked quite irked by what they had discovered.

"The palace has many servants," the latter solemnly proposed. "They move with a silence and swiftness worthy of my brethren, but it is very possible that they removed the belongings for some custodial reason."

"Or they didn't expect the boys to return," countered Humbart from the pouch.

Kentril felt defeated . . . and even more anxious than ever. "Is there nothing you can do, then?"

Holding up the dagger, Zayl muttered under his breath. The enchanted blade flared bright. The necromancer held the dagger before him, letting it sweep across the room.

"What're you up to?"

"I am trying to see if any useful trace at all was left behind. A single hair hidden under a chair, a scrap of cloth accidentally covered by a blanket . . ." No sooner had he explained, however, then the necromancer lowered the blade in mild disgust. "None of which I can find in this particular place. I am sorry, captain."

"Maybe we can—"

Before Kentril could finish, the door swung open, and Atanna appeared. "Why, here you are!"

She swept toward the fighter, Zayl seemingly nonexistent. Kentril accepted a swift kiss from her, then discovered himself being conducted out of the room.

"And you've changed back into that horrid, old outfit!" She *tsk*ed at him, sounding more like a mother hen than the desirable enchantress at which he stared. "You must dress before it's too late! Father already expects us there!"

"Where?" Kentril could recall no urgent matter.

"Why, for a formal introduction to the court, of course. You must be known to everyone before you officially take up the roles Father's promised you. It would be bad form otherwise."

"But—" Despite his uncertainties, despite the surmounting questions concerning Lord Khan, Captain Dumon found himself once again defenseless against the charms of the crimson-tressed princess. Atanna had come to him clad in a white-and-green gown fit perfectly to her well-curved form and designed, as it seemed with everything she wore, to utterly bewitch him.

"Now, you mustn't argue," she returned, guiding him to his own rooms. "I'll wait for you, but you must hurry! This is very important for your future here, Kentril"—her eyes seemed to shine like jewels—"and for *ours* as well."

And against that last point, his final defenses fell. Away went any concerns about the secrets of Gregus Mazi, about any subterfuge by Juris Khan . . . and any doubt that he would be Atanna's slave forever.

Despite some faint amusement concerning how completely overwhelmed the good captain had proven to be in the presence of Juris Khan's glorious daughter, Zayl otherwise worried about the man. Kentril Dumon surely had to feel caught between trust and betrayal, love and lies. Not trained as followers of Rathma were in the cultivation and control of emotions, the mercenary risked making a fatal misstep. Zayl hoped that would not be the case, for he knew that the captain remained his best ally. The giant Gorst could be trusted, yes, but lacked some of Kentril Dumon's battle-honed wits. As for Quov Tsin, if the Vizjerei ever proved Zayl's only hope, then surely they were all very much doomed.

But doomed to what? The key, he suspected, had something to do with the three missing men. More and more, the necromancer distrusted the notion that they had simply perished at the hands of common street thugs. No, he felt that there had to be something darker, something more ominous going on.

A check of the rooms inhabited by the other two missing mercenaries revealed the same lack of clues. Zayl considered mesmerizing one of the servants into revealing what had happened to the men's effects, but not only did that seem likely to earn him the watchful eye of their host, he could also not *find* any of the attendants. As the necromancer had remarked to Captain Dumon, they indeed moved as if trained by Zayl's own people, a curious thing to think about liveried servants. Yet another confounding piece of a puzzle whose image he had yet to divine.

"One hair, one piece of nail," he murmured as he finished his second search of the last set of rooms. "Not so much to ask, but apparently too much to hope for."

One single strand, one follicle, and he could have done as he had in the sanctum of Gregus Mazi. Zayl did not like being thwarted by such minuscule things; surely the forces that sought to keep the mortal world in balance did not intend such frustration. Zayl only wished that he could have—

The necromancer froze in the act of putting away the dagger, his mind suddenly aflame with a realization that he had been ignoring an entire path open to him all this time. Captain Dumon had actually brought it up, but, focused on the mercenary officer's actual reason for coming to him, Zayl had lost sight of it. The possible answer to all their questions shouted to be heard, and the spellcaster had been blithely deaf to it.

When first Zayl had sought the shade of Gregus Mazi, the latter had not been dead.

But now the sorcerer was . . . put down mercifully by the necromancer's party after discovering his horrific plight.

"I am a fool!" he uttered.

"Are you looking for argument?" came Humbart's voice.

He looked down at the pouch. "Gregus Mazi is dead!"

"Aye, and it's nothing to cheer, you hear me, lad?"

But Zayl did not answer him, already departing the emptied chamber for his own. He would set up the patterns, arrange the spell—

No! His room would never do. During the course of their search, the captain had told Zayl of Juris Khan's disturbing reaction during Tsin's spellwork. The necromancer suddenly wondered if seeking the ghost of the sorcerer would be a wise thing to do in the very sanctum of the one who had claimed, either erroneously or falsely, to have slain him.

At the very least, it would pay to perform the spell elsewhere, and Zayl could think of no better location than the mouth of the cave leading to where they had found what had remained of the unfortunate mage.

It took the necromancer little time to retrieve what he needed from his quarters and even less time to exit the palace by secret means. Zayl had memorized the layout to the edifice well, suspicious, somehow, that it would prove opportune later. Part of a calling held in mistrust and apprehension among most folk, he had done so out of habit. One never knew when an overzealous official might decide to make his mark by capturing and disposing of the "evil" summoner of the dead.

In some ways, escaping to the shaft filled Zayl with more assurance. Born to the jungle lands, he was distracted by the confining qualities of any building, even one so massive as the palace. Now, outside, he felt as if he could breathe again. His wits seemed to grow sharper, so much so that the necromancer had to ask himself again why he had not thought to attempt a new summoning of Gregus Mazi once the latter had actually perished. So much time wasted . . .

With the dagger to light his way, Zayl headed several yards into the shaft. Finding a fairly open part of the corridor, the necromancer squatted down and began to draw patterns in the dirt floor with the glowing blade. The spell Zayl planned would be virtually identical to the one he had cast in Gregus Mazi's sanctum, the only difference being some added symbols to increase the odds of success.

From out of the pouch he took Humbart's skull, three small candles, and a single strand of hair. Putting the skull to the side, Zayl arranged the candles, then placed the hair in the center. After pricking his finger and letting the necessary number of drops of blood fall onto the one hair, the necromancer lit each of the candles with the tip of his blade, then proceeded with the incantation.

A slight breeze arose in the shaft. Zayl quickly paused in his efforts, moving so as to block the wind before it could blow the hair away. Satisfied, he started his work anew.

Suddenly, the wind came at the display from the other side. Zayl frowned, recalling no such turbulent currents during his previous visit. He sniffed the air, seeking the scent of magic, but found none.

"Trouble?" asked the skull.

"A minor nuisance." Taking some rocks, the spellcaster built a small wall to protect everything.

Once more, he began muttering. This time, no wind interrupted. Zayl focused his gaze on the hair, thinking of the dead sorcerer.

As before, smoke arose above the hair where the blood touched it, the smoke then taking on a vaguely humanoid shape. As the necromancer advanced in his spell, the smoke swelled tremendously, growing as tall as a man and taking on more and more the characteristics of one. Zayl could make out a robed form, a man in a sorcerer's garb. The figure seemed to be reaching out, at the same time trying to speak.

"Gregus Mazi, I summon thee!" Zayl called. "Gregus Mazi, I conjure thee! I call upon thee to walk the mortal plane for a time more, to come to me and share your knowledge!"

And in the smoke, there formed an imposing, black-haired figure more like Kentril Dumon than either the necromancer or the Vizjerei. Broad of shoulder, determined of face, Gregus Mazi looked not at all like the viper he had been portrayed as and more like a legendary protector.

"Bit younger than when I saw him," Humbart remarked.

"Quiet!" Zayl had not yet bound the spirit to him, and until he did, any interruption risked breaking the summoning.

He muttered more, then with the dagger drew a double loop in the air. Mazi's flickering ghost solidified, becoming so distinct that ignorant onlookers might have believed that they could actually touch him. In truth, had Zayl worked hard, he could have created an even more substantial specter, but the necromancer had no need of such and respected the dead mage too much even to try to bind him so.

Soon, very soon, the spell would be complete. Then only Zayl would be able to dismiss the shade without the most extreme effort.

And as he became more a part of the mortal world, Gregus Mazi tried once more to speak. His mouth opened, but no sound escaped him. He continued to try to reach for the other spellcaster, but moved as if caught in some thick fluid. Only the eyes managed to express anything definite, and in them Zayl saw an urgent need to communicate a message, perhaps the very information he and the captain had sought.

"Gregus Mazi, let air once more fill your lungs! Let speech be yours as I permit it! Let the words you wish to speak be heard!"

The dead sorcerer moaned. With grim determination, he thrust a finger toward Zayl and at last forced a single word from his gaping mouth.

"Diablooooo!"

And as he spoke, Mazi's appearance transformed. His sorcerer's robe, briefly a resplendent blue and gold and covered with holy wards, *burst* into flames. The finger that pointed in warning shriveled rapidly, becoming skeletal. Likewise, the strong, determined visage melted away, leaving until the end the staring, warning eyes . . .

"Zayl, lad! Look out!"

Craggy, monstrous hands of rock suddenly thrust forth from the walls, catching the necromancer from both in front and behind. They forced the air from Zayl's lungs, and it was all he could do to keep from being immediately crushed to a pulp.

In his struggles, he kicked apart the display. Now bound to the necromancer, the monstrous ghost of Gregus Mazi should have remained fixed where it was, but instead it instantly faded away, the single word of warning still on its lipless mouth.

Zayl still had the dagger, but with his arms clamped awkwardly to his body, he could not raise it. With the vestiges of breath left to him, the desperate spellcaster shouted out words of power.

"Beraka! Dianos Tempri! Berak—"

He could not force anything more out. A rumbling shook the cave, and somewhere distant Zayl heard Humbart Wessel's voice calling to him.

The necromancer blacked out.

FIFTEEN

Juris Khan did not shirk when it came to rewarding the mercenaries who had chosen to depart. Kentril marveled at the riches he rained upon the men—gold coins, glittering diamonds, scarlet rubies, and so much more. The only limit to what the men received had to do with how much they themselves could carry, for the lord of Ureh had no horses or other animals to give them. That did not seem to bother Jodas and the rest, though; they found the bounty they had received more than sufficient.

"Come back to us again once Ureh stands among the mighty kingdoms of the world, and I shall make amends," Lord Khan informed them. "All of you are ever welcome here!"

The soldiers' host had arranged a ceremony in the grand chamber where once he had been imprisoned. A legion of courtiers clad in their finest flanked Kentril and the rest, clapping enthusiastically at various points during their master's speech. Kentril had met many of the nobles at least twice now, but still could not recall any names. Other than Atanna and her father, those in the palace seemed almost of a single kind, voices constantly in echo of the great Lord Khan. That did not entirely surprise the captain, of course, for powerful rulers often ended up surrounded by such, and in a realm as blessed as Ureh, what reason would anyone have to do otherwise? Juris Khan had seen them through the worst that anyone could possibly imagine.

Kentril himself bid the men farewell once the ceremony had ended. He reminded the six of the safest route possible through the jungle and emphasized the importance of avoiding the deeper waterways. "Once you reach Kurast, the way should be clear. Just try not to let anyone see everything you bring with you."

"We'll be careful, cap'n," Orlif bellowed.

Gorst clapped each man on the back, sending most staggering, and like a dutiful parent told them to remember everything the captain had taught them.

At a signal from Albord, the six saluted their commander, then headed out. Kentril and Gorst followed the party to the outer gate, wishing each man the best again.

Although the breaking up of a company always affected Captain Dumon more than he revealed, watching his surviving men depart now nearly shattered the mask of strength he generally wore at such times. Bad enough that so many would not be returning home, but the dark shadow cloaking the kingdom made him feel as if the six left in the dead of night. Both the men and their escort carried torches just so that they could see the steep steps. While Kentril knew that just beyond Nymyr the sun had only an hour before risen, he could not help worrying about nighttime predators or enemy warriors hiding in the dark. Even knowing such vile dangers existed mostly in his mind, it was all the captain could do not to go chasing after the others.

"Think they'll be okay?" Gorst asked suddenly.

"Why do you ask?"

The giant shrugged. "Dunno. I guess I always feel bad when others go."

Chuckling at this reflection of his own concerns, Kentril responded, "They're together, armed, and know where they're going. You and I made it back from the mountains of northern Entsteig with only one sword between us." He watched the torches, now the only visible sign of the party, descend into the city. "They'll do just fine."

When even the torches could not be singled out among all the other fires illuminating Ureh, the duo headed back to the palace. Lord Khan had given some hint of planning to speak with Quov Tsin about the work needed to settle the kingdom completely in the real world and remove the last vestiges of the vile spell. However, what interested Kentril more had been the knowledge that Atanna awaited him within. More than ever, he longed for her lips, her eyes, her arms. The departure of the others signified to him the end of his life as a mercenary and the beginning of something astounding. If not for the concerns he and Zayl had regarding the truth about Gregus Mazi, Kentril would have considered himself at that moment the luckiest man alive.

Thinking of the necromancer, he asked Gorst, "Have you seen Zayl lately?"

"Not since you tried to find out about Brek and the others."

When the captain had finally managed to ask Juris Khan what had happened to the quarters of the missing trio, the elder monarch had expressed complete puzzlement and a promise to have the matter investigated by one of his staff. He had spoken with such honest tones that Kentril could not disbelieve him. In fact, Kentril had even wanted to find Zayl afterward in order to tell the spellcaster of his certainty that Lord Khan could have had nothing to do with the clearing out of the mercenaries' belongings. Unfortunately, even then he could not find the necromancer.

"Keep an eye out for him. Tell him I need to see him as soon as possible."

Gorst hesitated, a rare thing for the generally sure-minded giant. "Think he's gone the way of Brek?"

Kentril had not considered that. "Check his room. See if his gear is still there." The Rathmian had few personal articles, but surely he would have left something behind. "If you discover his room just like theirs, come running."

"Aye, Kentril."

Now it was Captain Dumon who paused, his gaze turning to the flickering torches and lamps of eternally darkened Ureh. By now, Albord and the men would be well on their way to the city's outer gate. In an hour, two at most, Jodas, Orlif, and the other four would greet the sunlight.

"Kentril?"

"Hmm? Sorry, Gorst. Just wondering."

"Wondering what?"

The veteran mercenary gave his second a rueful smile. "Just wondering if I'll regret us not having left with them."

The gathered crowd cheered and waved as Albord and the others marched through the city. It looked to the young officer as if every citizen had come to see his fellows off. Never in his short career had he imagined such acknowledgment from others. Captain Dumon had warned him from his first day that a mercenary's life was generally a harsh, unappreciated one, but this moment made every past indignity more than worth it.

"Sure you don't want to come with us, Alby?" Jodas called. "Another good arm's always welcome!"

"I'm sticking here, thanks." Albord had few regrets about staying behind, despite his earlier desire to see his family. How better to return in, say, a year and show them what he had reaped as one of Captain Dumon's aides. Lord Khan had already announced as a certainty the captain's elevation to the nobility, his command of the military forces of the holy kingdom, and the upcoming marriage to the monarch's own daughter—possibly the greatest prize of all in Albord's mind.

"Well, maybe we'll come visit you again," the other mercenary returned with a short laugh. He hefted the sack containing his reward. "After all, this can't last forever!"

The rest laughed with him. They all had a king's ransom. Each man could live in wealth for the rest of his life and still have much left over. True, mercenaries were gambling men, but Albord doubted that the worst of them would go broke before a few years had passed.

"These jokers know the way to their own city gates?" Orlif grunted, referring to the six armored guards making up their farewell escort. Solemn and silent, they marched in unison even Captain Dumon's strict training had never managed to perfect among his men. "Seems like forever to reach it, and this load ain't goin' to get any lighter!"

"If those heavy sacks are slowing you down," Albord jested, "I'll be glad to watch 'em for you until you get back from Westmarch!"

Again, the men all laughed. Albord felt a hint of withdrawal; he would miss them, but his odds were much better with his captain. He had always sensed a greatness, and now that had been more than proven.

"There it is at last," one of the others cried. "Only an hour past there, lads, and we'll be smilin' in the sun! Won't that be a welcome sight?"

To Albord, the gates stood so very tall. When the party had first come to investigate the ruins, the gates had still been shut, almost as if yet trying to protect Ureh's secrets. Rusted relics then, the recreated gates now looked far more imposing. At least twelve feet high and so very, very thick, they could have barred an army trying to force its way inside. As with the doors of the palace, winged archangels brandishing fiery swords acted as centerpieces for each of the pair, and as with the other doors, those figures had been battered brutally by some force. Albord vaguely wondered again how the damage had occurred. Had some vassal of the sinister Gregus Mazi he had heard about taken to trying to destroy the symbols of Heavenly power?

The honor guard stopped at the gates, turning to face the departing soldiers. Their solemn, almost expressionless faces made Albord nearly reach for his sword, only at the last the white-haired fighter realizing how foolish that would have looked.

Then a strange silence fell over the crowd, a silence made all the more obvious by the distant sounds of continual celebration, the same sounds that had gone on without pause ever since Captain Dumon had set the magical gem in place atop the peak. Albord looked around, discovered that all the faces had turned to him, waiting.

Jodas and the other found nothing wrong with the scene and, in fact, eyed him impatiently. "Time to say our goodbyes, Alby. Got to be goin' . . ."

Caught up again in the moment, the departing mercenaries shared handshakes and back slaps with the young officer. Albord had to struggle to keep tears from showing and found it amusing to discover that Jodas and Orlif, among others, clearly suffered from the same affliction.

"Be better if you go off before we step out," Jodas suggested as the honor guard started to open the gates. "Good luck and all that, you know."

Many mercenary companies had a variety of superstitions, one of those among men from Westmarch being that if you didn't actually see your comrades walk out the gates, then there stood a good chance you would be seeing them again soon. Seeing them step through meant the definite possibility of never reuniting—and the likelihood that some had perished elsewhere afterward. Mercenaries lived too chancy a life not to take to heart whatever beliefs might help them survive. In fact, that had been in great part why their captain and second-in-command had remained at the palace in the first place.

Giving the six one last wave, Albord marched off. Still uncertain about his control of his emotions, he did not look back and suspected that the others imitated his ways. The continual noises of celebration began to get on his nerves, for he felt no reason for cheer at the moment. Even the thought of his own future in Ureh did not assuage him at the moment.

Louder and louder the merrymakers grew, the most adamant sounds coming now from behind him, where he had left his comrades. Albord quickened his pace; once he returned to the palace, surely his nerves would settle and he would recall all the good reasons he had chosen not to leave with Jodas and the rest.

But at that moment, a voice just barely audible over the raucous cries caught his attention. Albord paused, trying to understand what he had just heard. The voice had sounded like Orlif's—and the man had been calling the white-haired fighter's name.

Albord took a step toward Juris Khan's abode, but the sudden uncertainty made him pause. What harm would it do to go back and check? If he had heard Orlif, then surely they wanted something of him. If he had been mistaken about even hearing the man, there would be no trouble or danger of bad luck, for by this time surely the six had long vanished through the gates.

He turned back. It would take him but a minute or two to discover whether or not he had heard Orlif. At least, then, Albord could be satisfied that he had done all he could.

The shouts of merriment had risen so high now that they actually hurt his ears. Did these people never rest? Had they nothing more to do than celebrate? True, they had much reason for their happiness, but even a mercenary liked peace and quiet on occasion. The sooner Albord returned to the palace, the better. At least there he could find some escape from the carefree madness spread among the populace—

A short-lived scream cut through the air.

Drawing his sword, the young fighter raced the rest of the way to the gates. Perhaps he had been wrong, but he swore to himself that the scream had sounded as if torn from the throat of *Jodas*. Albord rounded the final corner—

And came across a tableau of terror that stopped him dead in his tracks.

A sea of horrific, shambling corpses—husks of bodies, to be precise—swarmed together like the hungry, vicious fish he had seen once in the jungle rivers. Clad in tattered, soiled garments, they madly fought one another as they all sought to claim some prize in their midst. Their gaping mouths, rounded and full of sharp teeth, opened and closed repeatedly. A few to the side could be seen feeding, their gnarled, skeletal hands gnawing on some bloody bit of meat.

From within the ever-growing mass, a human figure struggled his way to the top.

Orlif, his face ripped, his arms drenched with his own blood, cut with his sword, trying to reach freedom. From where he stood in shock, Albord could see that most of the mercenary's other hand had been either torn or bitten off.

Orlif saw him, and what Albord caught in that pleading gaze made him more terrified than he ever could have thought possible.

Then suddenly something tugged at the older fighter from within the hungering mass of fiends. Orlif let out one hopeless cry—and was dragged back down among them.

"No!" The shout escaped Albord before he could stop himself.

Empty eye sockets stared unerringly at the stunned soldier. Ghoulish shapes began to turn his direction.

Sense at last returned . . . and Albord turned and ran as fast as he could.

Throughout the monstrous, grisly scene, the music, laughter, and cheers had continued unabated. Albord looked this way and that as he ran, but of the merrymakers themselves he saw no sign. It was as if a city of ghosts celebrated around him.

Then, from an alleyway, one of the grotesque, shambling forms reached for him. Albord leapt aside, slashing with his sword as he hurried on. The sharp edge cut through one of the wrists, sending the clawed, cadaverous hand flopping to the ground. However, undeterred by the loss of its appendage, the ghoulish fiend followed after the mercenary.

The palace. If he could reach the palace, Albord felt certain that he would be safe. Captain Dumon would be there, and he would know what to do.

As he ran, the city itself began to change, with each second growing as twisted and deathly as its foul inhabitants. Buildings rapidly decayed or crumbled, and what seemed like thick blood slowly poured over rooftops onto cracked walls and parched earth. The sky took on a sickly color, and the smell of rotting, burnt flesh assailed the young fighter's nose.

In the distance, though, the palace of Juris Khan looked untouched. Albord focused on the one bit of sanity in a world now gone mad. Each step took him closer and closer to salvation.

Then, to his horror, he found the way blocked. A horde of desiccated, hungry corpses moved slowly and purposely toward him from the very street that would have led him directly to the stone steps. Rounded, toothy mouths opened and closed in anticipation of a new feast. The stench they exuded turned the frantic fighter's stomach, and it was all he could do to keep from falling to his knees and throwing up.

Albord looked left, finding an open side street. Without hesitation, he raced into it, hoping that it would open up onto a path leading to the steps.

Something in the shadows caught his arm. Albord found himself face-to-face with one of the ghouls, a mockery of feminine form, a dry husk clad in the shreds of what had once been a very feminine, very revealing golden outfit. Strands of hair draped around the horrific visage, and the mouth opened wide in anticipation.

"Come, handsome soldier," it rasped in a voice straight out of the grave. "Come play with Nefriti . . ."

"Let go of me, hellspawn!" With wild abandon, Albord struck at the demon, dealing only superficial damage. He finally cut into one arm, but then, recalling how not even that had slowed another of the creatures, he went for the neck.

The blade bit through the crusted skin and the dry bone as if through parchment.

The head of the demon dropped to the street, rolling several feet away. It spun for a moment, then stopped with the soulless face pointed in his direction.

"Nefriti hungers for your kiss," the head mocked. "Come kiss Nefriti . . ." The mouth opened and closed.

To his further dismay, the body continued to struggle with him. Albord managed to cut himself free, then for good measure ran the torso through. As the body finally began to collapse, the desperate mercenary fled.

The side street led to a major avenue that was, thankfully, deserted. Albord paused to catch his breath and decide on the best direction. Atop the hill, the palace, larger now, seemed to encourage him on. If he could get around the unholy throng, then the way would be clear.

With visions of Orlif to urge him forward, the young officer stumbled his way toward the hill. Now he knew what had happened to the three men who had earlier vanished. Surely this somehow had to be the work of the sorcerer their host had mentioned, the vile, corrupted Gregus Mazi. The Lord of Ureh had claimed to have destroyed the villain, but Albord had seen enough of sorcerers to know that they could create perfect illusions. No doubt Mazi had tricked his former master into believing his death and now sought his revenge.

Captain Dumon and the others had to be warned . . .

Laughter and music continued to assail his ears. Now the tones took on a mad quality, as if those who celebrated did so in an asylum. Albord wanted to cover his ears, but feared that to do so would slow him down, even if only by a fraction of a second. The sounds tore at his very soul, filled him with as much horror as the demonic horde behind him.

His pace picked up as he came within sight of the base of the hill. Only a short distance more . . .

His boot snagged on something.

Albord tripped, falling forward. He struck the stone avenue hard, sending waves of sharp pain through his entire body. For a few moments, he blacked out.

Forcing himself to consciousness, Albord saw his blade a few feet away. He reached for it, then pulled himself up.

Only then did he sense that he was no longer alone.

They came from the alleyways, the ruined buildings, and the streets. They moved as one, with one vile purpose. They plodded toward him, reaching, reaching . . .

Albord spun around, only to find every possible avenue of escape filled with gaping, hungering corpses. He glanced longingly toward the steps, toward the palace, and knew that despite his close proximity to the former, he stood no chance of making the final few yards.

Curiously, the voice of Captain Dumon suddenly filled his head. *Whenever possible, take the battle to the enemy. Better to fight and die quickly than to wait for the inevitable.* Captain Dumon had taught him that early on. The company commander had also taught Albord the facts about a mercenary's life, how for the vast majority death would prove almost a certainty.

Gripping his sword tight and raising it high over his head, Albord roared and charged.

As he collided with the foremost horrors, his blade bit well into dried flesh, crisp bone. Grasping limbs flew, and cadaverous bodies crumbled. Farther on, the palace continued to beckon, encouraging him to do his best.

They caught his free arm, then his legs. Grotesque faces filled his view. The sword was wrenched from his hand. Still, Albord struggled forward another foot, two . . .

At last, they brought him down, monstrous faces leering at him, hideous mouths eagerly working.

Albord screamed.

In the vast, silent library, Quov Tsin pored over the books left by centuries of predecessors, marveling at the work they had gathered for him. As much as he had savored the praises he had received from the courtiers of Juris Khan, the wizened Vizjerei loved his calling more.

Yet now he could not concentrate as well as usual . . . and for that he had to thank the fool mercenaries. Captain Dumon and the giant, Gorst, had left him with small but irritating doubts abut the veracity of their host's stories. Tsin did not like having doubts; Lord Khan had given him the entire library and made him high sorcerer for the most fabled of kingdoms. With such power, the Vizjerei could become known as the greatest of his kind!

"Damn you, Dumon!" Tsin muttered as he turned a page. "Damn you for not leaving things lie . . ."

"Is something amiss, Master Tsin?"

The sorcerer jumped. He glared at the newcomer, only to see that the fatherly Juris Khan himself towered above him.

"Nothing—nothing of consequence, my lord."

Khan smiled beatifically. "I'm so glad to hear that. You've done so much for the kingdom—and myself specifically—that it would disturb me if you were not happy."

Standing up, Quov Tsin surreptitiously studied his good host. How could the suspicions of the captain possibly have any merit? The man before him truly fit every aspect of the legend that the sorcerer had studied so closely over the decades. Surely he, Tsin, could better read the situation than a lovestruck, low-caste brute like Kentril Dumon! "I am most pleased by your gracious reward, my Lord Khan, and know that I live to serve you in whatever capacity as sorcerer you need."

"For that I'm very grateful, Vizjerei. It's the reason, in fact, I've come to see you alone."

Tsin's already narrow eyes narrowed further, almost becoming slits. "My lord desires my aid?"

"Yes, Master Tsin . . . in fact, I cannot hope to save Ureh without you."

The bold statement caught the diminutive spellcaster's imagination. *I cannot hope to save Ureh without you.* A flush of pride washed over Quov Tsin. Here at last was a ruler who appreciated his fine skills! More and more, the murky anxieties of the mercenary captain seemed but smoke. "I am at your beck and call, Lord Khan . . ."

The taller man put a companionable arm around the shoulder of the sorcerer. "Then, if you can tear yourself away from the books for a time, I need to show you something."

He more than had Tsin's interest. "Of course."

Juris Khan led him from the library. As they walked, the monarch of Ureh explained some of the historical aspects of the holy kingdom, telling how this ancestor or that one had helped gradually raise the realm to its ultimate glory. Knowing that his host simply sought to pass the time until they reached their ultimate destination, Quov Tsin all but ignored the other's words, instead noting such little things as how each guard stood at his most attentive when they passed or the way the servants looked in complete awe when Lord Khan simply acknowledged them with a nod of his head. The tall elder man ruled absolutely, and yet his people loved and honored him. Against that, Kentril Dumon's fears meant nothing.

Tsin quickly realized that he was being led to a part of the palace to which he had never been before. Near the grand hall, Juris Khan opened an unobtrusive door that the sorcerer could not understand having missed earlier. Within, a narrow stairway led down a passage only barely lit by a source undefinable. Deeper and deeper Tsin and his new lord descended into the underlayers of the vast edifice. The Vizjerei had expected that the holy palace had levels below ground, but he was astounded by just how far down they went.

No candles, torches, or oil lamps could be seen throughout the journey, yet the mysterious dim illumination prevented the two from having to travel entirely in the dark. Curiously, the dank, almost sinister aspects of his surroundings did not disturb Tsin, but rather heightened his anticipation. Surely what Lord Khan led him toward could only be a place of great importance.

And then he felt the forces in play, forces raw and chaotic. Even before they reached the thick iron door, Tsin already had some idea of what awaited him.

The savage, beaked head of a gargoyle acted as holder for the massive ring used as a door handle. Quov Tsin marveled at the intricate work of the head, so very lifelike that he expected the creature to snap at Juris Khan as the robed monarch reached for the ring.

"*Tezarka* . . ." whispered Khan as he touched the handle.

With a slight groan, the door slowly opened—to reveal the sanctum of a sorcerer extreme.

"My private chamber . . . a place of power."

Shaped as a hexagon, the room stretched wide in every direction. The

Vizjerei could have fit his own humble sanctum in this place a dozen times over. Shelf upon shelf of powders, herbs, and various rare items lined every wall, while books of arcana lay open upon three vast wooden tables. Jars with specimens that even the well-versed Tsin could not identify had been arranged on another set of tables to his right. Runes had been etched into various places around the chamber, wards against possible spells gone awry. From the center of the ceiling, a vast crystal illuminated all, its source of power that which Quov Tsin could feel permeating the entire place.

But most arresting of all proved to be the vast stone platform in the center of the room.

It stood at least as tall as the Vizjerei, and etched in the rectangular base were intricate runes, many of which even Tsin did not recognize. The platform, too, had been covered with such markings and, in addition, bore the symbol of the sun.

Without thinking, the gnarled Vizjerei stepped forward to inspect the platform. Running his bony fingers over the upper edge, he sensed the inherent forces that had been called up in the past . . . and still waited to be called upon again.

"This is . . . very ancient," he finally commented.

"Carved before the concept of holy Ureh had even been birthed in the minds of my ancestors. Built before any of the eastern realms, much less the western ones, existed. Created by the precursors of the Rathmians, my own people, and your worthy Vizjerei brotherhood, good Tsin. There are times when I question if those who hollowed out this sanctum were even human but perhaps instead heavenly servants sent to prepare the way . . ."

"So much power . . ." More than any of Quov Tsin's kind had ever wielded, even during those centuries when they had made pacts with supposedly subdued demons.

"It is here that you and I will undo the last of Gregus's curse, my good friend. It is here that I plan to restore Ureh fully to the mortal plane."

And Tsin could well believe that possible. Such primal forces proved tricky enough to manipulate, but if Lord Khan could do as he hoped, it would make all that the sorcerer had seen before seem like the spellwork of apprentices. Here existed a place of true mastery . . .

"I could do nothing," explained his host, "nothing at all while I was trapped. Yet I considered and considered well what would happen once someone of skill could free me. Thanks to the treachery of Gregus Mazi, all sorcerers were lost to me, save my dear Atanna." His expression shifted. "But, of course, as talented as she is, she is not you, Master Tsin."

The spellcaster accepted readily this obvious statement. Atanna did indeed have skill—enough so that if she had not already fallen for Kentril Dumon, Tsin might have approached her in the future himself for breeding purposes—but to manipulate such forces required great care, exceptional experience. In truth, without the Vizjerei, Tsin felt certain that any attempt by Lord Khan alone would have ended in abject failure.

"In this chamber," Juris Khan whispered, having somehow come up behind the short sorcerer, "with skills such as the two of us combined wield, there is no limit to what we can accomplish, my friend. Even beyond Ureh rising once more among the great kingdoms. The secrets of the world, and those beyond, could be open to us, if we are only willing to chance matters."

Quov Tsin could see all of it, all the glory, the power. He ran his hands across the runes, drinking in the forces each held. The wrinkled Vizjerei imagined all of them at play, all his to command, to wield . . .

Then he caught sight of a strange pattern at the very center of the platform, a curious, disquieting marking almost like a stain that someone had not quite been able to remove.

"What is that?" he asked.

Juris Khan barely looked at the marking. The tone of his voice when he responded completely dismissed the spot as unimportant.

"Blood, of course."

Sixteen

✳

Zayl . . .

He tried to move, but could not.

Zayl . . .

He tried to breathe, but could not.

Zayl . . .

If not for his training, he would have already been dead, his lungs completely deprived of air.

Zayl, you bloody young fool! You can't die on me now, damn it!

The necromancer tried to talk, but although he knew his mouth was open, no sound escaped it. He tried to open his eyes and at first they resisted. Only with arduous effort did he manage finally to raise the lids enough to see.

And only then did Zayl discover that he had been made like Gregus Mazi.

Even with eyes well-suited for the dark, Zayl could only just make out enough detail to know his terrible fate. He hung from a stalactite high above the first massive chamber that he and the two mercenaries had come across on their previous journey. Like the unfortunate Mazi's, Zayl's arms and legs had been pinned back tightly. Unlike the sorcerer, though, Zayl clearly lacked any purpose for being there. The power that had placed him there desired no sentinel, but rather merely wished the necromancer very, very dead.

Zayl *would* die, too—and soon. Already he could feel his body changing, becoming the same as the stalactite. Strange forces leeched into his body, altering his structure. Given time, he would become more a part of the mountain than even Gregus Mazi.

But before that happened, he would suffocate.

"Zayl, boy! You've got to still be able to hear me!"

Humbart Wessel's hollow voice echoed through the vast cavern, seeming to come from every direction. Straining, the necromancer managed just to make out the passage through which he and his companion had earlier entered. Somewhere within, the skull no doubt still rested, in many ways as trapped as he.

His hopes, which had briefly risen, plummeted. What could the bodiless Humbart do for him?

Zayl's thoughts grew murkier. An immense exhaustion filled him.

"If you're hearing me, I'm right where you left me, remember? You've a sharp mind! You see it in your head?"

What did the skull hope to accomplish? Zayl only wanted to go to sleep. Why did Humbart have to bother him?

"I think you're still listening, lad, or at least I hope so! Don't like the thought of sitting in this dank place the rest of eternity, so hear me out!"

Humbart's voice irritated the necromancer. He wanted to tell the undead mercenary to go away, but without legs, Humbart could hardly do that.

"Your dagger, Zayl! You need your dagger to help yourself!"

His dagger! Zayl's eyes widened. Did he still have his dagger?

His companion answered that quickly. "I can see it, lad! It's just a few feet ahead of me!"

And a thousand miles away, for all the good it would do. If the necromancer could have at least seen it, he could have summoned it to him. Zayl, however, had never mastered indirect summoning of objects, especially not under such dire circumstances. He had to see what he desired.

The urge to sink into oblivion grew strong again.

"Listen to me!" insisted the skull. "It's pointed toward me, with just a little bit of rock covering the tip. There's another rock shaped like a giant's tooth propping up the hilt area . . ."

Despite his desire to sleep, Zayl listened. In his mind, a picture of the dagger began to form. He even saw Humbart's skull, the empty eye sockets staring hopefully at the blade.

But why bother?

"You see it, don't you, lad? Damn it! If you're still alive and can hear, you've got to see it!"

And finally Zayl understood. Humbart had been with Zayl long enough to know the skills of the one who had animated him. He knew that the necromancer needed to see the dagger, so the skull sought to create a perfect picture for him.

It would never work—or would it? It would require what remained of the air trapped in his body, the minute particles here and there that enabled

Zayl to last four, five times longer without breathing than a normal man. Zayl would have to squeeze his lungs completely empty in order to draw enough strength for this one spell.

Meanwhile, Humbart went on with his descriptions, the skull either very optimistic about his companion's chances or merely not wanting to think yet about the alternative. If the latter, Zayl could hardly blame him, for thanks to the spell the necromancer had used, Humbart, too, would suffer. If someone did not find the skull, then unless the rest of the passage collapsed and shattered him, the former mercenary would be trapped in Nymyr forever, his spirit unable to move on.

"That's about it, Zayl, lad!" the skull shouted, Humbart's voice slightly more subdued. "You should have a good image now . . . that is, if you've heard anything at all."

Focusing on the dagger, Zayl quickly pieced together the image as the other had described it. He saw the rocks and how the blade lay upon them. He saw again Humbart's skull staring at the partially buried tip. The necromancer visualized each variation in the rocky walls, filling out his picture.

With every last iota of strength, Zayl fixed on the enchanted dagger, *demanding* in his mind and heart that it come to him.

"Zayl!"

Something gleaming flew out into the cavern as if shot from a crossbow. The trapped necromancer immediately focused on it. The object suddenly veered toward him, a beacon of light in the deathly dark.

The ivory dagger flew unerringly toward him. For just a brief moment, Zayl recalled what they had been forced to do for Gregus Mazi. Should he now will the dagger to come point-first? Should Zayl wish the blade to sink deep into his still-human flesh?

But the situation with Mazi had been different. Not only had the sorcerer been set into place with a purpose, but the spell had been given centuries to do its foul work.

Not so with Zayl. The transformation had barely begun. With the dagger to guide his work, he could still save himself—

The blade suddenly dropped. Struggling, the necromancer brought it back toward him. His concentration had slipped, and, worse, he felt his will ebbing. *Come to me*, he called in his mind. *Come to me.*

It did, moving with such swiftness that at first it seemed it would yet slay him. Only at the last moment did the dagger suddenly veer, darting around Zayl and the stalactite and forcing itself into the necromancer's encrusted hand.

The moment the hilt touched, Zayl found he could move his fingers. Gripping the blade, he channeled his strength into it. His lungs screamed, his heart pounded madly, but the imprisoned spellcaster would not give in.

As if struck by lightning, the shell around him shattered.

Weakened, Zayl plunged earthward. Had he been above the uppermost floor of the cavern, he likely would have died, but the stalactite upon which he had been bound had hung over the vast drop. That and that alone enabled him to recover enough to save himself.

As he fell past the ledge, Zayl managed to utter a spell. A gust of wind suddenly lifted him upward. With tremendous effort, Zayl managed to take hold of the cavern wall before him. His success proved timely, for the spell suddenly faltered, nearly sending him falling into the abyss.

Zayl managed to drag himself slowly to the upper floor of the cavern. Exhausted beyond belief, he lay there for some time, his breathing ragged and every inch of his body feeling as if someone had dropped Nymyr on top of him.

"Zayl?" came a tentative voice.

"I—I am—alive," he croaked back.

"You sure?" returned Humbart's skull. "You don't sound like it."

"Give—give me—time."

"It ain't like I'm going anywhere," mumbled the necromancer's companion.

Gradually, Zayl's breathing normalized. His body continued to ache, but at last he could at least move.

Under the glow of the dagger, Zayl discovered he had not escaped unscathed. His clothing had been reduced to shreds, and his skin had scars everywhere from where the spell had caused the stalactite and his body to begin to merge. Zayl had no doubt that his face, too, bore such marks, but he thanked the Great Dragon that his life had been spared.

On unstable legs, the necromancer finally returned to the passage in which the attack had taken place. The rock slide that he and Captain Dumon had discovered had all but vanished, almost as if it had been blasted away by some tremendous force. Zayl held the dagger before him just in case he might be assaulted anew, but could sense no danger.

Several yards in, he came across the skull.

"Ah, lad! Aren't you a sight for sore eyes—or just a sore sight, from the look of you!"

"I am not ready to join you in the afterlife, Humbart." Exhausted again, the spellcaster sat down on a large rock. "Tell me exactly what happened to me."

"After the two beastly hands clamped tight on you, you dropped the blade. I worried then that they might flatten you like a bug, but instead those rocky mitts began moving along the walls, heading toward the cavern. They ran you right through the collapse, sending more rock tumbling to me—you know I almost got cracked like an egg?"

Zayl could appreciate the skull's apprehensions, but he wanted to hear the rest. "Go on."

"That's it. You vanished from sight, there was a flash of some ungodly light, then I started shouting my head off."

"And I thank you. You saved me."

The skull somehow made a snorting sound. "Well, I had to! Who else is going to carry me out of this place?"

Zayl frowned as he looked past Humbart. What the skull could not see, apparently could not guess, was that farther ahead a ton of debris now sealed the entrance quite thoroughly. The necromancer doubted that he could either dig or magic his way through. That meant finding an alternative route of escape.

"Come, Humbart." He picked up the skull and started back into the cavern.

"You're going the wrong way, lad."

"No, I'm not."

A moment of silence, then, "Oh."

The pair entered the vast chamber. Holding up the dagger, Zayl surveyed his surroundings in every direction.

"We go that way," he finally said, indicating the mouth of a passage up near the very top of the chamber.

"That way? And by what route?"

Humbart had asked an excellent question. At first glance, there seemed no humanly possible manner by which to reach his goal. Zayl searched through the ragged remains of his cloak, but found that the rope he had earlier used had vanished. Still, according to the charts he had memorized, the gap above represented his best hope of finding a way out of Nymyr's gargantuan belly.

Staring at the slick surface leading up to the passage, Zayl took a deep breath and replied, "I climb, of course."

"Climb?" The skull sounded positively aghast. "Climb that? Zayl, lad, do you think—" The rest of his protest became muffled as the spellcaster stuffed him back into his pouch.

The necromancer needed no discouragement, his trust in his skills already quite limited. If he slipped on his way up, Zayl very much doubted that he had enough will to cast a spell sufficient to keep every bone in his body from shattering on the harsh surface below. Regardless of that risk, though, he had to try.

What Zayl had not told Humbart, what he had only come to realize from his own predicament, was that whatever secret existed in Ureh planned soon to reveal itself . . . and that could not, in any way, be a good thing.

Gorst came to see Kentril, the giant not at all in a good mood.

"Albord's not back."

Still trying to find some comfortable fit in the dress uniform, Kentril paused from adjusting the jacket to eye his second-in-command. "It's nearly the dinner hour. You check his room?"

"Aye, Kentril. His things are still there."

"Maybe he decided to stay in the city for a little while after the others left. Maybe their going made him a little homesick." The captain himself had felt so after bidding his men farewell. Even the pleasure of Atanna's company had failed to eradicate the feeling completely.

"Could be," Gorst grunted, not sounding any more convinced by Kentril's words than the captain himself had been.

For once, Kentril wished that he did not have to meet Atanna. Albord's absence did not sit well with him. "Scout the palace as surreptitiously as possible. Make sure that you've searched anywhere Albord might've gone. If I get a chance, I'll try to do some of the same."

"Aye."

"Any hint of Zayl?"

"His stuff's in his rooms, but he's still missing, too."

And that, in some ways, seemed to bode even more ill than the young mercenary's disappearance. Zayl did not seem the type just to go wandering off, not after the concerns the necromancer had expressed.

"Gorst?"

"Yeah, Kentril?"

"Go armed."

The giant nodded, patting the sword dangling at his side. "Always do. You taught me that."

Carrying an ax around would have drawn some suspicion, but a sheathed sword did not raise many eyebrows. Nor would the fact that the massive fighter wandered the halls of the palace seem too out of place. Clearly, as a foreigner, Gorst would be curious about the grand edifice, and, besides, for a giant of a man, the other mercenary had the stealth of a cat.

Gorst started to leave, then hesitated. "Kentril, if I don't find Albord in the palace at all, should I maybe go take a peek in the city?"

Captain Dumon thought it over, weighing options and lives. Finally, hoping that Albord would forgive him, he answered, "No. If it comes to the point of searching the city, we go together, or we don't go at all."

Alone again, Kentril tried to finish dressing, but this latest news refused to sit well with him. Now both the necromancer and Albord had gone missing. The captain gave thanks that at least Jodas and the others had left when they had. If not, how long before all of them would have disappeared?

Disappeared?

Albord had been last seen escorting the rest . . .

"No . . ." Forgetting his garments, forgetting even Atanna, Kentril burst from his rooms and ran to the nearest palace window that gave him some glimpse of the torchlit city. He stared down at the shadowed buildings, listened to the celebrating throngs, and tried to convince himself that the horrific thought he had just conjured up could not have happened. Surely the six who had chosen to leave had exited the outer gates and even now journeyed through the sunlit jungle. Surely they, at least, had reached relative safety . . .

Yet some churning feeling within would not let the captain accept what seemed a most reasonable possibility.

"Atanna." She would tell him what was going on. She would show him one way or the other whether his fears had merit.

He strode through the regal halls, ignoring the salutes of the helmeted guards he passed. Kentril had only one focus—Juris Khan's daughter—and for once he did not seek her for pleasure.

One of the almost faceless servants confronted him as he neared the grand hall. Before the pasty-faced man could say anything, Kentril seized him by the tailored collar and demanded, "Where's your mistress? Where's Atanna?"

"Why, I'm right here."

Startled, Kentril released the servant and turned. The beautiful crimson-haired princess wore a robe similar to the one in which she had been clad when aiding in the release of her father from his curse. Far behind her, Kentril vaguely noted a door he had never seen before.

"What is it you want, my love?"

He had the greatest urge to take her in his arms, to forget his problems, but despite how simple it would have been to do so, Captain Dumon could not forget his men. At least three had definitely gone missing and possibly seven more, excluding the necromancer.

"Where were you?"

"Helping my father," she responded offhandedly. Her lips pursed in concern. "You look troubled, Kentril. Have I offended you somehow?"

Again he had to fight the desire to drown himself in her. "I want to talk to you"—Kentril recalled the servant—"in private."

"We're quite alone," she said with a teasing smile,

Glancing over his shoulder, the captain discovered the liveried figure nowhere to be found. Truly they were swift of feet and as silent as the night.

Atanna suddenly stood at his side, her arm entwined with his. "Let's take a walk, shall we?"

She led him toward the balcony where Lord Khan had made his appearance after being freed by Quov Tsin. Kentril wanted to question her even as they walked, but Atanna put a finger to his lips and shushed as if he were a child. Gazing into those entrancing eyes, Kentril could do nothing but obey.

The air outside had a slight chill to it that caused the mercenary officer to shiver. How he looked forward to when Ureh could withstand the sun and the shadow of the mountain would only mean the aging of the day.

"I so enjoy it out here," his companion murmured. "I know we only sit upon a hill, but it feels like a mountain as tall as Nymyr!"

It could have been so easy to follow her lead, to let the mood take him. Kentril refused, though. He had lives to consider. "Atanna, I need to talk with you."

"Silly! You already are!"

Now he grew slightly angry. "Don't play games! This is important! At least three of my men are officially missing, and now another seems to be nowhere to be found. I'm even growing concerned about the six who left, not to mention Zayl. Too many people are unaccounted for, and that, in my book, means something terrible's going on."

She gave him an almost petulant frown. "Surely you're not saying that I did anything to them?"

"No, of course not. But something's amiss here, and I don't know what to think. Nothing is as it should be, not even Gregus Mazi—"

"*Gregus Mazi?*" Her gaze hardened. "What about that viper?"

Kentril decided he had to tell her. Surely Atanna did not know the truth. He gripped her by the shoulders. "Atanna, your father didn't slay him."

"What do you mean? Father said—"

"Listen to me!" He leaned close, letting her see in his eyes that he spoke only the truth. "Atanna, I found him . . . Gregus Mazi, that is. He'd been cursed, turned into a part of the caverns below, and used as some sort of hellish sentinel."

"What were you doing down there? How did you know where to look for him?"

Kentril glanced briefly over his shoulder in order to make certain that no one spied upon them, then answered, "Zayl found out. He'd been to Mazi's sanctum and there tried to summon the sorcerer's shade in order to question him about—"

Turning back to the view of darkened Ureh, Atanna muttered, "The necromancer . . . of course, he would be able to do it."

Frustrated, Kentril spun her to face him again. "Listen to me! You know your father best. Has he acted at all different? Is there anything about him that might be of question to you?"

"My father is exactly the way I expect him to be."

"But something's not right here, Atanna, and because of the two of us, I've ignored it much too long. Men who depended on me may be dead, and whatever took them could still be lurking in Ureh. If your father—"

She put a hand to his cheek, caressing him and making it hard for Kentril to concentrate. "Nothing can touch us here. This is the palace of Juris Khan. I have you, and you have me, and that's all that matters, isn't it?"

How simple it would have been to agree. Her very touch thrilled him, made all else inconsequential.

"No!" As he shouted, he grabbed her wrist. "Atanna! You've got to take this seriously! I can't stay here and pretend nothing happened! At the very least, I have to go searching for Albord and the others! They—"

"You can't leave! I have you now, and I won't let you go!"

Kentril gaped, caught unprepared for the vehemence with which the young woman spoke. Her eyes held a fury he thought not possible.

She took a step toward him, and to his surprise the hardened fighter backed up.

"I asked Father for you, and he said I could have you! All I wanted was you. I didn't want the others. Just you, don't you see?"

The fury had abated, but in its place Kentril discovered an unsettling look, a look that seemed to cut through him, see him inside and out. Without thinking, he took another step back.

Her face softened. "It was so lonely there . . . so lonely save for him and the few others . . . and when they were gone, I yearned for something more."

Every hair on Kentril suddenly tingled. As Atanna proceeded toward him, the wind seemed to catch her hair and robe, making the former flow wild and sensual and the latter pull hard against her curved form. Her smile promised everything as she eyed him under her lashes.

"I want you with all my heart, my soul, and my body, Kentril," she cooed. "Don't you want me, too?"

He did. He wanted her. He wanted to give himself to her in whatever manner she desired. The captain wanted to serve her, protect her . . .

But as Juris Khan's daughter reached out for him, something made Kentril throw himself forward.

The mercenary collided hard with Atanna. She let out a startled gasp, then fell backward, completely off-balance.

And dropped over the *rail*.

"Atanna!" Straining, Kentril tried to reach her, but already she had slipped completely out of sight. He stumbled to the rail, peering down in horror for some sign. Unfortunately, the deep shadow made it impossible to see anything. Kentril listened, but heard neither a scream nor the sounds of discovery.

He fell back, his heart seeming ready to explode. It had never been his intention to *kill* her! All Kentril had wanted was to break whatever hold she had upon him. He knew that she had been a wielder of sorcery like her father and that in her fear of losing him she must have thought that it would be all right to cast a glamour over him, make him love her more. If she had only understood—

Her father. Whatever concerns Kentril had once had about Lord Khan, they paled now in comparison to this situation. How could he face Ureh's master and tell him that his only daughter had plummeted to her death after having been pushed by the man she had loved? How?

Deep down, Captain Dumon knew that his mind still did not function properly. Contrary thoughts vied with one another, seeking domination. While a part of him worried over Atanna's death and its consequences, another part still battled the question of the disappearances and the truth about Gregus Mazi.

One way or another, he had to face Juris Khan. What Kentril had done could not be ignored. He had to face Khan.

He recalled the door he had seen far behind Atanna, the one from which it seemed most likely she had come. She had claimed to have just come from helping her father, which suggested that the elder monarch could be found wherever the door led.

Without hesitation, the mercenary ran from the balcony. The hallway echoed with the sounds of his booted feet, but nothing else. Of the servants and the guards, there existed no sign. Had they heard what had happened and gone to find their mistress's remains? Why had none of them come to the balcony to investigate what had happened?

Such matters faded in importance as he came upon the door. Throwing it open, Kentril saw that it descended deep into the lower levels of the palace. No torches or lamps lit the way, but some illumination enabled him to see a fair distance down.

Veteran reflexes almost made the captain reach for his sword, but then he recalled what had just happened. How would it look to come to explain Atanna's fall while wielding a weapon?

As he started to descend, Kentril thought about going back to find Gorst, but then decided that his friend should be no part of this. This had to be between Juris Khan and Kentril.

With great trepidation, the scarred mercenary followed the steps to their end. At the bottom, a gargoyle head with a ring in its mouth savagely greeted him from an ancient iron door. With nowhere else to go, Kentril tugged on the ring.

A cold yet soft breeze swirled briefly around him.

Tezarka . . .

Startled, he let go of the ring, then turned in a circle. Kentril could have sworn that he had heard Atanna's voice, but, of course, he had made that forever impossible. Any hint of her presence could only arise from his overriding guilt.

Reminded of why he had come down to this place, Kentril decided to try the ring once more. He already knew that it would not work, but at least—

With a slow groan, the iron door gave way.

Kentril stepped inside.

"Aaah, Dumon! What excellent timing!"

In the center of the chamber within, near a tall stone platform covered in mystic symbols, a smiling Quov Tsin reached an almost friendly hand toward the mercenary. The silver runes of the Vizjerei's Turinnash blazed brightly, and the diminutive figure seemed almost years younger, so enthused was his expression.

Baffled, Kentril slowly walked toward him. "Tsin? What're you doing down here?"

"Preparing for a sorcerous feat such as I could have only imagined! Preparing to delve into powers no other Vizjerei has touched in centuries, if ever!"

Kentril looked around, but saw no one else in the vast room. Even though he had interacted with sorcerers in the past, even visited them in their own sanctums, this place filled him with an inexplicable dread. "Where's Lord Khan?"

"Returning shortly. You might as well wait. He wants you here, too."

But Kentril paid him no mind. "I've got to find him . . . explain to him what happened to his daughter . . ."

Tsin frowned. "His daughter? What about his daughter? She left but a short time ago."

"I think the good captain fears that terrible harm's come to my darling Atanna," a voice behind the fighter boomed.

Startled, Kentril stumbled away from the door. Through the entrance stepped Juris Khan, looking stronger, more fit, despite his elder years, than Captain Dumon had so far seen him.

Lord Khan smiled benevolently at the dismayed figure. "She surprised you. She caused you to react instinctively. Atanna can be a creature of moods, good captain. You only reacted as was warranted."

"But—" Kentril could hardly believe that his host could speak so pleasantly about such a terrible accident. While it relieved him that the robed monarch did not hold him responsible, that did not change the fact that the man's child had fallen to the rocky landscape below. "But Atanna's *dead*!"

At this comment, Juris Khan chuckled. "Dead? I should say not! You're not dead, dear, are you?"

And from behind him stepped his daughter.

Captain Dumon let out a strangled cry and fell back against the massive platform.

"I didn't mean to make you upset before," she purred, the door through which she had just walked closing of its own accord. As Atanna moved closer, she wobbled some, for clearly one leg had snapped in the middle and the foot of the other twisted to the side. Her left arm bent at an impossible angle behind her, and the right, which reached out to Kentril, ended in a hand so badly mangled it could not even be identified as such. Dirt stained her torn robe, but, oddly, not a single drop of blood.

Her head bent completely to the side, barely held on by tendons from the neck.

"You see?" offered Juris Khan. "Broken a little, perhaps, but certainly not *dead*."

Seventeen

Gorst had been through nearly every level of the palace and had discovered a few significant things. Most important of them was that almost all of the servants and guards had vanished; only those he would have expected to see in the vicinity of his and Kentril's quarters seemed to be still active. When he secretly visited other floors, the halls remained empty, silent. Even the many courtiers who had clustered around the grand hall during Lord

Khan's announcements could not be found. It was as if only a skeleton crew manned the vast edifice.

The giant had not yet concluded his hunt, but had already seen enough that he knew he had better report to his captain. Kentril would understand what this all meant. Gorst admired his commander and friend immensely and trusted his judgment—except perhaps sometimes with Khan's daughter. Then it seemed that the captain on occasion lost track of matters. Of course, if she had focused her beauty on *Gorst*, the giant suspected he probably would have been even more befuddled. Battle was one thing; women were four, five, six complex things all at once.

He slipped past two watchful but unsuspecting guards near his own rooms, then, pretending to come from a side hall, nonchalantly walked into sight. Although he did not see their eyes move, Gorst sensed them suddenly take in his presence. They were good, but not good enough.

Reaching Kentril's apartment, he rapped twice on the door. When no one answered, he repeated the action, this time much harder.

Still no response. While it seemed very likely that the captain could be found with Atanna, Gorst nonetheless felt his unease grow. He could not imagine what he would do if now Kentril, too, had vanished. While he could certainly think for himself, Gorst worked best when given orders.

The giant had started to turn back to his own rooms when a hint of black at the back end of the hall caught his attention. He glanced in that direction, but saw nothing. Still . . . one did not survive long as a mercenary by ignoring such things.

Reaching the location without alerting the guards proved simple enough, but trying to find the source of the momentary patch of black afterward turned out to be much harder. Gorst soon began to wonder if he had imagined it. He could find no trace whatsoever in the hall, and unless it had somehow managed to melt into the wall—

And then the giant's sharp eyes noticed part of a door frame *ripple*.

Curious, Gorst reached out and gently touched the area in question.

The left side of the frame suddenly lost all but a vague semblance of normalcy, rippling so madly it almost seemed as if he stared at it through flowing water. A second later, even that vestige of reality faded away—and suddenly the battered, torn body of the necromancer, Zayl, fell toward Gorst.

The startled giant barely caught him in time. Zayl groaned slightly, clutching at him with what little strength remained.

"Get me—" the slim, pale figure gasped. "Get me—inside—room!"

Making certain that no one saw them, Gorst carried the spellcaster into the rooms set aside for him. He quickly lowered Zayl onto the bed, then anxiously looked for something to give the injured man.

"Open the pouch, damn it . . ."

At first, Gorst thought that the necromancer had spoken, but a quick check revealed Zayl's eyes were closed, the spellcaster's breathing slow but steady.

The giant finally recalled Zayl's disturbing companion and where best to find him.

It had probably been fortunate that the skull had spoken, for when Gorst reached for the pouch, he saw that, like the spellcaster's clothing, it, too, had been ripped in several places. Hints of its grisly contents could be seen through the tears, and if not for some luck, Gorst suspected the contents would have spilled out long ago.

Gingerly removing the skull, he placed it on the nearest table.

"My thanks, lad. Didn't think there for a while that we'd make it back in one piece."

Gorst tried to remind himself that he spoke with a fellow mercenary, not simply the skull of a man dead for centuries. "What happened?"

"Young fellow there tried to conjure up the spirit of old Gregus," Humbart Wessel explained. "Only, when Gregus did show up, he wasn't old, and he wasn't by far in a good mood! He tried to warn us, but right when he spoke, the very walls grabbed for poor Zayl . . ."

Humbart went on to tell of a most horrifying fate that the necromancer had only barely escaped with the skull's assistance, then the arduous climb out of the caverns and the exhausting return to the palace. The tale would have struck Gorst as half fanciful if not for all else that had gone on.

"Let no one tell you," the skull concluded, "that this young one's not as fit as a fighter for all his being a spellcaster, lad! Zayl'd be a good, sturdy man to have on your side in battle any time."

"Is there anything we can do for him?"

"Well . . . see if you can find a small red pouch among the things he left here."

Picking through Zayl's meager belongings, Gorst found the pouch in question. He held it up.

"Aye, that's the one. Now, if there's no curses or wards on it, open it up."

The giant obeyed, only after undoing the strings realizing just what Humbart had said. Fortunately, nothing sought to strike him down or reduce him to dust.

"There a small vial with a yellowish liquid in it?"

There was, right next to what looked like a dried eyeball. Swallowing, Gorst pulled out the vial, then immediately sealed the bag.

"Pour it down his gullet. I saw him use that kind of stuff once after a thorned hulk almost beat him into the ground— 'course, Zayl did manage to blast him to splinters in the end."

When opened, the thick, ugly liquid proved to have an odor well-matched to its appearance. Wrinkling his squat nose, Gorst went to the unconscious figure and, slipping his other hand under the back of Zayl's head in order to lift the latter up slightly, the mercenary carefully poured the contents into the other's mouth.

Zayl coughed once, then swallowed everything. Suddenly, the necromancer's entire body jerked wildly. Dismayed and startled, Gorst pulled back.

"Thought you said it'd help him!"

The skull did not reply.

The jerking abruptly ceased . . . and Zayl began to cough again. As he did, the peculiar wounds over every visible part of his body began to heal, then even fade away. The giant watched in amazement as, in but seconds, what little color the spellcaster had ever had returned and the last of the injuries utterly vanished.

Still weak but clearly recovering, Zayl eyed the soldier. "My thanks."

"And don't I get any credit?" grumbled Humbart Wessel. "Isn't like it's my fault that I haven't any hands, or I'd have fed you the stuff myself!"

"I definitely thank you, too, Humbart." The necromancer tried to rise, but could not. "It appears I need a few minutes longer. Perhaps it would be best if you brought Captain Dumon to see me. There is much we need to discuss."

"Can't find Kentril," Gorst admitted. "Can't find anyone but you so far."

The silver, almond-shaped eyes that did and did not remind the giant so much of Quov Tsin's narrowed in suspicion. "No one?"

"Albord's gone missing. That worried Kentril enough so he sent me looking around the palace. Couldn't find Tsin, couldn't even find hardly a soul anywhere besides on this floor. Seems the whole place is all but empty . . ."

"Yes, that is making more and more sense, I am afraid."

This brought a snort of disapproval from the skull. "Now, you said that once or twice while climbing out of Nymyr, and you still haven't explained to me just what you mean."

Zayl frowned. "And that is because I do not yet completely understand it myself."

Gorst knew he understood less than either, but one thing of which he felt certain was that his captain had gone missing, and that meant only one course of action as far as he was concerned.

"I need to find Kentril."

"It might be best—"

"Come with me or not," the giant said, determination hardening, "I'm going after my captain."

The necromancer forced himself up. "Give me just a short time, Gorst, and I will be more than happy to help you search. I think it might be best if we left Ureh and its shadowed past. The holy kingdom seems to me anything but."

Despite his impatience, Gorst agreed to wait. He knew that magic was involved and knew that against such he had little hope. He could wield an ax or sword well against any blood-and-flesh foe, but against magic he felt pretty much defenseless. Having Zayl with him would help even the odds. Gorst had already seen how skilled the man was.

It took the necromancer some minutes to recover his strength sufficiently and a few more minutes to do anything about his ruined garments. Gorst expected him to magic up some new clothes, but instead Zayl went to his pack and removed an outfit nearly identical to that which had been torn to shreds. Only the cloak could not be replaced.

"We shall have to find you a new pouch," Zayl commented to the skull. "I fear I do not have another large enough in which to place you, Humbart."

"Well, I'm not staying behind! If you don't—"

Gorst did not want to have to wait for them to finish arguing. "I've got a bag big enough. It can tie to your belt just like your old one."

Zayl nodded. "Then it is time to go find the captain and be rid of this place."

It seemed to Zayl that he had underestimated the giant. Gorst appeared far more clever, far more adept, than the necromancer had assumed. The information he provided Zayl concerning the layout of the palace not only matched the drawing that the spellcaster had studied, but corrected some errors caused by expansion and even evidently sheer mistake on the part of the one who had drawn the diagram.

The mercenary had used simple tricks to evade the notice of the armored guards, but Zayl felt that even such would slow their efforts too much. Thanks to the potion that Gorst had fed him—and whose contents the necromancer knew he had best never explain to the fighter—Zayl felt almost as good as new. His wounds had vanished, and the only remnant of his almost catastrophic finish consisted of a slight twinge in one arm. Still, the necromancer felt confident that he could now not only mask himself from the sight of the soldiers, but do the same for the giant as well. They would save much time by walking right past rather than inching their way along the sides.

While Gorst obviously did not entirely agree, he did not argue when Zayl began casting. Using the dagger to draw the fiery symbols in the air, Zayl strengthened his normal spell, then touched the mercenary with the tip of the blade.

"Nothing's happened," complained the giant.

"We are both tied to the spell. We can see each other, but no one else can see us. The same applies for most basic sounds, but I would not recommend shouting or sneezing as we pass. Abrupt and loud noises might penetrate the glamour."

Still a little reluctant, Gorst followed him out into the hall. Farther on, the sentries continued their motionless, tireless stare across the corridor. Zayl could not help but admire their training, so akin to his own. Each of the eight men stood tall and straight. Armed alternately with sword or ax, they almost could have been mistaken for very lifelike statues. Their nearly identical faces and expressions only served to emphasize that look and, in addition, had made Zayl early on wonder if they were perhaps all related.

He and Gorst slowly walked along, shoulder to shoulder, step by step. They passed the first pair, then the second, without any notice whatsoever. The mercenary seemed to relax, and even Zayl, who knew the power of his spell, felt some relief.

Then something about the next guard's countenance made the necromancer pause despite the urgency of the situation. Gorst gave him a worried, insistent look, but Zayl ignored it. He stared cautiously at the armored figure, wondering what about the man's face so bothered him. Unable to ascertain what it might be, he glanced at the opposing sentry, studying him.

It suddenly occurred to him what it was that he found so disturbing and yet so difficult to identify.

Neither guard had blinked. Zayl had waited far beyond reasonable human limit, and yet neither had reacted like a normal man. No matter how well-trained these guards might be, surely they had to blink at some point.

And yet they did not.

Zayl wanted to tell Gorst, but feared risking his spell. Once they were far past, he could tell the other of his disquieting discovery. For now, it behooved them to—

The unblinking eyes of one of the guards suddenly shifted in his direction, meeting the necromancer's widening gaze.

"They see us!" Zayl shouted.

Everyone moved at once. Gorst had his sword out and ready to confront any of the four they had already crept by. The one who had met Zayl's eyes leapt forward, ax swinging, face completely expressionless. The other three moved in behind him, similar blank looks on each.

Dagger before him, Zayl muttered. A black sphere briefly materialized, then shot directly into the chest of the first attacker. The armored sentry hesitated, then continued as if unhindered.

The results did not please the necromancer. Never before had he cast a spell of weakening and seen it completely fail. These guards were more than simply men—and, because of that, possibly more than he and Gorst could handle.

If he worried about such things, the gigantic mercenary did not show it. In fact, where Zayl's magical assault had failed, Gorst's considerable skill and strength made up for it. The first to reach the wild-maned fighter moved in with the obvious intention of quickly decapitating Gorst with his ax. Seemingly outfought already, Gorst waved his blade wildly about, leaving himself wide open.

However, as the ax neared, the giant did an amazing thing. He let the head and upper part of the shaft come within inches of his throat, then, with one meaty hand, stopped the ax in mid-flight and finally ripped it from the hands of its wielder.

Although disarmed, the guard charged forward. Keeping the handle foremost, Gorst slammed the sentry hard in the stomach. Metal bent in, and a gasp of air escaped the giant's otherwise emotionless foe. Not satisfied with forcing his enemy to double over, Gorst swung hard, using the flat of the ax to strike the guard solidly in the face.

A face that *shattered*.

The fragments fell away. Within the helm, utter darkness reigned. To his credit, the mercenary did not even wait for the pieces to hit the floor. Quickly twisting the ax around, he did as his adversary had intended for him, slicing off helmet, neck brace, and whatever might have held them in place.

The now-completely headless figure collapsed with a clatter onto the marble floor.

"They're not alive!" Gorst shouted needlessly.

"But they can be stopped," Zayl returned. Now that he knew better what they confronted, the necromancer felt more confident. Small wonder his spell had failed; he had based his work on the type of enemy he assumed he faced. These were not men, no. They resembled golems of a sort, and as a necromancer he had become well-versed in dealing with their like.

For the followers of Rathma, animating a construct—a figure of clay, stone, or some other substance—had been an art hand-in-hand with their dealings with raising the dead. In many ways, animating a golem required many of the opposite elements needed to summon a spirit or revive a corpse. With the latter, one brought back what had once been life. With the former, one imbued that which had never known life with a semblance of it.

Dodging the sword of his nearest opponent, Zayl ran through the spell for creating a golem, then reversed it. Hoping he would not misstep, he shouted the words not only in the latter order, but completely backward as well—everything to create the opposite effect.

The guard dropped his sword . . . and his hand . . . and his arms and legs and head and body. Armor scattered over the floor, and the face the golem had worn cracked into a thousand pieces as it struck the hard surface.

A second one nearly caught the necromancer while he stood admiring his work. The ax came within inches of Zayl's chest. Only barely did Zayl manage to spout out the altered spell again before the monstrous sentry could try a second strike.

Something different happened, though. The guard lost his ax, and his actions became uncoordinated, but he did not crumble as the first had. In fact, Zayl could see him slowly recovering, his movements returning to fluidity.

The golem had adapted to his spell.

Behind him, Gorst grunted as he lifted another adversary up into the air using the spiked head of the ax. Had the guard truly been human, he would have been impaled to death, but the golem only struggled, trying hard to reach the giant with his sword.

With massive effort, Gorst used the ax to throw the one construct into another. The force of his toss caused the one beneath to shatter when the pair hit the floor. However, the first rose again, a gaping hole in his armor where his chest should have been. He seized the ax left behind by his fellow and moved in to match weapons with the mercenary.

Zayl, meanwhile, found himself hard-pressed against his three foes.

Reacting instinctively, he summoned the Talon of Trag'Oul, which had served him so well in Gregus Mazi's sanctum.

The bone spear shot through the foremost golem, the one he had already slowed. The damage caused by both spells proved too much for the animated guard to overcome. The torso collapsed in on itself, then, as if a house of cards had been knocked over, the entire golem dropped in pieces.

Knowing he could no longer use the Talon, Zayl immediately summoned the Den'Trag, the Teeth of Trag'Oul. The combination had perfectly finished the carpet beast and surely would serve as well here.

But when the shower of swift, deadly shafts struck the pair, most *bounced* off.

The necromancer could scarcely believe what he saw; he had heard no tale of the Teeth ever failing. True, some of his missiles did pincushion the two golems and had even managed to disarm the one who had wielded the ax, but other than causing some slowness of movement, the projectiles had succeeded in doing little else.

It occurred to him then that the similarities between the Teeth and the Talon had enabled the golems to adapt to the former as well. Zayl cursed his stupidity, then sought some other spell not at all akin to any of those he had cast. He had to think fast, too, for although the animated sentries clearly respected the power of his dagger, its short length meant that they still had the advantage of reach.

As the one who had been disarmed bent to seize the ax again, the necromancer's remaining opponent thrust hard with his sword. The tip of the long blade came within an inch of Zayl's throat. He backed away, colliding with Gorst, who had been pressed back by his own remaining foes.

An idea occurred to Zayl, one he hoped would not prove wrong, or else he would be sacrificing both their lives needlessly. "Gorst! We need to switch opponents!"

"Switch? Why?"

"Just trust me! When I give the word!"

To his credit, the mercenary did not protest. Still back-to-back, Zayl could feel the giant's body tense as he prepared to follow the spellcaster's lead.

"Drive them back three paces, then turn to your left!"

Zayl himself dove forward, his sudden shift in tactics causing the golems to step away. However, the necromancer cast no spell, but rather simply did exactly as he had ordered Gorst. Spinning around, he abandoned his foes for those the giant had fought. At the same time, Gorst turned to confront Zayl's original pair.

Pointing the dagger at his two new adversaries, the necromancer unleashed the Teeth of the Dragon again.

The needle-sharp projectiles tore through the golems, completely puncturing the armor and shattering the guards into a hundred pieces that flew in every direction.

Zayl let out an uncustomary yell of triumph. As he had suspected, since these had not yet faced him in battle, they had not adapted themselves to his particular spells. By switching opponents, he had outwitted their creator's handiwork.

But that left Gorst with the pair that the necromancer had originally faced. Concerned that they might prove too much for the mercenary, Zayl whirled about, already putting together a spell that he hoped would at least slow the sentries down.

He need not have worried. Gorst had the situation well in hand—and one of the golems in hand, too. His weapon abandoned, the giant had one of his foes upside down over his head. Without hesitation, he thrust the golem toward the floor as hard as he could, and where Gorst was concerned, that proved hard indeed.

Helmet and false face crumpled into an unrecognizable jumble. The massive fighter tossed the rest of the body away, then turned on the final golem. Undaunted, the construct tried to cut a deadly arc with his sword. However, Gorst, moving far more swiftly than his form warranted, seized the wrist of the sword arm and tugged.

As the guard fell toward him, the mercenary slammed his fist through the emotionless mask with such force that his hand dented the inside of the back of the helmet.

Seemingly determined not to take any risks, Gorst ripped the helmet off, then he kicked with his foot at the creature's chest.

The last golem fell back onto the floor and broke, limbs clattering in various directions, bits of armor spinning about.

"Now what?" asked Gorst as he retrieved one of the axes.

"As you said, we find Captain Dumon."

They hurried down the hall again, the silence and emptiness of the palace doing nothing to ease Zayl's concerns. Surely the commotion caused by the battle should have sent more guards running to aid the others. Where were all those who had once inhabited this place?

More to the point, where was Captain Dumon? In a place so huge, with so many hidden passages, how could they possibly—

What a fool he had been! Zayl halted, Gorst nearly running him down in the process.

"Do you have anything of the captain's on you? Anything at all? If not, we'll have to return to his chambers."

The giant brooded over the question for a moment, then his face brightened. "Got this!"

He dug into a pocket and removed a small, rusted medallion with the picture of some bearded western monarch upon it. In badly worn script around the edges had been inscribed *For Honor, For Duty, For King and Kingdom.*

"Kentril got it from his father. Carried it with him for years. Used to say it brought him good luck. He gave it to me after I almost got my head chopped off about a year ago. Said I needed it more than he did."

Not exactly what Zayl had hoped for, but if Gorst's aura had not yet overwhelmed the older one set into the medallion by Captain Dumon, then it could still be of use in tracking the missing mercenary down. Unfortunately, their lack of time also demanded that the necromancer make use of a far less accurate spell, one with the potential to be more affected by outside influences such as the recent change in ownership.

Zayl had to try, though. Holding the medallion in his right hand, he dangled the tip of the blade over the center, all the while muttering under his breath.

Immediately, he began to feel a tug—but toward the watching Gorst. Irritated, Zayl focused on Kentril Dumon, picturing him as best he could.

Now the pulling came from another direction, an area near the grand chamber but in an area of which the necromancer knew little. Muttering a few more words, the necromancer tightened the focus his spell to make certain, then nodded to Gorst.

"Did you find him?"

Holding the rusted memento before him, Zayl checked the direction a third time. The invisible force continued to pull him toward the same path. "He is most definitely that way."

Ax gripped tightly, Gorst trailed close as Zayl followed the guidance of the bewitched medallion. As they proceeded, though, the spellcaster noticed an unnerving peculiarity about the lit torches and oil lamps nearby. The flames flickered rather oddly, and Zayl thought that the light actually looked *darker*, as if something drained it of its natural fury.

Their path led them to a secluded door, through which they entered without hesitation. Before them the pair found a passage descending below the main palace, a passage that neither could recall from the drawings. Gorst did not like the dim illumination that came from everywhere and nowhere, and even the necromancer felt a chill up and down his spine, but down they went, certain more than ever that there they would find the captain.

At the bottom, the duo came upon an immense iron door. The head of a fearsome gargoyle with features like those of the ones they had seen outside thrust out from the right side, a large ring in its mouth.

Gorst put an ear to the door, a moment later shaking his head. "Can't make out a sound." He tugged on the ring. "It's too strong for me. I'll just ruin the handle trying."

"Let me see what I can do." Slipping around the giant again, Zayl leaned close with the dagger. He sensed great forces in play not only around the door but beyond.

"Zayl," came the skull's voice, "I think—"

"Not now, Humbart. Can you not see—"

He broke off as the ring suddenly slipped from the gargoyle's beaky maw. A shriek echoed through the passage. The necromancer lurched back as the beak snapped at him, falling against Gorst.

A full-sized, winged, and taloned gargoyle leapt out of the door at them.

EIGHTEEN

"Atanna—" Kentril bit back the rest of what he had been going to say. This could not be Atanna, not this horrifying marionette.

Her head still tipped completely to one side, she gave him a macabre smile. "My darling Kentril . . ."

Juris Khan put his arm around her. With an expression akin to that on the face of any loving father, he said to her, "Now, my dear, you should go to your beloved looking your best, don't you think so?"

He gently put the arms in place, then ran his hand over the maimed limb. As Lord Khan's fingers pulled away, Kentril saw that Atanna's own hand had been restored.

Muttering words the likes of which the mercenary had never heard, the robed monarch took a step back. A fiery corona surrounded his daughter from head to toe. Atanna rose several inches into the air, and as she did, her legs twisted, reshaped, becoming once more normal limbs. The gouges in her face and form quickly dwindled, finally disappearing. Even her dress restored itself, all signs of damage vanishing.

"*Olbystus!*" called out Juris Khan.

Slowly, Atanna descended to the floor again. The shimmering corona faded away. Before Kentril stood an almost completely restored woman.

Almost . . . because her head yet hung to the side.

With a gentle smile, Atanna's father put her head back in place. Muscles, veins, tendons, and flesh instantly fused. The terrible wound sealed itself, all trace soon gone.

Juris Khan briefly adjusted her hair. "There! So much better."

"Am I pretty again, Kentril?" she innocently asked.

He could say nothing, could think nothing. In desperation, he looked to Quov Tsin, who seemed to be taking everything in with an eagerness that did not bode well at all.

"It's as you *said*," the diminutive Vizjerei almost cooed to their host. "The power to do almost anything, even to preserve life itself!"

"A gift of Heaven," their host returned. "A gift that can be shared."

"Heaven?" blurted the captain. "This is hellish!"

Khan gave him a paternal look. "Hell? But this is Ureh, my good captain! No beast or servant of the Prime Three can touch this holy kingdom—is that not so, Master Tsin?"

The Vizjerei sniffed. "Don't be so mundane, Dumon! Can't you even imagine the power of Heaven? Do you think Hell could preserve life so?"

"Preserve it? You call that *life*? She's *dead*, Tsin! Just look at her!"

"Why, Kentril, how could you possibly say that?" Pouting, Atanna stepped close. Her eyes glittered in that magical way they always had, and he could feel the warmth of her body even though she still stood a few scant inches away. Each breath rose and sank in fascinating display, enough so that even Captain Dumon had to start questioning his own fears. "Do I truly, *truly*, look dead to you?"

"Open your eyes and mind, captain," Quov Tsin urged, coming toward the pair. "You've always struck me as a little brighter than most of your earthy kind. You know the stories, the legends of the Light among Lights! You know how the archangels granted great miracles to the people, revealed to them things we can only just imagine!"

"But—but this?"

"Kentril is correct to be skeptical," commented Juris Khan. He extended his hands to take in the entire chamber. "Do not the archangels tell us to be wary of evil in the guise of goodness? Does not the world have tales about cunning demons seeking to corrupt humans at every turn? My good captain, the history of Ureh at the time when we sought the pathway to Heaven's sanctuary very much backs your suspicious nature. It is because of the subtle guile of Diablo and the many lesser demons that I prayed for a miracle, for a way to secure my kingdom completely from their evil. To my good fortune, the archangel did grant me that miracle, but in the meantime we more than once had to deal with cunning traitors and plots sinister barely recognizable as such. Yes, I applaud your skepticism, however misplaced it might be at this moment."

Tsin turned the veteran soldier so that the platform filled Kentril's gaze. The mercenary's eyes widened as he noted the glowing, pulsating runes. The urge to get as far away from the artifact as he could filled Kentril. Unfortunately, not only did the Vizjerei hold his arm, but Atanna stood right behind him.

"The archangel who had spoken to Lord Khan could not undo what had been done," the short sorcerer explained. "But he revealed to our host a possible escape should the proper elements come into play. They have."

Now Khan stepped around the platform, eyeing Kentril from the opposing side. "I had originally thought to make use of your fortuitous arrival to fulfill my original intention, to see Ureh at last rise to Heaven. However, your good Master Tsin rightly convinced me of our need to stay on the mortal plane, and, as it turns out, this works out so perfectly with what I've calculated that I cannot but believe that the archangel truly meant this route instead."

For lack of anything better to say, Captain Dumon muttered, "I don't understand."

"It's very simple, Dumon, you cretin! The archangel pointed out powers not bound by Heaven or Hell, powers of nature, of the world itself. What better than these to help bind Ureh to our plane again? The natural tendencies of such forces are to create a balance, to set everything into harmony. Ureh will become truly real again, its people once more able to go out in the sun, to go out and interact with other kingdoms, other realms."

At the moment, Kentril did not see that as quite the wondrous notion that Tsin clearly did. In fact, he regretted even having set the one stone in place. Ureh had not proven to be what he had expected—and his future not what he had thought it to be.

"What about Gregus Mazi?" the captain demanded, shaking off both Atanna and the Vizjerei. He could not forget the horrible sight he had seen.

"Lord Khan explained that simple matter to me, Dumon. You didn't find Gregus Mazi, but rather one of his acolytes. He tried also to destroy the Key to Shadow, but a protective spell cursed him so. The cretin brought it on himself. He now guards against others with equally vile notions, protecting Ureh's hopes . . ."

There were too many holes in the story, too many gaping holes, but for Quov Tsin, who had not been there, Khan's explanation seemed to make perfect sense. Not so for Kentril Dumon, however. He knew very well that Juris Khan had added another lie to the many already piled up. Everything that the captain and his companions had assumed about the holy kingdom had been wrong. They had come to find a legend and instead had unveiled a nightmare.

"And what about my men, Tsin? What about Albord and the rest—and even the necromancer, Zayl? A lot of good men have gone missing, and I've not yet heard a reasonable explanation for their disappearances."

Juris Khan came from around the platform. He seemed even taller, more foreboding, than previously. "The taint left by Gregus has touched some of my people, I admit. However, once Ureh is settled among mankind again, those who've done these terrible deeds shall be taken to account."

While a part of him wished desperately to believe the elder man, Kentril had heard too much he could not accept. "Tsin, you can stay here if you like, but I think I'll be going . . ."

Atanna was suddenly there at his side again. The captain felt torn between desire and revulsion. Here stood the woman of his dreams . . . the same one he had seen fall to her death, then return in most grotesque fashion.

"Oh, but you can't go, Kentril, darling, not yet!"

Spoken with honey yet still not sweet enough not to make him even more wary. Again pulling away from her, the veteran soldier readied his blade. "I'm going through that door. Tsin, you'd be smart to go with me."

"Don't be a bigger fool than I take you for already, Dumon. I'm not going anywhere, and you certainly can't. We need you most of all right now!"

"Need me? For what?"

The Vizjerei shook his head at such ignorance. "You're critical to the spell, of course, cretin!"

He looked from face to face to face—and turned to run. Against one spell-caster, Kentril Dumon might have defended himself. Against two, he might have even entertained some hope of victory.

Against three, only a madman stayed and fought.

But as Kentril ran toward the door, he abruptly discovered himself running toward the *platform* instead. With one fluid movement, the captain spun around, only to see the platform again.

"Do stop wasting our time with such games, Dumon!" snapped Tsin. "It isn't as if we plan to kill you."

Unable to make any progress toward escape, Kentril paused to listen. "No?"

"The amount of blood needed will hardly even make you dizzy, I promise."

Blood. . . .

"Damn you!" Still gripping the sword, Kentril lunged.

The weapon disappeared from his hand, reappearing but a second later in that of Juris Khan.

With an almost casual air, Atanna's father tossed Kentril's last hope aside. "My dear captain. You continue to misunderstand everything. Yes, we require you to lie down upon the platform, but this is hardly a human sacrifice. Let me explain . . ." An almost saintly look spread across his lined visage. "We deal with powers that are part and sum that which keeps the natural order in balance. In that natural order, life is most paramount, and in life, *blood* is the strongest representation. To bind the power, then, we need blood. The platform acts as a focus, which is why the blood must be drawn there."

A soft but cold hand touched his cheek. Jumping, Kentril once more faced the creature he had thought he loved.

"And they only need a few drops for that. The rest they draw, my love, is for *us*."

The caress both teased him and made his flesh crawl. "Us?"

"Of course, Kentril, darling! When the entire spell is complete, not only will Ureh be once more in the real world, but you shall never have to fear death again. Isn't that wonderful?"

Never fear death again . . .

They would make him like *her*.

He tried to flee again, but his body refused to obey his demands. Kentril could breathe, he could even blink his eyes, but his legs and arms remained frozen.

"Really, Dumon! The embarrassment you cause us both. You can certainly spare a few drops to save a city and the offer Lord Khan gives you—if it could be done more than once, I'd do it to myself."

To his minor satisfaction, the mercenary commander discovered his mouth worked. "You're welcome to it, Tsin!"

"I, regrettably, must assist in the spell. Besides, our good host assures me that when the conjunction of forces is correct again, he shall grant the favor. For now, you are the fortunate one!"

Kentril's legs began to move, but not by his choice. Next to the platform, Quov Tsin made walking motions with two fingers. As he did, the fighter's legs mimicked his actions.

"Damn it, Tsin! Don't you realize that something's wrong here?"

As he neared the Vizjerei, though, the captain noticed a faint, glazed look in the sorcerer's eyes. Up close, Tsin had the appearance of a man *entranced*.

"Up, please," the Vizjerei commanded.

Unable to resist, Kentril climbed atop the platform, spreading out as if his limbs had been bound by invisible cuffs.

Juris Khan loomed over him. In his hand, the monarch wielded a slim but serpentine dagger. "Have no qualms, Kentril Dumon. Ureh shall be eternally grateful to you."

As he raised the blade above his head and uttered words of power, the captain caught sight of Atanna smiling expectantly at him.

Soon they would be together again . . . and he would be just like *her*.

The winged gargoyle leapt out of the door, its entire body seeming to sprout from the iron itself. The beaked maw opened and roared, and the metallic talons slashed at the pair.

To his credit, Gorst placed himself in front of Zayl and began trying to slay the creature with his ax. Unfortunately, the ax bounced off the body of the beast with a loud clang, chipping the weapon's head in the process.

"What do we do?" asked the giant. The gargoyle stretched a good eight to ten feet from end of beak to tip of hind quarters. Zayl knew that even Gorst dared not get too close; the unliving sentinel would tear him to ribbons.

"Let me try a spell." The gargoyle seemed much like a golem, only in animal form. Perhaps, the necromancer thought, it could be dealt with in much the same manner.

He did as he had done before, reversing both words and spell, trying to transmute false life back into an inanimate object.

For a moment, the monster paused. It shook its head as if trying to clear its thoughts, then continued to advance unchecked.

Beaten for the moment, Zayl and Gorst withdrew, winding their way back up the steps. The gargoyle continued to follow until it reached the midway point between the top and bottom of the stairway. There it suddenly froze, iron gaze fixed upon the pair above.

"So . . . first and foremost, it protects the door," Zayl muttered, wondering what he could do with that bit of information.

Gorst leaned on the ax, glaring back at the beast. "We gotta get down there. Kentril's there for sure, and I don't like that."

The necromancer had to agree with him. For what reason Captain Dumon might be down there, he could not say, but surely it had to involve something dire. The longer the gargoyle kept the two of them at bay, the greater the likelihood that the captain would be murdered . . . or even worse.

"What goes on out there?" demanded a voice at his belt.

In all that had happened, Zayl had forgotten about Humbart. Of course, the skull could do little, but unless the necromancer responded, he knew that Humbart would only continue to rant.

"We face a gargoyle blocking the door through which we believe Captain Dumon can be found," he informed the contents of the bag. "Unless you have something to offer, I would suggest you keep still."

True to form, the skull paid him no mind. "You try one of your golem spells?"

"Yes, and it failed."

"What about—?"

Zayl sighed, exasperated as usual with his bodiless companion despite the good Humbart had done for him in the past. "This is hardly the time! I—"

"Only one question, lad! What about the Iron Maiden?"

"Iron Maiden?" grumbled Gorst, likely knowing the term only from the torture device.

"Another spell involving reversal. Why it should even be brought up I—" The pale necromancer hesitated. "But it could work, I think. It will involve risk, but if I am careful, I should be all right."

The giant shook his head. "If it's dangerous, use me."

"Gorst—"

The massive fighter would not hear him. "If it doesn't work with me, you can try something else. If it doesn't with you, what am I going to do?"

He had a point there, one that Zayl disliked immensely. Servants of Rathma saw themselves as the front line in the battle to keep the mortal world in balance. They did not generally gamble the lives of others in their place.

"Very well, but do not risk yourself needlessly."

"What do I do?" Gorst asked.

Already casting the spell, Zayl replied, "You must engage the gargoyle in combat."

"That all?"

From the skull came another response. "You could also try praying a bit, lad!"

Gorst grunted. Zayl finished the spell, explaining, "If it works as planned, whatever blow it strikes against you will damage it instead. If you feel the slightest pain, retreat quickly."

The giant said nothing more, not even commenting on the fact that if the gargoyle got one good strike at him, he would not have the chance to retreat. Hefting his weapon, the mercenary descended toward the metallic beast.

Nearly within range, Gorst suddenly paused. "If I strike him, does it hurt me?"

"No, you may attack at will."

The massive figure gave him a happy grin. "Good."

Nearly motionless while the two had stood atop the steps, the winged gargoyle suddenly stirred to savage life as the human approached. It snapped and slashed at Gorst even though the fighter had yet to get near enough. Despite his confidence in his spellwork, Zayl could not help feeling much concern for his companion. One never knew what spells might also surround the beast. He readied himself to protect Gorst the moment anything turned awry.

Barely a yard from the guardian, the giant suddenly raised the ax over his head and let out a war cry. The gargoyle roared in turn, leaping forward.

Metal clashed against metal. Despite the spell set upon him by the necromancer, Gorst fought as if his skills alone would save him.

Twice, three times, the head of the ax met the claws and savage beak of the gargoyle. The razor-sharp nails came within inches of the mercenary, but Gorst avoided them as he would have any attack.

With his prodigious strength, he dented the head of his adversary, but the toll of hitting the iron hide of the beast proved too much. The blade chipped and dulled, and each swing came slower and slower.

The gargoyle finally got one paw under Gorst's defenses. The fighter tried to retreat, but stumbled over the step behind him.

"What's happening?" Humbart called.

Zayl said nothing, poised to cast a spell even though he knew that it would not save the mercenary from terrible injury.

The claws tore at Gorst's right leg.

A horrible, metallic screeching sound rippled through the passage.

Gorst's monstrous foe suddenly tumbled to the side, its right rear leg shredded open. Seemingly unconcerned, the gargoyle pushed forward, trying with its beak to snap at the human's unprotected midsection.

Again the metallic shriek echoed throughout the area. Now the gargoyle did back away, although in rather haphazard fashion. In the area of its belly, a gaping hole now existed. A live animal would have already been dead or dying from such wounds, but the magic animating the winged terror kept it going, albeit without as much skill and fluidity of movement as in the beginning.

"It's working!" shouted Gorst. "I'm going in closer!"

Even seeing that his spell worked perfectly, Zayl did not relax. He also moved nearer to the struggle, watching for any possible threat or an opening of which he could make use.

Swinging the ax hard, the giant actually indented the gargoyle's left shoulder. Unimpeded by such a wound, the beast struck again, reaching for Gorst's right forearm.

The results were as expected. Instead of mangling soft, human flesh and ripping apart muscle and bone, the animated guardian only tore its own front right leg asunder. Suddenly stricken with two badly mauled limbs on the same side, the gargoyle teetered, falling against the wall. Yet still it did not give in.

"This is takin' too long!" bellowed the mercenary. "I'm gonna try something!"

He threw down his ax and leaned forward, presenting his face and throat for the beast.

"Gorst! No!" Even though the spell had so far protected the fighter, Zayl wanted to take no chances.

The metallic guardian, however, reacted too swiftly for the necromancer. With its good front limb, the winged creature slashed hard, aiming for the entire target. Claws that could have ripped away Gorst's face to the very bone came closer and closer . . .

With a savage squeal of wrenching iron, the gargoyle's own muzzle and throat tore off.

Little remained of the monstrous visage save a bit of eye. A ragged hole reminiscent of the damaged golems greeted the staring humans.

The gargoyle took an awkward step forward, choosing to stand on the ruined front limb. This time, it toppled completely to the side and seemed unable to right itself.

With almost childlike interest, Gorst leaned down and bared his chest to the one good forelimb. He then reached out and tapped the ruined guardian on the paw.

The paw instinctively attacked.

A great gouge appeared in the gargoyle's chest.

The metallic beast screeched once . . . then stilled.

"Nice spell," Gorst commented, rising. "How long does it last?"

"This battle is done," replied the necromancer. "It is gone now."

"Too bad. Can you cast it on me again?"

Zayl shook his head. "Not with any trust to its success. Besides, I suspect that such a spell will not help you down there."

The giant seized his battered ax again, not at all bothered by the other's answer. "Guess I'll just have to fight like normal, huh?"

With the gargoyle destroyed, the handle to the door had also been lost, but Zayl suspected that it did not serve as the true mechanism for entry. Such a place would not depend upon so mundane a device. The true key to opening the door had to involve magic—but how to discover that key?

He pulled the skull free. "Humbart, what do you see?"

"A red force blankets the whole thing. There's dark, greenish lines zigzagging over it from top to bottom, and in the center I see a kind of blue-yellow spot—"

That had to be what Zayl sought. "Guide the tip of the blade to it."

The skull did, urging the necromancer's hand left and right, up and down, as needed. "Right on the mark there, lad!"

A slight tingle coursed through Zayl as he touched the point of his weapon to the spot. Immediately, he began a spell of searching and unbinding. Without the unique properties of the skull, Zayl knew that he would have never been able to pinpoint the area so precisely, so cleverly had the wards been set in place.

His mind untied and unfolded the myriad patterns creating the lock, slowly teasing out the secret to its opening. Unbidden from his mouth came words even he had never heard before, old, old words of dark imagining. The necromancer considered pulling free, but that would have left him with no other options, and Captain Dumon most certainly in some dire strait.

Then, at last, a single word came to him, the final key and, if he had been privy to the knowledge of the original caster, the only one truly needed.

"*Tezarka* . . ." Zayl whispered.

With a slow moan, the door began to open.

The necromancer leapt back, joining a wary Gorst in preparation of the attack surely to come. The iron door opened wider, revealing light from within. A flood of varied and powerful forces emanated from within, enough to awe even Zayl.

Yet nothing burst forth to attack them. No guards, no golems, nothing.

Glancing at each other, Zayl and Gorst cautiously entered.

The vast, angled room immediately snared their attention, for here clearly stood the most private sanctum of a powerful spellcaster. The weighty tomes, the gathered specimens, powders, and artifacts—Zayl had never seen such a collection. He stared, for the moment caught up in the sight. Even Gregus Mazi's abode had not touched him so.

It took Gorst to break the spell over him, Gorst, who asked the question that had to be asked.

"Why is it empty?"

Nineteen

❋

They had left him unable to move but at least able to talk, and Kentril saw no reason to remain silent. "Tsin, Snap out of it! Can't you see how wrong everything about this is? You're under a spell yourself, damn it!"

"Do relax, Dumon," chided the Vizjerei. "Such an ungrateful cretin you are! Immortality, riches, power . . . I thought that was what a mercenary dreamed of."

It was no use. Quov Tsin could not see past whatever had been cast upon him. Lord Khan had preyed upon the sorcerer's greed, just as the captain himself had when first instigating Tsin to persuade their host to make Ureh part of the mortal world again.

Or *had* their host needed any convincing? It had been Atanna who had first broached the subject with Kentril, telling him that they could be together if her father did not decide to try once more to follow the path to Heaven. The mercenary realized that he had been *duped*; Juris Khan had no doubt sent his daughter to fill the gullible captain's head with such notions, knowing that Kentril would do his utmost to sway the Vizjerei.

Both he and Tsin had been played like puppets or, worse, fish on a line. Bait had been set to catch each, then the lord of Ureh had reeled them in with ease.

"It's quite ironic," commented the elder monarch. "I had only just sent my darling daughter to find you when you apparently came looking for her. I had meant to wait longer to cast this spell . . . but my children were so eager, so hungry, that I was forced to move the spell to this night."

Kentril looked to Tsin to see if he heard any of what their host had just confessed, but the short, balding sorcerer seemed quite contented preparing for the task at hand. The Vizjerei had begun to go around the edge of the platform, using mumbled spells to cause various runes to glow brighter. Whatever hold Juris Khan had over the sorcerer looked to be very complete, indeed.

"I had promised them your men when first we noticed your arrival, but I needed one of you for this precious work. I also needed another wielder of sorcery to aid in my effort, the others having been necessarily sacrificed to my sacred mission long ago."

"Gregus Mazi never tried to destroy Ureh, did he?"

The regal lord looked offended. "He did worse than that! He dared claim that I knew not what I did, claimed that *I*, Juris Khan, loving lord of all my subjects, *damned* rather than saved my people! Can you believe such audacity?"

Captain Dumon could believe that and much more about his captor. He saw now what he and the rest had so blindly missed. Ureh's master had gone completely insane, his desire for good somehow twisted into all of this.

"I admit, there were times when my beliefs faltered, but whenever that happened, the archangel would appear to me, bolster my will, and once more set me on the proper course. Without his guidance, it's possible I wouldn't have pressed on to the end."

This archangel Juris Khan constantly spoke of had to have been a product of his own mind—and yet, here stood the man who had nearly succeeded in reaching the sanctuary of Heaven! How could the archangel have been delusion, then? Only with the efforts of such a one could any mortal possibly have hoped to accomplish so incredible a feat.

"He warned me of the insidious efforts of the dark powers to influence those around me, that I could not trust any but myself. Even those who worked in concert to bring success to our goal might have become tainted . . ." Khan wore an expression of intense pride. "And so I cleverly planned to make certain that none of them would have the opportunity to betray me at the moment of our destiny!"

When the priests and spellcasters had gathered to do their part, they had not realized that their master had something else in mind in addition to their work. Devised in secret, Ureh's monarch had instituted a second spell, one so enmeshed in the principal effort that none of his underlings would take notice of it. Each would unknowingly assist in ensuring that there would be no attempt to usurp the holy quest.

Juris Khan had laid within the master spell a means by which to slay each and every one of those who aided him.

Their fates had been decided the moment they had begun. The spell that had sought to cast Ureh to Heaven had not only drawn from the innate magical powers of the world, but had also done so with equal force from the casters themselves.

"It had all been so well-planned, down to the most delicate of details," Kentril's captor went on. "I could feel Ureh's soul being lifted from its earthly shell . . . and the life forces of the corrupted ones being leeched from their treacherous selves."

But he had underestimated one among them, the one he most should have watched. Gregus Mazi, trusted confidant and nearly son to the elder ruler, a sorcerer knowledgeable and skilled. Along with the priest Tobio, Mazi had been the one who had most contributed to the breakthrough needed to make the great spell possible in the first place.

"I saw it in his eyes. I saw the moment when he comprehended what the spell sought to do to him. He didn't realize that I had done the altering, but he knew nonetheless the result. At the most crucial moment, at the most critical juncture, Gregus tore himself free from the matrix we had all created. With his remaining power he cast himself *out* of Ureh . . ."

The instinctive reaction had done more than save Mazi; it had also created an imbalance that had ripped the soul of Ureh free from the mortal plane, but, instead of sending the realm to Heaven, had left it in a shadowed, timeless limbo. With the aid of the rest of the kingdom's sorcerers and priests, Juris Khan might have been able to correct the matter and complete the quest for holy sanctuary, but his spell had done to them what it had failed to do to Gregus Mazi.

The one exception proved to be Tobio, whom providence had saved virtually unscathed. Lord Khan had decided that this had meant the priest had been chosen to live, and it pleased the monarch to know that one old friend of his had remained true. With Tobio, Khan had immediately worked to find freedom from their endless prison, but all plans had failed. The people had begun to panic, to fear that they would be trapped forever.

Juris Khan raised the dagger over Kentril as he talked, drawing invisible patterns. "And then, when our hour was darkest," he added with a grateful smile, "the archangel came to me in my dreams again. As you already know, he could not alter what had happened, but he could, at least, guide and—more important—assist me in fulfilling my people's destiny. The Heavenly One showed me how to open a door of sorts, let his power flood into me, let his wishes and mine mingle . . . and from there touch my children."

However, when he found out about this new gift, Tobio had proven to be a most jealous priest—at least in Khan's eyes. He had confronted his old friend, had claimed him to be not the recipient of holy powers but *tainted* by infernal ones. The priest had even had the audacity to attempt to restrain his lord, but Juris Khan had easily overwhelmed the misguided clergyman. With saddened heart, he cast Tobio into the ancient dungeons below, hoping that someday the priest would shake off the sinful thoughts and return to the fold.

Unhindered now, Lord Khan had acted upon the archangel's dictates, creating spells that would help preserve his precious children while he sought a more permanent remedy. The archangel showed him how to keep the people calm, how to open up each to the subtle ministrations of other angels, one for each person. He had Ureh's trusting ruler bring into the fold his own daughter, reveal to her the glory of the archangel and the gifts she would gain by helping her father and her people.

Pulling back the dagger from over Captain Dumon's chest, Juris Khan extended one arm to Atanna. The crimson-tressed princess came to her father, letting him envelop her in that arm. Atanna gave Kentril a loving, knowing smile, one filled with the certainty of the righteousness of her sire's cause.

"She was scared, my good captain, scared because she did not understand the blessing he wished to give her." The weathered but noble face beamed down at his loving offspring. "I had to be forceful. I had to *insist* . . . despite her unwillingness. It took much perseverance, even on the part of the archangel, but at last she opened herself up to him."

Atanna wore an enraptured expression. "It was so *childish*, my love! I actually feared what Father wanted! When the archangel entered me, I actually *screamed*, can you believe it? It all seems so silly now!"

To the captive mercenary, who had seen what such a blessing had created of Atanna and her father, it hardly seemed silly at all. Whatever their angelic benefactor had sought to accomplish, it had resulted in an abomination of everything holy.

"I believe I'm nearly ready, my lord," Quov Tsin suddenly announced. "There are but a few minor patterns to cast."

"I'm gratified, master sorcerer. Without your effort, this could not come to be."

Kentril chose to use the distraction as a chance again to test the mobility of his body. Unfortunately, even despite the Vizjerei's numerous tasks and Lord Khan's horrific reminiscences, the sorcery keeping the captain prisoner had not faltered in the least.

Atanna came to his side again, rubbing what would have been a soothing hand on his forehead if not for the fact that she used the same appendage that had earlier been mangled to pulp. The rich emerald eyes gleamed but did not blink. "You'll feel so silly yourself when this is all over, darling Kentril. You'll wonder just as I did why you made so much of a fuss."

He could not meet her gaze, not while the memory of how she had looked when she entered the chamber still burned harshly in his mind. Instead, the captain glanced past her at Juris Khan, who seemed to have finished with his tale and now intended to do the same to Kentril. "What did happen to Gregus Mazi?"

The pleasant smile on the robed monarch's kindly face became not at all pleasant. "I told you of the Keys, their making, and our earlier attempt to lock the shadow in place just as you eventually did for us. I also told you how Gregus came again to do the unthinkable, to betray us again. In all this, I did not lie, good captain. What I omitted, though, was that he had help . . . in the form of the misguided Tobio."

Gregus Mazi had secretly returned to Ureh and had learned of the crystals just as Lord Khan had previously said, but in the process he had also come across the still-imprisoned priest. Seizing on Tobio's madness and pretending to believe it, the sorcerer had informed his new ally that they had to remove or destroy the two Keys so that the holy kingdom could not remain on the mortal plane. It was decided that their chances would be double if each went in search of separate stone. Then, if only one of them succeeded, Ureh would again be cast into limbo.

But although he had entered the city unnoticed, Gregus Mazi did not escape his former master's attention when he sought out the Key to Shadow. The sorcerer had almost succeeded in stealing away the crystal, but Lord Khan had managed to catch him in the midst of the act.

They did battle, but the traitorous spellcaster did not know of the powerful gifts the archangel had given. Mazi fell swiftly, and in order to make certain there would be no repeat of such betrayal, Khan transformed him into the sentinel Kentril and the others had discovered. Before that happened, however, the lord of Ureh had wrung from his former friend the fact that Tobio had already started for the other crystal.

"You see, my dear captain, the Key to Light had indeed been set in place by brave martyrs. However, when I learned from Gregus that Tobio had gone to destroy my hopes for our eventual release, I admit I grew furious. Summoning the powers granted to me by the archangel, I transported myself to the shadowed side of the peak, there to find the misguided priest seeking to wrest the Key to Light from its anointed place." Khan paused, eyes momentarily closed in what appeared to be a moment of renewed mourning. When he opened them again, he told his prisoner, "I still cry for poor Tobio, corrupted by Gregus. His death I could not help. I gave him one good opportunity to see the errors of his way, to break free of the madness and come back with me to Ureh . . ."

Suddenly, Kentril recalled the grisly discovery he had found all but buried in the cold, hard soil atop sinister Nymyr. "But he didn't, did he?"

"Alas, no. Instead, foolish Tobio tore the Key free and stepped back into the first rays of the day. I admit I reacted without thought, only aware that he had stolen my children's freedom."

The weathered bone Captain Dumon had found had belonged to the determined priest, not one of the so-called volunteers. Uncorrupted, Tobio had been able to step into the sunlight, but it had not saved him from Juris Khan's wrath. Fortunately, the crystal had fallen to where even the lord of Ureh could not reach it. The madness that had consumed the shadowed kingdom had been kept in check.

That is, until Kentril and his men had come along.

"Even if the good Tobio had failed, I admit I would've still required the aid of a worthy sorcerer such as our friend Quov Tsin here," concluded Atanna's father, "but that would've been so much easier with the kingdom set in place, not resurrecting only once a day or two every few years." The smile returned. "But come! Time is fast approaching, and I've likely bored you with so much talk of the past. Now we must prepare for the future, when my people—my children—enlightened by the angels and no longer fearful of the sun, can go out into the world of men and spread the archangel's word to others."

But Kentril had seen those "children," the ghoulish creatures that now filled the city. The ghostly forms he and the others had first witnessed had been illusions to mask an even greater horror. Khan had played on the sympathies of the mercenary officer—and because of it, Captain Dumon had sent most of his men to terrible, monstrous deaths.

The vision he had seen twice had been no delusion caused by a thief's drug, no bite from a savage insect. It had been the truth, the reality of Ureh. The holy kingdom, the Light among Lights, had been transformed into something diabolic—*demonic*. All this time, Juris Khan had been manipulating him, preparing the way so that his horrific subjects could spread beyond the confines of the shadow, spread throughout the mortal lands . . .

Yet all the time his captor spoke of the wondrous archangel, the Heavenly figure who had come to guide him and his flock to the ultimate sanctuary. Again, Kentril wondered how everything had turned out so horribly. When had the archangel's word become twisted or usurped?

Or had there ever been an archangel in the first place?

Lord Khan had already taken his place, Atanna and Quov Tsin following suit. The towering monarch raised the dagger and opened his mouth—

"My lord!" blurted Kentril. "One last question, to ease my mind and enable me to accept this glory you offer! May—may I see what this wondrous archangel looked like?"

The Vizjerei, obviously eager to continue, only snorted at this abrupt question, but Juris Khan accepted it with pleasure, clearly believing that the fighter sought to understand. "Why, bless you, Kentril Dumon! If it makes all the difference, I can *try* to show you. You must know, of course, that I draw from memory, and so what you see, however magnificent, is but a dim, human representation of a being perfect in all manner. In truth, even I never saw him fully, for what mortal could stand the blinding glory of one of Heaven's guardians?"

Giving the blade to his daughter, he held his hands up high and muttered a spell. Kentril tensed more, although he could not be certain exactly why. Lord Khan would only be summoning a representation of the archangel, not the true being. The mercenary could hardly expect any aid from an illusion.

"Behold!" Juris Khan called, indicating an area well above the platform. "Behold a warrior of Truth, a guardian of the Bastion of Light, a sentinel of Goodness watching over all! Behold the Archangel Mirakodus, the golden-haired defender of mankind! Behold Mirakodus, he who has protected Ureh from the evils seeking its soul!"

And as his words echoed throughout the chamber, a figure formed for all of them to see. Atanna let out a raptured gasp, and even the jaded Tsin fell to one knee in homage. Juris Khan himself had tears in his eyes, and he mouthed silent thanks to the image of the one he had called his people's greatest protector.

Kentril stared in awe, too. Clad in glorious armor of the brightest platinum, intricate runes and sculptured glyphs decorating his breast plate, the tall, angelic form glowed as brightly as the sun. One arm held in it a flaming sword; the other reached out to the onlooker, as if beckoning him to come nearer. From the archangel's shoulders radiated a display of crackling, writhing tendrils of pure magical energy that in their continual frenzy created the illusion of massive, fiery wings.

The carved images that the mercenary had grown up around had always depicted the angels as hooded, faceless beings, but not so this one. The hood had been thrown back, revealing a visage of perfection surrounded by cascading golden hair. Captain Dumon at first felt some guilt for even gazing upon the heavenly features of Mirakodus, as if somehow the mercenary had not yet proven himself worthy to do such a thing. The broad jaw, the heroic cheekbones, the impossibly commanding visage—Kentril could never quite make out the specifics of any feature, but the overall impression left him momentarily speechless. No human being could ever hope to match such beauty, such perfection. Lord Khan had only managed to catch an earthly indication of Mirakodus, but even that proved enough to overwhelm the senses.

And then Kentril looked into the eyes and felt his awe suddenly supplanted by an entirely different sensation.

The eyes drew him in, snared him. He could not identify their color, only that they were dark, darker than even the most perfect black. Like a horrific vortex, Kentril Dumon felt as if Mirakodus drew in his very soul, pulled it into some bottomless pit. The urge to scream arose, yet at the same time the vision the mercenary beheld kept him in silent fear. An unreasonable panic such as Kentril had never suffered shook him. He wanted to rip his gaze away, but the eyes would not permit him that escape.

The captain felt himself dragged deeper and deeper into the archangel's eyes, deeper and deeper into a horror impossible to define yet in some way innately familiar. His skin tore from his flesh, and his bones danced free. Kentril felt the death of the grave and the unending torment of the damned soul.

Something within, some desperate push for sanity, for hope, at last enabled the fighter to tear his eyes from the figure above. As his mind slowly pieced itself together, Kentril tried to come to grips with what he had witnessed. Outwardly a messenger, a guardian of Heaven, but within, recognized perhaps even by the subconscious of Juris Khan, a thing that could not in any manner be associated with the archangels or their realm. Behind the facade that no one else seemed to see past, Captain Dumon had recognized a monstrous force, a thing of pure evil.

And in his mind, Kentril could only imagine one creature, one being, who could invoke such fear, such terror. The name thrust itself unbidden from the hardy fighter as he sought futilely to push himself away from Lord Khan's illusion.

"*Diablo . . .*"

"Yes," his captor said with an enthralled smile, seemingly ignorant of what Kentril had cried. "Mirakodus in as much his glory as an earthly mind can comprehend!" The image suddenly vanished as Juris Khan clasped his hands together in outright pleasure, his smile now turned toward the still dumbfounded soldier. "And now that I've shown you the wonderful truth, shall we begin?"

Zayl studied the chamber he and Gorst had so desperately sought to reach, the chamber where the necromancer had felt with complete certainty that Captain Dumon would be found. He stepped toward the center, all but unmindful of the massive, rune-covered platform as he tried to fathom what had gone wrong.

"Where is he?" asked the huge mercenary, eyes shifting warily from one part of the chamber to another. "You said he'd be in here."

"He should be." Zayl consulted the spell again, but the result came up the same. Everything pointed to this being the captain's whereabouts.

Yet, quite clearly, it was not.

He put away the medallion, trying to see what the dagger itself might reveal. Unfortunately, a full sweep indicated nothing.

Gorst wandered around, peering at every corner no matter how unlikely. "Think there's another door somewhere?"

"Possible, but not likely."

"Could he be below or above us?"

An astute question from the giant, but the necromancer had worked to focus his search spell in order to avoid that error. According to his results, their companion *should* have been right before them.

Shutting his eyes briefly, Zayl let his senses expand beyond his body. He suddenly became much more aware of the fearsome and wild powers at play and the fact that they most gathered near the stone platform just before him.

"You notice something?" Gorst asked hopefully.

"Nothing that clears up the question of what went wrong. I feel certain that he is supposed to be here."

The gargantuan fighter mulled this over for several seconds, then suggested, "Maybe Humbart could help."

A suggestion Zayl should have thought of himself. The skull had proven without a doubt its value, yet the necromancer ever hesitated. Zayl's instructors had always taught him the importance of independence, but when a tool such as Humbart Wessel worked, why not make the best of it?

He pulled the last bit of mortal remains of the older mercenary from the new pouch and showed Humbart the chamber. The skull made small, thoughtful sounds, but did not otherwise speak as his wielder let him view everything.

"I can't see hide or hair of him," Humbart announced when they had finished. "A real puzzle, that!"

"You see nothing?"

"Oh, I see a lot! I see a damned hodgepodge of colors and lines and other shapes and forms all swirling madcap about that big block of stone there. I see just about every rune on that thing glowing like lightning. I see enough signs of raw, earthly, and unearthly energy wrapping itself about that thing to make me wish I had feet again so I could hightail it out of here. But I don't see Captain Kentril Dumon *anywhere*!"

The necromancer grimaced. "Then my spell went awry after all. Despite my best efforts, it sent us in the wrong direction."

"It happens to everyone, lad. Maybe if you tried again?"

"I have tried enough. The results would be the same, I promise you."

This did not please Gorst at all. "But we can't give up on him!" the behemoth roared, slamming a fist on the nearest table and nearly upsetting an entire shelf of specimens nearby. "I can't!"

"Easy, boy!" snapped Humbart.

Fearing that the giant's growing rage might end up recreating Zayl's own near disaster in Gregus Mazi's sanctum, the spellcaster quickly said, "No one is giving up, Gorst! We need simply to think this through. Something is wrong here, something that I must consider carefully."

Somewhat mollified, the mercenary quieted. Zayl only hoped that he could live up to his words. He studied the various parts of the sanctum again, trying to find anything amiss. He stared at the shelves, the tables, the stone platform, the jars full of—

"Humbart, tell me once more what you see when you stare at the platform."

The skull did, recounting the furious forces and the glaringly bright and vivid runes. He told of the swirling energy, wild and monstrous, gathered over it. Humbart Wessel described a virtual maelstrom of sorcerous powers at play above and as a part of the stone structure.

"I don't see any of that," Gorst commented when the skull had finished.

Nor did the necromancer, and that interested him very much. He could sense them, yes, but not see them as Humbart did.

And from the skull's vivid description, it sounded as if the forces at play grew more alive, more violent, with each passing moment. They had to be building up to something, something Zayl could only imagine very terrifying.

Returning Humbart to the pouch, the necromancer stepped to the platform. Although he saw no life in the various runes, the feeling that they had been brought into play remained with him, so much so that when Zayl ran his fingers over several, he could swear he felt them pulsating.

"What is it?" Gorst asked.

"I do not know . . . but I must try something." Inspecting the runes, Zayl touched three he recognized for their power. He muttered a spell under his breath, creating ties between himself and those runes. Raw forces charged through his system, causing the necromancer to gasp.

The giant started toward him, but Zayl shook his head. Still struggling to keep the forces in balance, the spellcaster drew forth his dagger. The blade gleamed bright, and as he held the weapon over the platform, a rainbow of colors arose from various markings etched in the stone, creating an almost blinding display of power.

"Let the truth be known!" Zayl shouted to the ceiling. "Let the mask fall away! Let the world be shown as it is, our eyes uncovered at last! *Hezar ky Brogdinas! Hezar ke Nurati! Hezar ky—*"

Suddenly the necromancer felt a sense of displacement so great that he could not maintain his link. He fell back, his eyes seeming to lose all focus. He saw the entire chamber doubled—and yet also very different. While one version held Zayl and Gorst, the other revealed a different, barely visible scene with three figures standing very near him.

As Zayl stepped farther back, Gorst came forward. "I see him! I see—"

He got no farther. The room—all sense of reality—shifted again for the pair. The giant fell to one knee, and it was all the necromancer could do not to do the same.

The other version of their surroundings began to fade. Zayl struggled forward again, determined not to lose it. The vaguely seen figures did not even notice what happened around them. They appeared engrossed in something concerning the platform. One of them looked like Juris Khan, and another had hair the color of his daughter's. The shortest of the three put Zayl in mind of the Vizjerei, although what Quov Tsin would be doing here he could not say.

Planting his hands on two of the runes, Zayl barked out his spell anew. He summoned the forces to him. Something else sought to draw them away, but the necromancer persisted, certain that if he did not, it would result in disaster.

Again everything shifted. The two variations moved closer into sync.

A fourth form coalesced on the platform, the arms and legs spread as if bound.

The startling addition almost caused Zayl to lose his concentration a second time. Everything began to fade again, but he managed to keep it from disappearing altogether. For a third time, Zayl shouted the words of power while he demanded that the forces inherent in the runes obey his dictates.

The figure trapped on the platform came into focus. Zayl recognized Kentril Dumon, who did not yet see him. In fact, the captain stared wide-eyed at something above him, his expression so intense that the necromancer had to look himself.

Juris Khan loomed over them, eyes wide with anticipation. His hand had just begun a swift plunge toward Captain Dumon's chest—and in that hand a wicked blade sought the mercenary's heart.

Twenty

A simple spell had left Kentril unable to protest any longer, Juris Khan proclaiming that he needed the silence in order to cast the spell accurately. He actually apologized to his captive, assuring the captain that when all had been accomplished, he would make it up to him.

Atanna had come before the spellwork to stroke his forehead and kiss him gently on the lips. Now her mouth felt cold, dead, and the eyes looked glassy, a parody of life. Had someone long ago told the mercenary that the offer of a beautiful princess and immortality would someday revolt him, he would have surely laughed.

Now Kentril could only pray for a miracle.

Quov Tsin continued to ignore the obvious, continued to aid in this abominable plan. The Vizjerei began the first part of the spell, summoning forth forces locked in the runes and intertwining them with the raw powers emanating all around. Beside him, a blissful smile on her face, Atanna murmured words in what sounded like a backward version of the common tongue. She had her arms spread apart, the palm of one hand facing Tsin, the other facing her father.

Lord Khan himself presided over the prone Kentril, the sinister dagger held high and seemingly ready at any moment to strike. The monarch of blessed Ureh spoke in a combination of understandable and unintelligible phrases, both of which lent further fear to the prisoner.

"Blood is the river of life!" the elder man shouted to the ceiling at one point. "And we drink gratefully from the river! Blood is the sustenance of the heart . . . and the heart is the key to the soul! The soul is the guide to Heaven . . . and the guide to mortality . . ."

The dagger edged nearer, then receded as Khan started speaking in one of the cryptic languages again. Kentril wanted to faint, but knew that he if fell prey to such an escape, he might never wake up. Whether that would be preferable to the monstrous existence offered to him, the captain could not yet say. If he stayed conscious, at least some hope existed, however meager, that he would still find a way to free himself before it was too late.

But no avenue of escape presented itself to him. As Kentril watched wide-eyed, Juris Khan finally leaned forward and raised the dagger high above his captive's heart. The look in the elder man's eyes told the mercenary that this time, the blade would be plunged into its target.

Swirling tendrils of pure energy arose around Kentril, causing every fiber of his being to go completely taut. Quov Tsin guided the tendrils, from which Lord Khan then seemed to draw strength.

"Great servant of Heaven above, Archangel Mirakodus, hear this humble one! Blood, the harbinger of the soul, opens the path to the true world! Let your power guide! Let at last the might of Heaven undo what has been done! Undo the shadow's binding! Let the sun serve not to give death to your children! Let Ureh return to the mortal plane, and from Ureh let your children go forth and bring to their fellow men and women the truth you so dearly wish all to know!"

It all sounded so mad, but Kentril could do or say nothing to prevent the sacrifice.

"Blessed Mirakodus, with this blood, I, Juris Khan, do humbly beg this boon!"

The dagger came down—

A hand suddenly appeared out of nowhere and clutched Captain Dumon's right arm. Kentril paid it little mind, expecting that Tsin had simply wanted to make certain that the mercenary did not somehow manage to shift position. Shutting his eyes, Kentril waited for the agony, the emptiness of death . . .

"Captain, you must move quickly! I fear we may have little time!"

His eyes flew open. "Zayl?"

Sure enough, the necromancer leaned over him, one slim hand clutching the right arm. Farther back, Gorst watched them, his expression caught midway between relief and mistrust.

Of the other three, he could see no sign. All else in the chamber looked exactly as it should, but Khan, Atanna, and the Vizjerei had all *vanished*.

"What—?" he began, only belatedly realizing that the power of speech had been returned to him.

The necromancer cut him off. "Hurry! He may realize at any moment that I have usurped his spell. I must get us away from here before then!"

Zayl took his dagger and quickly passed it over each limb. As he did, Kentril felt the ability to move return. He needed no more urging from the spellcaster to leap free of the sacrificial platform.

"I am going to try something," Zayl informed him and Gorst. "With so many sources to draw power from, it may work. It may be our only chance!"

Not liking the thought of just standing around and hoping that the necromancer could save them, Kentril asked, "Can we do anything?"

"Indeed you can! Gorst, give the captain a weapon. The two of you must watch out for me in case our esteemed host realizes what I am now doing."

Kentril took the sword the other mercenary offered him, realizing at the same time that Zayl fully expected Juris Khan to return from wherever he had been sent at any moment. The two wary soldiers kept guard while the necromancer swiftly drew a complex pattern over the runes.

"This should do it," Zayl suddenly remarked. Without explanation, he pointed the dagger first at himself, then at each of his companions.

A sense of extreme lightness touched Kentril, almost as if he had lost every bit of weight. The mercenary officer almost expected to begin to float away, much as a cloud might. He opened his mouth to ask what the spellcaster planned—

The chamber vanished.

A wind-tossed mountain ridge materialized around him. Kentril reacted to this abrupt change of venue by planting himself against the rock face as quickly as he could.

Zayl had transported them to the most precarious edge of Nymyr.

The wind howled ominously, and thunder rumbled. Kentril looked up, saw that the sky had transformed. The nightmarish colors of his earlier visions had returned. He quickly glanced down at Ureh, to see now only a few sinister lights below. Captain Dumon could only imagine the scene within the city, the demonic denizens of the once-holy realm now stripped of any pretense of humanity.

"This was not where I planned to send us," muttered Zayl, his expression quite frustrated. "With the power I usurped from the runes, I should have easily been able to transport us to somewhere beyond the confines of this cursed shadow."

Kentril recalled the image of the false archangel. "Maybe that's not allowed. Maybe there is no escape from Ureh."

The necromancer eyed him closely. "Captain, what was Juris Khan doing when I appeared?"

"He said he had to cast a spell to ensure that Ureh would remain on the mortal plane, a spell that would allow his children to go forth into the world." With a deep breath, Kentril quickly went into what details seemed relevant. He described the monarch's clear madness, Tsin's entranced betrayal, the horrific incident involving Atanna, and the discovery that Lord Khan's archangel had been anything but Heaven-sent.

"This begins to add up, although not in any way I find comforting," Zayl remarked when Kentril had finished. "I think I understand. My friends, I think that Juris Khan did not nearly send his people to the sanctuary of Heaven . . . but instead all but condemned them to *Hell*."

The news did not surprise Captain Dumon nearly as much as it once might have. Such an answer would explain much of what they had confronted and certainly explained how he had felt simply staring into the eyes of Khan's interpretation of the mysterious archangel.

Zayl peered around carefully, almost as if he expected other ears to be listening on the godforsaken ridge. "This is my thought. In the days when Ureh stood above all others as a symbol of purity, that which spellcasters and priests knowledgeable called the Sin War took place. Little is known about its true form, but the powers of darkness were most active then, and such a place as the holy kingdom suffered many insidious attacks. Some of the legends you know hint of this, but hardly explain the full depth of the danger present to the mortal world back then."

"Demons attacked Ureh?" Gorst asked, his brow furrowing deeply at such a monstrous notion.

"Not as an army, but rather as forces seeking to corrupt those within. Generations of rulers worked endlessly to keep the corruption out, to protect the innocents from the Prime Evils . . ." The necromancer suddenly knelt and began drawing symbols on the ridge with his dagger. "Forgive me. I must work while I explain, or else we are all lost . . ."

"What're you doing?"

"Providing us with some protection from the eyes of our host, I hope, captain."

He drew a vast circle, then in the center put in place a series of runes. Although the necromancer appeared quite untouched by the harsh wind, both mercenaries had to continue to press against the mountainside to garner even some minute bit of security.

"Your tale fills many of the gaps in my own," Zayl went on. "I fear that while Juris Khan so carefully guarded his flock, he did not himself remain wary enough of the wolf. I believe that, as you indicated, something taking the semblance of a warrior of Heaven seduced the good ruler into believing that what he did would be best for Ureh. I believe, as you do, that this may very well have been *Diablo* himself!"

"But surely it can't be!" Kentril protested, not wanting to believe that he had seen the truth. "That would be just too outrageous!"

"Hardly. Ureh was the greatest prize of all. It would demand the effort of the greatest of demons. Yes, captain, I think that Diablo came in the form you saw, corrupted Lord Khan without him realizing that fact, and twisted everything good the man desired into worse and worse evil. Instead of

Heaven, he would have sent them to Hell, and only the timely action of Gregus Mazi prevented that. However, even limbo could not save them forever . . ."

Diablo, so the spellcaster suspected, had managed at last to touch once more the mind of his pawn. Slowly, he had made Juris Khan give both his people and his daughter to the demon lord. Ureh had become a corrupt nightmare, where the few who had perhaps resisted had become sacrifices or worse.

But the Lord of Terror had not been satisfied yet. Perhaps it had initially occurred to him when Ureh had first momentarily returned to the mortal world. Perhaps then Diablo had seen the opportunity for a true gateway through which his evil hordes could spread out into the world, unchecked by any barrier whatsoever.

"But Diablo required blood, untainted blood, to do this. Unfortunately, in his madness, Juris Khan had slain all other available spellcasters. He needed someone to aid him, someone of knowledge and skill. By either chance or fate, your party provided him with both."

"But you rescued me. We've stopped him."

Zayl arose, his solemn gaze meeting the captain's own. "Have we? The spell seemed quite advanced when I finally reached you."

"But he never drew any blood from me."

The necromancer nodded, but clearly took no comfort from that fact. "He still has Master Tsin."

Kentril gaped. Tsin had become Lord Khan's puppet, but, like the mercenaries, he had not been touched by either the original spell upon Ureh or its subsequent corruption. "But is that possible? Won't they need him for the rest of the work?"

"The Vizjerei has aided them in binding the forces that they need. It would be risky still, but I would not put it past our host and his true master if they grow desperate. Tsin's blood will do, if necessary."

Then, even though he had been rescued, Kentril and his companions had still failed. They had left behind them a demon-corrupted kingdom that would soon no longer be trapped under the shroud created by the mountain's shadow.

And when that happened, the horrors that had been visited upon Kentril would be delivered unto the rest of the world.

"No . . ."

"No, indeed," agreed the pale figure. "But I believe there is still a chance to prevent this horrific thing from coming to pass, a chance to send Ureh to its long-overdue and proper rest."

"But how? If Tsin's blood is already spilled, doesn't that mean that the city's already a part of our world again?"

"In order to work, the spell must be tied into the two Keys. It is my suspicion that they must still be in place when the sun touches the one atop this peak. Only then will the spell of blood tie itself to darkness and light and grant those within Ureh the ability to step freely beyond the shadow."

Gorst put the matter into simpler terms. "If the stones're in place, the demons can go free. If they're not, then Ureh turns back into ruins."

"Correct . . . but if the latter occurs, this time it will be permanent."

That made their path quite clear to Kentril. "Then use your sorcery to transport us to one of the Keys. We smash it, and all's done."

"Alas, captain, that would be unwise. I tried to use the power of the runes to send us to your original encampment, just beyond the shadow, but"—he spread his hands—"you can see where we ended up."

"So what do we do, then?"

Zayl toyed with the knife. "I have not entirely given up on using the vestiges of the power I usurped from the runes to transport us at least part of the way. I believe I can send you and Gorst near enough to the Key to Light to give you a chance. In the meantime, I will descend toward the Key to Shadow. One of us may succeed. That is all we need to do to stop this horror from expanding beyond Ureh."

That plan had been tried before, though, and for Gregus Mazi and the priest Tobio, it had failed miserably. Kentril pointed that out.

The necromancer, however, had an answer ready. With a grim smile, he explained, "I shall make myself much more noticeable. I suspect that Juris Khan will believe me the greater threat because of my skills. Besides that, he will have every reason to believe we all travel together."

"Illusion?" It hardly seemed likely to Kentril that Khan would fall for so simple a spell.

"Hardly. Captain . . . may I have a bit of your blood?"

After nearly having had it spilled already, the mercenary was surprised by the question. Still, he felt he could trust Zayl, especially under the circumstances. The man had saved his life.

Kentril thrust his hand forward, palm up.

Nodding, the necromancer reached forward with his blade, at the same time saying, "You, too, Gorst."

The giant obeyed with less trepidation, likely because of Kentril's own decision. Zayl pricked the forefinger of each, then had the pair turn their palms down.

Spots of blood stained the ridge. The ebony-clad spellcaster waited until each fighter had lost three drops, then ordered the two to step back.

He whispered for several seconds, waving one hand over the stained areas. Then, to both mercenaries' astonishment, Zayl pricked his own finger, carefully letting three drops fall upon each set.

"Under other circumstances, I would cast this in an entirely different way," he commented. "But this will have to do."

Again, he muttered under his breath. Kentril could see the strain in the necromancer's face and understood then that what Zayl sought to accomplish opposed everything he had been taught.

Suddenly, the ground before the captain began to rise up. A few inches at first, then more and more, in less than a minute the mound of rock and earth growing to half the size of a man and getting larger by the second. The taller the mound grew, the more it also took a defined shape. Arms sprouted from the sides, and from the arms grew individual fingers, then entire hands.

As the first mound rose, a second did the same next to it. This one outpaced even the first, quickly rising to become as tall as Gorst. In fact, the more Kentril studied it, the more it outwardly resembled a carving of the giant. Legs formed, and the outline of a torso developed. Even the thick mane of hair began to sprout forth.

And before the astounded eyes of the fighters, their very twins came into being.

The new Kentril and Gorst stood as still as the rock from which they had been born. Only the eyes blinked, but they did so at a uniform pace, not randomly like living people.

"A variation on the golem spells," Zayl told his friends. "Not an experiment to be tried first under such conditions, but at least it worked."

Gazing at his own face, Kentril asked, "Can they talk?"

"They have no true minds of their own. They can perform basic functions, such as walk and, to a point, fight, but that is it. Enough, though, I think, to keep the eyes of Juris Khan upon me until you reach the Key to Light."

"Zayl, you're setting yourself up to be a decoy—and not the type that usually survives the hunt!"

The necromancer's expression remained guarded. "I present us with our best odds, captain."

He obviously would not be talked out of it, and, in fact, Kentril could think of no good reason to turn down his plan. In truth, Zayl had more of a chance against Khan than either of the nonmagical fighters.

"We have taken enough chance here," Zayl went on. "I must send you away before he finally discovers where we are. I believe only because we did not end up where I expected did we avoid instant pursuit."

Once more, the necromancer focused his powers on the two. Kentril stood close to Gorst and tried to prepare himself for the sorcerous journey. That Zayl's last attempt had gone awry did not ease his mind about this second try. For all they knew, the mercenaries might end up dangling from the top tower of Khan's palace.

"May the Dragon watch over you," the spellcaster quietly called.

Zayl and the ridge vanished.

Juris Khan stared at the place where Kentril Dumon had been, stared at it in both pious anger and disappointment. The dark one had to be at fault for this, the foul necromancer he had been forced to accept as a guest in order to maintain appearances. It had disturbed him even to allow such a dealer in the magic of corpses to enter his beloved city, but he had forced himself to smile whenever Zayl had been near.

And now this was how the necromancer had repaid him.

"What in blazes?" spouted Quov Tsin. "What happened?"

"A misunderstanding," Khan returned. "A foolish misunderstanding."

Atanna had a look of intense disappointment on her face, something that only deepened the monarch of Ureh's fury at the unclean Zayl. "My Kentril!" she cried. "Father! My Kentril!"

He put a calming hand on her soft shoulder. "Calm yourself, my beloved daughter. The good captain will be returned to us. We may have to perform a different rite on him to make him ready for you, but rest assured, it'll happen."

"But what of Dumon?" the Vizjerei demanded. "Where did he go?"

"It appears I underestimated this Zayl. Not only did he see past the magical variation of this chamber I had long ago cast, but he used it to his advantage, reaching out from the other reality into this one and taking the captain with him."

"What of the spell, though? What of that?"

Lord Khan gazed thoughtfully at the sorcerer, but directed his words to his daughter. "Yes, what of that? Atanna, my darling, has our work been completely ruined?"

"Of course not, Father! I would never let you down like that. How could you even ask such a thing?"

"Of course, of course! My sincerest apologies, Atanna." He chuckled. The tall robed figure stepped within an arm's length of Quov Tsin. "And to you, too, Master Tsin."

The diminutive sorcerer squinted. "Apologies? For what, my lord?"

"For what I must do now." With shocking strength, Juris Khan seized the short Vizjerei and flung him atop the platform.

"My lord—"

"Know that your sacrifice will allow my children to spread across every land and open the way of Heaven to this benighted world!"

Tsin's mouth opened in preparation of a spell. Every rune upon his robe flared bright. The elderly sorcerer even sought to stave off Khan with his stick-thin arms.

None of his defenses, either magical or mundane, aided him against the power wielded by Juris Khan. With a prayer to the great archangel Mirakodus, Lord Khan drove the dagger into the Vizjerei's bony chest.

Tsin's eyes bulged. He gasped for breath but found none. His hands slid from the robes of the monarch, at last falling limply.

Blood spilled from the deep wound, racing over the garments and at last falling upon the platform.

A crackle of lightning shot up from the body of Quov Tsin, forcing Lord Khan back. More bolts quickly followed, creating an epic battle of forces in play directly over the corpse.

The master of the holy city fell to one knee in supplication. "Great Mirakodus, hear my humble plea! Let the world of mortal men be ours once again!"

A tremor shook the entire palace, but did not at all frighten Juris Khan. A sense of displacement swept over him, and momentarily he saw a hundred different variations of his surroundings. At last, however, they all began to merge, finally coalescing once more into the version with which he was most familiar.

The spell had succeeded. The soul and body of Ureh had been united again. The Light among Lights once more shone brightly on the mortal plane . . .

And all he needed to make it perfect was for the sun, only a scant time away from rising, to let its glory touch the Key atop Nymyr. That would seal the spell in place, remove the last impediment—

But no . . . there existed one more impediment, for surely the necromancer would attempt to stop him. Surely the corrupted one would persuade his friends to try to steal or destroy the stones, just as Gregus had convinced poor Tobio.

Zayl had to be removed. Without him, Kentril would return to the fold. The giant Gorst seemed an innocent, but if he could not be turned back to the light, then Lord Khan would have to remove him also.

"*Shakarak!*" A fiery ball materialized before him. Khan muttered another word of power, and the center of the burning sphere suddenly grew transparent.

The face of Zayl appeared.

"*Shakarog!*" The image backed away, revealing more and more of the pale necromancer and his surroundings. Juris Khan looked upon the corrupted figure with loathing. Hardly any color in his flesh and clad in clothes almost entirely as black as his heart. Truly an instrument of Hell, not Heaven. The archangel would have immediately commanded him destroyed for the good of all.

A second figure appeared behind Zayl.

Captain Kentril Dumon.

"So," he whispered to himself, "unlike Gregus and Tobio, these choose to travel together, the better to concentrate their efforts. A pity that it'll avail them nothing."

Atanna stepped up beside him, one delicate hand stretched out toward the mercenary captain.

"Kentril . . ." she cooed.

"I shall bring him back for you, my darling." He did not add that he would do so only if it did not prove necessary to slay the man. The spell that would have given his daughter the perfect mate could no longer be cast, and although

Lord Khan had promised her that Captain Dumon would yet be hers, more and more he realized how difficult that might be.

Still, he would try . . . but first he had to distract her, lest she wish to come with him. It would not do for her to see the captain slain, should that prove necessary.

"Atanna, my darling, I see no sign of the large one, the one called Gorst. I need you to keep watch on the Key to Light, make certain that he doesn't climb up and try to take it before sunrise. Understood?"

Fortunately, she had not heard what he had said about the group traveling together, nor did she see, as he briefly had, that the giant followed behind his fellow mercenary. "But I want to go to Kentril—"

"He would only become more confused, possibly even injure himself because of that. You know how torn he was. The necromancer will surely have turned his mind wrong for the moment."

Atanna obviously still wished to go, but she nodded her head nonetheless. "All right, Father . . ."

"Wonderful!" He gave her a hug, then kissed her forehead. "Now, be off with you. Soon we'll have this all sorted out, and the good Captain Dumon will be yours again."

"As you wish." She smiled, kissed him on the cheek, and vanished.

Any pleasantry vanished with his daughter. Grimly, Juris Khan glared at the figures wending their way down toward the Key to Shadow. They had condemned themselves with this sinful action, just as Gregus had. He would smite them down, even Atanna's beloved, if necessary. Their wicked deeds could not go unpunished.

Still, fairness dictated that he pray for the sinners even as he prepared to slay them. Just as he had done with Gregus and Tobio, Lord Khan whispered a few words, then ended with the phrase that always most brought him comfort.

"May the Archangel Mirakodus take up your souls."

And with a satisfied smile, he went to send the three to their final rewards.

Twenty-one

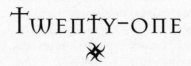

With the last of the power he had drawn from Juris Khan's sanctum, Zayl had managed to send himself and the golems to the very cavern in which he had so recently been imprisoned. The necromancer had dared not attempt another, similar spell, such magic risky at best and, under the circumstances, more foolhardy than helpful. From here on, it had to be with the aid of spells he knew well, no matter how that might limit him in the long run.

In truth, the necromancer did not expect to reach his goal unhindered—or possibly to reach it at all. Captain Dumon had suspected the truth; Zayl fully intended to sacrifice himself if it meant that the two mercenaries would manage to reach their own goal. Only one Key had to be removed before the sun rose, and the one atop Nymyr would serve as well as any.

Zayl had done everything he could to draw the attention of their foe, leaving a trail of sorcerous residue any competent wielder of power would notice, much less trace. That alone might not perhaps have sufficed, but the necromancer's companions surely erased any chance that Khan might turn his gaze elsewhere. Surely with his might, the ruler of Ureh would seek out his prey, beginning with the so-simply-detected spellwork of Zayl, then, through the arts, divining that the Rathmian did not travel alone.

The other two followed docilely along, almost like puppies trailing their mother. They wore determined expressions, but only because Zayl desired such from them. It would not do for Juris Khan to arrive only to see that the two fighters stared like empty-minded zombies. That would give away the truth much sooner than Zayl hoped. Every second extra granted to the captain and his comrade meant greater hope of success.

With the aid of a makeshift version of his original magical strand of rope, they quickly descended deep into the mountain's belly. The necromancer led each segment, showing the golems how it had to be done. Tied to his blood, they could repeat his actions exactly. The only danger other than their adversary remained any need for independent action. If they had to act for themselves, they risked falling and shattering.

"Are you sure of this?" asked Humbart as they drew nearer and nearer to their goal. "Maybe he went after them instead."

That had occurred to Zayl early on, but the pale spellcaster had not wanted to speak of such a disastrous turn of events. "He would surely come after me first, for fear that with my skills I would be the most logical threat."

"Aye, but logic might not have much to do with it, eh?"

"We shall hope for the best, Humbart."

The skull did not reply to that, answer enough in many ways.

Yet the deeper they descended, the more the concern grew. Had Lord Khan ignored the obvious and instead discovered the trail of the mercenaries? Had he recognized the necromancer's ploy with the golems from the very start? Question after question, uncertainty after uncertainty, plagued Zayl as they had never done in his entire life.

At last, they reached the level at which the enchanted crystal could be found. Keeping his dagger ready at all times, Zayl guided the golems along. The constructs had weapons identical to those of the men they had been designed to emulate, although these weapons had actually been forged from the same rock used to mold the bodies. How strong those would prove in combat, the spellcaster could not say. Again, all he hoped for was enough of a delay to give the others time to fulfill their own mission.

Nearer and nearer they drew, and still nothing impeded their progress. The slight frown that had early on creased Zayl's mouth deepened with each step. Already he noticed ahead the peculiar illumination radiating from the Key to Shadow's lair. So close, and still no sign that Juris Khan had pursued him. Would it be the necromancer who succeeded and the mercenaries who paid the ultimate sacrifice?

He paused. After a moment's thought, Zayl indicated that the Gorst golem should take the lead.

The massive figure stepped forward, ax in hand in much the same manner as the true Gorst would have held it. Every movement spoke of the fighter, a sign of how well the necromancer's quick spell had worked.

The false Gorst stepped into the very edge of the Key's unsettling light. He readied his weapon.

Nothing happened. The golem turned to Zayl, awaiting orders.

A howling form materialized over the construct, falling upon him.

The necromancer had never seen such demonic figures before, but he recognized well Captain Dumon's description of the ghoulish creatures that had been all that remained of Ureh's once-pious inhabitants. The dry husk of a body, the gaping, rounded mouth filled with edged teeth, the soulless black holes where the eyes should have been—even versed as Zayl was in the arts of dealing with the dead and undead, the corrupted humans of the fabled kingdom left him shuddering.

As the golem struggled with his monstrous foe, a second and third materialized around him. Zayl started forward, only to have another fiend leap out of the rocky wall and attack.

Under strands of loose hair, a face out of nightmare stared hungrily at the necromancer. The tattered remnants of a once seductive emerald dress barely clothed the shriveled, cadaverous form.

"*Kiss me,*" it croaked. "*Come enjoy my caresses . . .*"

Again, Zayl shuddered in open fear. Acting more on reflex than anything, he thrust.

To his surprise, the blade sank readily into the ghoul's throat.

The dagger flashed brightly as it dug into the dry flesh. The abomination let out a gasp that almost sounded relieved. For good measure, Zayl twisted the magical weapon, uttering a few quick words.

The throat wound flared. As the necromancer removed the blade, the flaring intensified, quickly overwhelming the macabre figure. The creature fell against the wall, curling into a fetal position. In but the blink of an eye, the entire body lay bathed in the furious brightness, the already shriveled form shrinking ever more in on itself.

Zayl watched a moment longer in order to assure himself that soon there would be nothing at all remaining. He then turned to face those already attacking the first golem and found that not only had their numbers trebled, but now they attacked from both ends.

He had been surrounded.

The golems did their best to hold the horrific band at bay, both fighting with the mechanical skill that they had inherited from the true mercenaries. The false Gorst chopped off the arm of one ghoul, while his counterpart ran another through the chest. Unfortunately, although both warriors were the products of sorcery, their weapons lacked the magical abilities inherent in the spellcaster's blade. True, with enough effort and time, they might be able to hack their foes to pieces, but the numbers and circumstances did not offer that as a likely hope.

That left matters to Zayl's skills.

In such tight quarters, he dared not use either the Talons or the Teeth of Trag'Oul, especially with Juris Khan no doubt lurking near, preparing to strike. Still, perhaps something similar . . .

Glancing quickly over his shoulder, Zayl cast the spell.

From both walls, the ceiling, and even the floor erupted thick bars of ivory, bars of actual *bone*. One of the demonic attackers collided with the barrier as it arose. Under a silent command from Zayl, the Kentril golem fell back just in time, barely avoiding being caught with the oncoming fiends.

Composed of the bones of a thousand different long-dead creatures, the wall very efficiently barred the ghouls' way. The gaping mouths snapped open and closed, and twisted, dried fingers madly but vainly sought the necromancer. With demonic fury, they struggled to get past his work, but, at least for the time being, the defensive wall held.

Yet for how long he could not say. Quickly turning back to those swarming around the Gorst golem, Zayl cast another spell. With the dagger, he drew a pair of curving lines in the air, at the same time reciting.

Two of the monstrous attackers had slipped past the construct, but they managed to come only a few feet toward the necromancer before the spell affected them. With almost human screams, they abruptly cringed, then swiftly backed away. Beyond them, those that had continued to fight the golem likewise suddenly cowered in outright fear.

One turned, fleeing into the darkened passage beyond. That caused the rest of the ranks to break, creating a scene both horrific and saddening. Each of these horrors had once been human, and in some ways Zayl regretted everything he had just been forced to do to them. They had not been at fault. Rather, they had been betrayed by the one they had most trusted, most revered.

Lord Juris Khan.

With the golems keeping guard, Zayl pushed on to the chamber of the Key. Whether or not he or his companions survived, at least one of the crystals had to be removed or shattered. If it proved necessary that this be the one, the necromancer would not falter.

And there it stood, exactly as he had seen it last. Beyond it, the dead form of Gregus Mazi still hung above, *his* nightmare, at least, at an end.

Keeping vigilant, Zayl started toward the Key. The rotting bodies of the winged fiends he and the others had slain previously lay all about, but no new danger reared its ugly head. Closer and closer the necromancer got to the dark crystal. His fingers came within inches—

A crackling sound drove him back, Zayl's first clue that the ceiling had begun to collapse. He looked up, saw no sign of any fissure or falling bits of rock, yet the harsh crackling sound continued.

Something farther back in the chamber moved.

The necromancer's eyes widened.

With movements akin to those of a marionette, Gregus Mazi tore himself free of his centuries-old prison.

But as Zayl stared into the eyes, he knew that Mazi himself had not stirred to life. The sorcerer had indeed perished earlier . . . but now his corpse moved at the will of the mad Juris Khan.

Body glittering from the many crystalline deposits covering it, the undead figure stretched out a crusted hand toward Zayl, who immediately stepped farther out of reach.

The hand suddenly shot forth, growing larger and longer as it neared.

The necromancer reacted too slowly. The elongated fingers wrapped completely around him, squeezing him tight much as the stone ones had done in the tunnel.

However, in contrast to that nearly fatal struggle, Zayl did not this time have to rely on himself alone. The golems, attuned to his will, strode into the chamber, weapons raised for battle.

The stalactite man thrust forward with his other hand, seeking to do with the false Kentril as he had done with Zayl. Commanded by the necromancer, the golem countered the assault with a swing of his blade. A good chunk of the outstretched hand dropped to the floor . . . but so did a part of the construct's blade.

"*Surrender to your fates,*" Gregus Mazi uttered. "*Repent your sins, and the archangel may yet accept you . . .*"

The mouth might have belonged to the resurrected sorcerer, but the voice and words truly could only be those of Ureh's mad monarch.

"*Kentril Dumon, my good captain,*" the macabre figure continued, the blank eyes fixing on the false mercenary, "*throw off the shackles of doubt and deceit forced on you by this corrupted soul! Immortality with Atanna awaits you . . .*"

Despite his predicament, Zayl's hopes rose. In those few lines, Lord Khan had revealed that he believed the construct to be the true captain. That meant that he had not noticed the two mercenaries climbing Nymyr. Even if Zayl perished, the chance still existed that Captain Dumon and Gorst could put an end to the threat posed by this city of the damned.

The Kentril golem did not answer, of course, that ability well beyond the necromancer's skills. Instead, he struck again at the reaching hand, chipping off one of its fingers but losing more of the sword as well.

Apparently seeing through the eyes of his undead puppet, Khan had not so far noticed anything odd about the golem, not even the peculiarity of the sword. The longer Zayl could distract him, the better.

"Captain Dumon listens only to me, my lord," the spellcaster retorted, putting as much condescension in his voice as possible. "So long as I live, his will is mine!"

"Then for the sake of his soul—and yours, even—you must die, necromancer!"

But although he expected to do just that, Zayl had no intention of falling prey to his adversary so easily. Juris Khan's interest in the captain had bought him necessary seconds in which to plan. The spell risked his own life, but if it succeeded, then Khan himself would have to take the stage.

He pictured a starburst in his mind, then overlaid it upon the crystalline form once inhabited by Gregus Mazi. With what air still existed in his lungs, Zayl shouted out a single word of power.

Gregus Mazi exploded.

The force of the explosion sent Zayl flying backward into the Kentril golem. A torrent of rocky missiles assailed the necromancer and his two puppets. The entire chamber shook, and the stalactite that had held Mazi for so long plummeted to the floor, impaling the earth there.

Zayl struck his head hard, becoming momentarily dazed. Rocks continued to pelt him, forcing the necromancer to cover his face with his arm. He had cast a variation of a spell that caused the corpse of one who had died violently to unleash in an awful explosion the anguish sealed in the body during its last terrible moments of life. Unfortunately, although Zayl had tried hard to focus the direction of that explosion, the size of the chamber had made it impossible for him to avoid some backlash.

With effort, the stunned necromancer rose to his feet. Neither golem moved to assist him, not having been told to do so. Zayl looked them over quickly, assessing the situation. Up close, he could see the damage that they, unprotected by any wards, had taken. Portions of each face had been completely obliterated, and chunks of rock had been broken off from the torso and limbs. Several vicious cracks now spread across both figures, hinting of further instability.

"There are no depths of evil to which you'll hesitate to go, are there, necromancer?"

Zayl quickly turned to the Key to Shadow—and, behind it, the sanctimonious face of Juris Khan.

The robed monarch gazed down fondly at the crystal, even placing his hands upon it as one might a favored child. Illuminated by the peculiar dark light, Lord Khan looked as monstrous as the creatures his people had become.

"To take a man's body, to destroy the house in which his soul had resided so crassly, so without care . . . truly your corruption is irrevocable!"

It proved tempting to remind the robed figure that he had seen no fault in seizing control of Gregus Mazi's corpse for himself, but Zayl suspected that

Juris Khan would have a ready rationalization for anything he did. In his own mind, however the lord of Ureh acted, he did so with the blessing of this not-so-Heavenly archangel of which he always spoke.

"I'm afraid," Zayl's former host went on, "that, for your soul, there is only the pits of Hell." His eyes began to shift to the Kentril golem. "But for the good captain and his friend, perhaps there might still be some hope . . ."

In the dim light, Khan had obviously not yet noticed the flaws and breaks in the two figures. Realizing that he still had a chance to stall the other a little longer, Zayl immediately leapt forward, brandishing the gleaming dagger.

"If I am going to the pits of Hell, then I shall take you with me!" he shouted.

Juris Khan reacted exactly as he had hoped, turning away from the constructs and focusing all his attention on the necromancer.

A wave of black light erupted from the Key, striking at Zayl.

He barely raised a magical shield in time. Still, the force with which the dark light hit sent the spellcaster flying against the wall. Zayl let out a scream as the pain of the collision jarred every bone in his body.

"Captain Dumon," the robed figure called out, "step away from him. Come to me. Atanna awaits you."

The golem, of course, did not move.

Leaning forward, face contorted with effort, Lord Khan repeated himself. "Step away from him. Come to me! Atanna—"

And as Zayl struggled once more to his feet, his head pounding and his legs almost ready to buckle again, Atanna's father realized the trick that had been played on him.

"Homunculi!" Khan shouted. Raising one hand, he pointed at the one resembling Captain Dumon.

The golem trembled. It took one step forward, only to leave the bottom half of its leg behind. The lack of balance quickly assailed the necromancer's creation, and it tipped forward. However, even before it could crash to the floor, the arms, the other leg, even the head, broke off, scattering in different directions.

Lord Khan formed a fist.

The golem lost any last semblance to the form of a man. A pile of fine dirt and crushed rock spilled over the chamber floor, the only remnants of Zayl's cleverly made puppet.

Zayl had not thought it possible for his adversary's countenance to grow any more grim, but the expression Juris Khan wore now caused even the stalwart spellcaster to regret standing so near.

"The mountaintop . . ." Lord Khan stared at Zayl with utter loathing. "They're climbing to the top of Nymyr!"

"M-maybe you should go after them. I shall w-watch the Key to Shadow for you."

"Do not taunt me! By the archangel, you *are* a thing of evil!"

The necromancer felt his strength returning, albeit slowly. If he could hold on to Khan's attention a little longer, then the mercenaries would succeed. "The only evil is the one you yourself let into Ureh, Lord Khan! You have succeeded in doing what demons and duped summoners failed to do for centuries. *You* brought eternal damnation to the holy kingdom. *You* corrupted your beloved people!"

"How . . . dare . . . you?"

Again, the wave of black light burst out of the crystal, but this time Zayl was better prepared for it. The attack pushed him against the wall, even made it hard for the struggling spellcaster to breathe, but it did not batter him as before.

Under his guidance, the remaining golem suddenly charged forward, swinging the stone ax at both Juris Khan and the stone.

Lord Khan redirected his power at the oncoming figure, beating at the false Gorst and sending fragments flying everywhere. The stone giant stumbled, but pressed on, driven toward his goal by the will of Zayl.

Forced to deal with two foes at once, Khan's effort against the necromancer himself flagged ever so slightly. It proved all Zayl needed not only to brace himself better, but to counterattack.

He did not seek out the elder monarch, however, but rather the Key to Shadow. Zayl did not know if he had any hope of destroying the artifact. If he managed even to damage it, so much the better. His greatest concern continued to be the success of Captain Dumon and Gorst. A servant of Rathma devoted his life to the struggle to maintain the balance; if Zayl had to give his now, it would only be his duty.

He sent forth the Teeth of Trag'Oul, hoping that one of the missiles would hit its mark.

Juris Khan waved his hand, and a shield of gleaming silver protected the Key from the horrendous rain of projectiles. The bony missiles went clattering in a hundred other directions, some of them even turning back upon the necromancer.

Gritting his teeth, Zayl dismissed the projectiles. As he did, his last golem finally crumbled, the Teeth finishing what Khan had begun.

"Spawn of Diablo!" The towering lord stepped in front of the protected crystal, seeming to grow even larger in the process. His eyes burned as red as those of any demon, an irony considering his opinion of the necromancer. Corrupted so thoroughly by the darkest of the Prime Evils, Juris Khan could not even see his own damnation. "Enslaver of souls! Accept your eternal punishment!"

"Would that punishment involve having to listen to more of your preaching, my lord?" Zayl taunted. His best weapon so far had not been any of his spells or even his golems. Words seemed to affect Juris Khan more than all else, especially those that placed him in anything other than the pious light he shone upon himself.

But this time, Ureh's master did not react as the spellcaster had supposed he would. Instead, Lord Khan shook his head in mock pity and replied, "Misguided fool. The evil that corrupts you makes you underestimate the powers of light. I know what you try, and I know why you try it!"

"I try it in order to keep you from continuing to assail my ears with your incessant sermonizing."

Again, Juris Khan did not rise to the bait. He chuckled quietly, looking down upon Zayl as if the necromancer were little more than a flea-bitten hound. "The last, desperate weapon of a defeated scoundrel. Your puppets served you better, Master Zayl, for they, at least, fooled me for a short time."

"They only needed to draw you here," countered the necromancer, "where I waited."

"And you think that you'll keep me here, occupy my time while your companions seek to reach the other Key. Did you believe I'd leave it unattended? Atanna watches over it; she will see when the mercenaries come, and she will do what is right."

Zayl allowed himself a slight smile. "Even against Kentril Dumon?"

Now, at last, he had caught Juris Khan's attention. "Atanna will see to it that he doesn't remove or damage the crystal. That is all she needs to do."

"She wants the captain, my lord. She wants him badly. Your daughter may be persuaded by her desire—her love, even?—to hesitate. That may be all he needs."

"Atanna knows her duty," the elder man countered, but his expression hinted otherwise. "She'll not betray the work of the archangel!"

As he spoke, Khan's hands suddenly crackled with energy. Zayl saw that the time for talk had passed; now, if he hoped to give the captain and Gorst any chance of success, the necromancer had to fight with all his might.

"It is time to confess your sins and ask absolution, necromancer," Juris Khan boomed, his face lit up madly by the powers he summoned. "And fear not for Atanna's heart. She is, after all, her father's daughter . . . and she will do what must be done even if it means utterly destroying *Kentril Dumon*!"

The high winds and fierce chill did not in any way touch the crimson-haired enchantress as she searched the darkened mountainside for the giant, Gorst. From her momentary perch atop a narrow, precarious ledge, she surveyed the rock face with eyes that saw in the dark almost as well as a cat's, seeking out the telltale signs of movement.

Only one other thought distracted her, burrowed into her mind with the savage intensity of a hungry leech. She knew that her father had promised not to harm her darling Kentril, but accidents did happen. In his misguided belief that the necromancer spoke truly, Kentril might sacrifice himself for the dour, pale figure. That would very much upset Atanna.

Seeing nothing out of the ordinary, she transported herself to another location. Atanna hoped to stay clear of the near-top of the mountain peak, even the night sky no protection. Only the black shadow, the comforting shadow, shielded her from a horrific fate that even the archangel's gift could not prevent.

Her concerns vanished in an instant as she immediately noticed a distant form below. It had to be the giant. Atanna prepared to move closer, the better to ensure that her strike would prove fatal the first time. For the sake of her Kentril, she would make his friend's death a swift one—

A second, smaller figure moved into sight.

"No!" she gasped. It could not be Zayl, whom she had seen in her father's vision, but neither could it be *Kentril*. He had been with the necromancer. How could he be here?

She would have to stop them. She would have to keep them from reaching the Key to Light. A simple spell would destroy the part of the mountain on which they climbed . . . and would *kill* Kentril.

Atanna could not do that. There had to be another way to stop them. Yet any attempt to block their path by destroying part of the mountain would also likely slay them.

"I cannot do it," she muttered. Yet to stand idly by would mean betrayal not only of her father, but also of the glorious archangel, Mirakodus.

Thinking of the archangel brought both love and fear to Atanna. She thought of his wondrous gifts yet also recalled with fear what had happened when he had entered her mind and soul. Atanna never wanted to go through that again. The memory still scarred her soul.

She prayed for an answer, and almost instantly her prayer seemed granted as an idea blossomed. Atanna could not raise a hand against her beloved, but neither could she betray all her father had sought. Therefore, she would have to place a challenge before her Kentril, a challenge that would prove whether or not he had truly been worthy from the start. Surely her father and the archangel would see the fairness of that. Surely they would understand what she did.

And if Kentril did indeed die . . . well, Atanna felt that he, too, would simply have to understand.

Twenty-two

✶

It had occurred too late to Kentril that he and Gorst would be at a great disadvantage when they attempted to climb Nymyr. When last they had done so, it had been with torches to guide them through the dark. The captain had only recalled that fact just as Zayl's spell had taken effect, but by then, the chamber and the necromancer had already faded away.

To his surprise, however, Zayl had evidently considered the problem, too, and dealt with it. Upon materializing on the mountainside, Kentril immediately noticed that the utter darkness of the shadow had given way to a deep gray, which enabled the mercenary to see at least some distance in every direction. Gorst, too, had gained this ability. The spellcaster clearly could not have altered the essence of the shadow itself, which meant that he had instead granted his companions a crude form of night vision.

Unfortunately, that gift had also shown them that Zayl had not been able to send them as near to the Key as they all might have wished. The two fighters had been left with quite a climb.

"We're probably gonna need some rope along the way," Gorst muttered.

Another thing Kentril had not gotten to mention prior to the necromancer's spell, and this time one that Zayl had also failed to anticipate. Kentril eyed the path above, trying to find a better route, but the ridge upon which they had been set offered only one direction.

"We'll just have to try, anyway," he finally replied.

Gorst nodded and said no more. If his captain intended to try to make the ascent without equipment, then so would he.

With the utmost caution, they began to wend their way up. Kentril had no way to estimate the hour, but if they suffered few mishaps, he suspected that they could reach the top with some time to spare. Of course, that also depended on whether or not Zayl could keep Juris Khan occupied long enough.

He tried not to think of the necromancer's potential sacrifice. The odds seemed very low that Zayl would survive. Kentril had witnessed the power of their treacherous host too often to believe that. Zayl would do what he could to keep Khan at bay, but sooner or later Ureh's mad monarch would kill the Rathmian.

Kentril could only hope it would be later . . . otherwise, they had all lost.

Up and up they climbed, and still no attack came. The captain had little time to think of much else, but as they drew nearer to the top of the peak, his thoughts went back to Atanna. Despite what she had proven to be, Kentril found some of his earlier memories too precious simply to discard. Perhaps if things had been different, if he had not learned the truth beforehand, he might even have willingly accepted her father's offer of immortality—but then he would have had to live with the results.

Pausing, he took a deep breath and tried to clear his head. It made no sense to keep thinking of Atanna. He had seen the last of her, the last of—

A robed figure stood atop a tiny ledge farther up. Even as distant as the figure was, Kentril could tell that he did not stare at Lord Khan.

"Atanna!" he shouted.

The wind blew dust in his face. Turning away, the mercenary brushed his eyes clear.

When he looked back, the figure had disappeared.

"What was it?" Gorst called from behind. "You see something?"

"I thought I saw—" But Kentril stopped. If it had been Atanna, surely she would have either come closer or destroyed him from the ledge. She would not have simply gone away. That made no sense whatsoever.

"Nothing," he finally answered. "Just my imagination."

They pushed on. Despite constant fears that they would eventually reach some spot that could not be overcome without equipment, the mercenaries' route continued to offer some avenue. Had Zayl somehow managed to send the pair to the easiest area upon which to climb? If so, then he had managed more with what power he had drained from the runes than he had given the fighters to expect.

"We're almost there," Kentril dared finally mutter to his friend. "Almost . . ."

Gorst grunted. *Almost* still meant quite a climb to go.

Reaching up, Captain Dumon seized hold of a promising outcropping, only to have the part he had taken crumble in his hand. Momentarily out of balance, he leaned toward the rock face. At the same time, his gaze went from upward to deep down.

Far below, something that resembled a swarm of ants moved with incredible swiftness up the side of the mountain.

The captain gaped. "Gorst! Can you see that?"

The giant stretched. "I see it. What is it, Kentril?"

"I don't—" So quickly did the shapes move that even in the short time in which the pair had talked of them, they now could be seen with a bit more clarity. They were large, each easily the size of a man and, in general, built like men. They had a grayish tone to them, although he saw bits and pieces of other colors on their backs, their arms, their legs.

Kentril swallowed. "It's Ureh's people. They're coming after us."

He pictured the hundreds of gaping mouths, the withered, cadaverous shells of what had once been human. He imagined those talonlike nails and the hungry faces. The captain could well imagine what had happened to Albord and all the others and understood that now the same fate rushed toward them.

"We have to get to the top, and quick!" But they could only move as fast as their surroundings permitted, and although the pair struggled mightily, it seemed that the voracious horde moved at more than ten times the pace.

The top beckoned yet was still too far up. Exhausted, Kentril and Gorst finally had to pause on a small ridge barely wide enough to accommodate both of them.

Gazing down at their pursuers, Kentril swore. "They climb as if born to the mountain. At this rate, they'll catch us just below our goal."

Gorst nodded. "We can't make it . . . but you can."

Kentril eyed the other. "What does that mean?"

With absolute calm, the giant began freeing his ax, which had hung on his back. "This is the best spot around. I'll hold 'em off here. You go on."

"Don't be a fool, Gorst! If anyone goes up there, it'll be you. I'll hold them off."

The other mercenary shook his head. He stretched one long arm out, the ax extended well beyond it. The weapon would have taken his friend both hands to wield. "You see? I got twice the reach you do, Kentril. We need that. I'm the best choice to stay, and you know it—besides, I owe you for the last time we climbed up here."

"Gorst . . ." Captain Dumon knew better than to continue to argue. Of all the men he had ever met, Gorst had to be the most stubborn. They could have argued until Ureh's abominations overwhelmed them, and still the wild-maned warrior would have stood his ground.

Taking one last glance down, Kentril nodded. "All right—but if you find a chance to save yourself, do it. Don't worry about me."

"I'll do what I can. You better get going."

Kentril put a hand on his friend's shoulder. "May your arm be steady."

"May your weapon be sharp," Gorst returned, finishing the old mercenary litany.

Steeling himself, the captain started up the final leg of the mountain. He pulled himself toward the top, trying not to think of what the giant would face and hoping somehow that they would both get out of the chaos alive. If he could make it to the top before the creatures reached Gorst, perhaps Kentril could yet save him. All he had to do was destroy the Key . . .

The encouraging thought pushed him to renewed effort. Closer and closer he came to the plateau. Rising above it, Kentril could make out the crystal's resting place. Such an irony that he now had to undo what he and his men had struggled so hard to accomplish earlier.

A hissing sound arose below him.

Cursing, Kentril pushed harder. The edge lay just a few yards up. Only a little longer.

Gorst let out a battle cry.

Despite knowing better, the captain had to look.

The giant stood at the edge of his small perch, swinging away with his ax at the first of the demonic creatures to reach him. With little room to maneuver, the abomination could not avoid the attack. The ax bit hard into its head, cutting deep.

The creature let out a horrific sound, then toppled backward off the ledge.

Wasting not a moment, the giant shifted his grip and used the very top of the ax to shove a second adversary off.

Despite those two rapid successes, though, a hundred more moved up, each trying to beat the rest to the lone defender.

Nearly frantic now, Kentril struggled to reach the plateau. However, each yard seemed a mile, and he felt as if he were climbing through molasses.

A very human roar of pain from below shook him to the core and made the fighter look down again.

The ghoulish creatures harried Gorst from every direction. Two had managed to get up on the ledge, and another sought a handhold near the giant's feet. A dozen others maneuvered for position around the lone mercenary.

Gorst landed a strong blow against one ghoul still wearing the battered remains of a breast plate and chain mail. The blade severed the upper part of the fiend's torso, but that upper portion still managed to wrap bony fingers around the upper part of the weapon's shaft.

Although he shook the ax as hard as he could, Gorst could not dislodge the determined ghoul. The effort also hampered his struggles against the others. The second demon leapt onto his back and tried to sink its horrific mouth into Gorst's neck.

Spinning around, the giant threw his ax down upon the one seeking a handhold. Both that creature and the one still clinging to the weapon plunged earthward, taking the ax with them.

Now unarmed, Gorst reached back and seized the monster latched onto his back. Unfortunately, it would not be as easily removed as the others, and while Gorst battled with it, four more made their way up to him.

Kentril continued his ascent, but with each step, his gaze flashed back to his friend. When next he glanced, it was to see the giant now hampered by *three* of the horrors, with more only seconds away. Gorst's shoulders were stained with blood, and despite his strength, he clearly had trouble standing.

The captain nearly turned back, thinking for a second that if he joined the other fighter, they could hold off the entire horde. However, common sense quickly pointed out the futility of his thought. Gorst had remained behind to give Kentril time to do what had to be done. To turn back now would be to waste the other mercenary's sacrifice.

Sacrifice . . . only now did the essence of that word truly sink in.

At that moment, Gorst let out a battle cry so loud it echoed well beyond Nymyr. As if his strength had suddenly been renewed by some magical means, the massive fighter straightened, raising one of his fiendish foes into the air. By this time, at least half a dozen more of Juris Khan's monstrous children had fastened themselves onto him, each ripping at his flesh, tearing away at his life.

Still roaring, Gorst suddenly charged forward.

"No!" shouted Kentril, his plea repeated over and over again by the mountains.

The giant leapt off the ledge.

Unable to let go in time, his many attackers fell with him. Gorst's leap, far less athletic than Captain Dumon knew the mercenary capable of, barely enabled the wild-maned fighter to clear his perch. However, Gorst had obviously had that very thing in mind, for as he dropped, he crashed into one climbing abomination after another, creating, in the process, an avalanche of monstrous forms raining down upon the shadowed kingdom.

"Gorst . . ." Kentril could not tear his eyes away from the dwindling figure.

Gorst had been with the captain longer than anyone. The giant had seemed invincible, unstoppable . . .

Tears struggled to be free, but Kentril could not let them come. Taking a deep breath, he looked away and began pulling himself up again, Gorst's last victorious charge burned into his imagination. The sun could not be long in rising. Kentril had to make certain that he had not just let his friend, *all* his men, die in vain.

Nearer and nearer he drew to the top . . . and below him, the horde closed the gap more quickly.

Zayl screamed, and not for the first time. He screamed loud and long, but he did not give in. His clothes were in tatters, and every inch of his body seemed to be either covered in blood or pounding in agony, but he did not surrender.

Yet neither had he come an inch closer to the Key to Shadow.

Seemingly untouched by every one of the powerful spells Zayl had tossed at him, Juris Khan approached the battered, half-dead figure. "Your determination, if not your cause, is quite admirable, necromancer. A shame that your corrupted soul shall be lost to Diablo forever."

". . . As yours is? . . ."

"Even until the end you persist in trying to twist matters, eh?" Lord Khan shook his head in a most paternal manner, something that all of Zayl's good training could not keep from greatly irritating the necromancer.

"Your blessed archangel is Diablo himself, can you not see that?"

But Ureh's monarch could not, so thoroughly had the demon done his work. Zayl even understood how it had happened, for Juris Khan clearly had been greatly full of pride in himself. He had been lord of the holiest of kingdoms, the symbol of piety and goodness, and because of that, he had not been able to comprehend that the most evil and cunning of demons had played him for a fool.

A *powerful* fool, however. He had taken everything that Zayl could thrust at him, taken it and shrugged it off. Little more remained to the necromancer save his dagger, which might have done him some good if he could have distracted his foe somehow. At least then, Zayl could have tried to circumvent Khan's defenses and perhaps wound the other.

What could he do, though? Every attempt had been more than met. There existed only words . . . and Zayl had few left of those, as well.

Still he tried, hoping against hope that Juris Khan would be wrong, that somehow Kentril Dumon and Gorst had made it to the other stone. Yet, if they had, would this battle still be going on?

"And where is your archangel, anyway, my lord? Perhaps if he were here, then we could prove once and for all whether I lie. Surely that is not too much to ask for, is it? Then again, maybe it is . . ."

"I need not ask of Mirakodus that he prove himself to me, unbeliever, for I have seen his gifts at work, and I have faith in his word. If he would choose to speak with us now, it would be by his choice alone, not yours or mine!" Juris Khan loomed over the necromancer. "Make peace with Heaven, thief of the dead, for in but a few moments, your tongue shall still forever, and so, then, shall end your lies!"

Zayl had no reason to doubt him. As the robed monarch approached, Zayl prayed that Trag'Oul would help guide his soul to the next plane of battle, not let Khan's true master seize it and drag it down to Hell.

And, as if hearing his prayer, a voice suddenly boomed, "Juris Khan! Juris Khan! I would speak to you!"

Both men froze. Khan's mouth opened and closed. He glanced at Zayl again, then looked up to the ceiling.

The voice boomed, "Juris Khan! Noble servant! 'Tis I, your benefactor, your archangel . . ."

The weathered face contorted into an expression of reverence and wonder. Lord Khan raised his hands above his head in a beseeching manner and called out, "Mirakodus! Great Mirakodus! You bless your humble attendant with your presence!"

Much quieter, the voice calling itself that of the archangel suddenly muttered to the necromancer, "If you've got anything left to give, lad, do it now!"

Needing no more urging, Zayl dove toward his foe, focusing his will entirely on the dagger he now thrust at the robed figure's chest.

The beatific look upon Juris Khan's countenance vanished in an instant, replaced by one of the darkest anger. He started to reach for Zayl, the monarch's hands blazing with fiery energy.

The dagger struck first.

A blinding flash of light enveloped the chamber as the necromancer's enchanted blade broke through Khan's defenses. With some initial hesitation, the tip sank into the brilliant robe, then continued unimpeded.

Gasping, Juris Khan struck Zayl a blow across the face. Fueled by both power and pain, he sent the necromancer again flying into the rocky wall.

Zayl felt something crack as he hit. Unable to stop his momentum, he bounced twice on the floor, then rolled to a halt at the very feet of his foe.

"You—you—" Khan seemed unable to find any words to fit his fury.

Through watery eyes, the necromancer saw the blood dripping from the other's wound. He had missed the heart, but certainly had come close enough to it to injure his opponent gravely.

"Where—where is your archangel now?" Zayl managed to spout. "He seems—to have—have abandoned you, my lord!"

"Impudent fool!" The insane ruler leaned against the shield he had created for the Key to Shadow. "I need but a few moments—and then I will heal myself!" Khan bared his perfect teeth. "A few moments you yourself do not have!"

A horribly familiar noise arose from the mouth of the chamber. Zayl heard the movement of many eager feet.

He forced himself to turn his gaze toward the entrance.

One of the ghoulish denizens of the holy kingdom thrust its macabre head inside. Two more quickly followed suit.

His strength on the wane, Zayl's bone barrier had finally given way, releasing the hungry fiends.

Juris Khan, his breath still ragged, pointed at the sprawled necromancer. "There he is, my children! There is the one you seek!"

Their rounded mouths opened in anticipation. The deathly gaps where their eyes had once been fixed upon Zayl. The horrific creatures reached for him, and Zayl knew that he did not have anything left with which to fight them.

With his little remaining physical strength, he weakly held the dagger before him, hoping that he would at least stop one before the rest ripped him to bloody shreds. Despite all his teachings, despite all his training, at that moment, the necromancer dearly wanted to live.

"Now there remains but one," Khan pronounced, his voice already much stronger than earlier. His wound clearly bled less, and his visage, while monstrous in its own right, did not show much agony from the near-fatal blow.

Zayl had guessed wrong. The power behind Juris Khan, the false archangel, protected well his valuable puppet. Diablo, if Captain Dumon had guessed correctly, desired Ureh to spread its gift to the world . . . and open the path for Hell's legions.

"Now there remains but one," the almost demonic figure repeated. He straightened in obvious preparation for his departure from the cavern chamber. "And who knows?" Khan continued, smiling piously. "Perhaps not even *one*, eh?"

And as the horde suddenly rushed to tear Zayl apart, Juris Khan *vanished*— to ensure, the doomed spellcaster knew, that his last question would become truth.

Had the sun yet risen? Under the shroudlike cover of the enchanted shadow, Kentril could not be certain, but he hoped and prayed that it had not done so. With Gorst and surely Zayl now also dead, it would be the greatest shame to have come so far and yet fallen short.

He managed to drag himself up onto the small plateau, but discovered that he did not immediately have the strength to stand, much less continue on. Lying on the harsh, cold ground, the captain inhaled, trying to catch his breath. Just a few moments more. That was all he needed. Just a few moments more.

The sudden clatter of rock from just below the edge warned him that even those few moments would not be granted.

Body shrieking, Kentril forced himself back to his feet. He staggered toward the final climb, knowing that his goal lay only a short distance up but wondering if he could climb so great a height at this point.

There came more clattering. The captain looked back to see a withered, dead hand reaching up.

He turned and ran toward it. A terrifying face came up, the grayish vision granted Kentril by Zayl making it appear even more deathly.

Mustering his courage, the mercenary kicked at it as hard as he could.

With a shriek befitting a damned soul, the ghoulish creature tumbled backward into the air, vanishing below. Kentril leaned over the edge, saw that four more were only a minute or so from reaching the top, with at least a dozen more right behind.

Dragging himself up to the rock formation, Captain Dumon started his last ascent. He had to make it. He *would* make it.

"Come on, you damned recruit!" he muttered at himself as he grabbed hold. "You can climb five times faster than this!"

Foot by foot, inch by inch, Kentril drew closer. From the east, he noticed no hint of the sun, surely a good sign. By now, he had to be near the very upper edge of the shadow, which should have enabled him to make out some light if any existed. That Kentril did not had to mean that the day had not yet dawned.

Then, shattering his rising hopes, he heard once more the all-too-familiar hissing. Kentril immediately looked down, knowing already what he would see.

The first of the demonic horde had reached the plateau.

They scrambled around at first, seeking him out. One looked up, noticed him. That was all the rest needed. The first of them scurried to the rocky tower, eager, no doubt, for Kentril's tasty flesh.

Fortunately, not every part of the outcropping presented a place for the ghoulish hunters to use to climb up. Some started along the captain's own route, while others tested paths elsewhere, seeking one that would hold them.

Their hunger for his flesh and blood clearly getting the better of them, a pair hurried to the western side, no doubt in the hopes of beating the rest to the quarry.

They did not get far. As Kentril watched in astonishment, the two suddenly flared bright, almost as if on fire. Their screams caused the rest of the monstrous pack to hesitate. The two started back to their companions, but as they moved, pieces of their dried flesh turned to ash, and the bone beneath began to sag as if made of ever-softening wax.

One fell, already a half-melted parody of human dead that became more liquid with each second. The other managed to reach what surely had to be the edge of the shadow, but not soon enough to save it. It, too, collapsed into a stomach-churning heap that proved so disturbing a sight that the rest of the creatures did what they could to avoid even venturing near it.

Kentril suddenly became aware that the ones just below him had started moving again. Cursing his own morbid fascination with the horrific destruction of the pair, he pulled himself up as hard as he could, trying to make up for lost opportunity.

He almost moved too slowly. A hand nearly caught his left foot. Kicking at it, the captain managed to shatter some of the fingers, slowing the ghoul down.

His own hand suddenly caught the uppermost edge. Heart pounding, blood racing, Kentril pulled himself up . . . and caught his first glimpse of the Key to Light's resting place.

It had not, of course, changed much. A thin layer of frost covered everything, including, by this point, the veteran fighter himself. Carefully checking his footing, Kentril headed toward his prize.

Something stirred up by his boot rattled toward the gem.

The bone he had earlier dug free. The last trace of his predecessor, the unfortunate priest, Tobio.

Trying not to think about how he might soon be joining the late clergyman, Captain Dumon approached the Key to Light. As he did, he noticed that its brightness had remained constant but not overwhelming. In fact, it seemed little more illuminating than its counterpart well below the earth.

Does it matter? Kentril chided himself. *Let it glow as bright as the sun or stay as dark as the caverns. Just grab the thing, and be done with it!*

He reached for the crystal—

Atanna's beautiful face suddenly filled his mind, filled it so much he almost imagined he could see it floating before him, covering the entire shadowed heaven.

My darling Kentril . . . the face said. *My sweet Kentril, how I yearn for your arms again . . .*

The captain hesitated, caught between duty and emotion.

Come back to me, Kentril, she went on, eyes glittering and mouth pursed as if hungry for his kisses. *Let us be together again . . . together for all time . . .*

All time? That notion stirred him to action again. He wanted nothing of Juris Khan's gifts, especially that one.

But despite his determination, he could not escape Atanna's siren song. As the captain touched the surprisingly warm gem, she filled his head with new words, more promises.

Darling, sweet, loving Kentril . . . there is so much we can give each other . . . I was so lonely until I saw you . . . and when you showed me the brooch . . . I knew that Heaven had promised you to me . . . come back to me, and all will be well . . . we will be one . . .

"Get out of my head!" Kentril snapped, shutting his eyes as he tried to force the image, the smell, the taste of Atanna from his memory. "Get out of my—"

A hiss barely alerted him in time. From behind came one of Lord Khan's vile "children," a hairless, gaunt cadaver dressed in the soiled garments of a merchant. A rusted medallion still containing a few valuable gems dangled from the neck chain half-buried in the ghoul's shriveled, hollow neck.

"Fine wares today!" it babbled. *"Good pots! Fresh from the kiln!"*

Whether the monstrosity knew what it said or not, its words unnerved the seasoned mercenary, yet another morbid reminder that what faced him had once been a fellow man.

Kentril swung hard with his left, landing a powerful punch to the chest. His hand sank in up to the knuckles, the dried flesh and old bone giving way. However, the blow only sent the horrific creature back a couple of steps.

Without hesitation, Kentril kicked with one foot. This time, he caught his adversary's leg, flipping the ghoul over.

Unable to control its momentum, the creature slid to the far side, slipping over the edge.

Again, Captain Dumon gripped the crystal. He ripped it free, then looked to the east. Still no sign of daylight. He had been early enough at least. Now all he had to do was destroy the artifact.

But Atanna's voice and face filled his mind once more, making it difficult to tell what was real and what was imaginary. Kentril had trouble recalling just what he had been intending to do.

Kentril, my darling Kentril . . . my one and only love . . . come to me . . . forget this foolishness . . .

She floated before him in a silver, gossamer gown, arms outstretched toward him, beseeching him. To Kentril, Atanna far more resembled an angel than even the false Mirakodus had. How breathtaking she was, how beguiling . . .

He took a step toward her.

A thing smelling of the stench of the grave fell upon him.

Kentril hit the icy ground hard, the crystal rolling from his grip. Both he and his attacker slid dangerously near the edge. The captain grimaced as the rounded mouth snapped at him, the ghoul's fetid breath almost as deadly a weapon as its teeth.

Managing to get his knee up, Kentril pushed the horror away. He scrambled for the Key, but his foe grabbed his arm and pulled the mercenary back. Beyond the creature, Captain Dumon saw with mounting dismay that three others had made it up and now converged on him.

Unable to pull his sword free, Kentril managed at least to draw his dagger. He stabbed at the hand that held him, chopping at the bone and decayed skin. The fingers loosened their grip enough on his arm so that Kentril could pull himself free. Dropping the dagger, the weary veteran drew his sword as he carefully backed toward his prize.

The larger blade did nothing to daunt the gathering fiends. They moved toward him as quickly as the slick surface enabled them. Kentril thrust at the nearest, then swung wide at two others following. He managed to strike one of the latter, but not enough to do any damage.

At last, he reached the Key to Light. Fending off the cursed citizens of Ureh, the captain scooped it up.

"Stop!" he shouted as best he could, the cold and his own exhaustion having taken their toll. "Stop, or I throw it off now!"

The creatures paused.

Kentril had them . . . but for how long? They would not simply wait until the sun rose and destroyed them. Even now, others could be heard wending their way up the other shadowed sides. It would take only a single lapse in concentration for Kentril to fall prey to one or more of them.

You would not do that, not when you so much wish to live.

A face appeared in his mind, but not Atanna's this time. Instead, Juris Khan seemed to stare at Kentril from within the fighter's skull, to see what the captain tried to hide from himself—that he very much *wanted* to live, wanted some way to escape from what clearly had no escape.

Kentril . . . my good captain . . . you can live and live well . . . love and love well . . . a kingdom can be yours . . .

Captain Dumon saw himself at the head of a magnificent force, his armor as brilliant, as majestic, as that of Lord Khan's archangel. He saw himself standing before cheering throngs, spreading the good will of Ureh to all. Kentril even saw himself sitting upon the very throne occupied by Juris Khan, Atanna at his side and their beautiful children perched near his feet . . .

Then the godlike figure of Khan swelled to life before his eyes, seeming to rise up all the way from the city far below, filling the sky. A gracious smile on his regal visage, the gigantic monarch reached forth a gargantuan hand to Kentril, offering him escape and all else the mercenary had envisioned.

Replace the Key, and come home, my good captain . . . come home, my son . . .

Kentril felt his will slipping away, felt himself ready to accept everything that the gigantic figure offered—even if that wondrous offer in truth masked an awful horror.

Then Kentril thought of Zayl, who surely had to be dead if Juris Khan had come here. He thought of Albord, Jodas, Brek, Orlif, and the rest of his company, victims of a monstrous evil into which the captain had blithely led them.

Most of all, he recalled Gorst, who had just sacrificed his life for his friend, his comrade. Gorst, who had not hesitated to do what had to be done.

Throwing aside his blade, Captain Kentril Dumon clutched the artifact to his body . . . and ran off the edge of the peak.

He closed his eyes as he did, not wanting to see the oncoming rocks below. The wind pushed at his face, his body, as if trying to tear the Key to Light from his death grip. Kentril imagined himself crashing on the mountainside, becoming battered to a pulp, the crystal shattering in the process.

Then the wind, the sense of falling, ceased.

The captain opened his eyes to find himself floating in air.

No . . . not floating. The ethereal hand of the giant Juris Khan held him, its ghostly fingers wrapped around his body. The look on the patriarch's huge face appeared anything but kindly now.

Put it back, Kentril Dumon . . . put it back now . . .

Staring at that gigantic visage, the mercenary could not help but think how much Lord Khan now resembled his sinister archangel. The eyes especially held that demonic intensity, and the more Kentril looked, the more the face seemed to shift, to grow less human, more *hellish*.

Put it back, and you may yet live!

But despite Khan's mutating countenance, despite the crushing fingers of the ghostly hand, Kentril would not. Better death, better every bone broken and his life fluids splattered across the earth below than to let *this* spread across the world.

He raised the Key to Light high, trying to throw it down upon the city. Yet his arms would not make the final move, no matter how hard Kentril tried.

The face of Juris Khan had lost all trace of humanity. Now he more than a little resembled the abominations his people had become. His skin shriveled, and his mouth took on a hungry, loathsome cut. The eyes burned with a fiery fury not of Heaven, but of well, well below.

Return the Key, or I shall shred your skin from your pathetic body, remove your heart while it beats, and devour it before your pleading eyes!

Kentril tried not to listen, choosing instead to concentrate on salvaging his mission. Where was the damned sun, anyway? How much longer before it finally rose?

He could no longer breathe, barely even think. A part of the mercenary begged him to take Khan's offer, even if that offer truly could not be trusted. Anything but to suffer longer.

Everything began to go black. At first, Kentril believed that he had started to pass out, but then the captain realized that Zayl's spell had begun to wear off. Kentril could still make out the ever more hideous form of his host, but little else. Ureh had become a dark, undefined shape, even the mountains nearby only murky forms. A bare hint of gray touched the eastern horizon, but other than that—

A hint of *gray*?

No sooner had Captain Dumon noted it than he felt a warmth in his hands. He forced his eyes upward, saw that the faint glow of the Key to Light had increased.

And as he quickly returned his gaze to the pinpoint of grayness far beyond the shadowed kingdom, Kentril knew that the night had finally come to an end.

With renewed determination, he held the crystal toward the gigantic, phantasmal form. Putting every bit of effort he could into resisting Juris Khan's control, Kentril shouted, "*You* put it back!"

He threw the Key.

The huge, ghostly hand reached for the stone, but as it tried to seize the artifact, the latter flared as brightly as the morning sun. The Key to Light completely *burned* its way through the ethereal palm, then sailed on unhindered toward the city below.

Juris Khan roared, a combination of rage and pain.

Fool! bellowed the giant in Kentril's head. *Corrupt soul! You shall be—*

He got no further, for at that moment the gleaming crystal struck against something.

It shattered—and from within burst forth an intense, blinding light that rushed out in all directions as if seeking to take in everything in its blazing embrace.

The area around the broken artifact erupted with day. Ureh, the mountain Nymyr, the surrounding jungle . . . nothing escaped the glorious illumination unleashed by the death of Khan's creation.

A wave of pure sun caught the scores of horrific pursuers still perched atop the peak or clinging to its side. The cursed folk of the once-holy city screamed and shrieked as they melted, burning away before Kentril's sickened eyes. By the dozens, those that had not yet made it to the top plummeted earthward, molten blobs that left fiery stains upon Nymyr's ever-more-battered flank.

And as the light coursed over Ureh building by building, those structures withered, crumbled, returning to the decayed, empty shells that Kentril and the others had first discovered. Walls fell in; ceilings collapsed. The effects of centuries of exposure to the elements took their toll once more, but this time in scarcely a minute.

From everywhere, the howls and cries of the damned souls of Ureh filled Kentril's ears, threatened to drive him to madness. He felt more pity than anything else for the creatures that had slaughtered his friends. They had been turned into abominations by the man they had most trusted, infested by demons who used their drained husks as a gate to the mortal world.

Perhaps now they could find eternal rest.

Then . . . Juris Khan, too, began to twist, to mutate. Kentril tumbled through the air, not falling but not exactly floating, either. He caught glimpses of the monstrous shadow figure as the first rays struck, watched as the corrupted lord of the realm was transformed. Juris Khan became even less than a man, more of a beast. Quickly went the face and form that had matched his people in horror. Now the elder ruler truly revealed the evil within him, the evil that could only be of *Diablo.*

And there, rising momentarily above the vanishing giant, a creature of Hell, a tusked, fanged figure of dread roared his anger at Kentril's desperate action. Ichor dripped from a scaly, barely fleshed skull that almost appeared to have been stretched long. Two wicked, scaled horns rose high above bat-winged ears. Over the deathly crevices that were all that formed a nose, the thick-browed orbs of the demon lord glared at the impudent human, the hatred and evil within them matching exactly that which the horrified mercenary had noted in the image of the false archangel Mirakodus.

Diablo thundered his wrath once more—and vanished as swiftly as he had appeared.

With a howl of agony, the vision of Juris Khan completely collapsed. The regal garments darkened and shredded. What skin had been left grew so brittle it fell off in thousands of pieces. Lord Khan put his other hand to his breast as if somehow he could stop the inevitable . . . and then the entire giant crumbled into a jumble of fragmented bones and scraps of cloth.

The last vestiges of Khan's image vanished.

Kentril found himself falling again.

Down and down he dropped, descending so fast he could scarcely breathe. The shattered ruins of the once-resurrected kingdom beckoned him. Kentril shut his eyes, praying that the end would be swift and relatively painless.

Just as he expected to hit, the terrified fighter suddenly halted once again. Captain Dumon's eyes opened wide. About a hundred feet or so below him, the roofless remnants of a rounded structure met his stunned gaze.

No sooner had this registered than Kentril began to drop, but at a slower, almost cautious rate. He looked around, trying to find the cause of this miracle.

The still shadowed palace of Juris Khan greeted him.

Somehow, the light of the crystal had managed to avoid the towering structure, but now true dawn had finally arrived, and the first rays of the day had already begun to eat away at the last of the false darkness. Kentril might not have thought more of the edifice's demise, but then he saw the figure poised at the very edge of the grand balcony, a figure with flowing hair of red.

Even so far apart, their eyes locked. Kentril saw in Atanna's a combination of emotions that left him so startled that at first he did not realize that she continued to lower him toward safety. Only when a brief, sad smile escaped her otherwise solemn expression did he understand *all* she had done.

The light began to pour over the palace. Kentril felt himself drop faster, but not so fast that he risked death. Atanna leaned over the rail, her arm outstretched toward him.

Although he knew that Juris Khan's daughter did not seek his hand, Captain Dumon could not help reaching for her. Atanna gave him another, deeper smile—

The sun touched her.

As it rose up her body, Atanna simply *faded* away.

At that point, the grand hilltop palace of Juris Khan collapsed in upon itself, quickly reduced to dust and ancient rubble. The hill itself seemed almost to deflate.

And without Atanna's spell to maintain his descent, Kentril Dumon dropped like a stone toward the ground.

Twenty-three

※

Voices pierced the darkness.

"Maybe it'd be better if you just raise him from the dead and be done with it, lad."

"He lives . . . although how that can be, I cannot possibly say."

Kentril wanted the voices to go away, to leave him to his eternal peace, but they would not.

"I will try something else. Maybe that can stir him."

A snort. "You should be using some of that power for mending yourself!"

"I will survive . . ."

A pinprick of light pierced the empty blackness, irritating the mercenary. Kentril tried to cover his eyes, but pain suddenly coursed through him.

"He moved, Humbart! He reacted!"

"Will wonders never cease!"

The light became insistent, glaring. It burned into his mind, forced him to look at it.

With a moan, Kentril opened his eyes.

Daylight greeted him, but it had not been the source of the glaring illumination. That proved to be the flaring light of an ivory dagger, a dagger held in the left hand of the necromancer Zayl.

The *only* hand remaining to the necromancer.

Zayl's other arm ended in a bound stump just above the wrist. The pale Rathmian looked even more pale save where his face had been scarred red. His clothing hung in pieces, and he looked as if he had not slept in days.

"Welcome back, captain," the spellcaster commented in a tone that for him almost bordered on the convivial.

"Lo! The dead rise!" chuckled the voice of Humbart Wessel. The skull sat perched on a rock next to the kneeling Zayl.

"Zayl . . ." Kentril managed to gasp. His own voice came out as more of a dry, hacking sound. "You're . . . alive . . ."

The necromancer nodded. "You are as surprised about that as I am about finding you. How is it that you are down here among the ruins when you had to climb up to the top of Nymyr to stop Juris Khan?"

Kentril forced himself to turn. As he did, his lower chest and left shoulder ached terribly.

"Be careful, captain. You suffered broken ribs and a dislocated shoulder. They can be healed a little better when I myself have recovered more, but it will take time."

Ignoring him, Kentril looked at all that remained of fabled Ureh. Even less seemed to be left standing than when he had first come across the place. The outer wall stood in fragments, and the roof of nearly every building within had collapsed. Ureh now looked less like a haunted legend than like just one more ancient city abandoned to time and the elements.

And of the palace, only the crumbling foundation yet existed.

"Tell me what happened, Captain Dumon," the necromancer urged. "If you do not mind."

Of all people, Zayl certainly deserved the truth. Accepting a flask of water from the spellcaster, Kentril went into as much detail as he could recall, from the initial ascent to the pursuit, Gorst's sacrifice, and finally his own decision to end the shadowed kingdom's threat even at the cost of his own life. As he spoke of Atanna, the weary fighter's throat closed, and his eyes moistened, but he continued his tale until his companion knew everything.

At the end, Zayl nodded sagely. "Perhaps a true archangel watched over you, captain. You timed it very well, especially where I was concerned. Another few seconds, and Khan's demonic children would have torn me to shreds. Only the knife and some skillful playacting by Humbart preserved me for that long."

"What did he do?" Kentril asked, glancing at the skull.

"Only pretended to be himself, their lord and ruler, calling to them to halt because the necromancer was needed for a spell. Did something like that with Khan, too. Maybe I should go on the stage after this!"

That brought a hint of a smile from Zayl. "Since neither our good host nor his corrupted people could see him, the idea bought a few precious seconds both times. Even still, the horde got over its confusion quite quickly"—he raised the bound stump—"as you can see."

"Is it all over, then? Has the danger passed?"

"Yes. Ureh and her people are at rest, and the gateway to Hell is sealed once more. Before I found you, I searched the area for any traces of the corruption. There was none."

Kentril peered up at the sky. By his reckoning, it had to be just after midday . . . but on *what* day? "How long was I unconscious?"

"Two-and-a-half days. I found you just before sunset of the first and have done what I could."

Two-and-a-half days . . . Fighting the pain, the captain pushed himself up to a sitting position. "How are my legs, Zayl?"

"They appear unbroken, but you would know best."

Testing them, Kentril discovered that although they ached, he could at least tolerate moving them. "If I can stand, I want to get out of here. I don't want to sleep within the walls of this place another night."

Zayl frowned. "It might be more prudent to wait another day or—"

"I want to *leave*."

"As you wish. I understand." With some effort, the necromancer rose. He put the skull in the torn pouch at his side, then moved to help the fighter.

As Kentril stood up, something clattered to the ground near his feet. Curious, he cautiously bent to pick it up.

Atanna's face looked back at him from the brooch.

"What is it?" asked Zayl, unable to see from his angle.

The captain quickly folded his fingers over it. "Nothing. Nothing at all. Let's go."

They headed toward the lush jungle. As they slowly walked, the necromancer informed Kentril of his plan for them. "We can make use of your old base camp tonight, then tomorrow I will guide us safely to some of the others of my ilk. They will be able to help heal both of us, and then you can be on your way."

"An outsider won't be a problem?"

Zayl chuckled slightly. "Not one who faced down Diablo himself. This will be a story they will want to hear."

Through the broken wall they stepped, leaving behind the Light among Lights forever. However, once well beyond the former limits of the shadow, Captain Dumon made Zayl come to a halt.

"Give me a moment, please," he requested.

In silence, Kentril looked back at what had become the end of both a dream and a nightmare. The wind howled through the crumbling skeleton of the lost city, sounding like a lament for all those who had perished.

"I am sorry about your friends," the necromancer said as kindly as he could.

Kentril, however, had not been thinking as much about them as about someone else. "It's done with. Best to be forgotten . . . forever."

He turned away once more, and they continued their trek. Yet, as he walked, Captain Kentril Dumon's hand slipped surreptitiously to a pouch on his belt . . . and dropped the brooch inside.

Behind him, the elements renewed their patient task of slowly and inevitably erasing the last memories of the kingdom of shadow.

Demonsbane

Robert B. Marks

I

THE NIGHT OF SOULS

✳

And the hosts of Hell looked upon man, and swore
vengeance for their defeat by the Vizjerei.
"No more will these creatures deny us," swore the Prime Evils,
"for we are greater than they." And thus began the Sin War.

—*The Holy Scriptures of Zakarum*

Siggard startled awake, the sounds of battle still ringing in his ears, as though he had just been in the midst of the bloodshed.

Exhausted, he lay on the bank of a road, the trees on both sides obscured by a light mist illuminated by moonlight. He tried to sit up, only to have his back explode in pain. For a moment he rubbed the sore muscles and kidneys, and then he struggled to his knees.

Blinking, he wondered where he was and how he had gotten there. The road did not look familiar at all, and there were no visible landmarks. He scratched his head, trying to think, and winced for a moment when his fingernails ran over a tender spot.

Siggard was a large man, well grown, with a full brown beard. But now his usually placid gray eyes were haggard and his beard was in a tangle. He shook his head; he knew he had been at the field of Blackmarch, a shield-man in the army of Earl Edgewulf. And they had been fighting someone, but who he could not say.

Groaning, Siggard gained his feet. He would first have to find his way to the battlefield and try to rejoin the army, but what he truly wished was to rejoin his family in Bear's Hill. That would have to wait until the fighting was done, though.

Taking stock of his gear, he noticed his sword was rather more notched than the last time he remembered, and his leather jerkin and trousers were ragged but intact. Where his coat of mail had gotten to, he had no idea. His wide shield was also missing.

Cloaked in a mist drawn eerie in the moonlight, Siggard tried to get his bearings, but no matter which way he turned, he couldn't tell where Blackmarch might lie. Finally, he picked a direction and began walking.

How long he walked before he reached the gallows, Siggard could not say, though it seemed hours. Regardless, he found himself facing a fork in the road. To one side of the road there was a three-way sign, but it was too dark to read it. On the other side stood a gibbet, a decaying corpse dangling from it by a worn hemp rope.

Unbidden, the words of one of his comrades in arms came back to him. "Hanged men have angry souls, you know," old Banagar had said. "That's why they hoist them at crossroads. That way they can't find their way back for vengeance." Banagar had always been rather morbid, he reflected.

Siggard shook his head, trying to ignore the stench of putrefying flesh. The road had to lead to a town somewhere, even if it was in the twice-damned underworld itself. So all he had to do was pick a direction and follow it.

He looked up at the corpse and smiled. "I don't suppose you'd know the way to Blackmarch, eh?"

The corpse's rotting head turned and glared at him.

Siggard leapt back in shock, drawing his sword and staring at the gibbet. The body dangled, lifeless, as it had before Siggard had spoken, and as it no doubt had long before the soldier had even arrived.

Siggard felt a chill go down his spine as he looked at the corpse. He prayed silently to the gods to let him see his family again, just one more time. He didn't want to die here, trapped among lost spirits.

His sword still drawn, Siggard backed down one of the paths, finally turning once the gibbet had vanished in the mist. The ethereal fog curled around him as he walked, Siggard mouthing a silent prayer with every step.

The path twisted and turned among the trees, and the dirt crunched under Siggard's boots. For a moment he wondered if he wasn't in some endless forest of the damned, forced to wander a haunted woodland for all eternity. He shook his head; if he was to find his way out, he would have to stop thinking like that.

Faint shapes appeared in the mist ahead of him, and for a moment Siggard could make out a horse and rider, standing under a large oak tree. He blinked hard, but the figure remained. He pursed his lips; whatever it was, it wasn't a figment of his imagination, though it did seem ghostly.

As he walked forward, he saw another figure appear in the mist. The newcomer drew a blade and, before Siggard had a chance to shout a warning, plunged it into the rider. Siggard rushed forward, his sword at the ready, praying he would not have to fight, yet as he ran the two figures faded into the swirling fog. Finally, he stood under the oak, but not even a footprint suggested that anybody else had been there that night.

"If this keeps up much longer, I'll go mad," Siggard muttered. "I might even start talking to myself."

He moved away until he had a respectful distance between himself and the oak, and then began to gather deadwood. After a bit of work, he reclined under an ancient elm, watching the flames dance on his small fire until he drifted to sleep.

*   *   *

Siggard stood in the shield wall at Blackmarch, watching the horizon. Earl Edgewulf walked from man to man, complimenting each on their standing and promising glory ahead. For his part, Siggard just wanted to see his family again. But he knew that the bloodshed was necessary; if they weren't stopped here, the enemy would be able to roam freely in Entsteig, spreading terror and destruction.

He closed his eyes for a moment, visualizing Emilye and his newborn child. His wife's golden hair had glittered in the sunlight when they had last spoken, and her crystal eyes had been unable to contain the tears she had been trying to hide. He had told her that it would be fine, that he would be back soon.

Thunderclouds scudded above, lightning arcing between them, followed by blasts of thunder. "It looks like it's going to rain," old Banagar muttered. Siggard grimaced at the elder man, running his eyes over the gray stubble surrounding a faint mustache on the wrinkled face. Siggard mouthed a silent prayer that the rain wouldn't turn the ground into a slick wasteland.

He stood on the bare hill, an army around him, like something out of a legend of the Mage Clan Wars, with every soldier clad in a shining coat of mail. They had taken the high ground, and had cleared some of the trees from the bottom of the hill. When the enemy charged, they would be completely exposed.

"Here they come!" one of the lookouts shouted. Siggard squinted and watched the treeline, looking for any sign of the enemy. Even after Earl Edgewulf had put them into formation, he still didn't know what enemies he would be facing. From the corner of his eye he thought he could see glowing eyes staring out from the shadowy woods, but when he looked directly at them, all he saw was darkness.

Then the woods began to boil, the trees themselves twisting and turning in torment. Siggard inhaled sharply as the enemy burst out from the tortured woodland with a shrill screaming, his gut churning in terror.

None of them were even remotely human.

Some were small and doglike, carrying bloodstained axes and hatchets. Others stood tall, their muscular bodies capped with the head of a goat, what little skin showing painted with demonic symbols. And in the background there were shadowy THINGS, defying any description.

Something shook him, and a voice said, "Would you mind if I share your fire?"

Siggard sat up, finding himself back beside the forest path. A cloaked figure stood above him, and Siggard could make out a sharp, but strangely kind visage in the shadows of the cowl. The fire crackled beside the man, and in the flickering glow of the flames and the waning moonlight, Siggard noticed that the man seemed to be clad entirely in gray.

"Help yourself," Siggard said. "I'm afraid I have no food to offer."

"That is not an issue," the man said, sitting down by the fire. "I have already eaten. Perhaps I can offer you something?"

Siggard shook his head. "I'm not hungry."

"There are many restless spirits out tonight," the stranger said. "As I walked, I saw several ghosts."

"I noticed that too," Siggard stated, scratching his beard. "For a while, I wondered if I had gone to Hell."

The man chuckled. "I can assure you, this is neither Heaven nor Hell. However, it is the Night of Souls, when it is said that in some places the restless dead will return."

"And what do they come back for?" Siggard asked.

"Some come for vengeance. Some come to see their loved ones again. And for some, they just cannot rest. Sometimes it is the earth itself that brings them back, remembering the life force that once was."

Siggard shuddered. "It is unnatural."

The man laughed, his voice strangely musical. "On the contrary, it is entirely natural! Life does not simply give in to death, and the soul is more than some abstract idea. These spirits merely walk their own path, most unaware of any others around them. But there are some, particularly in the forces of Hell, who would raise the dead, animating them so that they do not hold a spirit, but are merely an automaton. I think that is what you speak of."

Siggard shook his head. "I do not know if I should be terrified or awed by what you say."

The stranger lowered his hood, revealing eyes sparkling with life and a long mane of blond hair. "I think both would be appropriate. There are more things in Heaven and Hell than any mortal man could dream."

"And how would you know all of this?" Siggard asked.

The man shrugged. "I am a wanderer; I have seen more than most would ever imagine. That is merely my nature."

"Will you give me your name?" Siggard said.

The stranger nodded. "My name is Tyrael. May I ask your name?"

"Siggard."

Tyrael smiled. "Your trust does you credit, but be careful with whom you place it. I am safe, a traveler sworn to the light. But there are others who are sworn to darkness, and they do not reveal themselves unless they are forced to."

Tyrael leaned forward. "Tell me, friend Siggard, what brings you onto this road on this of all nights?"

Siggard shrugged. "I wish I knew."

Tyrael raised an eyebrow. "I don't understand."

"The last thing I remember is the battle at Blackmarch. If this is the Night of Souls, then that would be two days ago. I can't remember anything between lining up in the shield wall and awakening earlier this evening on the ground."

Tyrael nodded sagely. "Sometimes one will see something so horrifying that the mind will block it out, as though the soul itself cannot bear to remember it."

Siggard suddenly recalled the strange shadows behind the tree line at Blackmarch, and found himself nodding in agreement. "I guess I just want to find out what happened at Blackmarch and see my wife and child again."

Tyrael pursed his lips. "I have heard fell things about Blackmarch. I would not go there if I were you."

"I have to know what happened."

Tyrael shook his head, and for a moment Siggard thought he could see a great sadness in the man's eyes. "If you must go, then you must go. You are ten leagues south of Blackmarch as the crow flies. You can reach it in a couple of days by following the road north." He pointed back in the direction that Siggard had originally come. "If I were you, however, I would go south for one more league, and then take the fork west. It will take you back into Entsteig."

Siggard nodded. "I will consider your advice."

Tyrael smiled kindly. "That is all one could ask."

Siggard watched as the waning moon finally slid down under the treeline and the eastern sky began to brighten. "It will be dawn soon."

"It seems that the Night of Souls has come to an end at last," Tyrael mused. "All of the restless dead now return to their graves in the hopes of peace."

Siggard turned and stretched, wincing for a moment as his back ached. "I should begin my journey; I have a long walk ahead of me."

"May your feet be swift and take you into places far from harm," Tyrael said, still sitting by the dancing flames.

Siggard turned and looked at the road. "You have the tongue of a poet, my friend. I thank you for your good wishes."

But when he turned, he stood alone by the fire.

The mist was gone by the morning, burnt away by the autumn sun. Siggard carefully smothered the fire, trying to ensure that no billowing smoke revealed where he was. He still remembered the sights of the previous night with fear and awe, and wanted to ensure that he did not run into any restless spirits who did not respect the dawn.

Thinking back on the evening, he still wondered at some of what he had seen. He had never been a superstitious man, but the memories of the hanging corpse and the ghosts in the mist seemed too real to have been a vivid dream. And then there was Tyrael.

Was the stranger a ghost, come back for a friendly chat? Or was he something else? A figment from a dream, perhaps?

Siggard shook his head; at this point in time, it was useless speculation. Aside from which, he still had to find out what had happened at Blackmarch.

He checked that his sword was securely fastened to his belt, and began the journey north.

2
Encounters
✵

Alas, mourn for the open road!
For where there was once wonder and mystery,
now there is mistrust and death.

—Jiltarian of Khanduras, *Lamentations*

After only a couple of hours of walking, Siggard found himself once again facing the fork and gibbet. In the light of day, the hanged man was little more than a desiccated corpse, barely any flesh left on the pearly bones. The eyes that had seemed to stare so dangerously at him were reduced to empty sockets.

Siggard shook his head. It was amazing how easily the terrors of the night vanished once the sun rose. He was still left with the crossroads, however, one path leading back northeast and the other leading westwards. Either path could twist and turn, appearing to go one way when in reality it did the opposite.

Such is life, Siggard mused. Regardless, he had no time, and needed to get to Blackmarch. Scratching his beard, he finally chose the northeastern path, and began to walk.

As he traveled, the forest seemed to stretch on into eternity. At least the path seemed to be consistently taking him northwards; Siggard checked the position of the sun at what he thought was every hour, and everything seemed to be as it should. The path did weave, however, and when the sun finally sank into the west Siggard estimated that he had only traveled about five leagues.

Once again, he built a fire off to the side of the road. As he watched the flickering flames, giving the light mist around him an eerie glow, he suddenly realized that he wasn't very hungry at all.

Siggard blinked. Perhaps it was the concern he had for his friends in the army, he thought. Regardless, with virtually no food and nothing to hunt with, it was a blessing. Still, in some ways the hunger pangs would have been a blessing, too; the roads were known to be dangerous, and he could use the edge in staying alert.

As he watched the dancing flames, trying to remain awake, sleep claimed him at last.

* * *

Siggard broke into a cold sweat when he saw the demonic army approaching the shield wall. They literally boiled out of the trees, like some horrifying infestation. As if on cue, a bolt of lightning struck the forest, the crashing thunder deafening him.

For a moment, Siggard saw a small pheasant walking on the ground, oblivious to the men on the hill and the monsters approaching. It pecked at the ground, snatching at a worm. Then, prize caught in its beak, the bird took flight.

We are the interlopers, Siggard thought. All of us. And nature simply doesn't care.

"Barrage!" the lookout shouted.

Several rocks smashed into the ranks, flattening entire sections of the shield wall. Siggard watched in horror as one man tried to free himself from under a boulder, his entire lower body crushed into a bloody pulp.

But when he looked back at the demons, they hadn't moved. Strange shadows flickered just beyond the trees, and the creatures reared up, calling out with earsplitting screams.

As Siggard offered yet another silent prayer to see his family just once more, it began to rain, a drizzle at first, and then a downpour. After only a couple of minutes he felt as though he was soaked to the bone, despite the heavy leather and coat of mail. And, for some strange reason, he could smell a fire smoldering.

Siggard opened his eyes to find a cold autumn rain falling upon him. His fire lay smoldering, the last flames put out by the downpour. He shivered, wishing that he had a cloak to wrap around himself. He had owned one, he remembered, but where it had gone was yet another thing he could not account for.

At least there was no lightning, he reflected. That meant he could safely seek shelter in the forest.

But even as he forced himself to rise, the rain slackened and ceased. The soft light of dawn peeked through the clouds, and a bird sang in the distance.

Siggard was not at ease, however. In all of his experience a forest should smell fresh and magical after a rainfall, but the woods reeked of decay instead. For a moment he remembered all of the times he had gone hunting mushrooms with his wife during the early spring, just before the planting. They would venture into the forest, seeking their bounty and watching as the hares and squirrels went about their daily business. Once, they had even seen a great deer, but only briefly.

He shook his head. He still had several leagues to travel, and only the gods knew what had happened to the army. He began to walk, following the path even farther north, trying to concentrate on the task at hand.

As he walked, the forest became strangely silent. Other than the birdsong right after the rain, the only sound he heard was the crunching of his own boots in the earthen road.

"I'm going to have to get out of here," Siggard muttered uneasily, picking up the pace. As before, the path twisted and turned as he walked, but always bore northwards.

Finally, the sun began to set once again, and Siggard retired to the side of the road. He began to gather firewood, hoping that this time the flames wouldn't be smothered by rain.

"Excuse me, my dear sir!" called a voice. Siggard turned to see a tall, dark-skinned man with a bushy goatee regarding him. The stranger wore long light red robes, and carried a traveler's pack on his back. "Would you mind if I joined you? I would be happy to help in any way I could."

"How do you know I'm not a bandit?" Siggard asked.

"If you were a bandit, you wouldn't have asked that question," the stranger replied. "Besides, you have an honest face. Shall we trade names?"

"Siggard of Entsteig," Siggard said carefully. "And you are?"

The stranger bowed, his hands held together. "I am Sarnakyle of Kehjistan, a great land far to the east. I am one of the Vizjerei."

"A wizard?" Siggard asked.

Sarnakyle grinned. "Definitely not a shoemaker."

Siggard finished building his fire-pit and picked up a couple of dried sticks. Unceremoniously, he dropped them into the pit. "What brings you out on this road?"

Sarnakyle held up a hand. "Please, let me help you with that." He gestured quickly, and a spark leapt from his hand into the wood, lighting the fire. The wizard sat down, warming his hands. "I am a wanderer, friend Siggard. I have recently seen some . . . disturbing things, and I am trying to sort them out. And you?"

"I am trying to make my way to Blackmarch," Siggard stated.

"I do not believe I have been there," Sarnakyle said. "I have heard some terrible things about it, but I have not seen it. I think I will go, if you will have my company."

"Just so long as you don't slow me down," Siggard said.

"I can walk quite quickly," Sarnakyle said, still smiling. "Besides, you could probably use my help."

Siggard raised an eyebrow.

"No offense, my good sir, but with the exception of your sword you do not appear to be attired for battle. I am an experienced wizard."

Siggard grunted. "We will see."

Sarnakyle reached into his pack and pulled out some rations. Silently, he offered a bit of dried beef to Siggard.

"Thank you," Siggard said, taking the offering. When he bit into it, however, he found that he still had very little appetite. He ate half of the ration, and then wrapped the rest up in a leaf and put it in his belt.

"By the looks of it, you are not nearly as rested as I," Sarnakyle said. "Please, allow me to take first watch."

Siggard was about to object, but then thought better of it. After all, he only actually had a battered sword and a piece of dried meat to his name right now; nothing worth stealing at all.

*   *   *

For the first time in two days, Siggard didn't dream of battle. He was shaken awake by Sarnakyle, who told him that nothing had happened. He watched the wizard make some gestures at the ground, and then settle down to sleep.

He'd have to ask him what those were in the morning, Siggard thought. He watched the forest, his mind slowly wandering back to his farm, village, and family. Soon, he promised himself, soon he would see them again.

As his mind wandered, the eastern sky began to lighten, and finally the sun rose in all of its glory. Sarnakyle stretched and yawned beside him, and finally rose, scratching his goatee.

"That was a good night," the wizard said.

"You did something with your hands," Siggard said. "It was just before you went to sleep. What was that?"

Sarnakyle smiled. "A bit of extra protection. I set some magical wards earlier, and I just made certain they were still strong."

"If you can set magic wards, why did you need me to keep watch?"

"Magic is not as . . . powerful as many think," Sarnakyle said, and for a moment Siggard thought he could see a sadness in the wizard's eyes. "Sometimes a good sword arm can be as valuable as a hundred spells."

Siggard unwrapped the ration from last night and took a couple of bites. Somehow, he still wasn't terribly hungry. It could be simple concern; in less than three days, he had heard two people talk about Blackmarch as a dire place, and he was beginning to fear the worst for the army.

He wrapped the ration up again and looked over at Sarnakyle. The wizard sat on a rock, eagerly eating his breakfast. Well, Siggard reflected, at least this visitor hadn't vanished with the dawn.

"We should be going soon," Siggard said. "I want to be at Blackmarch as soon as possible."

"You should relax," Sarnakyle mumbled in between bites. "Blackmarch is a place; it won't go anywhere if we take an extra couple of hours."

"It is very important that I get there," Siggard insisted. "I am a soldier of the army of Entsteig, and I have to rejoin my companions."

Sarnakyle blinked and stopped chewing. He swallowed hard and stared at Siggard. "My friend," he began, "you are on a fool's errand. The army of Entsteig was annihilated at Blackmarch by a demonic force. It is said that fewer than ten men survived the battle."

Siggard found himself swimming in fear. If the army had been defeated, then the enemy could rampage amongst the countryside. And that meant that his family . . .

Siggard bolted upright, gathering his meager belongings and buckling his sword to his waist. "My family is in danger," he said. "I have to go."

"That army of demons was heading towards Entsteig, wasn't it?" Sarnakyle mused. "I'd better come with you."

"It could be very dangerous," Siggard warned.

Sarnakyle pulled his pack onto his back and smoothed out his robes. "I have more experience with demons than I would care to have, my dear warrior. Trust me, you are better off with me at your side."

"What is the fastest road west?" Siggard asked.

"A bit to the north there is a crossroads," Sarnakyle stated. "The western path will take us out of the forest and into Entsteig."

Siggard nodded. "It's about time we got out of this twice-damned forest."

As they set off, Siggard wished that he had the wings of angels, for every minute that they traveled brought the demons closer to Emilye and his child.

3
REVELATIONS AND SORROW
✳

Do not embrace hatred, for it can breed only destruction.
Embrace love instead, for those who love can change the world itself.

—Gesinius of Kehjistan, *Tenets of Zakarum*

As Sarnakyle had predicted, they came to the crossroads in the midmorning. A forlorn gibbet stood at the roadside, but not even a rope remained. For a moment, Siggard wondered how many had died at this place, their spirits returning on the Night of Souls to walk the earth in search of their execution-ers. He suppressed a shudder, and without a word began to stride down the western path.

As they walked, Sarnakyle talked of the wonders of Kehjistan, telling stories of the great temples and cities. He told of the Mage Clans in the east, and the dark magic farther south. It did not remove the horrible feeling from the pit of Siggard's stomach, but it did lighten the mood somewhat.

Much to the soldier's relief, by the time they stopped at sundown the trees had thinned considerably. Siggard breathed a sigh of relief; once he was out of the forest, he never wanted to return.

It only took them a couple of minutes to gather the wood they needed for a fire. Siggard tried to dine on some more of the ration Sarnakyle had given him earlier, but found he was too worried to eat.

"Are you feeling well?" the wizard asked. "You've barely eaten anything these last couple of days."

Siggard shook his head. "How could I be hungry when my family might be in dire danger?"

Sarnakyle nodded. "I understand."

They bedded down for the night, Sarnakyle first setting his wards with an abrupt series of gestures and then taking first watch. Siggard tried to sleep, but his dreams were filled with the screams of the dying and horrible visions of Emilye being tormented. Finally, Sarnakyle woke him up, and Siggard gladly took the watch. The minutes stretched into hours, and Siggard tried to think of anything but the terrors that could be occurring to those he loved.

Finally, the dawn came, and they smothered the last of the fire and began on their way again. The path twisted and turned, but finally the road led them out of the trees into the open fields of Entsteig.

Sarnakyle took a deep breath, wonder overcoming him as he saw the rolling green fields and sparse woodlands, each filled with the many colors of autumn. "What a beautiful country! Its natural beauty puts even the great temples of Viz-jun to shame!"

Siggard nodded grimly. "Let us hope that this 'beautiful country' is not being overrun by demons."

"Do you know the way to your village?" Sarnakyle asked.

"Once we get to the King's Road I'll be able to get my bearings," Siggard stated. "All roads lead to the King's Road."

With that, they walked westwards until the sun began to set. They camped near a copse of trees; after his experience in the forest, Siggard couldn't call these anything greater than woods. Sarnakyle wanted to make a campfire, but Siggard wouldn't have it; the demons could be anywhere, and the last thing he needed was to attract their attention with a pillar of smoke.

This time Siggard took the first watch, taking a little comfort from being in his homeland once more. He woke Sarnakyle just after midnight, and tried to sleep. Once again, his dreams were troubled, and it was a relief to be roused at the dawn.

By midday they had reached the King's Road, a wide path paved with rough-hewn stone. At the crossroads stood a large wooden sign, inscribed with simple letters.

"We have to go north," Siggard said. "My village is about a day east of Brennor, and Brennor is about three leagues northwards."

Sarnakyle smiled. "To Brennor we go!"

Siggard shook his head. "I almost think you are enjoying this too much."

The wizard shrugged. "What is the point of visiting new places if you can't enjoy yourself?"

"Under any other circumstances, I would agree with you," Siggard said, and began walking. Sarnakyle strode beside him, remarking on the freshness of the air, and comparing it to the stifling cities in Kehjistan.

"Don't get me wrong," Sarnakyle said. "Viz-jun is a beautiful and great city, and you should visit it someday. But there are so many people that the air can be difficult at best. I sometimes think that the ideal place to live is in the country."

The wizard suddenly stopped. "What is that smell?" he remarked, sniffing the air.

Siggard took a deep breath. Indeed, he could detect a bit of smoke, as though some fire close by had been smothered.

"Is there anything nearby?" Sarnakyle asked.

"Just a small village," Siggard replied. "It could be the harvest festival."

Sarnakyle licked his lips. "Now that is something to look forward to!"

As they walked, they found themselves facing a rise in the road, and behind the hill rose a curl of smoke.

"I hope we haven't missed anything!" Sarnakyle exclaimed. "It has been some time since I attended anything remotely like this!"

But when they crested the hill, Siggard's heart sank. The village itself had been fired, and in the town square, surrounded by the husks of burnt-out buildings, lay a pyramid of severed and decaying heads.

An investigation of the village revealed no life whatsoever. When the demons had passed through, they had killed every living soul. As they staggered out of the village, stunned to their very souls, Siggard and Sarnakyle saw the maimed and brutalized bodies of livestock at one of the local farmsteads. Siggard had no doubt the animals had been slaughtered to feed the army and then left to rot; after all, the demonic army would be able to move faster if it lived off the land than if it carried its food with it.

"We should travel through the night," Siggard said, regarding the horrifying pyramid. "With some luck, the demons won't have gotten to my home yet."

"Haste is important, but so is rest," Sarnakyle said. The wizard's playful demeanor was gone, replaced by a solemn determination that surprised Siggard. "The demons will try to cause as much destruction as possible, probably working in a circular pattern. If we travel directly to your village, we should be able to beat them."

"How do you know all this?" Siggard demanded.

"I am a Vizjerei," Sarnakyle stated. "One of the 'Spirit Clan.' I have summoned demons, and I have also fought them. I've seen these tactics used before by Bartuc, the Warlord of Blood."

"Could Bartuc be behind this?" Siggard asked.

"I sincerely hope not," Sarnakyle said. "I helped to kill him. Do you know a direct route from here?"

Siggard nodded. "I think I've been here before. If I'm right, this was Gellan's Pass, and that means that there is a path toward my village to the northeast."

"Damned demons," Sarnakyle cursed. "If only they hadn't killed all of the horses."

They found the path, and had managed three leagues by sundown, stopping for the evening at the side of the road.

That night, although Siggard managed to finish off the ration Sarnakyle had given him days ago, he could not sleep. The fear gnawed at his gut, and with every minute that passed he wished that the dawn would come.

As the sun rose out of the east, they set off again, Siggard walking more anxiously than he had even when Emilye had begun her labor pains. If only she was safe, he could be happy. Then he could take her away from all the madness into a walled town like Brennor, where they would be safe for eternity.

"We have the advantage, you know," Sarnakyle said as they walked. "We only have to move ourselves; whatever demon leads this army has to march thousands across the land. We can cover double the distance they can."

"It still won't matter if we get there too late," Siggard gritted, marching forward even more quickly. He finally slowed down when Sarnakyle jogged up beside him, puffing in exertion.

That night, Siggard reckoned that they had covered seven or eight leagues, and should be at the village sometime tomorrow. Sarnakyle had actually managed to catch a hare during the walk, and cooked it with a bit of magic. While the wizard ate with relish, Siggard found that he had no appetite at all, and left his share of the animal alone.

"If you won't eat, and you should," Sarnakyle said, licking his fingers, "tell me of your home."

Siggard thought for a moment, and then began to speak. "We own a farm, just outside of the village square. My father brought us to Bear's Hill when I was very young, and we did quite well."

"Bear's Hill?"

"My village," Siggard clarified. "I met Emilye when we were both children, at one of the village dances. She was absolutely radiant, and I, well, I was a rustic farmer. Still, she saw me, and I saw her, and it was love at first sight."

Sarnakyle grinned. "It must have been wonderful." He took another bite out of the rabbit.

Siggard nodded, and for a moment, there was a hint of a smile. "It was. When we got married, I promised her I'd always protect her. Whenever we could, we would go out exploring or picking mushrooms in the countryside, even when she was bearing our child. I tried to make her go gently, but she told me that she was pregnant, not fragile."

"Quite a woman."

"Yes," Siggard said. "The call to arms came only a couple of weeks after my daughter was born. We hadn't even decided on a name. I told her I'd be right back, and we'd choose one then. It's bad luck, you see, to leave a Naming for more than two months."

"I'm sure she'll be fine," Sarnakyle stated.

"I hope so," Siggard said. "By all the gods, I hope so."

They left their camp before the dawn, so eager was Siggard to get back to his home. They walked silently, Siggard trying at every step to convince himself they would arrive in time, and would be able to convince the village's Ealdorman to evacuate everybody before the demons came.

As they walked, Siggard touched his sword hilt, praying that the battered blade would serve if there was any trouble. The memories of the battle had become something secondary; all that mattered was getting to Emilye and his daughter in time.

Finally, they passed the engraved marker stone for the village, and Siggard breathed a sigh of relief. There didn't seem to be any damage to the outlying farmsteads, which meant that they had probably made it in time.

Still, there were no people about, which was odd for this time of year. It was the harvest, and at the least the Ealdorman would have had them preparing for the harvest festival. An uneasy feeling began to gnaw at Siggard's gut.

When they entered the town square, Siggard's heart almost stopped. Many of the buildings were burned, and in the center of the square lay a pyramid of severed heads.

Sarnakyle looked around in shock. "Perhaps she made it out in time," he suggested. "She might not have perished here."

Siggard almost grunted an agreement until he saw a glint of golden hair in the pyramid. He told himself that it had to be somebody else, it couldn't possibly be her. But when Siggard stepped forward, he saw Emilye's dead eyes staring at him from the pile, her face a mask of horror, the flies consuming her flesh.

He backed up, unable to speak. Then he fell to the earth, weeping. Everything he had lived for was now gone. Had the demons come at that moment to take his life, he would have had neither the strength nor the inclination to defend himself.

4
BETRAYALS
✴

How can I possibly stay? I have seen my own brother
die before the gates of my city, possessed by darkness.
I have seen all that I know changed beyond recognition.
I must leave, for my soul is empty of all but sorrow.

—Velinon the Archmage, *The Words of Horazon*

How long he wept, Siggard could not be sure. He sat by the horrific pyramid and sobbed until his eyes were bloodshot and dry, lamenting the loss of his wife. To make matters worse, he didn't know if his daughter was alive or dead.

Entirely spent, he looked around weakly. The world was cast in the reddish light of the setting sun. Sarnakyle sat on a fallen tree, regarding him with casual interest. How the wizard could remain unmoved, Siggard did not know.

"We aren't alone," Sarnakyle said quietly. "There are at least three people watching us from the shadows."

Siggard swallowed and stood unsteadily. "Demons?"

"I cannot tell," Sarnakyle said. "I have a spell ready, though."

"With luck, we won't need it," Siggard stated. He turned and called out to the deepening shadows. "I am Siggard of Bear's Hill! Are you friend or foe?"

"Siggard, is it you?" a familiar voice called. A gaunt, ragged man stepped out of the shadows, scratching his weathered face. Siggard's eyes widened in surprise.

"Tylwulf," Siggard breathed. He turned to Sarnakyle. "There are survivors!"

The wizard shook his head. "This does not feel right."

Tylwulf staggered forward, and Siggard saw dried blood caked on his face. "We heard the army was destroyed, and we feared the worst," he stammered. "Then the demons came, and some of us ran, and . . ." Tylwulf broke down into tears.

"My daughter, Tylwulf," Siggard demanded, taking hold of the man's torn tunic. "What happened to my daughter?"

Tylwulf shook his head, almost as if he was fighting with himself against horrible memories. "Dead, all dead. They ate the children, and killed all the women they could. Some of the men they took with them." He glanced at the pile of heads and immediately shied away. "We try not to think about it. If we're good, they might not come back."

"I don't like the feeling of this," Sarnakyle cut in.

Tylwulf looked at the wizard for a moment, his eyes widening in shock. "A Vizjerei! You travel with interesting friends, Siggard. This is one of the Spirit Clan."

"Is there a place we can stay for the night, Tylwulf?" Siggard asked. "It is getting late, and I would prefer to be indoors this evening."

"Camylle and I will put you up," Tylwulf stated. "Even your friend may come. Come, my farm was untouched."

After a short walk through the shattered village to Tylwulf's cottage, Siggard and Sarnakyle found themselves left to the tender mercies of Tylwulf's wife, who cooked a meal and set a hospitable table. But Siggard wished he could have been here under better circumstances.

He watched Sarnakyle sniff a plate of roasted beef cautiously, and then began to eat slowly, as if the wizard was tasting every part of the food. Siggard shook his head and ate a couple of bites, then put the plate aside. He was just too depressed to eat; the death of his family weighed heavily on him, a wound that might never heal.

"You should have some," Tylwulf said, eagerly tearing at some meat. "You'll need your strength to help us rebuild."

"I fear it will be an eternity before I have an appetite again," Siggard said. "I have lost too much, and seen such carnage . . ." He shook his head.

"What happened at Blackmarch?" Camylle asked, tousling her auburn hair.

"I don't remember," Siggard admitted sadly. "I remember the shield wall, and then the demons attacked, and something was happening in the forest. But then I must have blacked out and been carried off. I woke up alone in a forest in Aranoch two days later on the Night of Souls." He blinked. "At least, I think I was in Aranoch."

"And that is where you met the Spirit Mage?"

Siggard nodded, sipping some ale.

"A strange tale," Tylwulf muttered.

"How many survived here?" Siggard asked.

"Ten," Tylwulf replied. "We were able to hide while they did their work. They killed all of our animals, so at least we have meat."

"Have you sent warning to Brennor?"

Tylwulf shook his head distractedly and muttered something about not having time, and then excused himself. Oddly, Camylle gave Siggard a come-hither look, and then left for one of the bedrooms, her tattered dress falling around her legs.

Sarnakyle leaned over. "Something is very wrong here."

"What was your first hint?" Siggard snapped. "The pyramid of heads? Or how about the burning buildings?"

"I understand that you are grieving," Sarnakyle said quietly. "I respect that. However, please look around and see what there is to see."

Siggard scowled and looked at the plates of food, wishing he was sitting at Emilye's table and holding his child. But that would never be. He began to sob again, only barely aware of Sarnakyle standing and keeping a watchful eye on the door.

Tylwulf came through the wooden hallway bearing a torch. "Your lodgings are ready. I trust you are willing to share a room; we only have one to spare."

"That will be fine," Sarnakyle answered quickly.

Tylwulf led them down the hall to a small chamber with a large bed. To the side was a round table with a bright candle slowly burning down. Siggard thanked him and sat down on the bed.

"If you need anything, my wife and I are in the next room," Tylwulf said, closing the door.

"Prepare for battle," Sarnakyle said quietly. "There will be treachery tonight."

Siggard shook his head. "How could you possibly tell that?"

Sarnakyle sighed. "I know it is difficult, but you must see clearly. You are not asking the questions you should be. How did they survive when barely anybody else did?"

"How did I survive Blackmarch?" Siggard retorted. "There is such a thing as good luck."

"Next question," Sarnakyle began. "How did they know I was a Vizjerei?

And why did he call me a 'Spirit Mage'? Through your journeys with your father, you are well traveled, and you didn't know until I told you. Has this farmer honestly seen as much as yourself? Has he visited the east?"

Siggard shrugged.

"The words 'Spirit Mage' are only used by two groups of people, my friend. The first is by the other Mage Clans. The second is by the demonic forces themselves. Add this question: where are the graves? Have you seen a single fresh burial or body?"

A chill went down Siggard's spine. "What do you suggest we do?"

"Put out the candle and wait. And refrain from killing the one that attacks us."

Siggard nodded, and they silently stuffed their pillows under the blankets. As quietly as he could, Siggard drew his sword and snuffed the candle. He took position at one side of the door, while Sarnakyle stood at the other.

As they waited in the darkness, Siggard's mind spun with both hope and fear. Perhaps Sarnakyle was wrong, and the carnage in the town square had unbalanced him. Yet, at the same time, the wizard's concerns could not be dismissed. Siggard had known Tylwulf for years; they had even been friendly rivals for Emilye's hand. The only time the man had ever left the village was to go into Brennor for supplies.

Sarnakyle began to snore. Siggard started and looked over at the other side of the door, to see the wizard's eyes open and alert. He nodded and began to make a snoring sound himself. The ruse was worth a try.

So quietly that he nearly didn't notice it, the door began to open. Siggard watched as both Tylwulf and Camylle crept towards the bed. The two farmers took positions on opposite sides of the bed and raised their hands. There was a flash of steel, and Tylwulf brought a dagger down onto one of the forms under the covers, right where the heart would be.

With a shout of anger, Siggard leapt forward, followed by Sarnakyle. Tylwulf gasped in shock and dropped his blade as Siggard's sword came to meet his throat. There was a startled cry from Camylle, and Siggard looked to see Sarnakyle holding her tightly by the waist, a dagger of his own at her neck.

"Talk," Siggard demanded.

"They'll kill me," Tylwulf said.

"So will I."

"They came to free us," Tylwulf began. "They gave us power, but we had to give them everybody pledged to the light. We told them that the demons would show them mercy, and they surrendered. They didn't even fight when the demons started killing them. They just stood there in disbelief." Tylwulf leaned forward against the blade, drawing a drop of blood. He spoke again, a mad glare in his eyes. "I especially liked watching them kill Emilye. You never did deserve her. Then they let us have some of their spirit, and we got to share in the children. A freshly born babe is a taste to die for, you know, and we didn't waste a single cut of meat. Of course, they had to kill the livestock so that we could eat. After all, there aren't always people around to feast on . . ."

Siggard gasped in horror as he listened. As the traitor spoke, a reeking vileness seemed to clutch him. With an angry blow, Siggard struck Tylwulf's head off.

Then the rage took control. Screaming for vengeance, he pulled Camylle away from Sarnakyle and plunged his blade into her breast again and again. Then, once he finished watching her die, he roared in fury, stalking out of the house.

Eight people stood outside, all holding farm implements, and in each eye there was a dark madness. Siggard growled and attacked, not caring that he had once called them friends. The first one he slew was an old farmer from the western end of the village, who barely had time to raise his hoe. Siggard killed him with a slice to the throat, leaving him gurgling as the blood sprayed from his neck. He then turned on a woman with a cooking knife, spilling her intestines with a single stroke.

"Vengeance!" he screamed, sidestepping as the third one, the village leather worker, attacked. Siggard cut the hoe in half with his sword, then with his free hand snatched up the broken wood, driving the stake into the man's face. He growled in satisfaction as brains hit the earth.

He felt a piercing pain in his back, and turned to see a slight woman, the blacksmith's daughter. She was a girl no older than nineteen, still blossoming into womanhood. She held a long bloody knife in one hand, and her face bore a demonic smile. He thrust his sword into her heart, killing her with one blow.

The last four tried to run, and he screamed in fury as he cut them down. The last one turned and tried to fight, a fat man whose face was oily with sweat. When he struck the man's head off, his sword broke in half, as though it could take no more. He found himself once again in the village square, his hands and clothes covered in blood and gore.

Then the rage left him, and he felt a combination of horror and disgust. He collapsed to the ground, throwing up everything he had eaten in the last two days. Even when he had nothing more to vomit, he still retched, and finally he sat up, trying to spit the horrible taste out of his mouth.

"When you get angry, you don't do it by half measures, do you?" Sarnakyle said. Siggard turned to see the wizard sitting on the overturned tree again, watching him.

"I've done something monstrous, haven't I?" Siggard asked weakly.

Sarnakyle shook his head. "Although this won't make you feel any better, you did what had to be done. I have never seen a demonic possession ended without the death of the host."

"I feel so hollow," Siggard mumbled.

"This kind of killing does that," the wizard said. "You were not in the middle of battle, you were slaughtering those you might consider defenseless. But they were clutched by evil, and could not turn back. You probably did their souls a favor.

"When I was back in Viz-jun, I was called upon to investigate a possession. A small child, no more than two years old, had killed his parents. Even in the heart of Kehjistan, there was nothing that could be done. Finally, I had to kill the child to banish the demon. My reaction afterwards was almost identical to yours."

Sarnakyle leaned forward. "Had you not reacted this way, I would have wondered if you were still human."

"I have killed the traitors," Siggard said. "Why don't I feel as though I am revenged? Is vengeance truly this hollow?"

"Sometimes," Sarnakyle said. "In your case, I think you have not destroyed what you needed to destroy."

"What do you mean?"

The wizard pointed to one of the bodies around them, his orange-red robes billowing in the breeze. "These were victims themselves. These are the effects of the illness, but the ailment still lives. Their crime was to be weak-willed in the face of darkness. The death of your family, and all of this horror, has been ordered by the archdemon leading the demonic army. It is he who must die."

"How do you know there is an archdemon?" Siggard asked.

Sarnakyle smiled. "Armies like this are led by a baron of Hell. The lesser demons will not follow one of their own kind. Some greater power must lead them."

"I see," Siggard said. He stood up, his resolve giving him strength. "I swear, by the blood of my family, and the lives I have taken today, that I will find this archdemon and destroy it."

Sarnakyle nodded grimly. "That is a worthy goal, my friend. Come now; we should rest for the morning, but first I should tend to you, and make certain that none of this blood on you is yours."

5
Plans and Journeys
❋

Arkaine spoke,   opened his word-hoard,
"Fate will always aid   when one's bravery holds,
and when one's cause   is great and just."

—*The Lay of Arkaine*

"You're rather lucky," Sarnakyle said, bandaging Siggard's back. "You were wounded once, and it was very light. Already it is mostly healed."

Siggard stood and looked around. At Sarnakyle's suggestion, they had retired to Tylwulf's cabin, for, given the farmer's words, all of the village traitors were dead. Still, the wizard had insisted on placing wards around the cottage, just in case there were one or two others that Tylwulf hadn't mentioned.

Siggard donned his tunic, wincing slightly as his back strained against Sarnakyle's bandages. The flames from the torches mounted on the wall cast an eerie, flickering light, and for a moment Siggard just wanted to leave and be done with the place.

"It will be morning soon," Siggard said. "Perhaps a couple of hours until sunrise."

"We should rest in the time we have," Sarnakyle said. "But first, we should draw up a plan. Where do we go from here?"

Siggard shrugged. "We find the archdemon, and then we kill him."

Sarnakyle smiled, an amused look on his face. "That might just work, assuming our enemy's army has decided to take leave of him. If I might suggest another plan: when we were fighting Bartuc, he would raid the undefended villages, cut off the support to the walled towns, and then attack them. It seems to me that this demon would do the same; it makes strategic sense. Perhaps we should go to a fortified town, and let this archdemon come to us."

"Very well," Siggard conceded. "We'll go to Brennor, then."

"I will hold watch," Sarnakyle offered. "You look like you could use the rest more than I."

Siggard nodded and wearily stepped into the master bedroom. His eyes widened when he saw blood smearing the walls, and a demonic star painted on the window. He shook his head and walked into the kitchen lying opposite the room they had been attacked in.

"At least I might be able to sleep here," he muttered. He lay down on the wooden floor, fully clothed lest some harm come in the night, and fell into a slumber.

His dreams were a maelstrom of faces, most in torment. He saw the people he had killed, laughing at him as he struck them down again and again. And then he saw Emilye, her beautiful eyes filled with sorrow, as though in pity for what he had become.

He sat up, his body awash in a cold sweat. Sarnakyle stood over him, some fresh clothes in his arms. "It is midmorning," the wizard said. "I decided you should rest as long as you could." He passed the bundle to Siggard. "Try these on; they will suit you better than what you have now."

"Where did you get them?" Siggard asked, examining the clothes. He held up a warm-looking black-hooded cloak and some leather trousers. Both seemed to be of exceptional workmanship. Then he looked at the remains of the bundle, a long-sleeved gray tunic that seemed to be made of sheepskin.

"I found them in a chest in the cellar," Sarnakyle replied. "They seemed to be too large for either Tylwulf or his wife, so I can only assume they must have belonged to his father."

When Siggard paused, looking at the clothes suspiciously, Sarnakyle added: "I have checked them. There are no traces of magic on them, either good or evil."

"Were you able to find any weapons?" Siggard asked, fondling the cloak.

Sarnakyle shook his head. "I'm sorry."

Siggard nodded. "Thank you, my friend. If you will give me a moment to get dressed, we can be on our way."

The clothes fit Siggard almost perfectly, the only problem being that the trousers were slightly overlarge. That difficulty was easily fixed, though, by Siggard's sword belt, the empty sheath swaying at his side.

They strode west on the Queen's Road, a cobblestone path that Siggard remembered his father taking him along several times. The sky was overcast, and on occasion there was a brief burst of rain. It was enough that Sarnakyle stopped and drew a red cloak from his traveling pack.

"If we are to fight this archdemon," the wizard said as he pulled the cloak on, "I do not wish to die of a chill first."

Siggard gave him a slight grin, and then they began to walk again. It was difficult to tell how late in the day it was; the sky was completely cast over, and at best there was a brief ray of sun as the clouds scudded across the sky.

"I fear there may be lightning," Sarnakyle said. "I can feel it coming in my bones."

"Let us hope that we can find shelter before then," Siggard said. "If you hadn't let me sleep so long, we could have been there by nightfall. As it is, we will probably arrive sometime tomorrow morning."

"Are there any inns on the road?" Sarnakyle asked.

"I think there is one halfway to Brennor," Siggard replied. "This is a good road for travelers."

"Odd that we haven't seen any yet," Sarnakyle mused.

After a moment, Siggard realized that the wizard was right. They had been traveling for hours, and the daylight was fading. Yet they had not encountered another soul while they walked.

Siggard shook his head. This did not bode well: especially during the harvest season, there should be traffic along the main roads. With all he had seen, it was not a concern he could easily dismiss.

"Let us hope that the inn is still there," Siggard said, his stomach slowly twisting into a knot. Somehow, he dreaded the worst.

An hour later Siggard's fears were confirmed. There had indeed been an inn along the Queen's Road, but now it was reduced to a burning husk.

Lightning flashed in the darkening sky, the booming of thunder filling the air. Siggard and Sarnakyle pulled their cloaks closer to them and trod around the ruins of the inn.

"This can't have happened too long ago," Sarnakyle said, using a fallen branch to point at a maimed corpse. "These bodies are very fresh, and they have not been used for . . . other purposes. The archdemon must have been in great haste."

"Brennor could already be under siege," Siggard muttered.

Sarnakyle nodded. "The only way we can find out for certain is if we go there. We need a place to stop for tonight, though."

Siggard shook his head and pulled up his hood. "I think there might be a barrow-ground to the south, but that is all there is aside from Brennor itself."

Sarnakyle grimaced. "If that is all there is, then that is where we must go. I think I can protect us."

Siggard began to follow a small side road near the inn. "Come with me," he said, motioning. "The burial ground is this way, if I remember correctly."

"Have you ever taken shelter there before?" Sarnakyle asked.

Siggard shook his head. "We always stayed at the inn. My father once took me to see the mounds, though. He wanted to show me where the ancient kings rested. I remember some of the tombs being open at the time. It was many years ago, though."

Their walk became a jog as a heavy rain began to fall, quickly soaking both of them despite their cloaks and leathers. The thunder became deafening, and the only thing keeping Siggard from running was the fear of getting lost in the blinding rain.

Finally, they came to a large grove of evergreen trees. Inside the grove lay several mounds of earth, each grass-covered. For a moment, Siggard thought he could see vague shapes moving among the mounds, but when the lightning flashed, it appeared to be only his imagination.

Sarnakyle shook his head. "This is a place of the dead. I do not know how welcome we will be here."

"What choice do we have?" Siggard asked.

As if on cue, a bolt of lightning struck one of the trees. As the flaming branches fell to the earth, Sarnakyle shrugged and said, "On second thought, a barrow can't be that bad."

"We have to find an open one," Siggard shouted, his ears still ringing from the thunder. "There will be a curse on us if we defile an unbroken grave."

Siggard strode around one of the mounds, only to find the ancient stone door standing resolutely shut. A look at the tomb across from him revealed another sealed doorway.

Siggard suddenly felt himself being drawn. He walked towards one of the middle barrows and stopped. The wide maw of the open mound seemed to welcome him, as though it was where he belonged.

"Sarnakyle!" Siggard called. "I've found one!"

Siggard turned to see the wizard jogging up, his makeshift staff swinging in his hand. Siggard then turned and entered the tomb, disregarding Sarnakyle's shouted warning.

The inside was mercifully dry, and as Sarnakyle followed, he set his staff on fire, providing a crude torch. In the flickering light, Siggard saw several skeletons lying by the stone wall, their bones jumbled together. In the center of the mound lay a large stone sarcophagus, its sides ornamented with ancient runes and carvings of battle.

Something glittered in the torchlight, catching Siggard's eye. He stepped forward, to find a long, shining sword lying on top of the coffin. The cross-guard was shorter than he was used to, and the pommel was large and ornamented. On the blade itself several runes were carved into the fuller, runes that seemed to writhe with life in the torchlight.

"I wouldn't touch that if I were . . . in the name of Horazon!" Sarnakyle exclaimed. "This is a sword forged by Velund!"

"It is a special blade," Siggard mumbled, only half aware of his words. The sword drew all of his attention, and he wanted more than anything to pick it up. On the edge of his consciousness it seemed he could hear the whisper of a song coming from the blade itself.

"These swords were forged to be great allies," Sarnakyle said eagerly. "They choose their masters carefully, and serve them to the death. If it calls to you, and you can name it, the sword is yours."

Siggard turned to look at the wizard. Sarnakyle's eyes almost glowed with wonder, and then something drew Siggard's gaze elsewhere. Several of the skeletons had moved, or so he thought, and empty eye sockets seemed to gaze at the two.

Siggard slowly reached forward, placing his hands on the ancient leather of the hilt. As he touched it, the sword came to life, singing to him of glory and battle. It sang of armies of angels and demons, and battles at the gates of

Heaven itself. And throughout the song there was a single name, a name that Siggard only had to say once, and the blade would serve him forever.

Siggard turned and raised the sword. Around them, the skeletons shifted, the bones coming together, as though they might rise up to strike if the wrong words were spoken.

"Do you know the sword's name?" Sarnakyle asked.

Siggard nodded and called out at the top of his lungs. "Guthbreoht!"

With a clatter, the bones fell back to the earth, the skulls turning away from the two wanderers. Sarnakyle drew a breath in wonderment.

"They were the guardians of the blade," the wizard said, watching the last skeleton slump down and turn away. "Had you said the wrong name . . ." He shuddered.

Siggard sheathed Guthbreoht. "The sword has a new guardian now." He suddenly looked towards the entrance, listening. The rain had stopped, and the cloak of night was broken by a brief bird song and the chirping of crickets.

"I wonder how long you've been drawn here," Sarnakyle muttered.

"The storm is over," Siggard said.

Sarnakyle nodded. "Let us rest outside, my friend. This place has brought me much closer to the underworld than I ever desired to be."

Siggard nodded, and they left the tomb. For a moment, Siggard felt something watch him leave, but when he turned, the barrow was empty of all but shadows.

6
ARRIVALS AND SETBACKS
✳

Cherish all of Mankind, for Man has as much of the divine as the Archangels themselves. But unlike the Heavenly spirits, Man must overcome his failings, and chief amongst them is pride.

—*The Holy Scriptures of Zakarum*

They spent the night sleeping under the stars, Siggard holding Guthbreoht in his hands as he slept. The sword sang to him, and during its song, Siggard dreamed.

He stood again in the shield wall at Blackmarch, watching the demonic army break through the tree line. Giant boulders smashed into the ranks, flattening entire groups of soldiers. Still the lines held, the spearmen shouting insults at the demons.

Old Banagar smiled. "This is the way battle should be!"

"I'd rather be home!" Siggard shouted, raising his shield as the arrows started to fly. The goat-things stood before the army, holding great bows in their hands. Each time they loosed, a soldier fell, screaming in agony.

The smaller dog creatures and several of the goat creatures charged, bearing crude axes and clubs. They crashed against the shield wall, and the front lines became a struggle for survival. Siggard cut a goat-demon down with his sword, the force of the blow nearly unbalancing him. Something seemed strange about the blade, though, as if it wasn't really the one he should have . . .

The rush subsided, leaving the shield wall intact. Before the front lines lay a pile of bodies, some human, most monstrous. For the first time since the enemy came out onto the field, Siggard felt hope. Now that most of the demonic force was in the open, he saw that Entsteig had the advantage in numbers. More demons came out of the tree line, but they were outnumbered fivefold.

Once again they charged, this assault even more furious than the last. Siggard found himself barely able to think, his reflexes alone keeping him alive. As one creature came before him, he lifted his shield, the blow from an ax nearly knocking him over. His counterthrust took the creature in the belly, and the monster keeled over, screaming in anguish. As it fell, another took its place, and Siggard's blow almost severed the creature's head. The monster fell back in a spray of blood, a flap of skin the only thing holding its head to its neck.

"I think we might just win this battle!" Banagar shouted in triumph, raising his shield to mock the enemy.

With a fierce rustling, the shadows at the tree line parted, and a horrific monster strode into the open. Several of the Entsteigian archers loosed their arrows at it, but the shafts bounced harmlessly off the terrifying thing's muscular crimson chest.

Siggard gasped. The demon was a giant, easily dwarfing the goat creatures assailing them. Its eyes shone bright red, and horns protruded from its shoulders, elbows, and knees. It wore only a primitive loincloth and a belt, and it bore a giant sword. On its chest a strange symbol was emblazoned, and Siggard could not tell if it was a tattoo or something the creature wore.

"I am the favored of the Lord of Terror!" the creature bellowed, shaking the ground itself. "You will drop your weapons and submit to me, or all of you will die!"

A voice, tinny in comparison to the demon's, but still proud, called out. "We will never surrender to darkness. Go back to the underworld and trouble us no more!"

Siggard blinked, suddenly recognizing the voice. It was Prince Hrothwulf himself, the heir of Entsteig, a man beloved by the entire kingdom. He hadn't realized that the king had sent his son with this army, and for a moment he wondered if it was a good idea.

The demon smiled, and in that grin Siggard saw more malice than he had experienced in an entire lifetime. "Then all of you will die!"

The monster walked back into the trees, and the shadowy things moved again, covering its exit. There was a moment of silence, as Siggard and the rest of the army wondered what would come next.

"They're behind us!" came a startled cry from the rear of the line. Siggard turned to see several soldiers cut down, seemingly by nothing. Yet the blood spilled was real. Then a creature materialized, holding a long jagged knife, right in the middle of the shield wall.

Confusion reigned, and in that moment the demons attacked. This time, they broke through the shield wall, and Siggard found himself trapped in a sea of enemies. He fought like a madman, taking several of the creatures down, but there were still more, and the line was broken.

There was a gurgling cry from Banagar, and Siggard turned to face another of the materializing demons. With a great blow, he split open the creature's head, but more came, and Siggard found himself in a crush of men such that he couldn't move.

At that moment, sheer panic took hold.

He startled awake to see Sarnakyle standing watch. The wizard had draped his damp cloak over one of the tree branches, and seemed to be waiting for it to finish drying. The morning sun was still close to the horizon, giving off a pleasant heat tempered by a light breeze.

"It is a good day to be alive, my friend!" Sarnakyle said, motioning towards the clear sky. "This promises to be a great day."

Siggard stood and stretched. "I only hope that the people of Brennor agree with you."

Sarnakyle walked over, a piece of meat in his hand. "I was able to catch a hare last night. It was a bold creature; it almost walked right up to me."

Siggard took the offering with a nod and ate a small piece. Then he put the rest away.

"You really should eat more," Sarnakyle said. "This cannot be healthy."

"I found out only two days ago that my family was dead," Siggard pointed out. "How can you possibly expect me to be hungry?"

"If you don't eat, you will not have the strength to meet the foe, and you may end up joining your family before you can claim your vengeance," Sarnakyle chided. "Do not soil their memory by dying needlessly."

Siggard conceded the point and finished off the meal, even though he had no appetite for it. It seemed to settle, though, so he turned his mind to other things.

He stood and walked to the edge of the clearing, looking out at the barrows. In the morning light, they appeared old and decrepit, as though they were merely old tombs that would soon be forgotten. Perhaps one day they would fade into the land, and be passed by travelers who would mistake them for small hills.

Such is the way of things, Siggard thought. *All things must be forgotten in the end.*

"We should go," Sarnakyle said behind him. "The open road awaits."

Siggard nodded, turning away from the mounds. Somehow, he knew that he would never see them again in his lifetime. He pulled on his cloak, and joined the wizard as they ventured off towards the Queen's Road.

*   *   *

Around midday, they finally came to Brennor, and as with every other time he had been there, Siggard felt overwhelmed. The town was huge, surrounded by a large stone wall that was said to be impenetrable.

They stood at the gate, watching the guard allow a trickle of travelers inside the wall. The guards were impressive, their deep blue tabards and shining mail putting the entire army of Entsteig to shame.

"So this is your idea of a town," Sarnakyle mused. "Quaint. I like it, though."

"Surely you can't think this to be small," Siggard scoffed. "This is one of the greatest towns in the land."

"In Kehjistan, there are villages larger than this," Sarnakyle said. "But that is Kehjistan, and this is Entsteig. Standards are different."

"Let's go in and see the earl," Siggard sighed. He didn't want to get the wizard started on another long-winded story about the wonders of his homeland.

Sarnakyle held his hand up for a moment. "You saw how easily a demonic presence can lurk in a human form. We must be cautious, and tell only the earl what we know."

Siggard nodded. "Or the enemy might know our secrets. Don't worry; I understand."

As they approached the gate, the two guards lowered their spears to block the way. "State your names and business."

"Siggard of Bear's Hill, and Sarnakyle of Kehjistan," Siggard replied. "We are here to stay for the night, and then head southwards on the King's Road."

"Why are you heading south?"

Siggard pursed his lips, then spoke. "My friend and I are visiting some of my relatives in Gellan's Pass."

The first guard's mustache bristled. "You might have some difficulty with that. We haven't had word from the south since shortly after Blackmarch. Pass and be recognized."

They entered the town, immediately assaulted by a menagerie of sights and scents as they went along one of the narrow winding streets. The blocky stone buildings rose high above them, and several times they had to dodge a rain of reeking excrement as somebody emptied out a chamber pot.

"I suppose some people enjoy living like this," Siggard muttered, wiping some mud from a passing horse off his cloak.

"People like to dwell together," Sarnakyle said. "And in a city or town you can find artisans, craftsmen, all those trades that cannot flourish in a village."

"Art for squalor," Siggard said. "I wonder if the trade is worthwhile."

Sarnakyle smiled. "When you come to the east with me one day, my friend, you will see why it is. Now, do you know anything of this earl?"

"I served under the Earl of Brennor at Blackmarch, but I do not know if he survived," Siggard replied.

"We can probably assume that he didn't," Sarnakyle said. "I did not hear of any of the leaders living through the battle, and if any had, the bards would have spoken of them in their songs. Does he have a son?"

Siggard nodded. "Tilgar. Earl Edgewulf is a good man, who knows when and how to listen. I have not met his son, though. I have heard that Tilgar is brave, but not much else."

"We must hope that he is the equal of his father," Sarnakyle stated.

When they arrived at the stone castle that housed the seat of the Earl of Brennor, they were shown in to a small audience chamber. There they waited, Sarnakyle taking a close look at the tapestries on the wall while Siggard sat in one of the three chairs that had been provided.

"This is interesting," Sarnakyle said, pointing at one of the pictures. "This shows a battle between Heaven and Hell. I didn't think that mythology had spread so far."

Siggard blinked. "We have always believed in Heaven and Hell. We may even have learned of it first."

Sarnakyle chuckled. "Now there you must jest! No learning could equal the greatness of Kehjistan!"

The door opened, and a rotund man with a bushy gray beard walked in. Siggard looked at him closely, but it was not Earl Edgewulf. The man appeared too old to be the earl's son, though.

"I am Hunfrith, the steward of Brennor," the man said. "Please, be seated. I understand that you request an urgent audience with his lordship, Earl Tilgar."

Sarnakyle nodded and sat. "It is of the utmost importance."

Siggard blinked. "Not Earl Edgewulf?"

Hunfrith shook his head sadly. "His lordship was slain at the battle of Blackmarch. Earl Tilgar now holds the seat of Brennor."

"Our condolences," Sarnakyle said. "But we really must see his lordship now."

"Now, what this is about?" Hunfrith asked, leaning forward.

"It would be better if his lordship heard it first," Siggard said.

"Understand my position here," Hunfrith said. "You are asking to see his lordship, who is a very busy man. Not only is there now a food shortage, due to a lack of merchant trade, but the king's son, Prince Hrothwulf, was slain with the old earl at Blackmarch, a battle for which we have no reliable accounts. This means that there is now no successor to the throne, and now that his majesty has become ill every landowner who has rings to give away is trying to solidify his power. For all I know, you two could be assassins, or you could have news of minor importance at best. So I need to know that this is worthwhile."

Siggard decided to take the risk. "There is an army of demons raiding the lands around Brennor. My own village has been attacked and destroyed, and so have most of the settlements around the town. That is why no merchants have come with harvest goods."

"Their strategy will be to cut off your supplies and then attack the town," Sarnakyle added reluctantly. "I have seen this before in Kehjistan. From what you have told me, they already succeeded."

Hunfrith looked at them incredulously. "Do you honestly expect me to believe this?" he demanded. "An army of demons? I wish that was a new rumor; I think I preferred the stories of goblins and a dragon. This must be some sort of ridiculous joke."

"It is no joke," Siggard asserted. "I was at Blackmarch, and I saw what faced us. We were not fighting against men, but the foulest creatures of Hell."

"You were at Blackmarch," Hunfrith said.

Siggard nodded.

"And how did you survive the battle, may I ask?"

Siggard shrugged. "I do not remember. I just recall the shield wall breaking, and then I was in the forest with a giant lump on my head. I lost two days."

"It sounds to me like you are a deserter trying to cover your cowardice with tales of ghosts and goblins," Hunfrith stated.

"Siggard is no deserter, and we have important news," Sarnakyle said impatiently. "You may come under attack any night now. Will you kindly let us pass?"

Hunfrith stood up. "Absolutely not!" he bellowed. "You are lucky I don't order you two hanged for cowardice! Now get out of my sight before I change my mind!"

Siggard shook his head and stood angrily, turning to Hunfrith. "This is not over."

The steward smiled thinly. "Shall I have the guards escort you out?"

"We know the way," Sarnakyle said bitterly. With that, they turned on their heels and left.

They found a suitable inn shortly before sundown. The accommodations were acceptable, but barely, and it was the best they had seen in the northern side of town. At least the help didn't try to harass them while they ate.

"We will have to try again tomorrow morning," Sarnakyle said, supping on some thin vegetable soup. "If this town isn't prepared, the archdemon will simply walk through it."

"We'll need a way to get past the steward," Siggard said, ignoring his own soup and longing for some of Emilye's delicious mutton stew. The very thought of her brought a tear to his eye, and as he wiped it away he had to wrench his thoughts back to more immediate matters.

"Perhaps we can deliver something," Sarnakyle suggested. "Is there anything the castle is in desperate need of, besides a new steward?"

Siggard shrugged and stood up. "I have to get some fresh air."

"One moment," Sarnakyle said. "I'm almost finished." He downed the last of his soup, left a small silver coin on the table, and joined Siggard.

In the street, Siggard took a deep breath, but the air was not as fresh as he had hoped. Sarnakyle leaned against the inn's gray stone wall, and together they watched the few townspeople meander around, some looking as though they had some sort of direction, others appearing to be lost souls.

"Do you remember anything about the archdemon you fought?" Sarnakyle asked. "Anything at all could help."

"Lots of horns," Siggard replied.

"Most greater demons have lots of horns," Sarnakyle said. "I have no doubt that the Prime Evils themselves must look like balls of spikes. Anything else?"

Siggard thought for a moment. "There was a symbol on its chest. I can't remember what it was, though."

"A glyph," Sarnakyle said. "That could be very ill news. That means that the archdemon is enchanted in some . . . do you smell smoke?"

Siggard started and inhaled sharply. Indeed, an acrid stench now filled the air. He looked around to see a large pillar of smoke rising from the eastern side of town.

Siggard was overcome with dread. Part of Brennor was burning, and there was no thought of it being an accident; surely the demonic siege had begun.

7

FIRES AND DEMONS

What is bravery? Are those who fight in a hopeless cause brave, for they die for their beliefs? Are those who run from death brave, for it is easier to die than live? Or is bravery instead pushing aside one's fear to do what is necessary, be it to live or die?

—Godfrey of Westmarch, *Questions*

Siggard and Sarnakyle pounded through the streets of Brennor, desperately racing eastwards where the fire burned. As he ran, Siggard searched his memory for what was in that section of the town, from the few times he had visited with his father or wife.

There was the service entrance to the castle, along with the main barracks and armory . . .

A cold chill began to run down Siggard's back. If the demons destroyed the armory, the town would be lost. Brennor had already been cut off from any new supplies.

He cursed and skidded to a stop. They faced a dead end, terminating in a small shop selling wicker baskets. The shop was closed for the night, and a wooden sign hung from the oaken door informing all who could read when it would be opening the next morning.

They whirled about and raced towards a side street. "This place is a labyrinth," Sarnakyle called. "Do your people not plan their towns carefully, so that it is easy to get from place to place?"

Siggard panted and shook his head. "Most towns just grow in Entsteig. People find a good place and live there. I've heard the capital is even more of a maze than Brennor. There was a left turn back there. If we take that, we should be able to find our way."

His robes and cloak flapping, Sarnakyle shouted, "Right!"

They wound their way quickly through the maze of streets and alleys, passing several ladies of the night who barely had time to call out their wares even as the two passed. After several turns, always keeping the plume of smoke in sight, they nearly collided with a fire brigade.

"Damnation," Siggard muttered. "It's begun."

Siggard and Sarnakyle slowed to walk down the side street, passing the guardsmen. One of the guards turned and called after them to stop, but they both ignored him.

The street emptied out into a small square, where Siggard saw several soldiers crowded into a circle, desperately fighting for their lives. They were surrounded by froglike creatures that appeared strangely indistinct, as though they were here and yet not. Behind the battle stood the stone walls of the barracks, fire belching forth from every window to sear the air.

Siggard felt rage begin to take hold, and he drew Guthbreoht. The sword's song filled his being, fueling his fury, and he screamed an ancient battle cry whose words were older than the world itself.

He rushed into the fray, cutting down one of the demonic things with such force that the monster was sliced in half. His sword sang in exaltation as he turned to the next demon, quickly spilling its guts onto the cobbled road. Had anybody been watching, they would have wondered if he wielded the sword or vice versa.

He heard a shout from Sarnakyle, and a bolt of fire struck behind him. He turned away from the heat to see one of the demons staggering back, its body a living torch. With a quick thrust Siggard pierced it through, and turned again to barely dodge another demon's lunge. The claws of the thing scraped past him, and Siggard's blow severed the monster's spine.

He looked to see the soldiers forming into a shield wall and charging. His frantic attack had distracted at least half of the demons, giving the guardsmen a chance to rally. Two of the monsters fell to the soldiers' swinging blades, but the melee was not without a cost. One of the guards went down, clutching at his gaping throat as his lifeblood poured out in a scarlet rush to stain the ground crimson.

Siggard began to work his way towards the wall, suddenly realizing that if he didn't join the other soldiers, he could be surrounded and killed. Two more creatures fell to his sword, Guthbreoht's song becoming stronger with each demonic life it took.

Just before he reached the advancing shield wall, he felt an evil presence behind him. He reversed his grip and struck, feeling the sword pass through flesh and bone, but when he turned to look he saw that the steel impaled thin air. An ichorous blood began to run from the blade, and one of the creatures slowly started to appear, Guthbreoht transfixed in its neck. Siggard wrenched the sword clear, levering off the demon's head.

And then the shield wall overtook and engulfed him, and he took his place at its head. The soldiers continued to advance, cutting down every demon in their path. With Siggard in their ranks, they had become unstoppable, his sword destroying a monster with every stroke.

Several bolts of lightning struck down from the sky, killing the last of the demons. Siggard turned to see Sarnakyle nearly staggering from exertion, his face a sweaty mask. The wizard was reaching towards the heavens, and where he pointed a small cloud had formed. Finally, Sarnakyle lowered his hand, the thunderhead above vanishing into a bluish mist.

Even as the firemen rushed past them, the captain of the guard, a large mustached man with a slight limp, stepped up to Siggard. "Sir, I thank you. If it hadn't been for you, they would have destroyed us and burnt down the armory."

"So long as the armory is safe," Siggard said, feeling the exhaustion as the adrenaline left his system. He stepped over to one of the dead soldiers and said a small prayer, then wiped his sword clean on the body's tabard. He didn't know if blood would rust a blade forged by Velund, but he didn't want to take any risks. Strangely, the edge was not dulled at all, as though he had been cutting through cloth rather than flesh and bone. He sheathed Guthbreoht and sat on a wooden bench at the edge of the square, watching as the bucket brigade formed and dashed water on the billowing flames.

Sarnakyle walked over and sat beside him. "Given the clear skies, I didn't know if that lightning spell would work. I'm glad it did."

Siggard patted the wizard on the back. "You did well, my friend."

"Do you suppose the steward will allow us to see the earl now?"

Siggard raised his head and surveyed the square. The firemen continued to pour bucket after bucket into the rising flames and choking smoke. "They won't be able to put it out, will they?" Siggard mused, wrinkling his nose at the acrid smell.

Sarnakyle shook his head. "It is too far gone. I only hope that nobody was trapped inside."

"We should probably help."

"Probably."

"In a moment."

"Yes," the wizard agreed, wiping the sweat from his brow. "Once we're rested."

Two more people entered the square, both wearing tunics of office and rich cloaks. One, a tall red-bearded figure, wore an ornamental mace at his side. The other was shorter and rotund. They talked to the captain of the guard for a moment, who pointed first at several of the monstrous bodies lying on the ground and then at Siggard and Sarnakyle. They spoke a few words more, then the two newcomers strode towards the weary pair.

Siggard sighed in frustration when he realized that the first man was Hunfrith. He didn't recognize the second man, though. As they approached, Siggard stood, Sarnakyle following his lead.

"These are the men who sought an audience with me earlier today?" the strange man asked Hunfrith.

The steward nodded, and Siggard realized who the tall man was.

"It is an honor to meet you, your lordship," Siggard said, bowing. "Siggard of Bear's Hill and Sarnakyle of Kehjistan, at your service."

"From what Captain Hagan has told me, I owe both of you several debts of gratitude," Earl Tilgar said. "You may have saved our town. You may have however many rings you wish from my treasury."

"We have more important matters," Sarnakyle stated. "This town may be under siege by a powerful demon within a matter of days. We request an audience so that we may tell you what we know."

Tilgar nodded. "I will see you at midday tomorrow. Come to my castle, tell the guards your names, and they will bring you to me. Hunfrith will take care of any arrangements. If you will excuse me, there are several things I must do now."

Siggard and Sarnakyle both bowed as the earl turned and walked back to the captain of the guard. Hunfrith remained and wrung his hands uneasily.

"I believe I owe both of you a grave apology," the steward said. "Please pardon me. We have heard many strange stories about the death of the old earl and prince, and it is easy to be suspicious."

"I understand," Siggard said. "I too have witnessed many things that I would not have believed a month ago."

"I will see you both tomorrow then," Hunfrith said, bowing. "It would be good decorum to wear your finest. The earl is a royal cousin, and there are matters of politics to be aware of."

With that, Hunfrith returned to the earl. Sarnakyle shrugged to Siggard, and the two strode back through the winding streets to their inn. When they reached their room, Siggard removed his cloak, sword, and tunic, fell onto the bed, and within moments was in a blessedly dreamless sleep.

8
WARNINGS
✳

It is possible to have freedom, and it is possible to have peace.
It is rare to have both.

—Dil'Gerran of Kehjistan, *Sayings of the Northmen*

Siggard was up at the crack of dawn. He rose from the bed and opened the shutters to watch the town come to life. First the merchants began to open their shops, and then the apprentices came out, buying the items their masters would need to go about their business, cleaning out windows, and preparing the displays.

The street peddlers arrived next, jockeying for position to hock the passersby. After them came the retainers of the minor nobles' houses in the city, and the streets filled with the sounds of vendors calling out their wares.

From Siggard's few trips to Brennor, he knew that this was just the surface. Inside, the blacksmiths would begin to forge iron and steel, and bladesmiths would prepare new arms and armor for the city guard. There were also illuminators who would even now be drawing new illustrations on their manuscripts, artisans creating tapestries, bards composing the next saga of Arkaine, and any number of other artists and master craftsmen plying their trades.

With a start, Siggard realized that it was not just a fortified town that hung in the balance, it was an entire civilization.

He turned away from the window to see Sarnakyle beginning to stir, wiping his hands on his white under-robe. Once the wizard was up and about, they would go to the castle and seek their audience with Earl Tilgar. Before that, though, they would have to be ready.

Siggard picked up his tunic and frowned. The once-gray shirt had become covered with brown bloodstains. He would be able to wear it while he bought a new one, but it would certainly not serve when he went to see Earl Tilgar.

He watched Sarnakyle blink the sleep out of his eyes and sighed. There was so much to do, and so little time.

They were able to find Siggard some new clothes at a shop close to the inn. Once again, he found himself dressed in a gray tunic and black cloak, but of a much finer cut than he had worn before. Sarnakyle not only happily paid for it all, telling Siggard that it was the least he could do for somebody who had lost so much, but also handed him a small jingling coin purse. Although Siggard couldn't be sure, it seemed that there was something more on Sarnakyle's mind, but the wizard revealed nothing to him.

Sarnakyle wore his usual reddish robes and cloak. Siggard wondered for a moment if he would ever see the man dressed in any other color, but then dismissed the thought as unimportant.

They ate a light breakfast of milk and freshly baked bread at a local bakery, and then made their way to the castle. By the time they got there, the sun was high in a cloudless sky.

They gave their names to the guard, a massive man bearing Earl Tilgar's crimson colors. Siggard could only assume that he was part of Tilgar's housecarls, the earl's personal warband, rather than the city guard. The guard passed a message inside, and very quickly Siggard and Sarnakyle were greeted by Hunfrith, who led them deep into the castle.

They were taken up several flights of stairs to a bright office where Earl Tilgar and three soldiers were waiting. A large table stood in the center of the room, several maps spread across its oaken surface. From the window Siggard could easily see the battlements and towers of the castle and town walls.

"I am glad you are both here," Tilgar said. "Don't bother to bow; this is a war council, and I understand there is very little time. Please allow me to introduce you to my companions." He pointed at the first man, dressed in a deep blue, who Siggard remembered from the battle outside the barracks. "Captain Hagan, who commands the city guard." He pointed at the second man, a red-bearded warrior who wore Tilgar's personal colors. "Wulfgar, the commander of my housecarls." Finally, he pointed at the third man, a wiry gentleman in royal purple. "Guthwulf, the commander of the King's men stationed here."

"A pleasure to meet you all," Siggard said, bowing just in case. As he rose, he noticed a look of approval from Guthwulf.

Tilgar pointed to the map. "It has now been a week and a half since we have had any word from the villages around the seat of Brennor, and our scouts have yet to report. Our supplies are now running low, and we have perhaps a reserve of one month before people start starving. I understand that Siggard and Sarnakyle have information pertaining to this?"

Siggard nodded and stepped forward. "Your lordship, I fear that there is little or no relief coming. The settlements that supply the town have been destroyed by a demonic army."

Hunfrith raised his hand. "I will vouch for them. We have all seen the bodies found after the attack on the main barracks. They were not human."

"Your lordship, if I may," Sarnakyle broke in. "I fought at Viz-jun against Bartuc, the Warlord of Blood. He was one of our number who had become, for all intents and purposes, an archdemon. He followed a similar strategy against us. First he destroyed all the settlements supporting the city, and then he assailed the city itself. If this attack last night is any indication, the main army of whatever archdemon we face will be here within days."

Guthwulf looked at Siggard for a moment. "I understand you were at Blackmarch, and that we will be fighting the same enemy. What did you see there?"

"We formed a shield wall on the highest ground we could find," Siggard reported. "None of us expected a demonic army, but we were able to hold our own for a while. There were creatures that seemed to be walking goats, bearing bows, axes, and clubs. The archers were very accurate, and every shaft found its mark. There were also some smaller monsters resembling dogs, carrying axes. They seemed to have some sort of missile weapons, and there were these shadowy things near the archdemon. I didn't see what they actually did."

"What were the numbers like?" Hagan asked.

Siggard shrugged. "We seemed to outnumber each charge fivefold, but there were far more coming. I would guess we were facing about five thousand, but I cannot be certain. I got caught in a crush when they broke through the shield wall, and I don't remember anything after that."

"How did they break through?" Tilgar said, leaning forward on the map table.

Siggard shook his head. "I just don't know. The line was solid, then the archdemon appeared, and suddenly these creatures were among us, killing every man they could."

"We Vizjerei call them 'Hiddens,'" Sarnakyle cut in. "We don't have a better name for them. They were at Viz-jun, though. They were probably within the ranks before the battle even began, waiting for the archdemon's signal. Bartuc used that tactic as well. Those creatures we fought last night were also a sort of Hidden."

Tilgar scratched his beard. "Could we be facing this 'Bartuc' you mentioned?"

Sarnakyle shook his head. "The Warlord died two years ago at Viz-jun. I helped kill him, and I saw the body."

"So it is some other demon, using Bartuc's tactics," Hagan mused.

"Using his strategies," Sarnakyle corrected. "I do not know what this archdemon will do once the siege begins. The demonic forces are chaotic at best, and it would be very dangerous for us to assume anything. The only way the armies of Hell have ever been consistent has been in how they approach a walled town. They cut it off, then they attack."

"We'll need to prepare for a full siege," Tilgar stated, turning to his commanders. "Hagan, pull the catapults out from the armory and put a full guard on it. Also, put your men on alert; there may be more of these Hidden creatures to deal with. Guthwulf, I'll need some advance scouts to scour the land. Find out where this demonic army is, how many of them there are, and how long it will take for them to get here. Wulfgar, get the housecarls ready for battle, and prepare the tunnels underneath the town. We may have to evacuate the city if the worst comes to pass."

"There is one hope," Sarnakyle said. "The other demons are being kept here by the power of the archdemon. In order to exist on this plane, it will have had to possess a mortal body. If we can kill this baron of Hell, the other demons will be banished from this plane. Be wary, though; Siggard has told me that the archdemon is enchanted with a glyph of power, so it will be difficult to destroy at best."

"We will find a way," Tilgar promised. "The elder earl prided himself in his ability to keep his people from harm, and I am my father's son. If this archdemon attacks the walls of Brennor, it will die here."

The wizard smiled. "That is all one could ask."

Tilgar nodded. "I will have Hunfrith find rooms for you in the castle. With your experience, Sarnakyle, I feel it would be good to have you close by."

Sarnakyle shook his head. "With all due respect, your lordship, we already have suitable accommodations. The comradery of the inn will be good for both of us, I think."

Tilgar shook the hands of both Siggard and Sarnakyle. "Very well, then. You two should go and rest. Inform Hunfrith of where you are staying, and any news will be sent to you."

Siggard and Sarnakyle nodded, bowed, and allowed themselves to be shown out.

The waiting proved to be much worse than the fighting had been. They stood on the town wall and watched as the mounted scouts left the city, breaking off in several directions to search for the demonic army. And then the hours began to pass, the sun set, and Siggard was left tossing and turning in his bed, longing for the touch of his sweet Emilye.

He spent the next morning tending to Guthbreoht, whose song had become soothing and gentle. After the sword was oiled to a mirror polish, he sheathed it and walked downstairs to the inn's common room to wait for news. No word came that day, although several bards sang epics of the hero Arkaine, who had won some great victory in the east against demonic forces.

The mood of the town had changed overnight. Where before the inn's common room had been filled with life and laughter, now everybody was grim, waiting for the battle they knew would come. When Siggard watched Brennor come to life the next morning, after another nearly sleepless night, the denizens seemed to go through their daily business as though it was just a routine and nothing more.

He oiled his sword once again, went downstairs, listened to more epics, and waited for news. And, as another night fell, still no word came, and he was almost sick of hearing tales about Arkaine slaughtering demons with superhuman strength.

Sarnakyle was not much help. The wizard spent most of his time in the room, reading some old books he had stored in his pack. When Siggard had asked him what they were, he had been told they were spellbooks. The answer had been curt, though, unlike Sarnakyle's usually kind demeanor.

That night he dreamed of Emilye, but her face was ancient and decaying, and no matter how hard he tried to hold on to her, she slipped from his grasp and turned to dust. He awoke in tears, the pain of her death fresh once more, and silently wept for almost an hour before the sun rose.

That morning, after he had oiled his sword and gone down into the common room for a bite to eat, the innkeeper handed him a message.

"Just came in for you, sir," the innkeeper said. "Has Earl Tilgar's personal seal, it does."

Siggard handed the man a silver coin and opened the paper. He read it quickly, the elegant script suddenly reminding him of Emilye's gentle reading lessons, and felt absolute dread curl around in his stomach. He rushed upstairs, and threw open the door to their room, startling Sarnakyle, who was carefully going over a passage in his codex.

"Read this," Siggard said, handing the parchment to the wizard. Sarnakyle's eyes widened when he looked at the page.

"Army will arrive within a day from the east," he read aloud. "The demons number between three and four thousand. All nearby villages are destroyed, and all roads are blocked. We are completely isolated."

Siggard shook his head. "If we are truly cut off, then if the town is evacuated, there will be nowhere for the people to go. The demons will destroy them at will."

"I have not seen a situation this bad since Viz-jun," Sarnakyle stated. "We must prepare ourselves. Tomorrow, darkness falls upon Brennor."

9
Revelations
※

To fight the battle is easy.
To wait for it to begin is terrifying.

—Godfrey of Westmarch, *Quotations*

Siggard stood on the eastern town wall, watching the horizon for any sign of the demonic force. He fingered the leather-bound hilt of his sword nervously as he waited, his gut churning in impatience and fear.

Unbidden, his mind turned back to the horrifying carnage of Blackmarch. The archdemon stood clear in his mind, and he knew he would recognize it immediately when it came. Somehow, despite Guthbreoht's soothing song echoing in his ears, the thought of fighting the archdemon brought a shrill terror. Still, he thought, there was vengeance, and his heart hardened.

He heard soft footfalls behind him, and he turned to see Sarnakyle approaching. The wizard held one of his books, which he set down on the parapet.

"I thought you were in the inn studying your magic," Siggard said.

Sarnakyle shrugged. "I decided to get some fresh air. Besides, I couldn't stand to wait in the inn any longer."

"You wouldn't have missed anything," Siggard pointed out. "Tilgar has messengers waiting to find us as soon as anything appears."

Sarnakyle smiled and looked to the west, where the sun hung low in the sky, casting a shadow over the town. "And I suppose you just came out here for a brief midday stroll?"

Siggard grimaced. "Something like that."

"The warning is only a few hours old," Sarnakyle said. "To be honest, I think this demon will appear sometime in the morning. It does have a large army to march here, you know."

"Doesn't make the waiting any easier."

Sarnakyle nodded. "I know what you mean."

The wizard leaned on the rough stone wall, looking out to the darkening horizon. "If Tilgar is smart, and I believe he is, his catapults will strike the demons as they come close to the town, forcing them to camp far away."

"What good would that do?"

"It would give us some space," Sarnakyle explained. "The farther away they have to camp, the less likely it will be that they can completely surround us. And we can use any advantage we can get."

"We have your magic," Siggard pointed out.

"Yes, well," Sarnakyle muttered. "We do indeed."

"Here they come!" the lookout called. A horn blast sounded, and commanders barked orders to their soldiers.

He looked out over the parapet, squinting as he peered towards the horizon. Tiny shapes began to appear in the distance, bearing strange banners.

Siggard drew his sword, felt the blade's song infuse him with strength. He tried to make out the device on the banners, but they were too far away. He looked at Sarnakyle, who was leaning forward as well, lost in concentration. Beside them were several soldiers, weapons at the ready.

The wall was filling with men-at-arms.

"Archers!" one of the commanders called. "Wait for my signal!"

Siggard looked back at the boiling horizon. The demonic army literally filled the landscape, overwhelming the hills and fields outside the town. Finally one of the banners became visible, a horrifying depiction of a flayed corpse against a black moon, mounted under a human skull. Siggard's gorge rose, and he fought back a dizzying nausea.

"No," Sarnakyle cursed. "Anybody but him!"

"What is it?" Siggard asked. "Who do we fight?"

"Assur," Sarnakyle hissed. "The favored baron of the Lord of Terror."

Siggard jumped as a catapult loosed a ranging shot, the load flying overhead only to fall short of the approaching horde. Still onward they came, creatures of all sizes, and in their center, surrounded by shadowy things that could only come from a horrible nightmare, stood the giant archdemon.

"That can't be three thousand," Siggard muttered. "Maybe five, or six, but not three."

"He's brought help."

Another rock was loosed, the boulder falling into the demonic ranks, and a barrage followed. Several monsters fell, but the horde continued to advance, relentless as a force of nature. Each gap in the line the catapults made was immediately filled as more demons entered the crush.

"We have to warn Tilgar," Sarnakyle said, turning from the wall. "We have to evacuate the town."

"What is wrong?" Siggard demanded. "What is so special about this 'Assur'?"

Sarnakyle turned, and Siggard recoiled. The wizard's face was ashen, his eyes wild with fear. "There is no way we can possibly slay this archdemon," Sarnakyle said with absolute certainty, picking up his book from the parapet. "The battle is already lost."

They passed towards the castle, pushing past entire bands of soldiers heading to the eastern walls. No matter where they walked, they could hear the thudding of the catapults lofting rocks.

Finally they arrived, winding their way through several groups of guardsmen. Siggard tried asking many of them where Earl Tilgar could be found, but none seemed to know, telling him to ask somebody else. Siggard growled in frustration, but there was little he could do; the confusion was too great.

Eventually, they came across Hunfrith directing some soldiers to the castle walls. Sarnakyle tapped the steward on the shoulder, and the man turned abruptly.

"This had better be important," Hunfrith snapped. "In case you haven't noticed, we're in the middle of a siege."

"We have to speak with Earl Tilgar immediately," Sarnakyle demanded. "This is a matter of life and death."

"He's in the war room," Hunfrith said. "You'll have to find your own way there. I'm too busy to guide you."

Sarnakyle nodded. "I remember the way." Spinning on his heel, the wizard strode into the castle, Siggard struggling to keep up. With almost unnatural deftness, Sarnakyle picked a path through the crowds of soldiers and guardsmen, calling for space to move.

The gatehouse opened into a courtyard bustling with activity. Several soldiers were repairing a catapult, and archers were rushing to the walls. Sarnakyle ignored it all, and Siggard found himself running to catch up to the wizard after taking a quick glance around.

Without ceremony they entered the keep, Sarnakyle winding his way through the maze of corridors, Siggard close behind him. Finally, they reached the war room to find Earl Tilgar pouring over maps with his three commanders and one other figure.

"Our scouts have managed to destroy their catapults," one soldier said, pointing at a map. "So we have at least one advantage."

Siggard's eyes widened as he recognized the tall, gray-cloaked man with sandy-blond hair who rose from the table to greet him.

"Greetings, Siggard," he said. "I am pleased that you found your way out of the forest."

"Tyrael," Siggard breathed, remembering the man who had shared his fire. "I had thought you a ghost."

Tyrael smiled. "I am happy to say that I am no restless spirit."

Tilgar looked over at Siggard in surprise. "You know the Archangel Tyrael?"

Siggard raised an eyebrow. "Archangel? You didn't tell me you were an angel."

"You didn't ask."

"Lord Tyrael, it is good to see you again," Sarnakyle said, bowing. "Unfortunately, I have grim news. The archdemon we fight is Assur."

Tyrael nodded. "I know. It will be a difficult fight."

"Did everybody know Tyrael was an archangel but me?" Siggard wondered out loud, but nobody answered him.

"If you are here, Tyrael, does that mean that the Lords of Heaven will intervene?" Sarnakyle asked. "I fear that is our only hope."

Tyrael shook his head sadly. "It is very difficult for the most powerful of us to appear on the mortal plane. Even I cannot manifest myself for more than a night at a time. I can offer advice, but nothing else."

"Then we are already lost," Sarnakyle said, turning to Tilgar. "We must evacuate the town, your lordship."

Tilgar shook his head. "I do not understand. What is so special about this 'Assur'? From what I can see, even with his current numbers, we still have equal forces and the town walls to protect us."

"He is enchanted by a glyph that can only be cast once every millennium," Sarnakyle said. "He cannot be slain by any hands alive, be they mortal or angelic. No weapon we have could touch him."

"How could you possibly know this?" Tilgar demanded. "How can you be certain?"

"I am one of the Lords of the Vizjerei," Sarnakyle explained. "For decades I studied the summoning of spirits and demons, and came to lead many of my clan in the council. The demons do not give information easily, and often it is enveloped in lies, but recently we have learned the names of most of the barons of Hell. Their lords, the lesser and Prime Evils, we know only by title. Of all of the barons, Assur is the most feared. We know little about him, save that he is the favored of the Lord of Terror, and that he is enchanted with the Glyph of Invincibility."

"You can summon demons, correct?" Wulfgar asked. "Then can you summon monsters of your own to fight them?"

Sarnakyle shook his head. "My magic is not what it once was. When Bartuc, the Warlord of Blood, attacked the city of Viz-jun, we Vizjerei led the smaller clans into battle, believing that the demons we could summon, combined with the elemental magic of the lesser clans, would easily destroy the army of Bartuc.

"For centuries, we had summoned the creatures with ease, thinking that we could control them. At the siege, we discovered that for all these centuries we had been misled. The demons we summoned turned on us, savaging our own lines. When we attempted to banish them, we could not. If it had not been for the lesser clans, the city would have fallen on the first day. We had ten times the numbers of Bartuc's army, and a third of us died in the siege, most lost not because of the forces of the Warlord, but because of our own summonings.

"After the siege, we of the Vizjerei were shattered. Most of the clan lords, such as I, began to wander, trying to rediscover what was real. I have spent the last two years learning the elemental magic that saved us, but I am not nearly as powerful as I once thought myself. We cannot fight Assur with demons."

Tyrael nodded. "Lord Sarnakyle is correct. You must rely on your own resources in this fight. If at all possible, however, you must not let Assur take the town. This could be the most important battle ever fought in the mortal realm."

"I don't understand," Siggard said.

"Heaven and Hell have warred for millennia, but only recently have the forces of darkness taken an interest in the mortal realm. The realm used to be protected from the higher and lower planes, but the Prime Evils have used the Vizjerei to weaken that protection. If they can establish a foothold and keep it, then they will have a place that the forces of light cannot besiege, from which they can assault the very gates of Heaven. That is why they sent Assur; with him, they are certain they will be victorious."

"How can we fight him?" Sarnakyle said.

"You can try to kill him," Tyrael said. "Perhaps there is one among you who might succeed. But there is little chance of victory along that path. Instead, you should destroy his army. If you can drive it back, we will win this battle."

Tilgar looked down, his face ashen. "I was once told by a seer that I was touched by fate, but I do not wish to fight Assur in single combat." He raised his head to gaze at Tyrael. "And what happens to us if we lose?"

"An eternity of darkness," Tyrael stated calmly. "And that is why they must not take this place."

10
BATTLE

�֎

*Always respect the purity of battle. For only in
the heat of combat are all pretenses of nobility and quality stripped away,
replaced by survival and death.*

—Leoric of Khanduras, *The Craft of War*

As Siggard and Sarnakyle walked out of the castle, Siggard paused and struggled to don a shining coat of mail, a parting gift from Earl Tilgar. At last the byrnie settled into place, and Sarnakyle passed him his black cloak. As they walked, they heard the whistling of arrows and the screams of dying demons.

Siggard broke into a jog. "It has already begun in earnest." He didn't even bother to look if the wizard was following, but instead drew his sword. The runes on Guthbreoht's blade writhed as though they had a new life.

Sarnakyle finally caught up to him. "You are that anxious for your revenge?" he asked, then added, "Do not let your fury undo you."

Siggard stopped before the rough-hewn stairs to the wall and turned to face Sarnakyle. "Assur destroyed my village, my family, and my world. There will be blood for blood."

With that, he ran up the hoary stone steps, Guthbreoht's song becoming overpowering in his ears. As he crested the wall, he looked down into the roiling mass that had surrounded the town. The horde seemed almost infinite, despite the constant bombardment from the catapults, a rain of boulders that crushed all it touched. For a moment there was a silence as the demonic ranks surged under the wall.

Then the sun set.

There was a great roar from the monstrous army, and it rushed forward. The smaller dog creatures began to scale the wall, leaping from crevice to crevice with their claws. Guthbreoht took two of the creatures as they reached the top, splitting their heads like overripe melons. Still, a mass of the monsters leapt over the battlement, landing within the Entsteigian ranks with a shrill shriek.

A rush of flame singed Siggard's side, and the charred corpse of one of the demons fell beside him. "Somebody has to watch your back," Sarnakyle shouted, as even more of the foe poured over the wall.

Siggard screamed an ancient battle cry and advanced, gutting one of the monsters before it even knew he was there. Another leapt at him, ax at the ready, only to have Siggard strike, cutting the creature's head in half and spraying brains onto the stone floor.

There was a nearby cry, as housecarls struggled against a larger group of demons. With a shout of rage, Siggard charged, scattering the creatures and killing two.

And still the foe flooded over into the ranks like a foul sludge.

Siggard found himself strangely separated from the battle, watching himself act. There was no longer any thought in his actions. He and the sword acted in concert, as though they had always belonged together. As the demons came over the wall, the blade greeted them with joyous song, spilling guts and black blood wherever it struck. Time itself became meaningless, and soon he could remember nothing before the fighting.

He was beyond exhaustion. Somehow, he knew that Earl Tilgar had joined the fray with more of his housecarls, heard the man's hoarse war cries echo out over the wall. Although he was not certain how, he was aware of Sarnakyle sending spell after spell into the masses, the wizard protected by a ring of guards. As the red-tinged moon rose into the starry sky, the fetid stench of blood and death filled the air.

And then, abruptly, the demons stopped.

Siggard stood at the wall, his blade and mail-coat covered in blood and gore. Somehow, during the battle he had shed his black cloak. He suddenly wondered where it was, and whether he would have to get a new one.

"Are you all right?" Sarnakyle panted, stepping over several bodies towards him. "Are you uninjured?"

Siggard nodded. "I took no wound."

"That must have been the first wave," Earl Tilgar stated, leaning against the wall nearby, cleaning blood from his sword. "How long did that last?"

Siggard shrugged. "I've lost track." When he looked down, he saw vague shapes moving in the darkness, but nothing else.

"I'll try to get some light down there," Sarnakyle said, holding out his hand and chanting softly. A bolt of lightning split the air, landing just outside the wall. In the flash of light Siggard saw the still-roiling landscape, a pile of bodies lying beside the wall.

Siggard blinked, suddenly noting the unnatural silence. "What happened to the catapults?"

"They ran out of boulders a while ago," Tilgar replied. The earl then turned to one of his housecarls. "Have lit bundles of wood lowered down the wall. We need to be able to see more than the moon will allow."

As the soldiers carried out Tilgar's commands, Siggard wished Assur himself would attack, scaling the wall so that he could strike at the monster that killed his family. In that moment, Siggard did not care about the archdemon's enchanted glyph, or whether he himself would survive the battle. He shook his head clear of these thoughts to look over the battlement, the bottom now illuminated by flickering flames.

"Here they come again!" came a cry from the north, and Siggard looked over the parapet. In the moonlight, the goat creatures were attacking, carrying giant ladders to the hoary stone.

"Poles to the ladders!" Tilgar ordered. "Don't let them reach the top!"

Siggard joined the others in a desperate race to topple the ladders, long poles pushing them from the walls, demons screaming as they fell to their deaths, but for each ladder that fell, another took its place. Siggard came to one, only to have a grinning goat head rise before him. With a stroke of Guthbreoht, he sent the head flying, and then helped the pole-men knock over the ladder.

The whistling of arrows filled the air, and several of the housecarls fell. Siggard heard a grunting behind him, and he turned just in time to skewer a goat demon. Guthbreoht's song surged through him, and he began a dance of death, every step leaving a dead monster.

"They're gaining the wall!" came a shout, and Siggard turned to see a mass of demons scale the parapet close to Earl Tilgar. With a shout of rage, he charged. The first monster he cut down from behind. Another turned and attacked, and he first cut the creature's club in half, and then spilled its intestines onto the parapet.

Somebody shouted a warning, and Siggard turned, his sword raised. A demon was running at him, screaming for vengeance. With a thrust he put Guthbreoht through the creature's head, splattering pink and white brains onto a nearby guardsman. He withdrew his blade only to attack the mass of monsters again in earnest.

Three more goat creatures fell to his sword, and then it became quiet, Guthbreoht's song still throbbing in Siggard's head. Tilgar looked up, the earl's mail-coat torn and so blood-soaked that it no longer shone in the torchlight, yet little of the blood was his own. "Once again, I owe you a debt of thanks," Tilgar said. "You just saved my life. If you ever have need, come to me or my family, and we will see to you."

"If we survive this, I'll redeem your pledge."

Something twigged at Siggard's mind, though, something important that he should be remembering. But the only thing he could liken this situation to was Blackmarch, and that was a stand-up battle rather than a siege.

"Where's the third wave, do you suppose?" Tilgar asked.

Siggard shrugged, wiping sweat from his brow. How he was fending off exhaustion was beyond him, but he wasn't going to complain about the blessing. "I'm happy for any break we can get."

Tilgar smiled and nodded. He turned to a housecarl. "Have these bodies flung from the wall, and see what can be done about the blood. If we get attacked again, we'll be in greater danger of breaking our necks from tripping over the slain and slipping in their gore than from the demons."

"I am the favored Baron of the Lord of Terror!" came a bellowing roar from the demonic ranks. "You have seen the might of my army! Know now that I have many more ready for battle! I will give you a choice, pitiful mortals! If you give us the town now, only half of you will die! If you fight, none of you will survive! Give me your answer!"

Tilgar rose and stood by the wall. "It is you who will not survive, Assur, Baron of Hell! Know now that any one of us would rather die than serve you! Come to fight me, and I will kill you with my own hands!"

"You are a fool, little man, for no creature alive can slay me!" Assur cried. "All of you will die, mortals! For you have already lost!"

Even as the archdemon answered, Siggard's stomach sank in realization. The battle at the wall had been a diversion . . .

"By all that's holy, Tilgar, evacuate the town," Siggard cried.

Tilgar turned to him in shock. "Surely you aren't going to believe this foul . . ."

Suddenly, from the keep there was the hiss of arrows, and almost half of the soldiers still on the wall fell, struck down by the deadly bolts. A great roaring came up from the demonic ranks as they surged forward, bearing more ladders.

"The Hiddens took the keep while we weren't looking," Siggard said. "Give the signal to evacuate. This battle is lost!"

Tilgar gave Siggard a look of horror, his face pale as a ghost. Then he turned to the housecarl and nodded. The soldier raised a horn and blared several notes.

"Siggard, Sarnakyle, you are coming with me," Tilgar ordered. "The city guard knows what to do now."

"Are you sure we aren't needed here?" Sarnakyle asked, stepping forward. Siggard turned to see the wizard's face was flushed with sweat, the man swaying from exhaustion.

"Any man who stays on the wall now dies," Tilgar said, motioning to the men around him with his mace of office. The blue-clad soldiers were busy knocking over the ladders and loosing arrows on the keep. "The guards know what they must do, and they are all ready to make the sacrifice. We now have a sacred trust to the innocents in this town. They have already been taken into the tunnels. We must ensure that they are not followed."

Siggard nodded, and looked towards the demonic ranks. "This isn't over," he vowed, speaking above the hissing of arrows. With that, he and Sarnakyle followed the earl down, trying not to look back at the brave men on the wall, who knew that they would die that night but continued fighting regardless.

Tilgar led them through the maze of streets, Sarnakyle quickly snagging something from an abandoned shop as they walked. The sounds of the fighting had grown faint, although the arrows still flew overhead.

Finally, they came to a rough stone building in the town square. Outside stood Hunfrith, waiting impatiently, a sword in his trembling hand. "All of the remaining housecarls are inside," he said. "The King's Men have elected to stay and fight."

Tilgar shook his head. "The loss of life is wasteful, but it will buy us some time. Let us go."

As Hunfrith turned, something swooped out of the shadows. Siggard raised his sword, a cold sweat running down his back. One of those shadowy *things* from Blackmarch had arrived, and from its strange form emerged razor sharp claws.

"Go!" Sarnakyle shouted, raising his hand and uttering an incantation. A bolt of fire exploded from his palm, splashing into the creature to no effect. Then Siggard struck, slashing out with Guthbreoht while shouting a war cry. As he moved, he was aware of Tilgar and Hunfrith dashing into the building.

The thing recoiled as Guthbreoht touched it, and Siggard struck again and again, until the strange monster fell back and dissolved into the darkness. Whether it was dead or just mending its wounds, Siggard did not know. Regardless, he was certain the time had come to flee.

Siggard backed into the building, followed by Sarnakyle, who closed and barred the door behind them. He jumped as a hand touched his shoulder, nearly striking out with Guthbreoht, but something in the sword's song stopped him. "Come, the way is clear," Earl Tilgar's voice said, and he and Sarnakyle turned to find themselves facing a large staircase leading into the earth.

Tilgar led them down, a torch in his hand, and Siggard soon lost track of the number of steps they descended. When they got to the bottom, they found themselves in a large, torchlit tunnel. Deep in the tunnel they could hear a multitude of hushed but fading voices, as though a large number of people were moving away.

"Come with me," Tilgar said, and he took several steps forward. Then he wrenched one of the torches from the wall. There was a great roar from the earth, and several tons of stone fell down the staircase, sealing it.

"Now they cannot follow," the earl said, and led them into the tunnel. "These passages have been here since the earliest days of the town," he said, motioning to the rocky gray walls. His pale face flickered in the torchlight. "Recently, they were expanded into an escape route, and several of them were sealed off. This will take us well into the west, where we can begin to make our way to the capital. Hopefully, the archdemon will be too busy in Brennor to stop us."

"When were they evacuated?" Siggard asked. "There have to be ten thousand people in the town."

"We started evacuating people shortly after your warning," Tilgar replied, quickening the pace. "We had them wait in the tunnel, to avoid revealing its existence. A quarter of the housecarls went with them, just in case the tunnel was discovered. The signal I sent was the one to begin moving people out of the passage, not into it."

How long they walked, Siggard could not be certain. Deep in the musky earth, without sun, moon, or stars, he had no way of measuring time, and with his deepening fatigue, the entire experience seemed like a waking dream.

Suddenly, from behind them there was a dull rumbling, like a distant thunder. Earl Tilgar smiled grimly. "I do not think Brennor will be the fortress Assur had hoped," he said, but he would not say more.

Finally, there was a light at the end of the tunnel. Dawn's amber glow broke through the gloomy earth, and they emerged from a hill into the cloudless morn. Siggard shivered at the morning chill, and Sarnakyle pressed something warm and soft into his hand.

"I noticed you had lost your cloak during the fighting," Sarnakyle said. "So I got you a new one. If I can find the shopkeeper, I will pay him for it."

Siggard nodded wearily and pulled on his new black cloak, wrapping it about himself like a second skin. He looked around to see a large group of milling people, people from every age, craft, and discipline. They stood behind a cluster of hills that Siggard surmised must be large enough to hide them from the sight of any watcher from Brennor.

Siggard climbed the hill and peered over the rocky tor. As he looked toward the distant town, his eyes widened. The walls of Brennor were no more, lying in a crumbled heap. The castle still stood, surrounded by the abandoned town, and the windows of the keep shone with an unearthly red light.

When he came down, Tilgar smiled in grim satisfaction. "The final orders of the city guard were to bring down the walls. One of Brennor's great secrets is that any enemy who takes the place will only gain a small fortress. The King of Entsteig has never allowed one of his own towns to be used against him."

Tilgar turned to a housecarl, asking if Wulfgar still lived. When the answer came back as a negative, the earl shook his head sadly and began to give marching orders.

"Siggard, I would be grateful if you would stay with us," Tilgar said, placing his hand on the warrior's shoulder. "Your sword arm would be a great help."

Siggard shook his head. "I'm going to rest here, and then go back to Brennor at nightfall."

Sarnakyle startled. "Are you mad, my friend? What can you possibly hope to accomplish against a demonic horde?"

"I'm going to kill Assur," Siggard replied coldly.

"You know what that glyph means," Sarnakyle insisted. "Assur is invincible."

Siggard smiled grimly. "The murderer of my family is in Brennor, so I will seek him out and destroy him if I can. I know he can't possibly expect me."

"If you do this, you will probably die, Siggard," Tilgar said. "Are you certain that's what you want?"

Siggard affixed the earl with a cold stare. "Everything I love is already dead. If I must perish trying to avenge it, then so be it. But one way or another, I swear that Assur will die at my hands by daybreak."

I I
RECKONINGS
※

While an army can accomplish more than one man,
there are times when an individual can achieve
that which a legion cannot.

—Tobarius of Kehjistan, *Philosophies*

Siggard strode through the night, his hand resting on Guthbreoht's hilt under his black cloak. He was careful not to walk too fast, lest he attract unwanted attention from the castle of Brennor.

The refugees had left around midday, Earl Tilgar giving Siggard explicit instructions of where they would be going, and to find them if he survived. Sarnakyle had offered to help, but Siggard had refused. The last thing he wanted to do was endanger the wizard's life, particularly when Earl Tilgar would have a far greater need of magic protection than he.

After the refugees had departed, Siggard had cleaned the caked blood and gore from his sword and mail-coat, checking both for rust. He had oiled the sword, and blackened the mail with coal, removing as much of the shine as he could. Then he had waited for sunset.

Siggard finally reached what was left of the gates of Brennor. The wall truly had crumbled, and the air reeked of death. From the faint light of the castle windows, he made out bodies lying throughout the rubble. No doubt the crows and carrion eaters had eaten their fill during the day.

He made sure his cowl properly covered his face, and began to walk through the town. Most of the buildings he passed were scarred and hollowed out from the last of the fighting, and the corpses of guardsmen lay sprawled over the street. He slowly picked his way across the carnage, careful not to disturb anything.

A flickering fire caught his attention, and he stepped back into the shadows. Two of the goat creatures passed by, one carrying a torch, the other a severed head. As they passed, Guthbreoht's song became insistent, but Siggard held back. "Soon," he whispered. "Soon there will be vengeance."

He waited for another moment, and then took to the street again, carefully keeping in the darkness. He was certain that there would be guards at the castle door, but an idea was beginning to form in his mind. A vision of Tylwulf returned to the forefront of his memory, and he smiled grimly. The traitor would be helpful, after all.

But he still had to get into the castle.

He wound his way through the rubble of the town, sliding again into the shadows as he came to a campfire in the middle of one of the town squares. Several demons sat by the blaze, chortling and speaking in some guttural tongue. One of them held up a severed human arm and gnawed on the flesh.

Siggard forced down a wave of nausea and turned aside, slipping further into the darkness. The reckoning would come soon enough. He wrapped his cloak tighter about him and began to wind his way around the group at the fire, hoping he wouldn't attract their attention.

Finally, the fire lay in the distance, and he walked onward through the maze of crumbling streets, keeping the castle firmly in sight.

Before he could react, one of the dog creatures rounded the corner ahead of him. The creature rose to its full height of four feet and glared.

"What you want?" it demanded.

"Go away," Siggard growled, standing perfectly still.

"You tell me what you want or me call guards!" the creature shrilled. "Now what you want?"

"I've come to serve lord Assur," Siggard answered gruffly. "Now are you going to get out of my way, or am I going to have to hurt you?"

"You come with me," the dog-man said. "Me take you to others."

Siggard rolled his eyes theatrically. "Very well."

"Baron Assur need many men," the creature rambled, leading him to the castle door. "He need to call more demons, need more power. You give body, you give soul, you give power!"

The door appeared unguarded, but as they approached, two Hiddens emerged from the darkness, one on each side of the way. The dog-man spoke a few words, and they moved aside. Siggard followed the creature into the castle courtyard, taking careful note of where the Hiddens had placed themselves.

"You serve Baron Assur well!" the demon crooned, leading him past another pair of dog-men guarding the entrance to the keep. "You give him good soul!"

Siggard tried to ignore the creature's demented grumblings as he followed it through the passageways. As he walked, his hand flexed on Guthbreoht's leather hilt.

"Where is Lord Assur?" Siggard demanded.

"He in room with many maps," the dog-man said. "You no go there. Overseer take care of you."

Siggard stopped and looked down the corridor. It was empty on both sides, as far as the eye could see.

"Why you stopping?! You follow me!"

Siggard smiled coldly and struck. Guthbreoht flashed in the darkness as he drew and slashed in a single stroke, sending the dog-man's head thudding against the wall. Siggard began to walk purposefully down the corridor, hiding his sword under his cloak. He knew exactly where the war room was from here.

He made his way through the corridor, passing several demons who appeared to think that since he had gotten in, he must have some legitimate business. He smiled inwardly as he came to the door of the war room, a red light flowing from the crack between the hinges. It was seemingly unguarded, but Siggard knew better.

As quickly as he could, he slashed the air with his sword, and the heads of two Hiddens fell to the ground, the bodies appearing and crumpling shortly afterwards. He looked around again to ensure that there were no other demons in sight, and then opened the door and stepped in.

The huge form of Assur loomed before him, but the archdemon's back was turned. A second shadowy thing turned toward him, however, as if realizing he was not possessed, and charged, talons outstretched. As lithe as a cat, Siggard disemboweled the monster, and the creature faded, screaming in agony. Guthbreoht's song began to grow in strength.

Assur turned, fixing Siggard with angry black eyes. The archdemon drew a giant sword of his own from a sheath at the side of his loincloth.

"You are foolish, mortal," Assur rumbled. "No weapon wielded by the living can harm me, not even a sword of Velund."

Siggard held up Guthbreoht and began to speak, every word filling him with rage. "I am Siggard of Bear's Hill, whose family and village you slaughtered. Know now that I died inside the day my wife did, and my soul is empty of all but a lust for revenge. I will have my vengeance upon you, for you fight a dead man this day!"

Siggard roared in fury and attacked, his assault pushing the demon back. The two swords clashed with incredible speed, crying out with a ringing of tormented steel. Assur's face was a mask of amusement, but it quickly turned to anger as the onslaught continued.

"Die in truth, mortal!" Assur bellowed, counterattacking. He raised his blade and brought it down with all his might, Siggard barely blocking the deadly stroke. He thrust forward, forcing Siggard to dive out of the way. Snarling, Assur rounded on him, attacking again. The power of the blows drove Siggard back, every parry numbing his arm until he thought that it would take superhuman strength to defeat the demon.

Then Guthbreoht's song filled his spirit, and Siggard began to laugh. With an ancient battle cry, he lunged forward, striking the sword from Assur's hand. As the demon recoiled in shock, Siggard thrust, impaling the glyph and driving the steel deep into the monster's flesh.

Assur screamed, a cry of rage, fear, and pain. Blood poured from the wound as Siggard wrenched his sword, bringing the archdemon to its knees. With a cruel yank, Siggard freed his blade.

"Now it is over," he said, and with a great sweeping blow struck Assur's head off. It flew across the room, thudding against the wall and falling to the floor. As Siggard watched, the demonic face melted into the visage of a middle-aged man, a look of horror painted across his face. Siggard turned to the body to watch it topple to the ground. Silently, it changed into a human corpse in tattered robes.

He walked from the war room and strode down the corridors, exhausted. A pair of demons approached him, but even as he turned they gave a shrill cry of agony and exploded into flames. He stepped over to one of the windows and looked out across the ruins of the town. Brennor was alive with small blazes, dancing fires running around like creatures in torment and then vanishing.

"You slew our master!" came a cry behind him. He spun, sword at the ready, to find a guardsmen with mad bloodshot eyes lunging at him. Siggard side-stepped casually and slashed, cutting the possessed man down. Then he continued on his way out of the castle. If there were still some demonic forces in the town, so be it; he had his revenge at last.

Siggard sat on a hill near the crumbled walls of Brennor, watching the sunrise. He shook his head, trying to understand why he still felt empty and unfulfilled. His family had been avenged; surely that was enough to give him some peace, wasn't it?

And there were some other things that he had only just begun to think about. Little aspects of the last few days that had been nagging him, but he hadn't had time to consider. Horrible things, that could only lead to one terrifying conclusion.

"You've done surprising well," a familiar voice said.

"Tyrael," Siggard said, raising his head to gaze upon the placid face of the gray-clad archangel. "I thought you would come."

Tyrael nodded. "After Brennor fell and you stayed behind, I had to see what you would do. You should be proud; you've rid the world of a great evil."

Siggard tried to smile, but he found he just couldn't feel happy. "I've been thinking about some things. My missing days, my lack of appetite, how I was untroubled by wounds during the battle, those sorts of things."

Tyrael sat down on a rock and pursed his lips. "And?"

"Assur's glyph was absolute, wasn't it? No living hand could slay him."

"That is true."

Siggard wrapped his cloak around him and tried to stave off a chill. "When did I die, then?"

"At Blackmarch," Tyrael replied. "You were stabbed in the back by a Hidden during the last crush of the battle. The blade sheared through your mail-coat and slew you."

"And Heaven brought me back," Siggard added.

Tyrael shook his head. "No, we didn't. You did that all by yourself."

"I don't understand."

Tyrael leaned forward. "Very rarely, perhaps but twice in ten millennia, there is a soul so full of life that death cannot claim it. I have seen it only once before.

All I did was direct you to where you could do some good. Your timing, I am pleased to say, was excellent."

"Am I a ghost then, or a ghoul?"

"No," Tyrael replied thoughtfully. "It is difficult to say what you are. Death cannot claim you, but neither can life. You are trapped in between, until you find some way to rest your incredible vitality. And then, perhaps, death will find you."

"I suppose now that I've avenged my family, I can rest," Siggard said. "That's the way the ghost stories go, isn't it?"

Tyrael shook his head sadly. "You will not find your rest through revenge, no matter how hard you try. Vengeance is an act of hatred, and hatred never brings peace. No, if you are to discover some peace, you must do it through an act of love. I think you will find it, although it may take you centuries."

"Lovely," Siggard grumbled.

"Do not feel too badly about it," Tyrael said. "The way I see it, you have a choice. You can search for some act of love that will bring you peace, or wander the earth and help us in our fight against Hell." The archangel leaned back and regarded Siggard warmly. "You have quite a gift, you know. The only hand that could possibly still your heart is your own. This was but one battle in a much larger war. The Prime Evils now want dominion over the mortal realms, and they will continue to seek it. You would be an ideal soldier against them."

"It is a great deal to think about," Siggard said.

Tyrael smiled and began to fade away. "Do not worry," his voice echoed. "You have all the time in the world. May the light go with you, my friend."

Siggard sat for a while, considering. Then he stood, stretched, and began to walk back towards Earl Tilgar and his men. He had a long road ahead of him, but at least he knew his first destination.

EPILOGUE

Who can see the plans of Heaven or Hell?
Do not seek to know the unknowable, for fate will
reveal all when the time is right.

—Gesinius of Kehjistan, *Tenets of Zakarum*

The destruction of the archdemon Assur at Brennor in the year 302 would prove to be one of the most significant early victories of the Sin War, and the lands of Entsteig remained untroubled by the forces of Hell for at least two centuries afterwards.

Earl Tilgar reclaimed the town and destroyed the few demonic forces that had survived Assur's death. In the following years, after weathering a devastating famine that cost many lives, he founded the dynasty that ruled Entsteig until the capture and binding of the Prime Evils themselves, some six hundred years later.

Sarnakyle traveled in the western lands for another five years, finally returning to Kehjistan and leading the Vizjerei back into the practice of elemental magic. His death is not recorded, as twenty years after returning to his homeland, he again began to wander, and never returned. He was remembered as "the Red Wizard," and to this day the Vizjerei believe that in a time of great troubles he will come back to lead them.

Siggard remained with Earl Tilgar for several years to help rebuild Brennor. He then began to roam the world, fighting in many of the battles of the Sin War. It was said that he fought in battle after battle over the centuries, although what is truth and what is the bards' fiction is impossible to tell. After some five hundred years, however, he disappears from the sagas and epics. Whether Siggard finally found his peace or just grew tired of the conflict, none can say.

However, it is still held among the Entsteigians that if one goes to the ruins of a certain village on the Night of Souls, one will see a lonely figure standing a silent vigil in the mist, seeking a glimpse of loved ones long gone to dust.

About the Authors

RICHARD A. KNAAK is the *New York Times* bestselling author of some three dozen novels, including the *War of the Ancients* trilogy for *Warcraft* and the *Legend of Huma* for *Dragonlance*. No stranger to the *Diablo* world, he has penned three stand-alone novels, including *Moon of the Spider* and *The Sin War* trilogy. His other works include his own *Dragonrealm* series, the *Minotaur Wars* for *Dragonlance*, the *Aquilonia* trilogy of the Age of Conan, and the *Sunwell Trilogy*—the first *Warcraft* manga. In addition, his novels and short stories have been published worldwide in such diverse places as China, Iceland, the Czech Republic, and Brazil.

Currently, the author is at work on several projects, including *World of Warcraft: Night of the Dragon*, a sequel to *Day of the Dragon*; a second manga set; the *Ogre Titans* trilogy for *Dragonlance*, and more. His recent releases include background storywork for a recent game release by D3P and *The Black Talon*, first of the *Ogre Titans* novels.

MEL ODOM lives in Moore, Oklahoma, with his wife and children. He's written dozens of books, original as well as tie-in material to games and shows and movies such as *Hellgate: London, Buffy the Vampire Slayer*, and *Blade*, and received the Alex Award for his novel *The Rover*. His novel, *Apocalypse Dawn*, was runner-up for the Christie Award.

He also coaches Little League baseball and basketball, teaches writing classes, and writes reviews of movies, DVDs, books, and video games.

His webpage is www.melodom.com, but he blogs at www.melodom. blogspot.com He can be reached at mel@melodom.net

ROBERT B. MARKS is an author, editor, researcher, publisher, and Viking Age re-enactor living in Kingston, Ontario. He holds two degrees from Queen's University—the first in Mediaeval Studies, and the second in English Literature. He is the author of *Diablo: Demonsbane* (2000); *The EverQuest Companion* (2003); and *Garwulf's Corner* (2000–2002), one of the first computer games issues columns to appear on the Internet. Some of his recent nonfiction work has appeared in *The Escapist*. His new publishing company, Legacy Books Press (www.legacybookspress.com), published its first book, *A Funny Thing Happened on the Way to the Agora*, in December 2007.